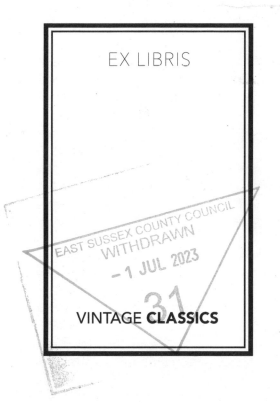

EX LIBRIS

VINTAGE **CLASSICS**

HARRIETTE ARNOW

Harriette Arnow was an American teacher, novelist, social historian and essayist, celebrated for her works on the populations of the Southern Appalachian Mountains. She was born into a family of teachers in 1908 and after studying at the University of Louisville taught for two years in a school in rural Pulaski County. These experiences provided the basis for her first novel, *Mountain Path*. After spending time in Cincinnati and Kentucky, Arnow moved with her husband and two children to a farm in Michigan. It was there that she wrote *The Dollmaker* in 1954, a book that would become a landmark in American fiction. It was at that same farm that she died in 1984.

HARRIETTE ARNOW

The Dollmaker

WITH AN AFTERWORD BY
Joyce Carol Oates

VINTAGE

1 3 5 7 9 10 8 6 4 2

Vintage
20 Vauxhall Bridge Road,
London SW1V 2SA

Vintage Classics is part of the Penguin Random House
group of companies whose addresses can be found at
global.penguinrandomhouse.com

Penguin
Random House
UK

This edition published by Vintage in 2017

First published by Macmillan Publishing Company Inc. in 1954

www.vintage-books.co.uk

A CIP catalogue record for this book is available
from the British Library

ISBN 9781784871871

Typeset in India by Thomson Digital Pvt Ltd, Noida, Delhi

Printed and bound by Clays Ltd, St Ives plc

Penguin Random House is committed to a sustainable future
for our business, our readers and our planet. This book is made
from Forest Stewardship Council® certified paper.

MIX
Paper from
responsible sources
FSC
www.fsc.org
FSC® C018179

1

Dock's shoes on the rocks up the hill and his heavy breathing had shut out all sound so that it seemed a long while she had heard nothing, and Amos lay too still, not clawing at the blanket as when they had started. They reached the ridge top where the road ran through scrub pine in sand, and while the mule's shoes were soft on the thick needles she bent her head low over the long bundle across the saddle horn, listening. Almost at once she straightened, and kicked the already sweat-soaked mule hard in the flanks until he broke into an awkward gallop. 'I know you're tired, but it ain't much furder,' she said in a low tight voice.

She rode on in silence, her big body hunched protectingly over the bundle. Now and then she glanced worriedly up at the sky, graying into the thick twilight of a rainy afternoon in October; but mostly her eyes, large, like the rest of her, and the deep, unshining gray of the rain-wet pine trunks, were fixed straight ahead of the mule's ears, as if by much looking she might help the weary animal pull the road past her with her eyes.

They reached the highway, stretching empty between the pines, silent, no sign of cars or people, as if it were not a road at all, but some lost island of asphalt coming from no place, going nowhere. The mule stopped, his ears flicking slowly back and forth as he considered the road. She kicked him again, explaining, 'It's a road fer automobiles; we'll have to ride it to stop a car, then you can git back home.'

The mule tried to turn away from the strange black stuff, flung his head about, danced stiff-leggedly back into the familiar sanctuary

1

of soft ground and pine trees. 'No,' the woman said, gripping his thin flanks with her long thighs, 'no, you've got to git out in th middle so's we can stop a car a goen toward th doctor's. You've got to.' She kicked him again, turned him about. He tried one weary, halfhearted bucking jump; but the woman only settled herself in the saddle, gripped with her thighs, her drawn-up knees, her heels. Her voice was half pleading, half scolding: 'Now, Dock, you know you cain't buck me off, not even if you was fresh—an you ain't. So git on.'

The great raw-boned mule argued with his ears, shook the bridle rein, side-stepped against a pine tree, but accepted soon the fact that the woman was master still, even on a strange road. He galloped again, down the middle of the asphalt that followed a high and narrow ridge and seemed at times like a road in the sky, the nothingness of fog-filled valleys far below on either side.

A car passed. Dock trembled at the sound, and side-stepped toward the edge, but the woman spoke gently and held him still. 'It won't hurt you none. It's a car like th coal truck; we ain't a stoppen it. It's a goen th wrong way.'

The mule, in spite of all the woman's urging, was slow in getting through his fright from the passing of the car. He fought continually to stay on the edge of the road, which was beginning to curve sharply and down so that little of it could be seen in either direction. The woman's head was bent again, listening above the bundle, when the mule plunged wildly toward the pines. She jerked hard on the bridle, so swiftly, so fiercely, that he whirled about, reared, came down, then took a hard, stiff-legged jump that landed him for an instant crosswise in the road.

The roar of a car's coming grew louder. Terrified by the strange sound, the unfamiliar road, and the strangeness of the woman's ways, the mule fought back toward the pines. The woman gripped with her legs, pulled with her hand, so that they seemed to do some wild but well rehearsed dance, round and round in the road, the mule rearing, flinging his head about, fighting to get it down so that he could buck.

She eased her hold an instant, jerked hard with all her strength. He reared but stayed in the road. Yellow fog lights, pale in the gray mists, washed over them, shone on the red sandy clay on one of the woman's shoes, a man's shoe with cleats holding leather thongs, pressed hard against the mule's lifted body as if it pointed to a place in the bridle mended with a piece of rawhide. It seemed a long time she sat so, the mule on his hind legs, the car lights washing over her, the child unshaken in the crook of her left arm while she talked to the mule in the same low urgent voice she had used to get him onto the highway: 'Don't be afeared, Dock. They'll stop. We'll make em stop. They dasn't take these downhill curves too fast. They'll have to stop. We'll all go over th bluff together.'

There was a loud, insistent honking; brakes squealed and rubber squeaked while the fingers of light swept away from the woman and out into the fog above the valley. Then, as the car skidded, the lights crossed the woman again, went into the pines on the other side of the road, swept back, as the car, now only a few feet behind her but on the other side of the road, came out of its skid. The woman's voice was low, pressed down by some terrible urgency as she begged under the screaming of the horn, 'Crosswise, crosswise; it'll git by us on t'other side.'

She jerked, kicked the mule, until he, already crazed with fright, jumped almost directly in front of the car, forcing it to swerve again, this time so sharply that it went completely off the road. It plowed partway into a thicket of little pines, then stopped on the narrow sandy shoulder above the bluff edge. The woman looked once at the car, then away and past the trembling mule's ears; and though she looked down it was like searching the sky on a cloudy day. There was only fog, thickened in splotches, greenish above a pasture field, brownish over the corn far down in the valley below the tree-tops by the bluff edge.

'You done good, real good,' she whispered to the mule. Then all in one swift motion she swung one long leg over the mule's back, looped the bridle over the saddle horn, turned the dazed mule southward, slapping him on the shoulder. 'Git,' she said. She did not look after him as he leaped away, broken ribbons of foam flying down his chin, and blood oozing from a cut on his left hind leg where the car had grazed him.

3

She hurried the few steps along the bluff edge to the car as if afraid it would be off again; but her hand was reaching for the front door handle before the door opened slowly, cautiously, and a soldier, his head almost to her chin, got out. He stared up at her and did not answer when she begged all in a breath: 'I've got tu have a lift. My little boy he's . . .'

The soldier was no longer looking at her. His eyes, blue, and with the unremembering look of a very old man's eyes, were fixed on the poplar tops rising above the bluff edge. He looked past them down into the valley, then slowly taking his glance away he reached for the handle of the back door, but dropped his hand when he saw that the window in the door was opening.

The woman turned to the down-dropping window and watched impatiently while first a hard and shiny soldier's cap rose above it, then a man's face, straight and neat and hard-appearing as the cap, but flushed now with surprise and anger. The mouth was hardly showing before it spoke, quickly, but with a flat, careful pronunciation of the words. 'You realize you've run me off the road. If you can't manage a horse, don't ride one on the highway. Don't you know there's a war and this road carries . . .'

The woman had listened intently, watching the man's lips, her brows drawn somewhat together like one listening to a language only partly understood. 'I know they's a war,' she said, reaching for the door handle. 'That's why th doctor closest home is gone. It was a mule,' she went on. 'I managed him. I had to make you stop. I've got to git my little boy to a doctor—quick.' She had one foot inside the door, the child held now in her two hands as she prepared to lay him on the seat.

The man, plainly irritated because he had neglected to hold the door shut, continued to sit by it, his legs outspread, barring her way. His hand moved slowly, as if he wanted her to see it touch the pistol in a polished holster by his side, let the pistol speak to her more than his toneless, unruffled words when he said, 'You must use other means of getting your child to the doctor.' He reached swiftly, jerked the door so that she, bent as she was, and with the heavy bundle in her two hands, staggered. Her head flopped downward to his knees, but she righted herself and kept one foot in the door.

4

'If my business were not so urgent,' he said, not taking his hand from the door, 'I would have you arrested for sabotage. I travel from'—he hesitated—'an important place on urgent business.' The voice still was not a man's voice, but the shiny cap, the bright leather, the pistol. It sharpened a little when he said, turning from her to the driver, 'Get back into the car and drive on.' He looked once at the bundle where one small sun-burned but blue-nailed hand waved aimlessly out of the blanket folds. Then, letting the door swing wide, he jerked it swiftly so that it struck hard against the woman's back, bent again as she searched for his eyes.

She straightened, put the hand under the blanket, but continued to stand between door and car. 'I'm sorry you're th army; frum Oak Ridge, I reckon, but I'd a stopped you enyhow.' Her voice was quiet as the voice below the cap. 'You can shoot me now er give me an this youngen a lift to th closest doctor.' And even in the man's work shoes, the long and shapeless coat, green-tinged with age, open, giving glimpses of a blue apron faded in strange squares as if it might have at one time been something else—a man's denim trousers or overall jumper—she held herself proudly, saying: 'You want my name; I'm Gertie Nevels from Ballew, Kentucky. Now, let me lay my little boy down. You cain't go . . .'

The officer had flung the door suddenly outward again. Still she did not fall when he banged it back against her, though in her attempts to keep from falling forward into the car and onto the child she dropped to her knees, her feet sliding through the gravel to the bluff edge. The officer gripped the pistol butt, and his voice shrilled a little as he said to the young soldier who had stood stiff and silent, staring at the woman: 'Get in and drive on. She'll have to drop off then.'

The other took his eyes from the blanket, still now. He saluted, said, 'Yes, sir,' but continued to stand, his body pressed against the car, his glance going again to the treetops below his feet.

'Back up on the road and drive on,' the other repeated, his face reddening, his eyes determinedly fixed straight in front of him.

'Yes, sir?' the other said again, unmoving. There was in his questioning acceptance of the command some slight note of pleasure. He looked up at the tall woman as if he would share it with her. Their glances crossed, but the trouble, the urgency of her need would let nothing else come into her eyes.

She looked again at the other. 'You want him to go over th bluff?' And her voice was weary to breaking, like an overwrought mother speaking to a stubborn child.

The older man for the first time looked past the woman and realized that what he had taken for a continuation of the brush and scrub pine was the tops of tall-growing trees below a bluff. He looked quickly away and began a rapid edging along the seat to the opposite door. It was only when he was out of the car and a few feet from the bluff edge that he was able to speak with the voice of polished leather and pistol handle, and command the other to back out.

The woman, as soon as the officer moved, had laid the child on the seat, then stood a moment by the door, watching the driver, shaking her head slowly, frowning as he raced the motor until the car shivered and the smoking rear wheels dug great holes in the sandy shoulder. 'That'll do no good,' she said, then more loudly, her voice lifted above the roaring motor, 'Have you got a ax?'

He shook his head, smiling a little, then his eyes were blank, prim like his mouth when the other told him to turn off the motor. The woman picked up a large sand-rock, dropped it behind one of the deeply sunken rear wheels. 'Have you got a jack?' she asked the officer. 'You could heist it up with a jack, git rocks under them wheels, an back up on th road.'

'Take your child out of the car and get on,' he said, his voice no longer smooth. 'We may be stuck here until I can get a tow truck. You'll be arrested.'

She glanced at him briefly, smoothed back her straight dark brown hair with a bended arm, then drawing the bottom of her apron into one hand to form a kind of sack, she began gathering rocks with the other hand, going in a quick squatting run, never straightening in her haste, never looking up.

The young soldier had by now got out of the car and stood by it, his back and shoulders very straight, his hands dropped by his sides so that a band of colored ribbon was bright on his dull uniform. The woman glanced curiously at it as she dumped a load of rocks by a wheel. The officer looked at him, and his voice was shrill, akin to an angry woman's. 'Hatcher, you're not on the parade ground.'

'Yes, sir,' the other said, drawing himself up still more rigidly.

'Get out the jack,' the officer said, after frowning a moment at the woman as if loath to repeat her suggestion.

'Yes, hurry, please,' the woman begged, not pausing in her rock gathering, but looking toward the child on the back seat. It had struggled until the blanket had fallen away from its head, showing dark hair above a face that through the window shone yellowish white, contorted with some terrible effort to cry or vomit or speak. Like the woman as she ran squatting through the mud, the struggling child seemed animal-like and unhuman compared to the two neatly dressed men.

The woman hurried up again with another apronful of rocks, dumped them, then went at her darting, stooping run along the bluff edge searching for more. The young soldier in the awkward, fumbling way of a man, neither liking nor knowing his business, got out the jack and set it in the sandy mud under the rear bumper. 'That's no good,' the woman said, coming up with more rocks; and with one hand still holding the apron she picked up the jack, put a flat rock where it had been, reset it, gave it a quick, critical glance. 'That'll hold now,' she said. She dumped her rocks by the wheel, but continued to squat, studying now the pines caught under the front of the car.

The officer stood at the edge of the asphalt, silent. Sometimes he looked up and down the road, and often he glanced at his wristwatch, but mostly his frowning glance was fixed on the car. He watched the woman now. Her hands had been busied with rocks and apron when she bent by the wheel; now one hand was still holding her emptied apron as she straightened, but in the other was a long knife, bright, thin, sharply pointed. The man, watching, took a quick step backward while his hand went again to the pistol butt. The woman, without looking at either man, knelt by the front of the car and, reaching far under with the knife, slashed rapidly at the entangled pine saplings while with the other hand she jerked them free and flung them behind her.

Finished with the pines, she went quickly along the bluff edge by the car, her glance searching through the window toward the child, still now, with the hand of one down-hanging arm brushing the floor. She watched only an instant and did not bend to listen, for clearly in the silence came the child's short choking gasps. She hurried on around the back of the car, and bent above the soldier, only now getting the jack into working position. 'Hurry,' she begged in the same tight, urgent voice she had used on the mule. 'Please, cain't you hurry—he's a choken so,' and in her haste to get a wheel on solid rock she began clawing at the muddy earth with her hands, pushing rocks under the tire as it slowly lifted.

In a moment the officer called, 'That's enough; try backing out now.'

Some of the woman's need for haste seemed to have entered the soldier. He straightened, glanced quickly toward the child, struggling with its head dangling over the edge of the seat, its eyes rolled back but unseeing. He turned quickly and hurried into the driver's seat without taking time to salute or say, 'Yes, sir'. The woman ran to the back wheel that had dug such a rut in the mud, and watched anxiously while the driver started the motor, raced it as he backed an inch or so. The car stopped, the motor roaring, the wheels spinning, smoking, flinging mud, rocks, and pine brush into the woman's face bent close above them in her frantic efforts with hands and feet to keep the brush and rocks under the wheel.

'Try rocking out,' the officer said. 'Pull up, then shift, quick, into reverse.'

The soldier was silent, looking at the emptiness in front of him. With the bent young pines cut away, the bumper seemed to hang above the valley. He moved at last, a few inches forward, but slowly, while the woman pushed rocks behind the rear wheels, jumping from first one to the other as she tried to force the rocks into the earth with her heavy shoes. The car stopped. The driver shifted again into reverse. The woman stood waiting between the side of the car and the bluff, her long arms a little lifted, the big jointed fingers of her great hands wide spread, her eyes on the back fender, her shoulders hunched like those of an animal gathering itself for a spring.

The motor roared again, the back wheels bit an inch or so into the rocks and mud, then spun. The woman plunged, flinging her two hard palms against the fender. Her body arched with the push like a too tightly strung bow; her eyes bulged; the muscles of her neck and face writhed under the thin brown skin; her big shoes dug holes in the mud in their efforts to keep still against the power of the pushing hands. The car hung, trembling, shivering, and one of the woman's feet began to slide toward the bluff edge.

Then her body seemed slowly to lengthen, for the car had moved. The woman's hands stayed with the fender until it pulled away from them. She fell sideways by the bluff edge so that the front wheel scraped her hip and the bumper touched strands of the dark hair tumbled from the thick knob worn high on her head. She stayed a moment in the mud, her knees doubled under her, her hands dropped flat on the earth, her drooping head between her arms, her whole body heaving with great gasping breaths.

She lifted her head, shook it as if to clear some dimness from her eyes, smoothed back her hair, then got slowly to her feet. Still gasping and staggering a little, she hurried to the car, stopped again but ready to start with its wheels on the hard-packed gravel by the road.

She jerked the door open and started in, but with the awkwardness of one unused to cars she bumped her head against the doorframe. She was just getting her wide shoulders through, her eyes on the child's face, when the officer, much smaller and more accustomed to cars than she, opened the door on his side, stepped partway in, and tried to pick up the child. It seemed heavier than he had thought, and instead of lifting it he jerked it quickly, a hand on either shoulder, across the seat and through the door, keeping it always at arm's length as if it had been some vile and dirty animal.

The woman snatched at the child but caught only the blanket. She tried to jump into the car, but her long loose coattail got under

9

her feet and she squatted an instant, unable to rise, trapped by the coattail. Her long, mud-streaked hair had fallen over her face, and through it her eyes were big, unbelieving, as the man said, straightening from pulling the child into the road a few feet from the car, 'You've helped undo a little of the damage you've done, but'—he drew a sharp quick breath—'I've no time for giving rides. I'm a part of the army, traveling on important business. If you must go with me, you'll leave your child in the road. He isn't so sick,' he went on, putting his foot through the door, even though the woman, still crouching, struggled through the other door. 'He seemed quite active, kicking around,' and then to the driver, quietly now, with no trace of shrillness, 'Go on.'

The woman gave the driver a swift measuring glance, saw his stiff shoulders, his face turned straight ahead as if he were a part of the car to be stopped or started at the will of the other. The car moved slowly; the officer was in now, one hand on the back of the front seat, the other closing the door. She gave an awkward squatting lunge across the car, her hands flung palm outward as when she had flung herself against the fender. One hand caught the small man's wrist above his pistol, the other caught his shoulder, high up, close to the neck, pushing, grasping more than striking, for she was still entangled in her coat.

He half sat, half fell in the road, one foot across the child. She did not look at him, but reached from the doorway of the car for the child, and her voice came, a low breathless crying: 'Cain't you see my youngen's choken tu death? I've got to git him to a doctor.'

One of the child's hands moved aimlessly, weakly knocking the blanket from its face. She gave a gasping cry, her voice shrilling, breaking, as if all the tightness and calmness that had carried her through the ride on the mule and the stopping and the starting of the car were worn away.

'Amos, Amos. It's Mommie. Amos, honey, Amos?' She was whispering now, a questioning whisper, while the child's head dangled over her arm. His unseeing eyes were rolled far back; the whites bulged out of his dark, purplish face, while mucus and saliva dribbled from his blue-lipped swollen mouth. She ran her finger down his throat, bringing up yellow-tinged mucus and ill-smelling vomit. He gave a short whispering breath that seemed to go no deeper than his choked-up throat. She blew in his mouth, shook him, turned him over, repeating the questioning whisper, 'Amos, oh Amos?'

The driver, who had leaped from his seat when she pushed the other through the car, was still, staring at the child, his hands under the older man's elbows, though the latter was already up and straightening his cap. For the first time he really looked at the child. 'Shake him by the heels—slap him on the back,' the young soldier said.

'Yes, take him by the heels,' the other repeated. 'Whatever is choking him might come loose.' And now he seemed more man than soldier, at once troubled and repelled by the sick child.

The woman was looking about her, shaking the child cradled in her arms with quick jerky motions. 'It's a disease,' she said. 'They's no shaken it out.' She saw what she had apparently been hunting. A few feet up the road was a smooth wide shelf of sandstone, like a little porch hung above the valley. She ran there, laid the child on the stone, begging of the men, 'Help me; help me,' meanwhile unbuttoning the little boy's blue cotton jumper and under it his shirt, straightening him on the stone as one would straighten the dead. 'Bring me a rock,' she said over her shoulder, 'flat like fer a piller.'

The young soldier gaped at her, looked around him, and at last picked up a squarish piece of sandrock. She slipped it high up under the child's shoulders so that the swollen neck arched upward, stretched with the weight of the head, which had fallen backward.

'Help me,' she repeated to the young soldier. 'You'll have to hold his head, tight.' She looked up at the other, who had stopped a few feet away, and now stared at her, wondering, but no longer afraid. 'You hold his hands and keep his feet down.' She looked down at the blue swollen face, smoothed back the dark brown hair from a forehead high and full like her own. 'He cain't fight it much—I think—I guess he's past feelen anything,' and there was a hopelessness in her voice that made the officer give her a sharp appraising glance as if he were thinking she could be crazy.

11

'Wouldn't it be better,' he said, 'to go quickly to the nearest doctor? He's not—he still has a pulse, hasn't he?'

She considered, nodding her head a little like one who understood such things. 'I kept a tryen to feel it back there—I couldn't on th mule—but his heart right now—it's not good.' She looked at him, and said in a low voice: 'I've seen youngens die. He ain't hardly breathen,' then looked down again at the child. 'Hold his hands an keep his feet down; they's no use a talken a gitten to th doctor; th war got th closest; th next is better'n fifteen miles down th road—an mebbe out a his office.'

'Oh,' the officer said, and hesitantly drew closer and stooped above the child, but made no move to touch him.

'Hold him,' the woman repeated, 'his hands,' her voice low again and tight, but with a shiver through it as if she were very cold. Her face looked cold, bluish like the child's, with all the color drained away, leaving the tanned, weather-beaten skin of her high cheekbones and jutting nose and chin like a brown freckled mask painted on a cold and frightened face with wide, frightened eyes. She looked again at the child, struggling feebly now with a sharp hoarse breath, all her eyes and her thoughts for him so that she seemed alone by the sloping sandrock with the mists below her in the valley and the little fog-darkened pines a wall between her and the road. She touched his forehead, whispering, 'Amos, I cain't let th war git you too.' Then her eyes were on his neck bowed up above the rock pillow, and they stayed there as she repeated, 'Hold him tight now.'

The older man, with the air of one humoring a forlorn and helpless creature, took the child's hands in one of his and put the other about its ankles. The young soldier, gripping the child's head, drew a sharp, surprised breath, but the other, staring down at patched overall knees, saw nothing until when he looked up there was the long bright knife drawing swiftly away from the swollen neck, leaving behind it a thin line that for an instant seemed no cut at all, hardly a mark, until the blood seeped out, thickening the line, distorting it.

The woman did not look away from the reddening line, but was still like a stone woman, not breathing, her face frozen, the lips bloodless, gripped together, the large drops of sweat on her forehead unmoving, hanging as she squatted head bent above the child. The officer cried: 'You can't do that! You're—you're killing. You can't do that!'

He might have been wind stirring fog in the valley for all she heard. The fingers of her left hand moved quickly over the cut skin, feeling, pulling the skin apart, holding it, thumb on one side, finger on the other, shaping a red bowed mouth grinning up from the child's neck. 'Please,' the man was begging, his voice choked as if from nausea.

The knife moved again, and in the silence there came a little hissing. A red filmed bubble streaked with pus grew on the red dripping wound, rose higher, burst; the child struggled, gave a hoarse, inhuman whistling cry. The woman wiped the knife blade on her shoe top with one hand while with the other she lifted the child's neck higher, and then swiftly, using only the one hand, closed the knife, dropped it into her pocket, and drew out a clean folded handkerchief.

She gently but quickly wiped the blood and pus from the gaping hole, whispering to the child as it struggled, giving its little hoarse, inhuman cries. 'Save yer breath, honey; thet little ole cut ain't nothen fer a big boy like you nigh four years old.' She spoke in a low jerky voice like one who has run a long way or lifted a heavy weight and has no breath to speak. She laid down the handkerchief, hunted with her free hand an instant in her back hair, brought out a hairpin, wiped it on the handkerchief, inserted the bent end in the cut, and then slowly, watching the hole carefully, drew her hand from under the child's neck, all the while holding the hole open with the hairpin.

The young soldier, who had never loosened his grip on the child's head, drew a long shivering breath and looked with admiration at the woman, searching for her eyes; but finding them still on the child, he looked toward the officer, and at once gave an angry, whispering, 'Jee-*sus*.'

The woman looked around and saw the officer who had collapsed all in a heap, his head on Amos's feet, one hand still clutching the child's hands. 'He's chicken-hearted,' she said, turning back to the child, saying over her shoulder, 'You'd better stretch him out. Loosen his collar—he's too tight in his clothes enyhow. Go on, I can manage.'

The young soldier got up, smiling a secret, pleased sort of smile, and the woman, glancing quickly away from the child, gave him an uneasy glance. 'Don't you be a letten him roll off the bluff edge.'

'No?' the other said, smiling down at Amos, breathing hoarsely and quickly, but breathing, his face less darkly blue. The soldier looked past the officer crumpled on the stone down to the wide valley, then up and across to the rows of hills breaking at times through shreds and banks of the low-hanging fog, at other places hidden so that the low hills, seen through the fog, seemed vast and mysterious, like mountains rising into the clouds. He waved his hand toward the hills. 'I'll bet hunting there is good.'

The woman nodded without looking up. 'Mighty good—now. They ain't hardly left us a man able to carry a gun er listen to a hound dog.'

'Where is—' the soldier began, then stopped, for the officer's head was slowly lifting, and at once it was as if the other had never looked at the hills or spoken to her. He straightened his shoulders, pulled down his coat, watched an instant longer. As the head continued to lift, he stepped closer, and after a moment's hesitation, and with a swift glance at Gertie, put his hands under the other's arms, standing in front of him so that the officer was between him and the bluff.

The woman gave the two a quick, worried glance. 'It's high there; watch out.'

'I'm quite all right,' the officer said, shaking the other's hands away. He lifted a greenish, watery-eyed face that seemed no soldier's face at all, only an old man's face. 'How's the little one?' he asked, getting slowly to his feet.

'Breathen,' the woman said.

'You've done a thing many doctors would be afraid to do without an operating room or anything,' he said, all his need for haste somehow dropped away. The other had handed him his cap, but he stood holding it, looking at the woman as if there were something he would like to say but could not.

The woman dabbed at the blood and mucus and pus bubbling through the hole. 'If that stuff runs down his windpipe an into his lungs, it'll be bad,' she said, as if talking to herself more than to the men. 'You can give a sheep pneumonie if when you're a drenchen it water gits down into its lungs.'

She looked about her: at the little pine trees, at the tops of the black gum and poplar rising by the bluff, then away across the road as if searching for something. 'Once I saved a cow that was choked—an in her windpipe I put a piece a cane.'

'What is it?' he asked, careful not to look at the child. 'It doesn't seem like plain choking.'

'It's—' She rubbed her bent arm up her forehead, back across her stringing hair. 'I disremember what they call it now; used to be they said membranous croup. I thought it was jist plain croup, bad hard croup like he's had afore, till Aunt Sue Annie come. She told me word come in th mail last night Mealie Sexton's baby was dead. We thought it had th croup when she come a visiten my mother when she come in frum Cincinnati—her baby an him, they was together.' She looked toward the young soldier, who stood in respectful silence a few feet behind the other. 'Could you hold this open and watch him; I'll have to git somethin to put in it. It'll take jist a minnit. They's a little poplar right acrost th road.'

He glanced as if for permission at the officer, but the other had turned away, looking greenish and sick again; and after a moment's hesitation the young one came with a fresh clean handkerchief of his own and took the hairpin and the woman's place by the child. She hurried across the road to a little poplar, and with one swift stroke cut a bough about the thickness of her middle finger, cut again; the bough with its yellow leaves unflecked with red or brown dropped away. Then, working as she walked back across the road, she stripped the gray bark from the short length of limb, glancing between each knife stroke at the child. She had crossed the road, when she stopped, knife lifted, to look at a red card lettered in black, tacked to a fairsized pine tree. Most of the print was small, but large enough for men in passing cars to read were the words: MEN, WOMEN, WILLOW RUN, UNCLE SAM, LIVING QUARTERS. Her knife

15

lifted, came down in one long thrust against the card. It fell and she walked on, the knife working now with swift, twisting cuts, forming a hole in one end of the wood.

'You shouldn't have done that,' the older man said, nodding toward the card at the foot of the pine. 'They need workers badly— as much as soldiers almost.'

She nodded, glancing again toward the child. 'But in our settlement they ain't nobody else they can git,' she said.

'Is your husband in the armed forces?' he asked.

She shook her head. 'His examinen date is still about three weeks off.'

'Does he work in a factory?'

'He hauls coal in his own truck—when he can git gas—an th miners can git dynamite an caps an stuff to work in th coal.'

'The big mines are more efficient,' he said. 'They need materials worse.'

'Th only miners they left us is two cripples an one real old.'

'But a good miner back here in these little mines—I've seen them by the road—would be a waste of man power, working without machinery,' he said.

She studied the cut in the child's neck, listened, frowning, to his short whistling breaths. She nodded to the man's words at last, but grudgingly, as if she had heard the words many times but could not or would not understand, and her face was expressionless, watching now the knife in the soft wood, now glancing at the child.

'It's like the farmers,' the officer went on, his voice slightly apologetic as he glanced toward the child, struggling again so that the soldier must lay down the handkerchief and hold his hands while the strain of holding the hairpin steady in the windpipe was bringing sweat to his forehead. 'They can't exempt every little one-horse farmer who has little to sell. A man has to produce a lot of what the country needs.'

She did not nod, but her lips tightened so that, as when she had cut the child's neck, her mouth was a pale straight slit below the long straight upper lip and the jutting nose. 'They warn't a farmer in all our settlement big enough,' she said, and her voice was low and sullen.

16

'Have you any relatives in the armed forces?' he asked, his voice somehow critical.

'Jist cousins an in-laws an sich—now.'

'Now?'

'Since yesterday mornen—I had a brother till then.'

'Oh.' His voice had changed, filled with a kind of proper sadness. 'Let us hope he is only missing and that—'

'Jesse—that's my man's brother—he's th one that's missen. Fer my brother th telegram said, "Kilt in action."' The knife was still, and she sat a moment staring out across the hills, repeating slowly, tonelessly, 'Kilt in action.' Then, still in the toneless talking-to-herself voice: 'These same leaves was green when they took him—an he'd planted his corn. Some of it he saw come up.'

'He was a farmer?' the man asked.

The knife moved in the wood again as she said, 'One a them little ones.' The knife fought the wood with sharp swift jabs, forming a hole the length of the short piece of poplar. The man, watching stiffly, uncomfortably, trying not to look at the child or the woman's face, said, 'You are very skillful with a knife.'

'I've allus whittled.'

'What?'

'Oh, handles.'

'Handles?'

She looked down at the hand that held the poplar wood, the back brown and wrinkled, fingernails black and ragged, then at the palm, smooth with the look of yellowed leather. It was as if the hand were a page engraved with names while, she looking now at the poplar wood, repeated: 'Hoe handles, saw handles, ax handles, corn-knife handles, broom handles, plow handles, grubben-hoe handles, churn-dasher handles, hammer handles, all kinds a handles—it takes a heap a handles. Sometimes I make em fer th neighbors.'

He was silent, his glance fixed on her hands. 'Handles,' he said at last. 'There wouldn't be much fun in handles.'

Her face for an instant softened, and as she looked up something that might have been hatred was gone from her eyes. 'I've never had much time fer whittlen foolishness. Oh, a few dolls. Cassie—that's my least girl—she's crazy over th dolls I whittle, but when I git all settled I'm aimen to work up a piece a wild cherry wood I've got. It's big enough fer th head an shoulders uv a fair-sized man if'—her voice was low again, wandering as if she talked to herself—'if I can ever hit on th right face.' She glanced at the soldier struggling to keep the child's hands from clawing at his neck. 'Hold out a little minute longer. I've about got this hole through.'

The older man stood so that if he looked straight in front of him he could see the woman but not the child. 'What kind of face?' he asked.

She shook the shavings out of the rapidly deepening hole, began on the other end. 'I don't know. I've thought on Christ—but some-how his face ain't never clear er somethen. Maybe some other—old Amos, I liked, or Ecclesiastes or Judas.'

'Judas?' And he gave her a sharp, suspicious-seeming glance.

She looked again at the child, then nodded, her eyes on the knife blade as she talked. 'Not Judas with his mouth all drooly, his hand held out fer th silver, but Judas given th thirty pieces away. I figger,' she went on after blowing the shavings out of the hole, 'they's many a one does meanness fer money—like Judas.' Her eyes were on the poplar as she spoke, 'But they's not many like him gives th money away an feels sorry onct they've got it.'

She looked toward the child and met the eyes of the young sol-dier—there was a head nod in his eyes—but he was silent, for the other was saying, 'You seem to be quite a student of the Bible.'

She shook her head. 'Th Bible's about th only thing I've ever read—when I was a growen up my mother was sick a heap an my father hurt his leg in th log woods. I had to help him, an never got much schoolen but what he give me.'

'And he had you study the Bible.'

'He had me git things by heart th way they used to do in th old days—poetry an th Constitution an a heap a th Bible.' She rose, and still whittling walked toward the child. She stood above him, work-ing swiftly until the hole in the tiny wooden pipe was to her liking, and then with the same gentle skill with which she had whittled she put the tube into the child's neck. She then wrapped him swiftly in the blanket, and with no glance at either man walked quickly to the car.

The officer pushed himself into a corner as far from the woman and child as possible. He sat stiffly, trying not to show his distaste for the big woman cluttering his speckless car, just as he tried not to look at the child or show that the inhuman gurgling cries it gave or the whispering bubbles of its breath nauseated him like the sight of the wooden tube beaded at times with pus and bloody mucus.

The woman sensed this and sat, trying to make herself as small as possible, her muddy feet unmoving by the door, her great shoulders hunched over the child, and slightly sideways. The driver stared straight ahead at the road. The woman mostly watched the wooden pipe. The officer looked first at one side of the road, then the other, unable to keep his glance from the child.

The road left the high pine ridges and followed the twisting course of a creek down into the valley of the Cumberland. Above them on the shoulder of the ridge lay a steep little clearing; stumpy first-year new ground it looked to be, not half tended. Even in the rainy twilight Gertie could see the leafless sprouts encircling the white oak stumps and the smallness of the fodder shocks—a woman's fodder shocks. Held up against the hillside on long front legs like stilts was a little plank house with a tar-paper roof. Chickens were going to roost in a crooked dogwood tree near the door, and a white-headed child came around the house, stumbling under the sticks of stove wood hugged in its arms, while on the high porch steps two other children, one too small to walk, played with a spotted hound.

Though it lay on the woman's side of the road, both glanced at it—the first house after miles of Cumberland National Forest. Then both saw the service flag with one star—blue—in the one front window by the door.

'What crops do they raise in this country?' the officer asked, as if he didn't much care but wanted to make some sound above the child's breathing.

'A little uv everthing.'

'But what is their main crop?' he insisted.

'Youngens,' she said, holding the child's hands that were continually wandering toward the hole in his neck. 'Youngens fer th wars an them factories.'

19

He turned his head sharply away, as if he wished to hear no more, but almost at once his unwilling glance was flicking the child's face where the blueness was thinning, and the eyes, less bulging now, showed their dark coloring through the half open lids. 'Your child needs a hospital,' he said, looking past her through the window. 'You'd better go with us until we reach one.'

'Th closest that ud take him with a disease like this is mebbe Lexington—an that's nigh a hunnert miles away.' She wiped a trickle of yellowish saliva from one corner of his mouth. 'He needs some drugs, like they give fer this, right now—he oughtn't to wait.'

'He needs oxygen,' the man said. They were silent again, and once more the sounds of the child's battle for breath filled the quiet car. 'Do you farm?' the officer asked in the same aimless, desperate, sound-making voice.

'A little.'

'I guess every family back in these hills has a little patch of land and keeps a cow or so and a few sheep.'

The woman turned and looked at him, her quiet gray eyes questioning. She gave a slow headshake. 'Not everbody has got a little piece a land.'

'I suppose you have.'

She shook her head again with a slowness that might have been weariness. 'We're renten,' she said, 'on Old John Ballew's place; he gits half—we git half.' She hesitated, then added slowly, in a low voice, as if not quite certain of her words. 'Now, that is; but—we're aimen—we're buyen us a place—all our own.'

'How nice,' he said, still making sound, giving a quick glance at the child. 'A place for you and your children to live while your husband is in service.'

'Yes,' she said. A warm look came into her troubled eyes as when she had spoken of the block of wood. 'Silas Tipton's went off to Muncie to work in a factory. He wanted his wife an youngens with him, so he sold his place. It's a good place—old, a long house—big an built good like they built in th old days. He sold it to Old John Ballew fer to git money to move on. Old John don't want th place. His boys is all gone.'

He nodded. 'So you'll buy it; farm it while your husband's gone.'

'Yes,' she said, speaking with more certainty than before, as if her words had made the land her own. 'My biggest boy, Reuben, he's twelve,' and her eyes were warm again. 'He likes farm work an he's a good hand.'

'You like to farm,' he said, not asking, glancing at her wide shoulders and muscle-corded wrists showing beneath the too short coat sleeves.

She nodded. 'I've allus farmed. My father had a big farm—I hepped him when I was growen up. My brother is—' She stopped, went on again, but the words were a thick mumble. 'Way younger than me.'

After a little space of level road, they were going down again, and the rainy autumn dark came swiftly down like a settling bird. There were sharp steep curves where the dripping limestone cliffs above gave back the sound of the car's horn, and below them lay a narrow black plain pricked with lights. A train blew high above them somewhere in the limestone walls. The child started at the strange sound, and the woman whispered, 'Nothen's goen tu hurt you, honey.'

On the low road in the village by the Cumberland, the lighted windows of homes were squares of brightness behind the shadows of the leafless, dripping trees. Then came sidewalks with store windows bright above them, and the driver went more slowly, looking first this way and that. The woman looked at the windows filled with many different things, and on them all were pasted white or red or blue or yellow sheets of paper that bore pictures of Uncle Sam, of soldiers, of sailors, of airmen, of pretty girl soldiers with neat hair; but all held big black words like the red sign on the pine tree: 'GIVE, RED CROSS—JOIN THE WACS—GIVE BLOOD—WORK AT WILLOW RUN.'

The car stopped in a wash of light from a broad window, while high above the road more lights made a brightness on the wet leaf-plastered sidewalks that lay on either side the street. The woman, as if unaccustomed to so much brightness, squinched her eyes and twisted her head about as she drew the blanket more closely about the child.

'Wait,' the officer said. 'Hatcher, make certain there is a doctor's office close by and that he is in.'

21

The woman watched the soldier go across the street, then glanced at the officer, who was looking out his window as he rolled it down. A door had opened on the street, and through it came a burst of jukebox music. The woman looked toward the sound, a shadow of girlish interest in her troubled eyes, then her glance went swiftly back to the officer's head, and not taking her eyes from him, she lifted the child on one arm, and with a quick and furtive movement reached into her coat pocket, her hand going down into the lining, searching. The man turned a little, glancing at her in his quick, impatient way, and her hand at once became still, and did not search again until he had turned away.

The hand was still again when the young soldier opened the door, saying, 'The doctor's in his office right across the street.'

The woman hesitated, moving toward the opened door, but looking at the officer, her hand, folded into a fist, coming slowly out of the bottom of her coat. She flushed, opening the fist, showing a worn and limp bill. 'I want tu pay you fer th ride,' she said, 'but I can't find th right change.'

The officer looked at the outstretched five-dollar bill, surprise and disgust reddening his face. 'I wouldn't think of charging,' he said, staring at the bill, so worn, so wrinkled, the five was hardly legible.

'But I aimed tu pay,' she said, touching his hand with the money.

He reached quickly for the money like one suddenly changing his mind. 'I can change it,' he said, and turning away from her drew out a wallet; but it was only after she was out of the car that he put bills, folded closely together, into her hand, saying. 'A dollar's fair enough, I guess.' And then, 'Good luck. Help her across the street Hatcher.'

'I can manage,' she said, dropping the money into her apron pocket.

The young soldier stooped quickly and picked up a small bright thing fallen from the folds of the child's blanket. He handed it to her as they walked across the highway. 'Keep it for the baby,' he said. 'Stars like that are kind of scarce.'

'Oh,' she said, 'th man's star—I didn't mean to tear it off. You'd better give it back to him; somebody'ull git him fer losen it. I've heared they're mighty hard on soldiers if their clothes don't look right.'

'Not on the likes of him,' the other said. They had gone a little distance down the sidewalk when the man pointed to a lighted doorway a few steps back from the street. 'There's the doctor's,' he said.

She glanced timidly toward the door. 'I ain't never been to a doctor before. Clovis, my husband, he's allus took th youngens th few times it was somethen Sue Annie couldn't cure.'

His flat, absent-minded eyes opened wide in astonishment. 'Lady, you can't be afraid of nothing. Just walk in.'

2

She stepped into a small square hallway and stood an instant hesitant before its two closed doors, then opened the one that looked most used. She walked into the room behind the door, then stopped suddenly, blinded by the unaccustomed lights and confusedly aware that what seemed to be a whole roomful of people sitting on chairs and sofas and standing by the walls had looked up at her coming. They now turned to her with the quick, interested glances of people so long hemmed together with their pains and troubles that any occurrence no matter how trivial, is a welcome diversion. They looked more intently now, for she was large beyond any woman most had ever seen, and there was from the rough clothing, disheveled hair, and mud-streaked face the crying need for help.

A thin hump-shouldered woman with a sleeping baby across her knees pressed herself into a corner of a small sofa to make room between herself and a teen-age boy in overalls with blood-stained bandages over most of his head and half his face.

Gertie backed swiftly away. 'Your baby might git this bad disease—an mine cain't wait.' She hurried back into the hall, knocked on the other door. A woman from the waiting room called in a sharp, city-like voice: 'Th doctor's busy sewing up a man's leg. You'll have to wait your turn.'

Gertie knocked more loudly. When no one came she opened the door and went into a small room furnished with a desk, two chairs, and books on open shelves. She saw another door, and was opening

24

it when a woman all in white came quickly through it. 'You must wait outside—or better, come back. Th doctor's—'

'I cain't,' Gertie interrupted. She pulled back the blanket, held Amos toward the woman.

The nurse looked down at Amos, studied his face an instant before she saw the blood-streaked neck set with the wooden pipe. She turned swiftly away, opening the door behind her. She was half-way across the next room before her voice came even and smooth, 'This way, please.'

Gertie followed through another small room lined with shelves filled with bottles and jars, past an open door through which she saw a man stretched under a bright light on a high bed-like table while over him a tall man worked. She heard groans and smelled something that made her think of whisky.

The nurse left her in a tiny room that held nothing but a high iron bed, one chair, and a bright white light in the ceiling. Near the foot of the bed was a window, and Gertie saw just past the glass, clear in the white light, the limb of a maple tree to which still clung a few pale rain-dripping leaves. 'Put the baby on the bed and undress him—if you can without hurting his neck,' the nurse said, and was gone. She was back with the doctor before Gertie had Amos out of his overalls.

He was a tall thin man with pale skin and pale hair, though his eyes, set in crinkles now, were the kind of bright quick blue that might once have gone with red hair. He considered Amos briefly, but unlike the nurse he let his eyes stop and stay on the wooden pipe. His mouth opened, then closed, opened again as he said to the nurse in a slow, seemingly unconcerned voice that he might have used to discuss the weather, 'I believe you'd better set up the oxygen tent.' And to Gertie, 'I believe we'd better use a different kind of tube.' And over his shoulder to the nurse, now tap-tapping away, 'We'd better rig up an IV, put what drugs we can in it. Break out that new box of serum—I used the last on that case in Hidalgo. Better bring it first.' And back to Gertie as he fitted a stethoscope to his ears, 'Been sick long?'

She flushed and said in a low voice, 'Three days.' Her voice grew even lower, more guilty-seeming, 'Ole Dave Sexton's hawgs got in our corn. Th fodder's stripped, but th corn ain't gethered, an me an th boys, we worked all day a tryen to save it—messed up it was, down on the muddy ground. I ought . . .'

She stopped, uncertain of whether or no the doctor heard. He had plugs in his ears and was listening to Amos. She stood pulling the knuckles of her left hand with her right, studying the doctor's face as though it were a page of writing in an unfamiliar hand.

He finished and looked at her. 'Diphtheria out your way?'

She nodded above her wringing, pulling hands. 'But I didn't know—till down in the evenen today. Sue Annie come an told me. Will he—' She looked toward the wooden pipe. 'Did I do—wrong? I couldn't jist stand an watch him.'

He took the hypodermic needle the nurse handed him, and shot stuff into Amos's hip. 'I believe you've done all right,' he said, but still she couldn't read his eyes or his voice, could only comfort herself with the realization that Amos was now more able to fight the needle than her knife. Still, when the nurse came in rolling an iron tube of a thing on wheels with one hand, the other holding a tray covered with a towel, and he told her to wait outside, she was more afraid than ever.

Gradually, she grew conscious of the sounds around her; she heard what she knew was a telephone ringing; the nurse would come and talk in another room and the ringing would for a little while be still. She heard often the words 'doctor' and 'busy,' and once the nurse said, 'He'll get there in time—her pains are still five minutes apart.' In between times she heard groans from the room she had come past, and now and then, smothered and low through the walls, the cries of babies, the low-voiced talk of the waiting sick people, the opening and closing of the outside door as more came in; and with each opening of the door there came, like the splatters of rain on the window, loud dance music from the juke box across the street.

The nurse was constantly hurrying back and forth, and once, when she passed with a bottle in one hand, a stand in the other, rubber tubing dangling down her shoulder, Gertie heard her through the open door: 'There's a boy outside wants you to come to his

26

father—pneumonia, they think; bloody vomit, pain, out of his head with fever, sick about a week, about six miles east of Sweet Gum in a bend of the Cumberland. He offered to bring a mule to the end of the graveled road. Dr Barnett, he said, had made it in his Model A with chains even in muddy weather. I told him you couldn't come; but he won't go away.'

'Dr Barnett's somewhere in the Pacific studying up on tropical diseases—hadn't touched a patient, the last I heard,' the doctor said and then sighed, a long shivering sigh that seemed to begin at the bottom of his belly. 'I guess maybe we'd better send some sulfa pills. Pills,' he said, and there was silence between them as they worked with Amos; and then, like a man finished with one thing and able to think of another, 'How's the Osgood business?'

'They've telephoned twice for you to come, but she's not had convulsions.'

'I don't like her blood pressure,' he said.

'But she was like that the other time,' she said.

'But this time the baby's been dead so long.' He was moving toward the door, and Gertie hurried toward him. He looked away from Amos, and if he saw the questions in her eyes he made no move to answer them, but asked, 'Up all last night and worked all today in the rain?'

She nodded.

'Sleepy?'

She shook her head.

'You'll have to sit all night by his bed and watch that tube. Don't let it plug up; if you doze and it plugs he'll choke. Don't go into the waiting room—half the children in this county haven't been immunized. I'll look in again, maybe around midnight.'

The nurse lingered an instant and smiled a tired smile. 'There's a place across the street sells coffee—some time later maybe I can stay with him long enough for you to run get a cup, or if I get a chance, I'll bring you some.' And she was gone after the doctor.

Gertie leaned a long time over Amos, looking down at him in the tent. She studied the needle in his arm, the bottle hanging above him, frowned over the new tube in his neck; such a flimsy little thing it looked to hold the windpipe open. After a while there was a drop on the end of it, and she reached through the tent flap and wiped it away; then quickly and with a guilty air she felt his pulse, but it was only for a moment; almost at once she took her hand away and smiled a faint but joyful smile.

She sat by the bed, stiff and still in the straight-backed chair, twisting her head at times, or shielding her eyes with her hand against the white down-beating light. She watched and listened to the child, but her empty hands were restless; they smoothed back her hair, straightened her coat, touched Amos, and at last began to pick the Spanish needles off the faded apron. The picking was too slow, and without looking away from the child she let one hand go into her apron pocket and bring out the knife, swiftly, already open and ready for work.

However, the knife, instead of scraping on the Spanish needles, hung idle above her lap while she reached in her pocket with the other hand and brought out the officer's change from the five-dollar bill, forgotten until now. She began to unfold the tight little wad with the thumb and finger of her left hand, but hardly was it half unfolded when the knife dropped into her lap and she seized the money with both hands. She unfolded the four bills quickly, staring hard at each. She sprang up. The forgotten knife slid to the floor and lay there while she held a bill under the light. She turned the bill over and over, felt it between thumb and finger, rubbed her eyes, looked again. Turn by turn she examined each bill, but always each showed a ten in one corner on one side, a ten in the middle on the other.

She stood a long time holding the money, looking about, glancing now and then at the child as if to make certain he was asleep. The man in the next room groaned, and someone spoke to him, a soft whispering, the words lost in the wall. Gertie glanced uneasily toward the door, hesitated; but like a mother whose eyes and hands cannot get enough of a newborn child she smoothed each bill between her hard palms, whispered the letters of the name, 'H-a-m-i-l-t-o-n.'

She remembered her knife, picked it up, and dropped it into her pocket. She sat down, watched Amos, but still her glance went often to the money as she spread it widely in her lap so that all of each bill showed. Now and then she looked uneasily over her shoulder, and always she listened. She heard cars on the highway, slithering in the rain. Twice they stopped, and there were feet running up the steps, then knockings on the doctor's door. Sometimes a train whistle blew, and once again there came a faint spattering of music.

Clutching the money, she got up to wipe another drop from the tube, and then was restless, pacing back and forth in the tiny room. She had stopped to watch the maple bough swinging, tapping the window in the spattering rain, when she heard a truck, loud, the motor coughing a little, coming down the highway from the south. She waited, her face tense with listening while the truck stopped and feet came up the steps, across the porch; there came then a loud, insistent knocking. Somebody answered at last and this time the feet did not go away. She heard them over the linoleum in the storeroom. Swiftly she shoved the money down into the secret place below the tornness of her coat pocket, shook the coat, gave the cloth a swift critical glance as if to make certain it kept its secret well, then stood straight and still and watched the door.

It opened slowly part way, and a man's voice, troubled for all its slow softness, asked, as if afraid of the answer, 'Well, how is he?'

'Better,' she said, not moving toward the door, but looking again at the coat pocket, then quickly at Clovis, his tall thin body stooped a little, his forever hunched shoulders hunched still more as they always were when he stepped through a strange door, for he was as tall as she, but without the bigness of bone or width of shoulder.

He continued to hesitate in the doorway, throwing his worried glance first at her and then at the tent over Amos with the half emptied bottle of yellowish liquid hung above it. The fright grew in his eyes. 'He's a goen to be all right,' she said, her voice reassuring, gentle as if speaking to a troubled child.

He drew a long shivering breath, came through the door, straightened, and tiptoed toward the bed. 'I figgered everthing ud be all right when old Dock come home jist as I was pullen in with th truck. I lowed you'd been lucky an got a ride quick.'

29

She nodded. 'Yes, I got a ride—quick.'

'Your mom wouldn't give in fer me tu leave her bed. I stayed till th worst uv her fainten spells was over. An anyhow I didn't have gas enough tu git all th way in—I had to go to th Valley an beg em fer gas like I was asken fer my life an . . .' His jaw dropped, and he gave a low whispered, 'I'll swan,' as for the first time he saw the cut neck. His long hand went to her shoulder, gripped it. 'I knowed he was bad er you wouldn't a gone runnen off to th doctor an yer mom a needen you so—but I didn't low he was that bad er I'd a left yer mom an come.'

Gertie's voice came kind and comforting. 'I'm th one ought to ha knowed—sooner. I was bad worried but kept a thinken all day— I'd run back ever little while to look at him an ask Clytie how he'd been—but I was still a worken in th corn a thinken it was croup when Aunt Sue Annie come an told me. "Git on thet mule an go," she said.'

Clovis's hand did not leave her shoulder. 'I hope you didn't have to stand an watch that doctor cut that hole.' He turned away, gagging, paling.

She hesitated, studying Amos, then slowly shook her head. 'I didn't watch.'

He stood half in and half out the doorway, bothered by the rough whistling breath as the officer had been bothered. 'I'll have to think up somethen tu tell yer mom. When I left her she made me promise to send you back to set out th night with her. I never had th heart to tell her Amos was kinda sick.'

'Whyn't you tell her th truth? The hawgs was in th corn an I had to save it.'

'Tell her that you was a worken when you'd jist heared your onliest brother was . . . I told her you was plum broke down with grieven.'

She looked away from him to the maple bough, tapping again. 'I felt better worken out in th rain—when old Uncle Ansel come riden an told me th word that Red Cross woman brung I couldn't set still. She'll know, or leastways Pop'ull know it was a tale you told. I never did break down.'

'You're like Mom,' he said, 'a waiten fer word on Jesse. Hearen this on Henley has kind a chirked her up. "They won't git two frum a little place like Deer Lick," she says. An it takes more'n I've got tu let on to her that a six-months-old telegram that says missen in action is about th same as—'

'It ain't,' Gertie said, and asked, 'How's Pop?'

'Holden up fine, I recken; to tell th truth I didn't see much uv him. Somebody said he'd done th barn work an was whittlen away on a ax handle.'

'White oak?'

'I don't rightly know.'

'He allus took to oak when somethen bothered him er his leg hurt bad. Anybody give him any supper an did he eat?'

Clovis was getting impatient with her questions. 'I tell ye, Gert, I never was away frum yer mom's bed. Somebody cooked. Ann Liz Cramer brung me an yer mom both big plates a grub.'

'Mom eat?'

He nodded. 'It tuck a heap a beggen, though. We all told her to eat an keep up her strength. She was mighty weak but she cleaned up her plate pretty good.'

'She ain't so bad off then, I recken.'

'Now, Gert, you know how weakly yer mom is. Why, this trouble ull lay her up most a th winter—she was a wonderen when you could git down to do th washen. It ain't like,' he went on after Gertie had wiped another drop from the tube, 'Henley was saved. She cain't git reconciled to him a goen without salvation. She's sent fer Battle John Brand tu come an pray.'

'Prayen cain't help Henley—now.'

'Yer mom wants Battle John to pray to God to give her peace. She cain't git reconciled,' he repeated, patient as if he talked to a child, but irritated by her lack of understanding. 'She cain't git reconciled,' he went on in a lower voice, glancing at Amos as if afraid he might hear. 'She cain't never meet Henley in heaven when he ain't been saved.'

'Mom could backslide an go to hell if she's so certain Henley'ull be there.'

Clovis looked at her an instant in silent horror, then gave a mournful headshake, his large light brown eyes troubled. 'Gert, you're so riled up with all this trouble at one time you don't know what you're a sayen.'

She was silent, her head bowed against the down-beating light as from a rain, her hands twisting as when she had stood outside the door while the doctor worked on Amos. 'Clovis?' she asked, her voice hesitant, apologetic. 'Couldn't you set with Amos fer a little minute while I run git me some cawfee.'

'It's a pouren th rain.'

'I know, an I cain't smell it er hear it. It's—it's like bean buried alive—an it's so hot in here. Somewhere's hid away they's a mighty big fire; th doctor's gone, th place could be a burnen down.'

Clovis smiled at her ignorance, moved toward the door, and stood with one hand on the knob. 'Take yer coat off, then. Th doctor's got a furnace down in th basement, fancy kind with a stoker. Many's th load a stoker coal I've hauled fer him. You need more'n cawfee. You ain't never in your life had a hamburger. I'll git you one; they're real good.'

She shook her head. 'I ain't hungry. I jist want cawfee.' She hesitated, then went on in a low, half ashamed voice, 'It ud be kind a nice to listen to that music while I drunk . . .'

'Music,' he said, and was horrified and troubled again. 'Music at a time like this—dance music. Gert, they's no use a diggen up old troubles—what's done is done—but, well, if'n you'd never a heared dance music you'd a been a lot better off—an—an Henley, too.'

'I recken,' she said, plucking Spanish needles from her apron, 'Mom's been a recollecten that time I danced in th square dances when Pop played his fiddle at Clem Sexton's—close to twenty years ago—a couple a years fore we was married, an that's fifteen.'

'Henley's goen brung it all to her mind afresh,' he said, half apologetically. 'Him a loven dancen an fiddle music an . . . Aw, Gert, you're all wore out an half out a yer head with grief an trouble. You know it was yer arguen an hunten through the Bible an a quoten what it said about dancen, stid a taken th preacher's word an asken forgiveness an repenten like a body—'

32

'Lemme go, Clovis, git out a this place fer jist a minute.'

He went through the door, saying over his shoulder, 'Gert, honey, you'd better let me go. You ain't looked in a looken glass lately; you've got mud splashes all over an yer hair's straggeldy.' He looked down at her feet. 'An you fergot to put on your Sunday shoes.'

She flushed; Clovis as always was neat and clean, for, as he said, he couldn't go around looking like a tramp when he hauled coal. The overalls of her starching were ironed to the smoothness of glass, cuffed neatly above his clean and mud-free shoes, and the new red and black checked woolen shirt he'd bought only three or four weeks before was clean with all its buttons. She looked from him to her own rough, muddied clothing, just as it was when she'd worked in the corn. She sighed. 'Don't be a wasten good money on fancy grub fer me. It'll take a heap fer this sickness.'

He smiled, half pleased, half troubled. 'You're fergitten I'll be goen on Uncle Sam's pay roll in a few weeks—you'll have money regular ever month.' And when he returned some time later, he brought two hamburgers in a paper bag as well as a mug of coffee. She took only the coffee, pushing the grease-stained bag away.

'You eat it,' she said, and with a last glance at Amos took the coffee and hurried out the back door. She walked slowly along the cement walk that led to the front porch, lifting her face to feel the rain, for after the bright whiteness of the hot little room, the cold rain and the dark were like old friends. She tried an instant to look into the sky to find the north star and so find herself, but the lights were bright and the clouds an even gray so that as she sat on the top porch step and drank her coffee she knew not where she was.

She drank the coffee slowly and tried to find the music underneath the rain and the passing cars, but if it came at all it was faint and far away as thunder when the clouds are lost behind the hills. The coffee was almost finished when a car stopped with a quick slithering squeal and a man got out and hurried up the walk, followed by a woman. She had risen and stood a little to the side to let them pass before she saw in the half darkness that it was the doctor and his nurse. 'How's the little one?' he asked, not bothering to look at her face but glancing once at her great size and then moving on.

'A sleepen like a lamb,' she said. He was past her, opening the door into the waiting room before the question in her head could begin to shape itself on her tongue. 'Doctor, tell me—how is it in th Army when a man—gits killed? In battle, I mean.'

He was opening his office door before she had finished. He turned slightly and looked at her. 'It all depends,' he said. 'In this war they kill men by different methods in different places; most, I suppose, die by . . .'

She came very close to him, the forgotten coffee mug held tightly in her hand. 'Oh, I don't mean, Doctor, if he was shot—or—or tore up in little pieces by a bomb or killed by his own gun a goen bad; but jist before he died did they pick him up—an take him to a—a hospital.'

The nurse was speaking behind her, speaking in a bright, reassuring tone, quickly, as if she had already said the same thing to lots of other people. 'All our fighting men when wounded get better care than any other soldiers in any other war. Stretcher bearers come almost at once and carry them to little hospitals right behind the lines. They give them—'

'Not always,' the doctor said. He had stopped and was looking at her, measuring her size and the jut of her nose and the way her forehead rose high and straight above it. 'Sometimes, when the stretcher bearers know they are dying, they leave them alone—outside—they don't bother them. Your maiden name was Kendrick, wasn't it?'

When she had nodded, he said, looking into her face that searched his own for bright, smart lies, 'When we heard about it, I remembered him—he was here several times to get medicine for your mother—and when I saw you, you made me think of somebody but I couldn't think just who. We'd talked sometimes of hunting and farming.'

She nodded. 'People allus said we looked alike. He couldn't abide bein shut up like—back there,' and she motioned with the mug

34

toward the little white room. But he was a doctor again, hurrying away with no time to waste on the dead. She made the bit of coffee last a while, then suddenly afraid Clovis might forget to watch the end of the tube and Amos would choke, she hurried back; but Clovis was by the bed, smiling down at the sleeping Amos.

'That doc give him some shots, an said he was a comen along jist fine, an said sean as how he was doen so good I could mebbe take you all home in a day er two—wrap him up good. He sure is a funny-turned man,' he went on, all his early terror given way to a gay talkativeness. 'When I told him I bet cutten that hole in a human's neck wasn't so easy, he give me th quairest look, an finally he kind a nodded his head an said, "Under th circumstances, it would be hard, very hard." Wasn't that a funny answer frum a doctor? They like to cut holes in people er they wouldn't be doctors.'

'They make big money,' Gertie said, stopping in the doorway. She hesitated, then turned into the storeroom, looking about her. She nodded with satisfaction when she saw a crate-like box, less flimsy than those used for the shipping of oranges, but made of some soft cheap wood unfit now for much of anything but kindling. She turned to Clovis, who had stuck his head around the door, curious as to what she was doing. 'Do you recken th doctor would mind me taken a board er two frum this? A little whittlen foolishness ud make th time pass.'

Clovis bent on her the same look he gave to the truck motor when it made one of its forever different sounds that usually betokened nothing more than old age and hard usage, but always a mystery until he had solved it. 'Nobody ud want that,' he said. 'But if'n you must waste elbow grease on whittlen, couldn't you make a ax handle er somethen somebody could use?'

'I ain't got no wood by me fitten fer handles,' she answered, pulling a board from the box. 'But any kind a whittlen foolishness is better than nothen. I'll make Cassie a real jumpen-jack doll—I been aimen to fer a long time.'

'Th way she's a acten up, she needs a switch stid uv a doll. Went off to th woods right atter you left an didn't git in till jist fore I got there—had Mom all worried—then come in frum getheren eggs an fell flat on th floor; never looked where she was goen an broke two and gommed up th floor. Clytie was a wanten me to spank her.'

'An eggs mighty nigh two fer a nickel at Samuel's,' Gertie said, then added quickly, worriedly, 'But you didn't switch her—did ye, Clovis?'

'Now, Gert, you know I didn't. Mom wouldn't let me no how—but that youngen is a aggravaten little thing.'

Gertie said nothing, and Clovis began wondering on what he should tell her mother to keep her quiet so she wouldn't go into her fainting spells again; and after listening with many headshakes to Gertie's advice to tell her all about Amos, the hole in his neck, the needle in his arm, the tent, and everything, so as to take her mind off Henley, he went away.

She stood near the door, listening until the sound of the truck was gone, she then closed the door gently, looked for a lock or thumb latch and, when she found none, she stood a moment, considering. Then in the same carefully noiseless way, she took the chair, tipped it, and wedged the back under the handle of the doorknob. She looked at the child, still sleeping his drugged, unnatural sleep, listened a moment to his breathing, then called softly, 'Amos?' She called again, and when he did not answer she took off her coat, sat flat on the floor, her legs outspread, her back against the uptipped chair, the coat across her lap. She put her hand down through the torn pocket, and slowly, carefully twisting her hand as if the hole in her pocket were almost the exact size of her hand, she began to bring out worn and grimy bills. Some were folded alone into tiny squares, others were folded two and three together, and many, like the four new bills, were crumpled hastily into tiny balls. Each she unfolded and smoothed flat on the floor with the palm of her hand, looking at it an instant with first a searching, then a remembering glance. Sometimes after a moment of puzzlement she whispered, 'That was eggs at Samuel's two years ago last July,' and to a five, 'That was th walnut-kernel money winter before last,' and to another one, 'That was th big dominecker that wouldn't lay atall; she'd bring close to two dollars now.' Of one so old and thin it seemed ready to fall apart at the creases, she was doubtful, and she held it to the light until she saw the pinhole through Lincoln's eye. 'Molasses money.' She was hurrying now, eager to have it all in a pile, counting, pretending she was uncertain how much there would be.

'Three hundred ten,' she whispered at last, leaning back, looking at it, 'Fifteen year, mighty nigh—an we've got more'n half enough to pay fer th Tipton Place.' Her words had been loud. She sprang up and looked down at the child; the waxy ear lobes were beginning to show a faint trace of pink.

'Oh, honey,' she whispered, 'no worken away an given half to th other man fer you like's been fer Reuben. Soon as your poor daddy gits in th army, we'll git us a place a our own.'

3

Gertie held the Bible open at Ecclesiastes. She stood with her back to the open front door, and faced the five children. Amos, still a shade pale and thin from his sickness of three weeks back, sat on a sheepskin rug near the heating stove. The four older ones, neat and quiet in their Sunday clothes, sat in a row between the two beds that stood, one in each back corner of the big low-ceilinged, small-windowed room. Her reading seemed a talking, for she looked more often at the children than at the Bible page, saying the words sometimes when her eyes went past the children to the rows of October-colored hills that lay behind the back window.

' "One generation passeth away, and another generation cometh: but the earth abideth for ever. . . . All the rivers run into the sea; yet the sea is not full; unto the place from whence the rivers come, thither they return again. . . . The thing that hath been, it is that which shall be; and that which is done is that which shall be done; and there is no new thing under the sun." '

She stopped, her finger under a word, cleared her throat, and looked at the children. 'What th old preacher—recollect he was a smart man—th son uv David, means, I allus thought, is to tell us that whatever kind a luck comes, good er bad, it has already come to somebody afore us. Right now they's trouble over all th world, an trouble right in our settlement—but it won't be ferever. It'll—' Twelve-year-old Reuben, her oldest boy, alone was listening. He searched her face, frowning, with one hand absent-mindedly pulling against the blanket roll of the old wild cherry bed. He had her eyes

38

and bigness of bone and cast of face—a straight mouth, and still gray eyes, solemn, that to a stranger might seem sullen.

'But th trouble cain't go away,' he said. 'Uncle Henley cain't come back.'

Clytie, the biggest girl, and two years older than Reuben, looked up from staring at a little silver guitar strung on a silver chain around her wrist, a gift of her Uncle Henley, and put on now for Sunday. Henley had sent her the bracelet when he wrote his last letter from a place in Texas. He had sent more things to her than to the others for she had been his favorite, though in looks she was not akin to him at all. Thin-boned and pretty, Clytie was, with her father's large shiny brown eyes and chestnut-colored hair, worn always in two thick braids, each formed of three smaller ones, so that now as she sat with bowed head, weeping, the braids coming away from the middle seemed like folded satiny wings upon her head; and her face, unlike Reuben's, was not ugly in sorrow, held no anger, no questions that would never be answered because there were no answers. She turned now to Reuben with a sisterly rebuke, 'It was God's will.'

'That they took Henley off an killed him. If he'd ha been a bigger, richer farmer—'

'Hush,' Gertie said. 'It's been happenen to men since th beginnen. Listen to old Ecclesiastes: "I returned, and saw under the sun, that the race is not to the swift, nor the battle to the strong, neither yet bread to the wise, nor yet riches to men of understanding, nor yet favour to men of skill; but time and chance happeneth to them all." Allus you've got to recollect, youngens, that a sober hard-worken man could go hungry an a good man go to jail, but—'

The children were not listening: Clytie sniffled above the silver guitar; Reuben thought of Henley; the others were most too little. Enoch, the nine-year-old, sat stiff and straight on a chair like a boy having his picture taken, his new overalls neatly creased from Clytie's iron as he had directed, his hair parted, his eyes on his mother, but with a critical, almost an accusing, glance. Amos, the baby one, and not yet four, studied two hickory nuts between his outspread legs.

Cassie sat on the block of wild cherry wood, as quietly as she was ever able to sit, wiggling, giggling, whispering. Gertie looked at her sternly until she sat consciously still, her thin legs, that looked even thinner above Enoch's last spring's shoes, held carefully straight and still by the block of wood, her arms folded over her stomach, her hair, the color of corn silk, escaped from its braids and fallen across her bright dark eyes, laughing now in spite of the prim straightness of her mouth.

Gertie went on at last, but only Cassie's eyes were upon her as she read: ' "For man also knoweth not his time: as the fishes that are taken in an evil net, and as the birds that are caught in the snare; so are the sons of men——" '

Cassie with a low laugh had slid from the block of wood, her bottom striking hard against the floor. She turned and hit the block of wood, crying in her laughter-bubbling voice, 'You mean youngen, quit a pushen me.'

Gertie folded her lips together, looked hard at Cassie. 'What am I a doen, Cassie Marie?'

Cassie flipped hair out of her eyes, the backward motion flinging her head against the block of wood; and leaning so with her head against the wood, she considered her mother's question. 'Why, I recken you're a tryen to preach at us like Samuel.'

Clytie cried, 'Make her behave, Mom, acten like a heathern,' and Enoch corrected:

'Mom cain't preach; she's not so much as a church member, crazy.'

'I ain't preachen,' Gertie said, 'but somebody's got to teach you th Bible. Don't you know, youngens,' she went on, 'that a long, long time ago, away back afore ever old John Kendrick—you recollect his grave's in our graveyard, an many's th time you've heard your granpa tell on how he rid a mule into th battle a Brandywine, an how that mule outswum them horses—well, away a long time back afore he was born his people warn't allowed to read their Bibles. In them days a Bible cost a heap a money an a body had to read em on th sly. But more than enything, them people—they was your people, recollect—wanted a place where they could read their Bibles when an how they pleased. An now jist because our preacher's gone to Oak Ridge an they ain't enough people left fer Sunday school, that's no reason to do without th Bible. We need it worse right

40

now in this evil-net time.' She looked at Reuben. 'Can you say th commandments any better than last Sunday?'

The children grew ever more restless as slow-tongued Reuben struggled through the Ten Commandments, helped at times by impatient promptings from Clytie, who already knew the commandments, the blessings, and the Lord's Prayer. Gertie looked once behind her through the open door and frowned a little on the shortening shadow of the house, but continued with the memory work. She listened while Enoch repeated the blessings, swiftly, tonelessly, going ever faster until when he reached, 'Blessed are ye when men shall revile you and persecute you and shall say all manner of evil against you falsely for my sake,' his words were blurred as those of a too swiftly played phonograph.

Clytie, carefully, and with a clear pronunciation, different from her everyday speech, recited the psalm that Gertie had suggested she learn: ' "God is our refuge and strength, a very present help in trouble; therefore will we not fear, though the earth be removed . . ." '

Clytie finished, and together they recited the Lord's Prayer. But before the prayer was finished, Clovis, long since through with his Sunday's shaving in the kitchen, cleared his throat impatiently; and hardly was the 'Amen' ended before the line of children broke apart, and Clovis reminded from the kitchen door:

'Gert, we've all got to be a goen. Yer mom's already taken it hard cause you ain't come sooner. An—well, you know—I've got to tell my folks goodbye.' He caught Enoch's troubled glance. 'Go visit with em, I mean. It ain't like I was leaven next week fer good.'

'Yes,' Gertie said, but was still, looking through the window toward the hills. Clytie was crying again. The other children were too silent, and Clovis, when he did speak again, was choked and hoarse, 'Aw, Clytie, honey, don't start a carryen on so. Pshaw, it'll mebbe all be over fore I go.'

Gertie drew a sharp quick breath, then turned to the children, 'Your Granma Nevels wants you all to come, too, today, when your pop goes to—' She managed to smile. 'Law, he's just goen fer a visit. A body ud think from all this carryen on that Wednesday he was goen acrost th waters stid uv jist fer his examination. An I don't

41

want a one a you to be a snifflen an a carryen on about yer daddy goen off in front a yer Granma Nevels. Recollect he's her boy, an she's got three gone.' Her voice hoarsened. 'I've got to go see my mother, yer Granma Kendrick. I ain't been to see her an Pop since your Uncle Henley—'

She couldn't go on; and anyway Enoch, looking ever more accusing, was saying: 'You're allus sayen that everything's goen to be all right; an Uncle Henley he's dead, an Uncle Jesse, he's been missen so long he's same as—'

'Alive,' Gertie said with loud conviction.

Clytie, recovered from her tears, looked accusingly at Cassie. 'Mom, cain't you take Cassie Marie with you? I jist cain't make that youngen behave. T'other day when you was gone with Amos, she kept asken Granma Nevels when was Uncle Jesse comen home—like she didn't know it was nigh six months ago that th missen-in-action telegram come, an that Uncle Jesse's most likely—'

'Alive,' Gertie repeated. 'Keep your Granma Nevels a thinken that. They wouldn't git two frum sich a little place. We'd better git goen now. Cassie Marie, honey, I guess you had better go with me.' She saw the disappointment in the child's face at losing the trip in the coal truck to see her favorite grandmother, and comforted, 'We'll have us a pretty walk through th woods.' Then to Enoch, pulling on his jacket as he ran to the coal truck. 'Recollect, no snifflen now. Be good, an make Granma Nevels happy.'

Reuben lingered in the doorway, 'Mom—cain't I go hunten? I seed Granma and Granpa Nevels Friday when I hauled em up some wood. Couldn't I go hunten an then hep Granpa Kendrick with his night work this evenen?' He looked hopefully, but doubtfully, at his mother, and then at Clovis, who was getting Amos into his coat.

'Yer Granpa Kendrick ud be mighty glad to see you,' Clovis said, 'but you know yer mom er me neither don't hold by hunten an carousen around on Sunday, specially when Henley's—when they's so much trouble in th settlement.'

Gertie looked through the door, past the rented ridge field to the hills, warm-looking and soft and kind in the yellow autumn sun after the frosty night. 'He's worked hard all fall,' she said, 'down at Mom's an here, a saven that hog-messed-up corn in th rain.' She drew a shivering breath. 'Henley would mebbe a gone hunten today.'

Clovis picked up Amos. 'Well, whoever's riden with me, come on,' he called, as he started for the truck.

Clovis was put out, Gertie realized, by her unreligious ways in letting Reuben hunt on Sunday. Still, she had no heart to forbid the boy to go. He had already gone for the little twenty-two that Henley had given him on his tenth birthday. Enoch ran to help Clovis with the business of filling the truck radiator, which he had drained the night before against the frosty cold, while Clytie got the many-layered jelly cake they had baked yesterday for Granma Nevels. Clovis poured a thin trickle of gas into the carburetor. In an instant, blue flame whooshed up. As always Cytie squealed, Gyp barked, the younger boys cried out in delight, and Clovis, his eyes beaming with gratification, exulted, 'She's started.'

Only Reuben, walking now through the last summer's cornfield where the thin blade-stripped stalks rose no higher than his shoulders, did not glance at the truck. 'Don't be a shooten me and Cassie, now, son,' Gertie called above the sound of the motor. 'Recollect, we'll be comen down through th woods past th old Tipton Place.'

He had walked slowly on, giving little sign that he listened to her warning, but at the words Tipton Place he stopped short, then turned and looked at her. 'That Tipton Place, it's pretty, Mom,' he said. He seemed eager to say more, but after a cautious glance toward Clovis lifting Amos into the cab he only looked a moment at his mother, his eyes narrowed in thought. He turned swiftly about then, and strode across the field.

Gertie watched him and nodded with satisfaction over the way he carried his rifle. Clovis and the other children were calling and waving good-bye. She stood a moment longer on the porch, and waved and watched the battered truck go lurching down the rutted lane.

A low laugh caused her to look behind her. She hurried back into the middle room, saying with more sorrow in her voice than chiding, 'Cassie Marie, quit kicken that block a wood. You'll be ruinen it.' She knelt and smoothed the wood with her apron, and examined it for scratches.

Cassie, who had been lying on the sheepskin, kicking the wood with her heels, was troubled, and patted the wood as she, kneeling now, leaned her cheek against it, whispering, 'I didn't mean tu hurt ye, honey, honest.' And to Gertie, with a contrite, hair-flipping headshake, 'I fergot she could feel it, Mom.'

'*Him*,' Gertie said, rising, but still looking down onto the top of the great chunk that stood high as Cassie's shoulders.

'*Her*,' Cassie said, her eyes gay again, teasing. She flung her arms about the wood, laughing, pushing hard to make her fingers touch on the other side. As usual they would not touch, and as always she cried, 'You're so fat—fat as Granma Kendrick's feather beds, you ole fat thing you; an your hair not braided yit. It'll git in yer eyes, Callie Lou, and you'll be cross-eyed, Callie Lou.' Still hugging the wood, she tilted her head far backward, looked up at her mother, begging, 'Part her hair an make braids, Mom.'

It was an old argument between them, the hair on the block of wood, for if one were close enough, looking down in good light, like now, when the early sunshine fell like a curtain by the southern windows, not falling through but making a brightness in the room, the shape of the top of a head with unparted hair swirling loosely away from the center showed clearly. The waving hair might have twisted into curls on its ends, but the curls, like the face, were buried in the wood. There was only the top of a head, tilted forward a little, bowed, or maybe only looking down, but plainly someone there, crouching, a secret being hidden in the wood, waiting to rise and shed the wood and be done with the hiding. Gertie bent, reaching for the sheepskin, and at once the top of the head with its wavy hair was lost below the protecting rim of the wood, and the bright dark block seemed cherry wood only. But Cassie continued to fondle it, begging: 'Take her out, Mom. It's Sunday—she wants out. She's been a waiten there so long—so awful long, ever since I was little.'

'Way before then,' Gertie said, smoothing the sheepskin over the wood. 'He's been a waiten there in th wood you might say since before I was born. I jist brung him out a little—but one a these days, jist you wait an see, we'll find th time an a face fer him an bring him out a that block.'

'An she'll never be whittled up into door locks—she was for door locks, but Granpa Kendrick give her to you; she's too fine fer door locks, th old man said to Granpa, such fine wild cherry wood.'

'They don't make wooden door locks with wooden keys, no more,' Gertie said, going for her coat, looking about her to make certain the room was fit to leave. She shook her head over the ugliness of the tin heating stove, looked with satisfaction on the other things: the rag rug of her mother-in-law's weaving, given to Clovis as a wedding gift; the ceiling-high wild cherry sideboard put together with pegs, the wild cherry bed in one corner, with the tops of the head-high posts carved into the shapes of acorns, bigger and heavier than even the black walnut with the pure round uncarved knobs in the other corner. All these wooden pieces had belonged to her father's grandmother and had been cast off from his house to the barn when her mother came there as a bride.

She was hurrying down the lane toward the gravel road before she realized that Cassie, instead of talking to Callie Lou as was her custom, was talking to her, almost in tears as she said over and over: 'But I've got a mem'ry verse, Mom. You never did ask me did I have a mem'ry verse. You learned it to me,' she added when Gertie turned and looked at her, 'all about shoes an gold an silver, what th old man that kept sheep said.'

Gertie took the child's hand, and Cassie began in her skipping, whispering voice, 'That we may buy the poor for silver, an th needy fer a pair of shoes . . . an sell—an sell—an sell their golden crowns.'

'Now, now, my girl, you're adden things to th Bible; th pore don't have crowns. "An sell th refuse of th wheat," it goes. It means, I recken, that th hungrier some is, th richer some others can git. Nothen much makes sense,' she went on, tucking a wisp of Cassie's hair into a braid, 'without th before an th after. But you done good, real good, to git some a old Amos by heart. When I read him to you all t'other night, I never thought you'd recollect him. You're a real smart girl,' she added, reaching for a cocklebur on the child's dress tail; but Cassie had darted out of arm's reach, and was now tip-toeing for a late-hanging crimson saw-brier leaf near the tumble-down rail fence by the lane.

'But I cain't learn to read,' Cassie said, holding the leaf above her head, and for an instant still, troubled. 'An Clytie an Enoch, they both learned to read fore they was as old as me—but I cain't learn.'

'Don't fret, you'll learn,' Gertie said, trying to put a hearty conviction into her voice. They had never in all their moving about as renters lived less than two miles from a school, so that even before the war she had taught the older ones much at home in bad weather, or when they had no shoes. Since the war had taken the teachers, she had taught them all almost entirely at home. The bigger ones had gone ahead in their books, but Cassie, who could learn anything by heart, had never, in spite of all Gertie's efforts, learned even her letters.

Cassie lagged again, and Gertie, hurrying down the lane, gave a slow headshake, as over a puzzle, as she listened to the child, now in the road, now hidden in the brush, trying at times to skip in the too big shoes, now and then singing snatches of her wordless songs that almost always ended in bursts of laughter or low murmurings. A moment's silence, then Cassie sprang into the road in front of her, whirled about and stood laughing, crying as she pointed to her shoes: 'Lookee, lookee. I've got red shoes like Tildy.'

She had, between the laces on the coarse, crooked shoes, stuck some freshly fallen black gum leaves that lay brilliant red along the road. 'They're sure fine shoes,' Gertie said. 'Where'd you git em?'

'Montgomery Ward, an they costed forty dollars.'

'Law, law, an how did you git so much money?'

'Callie Lou's man—he's gone acrost th ocean to th wars, an he makes good monies—Callie Lou, she brung me th shoes, an six more pairs—golden slippers with silver heels like we take in Needle's Eye.'

'An where's your own man?' Gertie asked, catching at her hand.

Cassie laughed and ran backwards ahead of her. 'Oh, my man, he ain't much account; he lives in th holler heart uv a big dead chestnut tree.' She was spinning about, running away, one hand held out, the fingers carefully curved, her face turned now and again toward the curved hand while some smiling talk went forth to the playmate who ran down the road by her side.

The child's prattle faded. Gertie heard the plop of a falling, frost-sweetened persimmon, the clop of her shoes in the sandy ridge road, and cowbells—her own Lizzie's near, the others far away and faint; but mostly she heard the silence. She walked even faster, running away from the silence, the emptiness; in it would come Henley—never the soldier. She had never seen her brother as a soldier. He had, like others from their settlement, been trained sixteen weeks and shipped across with never another sight of home. Always he came in the silence as the farmer, blue-shirted, a lock of black hair fallen down between his slate-blue eyes; and in the silence, like now, or at night when the work was done and she patched by the fire, there was his face with the questions: 'Why me? What have I done? Why am I dead? Why?'

Unable to answer, she was like a rock bluff, echoing his questions, 'Why?' up to the stars and into the silence of the still Indian-summer noons. 'Why?'

Many times at night, unable to sleep, she had got down the Bible, but mostly she sat in the lean-to kitchen, so as not to waken Clovis or the children, with the book closed across her knees. The old questions that had always been in the Bible for her came back with Henley's one question—Job's children, did they know or question why they died to test the patience of their father? And Jethro's daughter bewailing her fate in the mountains, had she ever, like Henley, asked, 'Why me?' Did Judas ever ask, 'Somebody has to sin to fulfill the prophecy, but why me?'

She walked faster, but slackened her pace when she heard Cassie's prattle, behind her, now. She looked back and saw her high in a wide-branched pine by the road, and called, 'You could fall, climben so high,' her tone kindly with no scolding, speaking less in fear that Cassie might fall than to fling some sound into the silence of road, pine tree, and sky.

'Callie Lou, she's th one that'll fall. She's clean to th tip-top branch. Cain't you see her red dress?'

'She'd better git down,' Gertie said, walking on.

'She's a looken out fer heaven,' Cassie said, but after a little argument with the strong-willed witch child she sprang down and ran after Gertie, walking now in the graveled road that led the six miles to the highway. 'Where's all th coal trucks, Mom?' she asked, coming up to Gertie.

'Them that hauled th coal an them that dug it has had to go to war,' Gertie said. She walked faster again, eager to be away from the empty road that, once so fine and new, tying their settlement to the outside world, seemed now only a thing that took the people away. She turned down the ridge side by a small red gully, crept since the fall rains into the road itself with a bit of the road gravel caught in its red, crumbly sides. Less than two years ago the gully had been the Tipton path. She followed it down through a stand of young poplars, each holding still a few leaves in its topmost branches, yellow as if each tree wore a golden crown. She smiled at one, higher and straighter than the others, as she stopped to listen to Cassie calling from the pine wood around the ridge side, 'Make me a pine cone turkey, Mom, please?' and an instant later the child came running, holding out a fat, fully opened cone.

'Not now. We've got to git on. Your granma's expecten us.'

'But this ain't th way to Granpa Kendricks'.'

'We're goen a new way, down by th old Tipton Place. You recollect th Tiptons; they moved off to Indianee, about a year ago last summer. They had six youngens, one about your size, recollect? Their pop got him a job in a powder plant, an they sold their place to Uncle John Ballew.'

Cassie made a great business of wrinkling her forehead, turned to Callie Lou. 'Can you recollect these little youngens that has gone to war?' Callie Lou must have answered, for the two were deep in conversation as they disappeared in the woods.

Gertie hurried on through the gloom of the young, close-growing pines, over a tumble-down rail fence and through the Tipton new-ground cornfield, a rocky, steeply sloping bit of hillside where the sumac and beech and oak sprouts grew high as her shoulders and the wild grapevines and saw briers caught at her coattail and made traps for her feet. Twice she stooped and scratched at the earth with her fingers. Each time she smiled, for the soil was black and loose still, almost as good as fresh new ground.

48

She crossed a second rail fence, tumble-down like the first, but mended with pine brush piled in the corners and two strands of rusty barbed wire. Below it stood ancient black-trunked dying apple and pear trees, almost lost in the sumac and scrub pine that were smothering the growth of sage grass. One tree with a few knotty red apples still clinging leaned tipsily like a tree not quite blown down, but on going closer she saw the gully, deeper than she was tall, a red wound in the hillside stealing the earth from the tree.

She threw in some fallen dead apple limbs and a few sand rocks, whispering as she walked away, 'That'll hold back a little dirt, an keep this hillside frum bleeden to death.'

She went on, throwing quick searching glances about her. She paused by a row of black gum beehives, most tipped over, their bees dead or moved away, but a few lengths of the hollow logs stood upright, each sloping roof board held in place by one great stone.

Past the beehives and the orchard, sheltered by the curve of the ridge side, and on a southern slope where the early sun struck fully, lay the flattish bench of ungullied land that held the house and yard and barns and garden spot. She smiled on the shake-covered roof of the old log house; the white oak shakes, weathered to a soft gray brownness, must have been rived in the wrong time of the moon, for they had curled in places, and in some of the little cup-like hollows moss had grown. Now in the yellow sun the moss shone more gold than green, and over all the roof there was from the quickly melting frost a faint steam rising, so that the dark curled shakes, the spots of moss, the great stone chimney, all seemed bathed in a golden halo and Cassie called that the house had golden windows.

Some of the golden light seemed caught in Gertie's eyes as she walked down and around and at last stood by the yard gate. It was a good little gate of white oak slats, built to last, like the old walk of limestone stepping-stones half buried in the sod, bordered with clumps of tansy and catnip and hoarhound, brightened by a great bunch of yellow chrysanthemums, so sheltered here on the southern slope that they were blooming still, like the artichokes that grew higher than her head by a porch corner.

Cassie was laughing, pointing. 'Lookee, Mom, th Tiptons is home.' Gertie for the first time noticed the three ewes on the porch, chewing their cuds, and looking for all the world like people who have just stepped out their door to see who their visitors might be. Cassie called, 'Oh, how do you do, Miz Tipton; we've come to set all day,' and ran up the walk.

Old John's half wild ewes went leaping over the three great slabs of stone that made the porch steps. Cassie ran across the porch and pushed against each of the two front doors, big stout things made of three oak planks and three crossbars, but the doors were nailed shut, like the boarded-up windows. Gertie touched the Tipton dipper, rusty now, with a cobweb across it, but hanging still on its nail in a porch post. She walked around the house, hoping for, but never finding, an unboarded window. She brushed twigs and leaves from the high shelf where the Tipton clabber had soured for churning in summer and sweet milk and fresh meat had stood in winter, but the porch shelf, like the puncheon wash bench and rusty tin pan, was empty, forgotten like the ungathered walnuts that lay thick in the grass by the back porch steps, fallen from the big black walnut a little distance up the hillside.

Cassie, running, looking, sniffing, pointing out the wonders of the place, filled her cupped hands with walnuts, and came running back to Gertie, pleased beyond measure that she, who so seldom had anything, now had something to give. She was looking at her mother when she stumbled and fell, her face striking hard against a washed-out walnut root. She sprang up and stood rubbing her mouth and looking down at the spilled walnuts. Gertie put an arm about her waist. 'Cassie, honey, learn to look where you're a goen. Didn't you see that root? You're allus fallen down.'

'It's my shoes, I reckon,' Cassie said, looking fixedly into her mother's eyes so close to her own, then pulling her head away but staring still.

Gertie pulled the laces until the tops of the shoes touched, but still they were loose about Cassie's thin ankles. 'I'm a goen to git you some new shoes one a these days—all your own,' she said, then added quickly, 'Some time along toward spring—it ain't like they was school an you needed pretty shoes. These old uns uv Enoch's can run you through th winter.'

Cassie wasn't thinking of shoes. She was crying now, 'I can see little girls in your eyes, Mom, little bitty girls.'

'They're little Cassies,' Gertie said, bending her head to look at a smear of blood on Cassie's teeth so that the little girls went away. She scooped her up on one arm. 'We'll go down to th spring, honey, an you can rinse that bloodied-up mouth in that good cold spring water.'

Cassie cuddled against her, one arm about her neck, her cheek on her shoulder, all her child for an instant; the other in the red dress was gone. They passed the old log barn, and Gertie lingered a moment to study it. The shake roof was almost gone, but the walls were good and sound, like the hollowed-out chestnut log feed troughs; and in two of the mule stalls, under the good part of the roof, there was such a deal of manure. Her eyes on the good manure were warm as they had been on the house.

They were going down the weed-choked spring path when faintly from the head of the creek they heard two shots, little popping sounds Gertie recognized as Reuben's twenty-two. 'Mebbe your brother's killed us a couple a squirrels,' she told Cassie, but Cassie was asking for a dogwood toothbrush. Gertie cut each of them a red-tipped twig from the little tree of Cassie's choice, and they chewed as they went along, savoring the sharp bitter clean taste of the wood.

The leaf-choked spring seeped from under a limestone ledge at the foot of a great poplar, left by generations of timber cutters because there was, rising up from the roots, a low wide hollow fringed with moss and filled now with fallen leaves. Gertie reached into the hollow where the cup had used to be, and after a little searching brought it out. Pressing it down through the pale poplar leaves, she filled it, rinsed it, gave water to the child, then drank two cups herself, slowly, enjoying the water. Cassie, seeing her mother's leisurely, time-taking ways, began begging again for a toy; but now, instead of the pine-cone turkey, she wanted a doll, 'a doll with a skirt, please, Mom.'

'We oughtn't to be a wasten time thataway,' Gertie said, but was still, looking up toward the house, smiling a little.

Cassie saw her indecision and begged the harder. 'It's nice an warm, now, Mom, here in th sun. We could set on that ole log an make a doll.'

Gertie studied the shadow of the poplar tree. It was still a good while till dinnertime. She looked at the friendly moss-covered log, then turned swiftly about, the knife out of her apron pocket and open in her hand. She searched until she found a smooth-barked little hickory sprout, so crooked it could never grow into a proper tree, and from it cut a piece not much longer than her middle finger but with a little branch on either side, that, no sooner were they shortened, than they seemed arms reaching above the shorter end of the wood, which was no longer the end of a hickory sprout but a doll's head.

Gertie sat on the moss-grown log, and with Cassie leaning on her shoulder she cut on each twig a tiny hand with thumb outspread and fingers close together like those of a child in mittens. Then on the main twig, she cut between the upraised hands a tiny face. Eyes, nose, grew on the face, and the mouth heeded Cassie's plea, 'Make her laughen, Mom.' And above the face she notched the bark to form a jagged crown. Then, far enough from the other end to leave a space for feet, she ringed the bark, and Cassie begged again: 'Make her pretty shoes, Mom. High heels like Gussie Duncan's been a buyen since they took her man off to war an gived her big money.'

'They'll be mighty little,' Gertie warned, as she cut out a little sliver for the space between the feet. Quickly the knife point made shoes grow on the doll—dainty high-arched things with tiny slender heels and the faint tracing of a buckle above each instep, the feet pointing downward like those of a dancer on her toes. 'You'll have to put th diamonds on th shoe buckles, yerself,' Gertie said, lifting her head from the work for a leisurely glance up the hill. She could see the house, and past the strip of shadow that fell slantwise of the yard, the bluegrass, green as grass in spring. The grass, the golden flowers by the house wall, the moss on the roof, the yellow chrysanthemums by the gray stepping-stones, all glowed warmly as if they, with the house on the sheltered southern hillside, were set in some land that was forever spring.

Cassie saw her mother's warm-eyed glances, long glances when the doll lay forgotten, and once, after a moment's peering up the hillside, she said, 'You think that old house's pretty, Mom?'

Gertie nodded. 'But pretty's th least uv it. It'll be warm in th winter an cool in th summer, an no matter how hard th wind blows that house'll never shake, an th hard north wind'ull never tetch it. Recollect, I used to come here when I was a little girl about your size a long time ago. An behind it in th hillside they's a cellar with a smokehouse, an nothen never froze in that cellar, an in th hottest summer weather that cellar was so cold it ud keep milk sweet from one mornen to th next.'

'An we'd put them pears an apples in our cellar, wouldn't we, Mom?'

Gertie nodded. 'An we'd pick blackberries, our own blackberries in our own fields—we'd never have to go a asken my mommie er Old John could we please pick berries. An we'd—'

'Will we have to give Uncle John much a what we raise?'

'Not so much as one blade a fodder. We'll have fat hogs an chick—'

'Mom, make her a curledy skirt.'

Gertie bent to her work again, slitting the bark above the shoes up to the waist in narrow little strips. Then gently with the knife point she lifted each strip free up to the lifted arms, so that there grew upon the doll a little skirt; but winter was in the wood and the bark was brittle from the fall frosts or maybe her mind was not with the knife, for often a fringe of bark was broken so that the skirt was ragged. Still, when the last strip was lifted and Cassie reached for the doll, Gertie held it a moment, smiling. So little, but there was about it something light and joyous as it smiled between its lifted arms above its dancing feet. 'It's a quair-looken thing,' she said, handing it to Cassie.

Cassie brushed the tiny smiling mouth softly against her cheek. 'You're awful late gitten in frum school—it's milken time an th sun's low down. An did you read your lesson good? My, my, ten pages. Ain't you smart?'

'Who's your youngen's teacher, Ma'm?' Gertie asked, dropping the knife into her pocket and getting up.

'Miz Callie Lou, an there ain't no youngen she can't teach to read. She's th finest—' There was a scurrying through the leaves down the hillside, and both turned, listening. 'It's Gyp,' Cassie cried, and began calling him.

Reuben yelled from down near the creek; and a moment later Gyp came, sniffing at Cassie's cheek, leaping on Gertie, who smiled on the big-jointed, high-behinded tree dog, and wanted to know if he'd helped Reuben get a mess of squirrels. But Gyp only shook himself and then lapped greedily in the spring branch. 'Mom, oh, Mom.' It was Reuben again, his calls loud and excited.

Gertie hurried over the rocky creek bluff toward the sound. Reuben wasn't fool enough to hurt himself with his gun, and he was too much at home in the woods for frights and falls, but now the strangeness of his screaming troubled her. She reached the last ledge above the creek, and looked down, and seeing him, unhurt, and with hands empty save for his gun, called in some exasperation, 'Son, you'll never be any kind a hunter a maken noise enough to tangle a flock a wild geese.'

Reuben looked up at her, his slate-gray eyes laughing, like Cassie's eyes. 'I done more'n tangle a flock a wild geese. I shot at a bear in thet pawpaw grove—th biggest ole thing you ever did see—an did he run!'

'A bear! Are you certain? Vadie Sexton said she seed th track a one out by her smokehouse but nobody believed her,' Gertie said, taking Cassie by the shoulders and swinging her down the ledge.

'It was a honest-to-goodness bear; Gyp knowed it wasn't no possom er coon—he give one little runnen growly bark—acten big like he was aimen to fight, an that bear growled an kind a swiped toward him. You ought to ha seen him, Mom. It was a sight! I shot twice to scare him—he never did run, jist kind a walked off. I wish I could ha killed it. Would they have put me in th penitentiary, Mom?'

Gertie listened, her eyes almost as eager as Reuben's. 'Th meat would ha been good an we could ha had us a bear rug—but it's off th game preserve. It's agin th law to kill it. What color was it, son?'

'Browny black . . .' He sighed, smiling a little, reliving the scene with the bear. 'I wisht I'd ha tried to kill it. Wouldn't that a been somethen? I wished Henley could ha . . .' His face was sullen again, as in the morning. He looked down at the gunstock in his hand, the muzzle pointing over his shoulder as Henley had taught him to carry it in the woods.

Gertie cleared her throat. 'Hunten an trappen'ull be good this winter, all up an down th creek, an this place is close enough to th river a body could run down ever little while an git a mess a fish.'

He looked at her, wondering why she spoke so, his thoughts still trying to grasp death, hold it, look at it. He could never tell Henley about the bear in the pawpaw grove. That was death.

'An these little cedar trees up on these ledges here,' she went on, speaking against this awareness of the dead, 'they're might nigh fence-post size.'

He looked up the bluff side, shook his head slowly, as when after her awakening shake in summer before daylight he tried to awaken. 'Ain't this Granpa's land?'

She shook her head. 'It used to be your great-granpa's. Your great-great-granpa Kendrick owned all th land tween here an th ridge road clean down to th river an up to th head a th creek—nigh onto four thousand acres, I've heared Pop say. This is th Tipton Place now.'

'Oh,' he said, and started up the bluff side.

Cassie, in no wise excited by Reuben's bear, for bigger bears chased Callie Lou, cried: 'Could we put bear meat in our cellar, too? An we'll can a million cans a blackberries an—'

'Not so fast, my girl; that was jist talk,' Gertie said, but turned again to Reuben. 'They's th best garden place an more manure an that new ground . . .'

'It ud be a deal a work to clean up—fer somebody else,' Reuben said, studying her face.

'Mebbe—it won't be fer somebody else.'

Reuben studied her a time in silence, afraid to believe. 'Pop wouldn't like it,' he said at last. 'It's too far frum th gravel. Anyhow, he'll be needen a new truck er new tires er somethin like allus.'

'He won't need nothen in th army,' Gertie said. 'He'll want us to have a place a our own—that is, onct we've got it. Pretty soon we won't be a haven to give away half a what we raise.'

'You been sayen that a long time,' Reuben said, but unable to hold the doubt on his face he plunged up the hill, not just walking through the woods, but stopping now and again to study a tree. And once, before he disappeared, she saw him take his pocket knife and cut a little crooked cedar away from a straight one so that the straight one could grow.

4

Cassie ran ahead of her down the long slope of the pasture field. Gertie stood by the rail fence and watched her grow smaller and smaller, but always a child running, until she disappeared behind the new barn that Henley had built to hold his tobacco. The barn was empty now. The old barn that had held the hay and his black beef cattle was empty, too.

Suddenly the timbered hills, the fields rolling down to the river, the white-painted house with its two stone chimneys, the barns with the smaller outbuildings huddled about them, all these were no longer as they had been. When she was a child her father's place in the valley with its fenced fields, many of them green with bluegrass, had seemed a world of its own, richer, flatter, greener than any other farm she knew. She had married and learned the chaos of yearly moving and the struggle to make corn grow—never all your own—on the thin worn soil of sandy ridges. Her father's farm with Henley running it had seemed finer still. Now the ragged, uncut hay fields, the pasture, empty of cattle, the beginnings of a gully in the lespedeza field below her, all cried out to her that her father was old, with a crippled leg, and that Henley was dead.

She hesitated a moment longer, looking down. Then, her eyes bleak and gray, her mouth like a gash across her face, she strode on, stopping only after she had gone onto the screened-in side porch where the family ate in summer. She stopped just past the porch door and stood, looking at first one and then the other of two doors. The door on the end opened into the kitchen; her father might be there. The other led into the new part of the house that her mother had had built when she came there as a bride. Intended for a dining room, it had through the years become her mother's room, the center of her mother's kingdom of crochet work and potted plants.

Cassie called from around the house, 'Mom, Mom, Granpa's out in his blacksmith shop,' and ran back to her grandfather, expecting her mother to follow.

Gertie, with an uneasy glance at her mother's window, turned swiftly, soundlessly, and opened the porch door she had just come through. Her foot was on the second step when there came a wailing cry behind her, and her mother rushed onto the porch, 'Oh, Gertie, Gertie, your own born brother dead in a foreign land, an never once do you come to comfort your poor mother a weepen her heart away. An when you do come, you cain't so much as come in an speak to your poor dyen mother. Oh, Gertie, Gertie,' and her mother, standing on tiptoe, caught her around the neck, kissed her wetly on the cheek, and fell to weeping on her shoulder.

Gertie stood like a stone woman, only her hands clenching and unclenching with the effort not to shiver at her mother's kiss. In a moment the older woman's sobs had subsided enough that she could speak again. 'Oh, Gert how could you do me thisaway; your sister Meg has been so good an kind, has writ me so many letters, an is aimen to come an see me at Thanksgiven when her man has a extra day off. All th way frum that minen town Meg'ull come fer a day er two jist to see her mother—but you,' and for the first time she lifted her head and looked fully at Gertie.

Gertie looked back at the face, pale beyond any face she knew, almost never touched by sun or wind, seeming always close to death and God. The eyes so big and dark and sad below the pale forehead; the eyebrows black by the little weak white hand that rubbed them now in the old gesture of unspoken suffering. Gertie watched, unable to think of anything to do or say, while the hand rubbed the forehead, went up and back into the dark, ungraying hair, then dropped suddenly and lifelessly while the head bowed slowly, eyes closing.

Her mother leaned an instant weakly against the house wall, then slowly, as if the effort were very great, she straightened but, still tottering, she turned toward the front door. Gertie watched her, clenched hands tight by her sides, the muscles in her thin cheeks corded over her clenched teeth. Her mother was going round to the front door that opened into the parlor. The organ she had used to play while Henley sang was there, and on the wall above it, his guitar. 'Please, Mom—let's—let's set in your room.'

Her mother turned and looked at her with curiosity, 'You sound like you'd been runnen.'

'I hurried—kinda,' Gertie said, her voice hoarse, sullen-sounding, defiance in her step as she turned back to her mother's door.

'Hurried,' her mother was shrilling, beginning again to weep. 'Three weeks since th word come for poor Henley. An I've had such a time, an everbody else has been so kind but my own born child. They got me through th fainten spells, somehow—but from God alone can I be reconciled. I wish I could believe like them that Meg writ about in th minen town. An like you—if you believe anything. They've got some a them in jail, Meg writ; they go around a claimen they ain't no burnen Hell fire, that our God would never allow it; that at th very worst them like Henley will only be destroyed, but—oh, Jesus is kind—but it says, "Th Lord thy God am a terrible God,"' and on the last 'God' her voice rose in a terrible wail of weeping as she looked up at her great daughter, who stood now as in childhood when her mother wept or scolded— silent, high-headed, straight-shouldered, stony-faced.

It seemed a long while before Gertie could think to open the door, and in a voice which was hoarse and harsh, instead of gentle-sounding as she would have it be, remind her mother that she might catch cold, running out as she had done in nothing but a little crocheted cape about her shoulders.

Her mother refused Gertie's hand on her elbow, but by clinging to the doorframe and then seizing a chair back she managed to reach the rocking chair, reserved always for her, on one side the fireplace. 'An what mightn't a terrible God do,' she moaned, flinging her head against the back of the chair and looking at the ceiling. 'I cain't bear to think on it. Henley, my onliest son, a flamen there in Hell. He never found that narrow gate, oh, Lord, that little narrow gate to eternal salvation an life everlasten. But he follered that broad road straight to perdition, a dancen his dances an a drinken his drop—infinite justice, infinite mercy, let me be reconciled. Seems like it'll kill me. How could God do this to me?'

'It was Henley He done it to, Mom,' Gertie said in a low voice, and added, 'He broke none a th Ten Commandments.' She had stopped just inside the door, and stood rigidly still, her shoulders hunched a little, her hands clenched at her sides, almost with the air of a frightened and defiant animal dragged into the warm, over-crowded room against its will.

Her mother made a little business of straightening her head and looking at her, a flame of something close to hatred brightening her tear-wet eyes. 'Maybe if'n it hadn't a been fer you, Henley would ha give hissef to God. You was th oldest; he thought a sight a you, too much, I've thought many a time. He seen you stand stiff-necked an stubborn in th face uv th Almighty God. You never repented a your sin a dancen. If you an your father, too, but mostly you, had set Henley a good example, he might ha been singen in heaven now.' The rocking chair gave an angry, impatient creak. 'What a you a standen there a glaren at me that away—mad as fire. Seems like you've been mad about somethin ever since Henley went away. I recken you wanted me to lie—say Henley was our sole support. He wasn't.'

'Pop ain't been able to do hard heavy work since—' Gertie began in a low hard voice.

She stopped when her mother's head fell upon the chair arm and she began weeping again, words of heartbroken moaning mixed in with the weeping, 'Oh, God, oh, God, thy ways with my children are past understanding.' She was silent then, chair still, bowed head slipping slowly off the chair arm toward the floor.

Gertie could only twist her hands, stare at the sagging figure, and back away. She did lift one hand to catch her mother's shoulder, but jerked it back. Her mother would shrink from her touch and shrug her hand away, as when she had tried to help her through the door. Her frantic glance quite by accident struck the camphor bottle on the mantel. She seized it, held it toward her mother, meanwhile begging in a hoarse and broken voice: 'Please, Mom, please; try yer camphor. Mebbe it'll keep you frum fainten.' Her mother reached blindly, without lifting her head, and Gertie put the bottle into her hand. Gertie watched concernedly as she sniffed and revived enough to speak:

'Gert, I recken you wanted th whole neighborhood, specially them like your mother-in-law, that ole Kate Nevels, with her three boys gone an Clovis called, to go around a throwen off on me a sayen I kept my onliest one at home tied to my apron strings.'

Gertie opened her mouth, but closed it. She was silent, staring at the fire while her mother gradually gained strength enough from the camphor to sit up and say with a little headshake: 'You ought to read yer Bible, Gert. It's all foretold. "I come not with peace but a sword," Christ said. An recollect how in Revelations it tells us we can't buy er sell "thout th mark uv th Beast"—that means these ration cards; they've got th Beast's number an mark. Christ is a scourgen th world like he scourged th temple, an in his mighty wrath he—'

'But, Mom, mebbe,' Gertie began in a low hesitant voice, turning to look at her, 'mebbe they's another side to Christ. Recollect he went to th wedden feast, an had time to fool with little youngens, an speak to a thief an a bad woman. An Henley was like Christ—he worked an loved his fellowmen an—'

Her mother's rocker gave an angry swish, and Gertie, whose voice had grown ever lower and more hesitant, fell silent. She looked past her mother through the open door, her eager glance hunting up the hill-pasture path she had walked a few minutes before, then pausing on the brow of the hill where the woods met the bright blue sky; and for an instant it seemed that her Christ, the Christ she had wanted for Henley was there, ready to come singing down the hill, a laughing Christ uncrowned with thorns and with the scars of the nail holes in his hands all healed away; a Christ who had loved people, had liked to mingle with them and laugh and sing the way Henley had liked people and singing and dancing. That Christ walked down the hill now and stood by the door asking to be let in, because it was Henley's home and he knew Henley.

He wasn't there, of course. It was only her mind made this Christ alive, the way Cassie made the witch child Callie Lou alive, or gave life and heart to the piece of hickory sprout.

She jumped, then strode with awkward quickness toward the door. Her mother was shivering, exclaiming, 'Gert, no wonder

Amos like to a died with th croup if you don't shut th doors at your place no better than here.'

Gertie opened her mouth to say that the croup was a disease Amos had caught, but tramped on her tongue in time. She closed the door, soundlessly, as she had been taught to do as a child. Forgetting to take off her coat, she sat down on the edge of a split-bottomed chair, a good distance back from the fire. She tried to recollect at least one of the many things she had planned for talking with her mother, pleasant things that would take her mother's mind from Henley in Hell. She couldn't remember them now for wanting to ask about her father, but she dared not show too much concern for him too soon.

She was glad when her mother broke the silence, saying with a sorrowful shake of her bowed head: 'Gert, I allus say let a body believe what their Bibles tells em to believe. But you're mighty close to bein' a infidel. You're bad as them people Meg writ about in th coal-minen towns. They're a claimen that, come Armiegeddon, this world won't be destroyed by fire an brimstone frum heaven like th Bible says. Some a them got put in jail fer not saluten th flag, claimen it was a graven image.'

Gertie's head came up; she looked quickly at her mother. 'They cain't put em in jail. Th Constitution says, "Congress shall make no law respecting an establishment of religion, or prohibiting the free exercise thereof; or abridging the freedom of speech or—"'

'Gert, Gert,' her mother cried, more angry now than sorrowful, 'don't you know they's a war on, an things is different? If a religion is unpatriotic, it ain't right. Yer pop *would* learn you th Constitution an some a th Bible—an you been spouten em ever since like you was a preacher an a lawyer, too.'

Her mother began sniffing the camphor again, and Gertie, desperate for conversation, said quickly and in an unnaturally loud voice: 'Mom, how's that bad pain in your side? Clovis was a tellen me you'd been mighty bad with that old pain.'

'Gert, darlen, do I matter so little you cain't even recollect what hurts me? It's not that old pain that come after th bornen a you nearly killed me.' She sighed a moment in remembrance of Gertie's birth, then continued: 'I'm mighty bad constipated, mighty bad.

Soon as I git a little stronger, an before they take Clovis fer good, I'm a goen to git him to take me to a doctor in Town. That doctor where you took Amos, it's got so his medicine don't do me one lick a good no more, not my constipation. I don't think he's as good as that little doctor at th Valley. He went off to war right away. Your doctor's a slacker an not patriotic, er he would already ha gone.'

'But people has got to have a doctor. I don't believe Amos could ha—'

Her mother was sniffling again, her head bending toward the chair arm. 'Gertie, Gertie, if you'd lost a son like me you'd know they was a war on. Amos jist had you skeered. Clovis said th hole in his neck wasn't bigger'n a marble. After my poor Henley went an give his life, I feel that ever man—'

'God didn't give Henley his life to give away; an he didn't give his life. They took him an he didn't—' Her mother began to weep— Gertie realized she was saying things she had made up her mind not to say. She looked about the room, hunting desperately for something of which to speak; but the room seemed as it had been since childhood, forever crowded with things she had seen many times, but forever alien territory that had from the beginnings of her memory made her seem even bigger, uglier, more awkward, more liable to break something than she had seemed in other places.

Here and there on the walls, in little wooden shelves contrived by her father, covering the low windowsills, set on the cedar chest, on the center table, crowding Henley's picture on top of the phonograph, were her mother's potted plants: geraniums, begonias, varieties of cactus, coleus, sensitive plants. Many were blooming, but in a sad, halfhearted way, as if they were tired of the red clay pots, tied with crêpe paper, that cramped their roots like too tight shoes. A whole corner of the large room was taken up with a dais-like piece of furniture built by her father. It had three broad steps rising on all four sides, each step wide enough to hold a row of potted plants, with the small square on top holding the king of her mother's plant kingdom, a giant maidenhair fern that seemed to have changed little since Gertie first remembered it. She had memories of trips to the woods for the black rich earth from generations of leaves dying on limestone ledges, for the dirt must

63

be scraped from a damp limestone ledge where other ferns grew, so that every few years the plant had been repotted and divided, with rooted fronds going out to all the neighbors. Not long after her marriage her mother had given her a good-sized piece of it, rooted in a large red pot. She had on the way home stopped by a limestone ledge above the creek and there set the fern where it belonged to be.

Hanging from ornamental pegs whittled by her father for her mother could never abide a nail in her wallpaper, were innumerable pincushions. Some were of patchwork, others, in the shape of knitted or crocheted hearts and stars and diamonds run with pale blue or pink ribbon, faded now into dusty grayness. There were old almanacs advertising remedies for the female troubles that had plagued her mother so much since Gertie's birth. There was a great watch that had come down to her father from his grandfather; a never used powder horn—filled with two crêpe-paper roses brought home nine years ago from Uncle Chrisman Ballew's funeral—alongside an unframed, faded picture of Joshua blowing his horn by the walls of Jericho. Everywhere, on the dresser, the mantel, under the giant fern, on the chairbacks, the curtains, the sewing machine, the cushions, were samples of her mother's handiwork. Covers, scarves, and doilies were all embroidered and edged with crochet work or tatting, and all starched and ironed until they seemed of the shiny stiff coldness of metal when a bit of one could be seen between the medicine bottles, clocks, lamps, and vases of artificial flowers that surmounted them.

They somehow matched the floor, laid years ago with one of the first linoleum rugs in the settlement, so fine that for fear of spoiling it her mother had put a rag carpet over it, and over the carpet, new then and one of the last to come from old Aunt Sarah Kramer's loom, lengths and pieces cut from the old red turkey carpet that had been in the front room when she came to it as a bride, and over the old carpet to brighten it a bit, small rugs she had from time to time ordered from Montgomery Ward. One of these, depicting a very pink-faced little girl with overly large eyes and butter-colored hair with one reddish-pink hand resting on the shoulder of a large yellow-brown square-nosed cur dog, the breed of which had at times thrown Gertie into long fits of silent pondering, her mother had always considered too fine for feet, and kept in front of the flower stand where almost no one ever stepped for fear of knocking over a plant or breaking a frond of the swelling fern.

Gertie fidgeted in her chair and touched the knife in her apron pocket, then quickly jerked her straying fingers away. Her mother had ever hated the whittling, even in her father—and in a girl it had seemed almost a sin. Strange how she could whittle, but never learn to do a bit of fancywork. In spite of all her mother's teaching in the little spare time Gertie had had from the farm work, even her plain sewing was poor—all but the patching. Her mother often pointed out that her buttonholes looked like pigs' eyes—and she made all her own dresses too big and too long.

She realized her mother had left off crying and was looking at her. She turned eagerly, trying hard to smile, even when her mother said: 'Gert, did you let anybody see you a comen down th big road a looken that away. You'll have beggar lice an Spanish needles all over th place. An why don't you take off yer coat? What ails you anyhow? You act like you was a stranger.'

Gertie got up, jerked off her coat, knocking the faded flower from a large begonia as she did so. She stood then, staring into the fire, and unconsciously fell to pulling her fingers till the joints popped, a childhood habit that had always slipped upon her when trouble overtook her with empty hands. Her mother, just beginning an account of her wartime trials with the buying of thread, interrupted herself to scold, 'Gert, Gert, you know that drives me crazy.'

Gertie's frantic glance struggled with the curtains. Maybe her mother could be led to talk of the curtains. They looked new. But were they? They looked exactly like all the other curtains in this room she could remember, thin and white and edged with her mother's crochet work. But the starched lace, fragile-appearing as rows of snow crystals sewed upon the curtains, only brought back Battle John Brand, stampeding the souls of his flock to Christ with his twin whips of hell and God. She could feel the torture of the lace again as it had used to be on those long hot summer Sundays of her girlhood when she would sit by her sister Meg in the meeting house and listen to Battle John Brand.

His hell would quiver like the heat waves through the meeting house, and she would sit trying desperately to think of other things, but never succeeding. She could smell her own flesh burning, rising like an incense to God in heaven, with her mother who was forever listening down the golden stairs, but never hearing her daughter cry: 'I love Battle John's God. I love the Sunday clothing my poor weakly mother works so hard to make for me.'

She never, no matter how hot the coals or bright the flames that Battle John made, was able to say such things, but sat on in sweaty-handed guilt and misery. Was she, like Judas, foreordained to sin, she'd wonder? She knew, but was unable to imagine, that the torture of Hell was a million times worse than the torture of her Sunday clothes. The starched embroidered white dress of dotted swiss or voile, always edged with her mother's crochet, seemed by its very daintiness to make her own body, brown, bigboned, big-muscled, brier-scratched from the man's work she did on the farm, even more ugly. Her thighs, that could endure the jolting of a mule's back or long hours on the iron seat of the iron-wheeled mowing machine, cried to her in church with unceasing agony at their confinement in the encircling bands of knitted or crocheted lace and tucks, all starched and ironed until each toothed edge seemed so much iron cutting into her sweating flesh. More starched lace chafed her breasts, her back, and her chigger-bitten armpits; the pains and discomfort of these, added to the too tight shoes and the layers of starched slips and petticoats, made the long sittings under Battle John a greater agony than any pain she had ever known.

The cuckoo in the clock on her mother's wall whirred and creaked, for it was getting old, then leaped from its little house and cried eleven times. Gertie had seldom heard a pleasanter sound. She started toward the kitchen, but paused, her hand on the doorknob, and asked somewhat timidly, for she had never been a cook to match either her mother or Meg, 'Mom, couldn't I git dinner this onct an save you th trouble?'

Her mother considered as she juggled a bottle of pills so as to make one and only one pill come from the bottle. She succeeded, swallowed the pill, gagged, shook her head violently at Gertie's suggestion that she get her a glass of water. 'Law, Gert, I recken in times like these you can cook about as good as anybody.' She paused to gag again before continuing. 'Many's th time I've wished here lately that I had th stingy hand with lard an sugar you've allus had since you got Clovis. We run out uv our own lard back in August, an that ration don't hardly give me enough fer biscuits, an till hog-killen time I'll have to cook with butter, an butter seasonen gives me th sick headache. I tried fryen a chicken in butter, but it tasted jist like beef to me. I couldn't eat one bite but th liver.'

Gertie stood in the doorway while her mother went into a long pondering on whether or not she should let Gertie get the dinner. She did feel weakly, but on the other hand somebody would surely come on such a pretty Sunday. She finished at last with the decision in favor of Gertie, who went quickly into the kitchen, closing the door behind her. She hung her coat on a peg, gave the hem below the torn pocket a swift, critical glance. It looked flat and empty, like the tail of any other old coat. She pinched it between thumb and finger, and was reassured by the soft whispering crackle of money.

She paused an instant looking round the great room. She glanced into the wide-mouthed fireplace where her great-grandmother had baked the bread and cooked all the Kendrick food, and smiled a little on an usually large Dutch oven, one her father had always prized. His grandfather had brought it back from Alabama one early spring when he and the other men of the settlement had returned from driving their hogs to market in the south across the mountains. She crossed the kitchen to the great cookstove with its high curving legs, and rolled back the warming-oven door.

She looked at the platter there with two pieces of ham left from breakfast, two fried eggs, and on one end a little mound of biscuit. It was for an instant as it had been before she married, when this was home and if she grew hungry at any time of the day or night she had only to come to the warming oven or go to the cherry cupboard, where a selection of jams and jellies and canned and baked goods, especially gingerbread, were kept. Endlessly replenishing the kitchen, like the widow's barrel, were the smokehouse, the spring-house, and the roothouse. Behind these were the hogs and cattle and sheep on the range, the timber on the hillsides, the little coal mines—worked by paid miners but good for cash money. And under everything was the Big South Fork of the Cumberland that each year in the time of tides laid a thick coating of rich black earth on the already rich land of her father's river-bottom fields, sheltered from the fiercest currents of the river so that sand and gravel never came on the flood tide, only black silt settling slowly down from quiet back waters.

There'd been no fried meat left at her table in a long time. She turned quickly to the woodbox filled with the only kind of wood her mother could abide: split maple, hickory, and oak, cut green and seasoned, with one small corner given up to split red cedar root for kindling.

When the fire was burning well, the stove crinking with the rising heat, she hurried soundlessly through the outside door, then down the lane toward the thin thread of smoke that rose from the blacksmith shop, a little log building that in the days of her grandfather had served much of the settlement, but was seldom used now save by her father for his own work.

She pushed open the door, but paused a moment looking; in the dim light her father seemed a stranger, some old man, older than her father, who was hardly sixty, too deaf to hear the opening of the door. His hair had the thin straggly look of an old man's hair, and his shoulders, bent above the freshly made ax handle he was smoothing with a piece of broken glass, had the tired look of an old man's shoulders. He scraped on, smoothing the wood, not looking up until she stepped across the threshold, questioning more than greeting, 'Pop? Oh, Pop?'

The ax handle fell from his knees as he got up, and with the piece of glass still clutched in one hand he pulled her tightly against him, whispering, 'Gertie, Gertie.' He held her away from him, looked into her face, repeating, 'Gertie, Gertie.'

The never spoken knowledge of childhood that her father, not her mother, was the weak and pitiful one, the one who needed help, came back to her, but now as then she could say nothing of what was in her heart, nor speak of Henley, who in dying had taken with him the Kendrick name, the Kendrick land. In a moment she was able to say, 'Pop, I've been a worryen on how you was maken out with yer leg in this rainy fall weather.'

68

'Pretty good, pretty good,' he said. 'I was lucky to have Reuben to hep in th fall work, an I got th Cramer boys a few days.'

'I heared they'd went away,' she said, picking up the ax handle and hefting it.

He nodded. 'Th oldest ain't seventeen, but they're big as men—so they took off fer Muncie an they'll kill theirselves in one a them factories.' He sighed. 'They won't be men enough left to dig th graves. Looks like they could ha left us Clovis. He could ha kept th mail car runnen.'

She tried to smile, 'Why, Pop, many's th time I've heared you tell about how th women managed in th War a 1812 when they wasn't a man above fourteen left in th settlement. I can do a man's work.' She studied the ax handle. 'I kind a kept a hopen they'd leave Clovis. I mebbe ought to ha let him a gone to Oak Ridge er some factory. I think he wanted to. He hated to leave his old people an sell th truck—but he would ha gone. Mostly it was me, afeared he'd want me an th youngens to foller him to some city.'

He patted her shoulder. 'Clovis, he'll be all right in th army.'

She nodded, repeating, 'He'll be all right,' remembering that other, 'He'll be all right.' She and her father had stood together in the barn; late spring it had been then, with the sun rising far northward. They had stood in the pale spring dawn with milk buckets in their hands and listened to Clovis's truck as it took Henley to the railroad, and they had repeated each to the other, 'Henley, he'll be all right.'

She watched him as he took the ax handle, settled himself slowly and cautiously into the chair, and commenced scraping again, looking over his spectacles at the oak wood. She saw the glass make a deeper mark than it should have, scratching the oak. He too was thinking of the other 'all right.' In a moment she was able to ask, 'How's yer leg, Pop, an yer rheumatism?'

'Aye, not bad; nothen to speak of.' He reached and gave the bellows string three quick pulls that brought first red glowing life and then pale flames to the charcoal in the forge. 'I been kinda baken myself, an that helps. I ain't so bad.'

'Why'n't you set inside, Pop? It's jist now beginnen to git warm in th sun. A forge fire's no good fer baken yer legs an back.'

'Aye, law,' he said, looking through the little window to the hills across the river, 'you know how it is. Th mess a my whittlen allus aggravated yer pore mother—an seems like since—since this trouble—I've allus got to be a whittlen, an a chewen an a spitten, too. An yer pore mother, th smell uv it an a sean me spit—why, t'other night I was a setten by th fire and she had such a gaggen spell she come nigh fainten. How's th little un? I wanted to ride over to see him, but yer mom's been so bad I couldn't leave.'

'He's fine,' Gertie said, studying his hand scraping the oak. Seemed like it wasn't steady; but maybe she only imagined it, like a minute ago when he had stood up, his eyes had not seemed quite level with her own. No, she didn't imagine it: she had been little, looking up at her father, the tallest man in the world, six feet four; then grown, looking into his eyes when it seemed his eyes alone were the only ones in the world high as her own; and now the eyes were lower. She realized she was pulling her fingers again, but did not stop. 'Pop—I ain't right certain—well, I'm almost certain, but soon as Clovis is in th army—they'll be money I can depend on fer a little while—I'll move closer an . . .'

'The Tipton Place?' he asked, and his eyes were eager, glad as Reuben's. 'It's good an—'

'Gertie-ee. Gertie-ee.'

They both jumped like guilty children at hearing her mother's calling, exasperated and shrill. Gertie hastily opened the door, but much to her relief and surprise her mother, in a fresh crocheted cap and apron, seemed pleased and relieved to find her with her father. She pushed Gertie back into the blacksmith shop, then closed the door with a great air of mystery. 'Th Reverend Brand is a comen down th big road,' she whispered, pleased, 'an this is th last chanct I'll have to see you by yerself all day.' She fished in her left-hand apron pocket that always held her current crochet piece.

'You've allus been awful good to us—in a way, Gertie,' she went on, pulling a handful of bills from her pocket. She opened the pocket wide, peeped in, took another, and then held out the loosely crumpled handful. 'Take em; they're fer you. Your father an me has talked it over. You hepped a sight back in your younger days—you

70

stayed with us longer than most girls—an me an yer pop, we'll git along—somehow.'

Gertie stepped backward, staring at the money. 'Law, Mom, you an Pop—you'll be a needen it worsen Clovis an me.'

Her father smiled at her. 'It's Henley's cattle money,' he said. 'He wanted you to have it—all of it,' and he gave a quick glance at the bills as if he would count them. Failing, he glanced sharply at his wife, who held the money half hidden in her hand. 'His last wish—all of it,' he said, insistent.

'His dyen wish,' her mother said, in the unmoved but intentionally dramatic tone she might have used to arouse interest in some unusual bit of neighborhood gossip. 'He writ to me not long afore they took him across th waters, that if'n anything happened to him, to hep Gertie. You raised him, he said.'

Gertie choked and moved hastily backward, knocking her shoulder against the nail shelf as she did so. Her mother sighed heavily. 'It ain't like me an yer poor father had long fer this world.'

'But there's insurance money comen in ever month,' her father said.

'Mebbe it's like he allus said,' her mother went on, shoving the bills into Gertie's apron pocket: 'if you hadn't been big enough to hep on th farm while he was growen up we'd ha lost th place. Take it,' she said, turning away.

'Oh, Mom,' Gertie said, and her bleak face became a hideous thing, breaking into twisted wrinkles and grimaces as she began to cry, giving all her big being to the crying, wholeheartedly, like a hurt child.

Cassie, who had peeped in when her grandmother opened the door, had never seen her mother cry. She was terrified past tears, and buried her face in Gertie's apron. The child stood shivering, clutching her mother's leg when her grandmother broke into a mighty wail of weeping, screaming as she flung her apron over her head and hurried toward the house: 'Gert, Gert, think a me. I can't stand to see you cry. If Henley's goen hurts you so, think on how your poor mother feels.'

Gertie cried on, her hands pressed against her face, the crumpled money spilling from her pocket. Just as she had been unable to tell

71

her father any word of how she felt for him, she was tongueless to tell her mother that sorrow for Henley did not cause her tears, but her mother's unexpected gratitude, never mentioned through all these years. Maybe her mother had loved her. What a sin to have doubted it ever! She cried afresh over her own hardness of heart— Clovis going to war, and she thought only of money.

She rushed out of the shop and away with long quick strides, unmindful of Cassie's frightened eyes peeping up from her apron, or the small hands pulling on her skirt. At last she noticed the drag on her walking, and picked up the child and strode on, her feet follow- ing a path of escape in childhood—up the hill to the spring.

She was halfway there before she noticed that Cassie's arms were clasped so tightly about her neck they were choking her, while the child shivered and trembled like a young lamb in a January rain as she said over and over in a low, terrified voice, 'Don't cry, Mama; don't cry.'

The shameful realization came to Gertie that she was scaring her own child the way her mother had used to scare her. 'I won't cry no more,' she said. 'I ain't hurt. I'm all right, less'n you choke me to death with huggen. "Miss Cassie hugged her mommie to death." Now wouldn't that make a pretty piece fer th paper?'

Cassie smiled and patted her mother's hair, but was troubled still. 'Where we a goen, Mom?'

'To th spring—you know th spring—yer granma's spring.'

'But you ain't got no bucket.'

'Jist to look around—an git a drink,' Gertie said after a moment's wondering on why had she come. She realized she was clutching the money, and through all her sorrow there came a panicky fear that she had lost some of it, and that she didn't know how much there had been. She hastily slid Cassie to the ground and counted it, smoothing each bill, laying them evenly one above the other—fifteen twenty-dollar bills. She wished she had her coat. She would sit in the sun up here where no one could see, and count it all—more already than John had paid for the Tipton Place. She wouldn't have to wait. She wouldn't have to depend on Clovis. She wouldn't have to ask old Uncle John for credit. She wouldn't have to ask anybody for anything.

She hurried a few steps further up the hill, her eyes searching hungrily ahead. When she had gone high enough so that she could see the gray-brown roof of the old log house on the Tipton Place rising above the cedars on the rocky creek bank, she stopped and stood a long time looking. Such a safe and sheltered place; if a body didn't know it was there she would never notice it among the leafless trees. It was close to her father, and her own, all her own. Never, never would she have to move again; never see again that weary, sullen look on Reuben's face that came when they worked together in a field not their own, and he knew that half his sweat went to another man.

She heard her mother calling her again, and remembered it was past dinner-getting time and a preacher come for dinner. The fire in the cook-stove would have burned away, and where was Cassie? She saw her at last, far up the field, the hickory doll on one arm while with the other she fought something with a dried stickweed longer than she was tall. Gertie heard her cries of 'Sooey, Sooey,' saw the stickweed break the air, but for all her fierce fighting Cassie was losing ground before the enemy, running backward at times down the hill.

Gertie called to her. Cassie whirled about, dropped the stickweed, and came running, laughing. Halfway to Gertie, she glanced over her shoulder, then ran the faster, screaming, 'Mommie, Mommie, throw out some yers a corn. These wild hawgs can eat them stid a my little youngen. They're a overtaken me.'

Gertie made great motions of throwing ears of corn to hungry hogs, stamped her feet, cried, 'Sooey,' then held out her arms to the flying Cassie. She caught her up with a cry of, 'Woman, you oughtn't to take yer little youngen out through a bunch a wild hawgs thataway.'

'Thar warn't so many,' Cassie said, settling herself on her mother's shoulders. 'Callie Lou chased em all but two ole sows off up the creek.'

'That Callie Lou sure is brave,' Gertie said, hurrying down the hill.

Cassie hugged her mother, and Callie Lou was gone. 'Mom,' Cassie whispered as they neared the house, 'I heared Granma when she come cryen onto th porch. Was that why you was a cryen—because a Uncle Henley cain't never go up to Jesus?'

'Pshaw,' Gertie said. 'A body don't have to go to Jesus. He's right down here on earth all th time.'

'Have you seen him, Mom?'

Gertie considered, looking up the hill, 'Well, it's kinda like you a sean Callie Lou.'

'You mean he's got black curley hair an black eyes like Callie Lou?'

'N-o-o. When I seen him walken over th hill—he jist looked like a good-turned man.'

'Like a preacher in suit clothes a carryen a Bible?'

'No. Seemed like he wore overalls like a carpenter. He made things like yer granpa.'

'Was he a carryen a ax to cut a ax handle?'

'I didn't see his tools. He'd been in th woods, though, a looken fer somethen, fer he was carryen a big branch a red leaves. I figgered he'd cut down a old holler black gum tree fer to make beehives, an th leaves was so pretty he took em with him.'

She gave the down-hanging feet and legs of the child a quick squeeze. 'Jesus walks th earth, an we're goen to have us a little piece a heaven right here on earth. Your pop has to go away, but he'll be back—he'll be all right.'

5

She was standing by her father's corn crib with a two-bushel sack of corn on her shoulder. She wanted to load it on Dock, but Dock wouldn't stand for it; every time she started to throw the corn behind the saddle he jumped away and the corn fell to the ground. Henley bent to pick it up. She saw his right hand reaching for it, his blue sleeve rolled to his elbow above the big sunburned arm where the dark hairs had bleached a golden brown, and on his reaching hand there was the ax scar between thumb and finger; but his hand was young-looking still for twenty-eight, the back less rough and brown, the palm less leathery than her own. As he stooped again to reach for the corn, he looked up at her, his hair, dark as her own, but not so straight, fallen across his forehead. Through it she could see his eyes, dark blue like her father's eyes, more laughing—they had used to be like Cassie's eyes—but not laughing now; sober-serious, asking, 'Why—why do this to me?' and he was both hurt and angry, picking up the sack of corn. He flung it hard across her shoulder, so hard it hurt her neck, and the corn poured out, spilling swiftly to make a golden pile by her feet. Sorrowful, she was staring down at the spilled corn, so sorrowful, her insides aching as if the corn had been a wasted pile of yellow gold; and Henley was so mad at her. She wanted to ask him why, but the sack hurt her neck and she could not speak.

She struggled against the choking weight, reached for it, found Clovis's hand, half open, limp in sleep, the back of it flung like a dead weight across her neck, high up against her throat. She lifted the sleep-heavy hand and laid it back across his chest. All the pieces of reality scattered into nothingness by her sleep drew slowly back together; but she lay for a moment longer, fighting to hold the dream. Henley was looking at her, and in a moment he would laugh and go riding away with the shelled corn. She lay, her eyes closed, but she could not bring back the shine of the yellow corn or Henley's eyes. They were back there now in her memory with all other things.

She rolled out of bed, careful not to waken Clovis. Barefooted, and with the long coil of her hair falling down her back, she went to the little window in the end of the loft, so low and so small she must kneel in order to see any sweep of the sky. Yesterday had brought a thin gray rain, changing to sleety snow at twilight, but it was clear now, with no wisp of fog or cloud between her and the stars. The cup of the Big Dipper was getting close to the top of the sky. It was a long time till daylight, not much past three in the morning, but she could get up now and have fresh coffee ready for Clovis when he got up. She looked a moment longer at the stars, crouching lower, tipping her head far backward, sending her glance higher until it searched the ceiling of the world. She lost herself in the thousands and thousands of cold lights, her mind empty as when she had slept, so that for an instant she almost recaptured the wondering look in Henley's eyes—a moment more and he would have spoken. Then it was gone, and the lights were stars saying that dawn would come.

She tiptoed across the rough wide-planked floor to the stair hole, unconsciously remembering to crouch and not strike her head on the eaves, for even in the center of the loft she could not stand fully upright. Clovis had complained at times because he and she slept in the loft. He agreed with her that it was indecent for parents to sleep in the same room as half grown children, but let the boys sleep up above, he'd say; but Gertie was afraid of fire in the little rattletrap renter's shanty with the kitchen stovepipe going out through a hole in the wall. She thought now as she climbed down the ladder-like stair, how she had told him her fears of fire, but never a word about the goodness of wakening to stars or the night sound of rain on the shake roof.

The children slept in the two big beds in the main room. She went to the walnut bed in one corner, put one of Cassie's wandering feet back under the covers, and took her tightly clutching arm from Clytie's neck, for Clytie complained often that Cassie choked her and kept her awake with overmuch hugging. The three boys, as always in cold weather, slept fitted together like three spoons in the great cherry bed. Reuben was in front to keep the smaller ones from falling to the floor. Enoch next in the warmest spot, and Amos last, his chin on Enoch's neck.

She straightened their quilts, and still without striking a light, went into the kitchen. She shook down the ashes in the great cookstove, her one new piece of furniture, and it a gift from her father. She felt in the corner of the woodbox where the fat pine in fine splinters lay and built the fire. Quickly the top of the stove took on shape and size. The caps were marked by thin circles of red light, while the grate openings made six squares of light on the wall. The stove light shone on the wash bench of her own making, and on the bottoms of the water buckets. One was of red cedar, made of pieces of wood fitted together barrel fashion and held together with copper bands. It was an old bucket and had, like most of the furniture which she had not made herself, been a cast-off from her mother's house.

Clovis quarreled often at the weight of the cedar bucket and the clumsiness of it, pointing out that a new tin one would cost only a quarter. The children seldom carried it to the spring, but filled it from the smaller buckets. But now, as Gertie broke the thin skim of ice on top and lifted dipperfuls of water from it to fill the coffeepot, she smiled on it, remembering the years she had had it, and was filled for a moment with a proud consciousness of ownership, something solid and old, known and proved long ago by hands other than her own. She smoothed the middle copper band, bright in the stove light from many scrubbings with ashes. She decided that when she moved to the Tipton Place she would keep the bucket on the porch shelf and quit using it for water; instead, she would keep garden truck or meat in it, as her grandmother had used to do.

She put the coffee on, and stoked the stove afresh. Then, as always in any weather, she picked up the red cedar bucket and went to the spring. She as usual in clear weather stopped when she had rounded the house corner, and looked at the morning star. It rode high and bright above Old John's pines on the ridge top, seeming hardly the morning star, for as yet no promise of the sun's rising had paled the east and washed away the smaller stars. Last year it had in winter hung in the bare limbs of an old sweet gum by the road gate on Samuel Sexton's place they had rented. The year Cassie was born she'd never seen it at all; they'd lived low down on the eastern side of the ridge.

There was no whiteness of rock or glimmer of starlight under the pines to mark the craggy path down the ridge side to the spring, but she followed the path with no more thought for her feet than she would use to cross the kitchen floor. The spring seeped into a hollowed-out sand-stone basin at the foot of a low ledge, and without being able to see where stone ended and water began she squatted by the pool and dipped the bucket in, then lifted it and drank easily and soundlessly from the great thick rim as others might have sipped from a china cup. The water, cold with faint tastes of earth and iron and moss and the roots of trees, was like other drinks from other springs, the first step upward in the long stairs of the day; everything before it, was night; everything after, day.

She rinsed the bucket, then drew it up brimming full and went back up the path. Though at the top of the stair-like climb her breath came slowly and soundlessly as ever, she stopped and shifted the bucket to her other hand, looking straight above her through the pine branches to the stars. Little of the blue-black sky could be seen, and the pine boughs were mixed in with the stars, as if the trees carried stars instead of cones. A pine tree was a pretty thing. They'd let Clovis stay around three or four weeks before they took him off for good, and with more than enough money to buy a farm, and knowing the army would send her more, she'd buy coal oil and keep the lamp burning. Nights she and Clovis would sit around the stove and she would whittle on a poplar biscuit bowl like she'd been needing. Around it she would put a ring of pine twigs and on the side one white pine cone. But when Clovis was gone and she was settled on the farm, she would work again on the block of wood, nights in the firelight. She'd waited so many years, and now there was no need to wait. She had her land—as good as had it—and the face was plain, the laughing Christ, a Christ for Henley.

She hurried back to the kitchen where the two front caps of the stove glowed red, the coffeepot purred and talked to itself, telling itself it was ready to boil, and in the red glow from the stove the steam rose pinkish white from the tea kettle. She climbed the stair ladder and shook Clovis into wakefulness. 'It's time to git up,' she said.

He roused, shaking his head, then lifted himself on one elbow, and looked across the foot of the bed, searching for the square of light that would mark the loft-room window. Seeing only the star-sprinkled sky, he dropped back to the pillow, pulling the covers around him. 'Consarn it, Gert. It ain't anywheres close to daylight.'

She drew a deep breath. 'It's your army examinen day, honey,' she said.

At that he was up, for the special bus taking men to Cincinnati for their army examination left Town at six-thirty.

She wouldn't sorrow now and be afraid, she told herself. The real army was a little while away, and even then it would be only the training. Maybe the fighting would be over before he had to go across the waters; and all the while he was away there would be dollars every month to build up the Tipton Place. No money would have to go out to keep an old truck running, no half of the crops they raised would go to another man for rent. She felt guilty, pleasuring herself with such thoughts. When she scooped her hand into the lard, she took an extra pinch, for Clovis liked his biscuit bread flaky with lard.

She glanced at him as he curved his long narrow body over the stove top, shivered, rubbed his hands, then stretched with a mighty gaping and reaching up until his fingers touched the sloping cross beams of the lean-to kitchen. 'Git yer coffee, honey, off th warmen oven; it'll warm you up. Then you'd better hurry; it'll be gitten late,' she said.

79

'Oh, Law, my old woman a wanten to be shet a me,' he said with the same bright-eyed teasing look she had known when they were boy and girl together. He hugged her with both arms about her shoulders, playfully pushing his chin into the back of her neck, jiggling her so that she tipped the wooden mixing bowl until buttermilk sloshed on the table.

She jerked one elbow back against him, and spoke sharply as she might have to one of the children. 'Aw, Clovis, look at the gome you've made me make. Now git on. You'll git there jist when th bus is a pullen out.'

His hands slipped from her shoulders, but he stood an instant, his chin pressed against her, like a child's head leaning. 'Oh, Gert, lots a time I think you don't love me, nary a bit.'

The words were the same he had used many times, but the tone was different, less teasing, almost sad. He'd have her blubbering in a minute, making a fool of herself, like down at her mother's. She tried to put a teasing into her voice as she hunched her shoulders to get his chin off, for his breath was dampening her back hair. 'Lord, man, you're a big un to talk a love. Tie me hand an foot in a burnen house an have ole Uncle Ansel come to tell you his ole grist mill was down agin—you'd run off first to see what ailed th mill.'

'Aw, Gert, you're jealous a machinery like it was another woman.' He looked about the ramshackle kitchen, his eyes on the bare, rough-planked, big cracked floor as he said, 'I cain't much blame ye—fer all my machine fixen an coal haulen it's been a pore do.'

He went into the main room to put on the clean overalls she had laid out on the rocking chair, but was back in an instant, shivering, reaching in the woodbox for kindling. 'The youngens'ull freeze when they git up.'

Gertie dumped the dough onto the biscuit board and frowned at him. 'Now, Clovis, they ain't a bit a use a builden a fire an a waken th youngens.'

'But I want tu tell em goodbye.'

'But, honey, it ain't like you was a goen off to war this mornen— jist th examination. Why—why you mightn't pass, an if you do they

80

won't take you right away. If'n it's too cold in there, put yer clothes on here in th kitchen. I won't be a watchen.'

Clovis did as she directed, but kept glancing toward the room where the children slept. 'Jim Whittaker, he never got back,' he reminded her in a moment.

'It was just cause he didn't want to come back an wait around,' she said.

He slapped his razor on the strop hanging from a nail by the kitchen door. 'That waiten won't be no fun. Since Uncle Ansel cain't git hands, an hardly nothen a what he needs to run his mine, they ain't no coal to haul.'

'We've got grub to run us an—we'll git by,' Gertie comforted. She felt guilty, and tried not to want to tell him of all the money she had saved. She punched out flat rounds of dough and laid them in the bake skillet, shoved the skillet into the oven, turned the sow-belly, pushed it to one side of the frying pan, and then got the now partially thawed eggs out of the warming oven and broke them into the hot grease. While the eggs cooked, she tiptoed into the middle room and took from a row of boxes by the inside wall a quart jar of her precious sugar-sweetened preserves. She then took the meat and eggs from the skillet, and put in flour for gravy.

Clovis wiped his razor, folded it, but frowned still at his face in the mirror. 'I look like I'd been shaved with a cross-cut saw. Wouldn't it be somethin now to have it like th people in Town—th electric lights an bathrooms.'

Gertie poured milk over the browned flour, and frowned as she always did when she heard Clovis wish for some one of the wonders of Town. 'Electric lights an runnen water won't make a empty belly full,' she answered shortly. 'I'll bet they's many a time Meg would ha traded her electric fer a week's grub ahead, an her man made big money in th mines—when he got tu work.'

'Meg's seen a easier life than you,' he said, sorrow come back to his voice. 'No heaven and sweaten fer her tu make corn grow in land that ud be better left in scrub pine an saw briers, an then not keepen all you raise.'

Gertie turned sharply away. In another minute she'd be telling him about the money she had, and of how she meant to buy the

81

Tipton Place. Then he'd want the money for a bigger and better truck when he got out of the army, like the time he'd sold her heifer for tires. He might even want her to use up all his army pay, quit farming, and live in Town while he was gone. 'It ain't been so bad,' she said. 'They's a heap a people has seen it worse.'

'I'd ought to ha give up a long time ago an a gone to Oak Ridge like Samuel, but you—an Mom, too—wouldn't ever hear to it.'

'But you allus said me an th youngens ud have to come too,' she reminded him. 'An I ain't a wanten to be like Meg, allus liven from hand to mouth.'

'But she's had it easier an her youngens has got good schools,' he insisted, carrying the lamp to the kitchen table. He sat down but did not help himself to food. He looked up at her, his eyes soft, shiny brown in the lamplight. 'An anyhow, Gert, I've allus hoped you could have it nicer, way nicer'n Meg.' He looked at the plate of eggs and sowbelly she put in front of him, 'You wasn't raised to eat sowbelly in a tar-paper shack.'

She poured coffee, set it by his plate. 'Eat an quit carryen on so,' she said, her voice hoarse, angry-seeming. 'Our youngens is learnen,' she went on in a moment. 'An anyhow this settlement couldn't hardly a got along without yer tinkeren; th grist mill an th mail—'

'I wish to goodness you wouldn't call it tinkeren,' he burst out, a spoonful of gravy lifted above his eggs. 'In lots a places people that can fix machines as good as I can makes big money fer it—an I'd ought to ha gone off an got a job at it soon as times got good.'

'Aw, Clovis,' she began, and stopped; she'd only say the same things she'd said so many times already when he looked longingly at some letter from the employment office in Town begging him to go to work in that powder plant in Indiana or Willow Run or some other place.

He stirred the biscuit into his egg and gravy. 'If I'd a gone off to work like I ought three years ago, th army mightn't a gitten me now, an you'd all be a heap better off.'

'Mebbe not,' she said. 'They could a got you anyhow, like they done Millie Neeley's man—left her high an dry in Cincinnati where

82

he'd got a job, an her not gitten enough frum him in th army to keep her an th youngens in a town, an nothen back home to come to. You won't ever have to be a worryen on how me an th youngens'ull git along. I can manage.'

'By doen work fitten fer a mule—an th youngens growen up knowen nothen but work,' he said. He took one bite of biscuit and egg and gravy, and got up. He picked up his cup of coffee, and stood finishing it, quickly, as he took the lid from the refilled tea kettle and tested the water. 'It's hot enough. I don't want it bilen; it might crack th radiator, an I got all th holes fresh soddered up jist th other day.'

Gertie was stooping by the oven door, two fresh biscuits held lightly between her tough fingers. 'But ain't you a goen to eat, Clovis? You've got plenty a time.'

'I ain't hungry,' he said, and took his coal-dust-, grease-stained mackinaw from its nail behind the kitchen door.

'You ain't a comen down with fever er somethen, not eaten thisaway?'

He looked at her in hurt surprise. 'Woman, a body don't go off fer to be examined fer th war ever day. I wish you'd a got th youngens up.'

'But it ain't like you was a leaven fer true,' she said.

'Mebbe not,' he said, sighing, buttoning his coat. 'But all th same, it's somethen like th enden a th beginnen.' He crooked one arm and looked at the coat sleeve over it with sharp disgust. 'Did you wash this thing, Gertie? It looks like a bitch had had her pups on it, an raised em there.'

'I tried to,' she said apologetically, 'but it's old an th grease an coal dust wouldn't come out.'

'I wish t'goodness I'd a bought me a new jumper,' he complained. 'It's bad enough to go looken like a piece a pore white trash th'out bein' dirty into th bargain.'

'You'll look jist as good as a lot a th rest, I bet,' she consoled him. 'Looks ain't everthing.'

He rummaged through his pockets. 'Oh, law, I've left my wallet on th dresser. Take this an th spring water, an let her be a kind a warmen up. Recollect to shut off that petcock—I drained her.'

She took the flashlight from the high shelf and with the water went out to the truck, parked in the middle of the road at the top of a little rise so that the roll down might save cranking the motor. She set the kettle on the ground, knelt to search for the petcock, and only then turned on the flashlight, remembering as she always did when she saw its jabbing circle of light, how much it had cost and how Clovis was always having to buy batteries for it. Lantern light was cheaper, and she liked it better.

She turned the petcock. Holding the flashlight between her teeth, she poured the warmish spring water into the radiator, then poured in a little of the hot from the tea kettle, mixing them so that the hot might not crack the metal or the cold freeze. She had emptied both vessels, and rushed to the spring and back for more water before Clovis came.

As she poured in the last of the water, he gave her a hard quick hug, and a quick kiss that might have touched her lips had she not at that moment turned her head to see about the radiator cap.

He sprang in, twisted together the ignition wires, then as Gertie jerked out the rocks that wedged the wheels, he stepped on the clutch. She gave a push and the truck rolled away, slowly at first, then faster. She stood, bucket and tea kettle in hand, listening, watching. If it didn't start she'd have to go help him crank; but when the truck was hardly three-quarters of the way down she heard the cough and then the shivering roar. Still, she did not turn immediately away, but watched the black shadow of the truck pushing a weak blob of yellow light ahead. She watched it climb the rise, go along the level space of the ridge crest, turn onto the gravel, then down again. The black shadow was gone; only the sound was left, smothered by the hill, a lonesome going-away sort of sound, different from the noise of the truck's coming home.

She shivered, for the first time conscious of the cold.

The shivers did not go away completely until she had sat with her feet in the oven door long enough to drink a cup of coffee. She frowned, considering the lamp. The flame was turned down almost to blueness, but still it wasted oil and smelled up the kitchen, and daylight was yet a long while away. She wished for a churning, some work she could do in the dark, but the cold snap had kept the clabber from souring. Her fingers longingly touched the knife in her pocket; while the children were asleep would be a good time to bring the back of the head out of the block of wood. It would make her feel better, the whittling, and the block of wood would be company. She got up quickly, lighted the lantern, and went off to the barn for the peck or so of corn she had sorted out to shell for hominy. Millions of men were gone in the dark, and their millions of wives couldn't sit idlehanded and wait for daylight.

Later, she was glad she had hit upon the hominy making. The work helped keep the children busy, with less time for troubling over Clovis. It was hardly daylight before Enoch came running into the kitchen, half awake like a child in nightmare, crying that his pop had gone off to war and he hadn't kissed him good-bye. He wakened the others, and tenderhearted Clytie began to cry, so that Gertie must make a little lie and tell them that Clovis had kissed them all in their sleep before he left. 'It ain't like he was gone fer true,' she told them. 'He'll be back, mebbe as early as midnight.'

Cassie's eyes were doubtful as she said: 'But, recollect, you told us Uncle Henley, he'd be back. An Granma said he warn't never a comen back—never no more till th judgment day. Never,' she repeated, staring at her mother with her big-pupiled eyes, as if her mother's face might hold some answer to this new riddle of never.

'But your pop, he'll be all right,' Gertie said, her voice loud, insistent.

The children left off their crying and their questions, but she could not wipe the doubt from their faces. She was glad when the silent, scantily eaten breakfast was done, and enough daylight had come that she could go do the morning's chores in the barn. There, the cow and the mule and the fattening pig did not know that Clovis was gone.

In spite of the clear sunny weather and the pleasant bustle of hominy making, the children complained much of the length of the day. At noon only Amos was hungry, and though Gertie quarreled at them all for having eaten so much half raw hominy corn they couldn't eat their proper victuals she knew it wasn't the skinned hominy corn that filled their bellies, but the same thing that filled her own.

More than once through the long day, when the shadows of the house seemed fixed on the ground, she thought of the block of wood. Once, during the middle of the afternoon, she found herself kneeling by it, knife open in her hand. She sprang up, ashamed of her time-wasting ways, and went back to the hominy corn, bubbling through its last boil in a lard can on the kitchen stove. A pale finger of the low autumn sun had come at last through the kitchen window. She watched it as she stirred the hominy, but so slowly did it widen, so slowly did it move, that it seemed a dead thing, a differently colored strip of paper pasted on the wall. The band of light gave no brightness to the smoke-grimed building paper, faded into a dull red, but lay pale and sad, sadder than any sunlight she could remember.

There was no need, she told herself, to stand and stir the hominy like it was apple butter about to stick. Seemed like, though, it was the only thing she could think to do. She stirred and stirred and stared at the shelf on the wall behind the stove and at the wash bench by the kitchen door. They looked strange today, different, somehow, from the way they had looked yesterday.

The hominy was through the last boil long before milking and night work time. A moment's terror came down on her as she wondered how she could keep busy until time to go to the barn. She was standing on the porch searching out the children, who had gone walnut gathering to the far side of the field, when her eyes happened upon the great pile of knotty dead chestnut chunks she and Reuben had sawed last week. Clovis, she remembered, had quarreled when she and the boys had snaked it up out of old John's woods. Sure, Clovis had complained, the chinchy old skinflint would give them that for stove wood; if they did wear themselves out and saw it up nobody could ever split it, he had said. She smiled as she took the single-bladed splitting ax and the heavy white oak maul from their porch corner. Tomorrow morning, she told herself, she'd show Clovis her pile of split wood.

She selected what appeared to be a perfectly level spot, picked up an especially knotty, two-foot-wide cut of the dead chestnut, and put it there. She lifted the ax, held it an instant, searching out with her eyes the exact center of the wood. She sent the ax deep into the wood at the chosen spot. Then, with one blow of the maul, she buried the ax blade. She waited an instant for the crackling sound of splitting wood, and when none came she took the blunt-edged triangular froe, and holding it with one hand tapped it into the chunk of wood with the maul, careful to keep the sinking froe in line with the ax. As soon as the froe was firm in the wood, she raised the maul high in both hands and, bending a little, swung it in a high wide arc, bringing it down with such force that the block of wood sank a little into the earth and the head of the froe flattened somewhat.

The children straggling home with sacks of walnuts gathered round to watch. Now and then they gave cries of encouragement, and always shouts of joy as each chunk came apart. All were troubled, even Clytie, who hated all outdoor work, when one of the blocks swallowed both ax and froe and still showed not even a crack. Gertie sent Enoch running for the old iron wedge she'd used when she made rails to mend the fence. Hardly was it driven halfway in when the chunk gave up and came apart.

When the last chunk was quartered, she went to the house for a drink, and saw with something close to despair that the house shadow on the eastern side was still a hand's breadth away from the palings of the garden fence. She shook her head over the earliness of it, but all the same went on to the barn. There, she took heads of cane from the pile in one of the stables, and sitting on the low log sill, used a length of old crosscut saw and raked the cane seed down into her apron, dropped sack-like between her outspread legs. The fat hens, gentle as were all her animals, came pecking into her apron with quick out-thrustings of their heads. One, saucier than the others, stood on Gertie's knee and pecked at the head of cane. 'Git away, you feisty girl,' she said, and when the hen did not move, except to turn her head and look at her, she scolded in mock anger: 'I'll bet you didn't lay me a egg today neither. An eggs is better'n three cents a piece, my girl.'

The hen jumped away; and Gertie, looking after her, thought she had spoken unkindly, for with her bright comb, big wide behind, and neat slender legs she looked to be a good layer. She smiled on them all when she gathered the eggs—thirty-one that day. At this rate she could easily put another dollar in her pocket this week. Another dollar? For what? It was still like a sudden awakening from heavy sleep, each time it came to her that she had money enough for the land. Dollars now could go for other things—dishes, grass seed, new shoes for Cassie?

When she had put in more corn for the fattening pig and listened toward the house to make certain the children were all right, she walked across last year's cornfield. She stopped on its highest knoll to listen for Lizzie's bell. She heard at last the faint faraway tinkle that told her Lizzie had broken through the old fence and gone to the steep, wooded banks above the creek. Dock, of course, was with her, for he and Lizzie were great friends, one always lonesome without the other.

As she returned from the barn with the bridle, she realized she was singing at the top of her lungs, 'I've got a home in glory.' She checked herself with the guilty wonder of how she could sing on such a day—the day they took Clovis. They would turn him loose for a little while, but he would still be theirs, like a sheep wandering free on the range but carrying its owner's mark in its ear. But if some sheep were marked for slaughter, like Henley, others, like Clovis, would be all right. He'd be safe and cared for in the army. Once she was settled with the land bought and paid for, he'd be glad. He'd be more than glad if she saved his army wages for a truck. He might quarrel at the three miles of dirt road fit for nothing but a sled, but she and the boys would help him fix that.

She walked faster. There was inside her another upsurge of singing, even though she kept telling herself that all her fine plans would come to nothing if Uncle John Ballew didn't want to sell the Tipton Place. She plunged down the steep hillside below the field where the land lay north and east. Last night's thin snow still lay in the cuplike hollows of the leaves and at the feet of the tall, light-hungry trees. The dark hillside, after the sunny ridge, seemed another world, cold and set forever in a blue twilight. Dock came eagerly up to her and sniffed in her jumper pockets as if looking for corn. Lizzie lifted her head from a clump of fern and watched as Gertie broke a dogwood switch, brittle with the cold. Then, as if she were thinking, The night is cold and corn and fodder are better than fern, Lizzie turned straight about and went swiftly home.

Gertie smiled as she neared the barn, and heard Cassie's calling: 'Good night, sun, good night. I'll see you in th mornen. Sleep warm, sun.'

Supper without Clovis seemed more natural than dinner and breakfast. Bad roads, flat tires, and long trips had often made him full dark, coming home, so that the bigger children often ate supper before he got in and the little ones were sometimes asleep. The hominy making, the gathering of walnuts, and their other regular chores in the clear sharp weather had given them all good appetites. Gertie, sitting at the foot of the table with a lard bucket of sweet milk on one side of her, buttermilk on the other, a great platter of hot smoking cornbread in front, and other bowls and platters within easy reach, was kept busy filling glasses with milk, buttering bread, and dishing out the new hominy fried in lard and seasoned with sweet milk and black pepper. It was good with the shuck beans, baked sweet potatoes, cucumber pickles, and green tomato ketchup. Gertie served it up with pride, for everything, even the meal in the bread, was a product of her farming.

They were just finishing up on molasses and honey when Clytie let out a disgusted cry and sprang away from the table so hastily that her split-bottomed chair tipped backward. Cassie, standing between Clytie and Gertie, put her hand over her mouth and looked guiltily at her mother, while angry Clytie cried as she ran for the dishrag: 'Cassie, you're the gommeniest youngen; allus a spillen things. You're half pig.'

Gertie sighed and pushed the spreading pool of milk along the oilcloth with her knife blade so that it might run to the floor and Gyp get the benefit of it. Enoch quarreled, 'You'd slap me, Mom, if I all th time went around pouren out stuff.'

'You're bigger than her,' Gertie said, and to them all, 'Quit measuren your own corn in somebody else's basket.' She looked at Cassie, turning away from the table to hide the tears spilling over her cheeks. 'Hush your cryen, honey. Don't you want some bread an butter an jam? Recollect them wild strawberries we all picked back last spring? Well, I've got some a that jam open; sugar-sweetened it is, too.' She went for the jar she had opened for Clovis. Since he had not touched it, she had put it back in the press, thinking to save it maybe, for some Sunday morning when they were out of flour, with nothing much but cornbread and molasses and butter to eat.

The other children fell on the little jar of jam and emptied it in a moment. Only Clytie lingered daintily over the sandwich she had made for herself; Cassie's bread and jam that Gertie had fixed and urged upon her lay on her plate, untouched except for one corner scalloped with the marks of her small teeth. Gertie, clearing the table, called Cassie to come finish it. Instead of an answer there came from the main room, through the hubub of the other children, Cassie's voice, and low elfish laughter: 'They've took your man to th wars, Miz Callie Lou, clean acrost th waters, but they'll send him back to you. Allus recollect, Miz Callie Lou, they'll send him back to you—nailed down in a box with nickels on his eyes he'll mebbe be, but they'll send him back to you. So don't be a blubberen and a carryen on, Miz Callie Lou.'

Clytie, not listening to Cassie, was crying, 'Mom, Mom, you're a goen to make the lamp explode, a holden it sidewise thataway.'

Gertie hastily set the lamp she had jerked up back onto the table, and quickly turned away, afraid Clytie would notice the flusterment in her eyes. 'Now, Cassie, you've been a listenen to yer old rattle-tongued Aunt Sue Annie,' she called, raising her voice in mock sharpness. 'You'll be a scaren Callie Lou. Git in here, an hope Clytie with th dishes. You know how yer pop hates to come home to a dirty kitchen. An,' she went on, looking about for the others, 'don't any a you youngens be a gitten dunder-headed an sleepy now. We're a goen to have some studyen soon's th kitchen's readied an we can have the lamp in th middle room. Reuben, you build up th fire in th heaten stove. No matter how late it is, we don't want yer pop gitten back to a cold house.'

It was in the barn, where she had gone, as was her custom each night after supper, to take the supper slop to the fattening hog and make certain that all was well for the night, that Gertie stopped in the midst of scolding the pig for wasting his slop to say, 'I'll buy another lamp with th egg money this week.' She pondered, smiling a little at the pig, who looked at her and batted his long-lashed eyes. 'Two lamps'ull mebbe seem kind a wasteful, but when th nights is long th youngens, specially that Cassie, kinda needs em.'

She stood a moment in the barn hall, listening. The steady *clink, clink,* of a bell told her that Lizzie was chewing her cud. She heard Dock move in his standing sleep; a hen dreamed, talking; and she came away, sighing a little as she wished for sheep. The Tipton Place would be good for sheep, and she would get a start when the money started coming in from the army. She stopped as she crossed the barn lane, and, though she told herself that Clovis wouldn't be home until maybe the half-light, she listened until even her body, toughened to all weathers, felt the cold.

Back at the house she heard, as she opened the kitchen door, Enoch's soft but precise voice briskly sounding words from an old reader Mrs Hull had loaned them a few days ago: ' "the policeman held up his hand. The children—" '

Silence, then Clytie, her voice dressed up as if it had put on Sunday clothes as she tried to sound like the young teacher they'd had down from Lexington for two months in the summer before the city school in which she was a regular teacher had opened, 'Surely, Enoch, you know that word—a little common word like that.' More silence. 'Well, it's "smiled." Now look at it so's you'll recollect it.'

'I can recollect th big words a heap sight easier than the little ones,' Enoch said before reading again.

She heard Reuben's pencil on her old slate, and smiled. Her mother had laughed at it, for even when Gertie was little slates had been out of style. But her father had ordered it from Montgomery Ward, saying a slate was a good thing, since a teacher could, by listening, know if his scholars were working.

Gertie brought in the red cedar churn of cream, clabbered now, and Clytie looked up with her finger under a word. 'Mom, you oughta switch Cassie. We could have a real good school if it warn't fer her. She won't try to read her primer. Look at her.'

And, sure enough, Cassie lay on the sheepskin, one elbow on her neglected primer while she explored Gyp's mouth, her fingers feeling his teeth, even the ones far back, while he obligingly held his mouth open, smiling on her. He would have clamped his teeth hard on a hand of any of the others could they have managed to get so much as a finger into his mouth, but for Cassie, whether wandering through the woods or lolling in the house, he was ever a patient, smiling friend, even when she put her bonnet on his head and called him Callie Lou's granma.

'Listen, Cassie,' Gertie said. 'You want to grow up ignerent as old Gyp. Now leave him be an git busy with that primer.'

Cassie understood her mother's voice and smiled up at her through her long black lashes. Gertie thought of some bright-eyed wild woods bird giving her an instant's notice before it flitted away. 'Gyp?' Cassie asked, giggling. 'Where's Gyp? This is a lion. He's about to choke to death on gingerbread. He eats it too fast, like Amos, an he's been a choken an I been a hopen him.'

'You're all mixed up,' Clytie put in with some tartness. 'Th lion I've been a readen to you uns about in that old language book had a thorn in his paw.'

'My lion,' said Cassie, 'is choked on gingerbread.'

'Cassie, you're th biggest idjet. I'll bet Pop, if he wanted to, could draw coffee on you,' Clytie said all in a breath, then realizing what she had said, looked at Gertie with shamed eyes that asked forgiveness.

Gertie sighed, but only said, ' "He that calleth his brother a fool is in danger of hell fire." ' She turned to Cassie. 'Come read in yer primer now. I'll teach you while I churn.'

Cassie walked to her mother's chair, slowly, as if some great pain awaited her there. The mingled look of shame and guilt and puzzlement that always came when she wrestled with the primer changed her at once into a timid creature who seemed no kin to the Cassie of a moment ago.

Gertie turned away from the churn, put one arm about Cassie's waist, pulled her against her knee, and after smoothing her hair out of her eyes opened the book to the first untorn page. She put a finger under the first word as a signal to begin. Cassie bent very close to the book, then twisted backward against her mother's arm, peering fixedly at the word while Gertie warned, 'Don't git so far away, honey; you cain't see,' but already Cassie was sing-songing:

' "Here, Bobby. You can play. You can play with my kitten. Look, Bobby, Look." ' She turned the page, looked at the picture, then went on with no pause for breath, faster and faster: ' "Come

92

here, Bobby. Come here and see. You can see my kitten. You can play with my kitten. I can play with you." '

'That'll do,' Gertie said. 'Now what's this word?' and she put her finger under 'play.'

Cassie frowned, bent forward and studied the word, then pulled backward still looking at it. 'Ball?' she asked in a low voice, studying Gertie's face more than the word.

Enoch giggled, and even Reuben's slate was silent while he listened. Gertie sighed. 'Oh, honey, you've got yer whole primer by heart. It's "play"; now look at it good till you can recollect it. Now, what's this word?'

Cassie whispered rapidly to herself, then said in her hesitant, questioning voice, 'Come?'

'That's right,' Gertie said, pulling her closer. 'You're a goen to learn to read good, real good.' And she went on, pointing to words. Sometimes, after looking at the picture and whispering to herself, Cassie gave the right answer, but more often she did not. Gertie grew more and more conscious of Enoch's jeering giggles, Reuben's disapproving silence, and Clytie's brisk attempts at helping. 'Mom, mebbe if you tried that sample primer thet teacher give us—'

'We're gitten along fine,' Gertie said. But when the child looked up at her there was such shame and sorrow in her face that Gertie closed the book. She pulled the churn between her knees, smiling meanwhile at Cassie. 'You'll learn, honey; you're kindly little yit; jist five a goen on six, and you ain't had no schoolen, but you're a doen fine an—'

'But, Mom, you learned me fore I ever went to school,' Enoch interrupted.

'If'n you say another word, I'll git yer daddy's razor strop,' Gertie said, and gave the dasher such a hard quick lick that clabber squirted out the top.

The children stared at her. Their mother almost never threatened a whipping, and when she did she usually gave it. She took Cassie's hand and felt the cold sweat on the palm; trying too hard she was, trying harder than any of the others; she would from now on teach her when the rest were not around. Gertie said quickly: 'Cassie can count good; better'n any a you at her age—clean to a hundred. Show em, Cassie.'

But Cassie did not begin her usual gay tripping off of numbers. Instead she looked at her mother, and she was the wise one now, teaching the foolish. 'Mom—didn't you know you cain't take Pop's razor strop to Enoch? It ain't there no more. This mornen Callie Lou—she was a acten up so, a jerken my little youngens out a their beds an a playen in th fire an a carryen on so, th meanest I ever did see her, so's I tuck her to show her th razor strop. "Feel it", I says. "It'll hurt on yer backsides," I says. An, Mom, it warn't there. Pop, he's tuck it clean away.'

'Yer pop'ull be in about midnight; he ain't—' Gertie dropped the lifted churn dasher, pushed back her chair, picked up the lamp, and turned toward the kitchen. It seemed a long way from the chair by the stove to the kitchen wall behind the wash bench; the circle of lamplight moved with her, black shadows melting in front, black shadows closing behind. The silent children followed close at her heels in a tight little huddle, as if the lamplight were a warm thing that could shield them from the coldness of the shadows.

She walked close to the wash shelf without stopping, holding the lamp so close to the wall she could see the faint stripe of darker pink where the razor strop had hung for almost a year while the rest of the once red paper faded still more. She bent and rubbed the brighter strip, her hands more then her eyes forcing her brain to believe the emptiness. Clytie was crying behind her in accusing sobs, 'You'd ought to a told us, Mom, an a got us all up to a told him goodbye.'

Amos looked at his sister and cried from sympathy. Enoch sniffed, but he sounded happy, satisfied, when he said, 'Pop's gone off to war—none a th youngens around cain't make their brags to me no more, an say, "Yer pop he ain't a helpen with th war."' Then he, like Clytie, began to sob accusingly: 'Mom, you'd ought to a told us; we might never see him agin no more.'

Reuben caught his younger brother by his overall suspenders, and shook him until the twigs and dust and weed seeds flew out of his turned-up pant legs, 'Don't be a talken that away—*don't*.' And his voice rose, shrilling, until his last 'don't' was more wailing cry than command.

'You're a hurten him,' Clytie said, catching Reuben's arm, then looked up at her mother's broad, unmoving back, and spoke to it as she said: 'But Enoch, honey, they's no use to carry on so. Fer all we know th war ain't a wanten Pop—leastways not right away—he's gitten kind a old. Mebbe he's gone to work awhile in one a them factories.'

Gertie whirled with such a quick fighting swerve of her big body that the forgotten lamp in her hand sputtered, the flame hissing down to a dark blue line so that her voice cried from a darkness, 'He'd be better off in th war than in one a them factories!'

6

Gertie passed the empty schoolhouse on its high legs by the road. The yellow daisies Cassie and the other little ones had made back in the summer during the two months of school they'd had still clung to the windowpanes, but the petals were faded, unglued, and curling away from the glass. Forever Saturday the school was now. The coal the county board of education had paid Clovis to haul lay untouched in the yard.

She gave a backward glance to make certain Cassie was following, then walked on. It was the first time she had walked the graveled road since the day she had gone to her mother's. Though early and a weekday morning, the road seemed even stiller now. Sometimes she saw the sign of the mail mule, and twice she saw a rabbit, motionless in the road, looking at her with more curiosity than fear. Once, a squirrel quarreled at her from a young hickory. 'Sass, sass,' she said. 'You think cause th men's all gone, they ain't nobody left to hunt. But ole Gertie can shoot, an so can Reuben.'

The squirrel sprang away, and Henley for a moment came up from the back of her mind, thinning out the troubled wonder on Clovis. Tuesday now, and he gone since Thursday a week ago, and never a word. She was for an instant dead still, as if the death of her brother and the absence of her husband made a wall she could not pass. In spite of her plans for the Tipton Place, the days had dragged. The bigger children almost never worried aloud, but looked too often down the lane. Nights, as they sat studying, she saw too often the lifted head, the listening eye, when the faraway sound of a train or an airplane brought the hope, at least for a moment, that it was the sound of their father's coal truck coming home.

Cassie came calling behind her, 'Where's all the coal trucks, Mom?'

'Them that drove th trucks has gone away.'

'Why?'

'It got harder an harder to git tires an gas, an anyhow, even your daddy—he was th last trucker left—found plenty a people wanten coal, but he couldn't hardly git a load to haul.'

'Why?' Cassie persisted, running backward ahead of her down the road.

Gertie gave a weary headshake. 'They took a heap a th miners to th army, an some, like th Tiller men, went off fer th big money, an then them few that was left was like the truckers: they couldn't git blasten powder an hardly nothen they needed to work with. I recken they figgered that th mines, like the farms, was too little to—' She realized that Cassie had disappeared into a pine thicket by the side of the road.

She walked on, and soon came opposite Lister Tucker's house, where the yard gate lay fallen across the stepping-stones that Lister's father had put there before Lister was born. The frost-blackened, wind-beaten morning-glory vines still clung to the strings Lister's wife had tacked to the porch last spring, before Lister gave up trucking because he couldn't get tires for his truck. He and all his family had gone to Hampton Roads, Virginia.

Jaw Buster Miller's house was just over the next rise, but further back from the road. It was a nice-looking house, with new paint and lots of windows, for Jaw Buster had long made steady money on the railroad section gang. But now the uncurtained windows shone blindly in the sun like the unseeing eyes of the dead, all save one, and it was broken. Some youngen had done that; she paused, wondering if it could have been one of her own. Her own and the Hull children were about the only ones left big enough to throw rocks. Jaw Buster's family had soon followed him when he left the section gang for bigger money in a steel mill at Gary, Indiana.

She stopped and shifted the basket of eggs to her other arm when just ahead she saw Samuel Hull's store and post office. She stared at the building for some minutes, frowning, her lips moving. She walked again, still frowning in thought, but whispering hoarsely now, 'Miz Hull, I don't recken you've heared enything about Clovis.' Her frown deepened. That didn't sound right, not to Mrs Hull, with her eighteen-year-old son across the ocean and her husband gone to war work.

She reached the turning in of the lane, and saw with relief that she wouldn't have to ask Mrs Hull to quit her work and come to the store. The store door was open, and sleeping in the sun by the store porch was a high-shouldered, sway-backed mule hitched to a homemade sled. The old mule never lifted his head nor left off his dozing when she walked up, but she nodded to him as to a neighbor; and to the thin spotted hound with the torn left ear curled asleep in the sled she spoke, her voice apologetic, touched with sorrow. 'I heared you two nights ago, Sugar Bell, but I couldn't come. Nobody's left to come now to th foxes you hole.'

The old hound lifted his head and looked at her with rheumy, sleep-dulled eyes. She smiled at him, then hurried up the porch steps. The small-windowed store and post office seemed dark as a cave after the bright sunlight, and for an instant she could see nothing, only hear the twittering voice of her mother-in-law, 'Thank goodness, it's Gertie.'

Then Mrs Hull's pleased welcome, 'You've come right when you was needed th most.'

The blackness cleared, and Gertie saw the two women, side by side, on a homemade bench by the stove, smiling up at her, but weary, troubled under the smiles. Clovis's mother, whom Gertie, like everyone else in the settlement, called Aunt Kate, seemed smaller, thinner, with whiter hair and browner skin than Gertie could remember. When she reached to pull a cockle burr off Gertie's coattail, the hand seemed some little brittle thing whittled from brown wood, but there was life and kindliness in her voice as she asked:

'You all well, Gertie? How's Cassie Marie? She didn't come with t'others that Sunday about a week ago. Amos was a looken good. I was plum ashamed I never did git out to see him, but I cain't allus be a beggen off one a Miz Hull's girls to stay with th old man.'

'Law, Aunt Kate, Amos was might nigh well when I brung him home. It was mighty good a you to come an stay with th youngens while I had him at th doctor's,' Gertie said, remembering all the times she had thanked Aunt Kate for help in time of trouble. At all the bornings of her children, it had been Aunt Kate who came instead of her mother. The children had all had whooping cough when Amos was a baby hardly six months old. Her mother had been too puny to come, but Aunt Kate had helped her through the nights with the choking little ones and the vomiting older children. But then, as now, there had been only stumbling words of gratitude, never the right words. She smiled on the older woman and wished for words, something easy and careless for asking about Clovis. She didn't want to add to Aunt Kate's worries; troubled enough she was now with three other boys gone, and the baby one Jesse missing for six months.

She was still hunting words when Aunt Kate, restless-tongued like her sister Sue Annie, asked, 'Your mother holden up pretty good?'

Gertie nodded. The childhood hope that her mother could live like other people instead of just 'holding up' had long since died to a wish.

'I heared Clovis didn't come back frum his army examination,' Aunt Kate said, getting up. 'That Sunday I kinda thought he acted like it was goodbye, th way he set around with th old man. You got any notion if'n he's went straight into th army er to one a them factories?'

Gertie shook her head. 'I'll shorely hear in this evenin's mail. It's better'n a week now.' She tried to hold her voice level and let it show nothing of the terror that had ridden her most of the time since last mail day, when she had decided that something bad must have happened to Clovis. Almost as hard to bear as the fear were the shame and vexation that came on her now with the calmly waiting women when her mind decided that nothing was wrong with Clovis except that he just hadn't bothered to write.

'A week ain't hardly long enough to hear,' Aunt Kate was saying. 'It'll be five weeks an two days since I heared frum Barney. An then it was one a them funny little letters a body cain't hardly read, like th last I had frum Jesse.'

99

'You'll be a hearen—a hearen real soon,' Mrs Hull said, getting up, smiling at the older woman, who now, like a restless bird, had flitted to the door, 'An anyhow, we've got one piece a luck—Gertie can help us load this sled.'

Gertie set the basket of eggs on the counter. She turned around and for the first time noticed, halfway between the stove and the back of the room, a sack of cow feed. The gay pattern of purple flowers and red-billed parrots of its covering seemed a thing from some gayer world, dropped by accident into the old store with its homemade shelves and counters and smoky-brown plank walls. There was something contrary about its plump brightness stretched on the floor between the two weak-backed women, neither of whom had ever been any good at lifting, and Mrs Hull with a baby hardly six weeks old.

'I've got to learn to manage this store thout a man,' Mrs Hull said. 'I keep a thinken a man'ull come along when I know they's no man to come,' and she watched with something like envy as Gertie picked up the hundred-pound sack of feed, and tossed it lightly to her shoulder.

Gertie smiled. 'I recken I'll have to be th man in this settlement. Aunt Kate, you'd ought to ha sent fer me er Reuben to git up this feed.'

'Law, I can manage,' Aunt Kate said, gathering up the reins. 'We've still got plenty a coal Clovis hauled us, an ever time Reuben comes he cuts more stove wood. I been so addled, I never noticed I was runnen out a cow feed. An sean as it was a pretty day, I thought a little walk ud do Jerry good; he's stood around so long he's gitten stiff.'

She turned to the hound, who had climbed out of the sled when Gertie threw in the sack of feed, 'You can git back in now, Sugar Bell. All at once seems like he's got old, an he won't hardly eat nothen. Any kind a little hunt runs him down fer three er four days till he cain't do nothen but sleep. I biled us all up a hen t'other day, an he didn't eat no more'n th old man. Jesse'ull be a thinken I didn't take good care a him like I said I would. If'n you git any lard, Mary, recollect to save me some—butter shortenen in th biscuit bread is a killen th old man. Gertie, I hate to run off like this, but if th house

100

was to burn down th old man couldn't hope hissef.' She saw Cassie with Gyp at her heels skipping down the lane and waving a bunch of red dogwood berries. 'Let her go with me, Gertie, she'll be a sight a company.'

Gertie hesitated. She seldom let Cassie go visiting alone, forever spilling things, falling down, wandering off into the woods, talking to herself and confusing her deaf old grandfather, she might be more trouble than company. But while she hesitated, Aunt Kate had stopped the sled, Cassie had jumped in, and was now commanding Gyp to come ride with Sugar Bell. There was nothing for Gertie to do but remind Cassie to be a good girl and help her granma, and call to Aunt Kate not to make another trip for the mail. She would bring it and get Cassie. 'Recollect,' Mrs Hull called, 'it'll be late; Uncle Ansel is a riden his mule.'

The mule had started again, and Kate followed, giving no sign that she had heard. 'I wisht she'd set on that sled an ride,' Gertie said.

'She cain't hardly set still a minnit,' Mrs Hull said. 'She keeps a thinken she'll hear frum Jesse; she won't give in to believen that missen in action so long could mean—' Remembering Gertie's uncounted eggs, she turned back toward the door of the store.

Gertie followed, then stopped in the doorway. 'My traden can wait till mail time. I come . . .' One finger popped and then another before she could bring out the words. 'To tell you th truth, I jist got so fidgety wonderen on Clovis I jist started out; I thought mebbe you, Aunt Kate, somebody—knowed—'

'It's th first few days that is th worst,' Mrs Hull said. 'About all a body can do is keep real busy.'

'That's one a my troubles right now,' Gertie said. 'I'm pretty well caught up on th fall work—an renten a place ain't like haven one a yer own to work on.' She looked at a small patch of ground that bordered the lane, a dead-looking spot that seemed mostly weeds. 'Miz Hull, couldn't I dig yer taters? I'd ruther be a doen somethen than visiten—er plain waiten.'

Mrs Hull looked at the little field, started to say something, but choked. Gertie remembered that Andy, her oldest child, had planted the potatoes, taking time out from high school in March—in May

101

he had graduated—and now in early November he was on the other side of the world. 'Where's a spaden fork?' she asked, more and more ashamed of her own weak ways when her turn at waiting came; and when Mrs Hull hesitated she insisted, 'Back in th old days everybody hoped th preachers do their work, an it ud be a sin to let em rot.'

'But you must let me pay you,' Mrs Hull said. 'Samuel's not a preacher—now. He's left God's work fer Oak Ridge.' She shivered. 'Whatever it is.'

'I recken he thought it was his patriotic duty,' Gertie said, as she went with Mrs Hull for the spading fork. She didn't like the accusing way the woman spoke of Samuel, for he among all the preachers she had known seemed closest to God. He worked with his hands like Jesus, but better yet she'd never heard him try to scare the souls of the people loose and herd them up to God like driving stampeded sheep into a locked barn.

She thought sometimes on Samuel and the other ones away as she worked, sending the prongs of the spading fork slowly down with her foot, then pushing gently backward with one hand on the handle so that the hill of potatoes came up with the earth, unscarred and whole. The shadows of the little mounds of earth she made, shortened, turned more northward, but lay a little westward still when Mrs Hull called her to the good and bounteous dinner she and Rachel, the oldest girl, had cooked.

She and Mrs Hull and the seven little Hulls of eating size sat about the long oilcloth-covered table in the kitchen, while the baby slept in a back bedroom, and the radio played softly in the front room. They ate with little talk. Mrs Hull was absent-minded, passing Gertie the fried fresh ham twice, and never the potatoes at all. Once she went to see about the baby, she said, but she must have looked at the clock in the front room, for when she sat down again she said: 'I allus hoped they'd never take Clovis. He could a kept that old mail car a runnen. When Uncle Ansel rides his mule seems like mail-day waiten lasts ferever.'

'Where's Andy?' Gertie asked, and hoped her voice would sound the way she would have it sound—easy and off-like, as if he were away visiting; not low and sad the way her mother had always wanted people to ask about her health.

'His letters come through New York, an frum th way they sound we think he's in France,' Mrs Hull answered. She had learned to manage her voice; 'France' to the listening children might have been a neighbor's place over the hill.

Gertie shook her head to Mrs Hull's after-dinner urging that she sit awhile and listen to the news broadcast that came at twelve o'clock. Mrs Hull's house, like her mother's and most houses, smothered her.

It was good to be alone back in the potato patch. But the sun had hardly started down the sky before she heard a woman's voice and children's chatter in the lane. She looked up to see Mamie Childers with a baby on one arm, a split basket of eggs in her other hand, the basket dragged down by a child hardly of good walking size, whimpering and stumbling as it hung on to the handle. Some distance behind came her oldest, no older than Amos, but big enough to carry the empty coal-oil can.

Mamie saw Gertie, started to wave, but remembered she had no hand free, and came on so fast the toddler let go the basket and stood wailing in the road. 'Has th mail got in yit?' Mamie asked, gasping, putting the basket of eggs on the ground, and letting her tired body sag against the fence. She didn't live much more than a mile away, but it was an uphill climb with such a dragging load.

'Uncle Ansel had to ride his mule,' Gertie explained. 'It'll mebbe be on th other side a sundown fore he gits in.'

'Oh,' Mamie said, and then again, 'Oh.' Gertie thought she was going to cry when she said, her voice still breathless, 'I cain't be dark a gittin back home.' She asked quickly, as if afraid of the answer, 'Is th ole mail car so tore up Clovis cain't fix it?'

'Clovis is gone,' Gertie said, bending to dig another hill.

'Lord, Lord,' Mamie said, her words a kind of troubled moaning. 'What'll I do when I run out a coal? I cain't cut wood to do no good. An what'll we uns do now if a youngen gits sick an nobody to take it to th doctor?'

'I tuck mine on a mule,' Gertie said.

'But you've got big youngens, big enough to leave by theirselves at home,' Mamie said. She was leaning heavily against the fence, as if the learning of the goneness of Clovis, the last man, had been the

103

last burden her tired body could bear; but her eyes, Gertie thought, looked more sick than tired. They were big and bright as the eyes of a child just coming out of a long spell of fever.

'Whyn't you go set with Miz Hull an listen to th radio? You look plum tuckered. We'll all git along, somehow,' Gertie comforted.

'Don't tell me to go listen to no radio,' Mamie said. 'Alec got me one afore he left. "It'll be company," he says. But I hate th thing.'

'They say th war news ain't so bad,' Gertie said.

'Oh, it ain't th news. An anyhow Alec ain't in Germany where Hitler is. He's in France, Miz Hull figgered frum his letters.' Her voice dropped to a whisper. 'It's th people on th radio. I cain't git used to em. I fergit.' She looked at Gertie, held her with her eyes. 'T'other night I was a comen in frum milken—it was a misten rain an already dusty dark in th valley—an I heard this woman a talken in th house. She didn't talk so quair-sounden like most a them on th radio does, an I thinks to myself, "Somebody's come a visiten, an they'll mebbe stay all night." I broke into a run, a spillen haf th milk, an was clean through th kitchen fore I recollected th radio, an knowed I was still by myself. Th youngens thought I was crazy when I cried. But it would ha been so good on that black rainy night to ha had some neighbor woman by fer company.'

'Law, woman,' Gertie said, moving to the next hill, 'you've got plenty a company—yer youngens. They's a sight a company in jist a little baby. An yer stock—a good milk cow is a kinda friendly thing. An all snug down there in th valley with trees close, an that creek to hear, an then th radio.'

Mamie shook her head with despair at Gertie's lack of understanding. 'But what if I got mistook agin when I heared people, real people, an I jist thought it was th radio, an it was somebody mean mebbe comen to kill me an th youngens?'

'But, honey, they ain't no men, nobody left in this whole country to hurt a body,' Gertie said, looking away from the woman's eyes, then back again, smiling. 'But if'n it'll make you feel any better, I'll send Clytie down tomorrow evenin to stay th night. An when th weather turns bad, she can stay with yer little youngens long enough fer you to come git yer mail.'

Mamie had flashed her a look of inexpressible gratitude when a wail from down the lane caused her to turn her head, then cry, 'Oh, Lordy, I cain't so much as talk fer these youngens.' She rushed to the two-year-old who had fallen into a muddy rut in the road, and now lay screaming, gommed from head to foot with mud and water.

Gertie hurried with her digging. If she wasted much more time in gabbing, she wouldn't finish the patch by dark. But as always she paused a moment at the end of the row away from the house. Samuel's ridge fields were even higher than her rented ones. Standing on the edge of the field, she could see across the valley of the Big South Fork where white-painted houses like Samuel's and her mother's shone on green lawns above brownish fields of shocked corn that stretched down to the willow-fringed river. Higher than the houses rose the hay and pasture fields, still green from the rainy fall. The fields went up the lower slopes of the front row of hills to meet the timber near the top; and past this first row of timbered peaks and ridges others stretched away for miles and miles.

She always hurried at the other end near the store where there was nothing to see but the little Hulls beginning to do their night work. She heard through the open front door the hum of Mrs Hull's sewing machine and one of the younger boys singing to the baby brother whom Andy, the oldest, had never seen; but louder than anything was Mamie's talk, a loud, excited, half laughing, half quarreling talk, the noise of a woman with her tongue hungry for talk.

More people came down the lane: children running, women with babies in their arms walking tiredly, old women like Sue Annie, hurrying, with no wind left for gossiping. They would see her and forget the old greetings of other days like, 'How's your mother a holden up, Gertie?' or, 'Law, Law, it's been a time an a time since I've seen you. When are you a comen to stay all day?' Instead, they all, young and old, asked with breathless abruptness, 'Has th mail got in?'

And she would shake her head and explain that old Ansel's car was broken down and that he rode his mule, and most likely wouldn't be in till past sundown. They were usually stricken silent, and would stand for a moment in the lane, uncertain of what to do, but always more slowly and often wearily, they would go on to Mrs Hull's house or the post-office porch. Some, hungry for talk like Mamie, continued to stand by the fence, but Gertie had worked her way almost across the little field, and the distance made conversations brief. Even Sue Annie could talk only a little after being stopped dead in her tracks by news of the lateness of the mail. 'An here I am,' she cried across the field, 'tuckered clean out frum a washen, rushed through dinner, an a hurryen up th hill—when I ought to ha been a butcheren my fattenen hawg. An by tomorrer mornen most like it'll be warm agin an a rainen, an Nellie Sexton a haven her baby.'

'Th wind's set in frum th north,' Gertie called back.

'But that won't hold back Nellie's baby,' Sue Annie cried, turning with a suspicious sniff toward the north. She tried to call out some opinion on the weather, but between the quick walk up the hill and her calling conversation even she was too breathless to speak loud enough for Gertie to understand. Yet, some minutes later, when Gertie had dug to the end of the row next to the post office, Sue Annie, all her wind come back, was carrying on about Clovis. What if Uncle Ansel's grist mill broke down and they had to eat boughten meal? The government owed them at least one man who could fix anything and never got drunk.

Gertie turned to the next row, glancing half hopefully, half fearfully, down the lane as she did so. It was too early for Old John, she told herself. He was no weak woman to come rushing for the mail before his day's work was done. Still, she looked again before she was hardly to the middle of the row, but saw only Ann Liz Cramer, Claude Cramer's wife, with the younger half of her family, come from across the Big South Fork. The woman waved to her; Gertie waved, then listened to Ann Liz's laughing account of the wild time they'd had on the high swift river in a little skiff overloaded with themselves and the eggs and molasses they had brought to sell.

The Cramers, her mother said, were getting rich out of the war. None of the boys or Claude had enough book learning to go to the fighting, but Claude and the four older children, one of them a girl, had factory jobs in Muncie and batched while Ann Liz and the younger ones farmed. Now, there was hardly a mail but what brought a package of some finery or house plunder for Ann Liz.

She thought on Ann Liz and her farming as she reached the far end of the row where far below her a narrow band of shadow like a black line on the blue lake of the river told her more than a clock of the turning down of the day. Standing there looking out across the world, the war with all it brought and all it took away seemed somewhere else, not near enough to shorten her breath and chill her hands as when she listened to Mamie or sat in Mrs Hull's crowded house. She had only to look up the creek from the shadow on the river to a place hidden in a fold of the hills, and all the twisting troubles would leave her. Sorrow there was for Henley dead and worry for Clovis gone, but even these could not take away the wonder of the thing waiting for her as the Promised Land had waited for the Israelites—the Tipton Place. Maybe in only a few minutes now it would be her own.

The shadows crossed the river, touched the willows and the red birch on the other side, then strode steadily up the westward hillside. One by one the white houses seemed to slip under a thin blue cloak of smoke that thickened on the river, though high above, the wooded hills stood warm-looking and faintly pink in the low red sun. Black coal smoke rose from the post-office chimney, and from inside there came the cries and jabbers of little youngens with snatches of talk from the women, still-sounding and scattered, like the talk of women in church before services begin. Even the older children were touched by the waiting. More than one would stop, the way her own acted now that their daddy was gone, be suddenly still in its work or play, head lifted, listening. Its face for an instant would be like the faces of the old women or the young ones with babies on their arms who came every moment or so to stand on the porch and look up the lane and listen.

There was still sunlight enough to make shadows on the high ridges when Old John came, walking slowly and stiffly. Gertie looked at him, eager yet afraid. Though people said he'd bought it just as a favor to Silas Tipton, who needed the money to move his family; what if he didn't want to sell the place? She waited, calling to him with her eyes, but he never raised his head. He walked on down the lane with his eyes on the ground, but not like a man studying the ground. His shoulders and his bent stringy neck bespoke a man so old and tired he looked at the ground because it was the easiest thing to do.

He looked so old, she sighed as she turned back to the digging. He had four sons and three sons-in-law scattered over all the world in the fighting, and even his children not in the war were scattered. The spading fork handle was sweaty under her hands. She studied him as he turned up the post-office steps; he looked like he was in a selling humor. Her father always said he would never have sold his timber if he hadn't had a bad spell of rheumatism and no child left to help him.

She realized that while she had been gaping after John, her peace and silence had been destroyed. All the Hull children, helped it seemed by everybody else waiting for the mail, had come into the potato patch loaded with all the Hull tubs, baskets, buckets, and old gunny sacks to gather the potatoes. She saw with some sorrow that Aunt Kate and Cassie were among them. She started to scold the old woman for wearing herself out with a useless trip to the post office when she could have taken the mail and got Cassie, but instead Aunt Kate scolded her for having done such a deal of digging.

'Law, Aunt Kate,' she said, lifting her head, smiling, flinging back her hair. She realized Old John was looking at her, and that in his eyes, dimming and bluing up with age, there was something of the warmth and gladness that had used to be his when he looked at a timbered hillside he had watched grow from saplings to tall timber. 'Gertie, you're about th best tater-diggen hand I've ever seen,' he said. The warmness in his eyes widened, spread until his hollowed, gray-whiskered cheeks wrinkled with smiles.

'Why, I bet I ain't a bit better'n Mary was at my age, an she ain't hardly half my size,' Gertie said.

He glanced around to make certain no one noticed, took a long reflective rolling chew on his quid, then spat with careful precision at a little sandrock. He stepped nearer, glanced quickly around again, then said in a voice hoarse with his attempt at whispering, 'Gertie, they's a little piece a business me an you ought to go into right away.'

She gripped the spading-fork handle, leaned on it heavily, and looked hard at the potatoes she had just dug. Her insides were all a tremble, like some colt of a boy who has just begged a girl into the bushes but won't let on how tickled to death he is and wants to make her think it's all her doing. She moved to the next hill, pushed the spading fork down, and got herself in hand. 'You mean you're a wanten me to move an kind a shamed tu say so. You needn't be. That place ain't fitten fer nothen. I'll have to feed mighty close to make th little corn I've raised run me till picken time, an you know I ain't hardly got no stock atall to feed.'

'Now, Gertie, you know I ain't a tryen tu make you move. I've allus said you was one a th best renters I ever had.' He spat again and looked at her sideways from the corners of his eyes, smiling a little. 'But if me an you could do a little traden, your renten days ud be over.'

She dropped the weight of her hand onto the spading-fork handle and wondered that he could not hear the jumping of her heart. 'Law, Law, Uncle John, what th old preacher says is th truth, "To every thing there is a season and a time to every purpose under the heaven." Right now don't seem like th time to talk about renten. Didn't you know they'd got Clovis an I'm all tore up?'

John spat with a gesture of disgust. 'Now, Gertie, I know Clovis is gone an you're his wedded wife, an you feel bad an miss him.' He glanced around again, made a still greater effort to whisper. 'But you ain't no Mamie Childers lost on a little farm 'thout a man. Now, I don't mean a word a harm—an I like Clovis an I hoped they'd leave him. He's got a good turn, an when it comes to tinkeren they ain't nothen on earth he cain't fix. But jist between you an me—an I mean no harm—when he was home he warn't worth a continental to you in th crop maken. His coal haulen wasn't regular, an his tinkeren didn't bring in much. He loved it too well—he'd tear down some feller's old car an set it up agin an mebbe never git paid.'

Gertie smiled at him. 'Them army wages comes in mighty steady. I won't be a haven to pray fer rain on some pore piece a corn on a sandy ridge top fit fer nothen but scrub pine. Why, I'm a thinken about renten Lister Tucker's house right by th road an never a botheren with no crops. It'll be handy to th school an th mail.'

Old John smiled. He knew she was lying. 'Now, Gertie, you know you couldn't do thout maken a little crop a some kind. An as fer bein handy to th school, why everbody knows that schoolhouse'ull set there cold an empty till th war's over.' He smiled again and patted her shoulder. 'I recken you was a thinken a renten Lister's place while you was a goen over th old Tipton Place—I seen yer whittlen sign where you'd set by th spring an tried to figger how you'd git it frum me fer haf its price, a knowen I never wanted it in th first place.'

Gertie, completely mistress of herself now, tossed back her head and smiled, then bent to another potato hill, speaking careless-like to the spading-fork handle. 'Law, Uncle John, I hadn't hardly thought a thing about it. A woman's got no business traden round without her man. But how much'ull you give me to take it off yer hands?'

He smiled at her as she straightened for the next hill. 'Many's th time, Gertie, I've wished you could ha been one a my own. You're mighty nigh as good a hand at farmen as I am, an if I don't watch out you'll git th better a me in this trade.' He looked at her a moment in silence, his head twisting upward a little, for she was taller than he. 'Do you know why I'm a doen this, Gertie, offeren you land fer th same price I paid fer it—somethen I ain't never done? Fifty years ago I bought cut-over timberland fer fifty cents a acre, but I sold it fer more. Some uv it I've still got growed up in timber.' He remembered the sold timber, the cut trees, and he was for an instant an old man unable to steady his wandering mind.

He looked away toward the hills, then back to Gertie. 'It's fer yer ole pop. I seed him t'other day.' He hesitated, looking at her, and Gertie, no longer able to act uninterested, nodded as he went on. 'I ain't a tryen tu meddle in yer business, but yer pop told me about th money they give you—enough he thought to buy th place, he said. He'd give his good leg to know you could allus be close by him—close enough that he could come set in your house sometimes.'

He cleared his throat, and spoke carefully, as if his words were unsteady feet on slippery ice. 'Yer pop ain't had a easy life. It's like Sue Annie says—Henley was his boy, too, his onliest boy. So that place is yours, Gertie, fer what I paid—five hundred. Whatever you want to give me down; th rest on time with interest—half a cent less'n th bank, five an a half.'

Gertie nodded, but it was a moment before she could speak, and then her voice came choking and halting: 'I can pay it—all, Uncle John. All these yers—' She thought she was going to cry. She stood a long time bent over a potato hill, unable to see the spading fork, the undug potatoes forgotten. It couldn't be true. So many times she'd thought of that other woman, and now she was that woman: 'She considereth a field and buyeth it; with the fruit of her own hands she planteth a vineyard.' A whole vineyard she didn't need, only six vines maybe. So much to plant her own vines, set her own trees, and know that come thirty years from now she'd gather fruit from the trees and grapes from the vines. She hardly heard old John as he talked on about the price of land. He didn't think land would ever get any cheaper. She was paying about eight dollars an acre with that good log house thrown in. Some would say that was high, the old ones remembering fifty cents an acre for cut-over land, but now there were more people but no more land. . . .

She realized he had grown silent, and looked up. She saw that he stood with one hand behind his ear, listening toward the road. She looked about and saw that the women and children, who a moment ago had been talking, all were stilled; even Sue Annie was like a frozen woman.

Gertie thought for an instant of a game the children played where on a signal everybody had to stop and hold himself exactly as he was. But hound dogs never played games, and now they stood, heads lifted, listening like cur dogs. She heard it then, the sound faint on some high spot on the ridge road far away. A strange car was coming in, not the grocery truck but a car. The only cars that came brought news.

It seemed like something was choking her. She stood, the spading fork gripped in both hands. She wanted to go on with her work, dig another hill, but could not. Maybe it was some coal truck the government had left by mistake out hunting a load of coal. Unless a man were lost or hurt or killed in the war, they didn't make a special trip to bring the news. She tried to reason, but ice-cold hands, stronger than any human hands could be, were squeezing her chest and back, pushing on her throat.

111

It wasn't her turn. Clovis had been gone only ten days. Her turn had come with Henley. It wouldn't come back. Turn by turn, she told herself. Still she listened, with her whole body, as the others listened, heads lifted, nostrils faintly flared for the thin wind. It was nothing, not a thing; they'd all been scared by a wandering airplane. Then Matthew, Samuel's oldest boy at home, and twelve years old, who stood by the fence, called to the older and those further down the field, 'It's a car—a good-runnen car that don't make hardly no noise—a comen thisaway.'

Old John's faded eyes searched the faces of those nearest him. He understood from them what was happening, though he had heard nothing. He straightened his shoulders, spat out his quid, buttoned his jumper, then stood, shoulders braced, hands hanging empty by his sides, and waited like an innocent man standing up to be sentenced in court.

Gertie looked at him and remembered his four sons in the fighting; from him her glance went to Aunt Kate, who had been kneeling, emptying the potatoes the children brought in buckets and baskets into a tub. The old woman knelt with an unemptied bucket clutched in her hand, her head lifted, her eyes fixed on the road. In her ashy face, the eyes were wide and bright, straining, fighting to know. They made Gertie think of Cassie's eyes when Cassie tried to read and could not. Her hands would be clammy cold like Cassie's. Of which boy was she thinking? It was enough to know the news cars brought was never good.

Gertie plunged the spading fork into the ground and went and took the old woman by the arm. 'Let's me an you go back to th store,' she said, and pulled her to her feet. Aunt Kate's weight, dragging on her hand, seemed hardly more than that of Cassie, but her steps were uneven and springless. She was old, older than the old ought ever to have to be, old like her own father, and John and Clovis's father, and all the other old ones with their young in the war.

Gertie led her to the store porch where Mrs Hull stood, looking down the lane as she rocked Mamie's baby in her arms. Mrs Hull's ears were dead to the child's crying, a weary frightened weeping as if some of its mother's long terror had entered into it before its borning.

112

Gertie put Kate on one of the benches in front of the store stove. Mamie's baby hushed its crying, and in the silence Gertie heard the car. It was round the bend by the schoolhouse, following the gravel clean to the end, plainly hunting someone. She sat for an instant by old Kate, and though their bodies did not touch she could feel the old woman's quivering through the bench. She got up. She wished she were back in the potato patch, digging hard and alone, able to look out toward the hills. 'My help cometh from the hills.'

She wanted to begin at the beginning and say it all to Kate, but when she looked at her she could not. The old woman's unnaturally bright and somehow pleading eyes were fixed on the stove, holding to it as if the stove, and not the bench she gripped with a hand on either side a knee, held her up. 'Couldn't I git you a drink er somethin, Aunt Kate?' she asked at last.

Kate shook her head with a slow quavering, but would not look away from the stove, 'It ain't turned off no place, has it?'

'Not yit.'

Old Sugar Bell, wandering in with other hounds and young children, came sniffing out Kate and laid his head in her lap. He looked up at her, and the old woman seemed to take comfort from his touch, and began to smooth his forehead as if he were a troubled child. Gertie left them so, looking at each other, and went to stand on the porch with the rest of the company gathering there.

The sound of the car came steadily now. In a moment Gertie saw the flash of metal in the low sun as the car came through a place in the ridge road where the pines were thin. Even Sue Annie and the frightened baby continued silent, listening, watching, waiting. All were like people huddled together in a wild storm, looking out, looking up, wondering what next the wind will take or the lightning strike.

Old Lucy Anderson, with her five sons gone and her husband away with the mail, stood stiff and still on the top porch step like a wooden woman. Old John, his hat in his hand, his thin shoulder blades like folded wings under his buttoned-up jumper as he tried to stand straight with lifted head, waited on the bottom step in front of the women to take the message the car brought. He would talk to the strangers in the strange car, not because he was John

113

Ballew, the richest man, the largest landholder in the voting precinct of three school districts, but because he was the man, the only man, among the company of women and children.

The car came out of the pines and down the road between Samuel's fenced fields. Sue Annie whispered, 'It's th same one brung word a Henley an Jesse.'

Mrs Hull, shivering like a woman very cold, whispered, 'Sh-h, Kate'ull hear.'

But a moment or so later, when the car turned down the lane, Sue Annie was whispering again: 'It's the same car, an I do believe it's th same woman. She wore a kind a curledy coat made out a th hides a black lambs.'

It seemed long enough for the sun to go down before the car came on and stopped in front of the porch steps. A fattish woman with a high bosom, a Red Cross marker on one arm, and dressed in a coat of black lamb hides as Sue Annie had said, opened the car door and got out, slowly, like a woman not much used to moving herself around. A youngish woman, bare-headed and bare-handed, continued to sit in the driver's seat, turning her head a little to look at the children gathered in a tight huddle by the empty gasoline pump, but never lifting her glance to Old John directly in front of her or to any of the company. Gertie, watching as the others watched, trying to read the faces, the hands, the way the fattish woman walked around the car, thought the news they brought was bad, very bad, else the young one would open the car door and speak, or at least look up and smile.

All eyes were fixed on the large black pocketbook the fattish woman held in her two hands, looking down at it, opening it as she walked. The message was in it, Gertie realized, and Gertie's eyes were like all the other eyes, fixed on the purse, twisting into it, searching out its secrets.

The gold thing on the purse was unclasped at last, and the woman drew back the flap and looked in, but without taking anything out. She paused, her fingers fishing in the purse while she looked up at the people. John said, 'Evenen, ma'm. You've brung us word?'

He stopped, forgetful of his manners and of what he would say, as he, like all the others, tried to find the word in the broad face

114

where a young girl's big red-lipped mouth was painted on under an old woman's watery blue eyes. The face looked sober, concerned, but more than anything taken up with the awareness of the importance of its business. John, failing to find anything there, pried at the purse with his eyes, and like the others pried and tore harder still with his glance when, after some rummaging, she brought out a yellow envelope. A little gasp went up from the crowd. A yellow envelope like that had come for Jesse back in dogwood-blooming time, and another for Henley a little after molasses-making time.

No one moved forward. It was as if by not stretching forth a hand for it, the death or the pain of wounds or the lostness waiting there would pass by, and go into some other hand outstretched for it.

The silence was so heavy while the woman looked at the name that Gertie heard cowbells in the Cow's Horn across the river and far away, and behind her in the door Aunt Kate's gasping, uneven breath. Then it was as if Aunt Kate, by making sound, had asked for the letter and taken it for herself, when the woman said, looking at John: 'We have a message for Lorenzo Nevels. Is he here?'

All the trembling and the weakness left Aunt Kate, and her eyes shone blindly wide and sick in her face, unseeing like eyes going through the dark. She stepped forward with outstretched hand, saying: 'My man, he cain't come. Give it to me.'

She walked alone across the porch steps while Gertie hated herself; for whatever had happened to Kate's own, something inside her snapped up and free like a young hickory held down by a swinging boy, leaping free and rising straight. It wasn't Clovis. The message would have come to her. In all the others, too, she thought there was this instant's sinful secret leaping up of hearts, 'Not mine. Not mine.'

The bluish-white ring that had an instant before framed Lucy Anderson's mouth was dissolved, and the redness spread like a fire over Mrs Hull's neck had faded. The stranger woman's painted mouth was widening, spreading, as she held out the yellow envelope. Her voice was grudgingly kind as she said: 'Last time I brought you bad news—and now I'm so glad to bring you good news, very good. Your missing son has been found. He is a prisoner of war.'

She handed Kate the yellow letter. Her bright voice went on and on—something about the Red Cross in Town and food packages and where to send them.

Gertie caught the word, 'Italy,' then forgot to listen with her worry over Kate. The old woman stood with the envelope in her hand, staring straight into the face of the other, but a body could tell that none of the strange woman's words were sinking in, for Kate was like a woman made of starch caught in the rain, knees bending, shoulders humping. At last she settled slowly down onto the porch step, still holding the envelope, carefully, as if it had been some precious and fragile thing, while she kept her head lifted, listening still, like a child hearing words it cannot understand.

The crowd listened less, but maybe understood more than Kate; at the words 'good news,' breaths had gone out in a long relieved gasp; some, like Mrs Hull and Lucy Anderson, were half crying, 'Thank God, oh, thank God,' while Sue Annie quarreled in a shrill whisper, 'Jesus God, what ails th fools a wasten good gasoline to skeer th liven daylights out uv us all?' and reached in her apron pocket for a chew to moisten her dry mouth.

The woman's talk came at last to an end. There followed a silence that seemed to last a long while, then the woman was saying, somewhat sharply, as if she had already said it once, 'Are there any questions, Mrs Nevels?'

There was more silence, until Sue Annie whispered shrilly: 'Kate, th woman's asken you is they anything you want to know. Thank her fer her trouble.'

Kate looked confusedly around, as if she'd never known she had a sister Sue Annie, then quickly back at the woman, as if wondering who she was and why she came. 'No'm,' she said at last, and again, 'No'm,' then added in polite, toneless words, 'I thank ye kindly fer yer trouble.'

7

Aunt Kate had revived somewhat, but her glance was still bewildered as it wandered about the room, crowded now with the wearily waiting women, many with babies sleeping across their knees. Gradually the old woman's eyes fixed themselves on a large map of the world that Mrs Hull had got by sending fifty cents to somebody on the radio, and then hung from the nail that had used to hold a fat roll of bologna. One could, by leaning across the empty meat counter, make out even the fine print on the map, and find where each man had gone.

Aunt Kate after several glances at it, got up, and with a timid and uncertain air went to look into the map's face. Her glance was confused and searching, as if she measured the face of some silent, suspicious-seeming stranger.

Mrs Hull took the lamp from the mail shelf and set it on the meat counter a little sidewise of the map so that Kate might see better. Gertie, like many of the other women, crowded round to look over Kate's shoulder. She, unlike Kate and several of the older ones, could, without too much spelling and effort, make out a map, that is, if it stood in a place known to her, like Samuel's store here.

As it hung on the wall now, north was somewhere in heaven and south down in hell, and east was opposite the morning star. She could, however, take the map in her mind and lay it on the floor, and then, remembering the north star, know in what direction each man had gone. She found many of the strange places the women mentioned now. Some spoke fearfully in hoarse whispers, awed by their own inability to imagine clearly the mountains, the oceans, the vast stretches of flat land, the time, and the weather that now lay between them and the man who only a little while ago had been no further away than across the table. Others spoke casually, as they had used to speak of the next creek or hill, of the Aleutians, New York, Paris, Calcutta, Hampton Roads, Okinawa, Louisville, London, Cincinnati, Kelly Field, Oak Ridge.

Though the map was quite new and a war map, the name Oak Ridge was not there. A strange place it was, Samuel had said, where people worked without knowing what they did, and never asked. The power lines there were so many and so big they seemed made to carry all the thunderbolts of heaven. Lutie, Mrs Hull's oldest girl, had made a little dot about where she thought Oak Ridge should be. This was the place closest home, though in these strange, troubled times the men in the factories and the training camps in the United States did not seem so far away. Even places straight across the ocean, like England and France, seemed close—after looking at India.

Aunt Kate's Luke and John's Cles were there in the hot country where missionaries went. No one knew if they had ever seen each other. Still, it was good to know they were in the same country. They never seemed so all alone as Lucy Anderson's baby son who'd volunteered before the war like Kate's Jesse to see the world. Lucy's boy had been at Pearl Harbor, and then moved on with the fighting from island to island. It was now more than three months since Aunt Lucy had heard, so that now she could only stare at tiny specks of islands far out in the Pacific and wonder.

Gertie stared a long time at Italy, where Henley had been. She wanted to touch the place, but instead only whispered, 'Italy.' Soft as the troubled word had been, Aunt Kate heard. She studied Gertie's face as she had studied the map. 'Italy, that's it. I been a tryen an a tryen to call it to mind.'

She pondered, looking again at the map. 'I hope it's warm there,' she said at last. She bent close to the map as if it were sky and she would read the weather. 'Mebbe they won't let him freeze to death like they done my Uncle Abner in th Civil War. They kept him two year at Chillicothe. He went in a well man an come out a skeleton with one foot gone, Granma used to tell me; an she said, he said—'

'Things is different now,' Mrs Hull interrupted quickly. 'In this war th Italians an th Germans treat our boys good, real good, like we treat their prisoners here in this country.'

Sue Annie nodded, 'We've got the Red Cross now, Kate. Them Italians, they'll keep Jesse warm an full a feed as a baby.'

Even Gertie, who wondered what the Red Cross was, nodded knowingly when Aunt Kate's eyes swept her face. 'They'll be good to him, real good.'

But the old woman was studying the map again. 'Clovis was a tellen me once he heared say er read they was mountains in Italy an rough wild country, mighty cold in th wintertime. An that th ground, what they was, was real steep an rocky an pore, not enough fer the people, an that they was allus hungry an—'

Sue Annie sniffed loudly. 'Lord, Kate, Clovis don't know a thing. You're fergitten everthing we learned in school together. Why everybody knows it's allus warm in Italy, an that mighty nigh all the land is flat an rich an black as river bottom. They never run out a hawg meat er corn bread, an butter, too, if'n a body wants it, an—'

Several voices were interrupting: 'That's right, Kate, you've fergot yer book learnen,' while Gertie, with the air of a disgusted woman, said: 'Now, Aunt Kate, you know they ain't a thing in Clovis's head but tinkeren. Who does he think he is, a tellen you all about Italy like he'd visited there?'

Kate, who was staring at the map again, seemed not to have heard. She looked a time longer, her eyes questioning, wondering. She turned away at last with a weary headshake. 'It makes me dizzy, th map,' she said, and sat down. Most of the others continued to look at the map, wondering, hunting, murmuring the strange, heathenish-sounding names.

Gertie, taller than the rest, looked over their heads. Her troubled wonderings on Clovis were sharper now. Her ears, like the other ears, were constantly straining away from the consciousness of things around her to the road, though her reason told her that the mail mule's shoes would, in their coming, make too little sound for her to hear above the murmur of talk in the store. Suddenly, however, she turned quickly away and slipped through the door and hurried to the top step at the end of the porch.

She held her breath, leaned forward, listening. Disappointed, she was just turning away when she caught the faint sound she had thought she'd heard indoors—the clink of a mule's shoe in the road. She clung to a porch post. Maybe soon, real soon, she could look at the map and find a spot for Clovis. But what if she didn't hear? She looked up at the stars, washed in a keen light wind from the north. They hung above her, hard and cold and bright. She wished she could know that Clovis was somewhere looking up at the stars. But Clovis had never been a body to fool with the stars or the moon. Henley had never seemed so far away, for she could pick out a star and think he was maybe looking at it too.

She heard the mule shoes again. Soon they sounded more loudly and more often on the gravel; then suddenly they were softer, as Uncle Ansel turned into the sandy lane. Others of the women and several restless half grown children had gradually followed Gertie onto the porch to listen. The listening silence was heavy as the uncertainty lasted a moment longer. The creak of saddle leather sounded clearly through the darkness. There came a little chorus of cries, less joyous than in the old days, for at once the relief that the long wait was ended was dimmed by forebodings of disappointment or bad news.

Women, hound dogs, and children—even the younger ones like Cassie who had gone to sleep and were awakening now in startled wonder—all rushed onto the porch.

Mrs Hull pushed the door open wide and set the lamp on the mail window so that a broad band of lamplight fell across the porch. Old Ansel dismounted from the tired head-hanging mule, and with many hands to help him took the worn leather bags from behind the saddle and handed them to Mrs Hull. There were also two bulging canvas bags of packages and papers, but few glanced at these, and no one save Gertie waited while Uncle Ansel undid the fastenings. The rest followed Mrs Hull with the thin bags of letters.

Gertie, when she had carried the package sacks to the mail counter, came back to stand on the porch where she could hear the calling of the names through the open door, and at the same time see the stars and breathe good clean air. Already Mrs Hull's clean store had begun to smell of overly warm hound-dog hide, wet-bottomed babies, and trouble—the smell of worried women sweating out the wait for the mail.

Inside it was so still while Mrs Hull opened the mail sacks that Gertie heard a hound dog snuffling in its sleep. It dreamed of hunting. If she didn't hear would she dream of Clovis? She had dreamed of Henley; but the dream-seeing was all the sight she'd ever have of Henley. It wouldn't be that way with Clovis. She could hear the crinking of the coal stove and the shuffling of the letters as Mrs Hull laid them by handfuls on the counter.

Then, different from the old days when letters, papers, and packages were properly sorted and put all together for each family, Mrs Hull began at once the calling out of the letters. Ann Liz Cramer, Sue Annie Tiller, John Ballew, Mamie Childers, John Ballew, Ansel Anderson, Kate Nevels, then her voice, rising, trembling: 'Lutie, Lutie, read it quick. It's frum Andy.' She went on through other names, her voice fluttering only a little, and paused but an instant when Lutie cried: 'Mom, he's all right. Feelen good.'

Gertie stood in the doorway, watching hungrily, as did some of the others who had no mail as yet to read. Their hopeful eyes fondled each letter as Mrs Hull picked it up, then lowered it into the circle of lamplight long enough to read the address. Gertie watched through many names. She heard Mrs Hull read 'Iva Dean Gholson,' then saw young Iva Dean, a bride of only a month or so when they took her husband, rush forward almost crying with joy for she had heard nothing for many weeks. Mrs Hull said softly, as she held out the letter, 'I wish it was different, honey—but it's a due bill er somethen from Ward's.'

The letter fluttered to the floor unopened. Iva Dean turned away, hump-shouldered, old-faced, and tired; less alive she looked than Old John reading one of the many letters he had stacked under the lamp. The girl bumped into Ann Liz Cramer, who now and then glanced wistfully down at two letters held in one brown, brawny hand. 'You want me to read em, Ann Liz?' Iva asked.

Ann Liz nodded, flushing a little. Iva Dean turned her back firmly and rigidly toward Mrs Hull and began reading in a low voice the letter Claude Cramer and his children had had Blare Tiller write: '"Dearly beloved ones, I take my pen in hand to write you. The rest are in good health. My stomach is some better, but it will not be cured till I can quit this city water and have some good corn bread. This Indiana meal ain't so good. Well, the CIO got Arthur like it got me. We both have to pay. He don't have it so hard. His work is from eleven to seven at night. We—"'

Gertie turned away, not wanting to listen to words that rightly belonged to Ann Liz Cramer alone. 'Mom—do them men that ride them airplanes like Lena Gholson's man—do them men ever hit the stars?' It was Cassie slipping a hand, warm and moist from sleep, into Gertie's.

'Nobody can hurt th stars, honey—they'll allus be there.'

Cassie blinked at the sky. 'What makes you like to look at th stars, Mom?'

' "The heavens declare th glory of God; an th firmament showeth his handiwork. Day unto day uttereth speech, and night unto night—" '

'But what do they say, Mom?'

Gertie stared up, considering the Little Dipper. 'Different things to different people; fer one thing they say, "We'll never change, an we'll never go away—all the nations on this earth with all their wars, they cain't cut us down like we was trees." And they say to Cassie Marie, "Little girl, if'n you lost all yer friends an kin you'd still have us an th sun an th moon." '

When would it come, her name? The pile of letters must be almost gone. She took comfort from Cassie's touch and smoothed her hair, then frowned, feeling the sweaty dampness at the back of her neck. 'You'll be sick runnen out in this cold, hot an sweaty, you'll . . .'

The 'Gertrude' had sounded so strange, she never turned until she heard 'Nevels.' Mrs Hull held out a letter, long with a heavy look, and lots of stamps. Gertie fumbled over it, blinking, half blinded by the sudden change from starlight to lamplight. 'It's registered, an you can sign when I'm all through,' Mrs Hull said, and added as Gertie continued to blink and fumble: 'It's from Clovis, postmarked Detroit. Money must be—don't tear it crosswise.' And Mrs Hull went on, talking now to herself as she held up some circular, ' "Nunnely D. Ballew." Don't they know th only Ballews left is John's family?'

Gertie stepped back from the mail window, tore off the end of the envelope carefully, then pulled out sheets of tablet paper with bills of money folded in their center. She never tried to read for looking at the bills—three twenty-dollar bills. She stared, unbelieving. All that from her mother, and now this. It was enough to get a little start of sheep or maybe a good one-horse turning plow like . . .

'Gertie, is he all right? They didn't git him in th army?'

She nodded, rousing slowly to Aunt Kate's question. 'He's all right,' she lied, ashamed to say to her man's mother that so far she hadn't read a word, only looked at his money. 'He's in Detroit,' she explained, 'so he cain't be in th army. Wait, I'll read it to ye,' and slowly she read, following Clovis's unfamiliar writing with difficulty:

' "Dear loved ones,

' "Well, Gertie, I passed the army. But they didn't want me. Not right away. The army said I wud not be called for a right good spell. But that imploymint office told me a long time back to go to a factory. I come to Detroit. It was near as close as coming back home. I got a job that suits me. It pays good. I sold the truck. You know I had not hardly made nothing with it. They won't be no more coal to haul till the war is done. The truck brang more than I paid. It was them good new tires. I owed Lister sum. And I paid it. I am taking sum. I will send you more when I have a pay day. Now, don't be stingy, Gertie. Buy what you need. You and the children needs clothes. I want you not to have it so hard. Write to me." '

There was a long address, words of love, rows of X marks for kisses for herself and the children. These she did not read aloud; and anyway Aunt Kate was pulling her sleeve, asking like a troubled child: 'Gert, you won't leave us an foller him there? Deetroit's so fer away—might nigh as bad as bein acrost th waters. He'll like it there. All that machinery'ull jist suit him—fer a while. It'll be all over one a these days, an he'll come back an git him another truck. But if'n you foller him he might never come back.'

Gertie patted the old woman's shoulder. 'Law, Aunt Kate, you know I'd never go up there. I'll save jist about everything he sends so's he can buy him another truck when he gits back. I'll have Clytie git him a letter off in th next mail to let him know they've found Jesse. It'll . . .'

Sue Annie held up a gaudily beflowered apron and cried, 'Lookee, lookee, they ain't fergot their old grandmammie.' She saw Gertie's letter. 'Clovis has took off fer one a them factories, I bet, like he's been a wanten to. If he stays at work like my boys, th army'ull never bother him agin. He's so old, an with all them youngens.'

'He'll have to stay, that is, fer a spell,' Gertie said. 'He's sold his truck.'

'You'll have to be a widder woman like me, Gert,' Ann Liz Cramer said, then added doubtfully, 'that is, if Clovis'ull give in to stay away frum you an th youngens. Some men is kinda foolish thataway.'

'We'll manage,' Gertie said, giving Sue Annie a worried pitying glance. The old woman had fallen into a brokenhearted weeping over a letter she had just started to read.

Kate looked at her sister in troubled wonder, for Sue Annie had grandsons, but no sons, in the fighting.

'Nancy ain't a comen home to have her baby,' Sue Annie sobbed. 'She's a goen to one a them hospitals,' and she cried on, more sorrowful than indignant. 'An allus before I've been good enough to bring ever grandchild an great grandchild I've got.'

'Times changes, Sue Annie,' John said, looking up from a letter, one of many he had received. He turned to help Flonnie Belle Keith at the map behind the meat counter, her baby on one arm, her free hand groping over the Pacific Ocean while she asked of the map: 'Where's England? My Loy's in England.'

Gertie stood by the mail window, waiting impatiently until Mrs Hull could get the slip for her to sign. She felt guilty among these tired and troubled ones; she was so strong and glad. Many had finished their letters and were gathering around the map while they waited for the newspapers and packages. They talked in low voices, using at times strange new words and phrases that stood out in the ordinary speech of the people like weeds in a field. 'Bombardier—Guam—he's a trainen in a tank destroyer—Wac—plane carrier—they call em babushkas—waist gunner—V-mail—cargo plane—bazooka—UAWCIO.'

She turned her back on them all and looked through the door. She felt again the loneliness like an old sorrow. Why couldn't she cry for Clovis the way Sue Annie cried for her daughter? Why couldn't Clovis and she have wanted the same things? He'd wanted Detroit since the beginning of the war. She'd seen it in his eyes when he looked at the signs on the pine trees. He'd made his plans to stay away for true while the war lasted. She couldn't blame him. There wasn't any work here for a man like Clovis—now. When the war was over he'd come. . . . Mrs Hull had put slip and pencil before her. She signed and turned swiftly away, not waiting to see if there be some catalogue or circular.

She heard as she turned away the whisper of limp bills falling into the split basket; and Mrs Hull, shoving a package toward Ann Liz Cramer, said: 'Take it. If'n you don't I cain't ask you to hope us agin, an I'll need it. You're about th onliest one not tied down with a baby.' And then her voice, worried, wistful, 'You won't be leaven us, too?'

'Law, no,' Gertie said, adding, 'but I don't like taken a preacher's money.'

She hurried out the door with Cassie running to keep up with her. She wanted to be alone under the stars. Some other time she would sorrow for the war, cry for the ones away, look up at God, and quarrel on the why of Henley, who had died with no sin but no salvation; but not tonight when she was firm on her own land. Henley was dead, but she and her children were alive, with a hearth of her own for them all, and a place for Clovis to come back to when the war was ended. She had an instant's understanding of why people shouted in church. They saw the things that Moses saw when he looked across the mountains to the Promised Land, or that the thief saw when Christ said, 'This day, thou shalt be with me in Paradise.'

Christ? It was Christ in the block of wood after all. Soon he would rise up out of his long hiding into the firelight, the laughing Christ with hair long and black like Callie Lou's, but not so curly. Her Christ had to be that way—a body's mind couldn't be willed and walled any more than the wind could be willed and walled. Wicked she had maybe been all these years because she could see only Judas in the wood—the Judas she had pitied giving back the silver. Pity, pity. Was pity for a Judas sinful?

125

She was somewhere on the graveled road near the schoolhouse before she realized that Cassie was gasping for breath from her efforts to keep up with her, while she herself went with long swift strides and sang at the top of her lungs, joyfully, as if it had been some sinful dance tune, ' "How firm a foundation ye saints of the Lord." ' She slackened her pace, but couldn't stop the song as she smiled at the stars through the pines. Her foundation was not God but what God had promised Moses—land; and she sang on, ' "Is laid for your faith in His excellent word! What more can He say than to you He that said—" ' What more, oh, Lord, what more could a woman ask?

8

'Now, don't go a fighten, youngens,' Gertie said in an uninterested, singsong voice unusual for her. She held the knife still above an almost finished ax handle, and looked at the angry Clytie and the stubborn Reuben. 'You've both worked mighty hard all mornen. Why, by time to go home this evenen we'll have our place might nigh ready to move into. We've already got th kitchen scrubbed an clean,' she went on, making a long thin shaving curve downward from the handle. 'I guess if'n I hadn't a had sich good steady youngens I—we'd never in th world a got us enough together to buy us a place uv our own, an would a gone on a bein renters all our days. Now don't spoil it all by fussen when we've took time out to rest.'

'But, Mom, curtains, real winder curtains, all white—pure white, four sets fer this room.' Clytie leaned forward across the open borrowed Montgomery Ward catalogue, and spoke in earnest pleading. 'It's not like I was asken fer somethin fine like them fancy ruffled things Ann Liz Cramer bought. But they'd be real curtains, not feed-sack things. I know they won't hep th farmen none, but'—she sighed, seeing starched curtains by clean windows—'they'd be so pretty. I'd go down to th river an git me some pretty straight canes fer poles. An anyhow Reuben cain't sow his grass seed now.'

Gertie smiled as she had smiled at all things on this day. If Clytie didn't get her curtains this week, she would soon. Clovis would be sending more money, and if he didn't she'd spare her some egg money. She wouldn't have to be so stingy ever any more. She had a place of her own, same as had it. Night before last she'd taken cash money to John. As soon as the weather cleared enough, he'd ride to the Valley and there take a bus to Town, where he'd record the deed for her. It was good to do business with Old John. She wouldn't have to waste a day's time trailing into Town to see about the deed or lose a minute's sleep wondering if he'd back out of the deal or lose her money. John didn't lose money or back out of deals.

There came a screaming and a banging from the big room on the other side of the fireplace wall. Clytie rushed to the noise, her feet faster than her mother's slowly rousing mind. 'It's that Cassie,' she called back. 'She's tolled Amos into th cubbyhole by th fireplace an turned th button an run off.'

When Gertie continued silent, only making another long shaving fall from the ax handle, smiling on it as if it had been gold, Clytie raised her voice in a kind of beseeching scolding: 'Cassie Marie, cain't you behave yourself, a locken up Amos thataway? Are you allus a goen to be this mean in our own home?'

Cassie laughed. 'I didn't do nothen. It was Callie Lou locked him up, and it warn't no more'n she ought to ha done. He come in drunk frum Indianee 'thout one cent fer his wife an youngens. He's spent all his money in an—in a—'

'It was his pay check in a beer parlor, silly. That's what Sue Annie said, an it was old Willie Sexton done it. Mom, Mom, Cassie's tellen lies agin. Cassie, don't you know it's sinful to go tellen lies? It's aginst th Bible.'

Gertie roused, but spoke without harshness. ' "First cast th beam out of thine own eye; an then shalt thou see clearly to cast out th mote out of thy brother's eyes." Allus recollect, girl, that when you think th Bible's on your side it's mebbe on th other feller's too.' She reached out, and for no reason at all give Clytie, big girl as she was, the warm hard hug she would have given a baby, then asked: 'Did you write yer pop a nice long letter? I meant to read it, but hunten ax handles an sled runners out a our woods made me so late there wasn't time to read an send it to th mail.'

Clytie nodded. 'I told him everything I could think on, Mom.'

'But not about our place?' she asked quickly.

Clytie giggled. 'No, I done like you said, saved it fer a surprise. Mom, wouldn't it be fun fer him not to know till he come walken in?'

128

'He'd git to like it,' Gertie said. She looked about the large bare room. Its low walls, covered with torn and faded building paper, were straight and solid under the hand-hewn oak rafters that held up the wide thick oak planks of the ceiling which also served as floor for the rooms above. Rafters and ceiling had never known paint or paper, and were weathered to a deep tobacco-colored brown. She considered the four windows; two on the east, one on either side the door in the southern wall. They were small and narrow but unbroken and deeply recessed in the thick long walls, hidden from the hot sun of summer afternoons, but set to catch most of its warmth on the short winter days. Never would the windows get the cold blowing rain from the northwest, no more than would the door. Made of three great oak planks with three cross battens it was a mighty door, big enough for her to step proudly through with the back log on her shoulder, a length of a dead sugar tree above the spring that she and Reuben had sawed down yesterday.

It flamed now in the fireplace with a good steady heat, and made a warm and rosy-colored light so bright there was at times a flicker of red like a blush on the walls. Outside, the gray November rain came down, not settled yet into a steady down dropping, but in gusts and squalls on the southwest wind that had risen with the red dawn. At each cry of the wind or spatter of rain, Gertie nodded a little and smiled. It was good to hear the wind and rain and never feel it in her house.

She made another long stroke, then left the knife across her knees, and with both hands grasped the ax handle, and swung it. Her gray eyes gleamed with satisfaction. A gust of wind, louder than the others, leaped against the house, cried in the pines on the hillside. Gertie looked again at the windows, and saw the pale gold of a late hanging poplar leaf plastered against the glass. She turned and studied the fire, and her look of satisfaction broke into a smile as she watched the smoke, untouched by the wind, rise steadily upward. 'I knowed this was a mighty good fireplace; the wind'ull never kitch in th chimbley an blow smoke all over creation.'

Reuben lifted his head from the white oak maul he was making and nodded agreement, and she asked: 'How you comen, son? Strange work allus seems hard at first.'

'I ain't no hand at whittlen,' he said. 'But mebbe I can make a maul.'

'If'n a maul ain't balanced jist right it'll make splitten out chunks fer them shakes twict as hard,' she warned, but added in an encouraging tone, 'You mebbe ain't got th knack a whittlen, but it's a good thing to learn enough to make yer own sled runners an sich.'

'Mom, I been thinken,' Reuben said, speaking slowly, straightening the words in his head as always, for poor Reuben had not one bit of his Aunt Sue Annie's quick tongue. 'Clytie ought tu have her curtains. It's pretty late tu sow grass seed. Come March I'll have more money. Granpa's aimen tu pay me fer hopen with th fall work. An this winter I ought tu make a heap frum trappen. They's nobody much left but me to trap.'

Clytie roused from her dreams over a page of dishes—willow-ware that was blue, and poppies in a garden, red and green, and yellow drooping-headed flowers. 'Reuben, you go ahead an git yer grass seed right now 'fore it's too late. I been a thinken—Mamie gives me fifty cents fer ever night I stay with her an help in th work. I was aimen tu save it an buy me a coat, but they ain't no place to wear it. So's I don't need it. Pretty soon I could have me enough saved fer curtains.' She looked down at the catalogue—'an mebbe some dishes, too.'

Gertie got up quickly, folded the knife, and dropped it into her pocket. When she had hefted the handle it seemed like it needed a little stroke or two more down next the head, but she couldn't sit still any longer. Dance: her heart wanted to do that. So would her feet, she guessed, if so many people like her mother didn't think it sinful. To sit by her own fire and burn wood from her own land with no debts like some—all this, and then such children. 'Law, youngens,' she said, when she could speak, 'they's no need fer neither a ye tu give in to t'othern. Clytie, you do need a coat. If'n I was you I'd save my money fer clothes a some kind. We'll have plenty a money. You're fergitten about th heaten-stove money. You said Angie Tucker when you seed her down at Mamie's ud give ten dollars cash fer hit. Well, I'm aimen tu put that an five more I think I can spare on furnishens.'

She wished, watching Clytie's face, that she could spare twenty-five dollars. 'Fifteen dollars ull buy a heap a house plunder. Why don't you look at the linoleums?' she went on.

Clytie sprang up and whirled on her toes, then stood still, her eyes sparkling up as she said: 'Oh, Mom, we could make this th prettiest room with curtains an linoleum. We could leave th beds out an have what they call a setten room—a front room they mean—like Miz Hull's, where a body don't eat ner sleep neither.'

Gertie chuckled and stroked Clytie's hair. 'Now don't be a gitten too fine right away, girl. I figgered that linoleum fer th kitchen. It'd save a heap a scrubben. I like them ole beds mighty good, but some day,' she went on, smiling at Clytie, 'fore you're big enough to have beaux, we'll make this into a nice front room. On our own land like this where we can keep ever bite we raise an don't have to be a moven ever year, we can git ahead a sight faster an—'

A thump, thumping, and smothered cries took her rushing to the stairway in time to catch Cassie as she rolled onto the narrow landing above the little door. She seized her, shook her, blew in her face, then ran with her to a window to see what bones were broken.

The limp little figure dangled over her arms; the head, with the straggling hair slipped as ever from its braids, flopped backward toward the dangling hand-me-down shoes. Gertie, shaking her, whispering in terror, 'Cassie, honey,' blowing breath into the open sagging mouth, remembered guiltily that with all her riches not one new thing had she bought for Cassie, and that in all the hurry to get to the new house before the certain rain promised by the warm, windy, reddening sunrise, she had not even combed Cassie's hair. 'Clytie, git a dipper a cold water—quick!'

Then the limber arms were flung about her neck, the sagging mouth was laughing, while the too big shoes flew to the far corners of the room as Cassie kicked her heels. 'Oh, Mom, you looked so funny. I got tired a this sinful Satan-ridden earth and I went up to heaven.' She sighed and slid from her mother's arms. 'I didn't like it so good—that Callie, she pulled them gold feathers out uv a big angel's wings an throwed away her crown. It went a bounden an a bouncen down them golden stairs clean down to this Satan-ridden world.'

Clytie, her face white with fury, torn from linoleum, willowware, and curtains, threatened to throw the dipper of water into Cassie's face. But Gertie was too relieved to do more than slap her bottom hard enough, as Clytie pointed out in disgust, to squash a fly, and threaten to beat that Callie Lou till she was pieded black and blue from head to toe.

Cassie ran back up the stair hole, Gyp at her heels. Gertie for the first time recollected the job she had given Enoch seemed like hours ago, and that from him she had since heard no sound.

She climbed the narrow stairway. Three steps there were below a wide planked door that fastened with a button, then, a little landing, and the stairs turned. She reached the top step, but instead of calling to Enoch in the attic above she stopped and for the dozenth time admired the upstairs. The log house had been built by the old pattern with the logs laid high enough for a real upstairs with windows and divided like that below into two main rooms. She went to the one that had a little fireplace just big enough to burn cookstove wood. She looked at a corner between fireplace and window; that was the place for the block of wood. Nights up here in the firelight, she'd bring the head out of the wood. She could do fine work when the youngens were asleep and Clovis wasn't around to talk, and now with her own land she'd never have to feel guilty about wasting time.

Such good rooms! Out one window she would be able to see the north star, and from the other she could look down the valley toward the Big South Fork and her mother's house. Almost every day she would see her father. His land touched her land—her land, *her* land. Then she remembered Enoch, and raised her voice. 'Enoch, you found any leaks, son?'

'She ain't a leaken,' Enoch answered after her second call.

'You been looken good? Don't wait fer drops. Look good—all under th shakes an see if it's a seepen enyplace.'

She waited, and hearing no sound of feet over the boards to token his searching, called again: 'You be keerful a thet lantern. What a you doen nohow, a bein so still?'

'Mom,' he said, as he came and stuck his head over the cubbyhole, 'I looked good, real good, but they wasn't no leaks.'

She saw the book in his hand. 'So's you've been a setten a wasten good coal oil a readen when you could ha been pullen them old nasty newspapers off'n our bedrooms. We're a goen to start moven in less'n a week.' She sighed and studied her second son with more sorrow and puzzlement than anger. 'Enoch, honey, what ails you? Everbody else is a worken an a plannen, an you go a setten a readen books 'stead a looken fer leaks.'

Enoch held out the book for her to see. 'Honest, Mom, I looked fer leaks real good. I saw all these books an I recollected you wanted us to study ever day like we was goen to school. So's I studied some spellen. They's a sight a books, but they're old an they ain't got pretty pictures.'

Gertie took the book, a narrow little thing, the back a faded blue, the pages yellow and worn. 'It's a old blue-backed speller,' she said. 'They quit usen them when yer granma was a girl, but all th same, many's th night yer granpa had me spell out a it.'

'An, Mom, they's a book with th funniest number problems.'

'Ray's higher arithmetic, I bet,' Gertie said, and reached for the armload of books Enoch held. She raised her voice. 'Clytie, Clytie, you've been a wanten books. Come an see what Enoch's found.'

Clytie and the others came running and explored the pile. The books were mostly readers with small pictures showing little girls with long ruffled panties and little boys with hats and hair long as a girl's. On most was the name *McGuffey*, printed large; inside were names in faded ink. The one most often seen was Maggie Gordon, the Maggie beginning with a great curling *M*. When the children wanted to know who was Maggie Gordon, Gertie fell into a long musing and remembering aloud of who had married whom before she realized that this was the Maggie Gordon who had married old Isaac Tipton and was the granma of Silas Tipton who had gone off to Muncie, Indiana. She was up in Deer Lick graveyard now with Uncle Isaac.

Gertie thumbed through one of the books. Many of the poems were familiar as old neighbors who, though moved away and not seen for years, seem neighbors still when seen again. 'Look, youngens,' she said, glancing up from 'Into the Ward of White-Washed Walls' with the guilty realization that she was wasting time, 'you all have been worken hard. Th rain's kind a slackened, I'd better go up in our patch a timber an hunt me a little hick'ry that'll do fer saw handles an a good big tough maul, fer we'll be haven to split some rails pretty soon. While I'm gone you all can do a little studyen till dinnertime. Clytie, you start gitten some poems by heart. Pick out somethen good, an th rest a youens practice readen an spellen.'

She caught the sorrowful, shame-faced look that always came to Cassie's face at the mention of reading. 'All but Cassie an Amos, an they can git a poem by heart. Cassie, they's a real pretty poem. I got it by heart when I was about yer size. Look through th second reader, Clytie. I don't think I recollect it all: 'Once there was a little kitty with paws white as snow—'

They gathered in a ring around the hearth, heads bowed over books, with Cassie whispering after Clytie about the kitten that frolicked a long time ago.

Gertie took the big double-bitted ax and went out into the wind and the rain. She climbed to the edge of the cornfield above the house and stopped and looked back. Gray rain and curls of fog from the rising creek and the river made the hills across the creek seem one black iron mountain smudged and indistinct. Her father's farm and the hills beyond the river were blotted out so that she could see little but her own. Just below her was her house with the blue smoke rising, and set in the curving sweep of grassland, as green almost from the warm fall rains as grass in the spring. She saw the apple trees, black-trunked, gray-twigged in the rain; the pear trees, the peach, and rising like an outpost in the fog, the great poplar by the spring, its arms held up as if reaching for the sky. She wished she could see the cedar bluffs above the creek, with more cedar for fence posts than she would ever need, and the old sugar trees with their gray scarred bark, and the beech trees with their thin fine twigs that would on winter nights make a lace-like pattern against the stars.

Saw briers pulled at her skirt, and rain-drenched sumac and sassafras sprouts slapped at her, but she continued to smile as she plodded on up through the old cornfield. Now and then she would stop to cut a sprout or a grapevine, whispering to it, laughing a little. 'Jist you wait till I git started. Away you'll all have to go to make way fer my grass an clover an corn.'

134

She came at last to the steeper part of the hillside, that had never been plowed. Among the brush and second-growth timber were several young hickories and an old one scarred by lightning. She paused, ax uplifted by the old one, but the ax came slowly back to her shoulder, and she smiled at the old hickory, 'You'd be good an tough,' she said, 'an yer heart wood's dead, but I'll leave you fer seed an hicker nuts fer th squirrels an my youngens.'

She considered some of the less thrifty of the small hickories, but always instead of cutting she only slashed away the nearby hornbeam or other useless brush, whispering to the little hickory as she did so. 'It won't be many years 'fore you'll be big enough fer the saw mill, er mebbe I'll be needen you in that new barn I'm aimen tu build.'

It was with a little sigh and a fleeting look of sorrow that at last she chose her tree. There was more than enough tough straight trunk for the big maul and the handles, but some winter weight of snow, some accident with man or animal or weather, had crooked the top so that it could never grow into a fine upstanding tree.

135

9

She looked at Gyp, outlined in the stove light as he stood by the open kitchen door. He whined into the darkness, then twisted his head to look at the shotgun high on its two nails above the eating table. He looked hopefully at her, then turned away whining again toward the sounds that came from the ridge field.

'Go on,' she whispered, with no pause in the churning, ''fore you wake th youngens. But I cain't go with you. I've got a big day's work ahead a me. Long as they's light to see, I'm goen to be down at our farm splitten shakes to fix that barn roof so's we can move our fodder an corn. It ain't no coon, nohow,' she went on; 'them hounds is hunten. They're a chasen a fox, I guess. But no matter what it is they'll be nobody come to their cryen.'

She held the dasher still and listened. 'It's ole Sugar Bell. He don't know that Barney cain't hear him or Jesse neither in that prison camp in Italy. An that's Lister Tucker's ole Thunder. He took up with Pop when Lister moved to Hampton Roads. Go on,' she said to the still hesitant Gyp, 'But they'll be nobody come to you.'

She churned again, but between the steady glugs of the dasher she heard the crying of the hounds. It seemed like she'd heard it all night, the crying. Sometimes like a fiddle hidden in the hills, now far on the ridges, now near across the rented cornfield, rising and fading like a wind, mingling with the wind until it was hard to tell which was hound cry and which wind.

She had lain there in her bed and heard it and felt alone in the hearing. There was nobody else in the whole country to hear the hounds. The ears for the hounds heard other things, if they heard at all. Maybe some heard in their sleep, dreaming as she had dreamed of Henley. She stared into the stove grate trying to remember. It seemed a long time since she had dreamed of Henley. And hardly a month since the word had come that he was dead, not five since he went away. Now there was little left of him but the lonesomeness in her insides and the land his blood had helped to buy.

She slowly shook her head. It was as if the war and Henley's death had been a plan to help set her and her children free so that she might live and be beholden to no man, not even to Clovis. Never again would she have to wait to bake bread till Clovis brought home a sack of meal. ' "I've reached th land of corn an wine; an all its riches freely mine; here shines undimmed one blissful day where all my night has passed away." '

The lonesome sound of the crying hounds filtered through the kitchen, but she sang on, softly, so as not to awaken the children, thinking, planning, selecting what to do first. Today she'd burn the lantern and do the barn work before daylight. Soon as it was light enough to see she'd go dig up two or three little white pines. There were no white pines on the Tipton Place, and of all the trees she knew, a white pine had, she thought, the prettiest voice, warm and kind somehow even in winter. Old John wouldn't mind if she grubbed up two or three out of the edge of the cornfield where the next renter might grub them out anyhow. She'd set them below the gate close to the two poplar trees she'd already set. A poplar was a lonesome kind of thing, not like a maple or a hickory, seemed like one would hardly grow at all without other trees for company.

Later, in the gray, cloudy dawn, she scolded herself for wasting time. She'd better be at the shake making or digging up something useful like a plum bush; but it was such a good time for digging trees. She'd dug up three good-sized white pines and two little dogwoods before she hardly knew it, and as she wrapped their roots in the balls of moss that Enoch and Cassie had gathered from a rocky ledge below the field, she smiled as she told Cassie, 'They'll be big afore you hardly know it.' She added, with a warning look, 'You mustn't be a hurten em now, an a tryen to climb em soon's they're big enough to git a holt on.'

Cassie laughed her quick bubbling laugh, then came very close and whispered up to Gertie: 'Don't say hit too loud. Do you know what that youngen Callie Lou ud do? She'd pull up yer little trees.'

'Our little trees,' Gertie corrected. She made a mighty frown that brought her brows together until their blackness met above her eyes. 'When I git these trees set with their roots spread out, Callie Lou er nobody else, not even a witch, can pull em up. But,' and it was her turn to whisper after a quick glance around, bending low to Cassie's ear so that the forever listening, watching, waiting Callie Lou might not hear, 'but if'n you see her a tryen to pull em up you let me know an I'll give that youngen a good switchen.'

Cassie blinked and considered, then rising on tiptoe whispered, her voice troubled: 'You won't make it too hard, will you, Mom? She ain't a bad youngen at heart, jist full a jumpy meanness.'

Gertie nodded. 'Mostly, I'll jist scare her. I'll break me a little twig frum our peach tree behind th kitchen—no hick'ry limb.'

'Mom! Mom!'

She looked up, listening, then dropped the tree and started running across the field. Something uncommon bad, like the house on fire or Amos hurt, had happened. She'd never heard Reuben scream so, worse than when he had seen the bear. She was past the barn and running down the muddy lane before she saw her father's white saddle mule, standing carefully still as she always did for her father, while a plumpish figure so coated and bundled and scarfed she could not tell if it be man or woman climbed slowly from the saddle and became for an instant hidden on the other side of the mule. Then quickly the voice came, crying with the same scolding anger, pain, and sorrow in the cry, the old cry of, 'Gertie, Gertie.' A moment later she saw her mother weeping with her face against the porch post.

The younger children had rushed out, but overcome by the sight of their invalid grandmother getting off a mule they stood in a silent little huddle by the door. Only Enoch could find his tongue enough to ask, 'Granma, is Granpa dead?'

Her mother broke off her weeping and patted him on the shoulder as she said with such pitying sorrow that even brash Enoch was troubled, 'No, no, honey, your granpa ain't dead. Pore old crippled, sad-hearted soul, but he'd be better dead. He's lived to see his own flesh and blood bring disgrace to his bowed gray head.'

Gertie's heart went out to her sister, Meg, gone so long. What had she done—lied, fornicated, danced, played cards? 'Mom, Mom,' she began, 'I don't know what Maggie's done but it cain't be much.'

'Meg?' her mother shrilled, lifting her head, anger bright in her eyes. 'Meg's a decent woman. She ain't a sneaken an a slippen around a conniven to leave her man an make her children father-less. Fatherless. Fatherless.' Her tear-brimming eyes had traveled slowly from child to child, resting an instant on each as she designated its condition, but now again her forehead pressed against the porch post as she went on, her words spaced by sobs, 'I give yer mammy money—yer dead uncle's money, her own born brother's money—fer to buy you decent clothes an all th things you need. Yer everloven papa goes away an is a stranger in a strange place—jist fer tu keep bread and meat in your mouths. There he is,' she went on, looking now at Reuben as if he were the guilty one, 'away off in that cold, dirty, flat, ugly factory town, a haven to mix up with all kinds a foreigners an sich, a haven to pay money to a union—him that's never been made to belong to nothen. He ain't got nobody to cook him a decent bite a victuals. He could be took in th army, an you'd never see him agin. An what does yer mom do?'

Reuben's shoulders stiffened. 'She bought us a place a our own.'

Her mother turned away, weeping now into the saddle blanket, talking both to the gray mule and to God. 'Oh, Lord, oh, Lord, she's turned her own children against their father. She's never taught them th Bible where it says, "Leave all else an cleave to thy husband." She's never read to them th words writ by Paul, "Wives, be in subjection unto your husbands, as unto th Lord." '

She managed to lift her head and look at Gertie, standing stiff and dumb as ever under her mother's words, 'I couldn't believe it last night when Rildy come over to spend th night an told me th tales that was a goen around. Sue Annie told her that Mary Ballew had said you was buyen that old hillside and that old house.'

'It's a good house,' Reuben said.

'Young man, you need a father's hand. You're gitten sassy. Do you want th whole country a talken about yer mom?'

'They don't talk about Ann Liz Cramer, an she's lived without her man fer two, three years,' Reuben said, and looked to his mother for help, but Gertie stood and looked like Cassie when somebody caught her in a piece of meanness.

'Ann Liz Cramer lives where her man left her, a keepen his house an his youngens, an a doen what Claude wants her to do—fer he's a born farmer at heart. Soon's th war's over he's a comen home. Yer pop,' she went on, looking at Reuben and speaking slowly, 'ain't no farmer. Yer mom knowed that when she married him. She's held him back all these years. He could ha been maken big money down at Oak Ridge but she wouldn't give in to go with him, an—' She stopped, listening to a gay and lively whistle that changed soon into Clytie's singing as she climbed the short-cut path home from spending the night at Mamie's.

She waited, watching. Gertie, watching her, thought there was something like satisfaction in her face as Clytie, still singing, not knowing she was being watched, came in sight, and then began a dance like skipping on the big flat sandrock at the top of the path. Gertie wanted to cry out to Clytie that her grandmother watched, but could not, not even when she changed again from singing to whistling, and then, no more thinking that any one watched than a squirrel, flung her arms out wide and did a lively tapping dance that made the ragged coat she wore seem even more ragged, while Reuben's old overalls unrolled themselves and flopped about her feet. The only thing about her that seemed new and clean and shining was a Montgomery Ward catalogue under one arm.

Gertie's mother nodded slowly, her eyes on Clytie. There was satisfaction in her voice, and sorrow, deep sorrow, when she said, all the anger gone now: 'Look at her, growen up like a heathen, learnen how to dance frum that trashy Mamie, dirty, ragged. I'll bet she ain't combed and braided her hair in a week. You know she wouldn't ha been goen to ruin if'n Clovis was home.'

'You sound like she was comen up with a bastard,' Gertie said. 'We've been awful busy.'

Her mother began crying again, sobbing about Gertie's vile talk. Clytie heard and came on, the dance steps gone from her legs, her eyes fixed worriedly on her grandmother, shame in her face as if she had done great wrong. The bright catalogue was clutched like a shield against her bosom, but when she had walked up to the white mare her grandmother lifted her head and managed a wan and kindly smile. 'What are you a fixen to order, girl?'

'Curtains,' Clytie said. 'White curtains with blue bands fer our new front room, and new—'

Her grandmother took her by the arm. 'Child, you don't need curtains, not now; not till you git to Detroit.'

'Dee-troit?' Clytie asked, doubt in her voice.

'Yes, Detroit. You know, honey, yer papa, he wants you with him. He cain't make a liven no longer by haulen coal. He's a hunten you a place. You know that, a place close to a good school an—'

'But Mom said we couldn't go so far away, an that soon's th war's over—'

Enoch was interrupting with cries of, 'Goodie, goodie, we can go to school agin, a fine, big school.' His grandmother nodded, smiling. But Clytie continued for an instant troubled, glancing toward her mother, who stood motionless by the porch steps. Amos, not yet dressed, stood in the doorway, laughing, repeating, 'Dee-troit, Dee-troit,' as yesterday he had repeated Santa Claus when Clytie told him of Christmas.

His grandmother, quite recovered now, patted him on the head, then shooed him back into the house, crying: 'Pore little feller, he needs somebody that'll take care a him. Runnen around barefooted this away, he'll be a gitten that ole croup agin.'

'He never got up till you come,' Reuben said. His voice was hoarse now, broken by a growing doubt. He looked from his mother to his grandmother, then back to his mother. The trouble grew in his eyes, but still he waited, watching Gertie, hopeful, unwilling to believe she would not speak up for their farm. She continued silent. Gradually the hope in his eyes died. His glance, fixed on his mother's face, was filled with the contempt of the strong for the weak.

It seemed a long while that they looked at each other, mother and son. Gertie opened her mouth, closed it. One hand twisted, pulled the joints of the other. She started up the porch steps, but stopped when through the open door she heard her mother. She was cheerful now, chattering to Clytie about the color of the coat she must order with some of Henley's money, the kind of little suit for Enoch. Next she was holding forth on the wonders of Detroit. They would have a nice home with the electric and running water, both hot and cold maybe. And the school—such a fine big school it would be with a basketball court in a real gymnasium, like Meg's children had. Here her voice lifted for Reuben's benefit; he for all his clumsiness was good at pitching goals in the outdoor court at Deer Lick School. There would be a fancy cooking place for Clytie, hot lunches for them all, and most likely a bus. But better than anything, she reminded, their father would make them a good living and they wouldn't have to be working themselves to death in some old cornfield.

'But 'twould ha been our own—all our own field,' Reuben cried toward the doorway, but his voice was too low and hoarse to carry past his grandmother's chatter. He stood a moment longer on the middle step, looking dazedly about him. He saw the gray mule, and with no more words and never a look for Gertie led the gray mule barnward.

His head was bent, and Gertie thought as he walked away he was crying. She took one step toward him, but turned back and went to the chopping block. She had already filled the woodbox with wood cut by lantern light so as to have all of today's light for the Tipton Place, but still she chopped lengths from a hard dead hornbeam she had snaked up with Dock a few days before. Cassie alone stayed with her, silent, and with the lonesome look that came sometimes when Callie Lou ran away. Gyp stood by her, and she scratched him under one ear as she asked, after a long silence, 'Mom, can Gyp go to Dee-troit, too?'

There was such trouble in the child's voice that Gertie dropped the ax and picked her up. 'We ain't gone yit, honey. Mebbe—mebbe it won't be so bad. Mebbe—somehow.' Her tongue was still in the face of Cassie's disbelieving eyes, but her mind raced on. Maybe somewhere there was something—somebody to keep her from having to go away. John? Her father? No, her father would never speak up. He wanted her close by, so that in speaking for her he would speak

142

for himself. He would cry out no more than Job's dead children. John had her money. Maybe he'd gone already and recorded the deed. John wouldn't back out; he wouldn't go back on his word. 'But, Mom, can Gyp go, too?' Cassie was pulling on her chin, turning her face about so that she might bolster up her mother's limp words with her mother's eyes. 'An can we take that woman in th woods, Miz Callie Lou?'

'Yes, oh, yes,' Gertie said, hugging the child, but not looking into the waiting eyes. 'In Detroit,' she went on, 'they'll be people, all kinds a people, thousands an thousands a faces like we ain't never seen, an th finest we'll pick fer Callie Lou.'

'But she's got a face already, you jist ain't—'

Cassie, like her mother, heard the mule's feet in the lane—a click on the rocks, a suck in the mud. Gertie never looked around. She knew it was John. She let the child slide from her arms. John would never come so early in the morning, when his legs were bad, to tell her he had recorded the deed.

She stood there staring out across the ridge top, and saw the sun had risen. It poured red light upon the northwestern side of the ridge. The beeches lower down, and the sugar maples, were shadowed still, but higher up, toward the cove top, the trunks of the tall young poplars were pink in the rising light. It came to her that maybe she had always known those other trees would never be her own—no more than the fireplace with the great slab of stone—just as she had always known that Christ would never come out of the cherry wood. Seemed like all week he'd cried for her knife in the firelight, and now he was gone. Instead, here was John, old and troubled and tired, leaning from his mule.

'We've both got to do our duty, Gertie. Yer Mom sent fer me yisterday evenen. Frum th way she talks a body ud think I was maken a mint a money out a sellen that land to you. Twict I thought she was a goen to faint dead away. I cain't let a piece a land come atween a woman an her man an her people.'

'I'd never thought on it,' he went on when she remained motionless, silent, staring into the valley, 'but Clovis wouldn't like it down in a holler away frum th highway. Mostly, I recken, I thought

143

on how nice it ud be fer you an yer pop.' He reached for his leather moneybag. 'A body's got tu give in tu reason. Recollect, when we made our trade, you thought Clovis ud be in th army.' He nodded toward the house from which came her mother's chatter, then looked down into the leather bag and sighed as he began to pull out crumpled bills. 'Th right's on her side. Yer youngens does need schools, an when Clovis is a maken you a good liven you ought to go to him if he wants it thataway.'

10

She'd done a thing she'd never done in all her life—slept till past sunrise. The sun was in her eyes, and Lizzie was bawling, but it was way past milking time. She was way late, but she couldn't get out of bed. Her legs ached, and on one side she was cold, but on the other she was steamy hot and sweaty. She rose swiftly; she'd better milk even before she built the fire.

Something hit her on the head. Cassie moaned and whimpered, almost skidding from her lap, but did not waken. Gertie caught her shoulder, wakened enough to realize she had hit her head on the iron baggage rack above her. Once more, as she had done for hours, she pressed her big body as far back in the seat as possible and against the window, where, in spite of two thicknesses of glass, the cold, like water trickling, seeped into her hip so that it ached from the cold as her arms ached from weariness. She had held Amos and Cassie, one on either knee, all the way from Cincinnati to make room for Enoch and Clytie, wedged into the other half of the red plush seat. She looked quickly about for Reuben, and found him only after what seemed a long search in the dim light. He was on the arm of the seat right in front of them, but across the aisle; asleep, she thought, his head bowed on his arm along the seat back, like the little sailor, not much bigger than Reuben, on the arm of their seat by Clytie. The sailor's hat had fallen on Clytie's lap; his head nodded, touching at times her shoulder, but sleeping or waking Gertie could not tell, for always he clasped with both hands the back of the seat.

It was the new suit that had made Reuben seem a stranger. Her mother had ordered it as she had ordered the rest of their clothing,

145

and paid for it with Henley's money. All that seemed so long ago. But it couldn't have been more than two weeks back, for only two days after her mother's visit there'd come a letter from Clovis. He'd found a place and wanted them to come.

Still, it seemed so long ago, everything so long ago and far away: the other train, this train, even the dimming of the lights when all the people—the loud-talking, laughing soldier men and sailors and soldier girls, the crying babies, the puking, whining children, the red-necked, loose-jointed older men in overall pants so new they still smelled of the dye, the women in rayon dresses and muddy shoes, almost all with children in their laps—all, both black and white, had gone to sleep.

She nodded, her head jolting with the motion of the train. Maybe she was dreaming; in a minute she would jump out of bed and hurry to the spring, for it was moving day and she had a lot of work to do. She'd go outside and smell the good clean air; there would be a melting snow smell and a pine smell on the ridge top, and by her own house the smell of cedar through the creek fog.

She gagged, water coming into her eyes. She shivered with the gagging until Cassie whimpered in her sleep, then was still, smiling. Gertie tried to keep herself still, and let the child have her dream and keep smiling. She struggled to hold back the stuff rising in her mouth. She tried not to breathe the air that was like a stinking rotten dough pushed up her nose and down her throat. There were bits of vomit in the air where the black babies and the white babies had puked. There was vomit from the red-faced, red-eyed soldiers, laughing—a kind of cursing, crying in their laughter—even as they puked. One had staggered laughing, then puked right in the aisle by them, so close and with such a splattering that Clytie had cried out he was ruining her new coat. There was the stink of cigarette smoke, old now, and worse than when it was new, with its blue curls forever around her head. Mixed in it were the smells of wet babies, of stale soda biscuit from Alabama, fried fresh hot meat from Georgia, all old and smelly now in the too hot car, but still less strong than the smell of too many bodies shut up together. No matter how much they'd laughed and joked and drunk, there was on them all the fear sweat smell like she'd smelled in Samuel's store.

146

She smelled it on herself, felt it on her oozy hands. She was a coward, worse than any of the others. If she could have stood up to her mother and God and Clovis and Old John, she'd have been in her own house this night. Oh, if she were back with the money in her pocket, she'd say No to them all and move to her farm, sin or no. She straightened, and sat unseeing. Her hands were fists across the bodies of her children, but they slept on, limp heads jolting as the steel wheels clicked over the steel rails.

She got up, and with some difficulty turned herself about enough to lay the children on the seat. Then, with one long step she got into the aisle, careful not to brush against the little sailor. He looked as if the least touch would make him sprawl into Clytie's lap. She hurried on, her big body seeming even bigger, more awkward in the narrow aisle, flung this way and that by the rushing of the train. She knocked against the sleeping feet, the nodding heads, the shoulders sagged across the arms of seats.

The word *Ladies* was like a promised haven, though as she went through the first little room, the one with mirrors and chairs, she saw that even here there were women and babies sleeping. But the toilet—Clytie had told her to call it that instead of the privy house— was empty. She flung up the toilet seat, knelt, and vomited. Cold air like water bubbling up from a spring came through the open hole. She knelt a long while, savoring the rushing air. It tasted of train smoke and was burdened with sound. Still, it was better than any she had known since leaving home. All the hours they had waited in Cincinnati had been in a house-like thing, big and high above them, but smothery crowded down below, with people fighting for standing places in the lines before the gates.

She came out at last into the little room, which after the crowded car and the train noise from the open toilet seemed still and empty, with only two women and two babies, all of whom looked to be asleep. One sat, her head nodding above a young baby, face downward across her knees. The other lay on the bench under the looking glass, one sun-browned hand clutching an imitation patent-leather purse, the other cradled about a pale-haired little girl in a blue rayon dress, its ruffles smeared with chocolate and orange drippings. The woman's shoes, new and of the same shiny imitation patent leather as her purse, twinkled in the light, that is, all but one heel, and on that there was a smear of reddish mud. The mud was strange to Gertie, redder than any earth she could remember, and sandy, from the looks of it. She bent closer to look, and wanted very much to touch it, to know what it was and from where it came. It looked as if it would grow sweet potatoes and peanuts.

She rubbed the heel gently with her thumb, and a tiny piece of the red gold stuff broke away and fell into her palm. She touched it with a forefinger, pleased that she had been right. Sandy and poor it was; scrub pine and saw briers would grow in it, but so would sweet potatoes.

She was holding the mud, staring down at it, not wanting to throw it away, when she realized the other woman, the one she had hardly noticed and thought asleep too, was looking at her. She had made no sound that she had heard, and her head was still bowed above the baby on her knees, but Gertie knew she was look- ing, sideways of her eyes, the way Judas looked when he whispered about Jesus. And she remembered with something close to com- fort that she had brought the block of wood, brought it in spite of her mother's scorn and Clytie's gentle objections. Only Cassie had begged for the wood, hugged it as if it had been human. The woman kept on looking, watching slant-wise out of her eyes, and Gertie felt awkward and foolish, staring at the mud in her hand, remembering the good money she had spent to bring the block of wood—Judas wood it seemed now. Jesus would never come from it. But there were faces in Detroit.

'It looks like good dirt fer growen sweet taters,' she said at last, flushing, then looking fully at the woman, who smiled and said in a soft rich voice:

'That Georgia mud is good fo that.'

'I wonder,' Gertie said, speaking softly, for she had no memory of having spoken to a stranger woman except the nurse in the doc- tor's office, 'what th ground around Detroit is like? Will it grow sweet taters?'

The woman's head swung slowly, lifting fully into the light, and Gertie realized she was a Negro. She had never seen a Negro until, in Cincinnati, they had left their separate places and mingled with the whites. She'd heard Clovis say there were Negroes in Town, but she had so seldom been there she had never seen one. This woman did not look the way she had thought a Negro would—pure black with great thick lips and a mashed-down nose. Her skin was brown and full of gleams that made Gertie think of the cherry wood. Her eyes were large below a high, thin-templed forehead; and when she looked at Gertie all her face and the proudful way she held her head were somehow queenly, but bigger than anything else about her was the joy inside her that curved her lips into smiles and brightened her naturally somber eyes.

The baby, hardly two months old, Gertie judged, wriggled, twisting its head, then at last got a fist up to its mouth. The woman's smile widened, dancing through her eyes and across her forehead as she chucked it gently under the chin. 'Don't you go fallen off my lap, yo little ole booger, you.' She looked at Gertie, then back to the baby. 'She ain't been sleepen so good, poh thing; she's been sleepen on mah knees thisaway since day befo yesterday.'

'She'll be all right,' Gertie said. 'I'll bet she misses her bed less'n you do.'

'She misses her granma's singen, thas what she misses away off up heah—an I ain't so good at singen.'

Gertie nodded. 'Upon th willows in th midst thereof, we hanged our harps, and they that wasted us required of us mirth, saying, "Sing us one a th songs a Zion." But how shall we sing th Lord's song in a strange land?' She flushed. She hadn't meant to say that. But it had run in her head so, since early this morning on the other train, when Cassie had wanted her to sing right before a trainful of people.

'Them's pretty words,' the other said, then added somewhat defiantly, 'but ah don feel wasted. Detroit's goen to be nice.' A brooding, remembering look came into her eyes, but smiles shattered it when she looked down at the baby. 'She can go to a good school, an when she's sick they'll be hospitals for her like fo—' She had looked at Gertie and remembered. 'Like fo anybody else. She'll have a better raisen than her mammy or her pappy had,' and the joy came over her and would not let her be still, so that she seized the child, half sleeping as it was, and swung it above her head, smiling

149

at it, shaking it playfully, begging with her eyes for it to share in her joy, and when it could not she turned again to the silently watching Gertie. 'My man's got a place fo me—rent paid fo a month. Th street's in a place they call Paradise Valley, he wrote me. Paradise Valley,' she repeated softly to the baby.

The baby was too little to smile back. But Gertie managed a smile for the woman, though it seemed so long ago that she had felt as the woman felt now—going to a place that would be paradise. Paradise: it was a pretty word. She'd never thought how pretty it was until now. When the woman spoke it in her soft rich voice, it made her think of peaches, pure gold on one side, red in the gold on the other, soft, juicy, warm in the August sun, warm-tasting like the smell of the muscadines above the river in October. 'It's a pretty name,' and remembering, twisting the hurt inside her, she said to the woman what she had said to herself, ' "This day thou shalt be with me in paradise." '

The woman laughed. 'That's what mah man said to me, only in different words.'

Gertie nodded, and her voice was defiant. 'I'll allus think that a body oughtn't tu have tu die first to git it—that is, at least a little—a paradise on earth.' She turned from the woman's troubled puzzlement to look through the window. She pressed her face against the glass, determined to see what kind of country they whirled through. But this window showed no more than the one by her seat—steamy on the inside, crusted with smoke and dirt on the outside, and stout as for a prison, with two thick panes of glass. As if through all the night hours this train had stood still, she always saw the same things: lights, streaks of dirty snow, roads, telephone poles, a few cars, and earlier in the little towns the cold shapes of hurrying people, and once, across what had seemed to be a vast reach of palm-flat land, smudged lights that might have been stars.

In spite of the double glass she felt the hard cold seeping through, and turned away, but continued to stand, hunch-shouldered, lax-handed, looking about the room. It didn't seem that she could go back to her cramped smelly place in the coach, and anyway the youngens needed the extra room. The long woman on the bench still slept, and the brown one on the chair sat again as if asleep, nodding above the sleeping baby.

She fingered her knife, familiar in the strangeness of the new coat pocket. There was a metal wastebasket at the end of the bench, and she looked down into it, hoping to find something, a corncob, a bit of wood, anything her knife had known. She smiled when she saw in the debris of lunch wrappings, facial tissues, and orange rinds a large hickory nut cast off for lack of a cracking tool.

She heard a gasping, gulping 'Jesus!' from the brown woman; scared, she sounded, like her baby was choking to death. Gertie turned, stepping forward to learn what was her trouble. The girl sprang up, the baby clutched tightly in her arms, her body bent over it as if she would protect it from some lunging animal. Her wide eyes darted wildly, now up at Gertie's face, now at the knife, which all unknowing Gertie had opened and held ready in her hand. 'Don git no closah, woman,' she whispered as if her tongue were dry. She did not take her eyes from Gertie, and backed away until she was pressed against the window.

Gertie looked at her, her mind for an instant too pleased at the prospect of doing a pleasant and familiar thing to understand what ailed the other's mind. She thought for a moment that the brown woman might be crazy. They stood so for a long moment, staring at each other without speaking. Gradually, the brown woman's eyes leaping toward the knife made Gertie flush with understanding. The thought that someone could or would think that she would fight with a knife like a drunken Cramer was slow in coming. She folded the knife but continued to hold it, as she tried to smile into the wide eyes that shone whitely in the brown face. 'I'm sorry I skeered you,' she began, and motioned toward the wastebasket, hoping the woman would understand about her whittling. In glancing at the basket, she saw a huge and ugly woman, flat-cheeked, straight-lipped, straggeldy-headed, her face grayed with tiredness and coal dust, even her chapped lips gray. The straight, almost bushy black brows below the bony forehead were on a level with her own, and she realized she was looking at herself—the same old Gertie who had made her mother weep.

She laughed, a long laugh, a good laugh. It seemed she couldn't remember when she had laughed, not since corn-planting time when Henley went away. The big gray-faced woman was uglier laughing than sober. Her teeth shone whitely behind her gray lips. She laughed the harder, watching the big woman brush back her straight lank hair with a bended arm, but conscious that the brown woman was still staring at her, though now seeming more puzzled than afraid.

Gertie held up the hickory nut, hidden until now in her great hand. 'I don't wonder,' she said, speaking into the mirror, 'that a stranger woman like you is afeared a me. I jist happened to see myself, an skeered myself.' She stopped, but after the laughter the explanation seemed less hard. 'Some women pieces quilts an some crochets to pass th time. But me—I growed up with my pop. An I took to whittlen jist like him. I was aimen to whittle a basket out a this hicker nut I found, to kind a pass th time.'

She put a chair under the light by the mirror, and turning her back somewhat on the other, thinking maybe she hated to see a body whittle the way her mother hated it, she went to work on the hickory nut. The knife blade winked in the light, jiggled now and then by the rushing, clacking train; but the basket grew, a split basket, the splints marked clearly in the hard nutshell, the handle smooth, curving at the top as the nut had curved, while the sharp peak at the bottom of the nut grew smooth and became the bottom of the basket.

Gradually the brown woman, instead of darting sharp, suspicious glances, pulled her chair closer and closer and watched as Cassie would have watched. Sleepy-headed women coming in to change whimpering, wet-bottomed babies paused to watch, and two little soldier girls who didn't look much older than Clytie came in and smoked cigarettes, and lingered a long while watching.

She made the basket markings fine and tiny so that the work might last a long while. But the windows were always black, untouched by any gray of dawn when she looked at them. She realized with something close to despair that the basket would end before the night.

Several times she left off her work to see about the children. They were always the same, asleep in a tangle of arms and legs. The little sailor slept with his head on Clytie's shoulder, and Clytie clung to his upper arm, dreaming, Gertie guessed, it was Cassie back home, forever about to slide out of the high feather bed. The rest of the car slept the smelly, moaning, coughing, muttering sleep of cattle penned too closely in a strange barn.

Once when she got back to the rest room her seat was taken by a little baby-faced girl in a bright red coat nursing a baby. She kept talking about her soldier man at a place called Grayling, past Detroit, and wondering if it would be cold for the baby.

The brown woman offered her a chair, saying she was tired of sitting, but Gertie refused and whittled standing. Then the brown woman complained that she couldn't watch the work. 'You're worse than my Cassie,' Gertie said, smiling, 'fer wanten to watch things. Tell me th baby's name. I'll put it on this an give it to her fer a keepsake a me.'

The woman's eyes grew bright with pleasure, as when she spoke of the place called Paradise. 'I was hopan you'd sell it to me. Her first name is Beulah. I hope it ain't too long,' she added, glancing anxiously at the basket. 'But I want to pay yo.'

'Pay fer whittlen foolishness!' Gertie looked at her in amazement.

The girl nodded. 'I'll bet yo could make big money whittlen. City people sometimes loves handmade stuff. It's worth mo'n a dollah— way mo'n that if you count th time.' She opened her hand, and Gertie saw the green of money that from its crumpled, sweaty look she must have been holding a long time.

'Yo take this dollah,' she said. 'Keep it like a good-luck piece— an then it won't be pay. An Beulah Mae can always keep this fo a good-luck token.'

11

Gertie had no time to think of where she went or why. The press of people so hurried her up the long steel ramp that Cassie, clinging to her coattail, screamed with fright. Though she already had two split baskets on one arm and Amos on the other, she tried to pick up the child, but could not bend among the pushing, tightly packed bodies.

The crowd bore her through the gate, and at once there was more room, but no Clovis and no sign of the other children. She backed away a little, got Cassie out of the jam, and stood looking about her with quick, frightened glances. Where were the children, and where was Clovis? Panic overtook her when she realized that the last of the people were off the train. The rushing now was toward the train gate. Maybe the youngens had got scared and turned back. She wanted to rub her eyes, but realized that neither hand was free. How did the children look? The colors of their new clothing had evaporated from her head.

She took an uncertain step back toward the gate, and stood on tiptoe trying to see down the ramp. Something hit her on the shin. She saw a little cart of suitcases pushed by a man in a red cap. He gave her a mean look and said, 'Look where you're going, lady.'

She stepped backward. One split basket hit something. She turned, and a woman's eyes under a red scarf glared at her, and a wide red mouth said, 'Hillbilly,' spitting the words as if they shaped a vile thing to be spewed out quickly.

Then almost under her elbow a voice was crying, 'Mom, you've ruint yer new hat. It's knocked ever which-away.' And an instant later: 'Mom, can I go git me a Coke? Reuben won't let me go an they's a Coke place right by.'

She tried to put a tone of authority into her voice. 'Enoch, hush an grab holt a Cassie here an git her out a this. Let go a me, honey, an take Enoch's hand. He'll git ye out. Enoch, where's Reuben an—' Her eyes had chanced upon Reuben and Clytie. They stood on a bench, looking at her over the heads of the people.

She reached the bench at last, and the children got off and gave her the place they had saved for her. She dropped upon it and sat breathing hard, with the baskets still on her arms, though Amos slid down and stood by her knee. The older children stared at her, more surprised by her strange weak ways than by all the goings on around them. Clytie reached and straightened her hat, took the baskets from her, and set them on the floor. 'You look peaked, Mom,' she said. 'You ain't a gitten train sick like Cassie?'

Gertie shook her head. 'I'm all right, but I thought you youngens was lost.'

Clytie smiled at her mother's fear, hesitated, then looked to Enoch as if for help. He nodded, and she said, 'Mom, you need some good hot cawfee. Couldn't we uns take some money an buy somethen an set on one a them stools an eat it? I seen their prices, an you can git a bowl a oats fer a quarter, an—'

Enoch begged, 'Aw, come on, Mom, but me, I'd ruther have a Coke.'

'You can buy a whole box a oats fer less'n—'

Gertie felt the shivering Cassie, met Reuben's interested look. They did need some hot food. The half-bushel basket of cake and pie and fried ham and chicken sandwiches Aunt Kate had fixed for them yesterday morning was still half full; but the basket food, warmish, slightly smelly, had gagged her even when it was fresh, and Cassie would never touch it.

Amos tweaked Clytie's coat. 'Oats,' he said.

Clytie understood her mother's face, 'You come, too, Mom.'

Gertie shook her head, 'You uns go on an eat.' She fished in her pocket, brought out a dollar bill, and then a quarter. She looked an instant at the money before handing it to Clytie. 'Back home that ud keep us in oats an sugar fer sweetenen more'n a month.'

155

'Detroit's diff'rent,' Clytie said, then comforted, 'an recollect Pop's a maken big money.' She took Amos with one hand, and reached for Cassie with the other, but Cassie clung to Gertie.

'I ain't hungry,' she said, her teeth chattering.

The others went away, then overhead, like thunder speaking unknown tongues, voices boomed. Though they had heard the same in Cincinnati, both jumped and looked up. Cassie snuggled against Gertie, buried her face in her lap, shivering, whispering, 'What is it, Mom?'

'Jist some kind a contraption to tell people about trains, I recken,' Gertie said, and pulled the child close against her. 'Don't be afeared now. Pretty soon your pop'ull be here to take us to our pretty new home.'

'Will Gyp be a comen pretty soon?'

'In a little while—mebbe. But he'll be fine with yer Granma Nevels. Sugar Belle needs a little company. But soon as we git settled in a place with a big yard, we'll send fer him, that is, if we don't go back right away.'

Cassie was silent, her face pressed into Gertie's lap. Her shoulders shook with sobs, or maybe it was only shivers; it was so cold. Gertie's feet were cold on the dirty cement floor, puddled with snow water. Gusts of cold from opening doors hit her legs and went up her dress tail like wandering icicles. She missed the heavy man's shoes, the heavy socks, the longtailed, full-skirted dresses of her own making; the new coat was skimpy, the rayon dress also ordered by her mother was skimpier still.

She was glad when a tall raw-boned woman weighted down with children and baggage plopped down almost upon her. It gave her an excuse to take Cassie on her lap and press her tightly against her body. This, and the wrapping of her own coat over Cassie's bare blue legs, seemed to warm them both. 'You'll hafta be gitten her some snow pants,' the woman said when she had got her breath a little, shifted the baby to her other arm, clamped the child of walking size between her knees, and looked at Cassie.

Gertie turned to her, the beginnings of a smile thawing some of the frozen terror from her bleak eyes; for the voice sounded like back home, booming out through the nose like Ann Liz Cramer's as the woman went on, 'It's terrible cold up here right on till summer.' She looked at the split baskets by Gertie's feet, shook her head over Cassie. 'Pore little thing, her runnen an playen days is over.'

'Mebbe not,' Gertie said.

'She'll git killed in traffic, then.'

'Traffic?'

'You know, everything's on wheels; that's traffic. Detroit's worse'n Willer Run. It ain't no place fer people.'

Gertie nodded, remembering the red sign on the pine tree. 'They tried to bag ever man in our country off up to that place. But I recken they give em good money, an mebbe don't work em too hard.'

'Work? They about kilt my man.' She glanced about her, then moved so close to Gertie her breath came in her face. 'He's a big strong man. There never was a team a mules he couldn't outlast a breaken cotton ground—we're frum west Tennessee. He went to jine up, come Pearl Harbor, but th fools wouldn't have him; said he was deef in one yer.'

She sighed, then went on: 'They claimed it was his patriotic duty to go to this Willer Run. He wasn't one a them big farmers. An atter this youngen come,' she tapped the older child, 'he bagged me off up there too. Said he was goen crazy; said they was killen him. Soon's I could wean this biggest un, I got me a job an drawed wages—worked some. Th neighbor women an me, we took turns minden youngens, an I worked till six weeks afore this baby come.'

She was silent a moment, gathering words, remembering. Then after a kind of sigh and headshake, like a person who has been too long under water, she began again. 'An I expect they are a killen him. But I couldn't stand it no longer, jist couldn't. An anyhow we'd saved up enough to git us a tractor. But, Lord, it took some saven. An, God, th way we've lived. No water, no electric inside our shack at first. An swampy with mosquiters in summer, you couldn't set still. An then all winter you froze. Lord, it was awful.'

She stopped again, sighing, shaking her head. 'Ever night he'd come home looken peaked an wore out as a colicky baby with a touch a th sun, an I'd say, "What they have you a doen today, honey?" An he'd say, "The same damn' thing, a walken ahint some

157

superintendent that didn't know where he was a goen." Er mebbe he'd say "Jist a standen till they needed me." Lots a nights he'd git in at midnight an I'd say, "Well, honey, I bet you stretched then muscles on overtime." An he'd say, "Time an a half I've made this night fer waiten overtime. They sure made plenty a plus on me this day." '

'Plus?' Gertie asked.

The woman nudged her with one bony elbow. "Don't say hit so loud. Depots like this is jist lined with FBI. But you knew what th men say when they make em stand around: "Th more cost, th more plus." ' The woman's voice had dropped to a hoarse whisper. 'These big men that owns these factories, th gover'mint gives em profits on what things cost—six cents on th dollar I've heard say. So ever time they can make a thing cost two dollars stid a one'—she winked slowly at Gertie—'they're six cents ahead, an everbody's happy. Th more men, th more plus fer th owners, th more money an more men fer them unions. I figger,' she went on after a moment's reflective smoothing of her dress, 'thet Luke, he's jist a plus. He cain't hep it. His baby brother's kilt already.'

'Th county paper an th radio an them signs on th trees allus said them men was bad needed at Willer Run—tu win th war,' Gertie said.

'To make more plus.' The woman's voice dropped even lower. 'Whar's th bombers they've made. In their coat pockets?'

The voice in the roof was booming again, and the woman exclaimed, 'Lordy, I'd better be a gitten in line er I'll be standen, holden this youngen all th way to Louisville like I done with his brother a comen up. Mebbe,' she went on, standing now, the baby's head wedged into her shoulder to protect him from the jolting crowd, her purse clutched across his stomach where she could see it, suitcase handle and the child's wrist gripped in the other hand, ticket pinned with three small safety pins on her coat lapel, 'you'd better jist turn around an go back home with me.' She lingered a moment, her eyes more kindly than prying as they went from the split basket to Gertie's hard palmed hands then up to the new hat, 'It'll be gardenen time afore you know it, back home, an—well, recollect you ain't on no cost plus.'

Gertie managed to smile, though her voice was husky as she said with a little headshake, 'Mebbe I'll have a good garden patch up here—if we stay till spring.'

'I hope so,' the woman said, walking away now. She glanced once over her shoulder, then a hurrying soldier bumped her, a sailor fell in behind her, and she was gone.

Gertie realized she was shivering again. She sprang up, and was standing looking first this way and then that when she saw Clytie carrying coffee steaming in a paper cup. In her bewilderment Clytie seemed to be returning from a direction opposite to that in which she had gone. 'Drink it quick, Mom, fore it gits cold,' Clytie commanded, 'an you'll feel better.'

'I don't feel bad,' Gertie said, but drank the coffee gratefully, though it was weak with a dirty, dishwatery taste, and they had put sugar in it. The others came back, Enoch last, running, shrilling in breathless excitement: 'I seed Dee-troit, Mom. It's a snowen like I ain't never seed. Th snow in Deetroit don't fall down. It goes crosswise. An it ain't cold like we thought, fer th snow's melten. An, Mom, I seed a million cars. Let's git goen.'

'I'm waiten fer yer pop,' Gertie said. 'Shorely he'll knock off frum work long enough tu come an meet us. We don't want tu be gone when he comes.'

'Pop didn't sound pime blank certain in his letter like he'd meet us,' Clytie said, and the same eagerness that overflowed Enoch was reflected in her eyes as she insisted, 'That's why he give us th address an told us to git a cab.' The children's eyes were now all upon Gertie, waiting, expecting her to get the baggage that Joe Lee, the ticket agent at the Valley, had taken after putting a ticket on each piece and giving her a ticket to match. She had seen none of it since. Where was it now? Where were the bedclothes, the dishes packed in boxes, and above all the block of wood she had sent by express. These things she had understood were not to come for some days, but were they lost? Was everything lost? She looked wildly about her, fixed her glance at last on Enoch, who was begging: 'Give me th tickets an me an Reuben can go. We can carry it all. I seed the people a standen in line.'

Clytie shoved in front of Enoch. 'Let me go, Mom. I'm the biggest.'

'I can do it good as you can,' Enoch cried, and while he and Clytie argued Gertie laid down the new handbag of her mother's buying and fumbled in her coat pocket. She had pinned the ticket stubs and baggage checks in one pocket along with what had seemed money enough and to spare for the journey, but now in her confusion all were mixed in the mental map of her pocket. Clytie watched her fumblings with shamed embarrassment and scolded, 'Mom, you'd ought to use your new purse.'

Enoch looked at her and giggled, speaking so shrilly that a drowsing soldier roused enough to look at them and smile. 'Mom, you look like a body out a th funny papers, an yer hat's still crooked.'

' "Honor they fath—" ' she began. She found the baggage checks. 'Git it,' she said, shoving them toward Clytie.

The three older ones went away after Clytie had pointed out a door near which she was to wait, and brushed aside Gertie's feeble arguments that maybe they had better wait a little minutes longer for Clovis. Gertie, however, continued for a few minutes longer where Clytie had left her. She craned her head, searching in all directions, but looking longest and most hopefully toward an outside door through which a constant stream of people came and went. At last, with a troubled headshake, she loaded Amos on one arm, the baskets on the other, directed Cassie to hold her coattail, and went to the door by the sign directing people to the cab stand, the one Clytie had pointed out to her.

She waited near the swinging doors that let the sharp cold in, and where the passing people were constantly knocking against the baskets and bumping the children. Once again she heard, in the sharp, broken-into-pieces language, the word 'hillbilly.' A clock above the door told her it was only a little past nine, but it seemed it must be dinnertime before the older children came.

She took a rope-tied orange crate packed with clothing and cookware onto her hip, and with the baskets on her other arm followed Clytie through the door. Cold winds like snatching hands tore at them.

Her hat went blowing, rolling in front of her. She grabbed it at last, jammed it hard down into the basket, and strode on. The wind, as

160

if it had fingers, unbuttoned the new coat that billowed first behind her, then whipped about her legs as if in this place all directions were north. All around, sharp and cutting as white sand flying, the snow whirled, making it hard to see as they hurried down a sloping sidewalk. She knew only that all her own were there. Reuben was in front with her mother's round-topped trunk made of tin pressed into the shapes of roses on his shoulders, Enoch next with Clovis's old paper suitcase, split down one corner and tied with fishline, then Clytie staggering with the weight of a fruit-jar box of clothing under each arm. Gertie followed with her load, and behind her came the younger children, who tried to shield themselves from the wind and snow by burying their faces in her coattail.

They stopped at the end of a long line of silent people. They were people who looked much like those she had seen on the train: women like herself, clutching boxes and babies, shivering in huddles of toe-hopping, teeth-chattering children; the girls especially suffered, dressed as they were, like her own girls, in shortish coats and flimsy rayon dresses, their unbooted feet in low shoes and socks. The men and boys with pant legs between them and the cold were somewhat warmer but all seemed, like herself, cold, bewildered, dirty.

Two slowly moving cabs passed on their way toward the head of the line. But one stopped when a red-jowled man with a small bag and a large stomach ran out the door and down the walk, waving a bill which he seemed to have had ready in his hand. The man who had never waited was taken into the cab and driven away, followed by the angry cries and even curses of many in the line.

A gust of wind, wild as March and cold as if the sun had died, whirled words and cries away. Gertie put down her load, caught up Cassie and put her under her coat. The skimpy thing would not button over the two of them but she held it together as best she could with her arms crossed widely over her bosom. Her ears that had at first tingled, then hurt, were now so numb she could no longer feel her hair blowing about them.

She slid Cassie to the ground, and from the Josiah basket took an old woolen baby's blanket of her mother's crocheting. She was folding it diddy wise to put on her head when, through a lull in

161

the wind, she heard a shivering sobbing. She looked around and saw, only two people away in the ever-lengthening line, the little-girl mother from Georgia who had wondered on the train if it would be cold up in Grayling where her man was. She was trying to bundle herself and the baby, wrapped only in a sleazy cotton blanket, together under her thin coat, not much longer than a man's shirttail. Her words to the woman in front of her came in a shivering whimper, 'Who'd ha thought it ud be so cold in th fall thisaway?'

'Here, put this over that youngen,' Gertie called above the wind, and reached the blanket to her. She saw, more than she heard through the wind, the girl's shivering, 'Oh, thank you,' and again, 'Thanks.'

Cabs came slowly in, and the line moved slowly ahead, though soon Gertie's feet in the new thin shoes and rayon stockings grew so numb it was easier to stand still than to move. Amos and Cassie took turns crying, and even Enoch, who kept insisting it couldn't be cold because the snow was melting in the street, got so shivery he could hardly talk. Though the early-morning grayness had never lifted from the town, it seemed it must be milking time when at last their turn for a cab came. They were hardly inside before the driver, a little weazened black-eyed man, was asking, 'Where to, lady?' He did not look at them again as he pulled away from the curb, steering with a forearm while his hands unscrewed the red top from a vacuum bottle.

Gertie began another frantic fumbling with numb fingers for the address pinned down in her pocket, but Clytie said, smooth as a preacher, '18911 Merry Hill.'

'And where is Merry Hill?' the driver asked, able to use one whole hand now for steering. One was enough to hold the vacuum bottle while he drew the stopper with his teeth.

'It's clost to where my pop works, an he works at th Flint Plant,' Enoch said.

'Old man Flint's got plants all over town, all over th world,' the driver said. He stopped the car, then holding the bottle low, close to his chest with one hand, the red cup in the other, said, 'I gotta have a li'l drink u coffee.'

Then he was unable to pour for the laughter shivering his shoulders when Gertie begged: 'Don't put us out. Somebody must know where is this Merry Hill.'

'Lady, they's cops watchen this light,' he answered, the soundless laughter subsiding enough that he could pour.

Gertie saw the light like a red eye blinking through the whirling snow, and sat silent, mystified. But Enoch, who sat in a strange little seat next to the driver, though backward to him, squirmed around to look, then nodded knowingly. 'It's like the second reader, th red lights an th green. An look, lookee, Mom, they's two policemen in a car. I'll bet pretty soon we see one a standen on a corner like in th story.' And Enoch bounced on his knees with excitement until the driver turned on him in exasperation, reminding him that he was trying to drink coffee. 'It don't steam like hot coffee,' Enoch said, considering the red cup.

'It's cold,' the driver said, swallowing coffee, turning to look at the policemen in the nearby car.

'It don't smell like coffee,' Enoch said, wrinkling his nose with a sniff.

'Th smell froze,' the driver said, holding the coffee with one hand, driving under the green light with the other.

'It's not cold,' Enoch said, 'not real cold. The snow's melten.'

The driver's shoulders quivered again; the laughter so hard it made his head bob close to the steering wheel. Enoch never noticed the shaking shoulders; he was exclaiming, 'Lookee, they's three policemen in that car, but in th second reader they're a walken a beat er a standen on a corner.'

'Detroit don't go by no second reader, bub. You'll hardly never see one policeman, butcha'ull see a million in Detroit. Since u riots they go mostly in prowl cars, three by threes, sometimes two by twos.'

'What's a prowl car?' Enoch wanted to know.

'It's u car cops prowls in. Cops gotta prowl.'

'But what do they prowl after?' Enoch insisted.

'Mean people, of course,' Clytie said.

The driver nodded, laughing. 'Sure, sure that second reader's right. Cops, they never go after nothen but mean people.'

'But didn't you learn that in th second reader?' Enoch insisted. 'Don't they teach it up here?'

'I wouldn't know,' the driver said. 'When I went through that second reader forty years ago down in Alabam, they didn't teach us how to live in Detroit like they do little Kentuckians now.'

Clytie giggled. 'How'd you know where we was frum?'

'I've met youse atta station through two world wars. I oughta know.' His mocking eyes searched the mirror in front of him for Gertie's face. 'An I bet youses gonna go back pretty soon with money enough saved futu buy a farm, one a dem big bluegrass farms. Huh?'

Gertie tried to look away, but the cab windows, except for the bits of the windshield kept clean by the wipers, were so coated with snow and frost that for all the view they gave they might have been steel. She could only stare straight ahead, feeling the eyes on her face, sharp like the cold when Clytie cried: 'Mama's crazy after land uv her own. How'd you know?'

'Everbody is. Th Japs and u Germans, too. I figger,' he went on, stopping for another light, 'that about a million people has come to Detroit, all gonna git rich an buy u little patch a land back home.'

'I don't want nothen fancy,' Gertie said, somehow goaded into speech. 'I know we can save enough—more than—' The black eyes were laughing, a laughter without mirth, not mean, not making fun of her; more like he laughed at something she could not see—or imagine.

'That's fine, lady,' he said when they were moving again. 'Keep on knowen youses gonna have land. But if you do forgit, yukun remember land is free in heaven like that pie inu sky.'

'What's pie in th sky?' Enoch asked.

'Gotta keep shut, kid. Th Red Squad would have us both inu clink; me fu propigating un-American doctrines, you fu listening.'

'What's th clink?' Enoch asked, and immediately after, 'What's th Red Squad?'

'Things yu don't learn about, not even inu sixth reader, an soyu don't needu know. Now where inu hell is Merry Hill? Inu housing project.' He was driving slowly now, in a great press of cars.

Gertie shook her head over the strange words, but Clytie nodded, 'I recken it's a great big house like where city people lives, three, four stories high.'

'An we'll ride th elevator,' Enoch said, 'like in that story about th city children in th third reader.'

'Yeah,' the driver said, drawling the word, laughing again.

Gertie looked at him and pressed Cassie more tightly against her. All of them, even Enoch, were silent, staring straight ahead through the snow, where there was little to be seen but the red eyes of cars moving away in the grayness and the yellow eyes of cars coming on. Gertie scratched a hole in the frost on the window, but when the frost had swallowed the hole she did not scratch again.

She had wanted very much to see the sky, or if not the sky at least some bit of brightness. There should be the warm-looking, lighted windows of stores, and crowds of people. Instead, she saw only a few gray wind-battered shapes hurrying down dirty streets past dead-faced gray buildings. She wished Enoch would hush. He was asking the driver now if airplanes could fly in such weather.

'Sure, sure,' the driver said, and then asked, 'That new home close tudu airport?'

'Real close, my pop wrote.'

The driver nodded. 'We're inu right direction, bub. East side. Dey've been builden housing projects close tudu airport.'

'What's a housen project?' Clytie wanted to know.

'Houses th gover'ment builds fu war workers that don't need elevators.'

'Like coal-camp houses. My aunt Meg lives in one, an it's not so bad. She's got a big porch an a pretty good garden, but it's kind a smoky.'

The little man considered. 'Double th smoke, leave offu porch, halve u house, bury u garden, they'd maybe be about u same. I wouldn't know.'

The children fell silent as the driver, after much slow turning and slow driving through the narrow, crowded streets, came at last to a straight wide street, half buried in the ground, bounded by gray cement walls and crowded with cars and monstrous truck-like contraptions such as none of them had ever seen. Here there were no

165

lights to stop them, and they went so fast that Gertie could only sit, shivering, staring straight ahead, or blinking and crouching over Cassie when they shot under bridges carrying more cars, buses, and even trains. The wind pried at the doors and the windows, finding every crack; and as there seemed to be no heat in the cab all of them were as cold, almost, as when they had waited on the sidewalk.

The unbroken rush past the gray walls and under the bridges ended at last. There followed more turnings down narrow streets, strange streets that, though crowded, seemed set at times in empty fields until one saw a slowly moving switch engine or a mountainous pile of coal blown free of snow. The smoke thickened, and through it came sounds such as they had never heard; sometimes a broken clanking, sometimes a roar, sometimes no more than a murmuring, and once a mighty thudding that seemed more like a trembling of the earth than sound. 'Boy, I'd hate to live by one a them big press plants,' the driver said, then asked of them all, 'Don'tchas know where youses at? Right in u middle a some a Detroit's pride and glory—war plants.'

Enoch kept twisting around to see, but there was little to be seen save blurred shapes through the snow and smoke. The railroad tracks multiplied, and twice jangling bells and red lights swinging in the wind held them still while long freight trains went by with more smoke rolling down and blotting out the world. It seemed suddenly to Gertie as if all the things she had seen—the blurred buildings, the smokestacks, the monstrous pipes wandering high above her, even the trucks, and the trains—as if all these were alive and breathing smoke and steam as in other places under a sky with sun or stars the breath of warm and living people made white clouds in the cold. Here there seemed to be no people, even the cars with their rolled-up windows, frosted over like those of the cab, seemed empty of people, driving themselves through a world not meant for people.

They drove for a long while through the sounds, the smoke and steam, past great buildings which, though filled with noise, seemed empty of life. They were stopped again on the edge of what looked to be an endless field of railroad tracks, to wait while a long train of flat cars went by. Each car carried one monstrous low-slung, heavy-bodied tank, the tank gray-green, wearing a star, and holding, like the black feelers of some giant insect reaching for the sky, two guns. Gertie, hoping for something better to see, scratched another hole in the window frost. She was just turning away in disappointment when the whirling snow, the piles of coal, the waiting cars, the dark tanks moving, all seemed to glow with a faint reddish light. The redness trembled like light from a flame, as if somewhere far away a piece of hell had come up from underground.

She rubbed her eyes, then turned and looked through the windshield, but saw in puzzled wonder the redness still. Then Enoch was crying, all in a jiggle of excitement, 'Lookee—they's a fire.'

'That's white-hot steel, bub,' the driver said. 'They're maken a pour. Yu needn't be in such u hurry to see. I'll bet that steel mill's one a yu closest neighbors. Were gitten close to Merry Hill.'

'I hope it's a high hill,' Enoch said, 'where I can see all over th country.'

'Oh, it'll be a hill all right, covered with cattails an weeping willers.'

'Weepen willers don't grow on hills,' Enoch said.

'Detroit willers grows on Detroit hills,' the driver said.

They went on again at last, but the red glow followed them. The frost on the car windows was at times a reddish pink, as if bits of blood had frozen with the frost. They crossed another railroad, only two tracks this time, and past the tracks she saw no factories, only the cars moving between what seemed to be snowy fields on either side. The driver turned into a side road, then cursed as the car skidded in the powderlike snow, unmelted here. He rolled the window down, and drove more slowly, looking.

Gertie looked as he looked, and through the twisting, whirling curtain of smoke and snow she saw across a flat stretch of land flame and red boiling smoke above gray shed-like buildings. Closer were smaller smokes and paler lights about black heaps of rock-like stuff strewn over a gray wasteland of rusty iron and railroad tracks. She jumped, Cassie squealed, and even Enoch ducked his head when there came an instant of loud humming, followed by a bone-shattering, stomach-quivering roar. The plane was big, and seemed no higher than the telephone poles as it circled, fighting for altitude. There were several loud pops, but the roar gradually lessened as the plane climbed higher, then was drowned in the clank and roar of the steel mill.

The driver was shaking his head. 'Boy, if that thing fell it would flatten out all a Merry Hill.'

'Merry Hill?' Gertie asked, looking round her.

'This is it. Them houses is all Merry Hill, and if u sign's right we go back toward u railroad tracks an u steel-mill fence.' He nodded toward a battered sign on a gray pole, holding no words, only rows of numbers.

Gertie for the first time really looked at the rows of little shed-like buildings, their low roofs covered with snow, the walls of some strange gray-green stuff that seemed neither brick, wood, nor stone. She had glimpsed them briefly when they turned into the side road, but had never thought of them as homes. She had hardly thought of them at all, they were so little and so still against the quivering crimson light, under the roaring airplane, so low after the giant smokestacks.

Clytie, after one long look, gave a quivering sigh of disappointment; then in a moment she was Clytie again, forever looking at the best. 'They ain't got no porches or fenced yards, but they're long. They'll be plenty big fer us.'

'Fuyu an five more families—count u doors. Youses lucky to git a good place like this. Town's full u people sleeping twelve tu u room, in shifts three to u bed, an—' The driver was laughing so hard as he turned into a narrow alley that he scraped a tipsily leaning trash can, spilling tin cans and cindery ashes onto the snow.

A few feet farther on, the car stopped, but Gertie, thinking the driver was still searching, did not move. She stared straight ahead past the dirty alley snow, littered with blowing bits of paper, tin cans, trampled banana skins, and orange peels, at a high board fence. Past the fence she saw what looked to be an empty, brush-grown field; but while she looked a train rushed past. Everything was blotted out in the waves of smoke and steam that blew down; tiny cinders whirled with the snow against the windshield, and the smell and taste of smoke choked her. The noise subsided enough that she could hear the driver say, 'Well, this is it.'

The children, who had been gaping at the train, turned and looked, and like Gertie sat silent, looking. A few feet away across a strip of soot-blackened snow were four steps leading to a door with a glass top, set under low, icicle-fringed eaves. There was on either side the door a little window; in front of one was a gray coal shed; in front of the other a telephone pole, and by it a gray short-armed cross. The door was one in a row of six, one other door between it and the railroad tracks. Gertie turned sharply away, and across the alley her glance met another door exactly like her own.

12

Gertie stood, her outspread hands pressed against the door, closed behind her. She realized she stood in the kitchen of her new home, but it seemed more like a large closet with rows of uncurtained shelves above a sink, and smotheringly crowded with curious contrivances. A few feet in front of her was a doorless doorway into a small hall-like living room. In this room, no more than a dozen feet past the doorway, was another outside door, exactly opposite and exactly like the one behind her. The place seemed all halls and walls and doors and windows.

'It's so little, Mom. We cain't never cook an eat an—' Clytie's voice wavered, then died as she stared at a large black heating stove in a corner by the doorway.

Gertie continued to stand a moment longer, staring, choking, swallowing hard to prove to herself that she was not choking. 'I figger,' she said in a moment, 'that it's about twenty-five feet frum inside to outside. If it jist wasn't broke up so, but we can—' Clytie, she realized, had disappeared like the rest of the children. She heard their cries and comments of exploration behind the kitchen walls. She drew a deep breath, then took the few steps to the other outside door. She opened the inner door, and scraped a hole in the dirt and frost on the outer door. She saw across a narrow strip of soot-blackened snow another building exactly like her own, telephone wires and poles, smoke, steel-mill light, and steam. She suddenly bent close to the glass, smiling. Quickly, she scraped the hole larger, then looked again; dim it had been through the steam and the smoke, and far away on the other side of the railroad fence, but

170

it was a hill. She turned away; when seen more clearly the hill had become a great pile of coal.

She struck her shin bone against a chair as she closed the door. She bent to rub the pain, sharp in her half numb leg, and in bending her hips struck a corner of the low head of a cot-like bed. There was between the door and wall room for the head of the narrow bed, and on the other side of the door almost room for a chair. Touching the chair was a sofa, holding three cushions of some slippery, rubbery material. The wood of the sofa, like that of the chair, was a pale but shiny oak.

She stood a moment, her hands clenched by her sides, then carefully walked through the narrow space between bed and sofa. Two halls, scarce wider than her shoulders, led to the bathroom and the three bedrooms. Two of these were big enough for a double bed and four chairs each. The other was smaller still, but into it two single beds were jammed so close together there was no room to walk between them.

Clytie bumped her as she turned away. 'Mom, they ain't no dressers, an no looken glass, but I bet they's twenty chairs, all alike. An jist one table fer all our cooken an eaten.'

Clytie's voice had grown closer and closer to sobs, and Gertie patted her shoulder. 'I recken th gover'ment thinks people won't be a doen much in their houses but setten an sleepen. An anyhow it won't be fer long an—' she was comforting when Enoch's laughter and Amos's frightened scream came from the other side of the kitchen. She bumped into the stove as she whirled toward the sound. Amos, water dripping from his hair, came running, with Enoch behind him, explaining between giggles, 'He clumb into a little box uv a thing, Mom, an turned a round thing an water squirted all over.'

Cassie trailed behind them, whimpering, 'Th water stinks, Mom.'

'It's city water, silly,' Clytie explained. 'It's purified like in th health books, and that thing in th bathroom, it's a shower, like in th catalogue.'

Gertie tried a glass of water, but after one taste emptied it into the sink with a suspicious frown. 'They's somethen in it besides water. It's worse'n that on th train.'

Enoch was holding a match he had found above the kitchen sink and begging: 'Light th gas, Mom. It'll warm up Amos, an we're all freezen.'

Gertie turned to consider the little cooking stove in a corner of the kitchen. The top was hardly a fourth as big as that of her range cookstove back home, and no warming oven at all. Enoch climbed on the edge of the sink to watch, pointed out the knobs she must turn, while Clytie warned, 'Watch out, Mom. Vadie Tucker—recollect she'd been in Cincinnati—said a body had to be mighty careful a gas.'

Gertie struck a match, and held it waveringly, looking first at the row of small black handles, then at the blank wall behind. 'It ain't got no pipe. Mebbe it ain't ready to light.'

'I'll bet gas stoves don't need pipes. Go on, turn one,' Enoch urged.

'I don't know which is which,' Gertie said in a whimpering voice, new to her.

Enoch turned a knob just as her match went out. She reached for another, while Enoch cried: 'Hurry up, Mom. I'm turnen em all on.'

She struck the match and held it toward the burners, all hissing now. Flames leaped at her; the corner of the kitchen seemed a wall of flame. She, like the children, jumped away, but her head struck a corner of the row of open shelves across from the stove. She saw stars and whirling lights, smelled smoke, and heard the screams of the children. Then Reuben was slapping her forehead. Clytie was throwing a glass of water on her, and Enoch was laughing. 'Mom, you look so funny. Your hair's all swinged.'

Gertie was silent, rubbing the back of her aching head while she stared at the stove top, where four circles of flame flickered and leaped with a faint singing. Enoch reached for another match. 'Lemme light th oven thing, Mom. I'll strike th match an hold it by th holes 'fore I turn it.'

'I ain't a wanten you burned up alive,' she said, and took the match and squatted by the open oven door. She bent, searching, until her hips touched the opposite side of the cubbyhole and her hair brushed the floor, and saw at last a ring of little holes. She told the children to get a safe distance away, struck the match, and held it under the holes, while with her other hand she tried to turn the knob marked 'Oven.'

Her fingers pulled and twisted, but the knob would not move. The match went out; she lighted another and tried the knob again. Still the shiny bit of plastic would not yield. Two more matches, two more tries that made even her tough fingers ache, but the little thing was her master still. She stared at it a moment, then got slowly to her feet. 'I cain't do nothen with it, youngens. I'll build us a fire quick in the heaten stove an git th place warm.'

A large bucket that had once held paint stood by the stove, filled with coal. Gertie looked about for kindling. All over the place there was sign of Clovis—the bed with new sheets and blankets in which he had slept, his battered tool chest in a corner, new dishes and a coffeepot, groceries—but no kindling.

Reuben went out to the shed, but after what seemed a long while came back empty-handed and shivering. The little woodshed by the coalhouse had been so covered with snow he could hardly find the door, and when he had found it and clawed the snow away there had been nothing in it but beer bottles.

The tired, hungry, shivering children looked at Gertie, their eyes asking and expecting of her the warmth and food she had always given. She stood helplessly staring, first at the little knob marked 'Oven,' then at the cold heating stove. 'Jump around a little,' she advised at last. 'That'll kind a warm you up. I'll find—' Right behind her, seemed like, sounded a thumping, bumping thud, and then a child's scream. She whirled, thinking one of her own was hurt, but they were all looking as she looked, toward the wall of their bedroom by the kitchen.

They were all silent, listening, staring at the wall until the screams subsided. 'If we can hear them thet away, they can hear us, everthing we do an say,' Clytie whispered at last.

Gertie turned again to the heating stove. 'Whatever they are, they're people.' She got a starched apron of brightly beflowered feed sacking from the trunk, and said as she tied it tightly about her waist, 'I'm aimen tu try tu borrie some kindlen frum them—strangers er no.'

Clytie looked at her mother's singed and wind-tangled hair, the smear of gas soot on one cheek. 'I'll go, Mom. Nobody ud shorely mind loanen a little kindlen.'

173

Gertie frowned over Clytie's bare legs, smoothed her own tangled hair, and at last turned to Reuben. 'Son, couldn't you go? You're better fixed fer th weather than she is.'

The sullen look on Reuben deepened, but after a moment's hesitation he went out through the ice-struck creaking kitchen door. Gertie, with Clytie helping, began to unpack the boxes and baskets. She had got a quilt and put the three younger ones under it on the bed in the room across from the bathroom, when Reuben came back. She saw that he had no kindling, and watched worriedly as he closed the door, and stood a moment with his back to the room. Then, with no glance at her, and stumbling over the things scattered on the floor, he rushed into the little living room like a chased wild animal, hunting a place to hide.

He pressed his face against the glass of the other outside door, and stood there for what seemed a long while. Gertie followed him and patted his shoulder, and at last he was able to tell her in a choked and halting voice what had happened. He had gone first to the door on the side where the child had cried. The blind was pulled on the door, but all the same he had knocked. Finally, after he had knocked a second time, a little girl some bigger than Cassie had come and lifted up the blind and looked at him. She'd frowned and shaken her head, and then gone off again without ever opening the door.

He had gone next to the door on the other side. Memories of what had happened there caused him to choke and clench his hands in anger. 'Mom, I hadn't knocked real loud, but before I was through a funny-talken man yelled somethen, like strange swear words, an he sounded madder'n a hornet when I hadn't done a thing but knock. An all th time that same little old youngen that watched us when we come in, why he was a watchen me, a grinnen, an when I turned around to come home, he throwed a snowball right in my face, an then run off.'

'Now, now, honey,' Gertie said, 'it won't allus be like this. Recollect we'll mebbe not be here no time atall. But anyhow pretty soon you'll be goen to a big fine school like Meg's youngens has got. Now, chirk up. You'll have th little uns a feelen bad.' She looked around, her sad gray eyes a little brightened when she heard Amos's

174

loud laughter as Enoch with a great spluttering, whooshing, and banging of chairs drove one of the big trucks he had just seen. She heard the creaking of the bed. Cassie knew she mustn't jump on the bed, but this once would warm her up, and she was happy now, calling with the little gurgle like the old Cassie: 'Look out, big truck, look out. They's a red light.'

The sounds of the children were suddenly swallowed in a mighty thumping on the wall by the bed, while a voice boomed: 'Shut off u racket, kids. I gotta sleep.'

The children scuttled out, bumping into Gertie as she rushed to the bedroom. Cassie gave one last terrified glance toward the wall that had roared, then buried her face in her mother's apron. Enoch, defiant, wanted to know, though in a whisper, why any man would be sleeping in the daytime, and Reuben, his voice hoarse with anger, explained: 'That's him, Mom. Th man that yelled at me.'

Gertie picked up Cassie and Amos and went into the living room, since it like the kitchen was in the middle, farthest from the listening walls. She sat with the children on the sofa, the older ones gathered round her, even Enoch was meek as a sheep, and silent. Reuben continued to stand by the front door, but was turned about now, looking at her. Even in the pallid light there was something worse than anger in his eyes. Pleasure? Did he want to say, smiling, 'It serves you right for not buying the Tipton Place?'

A gust of wind cried in the telephone wires, then shrieked in the chimney, and Cassie snuggled against her, begging: 'Let's go back home, Mom, please. It's cold.'

Clytie, already troubled and half frightened by Reuben's story, suddenly flopped down onto the cot, and dissolved into sniffling sobs, while Amos screwed up his face and got ready to break into his lusty bawl. Gertie knew it was a sin to waste any kind of light in the daytime, but maybe some light would make the cold gray place warmer. She pulled the cord hanging from an unshaded bulb in the middle of the ceiling, and at once the hard white light fell over them, and their shadows lay sharp and cold on the bare floor. The cardboard walls shone smooth and dull, of some pale gray-green that made her think of a potato sprout that had never seen the sun.

In the light the stove seemed even bigger, colder, and uglier with its short bent pipe and strange rusty tin skirt.

She sprang up, a child on either arm, and turned back toward the bedroom. 'I'm aimen to put you youngens back in th bed. You've got yer shoes off an you'll freeze. I'm aimen to git some kindlen—somehow.'

Her voice had dropped to a whisper as she entered the bedroom and slid Cassie to the bed. 'Now be real quiet,' she whispered, giving Cassie, who still clung to her arm, a little push, and at the same time sliding Amos down with her other arm. 'You uns don't want that man to—' Cassie's hands had tightened on her arm, and Amos had begun to scream, 'I'm afeared, I—'

The fist—she knew it was a fist, and a big one, bigger than her own—banged again until it seemed the thin cardboard wall must crack, and the voice roared: 'Can it, kids. Can it, now. I calla cops. I gotta sleep.'

Amos screamed more loudly than ever, and the fist banged again. Gertie, with the two of them in her arms, started back toward the living room. Suddenly she turned short about and looked at the wall, still trembling from its blows. 'They're afeared an they're cold,' she cried, her voice so loud Clytie began a worried shushing. She heard the creak of a bed, a windy sigh. 'Don't be allatime scaren li'l kids, 'sbad—build um a fire,' the voice roared back at her.

'I cain't find no kindlen,' she cried.

More sighs, then a knocking, low now as if to call attention to his presence. 'Dey's boards in mu shed. Butcha gotta split um.'

'I'd be much obliged,' Gertie said, knowing more from the tone of his voice than his words that he offered what she needed. She shook her head in wonder over the 'Hokay' that followed, but whispered to the children, now more mystified than frightened, to be still and let the sick man sleep.

She took from his shed that adjoined her own, three good-sized, strangely shaped chunks of maple wood, harder and finer-grained than any she had ever seen. She got the hatchet from Clovis's tool chest, and went out to do the splitting.

She had just finished one of the chunks when she realized that the same redheaded child who had watched their coming in now

176

stood bare-headed and coatless as he watched her over a bottle of Coca-Cola tilted to his mouth. His blue marble-like eyes were accusing as he said, taking the bottle from his mouth: 'Yu got dat outa Victor's shed. He'll gitcha.'

'He knows,' she said, annoyed by this new business of being watched. 'I've got to git my youngens warm.'

'Maw keeps her oven on when her ain't got no coal.'

'I couldn't,' she said.

He finished the dirt-colored liquid, then looked about for a bit of windswept sidewalk. He found a bare spot, and flung the bottle hard against it. He did not smile, but something like satisfaction glittered in his eyes as he looked from the sharp-edged fragments to Gertie, staring at the glass with her mouth open, the hatchet uplifted. 'Won't burn,' he said, now studying the wood that was damp. 'Hillbilly,' he went on, looking again at Gertie, unsmiling, nodding a little like a child who has just got the right answer to a problem in arithmetic. 'But I'll tell Maggie youses cold,' he said, running away.

Gertie was gathering up the kindling when she realized that just behind her was someone else, watching. She looked around and saw, standing knee-deep in the drifted snow between her door and that of the man who had pounded, a smallish girl-like woman, her face rising above two sacks of groceries, clasped one on either arm across her stomach. Her eyes, large, and of a peculiarly light, almost golden brown, were fixed on Gertie in a speculative sort of way. She held her head tipped slightly sideways as she looked at her, gum still between small front teeth, sharp-looking and white, like those of a child, behind the softly curving woman's lips.

A gust of wind screamed down the alley banging unhooked storm doors in and out, whirling snow about the woman so that she for an instant seemed a face only, peering at Gertie through the snow. Gertie stooped for a bit of kindling, and behind her the woman's voice came, low and pretty, after the sounds from the child and the pounding man, 'Whatcha dream about last night?'

Gertie turned and looked at her while she repeated, 'Whatcha dream about last night?' The girl was past her indecision now, the speculation gone, the gum moving, then still as she said, almost plaintive, 'I gotta have a dream.'

Gertie considered, staring at her; little she was, and dressed in boots, pants, and a plain dark blue jacket, but even with the wind blowing snow over her and the groceries hiding her breasts the womanliness of her was plain. She made her think of a heifer she'd had once; even when the heifer was little and unbred a body could see the femaleness of it across a wide field. 'I didn't,' Gertie said. She hadn't slept; she couldn't dream; but the eyes needed a dream. The brown woman was like a dream—now. 'Paradise,' Gertie said.

'Paradise,' the other repeated, rolling her gum once, then holding it still. Her eyes were speculative again. But almost at once the girl was satisfied, taking the dream. 'Paradise,' she said, nodding. She turned toward the steps behind her, then called as she fitted a key into the pounding man's lock, 'Yu got salt?'

'Salt?' Gertie asked, gathering up the last of the kindling.

She never answered, but was out again in a moment, a shiny pot in her hands. 'Rock salt,' she said. 'Yu gotta saltcha steps, or yu'll break yu neck,' and she flung the little salt rocks on the steps and up and down the walk.

Gertie remembered later that she had thanked her for neither salt nor kindling. Enoch had stuck his head out shouting: 'I fixed that ole contrary bake oven, Mom. You push in thet knob uv a thing, an then she turns. Lookee.'

Gertie, coming in with the kindling, smiled. There was room for only one chair, and that sidewise to the oven door, but on it Clytie sat with Cassie in her lap and Amos in Cassie's lap, so that three pairs of cold feet were on the let-down oven door.

The taste of fresh outdoor air only resharpened the close, sickly smell of the indoors, thicker now with the oven going. Gertie hurried to start the fire in the heating stove. She had put one match to the damp pile of kindling, watched it go out, and was lighting another, wishing for a little coal oil, when someone knocked on the door. Even Enoch looked worried, and Clytie scolded in whispers, 'You youngens has been a maken too much noise.'

Enoch had the door only partway open when there came soft bubbly laughter that made Gertie think of Cassie, and then, more as if blown in than walking, came a slim girl, with a white cloth tied

178

over hair, black as Reuben's, but fine and soft and curling down almost to her waist when she shook her head quickly to make it right itself after the wind. 'It's wild out there,' the girl said, smiling as if she loved wild weather.

Gertie struck another match. 'It makes a body need a fire.'

'Francis—he's my little brother—said you was cold.' She came over to the heating stove and peered in. 'I couldn't find no kindling, but I gotcha some newspapers an bacon grease—that's what we use—from Mrs Bommarita.' She handed Gertie newspapers and small pieces of some flimsy dry wood. She then dropped a piece of cardboard holding a great gob of bacon grease, good enough for biscuit making, down into the stove.

Gertie frowned on the waste of good grease, and her knife hesitated above the gift of wood. 'Honey,' she said, studying it, 'ain't this a piece a some kind a toy?'

The girl shrugged her shoulders. 'It's not no good, just part of a old doll bed.' But when she looked up at Gertie, there was in her eyes—bright blue and set under lashes as long and black as Cassie's—a something like sorrow for the broken bed, and her voice was impatient for the hurt to be finished quickly as she insisted: 'Go on, break it up. It'll make good kindling, dry like it is. I'd kept it onu top shelf inu hall where du kids couldn't find it; I meant some day to try to glue it back, but now I'm too big fu doll beds.'

'Why, honey, you're not so old,' Gertie said. She broke the flimsy wood, but glanced swiftly at the face downbent as the eyes followed the broken toy into the stove. The girl watched an instant, then turned sharply toward the kitchen door.

She seemed a very little child when, after looking through the half of the kitchen window left from the icebox, she exclaimed: 'Yu know, if yu don't look high up yu can think yu gotta tree there an notta telephone pole. Some a th units does have trees—close. Onu other side a da through street they's real big trees. An one amu girl friends, she's got two big trees right inu yard—all her own. But her folks is gotta private.'

'Private?' Gertie asked.

'Yu know, a real house, all by itself. I'll bet you're glad to get out ina big place like this—lots a room an kinda quiet.'

179

Gertie gave the laughing, crying eyes a quick suspicious glance. 'I wouldn't call it so big ner quiet neither,' she said. 'An sean as how we started out to it, I reckon we're real glad we're here.'

'Yu outta be glad,' the girl said. 'I betcha yu got pull. Yu come to Detroit straight to a big three-bedroom place like this. These houses, they're good an warm anu rent's cheap, an they're the only places in Detroit where they keep u niggers out, really keep um out—sagainsa law. The niggers got into u last neighborhood where we lived and—' There came a banging on the door that threatened to break the glass, and a child's shrill cry of, 'Tell Maggie Daly if her's here her'd better git . . .'

The girl reached for the door, but before she could open it the bottle breaker had swung it wide, and was shouting, 'Git home, Maggie, git home. Pat and Jim's inu water fight. Water's all over. Youse better git.'

'I'll be there,' Maggie said, unflustered, smiling as she turned and explained to Gertie that her mother had gone shopping for the day, and she was staying home from high school to mind the younger children. She pulled a small pink slip of heavy paper from her jacket pocket, held it out to Gertie. 'Wouldn't cha like u ticket to the bingo party? They's door prizes an everything—donation's only twenty-five cents. It's all fuda good sisters—a new piano they need.'

Gertie started to shake her head, then remembered the grease and the doll-bed kindling. Reluctantly she reached into her pocket and fished out a quarter. Maggie hurried away, for Francis was screaming again.

The children crowded around and studied the card when the girl was gone. But to all their questions of what was bingo, who were the good sisters, what did Maggie have on the little thin chain around her neck, Gertie could only shake her head. Clytie said, looking happier: 'Wasn't she pretty, Mom? An not a bit stuck up. Can I have some overall pants like hers? They'd be good to keep a body's legs warm.'

The fire was singing soon, not loud, as the wind in the telephone wires, but with a good hearty crinking of iron and hissing of flame; and Gertie began the job of feeding the children out of the curious packages Clovis had left on the kitchen table. Tin cans she had seen, but never milk in a bottle. The children, warmed now, and all, even Reuben, happier after the coming of Maggie, crowded round her, hungry for bread and milk. Clytie got glasses, and the three quarts of milk and two loaves of bread were gone in an instant. Only Cassie wrinkled her nose and declared the milk tasted funny. 'It's pasteurized, silly,' Clytie said, 'like in th health books at school.'

'An it's made in a factory,' Enoch said.

'But they's a cow somewhere's behind it,' Clytie said, and while they argued there came another knocking, low down on the door, like a kicking, sharp and insistent, as if the person were in a great hurry, but hurry or no, determined to come in.

Gertie shoved the outer door open just as a small foot in an open-toed high-heeled slipper below a bare ankle hooked itself around the corner and began to pull. A dried up, puny-looking little woman came through the door, a steaming pot in one hand, a steaming skillet in the other. The arm of the hand that held the pot held together a bathrobe of some blue silklike material quilted into a design of flowers and embroidered with golden peacocks. In spite of her eyes being squinted against the smoke of the cigarette in one corner of her mouth, she managed to smile as she held the pot toward Gertie. Her hand, freed of the pot, took the cigarette, and she blew two long rolls of smoke down through her nostrils, rolls so long that Enoch looked at her in awed admiration.

Clytie stood still with a glass of milk halfway to her mouth, choking a little from a too hasty swallowing of the soft bread, and stared at the woman's toenails; bright red pink they were between the golden bands of the slippers. Even Cassie edged closer for a better look at the golden birds. Gertie, as she took the pot and smiled, stared in wonder at the woman's hair. Permanent waves with many tight little curls such as this she had seen but never the color. It was a rich pinky gold under the buckshotty drops of snow, but the strangest thing about it was that the color seemed familiar. She remembered at last the fat-faced child with the yellow cur dog on her mother's rug. The woman's hair was the color of the cur dogs.

Gertie realized she had not thanked her for the pot, though now she was holding out the skillet, saying through the cloud of her smoke: 'Here's some corn bread to go with them beans. Th only

181

kind a meal we can git round here comes in them little round boxes, an it ain't no good. An th beans ain't much. I run out a ration points and Clovis didn't have none. I had a little bacon grease, an put in a dab a cooken oil.'

'It was shore nice a you to go to all a that trouble,' Gertie said, and added in genuine admiration, 'Your bread's bound tu be good; it's mighty pretty.'

'Oh, Law'—the woman had glanced at the heating stove—'I'm plum ashamed a myself. I told Clovis I'd start you uns a fire this mornen when I got up to git th youngens off to school, but I laid back down a thinken, "Pretty soon I'll git up an hunt some kindlen an git um a fire started." Th next thing I knowed, I was a smellen them beans. A little minute more an they'd ha burned.'

Gertie tried not to look at the sleazy pink rayon nightgown, its lace-edged bottom trailing some inches below the bathrobe, as the woman continued after a long pull on the cigarette: 'Then soon's I got up, Wheateye, she told me, "Mommie, a strange boy come a knocken while you was sleepen," an I knowed it was one a you uns, an—'

'Butcha said yu'd knock my head off if I worked yu up agin,' and a skinny, pale-haired little girl stuck her head around the half open inner door.

'Git, Wheateye,' the woman said. 'I toldcha to stay home an start gitten ready fer school. Claude Jean an Gilbert,' she was talking again to Gertie, 'them's my boys—they'll be gitten in fer lunch right away. If you uns needs anything like somethen frum th store er anything to borrie—holler. I live next door. M'name's Meanwell—Sophronie, an I'm right sorry that fu th first time in six months when somebody does come a knocken an th youngen don't come a waken me screamen, "Mommie," it hadda be one a you uns.'

And she was gone, the golden slippers tripping through the snow, golden peacocks, smoke, and cigarette sparks whirling in the wind. Gertie stared after her, the pot in one hand, the skillet in the other, until Clytie said, 'Wasn't she dressed pretty, Mom?' and Enoch, said, 'Mom, I'll bet she's frum somewhere's back home. She kinda talks like us,' and Cassie whispered, 'Mom, I bet that's th kind a shoes th angels wears.'

182

Reuben came sniffing hungrily at the beans, but Gertie was silent, shaking her head, staring at the door as if she could still see the woman past it. Clytie took the skillet and asked: 'What's th matter, Mom? Wasn't it nice a her to come over. Don't you like her?'

Gertie spoke as if to the door. 'I was jist a thinken Mom was right. I ought to be up here with yer daddy. An that nightgown—a wearen a nightgown this time a day. A body could see right through it an—' She realized that Clytie was listening with too much attention. She turned away from the door too sharply, and struck her hip on a corner of the sink.

Her uneasy wonderings on Clovis were smothered out by an ever growing awareness of the pale walls, the overcrowded little rooms, and the air that with the unventilated gas stove going grew even worse than that on the train, something thick and dirty that burned her nose and gave her eyes a heavy, sleepy feeling. Several times she tried opening the outer kitchen door for a bit of breath, but each time the wind knocked it back and forth so violently the glass seemed ready to break. The windows seemed to have been made to let in light only. None of them would open at the top at all, and only two of the bottom sashes were neither stuck nor frozen shut. Once these were opened, there was still the second pane of glass; true, a body could open three little holes in the bottom of the frame, but the bit of wind that came through seemed only to make the floor colder without freshening the air.

She had turned the oven off as soon as the coal stove began to throw out heat, but during supper getting she not only had to turn it on again to bake the corn bread, but also keep most of the burners going. Soon, some curious moisture in the air made the kitchen wet as a dripping stewpan. Condensing steam ran down the windows in rivulets and dripped from the gas and water pipes that ran through the kitchen, the bathroom, and one bedroom; more water made an oozy sweating on the walls.

The cookstove itself turned out to be a contrary little thing: she was always turning the wrong knob, and twice she burned her fingers on pot handles that had got across the next flame. Worse, she was always hurrying up to it, thinking she had let the fire go out. She would stoop, reaching for wood, each time remembering only when, instead of the woodbox back home, she saw the gray cement of the floor.

She was continually bumping into the children, especially Cassie. She had just shooed her from underfoot again when a brassy-voiced man cried from the bedroom behind the kitchen, 'Now, don't forget, tell your mother about Tootsie Rootsies, the cereal our soldiers eat.'

Gertie sprang toward the sound. Some crazy man must have broken through the thin wall on Sophronie's side. She almost fell over Cassie, terrified into muteness, followed by Amos screaming with fright. Last came Enoch, doubled up with laughter. 'They thought it was a man, Mom, a real live man,' and then the greatest thought of all came over him, and he jumped up and down crying: 'We've got a radio, Mom. We got a radio. Pop had it hid.'

Clytie, too, jumped up and down and cried, 'Oh, goody,' but Gertie cried above the radio:

'Shut that thing off—all that racket in this little place.'

'Aw, Mom,' Enoch said, making no move to obey, 'everbody—'

His voice was drowned by that of the radio, which, under Clytie's inexperienced manipulation, had grown louder instead of softer.

Gertie was crying in agony, 'Make it quit, Enoch. Make it quit,' when on the other bedroom wall the same banging fist sounded.

'Damn. Go-od damn. Yu make da noise too much.' And the fist banged again, until Gertie, who had run to the sound, stood blinking at the wall, expecting to see the fist, hairy and huge as that of a Goliath, come crashing through.

Enoch hastily turned down the radio. Silence came to the wall, but Gertie continued to stand by it, held by her memory of the man's outcry. The tone had been more begging than commanding, a weak helplessness in misery, hopeless, the man a Samson with his hair grown long again—but blinded; a man like herself.

There came a banging on the kitchen door, but before she could reach it in six steps and three bumps, the door was shoved open, and a big chunk of a red-faced, eyebrowless man took the two steps between door and icebox. He jerked open the top door, and with no glance at either the milk or at Gertie, when she cried to him to watch out for it, swung ice from his shoulders, shoved it in, and strode out again as she reached frantically for a tipped-over bottle.

She was sopping at the gome the milk had made, run as it had down through the wooden slats into the bottom part, when he came back with a smaller chunk of ice. Giving her no time to get out of his way, he swung it over her head and wedged it in with the other chunk, pushing hard with one huge red-haired hand. It took a still harder push to shut the door on the ice, but it immediately popped open and a trickle of sawdust, coal dust-laden water began to drip onto the floor. 'Forty-six cents,' he said, holding out his hand.

'You've spilled my milk an crammed that box so full th door won't shet, an I didn't ask fer none,' Gertie said.

'Huh?' the man said, his blue child-like eyes opening still wider, as he repeated, 'Dat's forty-six cents, lady.'

'But I didn't ask fer no ice.'

The 'Huh?' that seemed more belch than word came again as he looked at her. 'Lady, youse gotta have ice. I gotta sell. Youse gotta buy.'

'Pay him, Mom,' Clytie whispered. 'We have tu have ice. It's so hot in here everthing'ull ruin.'

Gertie went to her coat for another dollar bill, while the man stood in the door and filled the alley with his mighty belching roars of 'Ice. Coal.' As he took the money, his glance rolled slowly, appraisingly over her face. 'Any t'ing else yu want? Coal?'

She shook her head, but he continued to study her face, his tongue reflectively licking his back teeth made a bulge in a jaw, 'Yu wanta—chance? Yu wanta make money, yu gotta take a chance. Yu know—yu wanta slip?'

'Slip?' and when he continued silent, tongue rubbing cheek, Gertie nodded toward Maggie's bit of cardboard on a kitchen shelf. 'Like that? I've already got one—tu help th good sisters.'

He glanced at the pink card, then studied her face a moment longer. He slowly shook his head, 'Naw,' he said, the sound rising in his stomach, falling down his nose. He went, then, crying 'Ice' into the snow.

The dusk had deepened until the flickering steel-mill lights made a bloody brightness on the windows, when there came another banging on the door. Clovis. He looked peaked, she thought, but hardly had a chance to look at him before the children came swarming over him, so crowding the tiny kitchen that she backed against the icebox, watching. Clytie was almost crying, and even Amos, little as he was, remembered his daddy as if he'd never been away.

She felt a sharp thrust of guilt. It was in truth like her mother said: the children had a right to live with their father. Seemed like sometimes they loved him better than her, especially Enoch and Clytie. But then she'd always been the one to give them the work and the scoldings. Clovis had brought the fun—trips in the coal truck, the river in summer, grape hunting in the fall. She'd never had the time.

In a moment he looked across their heads and smiled. 'Supper ready, Gert? I'm starved fer some a yer good cooken. I ain't had a bite a fried meat, seems like, since I got up here.'

'I ain't got no fried meat,' she said, 'but I've got supper.'

'I'm figgeren on some good eaten. You ought tu have a heap a ration points. You never used none at home.'

They pulled the table out from the wall, and there was room for Clovis and the older children to squeeze into their chairs, with space enough left at the corners for Amos and Cassie to stand. Gertie never sat down, but, as she had often done at home, stood between table and stove waiting on them all. Clovis, she saw, was displeased with the food. He looked resigned and disgusted as he had used to be when she left eggs out of the corn bread in order to have a few more to sell. Some of Sophronie's beans were left, and they were good, better than her own scrambled eggs and corn bread. The eggs had stuck for lack of grease and the bread, badly baked to begin with, was dry and hard and lifeless, as the meal that had gone into it.

He chirked up when Clytie praised the new dishes, and Enoch started carrying on about the wonders of the radio, and Cassie admired his new work clothing. Gertie, sorry that after he had bought so many things for them she didn't have a better kind of supper, said, trying hard to act pleased, 'You've done good, real good, Clovis, to buy so much stuff, an send us th truck money besides.'

He looked at her with a great showing of surprise. 'Law, woman, you shorely don't think I've paid fer all this. Up here everbody buys everthing on time.'

She had fixed herself a plate of corn bread and beans, set it on the rim of the sink, and started to eat, standing up. But now she turned away from the food, asking, 'How much we owe, Clovis?'

'Gert, don't start a worryen. Jist git it into yer head that I'm a maken big money. I ain't no sweeper maken th lowest. I done what I aimed to do, got on as a machine repair man. An it shore took some tall talken, an a heap a white lies. But it was worth it. I git in a heap a overtime, too. Do you know what my pay check-ull be this week?' he went on, laying down his knife and fork and twisting about in his chair to look at her, 'Why, better'n a hundred dollars.'

She heard the admiring gasp of Reuben, hurt and sullen as he still was from his attempts to borrow kindling. Big as he was, he'd worked many a day for seventy-five cents. Clytie, her voice all jerky with surprise and delight, was exclaiming, 'Oh, Pop—why we're rich. That's way more'n a schoolteacher makes back home in a month.'

'I don't make it ever week,' Clovis explained, 'an recollect that's afore hospitalization, an union dues, an OAB, an taxes. An right now, with everything tu buy, it ain't no fortune. It took saven to git a down payment on all this an on a car, too.'

Gertie backed against the sink, heard her plate of beans and corn bread flop off the rim into the dishwater, but did not look around, 'But Clovis,' she began haltingly, not wanting to darken the family joy, 'if'n you've already run intu debt 'fore me an th youngens comes, why how can you manage with us? An we cain't, jist cain't keep on a liven in this little hole. Cain't you git along without a car?'

He pushed his plate away. 'Gert, we ain't hardly seen each other 'fore you start a quarrelen about money an th place I got fer ye. What was you expecten—a castle in Grosse Pointe where them rich dagoes lives? I was lucky, mighty lucky, tu git this. They ain't hardly standen room in Detroit—I'd meant tu surprise th youngens with a ride when th weather was fitten.' He held out his cup for more coffee. 'But I've already got me a car. It's in th parken place now. A body cain't git along in this town thout a car.'

The delighted squeals of the children, all save Reuben, only subsided under his animated discussion of the car, especially the sweetness of the motor's running, now that he had worked on it. Gertie had heard little past the words 'got me a car.' She turned and looked down at the gray dishwater. If just for one minute she could walk outside, go to the barn, the spring, somewhere—walk, see her father, get away from the gas smell, the water smell, the steamy heat, the hard white light beating into her eyeballs. She turned toward the outside door. A corner of the pulled out table barred her way. She looked toward the passway. Clovis's chair was there. Her empty hands found the dishrag. Somehow she washed the dishes. Hemmed in, shut down, by all this—and debts.

The evening in the hot, overcrowded, noise-laden place seemed endless. She answered questions about back home, learned that Sophronie's man, Whit Meanwell, worked in the same Flint plant as Clovis, though on a different job and shift. She wanted to ask Clovis questions: how much did they owe, how much was the interest on the debts for the car and the house plunder, where was the school, and how far away? But the radio was on, and she talked but little.

As soon as the children were asleep, Clovis had no thought for answering questions. Amos had been put to bed on the cot in the middle room, so that Gertie and Clovis were alone in the room beside the kitchen. Still, she was conscious of the restless sleep of the children on the other side of the thin walls. They were all so close together it didn't seem decent. The whole place wasn't as big as either of the two main rooms at the Tipton Place.

She shut her eyes and tried to think that she was there when Clovis fell quickly into a deep, satisfied sleep. She drowsed and dreamed of pines talking. The talking rose, became the roar of a fast through train, its screeching whistle rising above the roar as it neared the through street. This was followed at once by the tumultuous sound of its passing, so close it seemed in the very house. Amos and Cassie screamed out in fright, then as the sounds subsided they sank gradually into a whimpering half-sleep. There remained only the quiverings—the windows, the steel springs of the bed, the dishes, a chair touching the wall.

There came at last a silence so complete she could hear the ticking of the clock under the bed, and the snoring of Sophronie's children behind the wall of the girls' bedroom. The feeling that had followed her at times since she had got on the train came back in the silence— she had forgotten something, something very important. But what? She was sorting out the things she'd left behind when she found herself lifted on one elbow, listening.

Someone was moving about on the other side of the wall. She heard running water, the soft thud of a pot going over the gas flame, the creak and slam of an icebox door—breakfast getting sounds. Soon she heard the opening and closing of the outside door, and whoever it was did not come back. He had not taken time to eat his breakfast. He was most likely the husband of that Sophronie in the sleazy nightgown. She was too lazy to get up and cook breakfast.

She drowsed, but sleep enough never came to drown the strangeness of the bed or the closeness of the air. It seemed only a little while before she found herself listening again. A singing it was in the alley now. Tipsy he was, and a tenor, 'They'll be pie in a sky—' A woman's voice cut him off, something like the girl Maggie's, but near crying, 'Please, Joseph, please. Du neighbors—'

'Quitcha tucken,' the man said, and a door on the other side of the alley slammed.

'Tucken.' What was 'tucken,' she wondered. Then the door next her own was opened quietly, but slammed shut so loudly that Clovis turned in his sleep. She heard the opening of the oven door, the little whoosh of the lighting gas, then the opening and closing of the icebox door. A chair was pulled out followed by the hissing sound of the cap jerked off a bottle of something fizzy like pop. She heard a chair tip back against the wall, so close through the thinness seemed like she could feel it. She could see the man's chair leaning against the wall, his cold feet warming in the oven, as he drank from the bottle. She heard the soft clink of glass on steel as he put it

189

down. But where had he been and why, at this time of night? She sat straight up in bed with wonder and surprise when the voice came, low, more like a sigh than a voice, 'Oh, Lord, that moven line,' for the voice was a woman's voice, Sophronie's.

The sounds on the other side of the wall or her own abrupt movement awakened Clovis enough that he mumbled sleepily: 'Don't be afeared, Gert. Th doors locks good.'

'Oh, I ain't afeared,' she whispered. 'It's that Sophronie. Why, she's jist got in home.'

He clamped one ear against the pillow, put an arm over the other. 'When else would a woman on th three-tu-twelve shift git home?'

190

13

Eat yer oats, Cassie—you'll git mighty hungry in school.' But Cassie only gagged and stared at Gertie with frightened, beseeching eyes.

'I don't want to go—to . . .'

'Kindergarten,' Clytie put in briskly. 'An Pop said you had to go. All th other little youngens goes. You'll like it, Cassie.'

And later Gertie repeated, 'You'll like it, Cassie,' as she got the child along with the others into what seemed the numberless pieces of clothing Clovis had bought for them all, when, after some cross questioning, he learned she still had left from the Henley money and what she had got from the sale of her stock and little store of molasses, corn, and potatoes, better than two hundred dollars.

Struggling now with the heavy woolen pants of Cassie's new snowsuit, she thought again of the money. She didn't begrudge the children clothes—boots, scarves, more underclothing, snowsuits for everybody but Reuben, boots for herself, and a woolen head rag. But most of the money she had meant to keep for getting a start of livestock when they went back home was gone. Only the money for land was left, the secret money gathered through the years. She had told Clovis of Henley's gift, knowing he would learn of it from the children, who had learned from her mother, but the new coat carried the secret of her savings as well as the old.

She roused to call to Enoch, who, all eagerness to see the fine new school, was dashing outside. It was only a few minutes past eight, and Sophronie had told them that school children were supposed to leave home between eight-twenty and eight-thirty, not a minute sooner or a minute later, else the safety-patrol boys would be gone.

But now, just as she started to open the door to remind Enoch of the time, he turned and screamed, 'Mom, Mom, we'll be late. Maggie's brothers an a lot more youngens is already a goen,' and without waiting for an answer he ran into the little crowd of children, hurrying down the alley.

'Less'n this clock's wrong er that woman's mistook, it's a way too soon.'

Enoch paid her no mind but walked on, following a few steps behind the children. Though no one of them turned to speak to him, some whispering, giggling talk went between them, and a little girl with long black curls turned and walked backward the better to see him, giggling all the while. Suddenly, as if by a signal, they all stopped and turned and looked at him. Gertie saw, even in the smoky early-morning light, the red flush rise on Enoch's cheeks. He hesitated an instant, then came on, but more slowly now, up to the watching children.

She watched Maggie's redheaded brother, the biggest one, bigger by far than Enoch, step out from the others. Then, so quick she hardly saw it, was the fist swung hard on Enoch's shoulder, and the expertly tripping foot that sent him sprawling on the alley ice. A smaller one, the boy who had thrown the Coca-Cola bottle, grabbed Enoch's fallen-off cap, new, with ear muffs, and flung it into the trash can, crying over his shoulder as he ran after the others: 'Go to yu public school, yu hillbilly heathen, youse. We don't have to go to school with niggers an Jews an hillbillies.'

She started down the steps, but hid again behind the storm door when Enoch got slowly to his feet. She watched him brush the black snow from his clothing, take his cap from the trash can, and then, with a smear of dirt on his cheek and limping a little, come back to his own walk, where he stopped and gave a quick suspicious glance all around, as if to make certain none had seen his humiliation.

She wanted to ask if they had hurt him much, but did not. Enoch would rather have her belief that he could take care of himself than her sympathy.

Clytie called to remind her that it was fifteen minutes past eight. She gave Enoch one last pitying glance, and hurried back to the job of getting the younger ones into the strange seeming outdoor

192

clothing, sending each child, as soon as it was booted, buckled, and zipped, outside to wait with Enoch. Then there was nothing to do but the thing she had dreaded since coming, and dreaded still more after watching Enoch in the alley—put on her own outdoor clothing, take the birth certificates and the shot papers from County Health as Sophronie had told her to do, and go to the strange school with the children. She pulled on the great knee-high boots Clovis had bought for her, but stood an instant longer in the kitchen. The Josiah basket, under the table because there seemed no room any place else for it, caught her eye. She picked it up, dropped the papers into it, and as she went out the familiar feel of the basket dangling from her arm was a comforting thing.

The children stood waiting in a silent little huddle against the coal-house, which gave some shelter from the keen-fingered north wind. Clytie frowned on the basket, whispering, 'Mom, I don't think people up here carries baskets.' But Gertie only pressed the basket against her as she stood by the telephone pole and looked about her. The sky, unlike the skies back home, told her nothing. Was it the even gray of clouds, of smoke, a cloudy dawn, or a cloudy sunset? It seemed early, very early, more like milking time than school time.

She heard a train, the clank and hissing roar of the steel mill, and sounds of traffic on the through street, one row of houses away, but there was no sight nor sound of people. She had a sudden distrust of the clock; maybe it was night still. She looked at the shivering, frightened children. Even Enoch was afraid, his cap twisting in his hand, an old-man look on him as he stared straight ahead.

Then he and the others looked up eagerly as a half starved sheep when the Meanwell door next their own was flung open and Sophronie's Claude Jean and Gilbert ran down the steps. Enoch looked toward them but did not move. Claude Jean, the smaller, a pale-eyed, white-headed boy of about his size, ran a little distance down the alley then stopped suddenly and called back, 'C'mon, kids, ain'tcha goen to school?'

Enoch's smile was a warming thing to see. He ran after them at once, followed a moment later by Clytie, with Reuben going last and more slowly. Gertie was leading Cassie and Amos into the slippery alley when the Meanwell door was flung open again, and

Sophronie, shrouded in clouds of steam, came onto the stoop with a freshly washed sheet in her hands, a cigarette in one corner of her mouth, a clothespin bag over her arm, and calling, 'Hey, you.'

The golden peacocks fluttered about her feet, as with one eye squinted against the cigarette smoke she began to hang the sheet on the clothesline, pushing down pins with sharp, swift jabs, fighting to get the sheet hung before it froze. 'Leave that little youngen uth me,' she said, when one hand was free and she could take the cigarette from her mouth. 'No needa draggen him all thataway through this cold.' Her still blue eyes went to Amos, smiled. 'Don't-cha wanta play uth Wheateye? You uns can have th best time.' The last pin in, she turned, pulled open her door, gave Amos a little push as she called, 'Wheateye, they's a little boy come to see you.'

Gertie had a glimpse of checked linoleum, flowerdy curtains in a kitchen so crammed with a washing machine and other furniture that there seemed no room for a woman of even Sophronie's size. She was considering trying to explain that Amos might cry with a stranger when the closing storm door for an instant framed Sophronie's face, blowing smoke, whispering, 'He'll be all right.'

Gertie tried to find Amos through the steam-blanketed glass, and failing, turned to the puzzled Cassie. 'It don't seem right leaven your little brother thisaway with a stranger woman, but we ain't got time to argue.'

Cassie only shivered and said nothing as Gertie hurried away, realizing the others were out of sight and that with no one to show her she had not the least notion of how to find the school. However, when she and Cassie had turned into the big alley by the railroad fence they found themselves at once in a swarm of children all headed for the through street.

They walked on what, Gertie thought, must be a cement sidewalk under the layers of snow tramped into ice. The through street by which they walked was clean of snow, though great banks of dirty ice and snow from the snow plows overflowed onto the sidewalk. Broad as the street was, it was crowded with cars and trucks and busses, with many flashing by so close the children were splattered from the piled-up slush.

194

She was hurrying along, trying to avoid the splatterings, and worried over Cassie, who walked with less and less eagerness, when a boy in a white belt stepped in front of her with his arms outspread. 'Watch out, lady.'

She stepped back, seeing for the first time, railroad tracks running right across the street, then saw, not twenty feet away, a train grinding toward her. The trucks and cars had been making so much noise she hadn't heard either the signal bells or the train.

The cars, loaded mostly with rusty scrap iron, moved ever more slowly past. Cassie began to whimper and shiver with the cold. Gertie's nose and cheeks began to sting, and in spite of the boots her feet were cold. It came to her that instead of stomping around in angry silence last Saturday when Clovis came home with her money spent and the car half full of new clothing she ought to have thanked him. The children had to have the strange heavy clothes, if on their way to school they had to stand still like this in what must be way below-zero cold. The train stopped, and Gertie wished the thing were human and she could hit it. The children were piling up like leaves against a cedar tree, and the cars and trucks were stretching out as far as a body could see, but the train stood there puffing like some great iron beast with no skin to hurt in the cold.

The children stood without complaining, accepting the train and the cold and the smoke and the smell of the cars as if they were a natural part of God's world, all but Cassie, who stood with trembling chin and brimming eyes. Gertie realized there was something the child wanted to say, and bent her head to hear the tremulous whisper, 'Please, Mom, let's git home out a all this racket. I cain't learn to read nohow, an I'm freezen cold.'

Gertie turned her away from the train. 'Listen, honey, we'll git goen agin pretty soon, an then you'll see this big fine school. Law, it is th prettiest, finest place. They'll be a gymnasium where you all can learn to do tricks an Reuben can show em how good he can play basketball, an a big fine lunch room, an a room with nothen but books, pretty books like you ain't never seen, an a place fer Clytie to learn cooken an sewen . . .' She realized that both the train and the traffic were still, and that around her the children, too, were still—and listening.

She pressed Cassie's face close against her coat, laid her hands on her scarf-wrapped ears, all the while conscious of the watching, listening children. Her glance happened on a boy, bigger than Enoch, maybe as old as Reuben, and not one of her own kind of people. There was a strange dark look about him, something sullen and mean in his face, she thought. He would, in a minute, call her hillbilly. The others would laugh as they had laughed in the alley. She stood bent protectively over the face-hidden Cassie, her glance more beseeching than commanding as it went round the half-circle of silent, watching children. She looked longest at the boy, begging him for his silence. But his black eyes stared back into her gray ones, his eyes accusing, condemning, she thought, as if she had committed the unpardonable sin. He continued to stare at her, condemn her, all the while he was taking off one ripped leather glove, then searching through his jacket pockets. He found at last what he hunted, and only now taking his glance from Gertie, he stepped up to Cassie and tapped her on the shoulder.

'Here, little girl, is something nice,' and he pushed two tiny paper-wrapped squares into the hand that clutched Gertie's coat. He bent and put his face close to Cassie's pressed down one as he said: 'It's gum, little girl. My mom gimme ut, bubble gum. Chew ut, and don't be afraid, little girl. Kinnergarden is nice.'

And behind the boy and all around him were little calls like the twittering of birds. 'Don't be scared, little girl. Miss Vashinski, her real nice. Youse don't do nutten in dere but play allatime. We singed lotsa songs.' And somewhere a voice unknown but familiar: 'Don't be afeared, honey. Good little youngens don't never git no spankens in kinnergarten.'

Cassie did not lift her face, but one hand let go its grip on Gertie to close over the red wrapped chunky squares, and disappear between Cassie and her mother's coat.

The boy smiled at Gertie, a triumphant smile that washed all the sullenness away, and now he looked like a tired and sleepy child, maybe no more than nine years old. In a moment he did lift his arms and yawn with a long stretching, but his face was accusing again when he said in a careful whisper, 'Butcha oughtn't to tell her such big lies, lady. S'no way to start um out. I hadda time uth Xavier all on account I lied to um.'

196

Gertie in spite of her shivers smiled. 'You took him to kindergarden, I bet, fer yer mama.'

'Naw, nursery school. Pop's a waist gunner in u Pacific. Mom works du seven-to-three shift way over at Grigg's Nummer Ten.' His eyes grew bright with pride. 'Her runs one a them big presses, good as a man. Her got in fourteen hours overtime last week.'

The train was moving again, and he took Cassie's hand. 'Rita, her goes to school, first grade, morning shift, but Xavier and Mary, I gotta take to nursery school on account a Mom, her leaves too early. Xavier, he start crying da first morning I took um. 'Mom, her'ull be back an gitcha right away,' I tells du kid. Mom hadda work overtime. I hadda go to da store after school. I never got du kids till five o'clock. Next morning when I try to leave, Xavier, he grab my leg, wrap his arms around it and wouldn't leggo. Nutten shadup his screaming—gum, sour-balls, nutten.'

'Ain't it awful cold on a little youngen so early in th mornen?' Gertie asked. 'Here, th stars ud still be bright as midnight.'

'Stars?' the boy said. 'I put plenty clothes on um.'

The train broke apart at last, and the little boy in the white belt waved them forward. Gertie went on, the wide-bottomed split basket riding above the bobbing heads of the children, who flooded out across the tracks and overflowed the walk, with many wading knee-deep in the slush by the road. She searched anxiously over their heads, hunting out her own, but could find no one of the three, and wanted to go faster but could not for the press of children.

She wanted to ask the boy what was the lie he had told, but the hurrying, crowding children gave her little chance to talk, not even when they were stopped again by more boys in white belts, stationed where they were to cross the wide through street. She began shivering again; maybe it was the cold, maybe it was the fear. Crossing the tracks had been easy, but here it looked as if they could never cross. Cars, trucks, gasoline tank trailers, many-wheeled Diesel-powered steel carriers, busses, all had piled up waiting on the other side of the railroad crossing, and were now going again, speeding to make up for the lost time, a roaring, belching, smoking, steaming river on wheels. She looked hopefully about for a signal light or a policeman on a corner, like in the story book, but there was neither.

197

At last the train-dammed traffic thinned. The little boys crept further and further into the street, and soon the children surged across. They hurried between a mighty truck with wheels higher than their heads pulling two red tank trailers with the word *Danger* on their sides, and a stubby-nosed thirty-two-wheeled steel carrier loaded with one great round of steel lashed down with ropes big as Gertie's wrist.

The boy still kept his grip on Cassie and, as they crossed the street and went through the deep slush at the curbs, Gertie realized that he didn't have high rubber boots like her own and most of the other children. His leather ones were old and cracked. Plainly they would not hold out water, and the laces were not stout rawhide but broken strings. Still, he had money for gum. Shoestrings didn't cost any more than a package of gum; maybe there wasn't money for both. She glanced at Cassie clutching the gum as if it had been the little hickory doll. It was of course better to spend money for shoestrings than for gum, but—

The 'but' still troubled her when, after walking for what seemed a long while by traffic-crowded streets, they stopped again for another crossing and she looked about her at the children. She saw here and there a child shivering in an old coat or ragged overalls. There were red mittenless hands and unbooted feet in low shoes that were not new. She gave a slow head-shake of wonderment. There couldn't be any poor people, not real poor, in Detroit when they were making men come out of the back hills to work in Detroit's factories. This boy, now, there ought to be lots of money in his house, money from the army and the factory job too. Maybe it was like she'd heard her mother say when somebody pitied Meg; factory workers, coal miners, and such were a shiftless, spendthrift tribe.

An old man with a bad limp helped the boys stop the traffic here, for with no bumpy railroad tracks to slow them down the wheeled things flew ever faster. Gertie then went down a narrow side street, bordered by low factory buildings on one side, and on the other by a row of little ramshackle paint peeling houses crowded close together, but with the look of homes.

She turned another corner, and all unconscious of the children pressing round her, the boy pulling on Cassie's hand, Gertie stopped in the snow and stared. High above the river of bobbing heads she saw a flag, clean with a golden tassel, flying straight out in the northern wind like a flag painted on tin. Below the flag she saw a black roof streaked with snow, and under the roof two rows of empty windows set in the dark soot-stained walls of a two-story brick building that rose high and straight out of the dirty, trampled, paper-littered snow. The bit of yard was separated from the street by a high iron fence, like the fences she had heard were about penitentiaries.

Getting closer, she saw that by the big building, so low she had not at first noticed them, were two little flimsy-looking houses. Built of gray painted wood, they made her think of the makeshift railroad workers' houses she had seen in the Valley. As she walked past them to the main building, she saw a window broken and mended with a board, walls spattered with mud and dirty snow, and under the eaves of one, not much higher than her head, a piece of gutter pipe loose and creaking in the wind. 'Dem's a portables—du kids in shifts goes in um,' the boy explained, and pulled Cassie onward.

Gertie's eyes jumped back and forth across the strip of trampled snow that made the school yard. There must be a tree. One tree for the children to see come spring, some flowering bushes, like the mock orange they'd set by Deer Lick School when she was a girl, some flowers, something. They went up steps, through a door into a hall tracked with snow water and filled with children and the smell of coal smoke. In front of her were steps going up and steps going down, and she hesitated. Somewhere a bell clanged that made her think of the railroad signal bells, and the boy said, 'We're almost tardy on account a du train.' He pulled his hand from Cassie and looked back at Gertie before plunging into the stream of children. 'Yu can't go no place tilla kids is ina home rooms. One a dem girls,' and he pointed to a tall girl with a band on her arm, 'can show where isa kinnergarten.'

The sea swallowed him, and as Gertie stood pressed against the wall a growing uneasiness laid hold of her. Maybe the others had got lost on the way; but that, she told herself, could have happened no more than if they had been logs coming down a swift smooth river. She was glad of the gloves she wore. Cassie, clinging to her still, couldn't feel the clamminess of her hands as she thought of Enoch in the alley and the word 'hillbilly' in the railroad station. If she could go for them all, but especially for Cassie, she . . . Someone touched her arm, and she saw it was the tall girl to whom the boy had pointed, and she was smiling, friendly-like.

'Yu Mrs Nevels that want's to enter u kid in kinnergarden?'

Gertie nodded, and when the stream of children had thinned somewhat she followed the girl across the hall into a large room where she saw many little chairs and tables, a fireplace, and a piano. But mostly she saw children, all kinds and colors and shapes. Seemed like there were more little youngens in this place than in all White Lily voting precinct back home.

Slowly, with the girl making a path for her, and Cassie clinging to her hand, Gertie made her way through the children. She was at last stopped completely by the great swarm about two women by the desk, and she stood throwing quick, searching glances at the women. One, dressed in dark blue, was small and old with gray hair. She had a nice smile and looked to be a good woman. It was hard to say about the other. Her hair was curled and her face painted, and worse, she wore long earrings that Gertie saw when she got closer were shaped into little birds, with blue jewel-like eyes, swinging from a vine. The birds were swinging as the woman bent her head above a little boy, and Gertie realized that the little boy and not the teachers was the center of attention, for all the children crowding round looked at him. The painted teacher was bent above him, saying, 'We're so happy to have you with us, Garcia. Garcia— is that right?'

But the boy, dark-haired, dark-eyed, small, dressed all in clean new clothes, neither smiled nor answered. He only studied the swinging silver birds with bright bird-like eyes, and the faded teacher watching smiled, a kind of sighing smile. 'I think we'd better try to get him into a special school. He doesn't understand a word.'

But the other, younger, shook her head until the birds flew past her cheeks. 'His family would never send him. A neighbor brought him. His mother works the day shift. He understands. I know he understands—a little.'

She turned toward Gertie when the tall girl said, calling across the heads of the children, 'Miss Vashinski, this is Mrs Nevels.'

The tall girl went away. The older woman went to the other side of the room, gathering children on the way so that the group thinned enough for Gertie to reach the desk. She swallowed, gripping Cassie's hand. In a moment she too would have to leave. The painted lips smiled at her briefly. The silver birds jangled as the yellow curls bent above Cassie. 'How nice, to have a great big girl like you.'

Cassie was silent, her glance leaping from high-piled yellow curls to silver birds to red fingernails. Miss Vashinski saw the gum twisting in the mittened fingers. 'And when you first come, we let you chew your gum. Wouldn't you like to unwrap it?'

Cassie loosened her grip on Gertie, and took the gum in both hands.

'If you take off your mittens you can do it better,' Miss Vashinski said.

Cassie was lifting the gum to Gertie for holding while she took off her mittens when there came a soft, hesitant, half questioning, half pleading, 'Chicle?'

Miss Vashinski turned quickly. The other woman, in the midst of a lipfingered sh-sh, heard above what seemed to Gertie a thousand children's voices, for she too turned quickly, smiling, nodding, when Miss Vashinski said, pleased as if she'd found a wad of gold, 'Garcia has spoken.'

Garcia, on hearing his name, looked up, but his eyes came back to the gum. He made Gertie think of a diddle, run with the mother hen all summer, knowing only her call, stopping for the first time to study an apron folded up with corn, and consider, making at last the first step to come alone for corn. 'Why don't ye give him one piece, Cassie?' Gertie asked handing back the gum into the now bare hands.

Cassie hesitated, then unwrapped the gum with her awkward fingers that had never before unwrapped gum. She gave her sudden quick smile, and handed one piece to Garcia, while a dozen or so children who had unburdened themselves of the other teacher's sh-shushing, drifted back to make a watching circle. 'Thank you

201

for the gum, Cassie,' Miss Vashinski said. There came a little chorus of children's voices, well behaved voices, as if they were doing what they thought they should do, 'Thank you for the gum, Cassie,' though in and out through the chorus were cries and comments, 'Can he bubble it?' 'Mom, her bringed me a whole package frum u shop.'

And one, a little girl with what Gertie thought must be a permanent wave and what she knew was a dirty rayon dress with no petticoat under it, seized Miss Vashinski's hand. 'Yu fingernail polish—it's like wot Mom's got.' Another, jealous, cried, 'M'mudder's got u same kind u perm'nent.' A blue-eyed little boy with almost no front teeth tweaked her smock, begging, 'Miss Vashinski, please, wear du yellow boid dress.'

'I am your away-from-home mother, children,' Miss Vashinski said. 'Now, please go back to your seats. Mrs White is waiting,' and as one hand began a gentle but determined pushing of a T-shirt-clad shoulder, the other picked up a pink card. The quick eyes, calculating, Gertie thought, not matching the red lips or the yellow curls, flicked over Garcia chewing his gum with an expert rolling motion not devoid of sound, then Cassie, chewing experimentally, slowly, as if constantly reminding her tongue not to swallow. The child's shoulder moved away from the hand. The hand went into the big pocket of the bright smock, came out with a fountain pen. The eyes flicked Gertie while the head flipped toward Cassie, 'Name?'

Gertie hesitated. 'Keziah Marie—but generally we call her Cassie. . . . She don't give much promise a liven up to her namesake.'

'Namesake?'

'Yes—you know, that other Keziah was among th fairest in th land.'

'Oh,' Miss Vashinski hurried down the list of questions while Gertie put on her desk Cassie's birth certificate and the little papers showing she had had her shots from County Health.

'Good,' Miss Vashinski said. 'It's nice you had your doctor do all that. Now Cassie won't have to start in a strange school with a sore arm.'

She talked rapidly, and her voice was filled with the hard sharp sounds Gertie had heard since coming to Detroit. School seemed broken into two hard pieces, 'skoo-oal,' and doctor seemed almost 'doct-tork,' but not quite. It was all so strange, that Gertie was silent, first getting what the woman had said into her head, then straightening her own answer in her mind—that all a body had to do in Kentucky was send their youngens to school the day the County Health people came. Then she happened to look toward Cassie and Garcia, and forgot everything she had meant to say.

Cassie's lips were shaped as when she kissed Callie Lou, but on her lips was the gum. Her eyes, puzzled, admiring, piqued too, were fixed on Garcia's face. Instead of a mouth he wore a large pale gray bubble, wonderously thin, round, beautiful like a balloon. Cassie watched, breath held, while it grew larger; she squinted her eyes, waiting for the burst but, lo, none came. The bubble went suddenly into his mouth, neatly, leaving no smear. Then there came such a pop that Cassie jumped and then drew closer as if she would see into his mouth.

Gertie squinched, and even Miss Vashinski looked around from the card. 'It's terrible stuff, but really quite creative,' she said, turning the card over, making check marks. Finished, and with her finger on a spot, she pushed the card toward Gertie. 'Sign here.'

Gertie hesitated. She had never put her name to anything, joined anything, promised anything. 'Could your husband sign?' Miss Vashinski asked, smiling, moving toward the door.

Gertie flushed. 'Oh, I can sign,' she said, and wrote her name with the fountain pen. She looked yearningly toward Cassie. Cassie was watching another gray balloon come out of the boy's mouth.

'The door's this way,' Miss Vashinski was saying, and Gertie followed the brisk tapping heels. 'She can come mornings.' Miss Vashinski was opening the door. 'There's only fifty-six in the morning group—sixty-three in the afternoon. The women on the three-to-twelve shift insist on sending their children in the afternoon. You have an older girl to call for her at noon the first few days? Good.'

The widely opened door into which Gertie had backed was closing. She turned determinedly back to the room. 'I'd better help her out a all that riggen.'

'We teach them that; she'll adjust,' Miss Vashinski said, with a big bright smile on her bright red mouth and an uneasy glance toward the room where Mrs White's voice sounded thinly above an ever increasing babel.

The door pushed gently on Gertie's shoulder. She found herself in the hall staring at it while behind her the young girl voice was saying, 'This way to the principal's office, Mrs Nevels.'

Gertie, after one long backward glance at the closed door, followed the girl up a stairway and down a hall, past open doors giving glimpses of child-crowded rooms. Nobody noticed their passing except a small man in spectacles happened to look round from something he did on a blackboard. He stopped, chalk uplifted, and stared at her as she went by.

The principal's office was smaller than her new kitchen, with nothing in it but books, a table, and a telephone into which a girl was speaking slowly. 'I know, but Mrs Zigorski, we can't send a kid home on telephone orders. It's againsa rules. Gimme your number, please . . . I don't unnerstand . . . The principal,' she went on, speaking slowly and resignedly, as if she had already said the same thing many times, 'is down in u sewing room. It's inu basement. He can't come—not right now on account a so many steps. Wait—Suse.' She was calling now to the blue-banded girl walking away from Gertie. 'Canyu unnerstand Hungarian? It's gotta be Hungarian. It ain't Polish; it ain't Ukrainian.'

The girl called Suse shook her head. 'I don't know nothing. Half u time no more I can't make out Granma. S'Greek, maybe. I'll go hunt Sophie. Mrs Nevels here wants to enter her kids. Yu sure now it ain't Ukrainian?'

'Sure.' She turned to Gertie as Suse walked away. 'Yu kids is all entered, everything but u family physician.'

'We don't have none.'

'Put down ours. We live close to yu on Merry Hill.'

Gertie gave a slow headshake, and wished she could see the principal. 'It don't make no difference, nohow,' the girl said. 'Them doctors, they've got a strong union, stronger than u CIO. They'll come if they wanta an yu ain't got seven dollars, an if they don't wanta come yu seven dollars don't do yu no good.'

Gertie stared at the telephone receiver that now and then gave little sounds of bewilderment and trouble. The girl talked into it again and the sounds ceased. She turned again to Gertie, 'S'all right to put that doctor down. S'cards gotta be filled.'

Gertie nodded at last, then watched the girl write on the cards, already quite well filled with Clytie's neat writing. 'Sign,' the girl said.

And Gertie signed again, three times, then took the rest of the birth certificates and shot papers from the split basket and left them on the desk as the girl directed. She stood an instant looking about her. School letting out time in the afternoon seemed far away. She remembered Cassie was to come home. Clytie would have to leave off lunch in a real school lunchroom—she'd given them all a quarter apiece, just for the first day. 'Is they any way,' she asked, 'you can git word to my biggest girl to bring her little sister home at dinnertime?'

'She knows to stop at th kinnergarden door,' the girl said. 'Allu kids hafta go home at noon. It's againsa rules to bring lunch. S'no place to eat it.'

'You mean,' Gertie said, 'you ain't got no hot lunch? An all th little youngens has to backwards an forwards in this weather?'

The girl shook her head. 'Th little kids don't come but half a day nohow.' She looked at her fingernails, of a red even brighter than Miss Vashinski's. 'This school ain't got nothen but teachers an kids. I went to one once in Hamtramck that had everything—even a liberry; yu know, a room with nothen but boo—uks.'

'They ain't no gymnasium with a basketball court, an no pretty cooken place?' Gertie asked, more and more troubled.

The girl shook her head. 'We ain't got no basketball on account we ain't got no room; we gotta take gym down inu little room inu basement.'

Gertie turned away, then turned back when the girl called after her: 'Oh, Mrs Nevels, I forgot; yu kids gotta bring soap—strong soap, if they wanna wash. Th water's awful cold in winter, anu furnace smokes.'

Gertie tried to smile, but could not, and strode swiftly down the hall toward the stairway. 'Mrs Nevels—Mrs Nevels.' It was Suse again, running down the hall. 'Mr Skyros wants to speak to you, please.'

Hurrying behind Suse was the same little baldheaded man in glasses who had stared at her. Behind him was a slender girl with yellow braids worn round her head like a crown. 'Mrs Nevels,' the man said, putting his hand on the basket, 'pardon, please, this interruption, but we wanted to ask about this beautiful basket. We have never seen one like it.' He spoke slowly and carefully, like a man who has talked to a lot of people who didn't understand. 'Is it Polish?'

Gertie shook her head. 'It come frum back home. Ole Josiah Coffey made it, one a th last afore he died.'

'Back home?' he asked, head tilted as he considered the fat sides of the basket.

'My country is Kentucky.'

'Oh,' he said, 'I didn't know they made baskets in Kentucky. What is it? It's not reed or willow or grass or bamboo.'

'White oak—splints. You know, you split em like house shakes, only finer, way finer,' she said, sliding the basket from her arm, then handing it to him.

'And there's not a bit of metal in it,' he said. He held the fat round sides with the tips of his fingers. 'It's such a beautiful brown. You've never stained it or anything, have you?'

'Oh, no. Oak weathers thataway. I allus liked th color a clean weathered oak wood. It's as pretty as tubaccer when it's hung up to cure.' She stopped. He was laughing—no noise—just his eyes dancing like Cassie's. Children were in the doorway of his room gaping at her. She heard a low giggle and then a snicker. He was so little, hardly to her elbow.

'Isn't it beautiful,' he was saying. 'Tobacco. I saw it only once— one autumn over in Canada. It was curing—all shades of brown.' He for the first time noticed the two acorns and the oak leaf, marked with the light strokes, the few lines with which Gertie made her pictures on wood. He studied it, smiling, then held it out for the girl Sophie to see. 'Did the old man do this?'

The laughter in the doorway was growing louder. 'It's a little old picture I done years back one day when I was a setten a waiten at th mill.'

'Oh, you carve?'

206

'Carve? Oh, you mean whittle—ax handles an sech, but sometimes a little foolishness like a doll fer a youngen.'

'You must some day carve something beautiful and fine.' He studied her for the first time. 'A human head. I believe you could.'

She wanted to tell him about the block of cherry wood that she was afraid was lost by now, but the children were laughing so. One kept running to the door, peeping then laughing and running away. And if he asked how she planned to make the face, she would maybe let her tongue run on the way she had with the man who wore the star. 'Did you want to borry th basket to look at?' she asked, backing away a little.

'Oh, thank you. I wanted to sketch it,' the girl said.

'Are you sure you don't mind leaving it. I guess it's an heirloom,' the man said.

Gertie smiled. 'I've left four youngens here. I oughtn't to mind leaven a old split basket.'

'They'll be all right,' the man said. 'They will'—now he didn't seem himself at all, but was like Miss Vashinski—'adjust. This school has many children from many places, but in the end they all—most—adjust, and so will yours. They're young.'

'Adjust?' One empty hand pulled a finger of the other empty hand.

'Yes, adjust, learn to get along, like it—be like the others—learn to want to be like the others.'

'Oh.' She pondered, looking down the hall—ugly gray—and at the children laughing in the doorway, then turned to him with a slow headshake. 'I want em to be happy, but I don't know as I want em to—to—'

'Adjust?'

'Leastways not too good.'

He looked quickly about him like one preparing to share a secret, then drew closer. 'Maybe they won't adjust at all.' His dark eyes looked up into her own and were somehow ashamed, sorrowful, like Judas giving back the silver. 'Most of us do, but there's always hope that one—' He jerked a shoulder toward the girl walking away with the Josiah basket, her head tilted, smiling a little as she studied it. 'My other talented one has adjusted—perfectly. He's drawing

207

me on the blackboard now—such talent. He never saw you or the basket in this ugly hall. He has adjusted—cartoons of the teacher—perfect adjustment, exactly what he is supposed to do—according to the comic books.' He patted her forearm. 'Your children will be all right. They will, I fear, adjust better than their mother.' And he turned and went quickly.

As Gertie was going down the stairs, her eyes chanced to look over the banister. Directly below her, coming slowly up from the basement, was a man she thought must be the principal. She couldn't see his face, mostly just the top of his head, with a pinkish, balding spot hidden like a secret in the center of his light brown graying hair. He walked slowly, like a man who has climbed many stairs and knows he will climb many more. His outspread hands, held carefully away from him, were smeared with black streaks. Gertie, looking down, was puzzled until she remembered the sewing machines, old and broken down. An old sewing machine was a contrary nasty thing. But somehow, from the look of him, she thought he had fixed it. No, the other word—adjusted.

She wanted to turn at the foot of the stairs and stop by Cassie's door, but forced herself to walk on. Once outside, she stopped and turned around and stood a long time staring at the gray building in the square of dirty snow. A look of listening was on her face, for from it there came between the sounds of distant trains and traffic a faint humming—like that from factories she had passed.

14

Four mornings gone now, and this, the fifth. As usual, the alarm had gone off at six o'clock, so that Clovis could be at work by seven. Six o'clock, she understood now, was four back home; too early for getting up in winter. Clovis, never eating enough at breakfast, seemed like, to keep a working man alive, went away in the dark with a bottle of coffee, sandwiches, a piece of pie, and beans in his lunch box. Six-thirty to seven-thirty was pure dark still, like the middle of the night. It was a lonesome in-between time when her hands remembered the warm feel of a cow's teats or the hardness of a churn handle, or better beyond all things, the early-morning trip in starlight, moonlight, rain or snow, to the spring—the taste of spring water, the smell of good air, clean air, earth under her feet. Her feet remembered the soft earth when they took the few steps over the ice and cement for a bucket of coal. She never lingered searching for the stars. Unless it were quite windy there were no stars, and even in winds so bitter they brought tears, the alley smelled still of smoke and fumes.

Two mornings now, after searching for some quiet work that would not waken the children, sleeping so close behind the flimsy walls, she had sat in the kitchen whittling on a piece of scrap wood Clovis had bought for kindling. This, like the borrowed kindling, was a maple, harder and finer grained than any she had known. It came in curious little chunks and squares that Clovis had said was scrap from some kind of war plant.

One little piece had seemed familiar in all the strangeness, and she had began whittling on it. Slowly and aimlessly at first, she had worked, not able to forget the knife, herself, everything except the thing growing out of the wood, as she had used to be in stray moments of time back home.

The hard white light overhead hurt her eyes and made a shadow on her work. The night sounds of Detroit came between her and the thing in the wood, but worse than any noise, even the quivering of the house after a train had passed, were the spaces of silence when all sounds were shut away by the double windows and the cardboard walls, and she heard the ticking of the clock, louder it seemed than any clock could ever be. She had never lived with a clock since leaving her mother's house, and even there the cuckoo clock had seemed more ornament than a god measuring time; for in her mother's house, as in her own, time had been shaped by the needs of the land and the animals swinging through the seasons. She would sit, the knife forgotten in her hands, and listen to the seconds ticking by, and the clock would become the voice of the thing that had jerked Henley from the land, put Clovis in Detroit, and now pushed her through days where all her work, her meals, and her sleep were bossed by the ticking voice.

Now, between strokes of the knife, she would glance at the clock to make certain that it was not time to waken the children; and the thing in the wood would seem wood only, and not her big-behinded hen that had eaten corn from her lap. But little by little, the hen mastered the clock, and by Friday morning was there waiting in the wood for the knife to free her, a good hen, ready to lay many eggs.

Gertie was working on a feather of the upcurving tail when a passing train brought back the world of the clock. She glanced at it, then sprang up, and hurried to awaken the children.

Cassie, though the many strange sounds at night often caused her to cry out with fright, awakened of mornings more slowly than the others. Twice, in her half-sleep, she had run to the door in her nightgown, crying she had to go outdoors; then, awakening quickly to Enoch's jeering laughter, she had gone silent and ashamed to the bathroom. Quiet, forever quiet, was Cassie. She showed no sign of loving school and feeling at home there as did Clytie and Enoch, or of half hating it like Reuben. More lost and lonesome than afraid, she always seemed like a child away from home.

This morning's breakfast was like her others in Detroit. Meekly she sat and put bites of egg and biscuit into her mouth, chewed, swallowed, then took a sip of milk, gagged, set the glass down hastily; then came the trembling, guilty whimper: 'I'm full, Mom. I cain't eat no more.'

'Aw, Cassie,' Gertie began, and stopped. Scolding her for taking food on her plate and not eating it was no good. She'd have to find something the child would eat. She looked at the half eaten egg, flat-yolked, gray, rubbery white, the biscuit burned on the bottom, too pale on top, smeared with margarine instead of butter. She wasn't any good at coloring the stuff, but butter cost so. None of them ate the way they had back home. Enoch was gone from the table, his egg unfinished. But he could snack off and on all morning, for Enoch, like the other third graders, went only half a day, his shift in the afternoon.

Gertie remembered the clock, looked, and quickly started the job of getting them off to school. Cassie, as always, was tangled up in her snow-pants. Clytie was complaining that she could find no clean handkerchiefs. Enoch was reminding her that it was the day for Cassie's milk money. This made Clytie recollect that soon the mothers club would have their Christmas bake sale, and couldn't her mother come and bring something for the sale; and wasn't there anything she could take for the Christmas basket drive; and how much money could they have for TB seals? Couldn't they each have at least a dime?

Gertie took change from the high shelf. She gave milk money, TB money, a can of pork and beans to Clytie, a can of tomatoes to Reuben for the food drive. Each child kissed her with a quick dabbing as it went out the door, hurriedly, for in the alley children were passing. Mike Turbovitch was begging Enoch to come play on the hockey pond, and behind him a girl in a bright red coat was calling Clytie. Even Cassie ran down the steps. Cassie had never told her, but Clytie had said that in the kindergarten room, right up on the wall where everybody could look at it, was a big picture Cassie had painted—a green hill with a black tree.

Gertie closed both doors on Reuben, the last as always. She looked down at her hand. One nickel was left over the fifteen cents for Enoch this afternoon. Last night at the big store there'd been all that silver left. She had watched the machine and thought a twenty-dollar bill would do it. Then the girl had punched on the sixty-cent tax, and Clovis had reached in his pocket again, brought out a one, and paid it all without a word.

She had been silent, shaking her head in weariness and wonder, as they drove homeward through the ugly, dimly lighted streets. 'I wouldn't mind so much,' she had complained at last, 'if'n all that money ud buy a egg that was real fresh er some good fresh meal.'

'Aw, Gert,' Clovis had said, 'they's millions an millions a people never tastes nothen but what they git outa stores. They've never tasted read good corn bread with butter an fresh eggs, so's they don't mind eggs that ain't never fresh, an store-bought bread with oleo. If'n,' he had gone on, half teasing, 'spenden a nickel's goen to be like losen a drop a blood fer you, why you'll be bled dry in no time atall.'

She remembered now, looking down at the nickel, that she had forgotten potatoes. The buying of potatoes was a part of the never ending strangeness. Back home, no matter what the season, she had always raised enough to carry her from one potato-digging time to the next. Now she would either have to go to one of the small stores near the project, where, Clytie had said, there were strange-talking clerks that a body couldn't understand at all, or buy from the man she had seen in the alley, selling stuff from a truck. He was maybe cheaper.

It was almost school letting out time in the afternoon before she heard the calling like a crying in the alley, and remembered with a sigh that she needed onions and cabbage as well as potatoes. She waited in the snowy alley, standing somewhat apart from the other women, many with babies in their arms, and all seemed like with young children who came crowding round the track crying: 'Mom, I wanta apple. Gimme grapes, Mom, gimme. Buy um, Mom, buy oranges.'

'Buy um, Mom. Buy um.' Amos, loud and brash almost as the Dalys, was yelling for some great greenish-blue grapes, the like of which she had never seen. So much foolishness. Youngens didn't

212

need grapes in December, or did they? Shoestrings or bubble gum? She stared at the grapes, conscious of the quick, mildly interested glances of some of the women, more conscious that most noticed her not at all. All were buying, crowding round the truck, and she felt foolish and stingy hanging back with Amos pulling at her coat, begging, 'Git grapes, Mom, please.'

She felt more stingy still when a little redheaded Daly came, grapes spilling from his cupped-up hands, holding the grape-heaped hands in front of Amos, commanding: 'Yu want grapes? Here.'

Amos helped himself as if they had been free from his grand-mother's vines. Money enough to buy her youngens a mess of grapes would buy a vine. 'What do you think of us? Are you getting all settled?'

Gertie realized the questions were being put to her. She turned from her pondering above the proffered grapes to see a fairly tall, well shaped young woman with long hair braided and wound round her head, and with a snow-suited baby on her arm. The woman was looking at her, and there was in her large, rather roundish brown eyes the same look that came over Clovis when he went into the insides of a strange car. 'I'm your neighbor you'll be seeing the most of, for I live straight across the alley from you. My name is Anderson.'

Gertie nodded, puzzled by the woman's voice. The words told, but the voice, like the eyes, asked, even when she gave her name.

'Her name's Nevels. She's got, I think, five kids, an her man works inu Flint plant. That right?' And the same face that had asked for a dream nodded to her, then smiled at Mrs Anderson.

'Why, hello, Max,' Mrs Anderson said, recovering quickly from an instant's confusion, but still unable to return Max's teasing smile. 'How's the job? I've wondered how you were; you went back to work so soon.'

'Yeah,' Max said, turning back to Gertie.

Gertie smiled at her. Though it was only now that she had heard even a part of her name, she knew her better, in a way, than any woman she had known back home. It was too much to know of any body, but she couldn't help what she had learned there behind the tin walls the night Enoch coughed so. They'd all taken what Sophronie called Detroit colds, and Gertie had been rubbing Enoch's chest with turpentine, kneeling by his bed, her shoulder almost touching the other wall.

She'd heard the woman come home—earlier than common it must have been, for Victor was still home in bed, and usually he seemed to be gone when she came home. Gertie had felt his eagerness through the cardboard walls, and heard the woman's laughter, soft, giving, nothing held back as in her smile to the woman now. She had left Enoch with his chest half greased, and let him cough until she heard Victor leave for his work.

She'd gone back to finish her rubbing of Enoch's chest, and it was then she'd heard the crying. Hopeless it had been, in a way like the roaring cry of Victor himself, but filled with sorrow, lostness, aloneness, the aloneness more than anything. She had heard without listening, but unable to leave the crying, and hardly knowing, she had fallen to talking, as if the chest she rubbed and the hurt thing through the wall were one. 'Don't cry, honey; don't cry. It won't allus be like this.' Gradually the crying had lessened, and it was like a listening there behind the wall. She had said aloud the words that for days and days she had heard in her head, ' "As a bird that wandereth from her nest, so is a man that wandereth from his place." '

The girl's voice had come then, apologetic, sorrowful, 'But I don't wanta nest.' The crying had begun again, softer, but more hopeless.

Gertie had tried hard to think of something. She must have drowsed, for it seemed suddenly she was hearing the cry of the old preacher: ' "For to him that is joined to all the living there is hope: for a living dog is better than a dead lion." '

Silence, and then the childlike giggle, 'But th lion ain't dead.'

The crying had not come again. Gertie had gone back to bed and fallen asleep while hunting a dream for the girl, a pretty dream for one who did not want a nest. Next day, when they had met by the coalhouse, she had given, 'Sky, a wide, wide sky filled with stars.'

The girl had taken it, smiling the gay kind of smile she gave now to Sophronie coming down her steps, booted, blue-jeaned, and lipsticked, ready for work, unable to linger when Max asked, 'How yu doen, kid?'

'Fallen down,' Sophronie said, not taking the cigarette from her mouth, for her hands were busied tucking wisps of hair under a blue bandana as she hurried up to Joe's truck. She did not look up when Mrs Anderson, who continued to stand by Gertie acting like a person trying hard to think of something to say, glanced at her face, then asked: 'Oh, what happened? You've hurt your head.'

'I fell,' Sophronie said, hefting a head of lettuce.

'How?' Mrs Anderson asked, giving the strip of adhesive tape a closer look.

'Off th merry-go-round, I guess,' Max said, moving toward the truck.

'Oh? What is that—this merry-go-round?'

'A thing that goes round an round. What else?' Max said.

'But this time of year? I don't understand?' Mrs Anderson shifted her baby—it seemed cross, like one just beginning to teethe—to the other arm, and looked at Max. She learned nothing there, and after a quick, worried glance toward a child reaching with a mop handle for an icicle by Gertie's kitchen door she concentrated again on Sophronie. 'What is it? Something in the factory?'

Sophronie nodded as she studied spinach. 'Jist like 'sembly, only it goes round. You go with it. Walken thataway made me dizzy.'

Joe, Gertie realized, was smiling at her, rubbing his hands, asking. 'What for you, ladee?' Mrs Anderson asked for a smaller piece of Hubbard squash, and Joe called over his shoulder into the truck some words she could not understand.

Mrs Anderson looked quickly up when the strange words came. 'Who's your helper, Joe? I thought your boys understood English?' And she stood on tiptoe peering into the truck. Gertie, standing behind her, saw in the dusky interior of the closed truck, the moving brightness of what looked to be a red and yellow coat. 'Is it another nephew, Joe?' Mrs Anderson persisted. 'He looks like a grown man? Is he a brother to the little one last fall who shivered so?'

'Tangerines nice today,' Joe said, holding out three in his wrinkled, calloused hand for her inspection.

She glanced briefly at the tangerines, then back into the truck. 'Has your nephew been discharged from the army, Joe, or is he like your boys? No citizen so he won't have to go?'

'Nice,' Joe said, listening now to Max, who was asking about green beans, nodding his head, repeating. 'Nice, today—tender,' busy taking things from outstretched hands for weighing, then calling again in his own language over his shoulder.

Mrs Anderson listened with a look of utmost concentration, then gave up at last with a little headshake and said, 'He must not have been over here long if he doesn't speak English yet. I'll take a dozen tangerines, Joe, if they're nice, and a green vegetable—broccoli, I think, and don't forget the squash.'

Joe, busied with her order, did not reach at once for the sack of Max's green beans held out to him from the inside of the truck. The hands, as if eager to be out of the truck, reached further, waving the sack, searching for its owner. Gertie saw a young man's face, eager, smiling, the dark eyes leaping from woman to woman until they found Max on tiptoe, one hand reached up for the beans. They searched no further, but now the eyes were like hands going over her body, caressing, pleased with what they found. Max, however, was hunting lettuce for Victor. She took the sack of beans without looking higher than the hand that held it. The boy's glance lingered on her a moment longer, hoping, but when Max only reached past his feet to the celery, his thirsty eyes went on. They went swiftly over the other women. Gertie's great size, the smallness of the Japanese woman, checked them for an instant, then they swept away on down the alley. Soon the eyes stopped and held something, smiled on it and caressed it as they had caressed Max.

Gertie, curious, turned and saw that it was Miller's car. Unlike Enoch, who by now recognized the cars of the neighbors as back home she had known the mules and the horses for miles around, Gertie knew only this one car because it was the longest and shiniest in the alley, loaded down with more contraptions than she had known existed. The young man continued to look at it, and it was only when old Joe spoke harshly to him, twice commanding him to do something, that he turned back into the truck, and then only his body. His eyes reached for the car still, until Joe whirled and yelled, such fury in his hissing spitting words that Gertie thought he was going to bite him.

Joe seemed even more angry when Mrs Anderson, who had been examining a basket of loose bananas, asked in her quick, excited way: 'Can't he understand English at all, Joe? Isn't it odd how he could come over here with the war on?'

'Bananas cheap today—nice.'

'Is the little one, the one that shivered so, his brother?'

'This piece squash, hokay?'

'Is the little one learning to speak English?'

'He learn. Lady, yu wanta squash?'

'Does he go to public school? Oh, yes, yes, I'll take that piece. Does he go to public school?'

'Da good sisters. Cranberries nice today.'

'Don't you like public schools?'

The words came in a quick angry hiss: 'Public school no good. Communist.' His voice smoothed like a starched shirt under a hot iron as he spoke to Sophronie, 'Green beans nice today?'

Sophronie shook her head. 'Them nice ones last week was tough,' but she bought freely of grapes, oranges, tangerines, and, urged on by the insistent Claude Jean, who went to school only of mornings, she bought ripe tomatoes and fresh pears.

Mrs Anderson watched her buying critically, and when she had gone turned with a little headshake to Gertie and Max, the only customers remaining. 'It's pitiful the way that woman works, and the way she spends her money. Pears, compared to dried peaches, are terribly expensive, and have almost no food value or vitamins. And such junky clothes. Rayon dresses for her little girl; they don't wear half as well as cotton.'

'Maybe Sophronie don't want vitamins or clothes that lasts forever,' Max said, her eyes smiling.

'But her children need them,' Mrs Anderson said, laying money in Joe's hand, looking to Gertie for support.

'Yeah,' Max said, yawning, stretching her arms, her breasts rising, pointed, pushing against the navy-blue jacket. 'Who's gonna say what I need. My pop said that once to a damned social worker when—' She had grown conscious of the pleased eyes of Joe's helper fixed on her bosom. She was for an instant angry, looking at him, then smiled. 'Hiyah, kid. You're already acting like a good American man. I'll betcha end up in u mansion in Grosse Pointe.'

'Grossa Pointa,' he repeated, flushing, stammering, There was in his face more than the simple pleasure of hearing a pretty girl say the one word of English he apparently knew. His eyes glowed as he nodded, smiling, his face ecstatic as if the place Max had mentioned were heaven, but a heaven on earth within his reach. Gertie, watching, thought of the brown woman on the train. Her eyes had been like the boy's eyes now, when she had repeated, 'Paradise.'

'Grosse Pointa?' The boy was puzzled now. He jerked his shoulder toward the low gray barracks behind him, as if to understand how one like Max, who lived in such ugliness, could know about a place like Grosse Pointe.

Max studied him an instant, her head tilted, her gum still, then laughed. 'It's America, kid. They taught me to read. I can read about it and see them people in th society section.' Her eyes narrowed. 'Say, kid, how come yu know about Grosse Pointe?'

But the boy could only repeat, smiling, 'Grossa Pointa.'

Joe, who after reaching into the cab of the truck had turned toward Max with something under his coat, stopped on hearing the word spoken by the young one. His smoothish eyes, that made Gertie think of over-roasted coffee beans, blazed. His seamy face paled with wrath as he spattered the boy with an outburst of short sharp sounds.

The boy scuttled into the truck guiltily, like one who knows he has done wrong. Joe's anger hardened into surliness as he figured the cost of Max's purchases. Finished, he darted a black, vicious glance from under his thick brows towards Mrs Anderson, who, though burdened with baby and vegetables, still stood watching and listening, but now with the look of a person who has solved at least one problem. 'Four ninety-three,' Joe said to Max.

'Yu put um up on me, Joe,' Max said, handing him a five-dollar bill.

'Twenty-six today, everybody,' Joe said, surly, making change.

'That's a heck of a lot for cigarettes,' Max said as she took the package.

'No wanta. No buy,' Joe said, reaching for the package, shrugging a shoulder.

'Oh, I'll take um, Joe. Whatsa nickel? Whatsa dime? Whatsa dollar? Whatsa million dollars? I made forty in tips last night. You make a hundred today with this new price. Old man Flint makes another million on machine guns that blows up an killa th wrong guys. Like my pop used to say, "Blood's th cheapest thing on earth, but they's money in it."'

'Investigation has revealed it was not Flint's fault,' Mrs Anderson said, somewhat sharply.

'Yeah?' Max said, loading her arms with vegetables. 'I forgot who's butter'n your bread. Old man Flint come off luckier than Christ. Somebody found Him guilty.'

'Oh, Max, don't always—' Mrs Anderson's eyes narrowed as she considered the oblong paper-wrapped package. 'Is that a carton of cigarettes? And you said twenty-six cents. That's above OPA.'

Joe reached for Mrs Anderson's broccoli. 'Help you home, ladee?'

'No, thanks, wait on her,' and still scrutinizing the package, Mrs Anderson nodded sidewise toward Gertie.

'Twenty-six cents?' Max was asking. 'Why, that ain't high for imported cork-tipped cigarettes. They're specials,' she went on, smiling, 'BM.'

'Really. I've heard of PMs, but never BMs,' Mrs Anderson said.

'We all gotta lot to learn,' Max said, turning toward her steps.

'Some a th potatoes,' Gertie said into Joe's asking eyes. 'About a peck.'

She bought, or tried to buy, the things she might have had this time of year at home—cabbage, onions, and a few apples. She only looked longingly at the sweet potatoes. At two pounds for twenty-five cents, a mess of baked sweet potatoes would cost almost a dollar. Back home she'd sold near twenty bushels for fifty cents a bushel. She wished the molasses, somewhere on the way like the block of wood, would come. It seemed a year since she had seen the wood.

Mrs Anderson hurried toward the through street after suddenly remembering that she had not seen her young son Georgie for the past five minutes. Gertie realized the others were all gone. Joe had shut the doors in the back of his truck, and was now looking under it for stray children and dogs. Still Gertie lingered, the heaped Josiah basket on her arms. She stepped up to the dark surly man just as he was getting into the cab. 'They's somethin I want to ask you.'

'Cigarettes all gone,' he said with a swift impatient glance at her, his hand on the door handle.

She shook her head. 'I mean—I wondered—I jist got here. Did it take you long to—well, to kinda learn to like it, this country. I figger it's so diff'ernt frum mine—it must ha been worse fer you.'

He had listened, his thick black brows drawn somewhat together with his efforts to understand. At last he smiled, shrugged one shoulder. 'I did not come to like.'

15

Gertie glanced over her shoulder to make certain Amos followed. She shifted the Josiah basket to her other arm, and then walked slowly on, head bent as she stared at the snow under her boots. Her thoughts were on the Tipton Place. She was all moved now, her corn and fodder were in the barn, for she had rived shakes and mended the roof. The hens had learned to lay in the nests she had made and lined with fresh hay, the hay so fresh it smelled still of hay instead of hen; and before the hen had put down her egg she'd turned round and round, shaping the nest to her bottom. Up at the house, in the big middle room on the hearth, was her red cedar churn filled with clabbered cream. When she had churned and molded the butter, it would be firm and yellow with little drops of water oozing out. The curving lily flower in the mold her father had made would rise clearly on the butter, and Cassie as always would cut off the lily flower and say, 'They's nothen so good as lily flowers, Mom.'

And she would say, 'One a these days I'm aimen to fry you a mess a butter-lily flowers, Cassie Marie,' and Cassie would giggle and . . .

'May I give you God's word?'

Gertie lifted her glance past the outstretched booklet up to the woman's face. She saw, below white hair, calm brown eyes, somewhat like Max's eyes in color but filled with a peace and a certainty that Max did not know. 'Read God's word,' the woman went on. Her voice was low and somehow pretty, but more than anything it was smooth and even. It told a body nothing but the words as it said, 'Find God and Jesus, and you will find yourself.'

Gertie cleared her throat and did not reach for the booklet. 'I've been a readen th Bible an a hunten God fer a long while—off an on—but it ain't so easy as picken up a nickel off th floor.'

'Evermore learning but forever from the truth,' the woman said, walking beside her. 'You need a teacher to help in the search. Find him. He is coming soon, very soon. The prophecies are almost fulfilled.'

'Paul said that nigh two thousand years ago,' Gertie said, and they were silent as they walked together down the bit of empty alley between the end of the six-unit building just ended, and the beginning of the building that held Gertie's unit. The woman turned away and knocked at the first door.

Gertie walked slowly on, watching the woman, keeping almost abreast of her, for no one came to her knocking at the first two doors. At the third door in the row of six, a woman was just coming out with broom and bucket, taking advantage of the thaw to scrub her steps. She did not look about her, but at once dipped the broom into the pail and began to scrub so vigorously that her broom spattered dirty water onto the next stoop, which was clean.

She was a little woman, faded and dumpy, puffed in the wrong places, Gertie thought, like a piece of bright but cheap cloth, washed and boiled in overly strong lye suds. She was the mother, Clytie had said, of the girl Maggie and of the boy who had knocked Enoch down. It was hard to believe, though, that this woman could be kin of Maggie. Her hair might have been red and curly once, or it might have been black and wavy. It was fuzzy grizzled now, matching the red, chapped hands on the broom handle. She looked like she might be pretty far gone in the family way, but it was hard to say. She was so dumpling.

When the gospel woman paused at the foot of the steps, a book held out, the little woman did not look round but continued to scrub as if she and the broom were alone in the world together. But Gertie, watching in swift sidewise glances, felt she knew that someone waited by the bottom step.

There was at the moment one of those sudden lulls of silence that now and then dropped into the alley; even traffic, held back by switching trains, was still. Gertie heard the gospel woman say,

'Could I leave some of our literature with you as a gift? It might help you through these troubled times.'

The little woman soused her broom up and down in the bucket, giving the other an angry, suspicious glance as she did so. She bent again to the scrubbing. 'Would you be interested in—' The gospel woman's words were broken off by a spattering of dirty water, some of which must have gone into her face. Still she advanced to the second step, and her voice continued pleasant, 'In this book are many of Christ's teachings that will help you through these tr—'

A broomful of scrub water well aimed, with no pretense of accident, flew about the brown shoulders and the dull scarf. Gertie thought it must have hit the woman in the mouth, for she heard a choking gasp, saw her elbows move as if she were wiping her face; but in a moment the woman was able to say, turning slowly away, ' "Do unto others as—" '

The Bible verse was cut in two by the pail of dirty water flung over her shoulders and head. Gertie saw it trickle down the coat, both front and back, as the woman turned about, wiping her eyes. The other cried with a furious shaking of the bucket: 'Some people that don't move fast enough when Kathy Daly gits ready to t'row out her scrub water gits dirtied. And if,' she went on, dropping the bucket and seizing the broom, 'good people like Father Moneyhan had th say-so in this country, yu'd git worse'n scrub water. Hitler knows how t'handle u likes a youse along wit u Jews.'

'Yes,' the woman said, still rubbing her eyes as she turned back to the other, 'the prophecies are being fulfilled. All over the earth we are persecuted. Hitler kills us, but here we are only beaten by mobs and put into jail.'

Mrs Daly flourished the broom. 'I mean git. I'll call a cops; da red squad. Youse can't talk about u gover'ment thataway in front a Kathy Daly, see? I'm a good patriotic Christian American. See? No nigger-loven, Jew-loven, communist's gonna stand on mu steps and tell me wot I gotta do. Don't think I don't know th likes a youse, communists, not saluten du flag, an—'

'Bow down to no graven image,' the gospel woman said, turning away again, but awkwardly, like one unable to see.

223

'Wotta yu mean, graven image?' And the broom came hard down on the blinded woman's head. Gertie had not known she was so close, but when Mrs Daly ran down two steps and brought the broom down a second time, it fell on her own outstretched hand. She held it and looked into the angry blue eyes above it. The eyes told her the woman was Maggie's mother, though they were red now, as if from old weeping, and set about with flabby wrinkles, faded as if the eyes along with the wrinkled, freckled forehead and pouchy cheeks had been left too long in the too hot, too strong suds. The loose-lipped mouth showed ragged, broken teeth as the woman cried, pulling on the broom: 'Youse jist got here, yu hillbilly heathen, an so help me yu think you run du town. Leggo this broom, yu big bitch. I'll calla cops.'

Gertie flushed, but hung on to the broom as she turned to the gospel woman, who was still wiping her eyes, her face twisted with pain. 'I live jist a little piece ahead. Go up to my place an git dry.'

'I can't see,' the other said.

'Youse ain't blinded,' Kathy cried, struggling with both her small hands to free the broom from Gertie's one big hand. 'I give youse a little Roman Cleanser inu water's all. But come close t'my house anudder time an youse'ull git a pot a lye water. Keep them books an that talk away frum mu kids, see?' Her voice grew louder, shriller, and her talk unlike anything Gertie had ever heard. It became a mixture of swear words such as Sue Annie might have used in her worst moments, coupled with others Gertie had never heard, all mixed in with prayer-sounding pieces of talk to the Virgin, Father Moneyhan, and various saints. Amos stared at her in wonder, as he had stared a few moments earlier at the strange-talking man in the little grocery store.

Gertie held the broom off with one hand, turned the blinded woman about with the other. The door next to Mrs Daly's opened, and a large dark woman in a starched pink apron came out to her stoop and stood watching. Gertie gave her one quick pleading glance, then turned away without asking for help. Something in the dark face under the neat rolls of hair in curlers made her feel that if the woman took anybody's part it would be Mrs Daly's.

'Is she badly hurt?' It was Mrs Anderson running down her steps, her baby bouncing on her arm.

224

'I'm fine, thank you, except that I can't see so well,' the woman answered, holding her hand out toward the voice.

Mrs Anderson ran up and piloted her out of Kathy's reach, and then, while Gertie continued to hold the broom, rushed back. Murmuring, 'How terrible, how terrible,' she ran stopping to pick up the booklets and the gospel woman's purse. It was a worn and shoddy thing of imitation leather, its flimsy clasp fallen open, with a few pieces of silver, but mostly nickels and pennies, scattered in the slush.

Max, in a full-skirted housecoat and with the rumpled look of one just awakened, ran down the alley and led the woman away. Gertie saw her in swift sidewise glances, as she saw Mrs Anderson, but mostly she looked into the eyes at the other end of the broom. The angry, troubled eyes made her want to say something, beg forgiveness for doing a thing she had to do. She had to hold one end of the broom, but Kathy Daly had to hold the other. Why? In front of her a whole houseful of little youngens was spilling through the door onto the stoop, and from somewhere inside she heard the crying of a baby—so many youngens. Counting these and the ones gone to school, there must be ten. They all screamed at her, repeating fragments of their mother's curses, along with such words as 'old bitch, hillbilly, Jew, communist,' the last word most fiercely and most often repeated, as if in it alone were gathered all the evil that could be put into all the curses. At last a little boy darted out and struck her on the thigh, crying, 'Hillbilly. Go back home, youse hillbilly communist.'

The voice was familiar, and looking at him she remembered the grapes he had held out to Amos only a few days ago. 'Let th rest be,' she said in a rough hoarse voice to Mrs Anderson, and dropped the broom and darted away.

She did not look back when Mrs Daly called: 'Youse needn't run. I wouldn't hurt a little ting like youse.'

The children in the doorway laughed so hard they could no longer call her names. Ahead of her she heard laughter, and looked up to see Max bending with laughter, her face twisted with the laughter as if it were for her some unaccustomed thing she did not quite know how to handle. 'Whyn'tcha pick her up an throw her inu trash can?' she asked when she could speak.

'I couldn't,' Gertie said, turning toward her steps, but stopping when Max motioned with her arm.

'Come on in. Expressman broughtcha some stuff. I got it.' And then to Mrs Anderson, just behind Gertie, her hands and arms overflowing with baby and booklets, 'Come on in my place. She's ina bathroom. Victor's worken double shift. They's somethen in my kitchen yu gotta see. It gives me th willies.' She motioned again to Gertie, explaining as she opened the door, 'Sophronie an me was drinken coffee when Kathy Daly went to war.'

Gertie followed Max and Mrs Anderson into the tiny kitchen that to her flustered glance seemed smothery crowded with fancy furniture. Sophronie, sitting at the table over a cup of coffee, smiled up at her, then lifted her peacock-draped arms in a long stretch, the cigarette between her fingers pointing ceilingward while she yawned with a long and yearning yawn.

Then, in the passway into the living room Gertie saw the block of wood. She crowded past the women until she was close enough to touch it; and there in the little empty space in front of the stove she knelt and studied it, both with her eyes and her hands to see if any hurt had come to it. But it stood unscratched and undented, marked only by the pasted papers to guide it on its journey. The top of the head was bending, searching for the face, waiting, as it had searched and waited all these years.

All unknowing her hands went under her coat into her apron pocket, opening the knife. If right now she and the wood could be alone together, she would bring out the face. His face was so clear—Christ coming down through the October field with the red leaves in one hand, an ax in the other. It was so plain, a little like Henley's face, a little—no—not exactly. Her hand came away from the knife, and dropped again onto the wood. How had it been, the face? She wasn't seeing. She was recollecting what she had seen. The only face she could see now was Kathy Daly's, the eyes looking at her with such hatred. A sin it was to make another sin with such hatred and such talk—but Judas had to sin. She saw that Amos had followed her, and now stood tongue-tied in the doorway behind Mrs Anderson who asked, looking over her baby's head: 'What is that? Do you carve? Did you do that?'

226

'It's what I wanted yu to see,' Max said, busily hanging the woman's dampened clothing on the overhead pipe. She turned to Gertie. 'I wanta see his face. He gives me th willies. Seems like all he's gotta do is raise his head an there he'd be.'

'It's quite a work of . . .' Mrs Anderson's tone, which had been one of grudging praise handed down with authority, changed to troubled pleading: 'Georgie, darling, please don't—do leave the poor woman's clothing on the pipe. It won't dry on the floor. Let Mother take off your snow suit while you're in the house.' The dark-eyed, smooth-faced child was still an instant while she, working awkwardly with one hand, unzipped zippers and unbuckled buckles. She had not quite finished when he darted into the living room after Amos and Wheateye. She did not call him back, but shifted the baby, and after another frowning glance at the block of wood turned her attention to the woman's clothing. She shook her head in pity. 'Poor thing. That coat must be twenty years old, and I guess it's her only outdoor garment.'

'Oh, yeah,' Max said, taking cups and saucers from a shelf above the sink. 'That coat's just like what th poor woman wears ina movies, but lookut them hose—Hudson's best brand a nylons—service weight.'

Mrs Anderson sat down and rocked the baby, beginning to whimper now, back and forth in her arms in a weary sort of way. 'Somebody's given them to her—poor woman.'

'Yeah?' Max said, pouring cream off a bottle of milk into a small pitcher. 'Who's got nylons to give away? And yu oughta see her slip, pure silk, real lace. People don't cast off slips like what she's got on—and make um fit. But so what? It's her business, ain't it?'

'Max,' Sophronie warned in a whisper, just as the gospel woman came into the passway. Gertie, pressed into a corner, aware as always since leaving home that she took up more than one person's share of room, gave the petticoat, showing a little under the housecoat Max had loaned the woman, a quick appraising glance, as did the others. She saw the lace was in truth handmade, and finer than any her mother had ever done. Still, it seemed to belong on the woman, who, without her hat and under the bright overhead light, looked older than she had looked in the alley, maybe as old as her mother, but unlike Sophronie, she looked neither tired nor faded without make-up, even though one eye was still faintly red from the scrub water. Her hair had plainly never been ruined by permanent waves and lack of care like Mrs Daly's. There was something about its soft whiteness, set in gentle waves and curling wisps around her ears, that bespoke an easier, kinder life than the alley gave.

There was the same look about her small white, uncalloused hands; and when she thanked Max for the coffee her voice was plainly a stranger to all alone weeping like Max's voice or mad screaming like Kathy's. She sat with the others about the table, silent, sipping coffee, smiling now and then at Mrs Anderson's baby, growing ever more restless. She gave it one of Max's bright silver spoons and a bit of coffee cake, which Mrs Anderson, with a horrified look, immediately took from the child, though not before she had got a few small crumbs into her mouth. 'It's not on her diet,' she explained as the child smacked its lips, then screamed, reaching for the cake.

'You have a pediatrician, my dear?' the gospel woman asked.

'Oh, yes. Yes, indeed,' Mrs Anderson said, looking somewhat startled, then composing her face to add, 'a very good one, highly recommended by two of my husband's bosses.'

'Really. And may I ask where your husband works?'

'In one of Mr Flint's plants—temporarily. He majored in sociology and did government work in employment down in Indiana before the war. But now he does something about personnel. I don't know just exactly what it is.'

'Neither does anybody else, I'm sure,' the gospel woman said. She smiled at Mrs Anderson, then looked at Gertie, still standing pressed into a corner of the passway. 'I can't begin to thank you,' she said, setting down her coffee cup. 'Not just for helping me, but for not hurting the other and for not saying anything.'

'She was too little, an I ain't much on talken,' Gertie said.

The other nodded, 'Talk—human talk—is no good. She needs Christ.'

'Yeah,' Max said, flipping a package of cigarettes across the table toward Sophronie. 'If Christ come knocken on her door, an he couldn't say his beads with a Irish brogue, she wouldn't let him in. If he told her about the man with the two coats, she'd call him a communist, and if his beard wasn't blond like the images she'd call him a dirty Jew.'

The gospel woman sighed. 'Poor thing—such hatred, such hatred. She needs a teacher.'

Gertie cleared her throat. 'Seems like she's got one—this Father Moneyhan she kept a quoten.'

'He's terrible—some say his teachings here in the United States have helped Hitler a lot,' Mrs Anderson said. 'He's fascist through and through.'

'I don't know this Father Moneyhan,' Max said, 'but whatever he is, if he's a Catholic he'll love Hitler an huggle up to Mussolini an hate th Russians worse'n th Germans,' and her eyes were no longer cool but hotly bright.

Mrs Anderson looked apprehensively at Max, and spoke soothingly, 'Now, Max, they hate the Russians because they're communists.'

'Yeah,' Max said, 'they hate th Russians for what they ain't, not for what they are. Kid, I'm educated—my mother-in-law's taught me more about some things than your man will ever know when he finishes that paper for that degree. Th pope's hated th Russians an th Russians has despised th pope from a long time back when there wasn't no communism, nothing but kings.'

'And the pope,' the gospel woman said.

'Max,' Mrs Anderson began, putting the baby over her shoulder, 'historically you're partly right; but still they don't hate the way you—'

'Oh, yeah?' Max leaned forward, an unlighted cigarette between her fingers. 'Maybe yu do know history, but yu're not married to a Catholic—or yu thought yu was married till yu learned different—a Polock Catholic. I know. See?'

'My dear, don't hate him or any Catholic,' the gospel woman said. 'You need—'

'Yeah?' Max asked, her voice rising. 'I know wot I need. If I quit hating them—him and her, th priest that done it, that lying sister that letum carry her away—if I quit hating them, I'd hafta hate myself—see?'

Mrs Anderson was looking worried. 'Please, Max, don't get all—'

'Hell, I'm not worked up,' and Max's voice from being shrill and hard was low, almost a whisper as she looked at the gospel woman. 'I gotta hate, see. Them Catholics killed my baby.' She sprang up so hastily her chair tipped backward. She jerked it upright, crying to it as if it had been human: 'Damn yu, yu God-damned chair. I hate loose chairs, allatime falling down.' She looked at the gospel woman, 'But Victor, he would have a house for th kid, he said. Then he helped um kill her. She was three months old day before yesterday, and three days old when they killed her.' She whirled, caught up one of the booklets. 'Yu don't think this—a million a these, a million Bibles, Jesus Christ hisself—can make me stop hating um. It wouldn't be doing right by her if I stopped—see?'

'Max, please,' Mrs Anderson said in a worried, pitying voice, 'they didn't kill your baby. It was weak—very weak. They didn't tell you at first—but I talked to Victor when it was about a day old. He was badly worried, for they had it in oxygen, and . . .'

Max was crying in a shrill voice that held no tears: 'They did kill it. Victor wanted a boy was why he seemed worried to you. Victor's mother wanted it to die. She called it a bastard, and me married more'n a year. She'd seen our marriage certificate made out in Pittsburgh.'

'But the baby was weakly, Max,' Mrs Anderson insisted.

'How inu hell do yu know so much?' She shook her head emphatically. 'She wasn't weakly. She had u strong cry. She was fine an strong till they carried her away. At his mother's own church it hadda be, not inu hospital chapel—to be baptized—sneaked her off. I didn't know till his mother told me. She knowed enough English to say that, to come bragging to me, "Da child's no bastard now," she says. Two days later it was dead—pneumonia. They lied to me; not strong at birth, they said. They oughta told th truth—Victor an his mom, they'd rather have a dead Catholic than a live, free kid.'

She turned to Gertie as if for support, begging her to bear some of the burden of the hatred, 'She was strong. I took care a myself, good. I never touched a drop a liquor, and only ten cigarettes a day—but the Catholics, the damned, damned Cath—'

'My dear, my dear,' the gospel woman interrupted, 'can't you see you've let them ruin your young life with hatred. Their few drops of water didn't kill your baby or change it in any way. Many are kind people with much love.'

'Yeah? Yu think they hang together on account a their love—their hate fer niggers an Jews an Russians an Protestants holds um together.' She gave the well kept hands, the gently waving hair, a quick, contemptuous glance. 'Wotta you know about hate?'

The gospel woman considered, staring down into her empty cup, and Mrs Anderson turned to Max and began an explanation, quick-spoken and somehow dreary, as if she had already said the same thing to her many times, of how the baby must have been puny from the beginning or they wouldn't have baptized it so soon, for usually they waited.

Max whirled from an absent-minded arranging of the gospel woman's books left by the sink. 'I've toldcha a million times they couldn't wait. They knowed that once I was home with her I'd never let um take her away. I was flat on my back.' Some word or title on the cover of a booklet caught her eye. She stopped to study it an instant, and when she spoke again her voice was more calm. 'I wanta buy about a dozen a these. I'll put um all over th place, this about Catholics. One I'll lay at th feet u his blessed Virgin.'

The gospel woman sighed. 'My dear, these tracts were never meant to be distributed in such a spirit of—'

'Hate. Sure I hate him. He knows it. He cheated on me when he begged me into marrying him in Pittsburgh. There, he made me think he was a man. He ain't no man, not here in Detroit. He's his religion an his job an his mom's boy. He's got a good Polock mom. She never let her kids go to public school or hear anybody talk English at home. He got away from her for th first time in his life, and learned he hadda have a woman. So he picked me.' She stood, hands on hips, looking down at the gospel woman. 'And they call it love. *Love.*'

'Everything has to have a name,' the gospel woman said. 'Try not to take it all so hard. You are very young, but some day you will—well, grow up, get more confidence in yourself so that you will quit being afraid.'

'Afraid? Victor's not gonna hurt me, none. He wouldn't.'

The older woman finished her coffee, turned about in her chair, and considered Max with a little headshake. 'Oh, I don't mean he would beat you or anything like that. If he did it might be easier. You could then, perhaps, make him hate himself for having done such a thing. But don't you think,' she went on, speaking slowly, carefully, 'that—well, at least sometimes, we are more afraid of what people might make us want to do ourselves, to change ourselves—that is, when we can see through them enough to know. Some of us are more afraid of that than anything they could possibly do to us.'

Max pondered an instant, her gum still, then nodded. 'Yu said it, sister. Damned if I'm gonna let anybody make me wanta be nothen but another piece a Hamtramck.'

'But you're very much afraid you'll start wanting to please, that's why you hate. You'll have to learn at least to cover it all up, so that they won't know and be, well, shall we say, tempted?'

'But how inu hell do you cover up somethen that's burnen a hole inyu?'

The gospel woman looked politely impatient. 'Just make up your mind. Be certain. Hatred, my dear, is an emotion. Usually we hate things or people with which we have some emotional involvement, such as—'

'Love?' Max whispered, when the other seemed to hesitate and hold back from the word. She nodded, and Max came very close to her chair, and looked down into her face, asking, 'But wotta yu gonna do?'

'Some manage one way. Some another. I have decided that Amnon's way was best after all. Remember, "Then Amnon hated her exceedingly; so that the hatred wherewith he hated her was greater than the love wherewith he had loved her. And Amnon said unto her, "Arise, be gone." A woman would have to manage differently.'

'It ain't that simple,' Max said, turning away.

'It's all a case of making up one's mind,' the gospel woman said.

'An when we've changed an tried to please em, we hate em worse than ever.' Gertie had spoken in a low voice, startled by her words, wondering why she talked. But here it wasn't like back home.

Talking to this woman was like singing to the wind. She would be gone, and what a body said to her was finished, not like talk to Sue Annie back home. There the words, always living, remembered, could be repeated twenty years later.

The gospel woman looked at her with interest, and seemed ready to say something, but at that moment Max happened to glance at the clock. 'Lordy, Lordy,' she exclaimed, turning toward the bathroom, 'I gotta go to Zadkiewicz's. I gotta find some soap powder a some kind.' She glanced at Gertie. 'Couldja git anything, or didn'tcha git nothen but th "nah"?'

Gertie smiled. The memory of her failure in the store hurt less now. Even the only half whispered jeer of 'heel-beely,' of a fat woman in a yellow scarf and a red coat, stung less. The woman, like many others, had watched while Gertie stood sweaty handed and dumb, pointing to this and that in the meat counter where the strange piles of sliced stuff seemed no kin to the hogs and calves and muttons she'd butchered back home. Worse, she had been unable to understand any word of what the man behind the counter said; angry and impatient he had seemed because he couldn't understand her. Suddenly, looking at the women around her here in Max's kitchen, it seemed almost funny. 'I did see him hand out some washen powders an soap—that good yaller napthie kind—but when it come to me I got th "Nah,"' and smiling more widely she flung out her hands as Zadkiewicz had done to show their emptiness.

'Yu gotta learn him,' Max said. 'Him an his "Nahs." I gotta buy soap. He's gonna sell me soap,' and she hurried away to dress.

'I'd like to watch and listen,' Mrs Anderson said. 'He will never sell me anything that's scarce.'

'An take notes for Homer?' Max called over her shoulder.

Mrs Anderson flushed, Sophronie smiled, and though the gospel woman looked at her, plainly curious, Mrs Anderson said nothing. They were silent until Mrs Anderson whispered under the sound of water running in the bathroom: 'Max, poor thing, has such a fixation. I've tried to tell her that 3 percent of all babies are stillborn, and that in spite of modern medicine a great many die shortly after birth.'

'Have you ever lost a child?' the gospel woman asked.

Mrs Anderson looked surprised and shook her head, and continued silent, staring at Gertie's block of wood until Max came back, dressed for the street in boots, blue jeans, and jacket. 'Good luck,' the gospel woman said.

'You need u luck,' Max said, opening her purse and taking out a five-dollar bill. She shoved it across the table toward the other. 'I ain't quite certain just what is your racket, lady, but whatever it is I bet you're out for something better'n a fast buck. Take it,' she insisted when the other looked at her but did not reach for the money. 'I had a houseful a drunks last night. Tips was good, but so was th pinches. Oh, them judges.'

'Thanks,' the gospel woman said, and straightened the hem of Max's tightly belted jacket. 'Poor judges,' she said, 'if I were a man I know I'd whistle when I saw you.'

Max jerked off the jacket belt and flung it on the table. 'If I could quit looken like a female, maybe they wouldn't try to go no further than whistlen. Allatime they're tryen to git me in cars, or crowden up on u street cars, an then, at work, th pinches. Detroit is th woman-hungriest place I've ever seen.'

Sophronie sighed. 'Ain't it th truth? They must be short a women in this town. On this shift I allus run out in the middle a th street, ever step a th way frum th bus, scrawny as I am. I'd ruther take a chanct on bein' knocked down by a car than took by a man—'

Max, her hand on the doorknob, was interrupting. 'Kathy Daly's gonna have another fit. They's a nigger woman inu alley. Acts like she's lost.'

The gospel woman sprang up, uneasily asking, 'Is she quite tall, slender, coffee-colored?'

'Yeah, lotta cream inu coffee, though. And she looks like something that don't belong in this alley—a lady. Yu want I should run tell her you're here.'

'Please,' the gospel woman said, after one glance through the door. 'It's Johala.' She considered, for an instant, her dampened clothing on the gas pipe. Then, like a child, ordinarily good and so unwilling to be caught in some meanness, she gathered everything in one swoop and hurried to the bathroom.

Max, who had run down the steps and called to the woman in the alley, opened the door, holding it wide as she said: 'Go right in an make yourself at home. She's okay. Hadda little accident. I gotta go, but I'll be right back.'

In spite of Max's welcome and Mrs Anderson's murmured, 'Come in,' the tall, straight, only slightly dusky woman hesitated in the doorway. She did not seem afraid, more like one who has learned that the entering of a strange door is not always a pleasant thing. Her large eyes went quickly over the women's faces, searched swiftly about the kitchen until she saw on the sink shelf by the door the gospel woman's purse. Like the tracts stacked close by, it showed traces of Kathy's scrub water. The woman gave a low, troubled gasp.

'Is she hurt?'

'Oh, no,' Mrs Anderson said. 'Her clothing got wetted, that's all.'

Sophronie smiled and flicked on Max's coffee-making machine. 'She's inu bathroom changing back into her clothes. Run an see about her if yu wanta, then set an have some coffee. I'll bet you've been a looken around these alleys in this weather fer a spell.'

'Not long,' the woman said, smiling at Sophronie. All the suspicion was gone from her face now, though she hurried a little as she went to the bathroom.

Any talk she and the gospel woman might have had was blotted out by an unusually low-flying airplane. The place was so filled with the stomach-shaking roar that Amos came running to his mother. Gertie, as always when he or Cassie was frightened by a plane, pressed his face against her bosom and clapped her hand over his ears, for she herself was never able to keep from cringing and shivering at the sounds. Holding him so, she felt some strange hardness against her bosom, and when the plane had gone she asked, 'What you been into, son?'

'Playen,' he said, 'with this sick man on this necklace.'

Sophronie looked and said: 'Oh, Lordy, them youngens has been into Victor's holy images. You'd better give it to me, honey, an I'll put it back. He allus keeps that on u table by his bed.'

Gertie studied the cross-shaped Christ on the string of beads, and asked in a low voice, 'Why would he want a necklace?'

Sophronie smiled. 'Don't let them like Kathy Daly an Miz Bommarita, let alone Victor, hear you a callen that a necklace. They'd putcha down fer a heathen. It's a rosary. I never seen one neither till I come up here.'

Gertie continued to look at it. Here was a Christ, she thought, her mother would have liked: the head drawn back in agony, the thorns, the nails, each with a drop of crimson below it, a great splash of scarlet for the wounded side, the face bearing many wrinkles to indicate agony. Sophronie saw her curiosity, and said, as she turned with it to the bedroom: 'You'll see plenty jist like it. They're all over this town, them Christs on crosses.'

Mrs Anderson's fat Georgie scuttled into the room clutching, as if he would never let it go, a china doll dressed in a gown of a soft and shining blue that made Gertie think of the Cumberland on a still October day. Mrs Anderson, in spite of the heavy baby, sprang up in horror. 'Georgie, darling, do be careful. You might break it. It's Victor's Child of Prague. His grandmother brought it to this country when she was just a little girl. Give it to Mother now.' She made a quick but futile snatch for the doll.

Georgie whirled back and dived into the passway, narrowly missing the stove, screaming: 'I wanna dis, I'm gonna have ut. I'm gonna.'

His mother snatched again. He jumped backward and bumped into the gospel woman, just returning from the bathroom. She took the blue china doll before Georgie knew what was happening. 'Thank you, my dear,' she said.

Georgie screamed, leaped for the doll, couldn't reach it, then kicked the woman sharply on the shin. 'Your foot slipped, my dear. You'll never play football unless you learn to manage your feet better than that,' and she smiled at him as she handed the Child of Prague to Sophronie.

Johala came and drank the coffee Gertie gave her, but the gospel woman lingered in the passway, bent above the block of wood, peeping as if she would see the hidden face. Mrs Anderson had shifted her now lustily bawling baby to her left shoulder, the better to seize and hold Georgie with her right hand. The effort reddened her face and corded her neck, for Georgie was kicking back and forth and up and down like a prancing pony, trying to get the gospel woman's attention as he cried: 'I can, too, make my feet mind. I wanta kick yu—yu old—youse old—' It was only after the fourth try that he remembered the word he had just heard in the alley. 'Bitch,' he cried triumphantly. 'Youse old bitch.'

Sophronie stood in the bedroom doorway, twisting her head about to send her voice above Georgie's screams to Gertie just around the corner from the door. 'Thank th Lord they ain't hurt none a Victor's pretties. But it's a wonder. One a them—I figger it was Wheateye—clumb up and got down his Virgin Mary.' The gospel woman glanced up from the block of wood, and Sophronie directed her glance to the bedroom in front of her. 'Ain't that a fancy place in there? Never a week goes by but what that man buys that woman somethen. That quilted rayon bedspread jist last week, an I bet it cost twenty dollars if it cost a dime. An,' Sophronie added, as if it were some unheard-of thing, 'he allus pays cash.'

The gospel woman nodded, but she seemed absent-minded, and looked again at the block of wood. Then as Mrs Anderson gradually got Georgie out of the passway toward the outside door, she moved a step nearer Gertie. 'You did that, I believe,' and when Gertie had nodded, she said, 'You must finish it, make something fine and beautiful.'

'A graven image?' the Negro woman was asking, drinking coffee, her face somehow the face of Peter exploring the wounds of Christ.

'Not a graven image, Johala,' the other said, 'but just a thing of beauty in this ugly world. Isn't that right?' and she turned to Gertie.

Gertie flushed. 'I don't know nothen about things like that. Mostly—well, mostly I jist like tu whittle.'

The gospel woman had listened closely to the halting words, and waited a moment, still listening, as if she hoped there would be more. But Gertie turned toward the wood, and Johala spoke politely, but with a hint of impatience: 'Mrs Mac—Bales, Floyd's waiting over on that through street. He might get a ticket.'

'That would be interesting,' the gospel woman said, listening to Mrs Anderson, who was explaining somewhat guiltily to Sophronie that she'd decided to take Judy home and feed her, though it was still almost an hour ahead of schedule.

'Did you ever try feeding a child when it was hungry? Breast fed?' Mrs Bales came closer and smiled at the hungry Judy.

Mrs Anderson looked horrified, 'Oh, no, all pediatricians know it's very detrimental to a child's emotional and social development to breast feed it after it's six months old. They gain much faster on formula.'

'Really?' Mrs Bales said, beginning to draw on her boots.

Sophronie draped her robe more tightly about her bony hips, picked up Gertie's rope-tied carton of bed clothing, and said to the coatless Wheateye, 'Git, honey.'

Mrs Anderson, with the hungry Judy screaming and gnawing her shoulder, was stalled on Max's steps because Georgie, good-humored now, had threatened to get mad again if his mother didn't stand and watch him be a snow plow. She looked enviously toward the thin Sophronie and her thin child, and said to Gertie, who was coming down the steps with the block of wood: 'If I let Georgie run around in this weather without a coat, he'd be hospitalized for a week. Her children are almost never sick, but they've never heard of cod-liver oil or vitamin pills,' and she gave a puzzled headshake.

Mrs Bales, walking ahead, smiled over her shoulder. 'Neither did Paul nor Thomas Jefferson. Goodbye, my dear; things will get easier.' She turned to Gertie. 'Thank you again. Search on and you will find—' They had covered the few steps to Gertie's walk when Mrs Bales stopped. She glanced uneasily toward Johala, who had also stopped and was waiting with the polite but impatient air of a busy woman forced to spend time at some foolish party. 'A face,' Mrs Bales went on, touching the block of wood, 'the perfect face. The top of the head, and the hair, the way it swirls, they're beautiful,' and she stood on tiptoe in order to see the top of the head again. She asked, without looking away: 'Did you see it, Johala? Did you see?'

Johala nodded, searching Gertie's face, 'Christ?'

Gertie nodded. 'I've allus kind a hoped so—but I cain't seem tu find a face.'

'Maybe,' Johala said, and she was smiling a little, 'you'll find it in Detroit. In Detroit there are many Christs.'

238

'Seems like they're all dead an hung on crosses,' Gertie said.

'I guess it's easier to live with a dead Christ,' Johala said.

Mrs Bates protested. 'Oh, Johala, Christ is alive. He is risen. His spirit struggles continually in Satan's world.'

'Yes'm,' the dark woman said, and moved on down the walk, for Georgie, plowing snow in her direction, was flinging the dirty snow onto her boots.

16

Saturday again, and all morning the alley had been first a knocking and then a reaching hand, cupped for the down-dropping silver, thumb and fingers reaching for the bills. Silver enough she had had for Casimir the ice-man and for the paper boy who collected each Saturday. Six loaves she had asked of the bakery man, wondering if only that much bread would run them till Monday, but still the dollar bill had been too little and she must break another. The milkman came with his milk and his bill for the seventy quarts they'd used since the Saturday two weeks back. She had held out to him a ten and a five, her lips moving over the figures; two ones and forty cents would be left in change. She had questioned with her eyes, opened her mouth to protest when instead of the forty cents there were two pennies. She remembered the sales tax. She was always forgetting the sales tax. Enough to have bought two more quarts of milk, and there was never enough for milk-hungry Reuben.

In between there'd been the peddlers and the children. 'Lady, any small children in the home?' An older woman shoved sample pictures into her face. 'Large photographs or postcard size for the father in the service. No? Friends back home, then? Remember them with a picture of loved ones.' She had hurried away after Gertie's three headshakes. Next came two little girls giggling with shyness, 'Lady, buy a chance on this beautiful radio. One punch, onli ten cents; git a box u candy, perhaps, even if yu don't gitu radio. Butcha can't lose, lady. Yu'll help u good sisters buy equipment fudu playroom.' There had come a boy thrusting a too bright wreath into her face. 'Why, lady,' when she had shaken her head, 'if I didn't tell yu it was paper, yu'd think um fresh frum u tree.'

Then came a man with a suitcase, opening the storm door and knocking on the inside door as if he owned the place. 'But I don't—' she began.

'Three sixty-five, Mrs Nevels, on your little account.' He came through the door and waved the card to remind her, the waiting cupped hand in his eyes. The suitcase was quickly opened on the floor, and more quickly still out came the purple curtains, the pink bedspreads, the flowered tablecloths, the towels, bathmats, pot holders, chenille rugs. They were a flood over the table, the chairs, and the board on which Gertie tried to iron, and over them the flood of words: 'Now, lady, any small thing for your home. Yu credit's good with us; so little, so little each week. Yu'll have more linens den u Hotel Statler an never know yu've spent a dime.'

Clytie heard and came running. She saw the length of blue-dotted ruffled curtains in his hands. 'Oh, Mom, they're prettier than th ones I was goen to order back home.'

The man seized more curtains, pink ones now. 'Just what the young lady needs for her bedroom; these flowers fudu kitchen; lace here fudu living room—dignity yet, but good.' He bent across the ironing board, looked up at Gertie, perspiring, backing away. 'Youse ez lucky, a chance like this on such a buy—pure cotton, regulation PY 47 goes on next week. No more cotton. Du navy's short on doilies. Yu gotta not git caught short.'

Gertie mumbled something about getting his money, and fled. His voice followed. 'Think a yu kids, lady. Kids gotta have curtains, rugs, bedspreads . . .'

Gertie closed the door behind her, and his voice and Clytie's voice were lost in the steel-mill sounds. She remembered, leaning against the door, breathing hard as if she had been running, that in this room there was no money. This was a kind of sanctuary, and often she fled to it. Victor and Max's bedroom was on the other side of the wall, and it was most always still of days except when Victor's radio played music, and though the music was different from any she had heard, she liked it. Here, too, was the block of wood. It stood on a chair because there was no room for it on the floor.

Cassie had wanted it in the room with the two little beds where she and Clytie slept, but Gertie had been unable to wedge it in.

She was smoothing the top of the head when Clytie came, begging for curtains at least for the living room, reminding her, 'Pop was quarrelen t'other night, sayen we was th onliest people in th alley 'thout curtains but Miz Anderson; an Georgie swings on hers.'

Gertie drew a deep breath. 'But they're so skimpy an flimsy—an they'll make th place seem littler. An all that money. Git that five-dollar bill from th high shelf. He'll have to have a down payment.'

Cytie said, 'Oh, goody,' and skipped away.

Gertie ironed again, but her thoughts wandered, as they so often did. She forgot, as she had forgotten many times since Clovis had brought her the always hot electric iron. She set it on the stove, and even bent to get the wood before she remembered.

She was in the middle of Clovis's good white shirt when there came another knocking. Too weary to walk round the board and open the door, she called the knocker in, though Clovis had warned her that in Detroit it was a dangerous thing to do. However, it was only Maggie Daly, holding out a box of Christmas cards, explaining she sold them to help the good sisters of Crimson Blood High buy batons for the class in baton twirling.

'Yu know you're gonna send cards to your folks back home,' Maggie said, spreading the cards on the table so that Gertie might buy without any interruption to the ironing, 'so buy these an help u good sisters.' And she showed cards with fat baby Christs that made Gertie think of the cur dog on her mother's rug. There were fat little angels that might have come from the ads for baby foods in the paper, and many prim-mouthed mothers of God, all blonde with the permanent-waved, neat-handed look of the women in the frozen-food ads. All seemed at least one heaven away from the tears and sweat and blood of the many childbirths and the work the Mother Mary had. Maggie was disappointed when in the end Gertie bought only three, and these, fat angels.

She ironed again, and not long after Sophronie came, whispering above her package-filled arms: 'Is your youngens all out a th way? I've got Santie Claus stuff—I meant to go to Max's, but Victor's home.'

242

'They're all out in th snow,' Gertie answered.

Sophronie turned and motioned with her head toward the battered car in the alley, then hurried across the kitchen, while a tall man, almost as tall and slim as Clovis, got out from the driver's seat. He loaded up with bundles, taking last from a box in the back a bottle of beer. 'Santa Claus,' he said, smiling as he came to the door, his voice soft and slow.

Gertie tried not to show the scorn she felt for such a foolish waste of money. A little stuff for Santa Claus, maybe, but not so much. Under the wrappings she caught glimpses of a sled, shiny contraptions on wheels, and boxes of all sizes. She saw on one the words *Hockey Skates,* and remembered with a twinge of guilt that Enoch had wished for just such skates. Amos would love a contraption on wheels. 'I ain't bought a thing,' she said, half defiantly, half apologetically to Sophronie as she helped her stow the stuff in the scant space under the bed in her room.

'You'd better be a layen it in,' Sophronie said. 'War's maken stuff so scarce they won't be nothen left by Christmas. Most a th stores'll let you have it on time, like clothes er anything else. An it's like Whit says, they ain't never little but onct.' The top fell off a flimsy cardboard box, and a tiny red cup rolled out. Sophronie reached for it with a worried, 'Oh, Lordy, I hope none uv em's lost,' and she opened the box to examine the set of dishes, little and dainty and red.

Even Gertie smiled on the little things. 'My Cassie'ud set a big dinner with them,' she said.

'You can git um in Hamtramck—two seventy-five. I allus, when I was a youngen, wanted a little set a dishes.' And she squatted a moment, staring at the cup, her usually expressionless eyes looking back at the little girl who had wanted dishes. She smiled up at Gertie and put the cup away. 'But we ginerly got our part a th cotton money along about Christmas, an by the time Pop paid up at th store they wasn't much left.'

'Hurry,' Whit called from the kitchen, 'they's a great swarm a youngens a comen this away. It's all right,' he called a moment later as the women hurried to hide the toys. 'They ain't a comen in. Looks like somebody's cleaned up ona Dalys, they're all a runnen in home. That biggest un's a bleeden some. Mebbe fer onct our kids didn't git th dirty end a th stick.'

The women came into the kitchen. Whit looked around from the door and smiled at Sophronie, satisfaction in his pale blue eyes. Gertie saw that two of his front teeth were broken, with only stumps remaining, and that running up from the broken teeth was a crooked scar, showing ugly across one temple, reaching up into his pale thin hair. Though she knew him to be younger than Clovis, his eyes looked old, holding something of the filmed and rheumy look of a very old man's eyes, but his laugh when he looked out the door again was young enough. 'It must ha been Claude Jean done it. He's a comen thisaway.'

Sophronie looked through the glass and gave a sharp gasp. 'They've hurt him agin. Look how he's a bleeden frum his mouth. Four a them, allus four a them on my two—an then th least uns clawen um while the big uns holds um.'

'Yeah. But recollect ours gits help sometimes.' Whit took a sip of beer, studied Claude Jean in the alley. 'He don't look like he'd got his feelens bruised up none.'

Gertie looked over their shoulders, but could not find Claude Jean or any of her own, for the alley seemed one churning, wriggling mass of children, tempted out on this warmish Saturday by the freshly fallen snow. She saw Georgie pulling his sled upside down. Following Georgie was a plumpish man in horn-rimmed spectacles and an overcoat, who at every step or so stooped, and with a quick furtive motion tried to put the sled right side up. The man always straightened quickly and stood helplessly watching each time his son turned and saw what he was trying to do, then stamped his foot and screamed.

A huddle of little girls was building a snow man across from Max's place who from their giggling squeals and cries loved the snowballs flung by little boys more than the snow man. Gertie wished that Cassie might be with them, laughing and squealing and hiding her face. She saw Cassie at last, but alone as always, running into the alley at the end by the railroad fence. She was not alone either, for in one mittened hand she held Callie Lou's hand, while with the other she caught up a handful of snow and tried to fling it into the witch child's face. She failed, but laughed and ducked her head when the other, using Cassie's hand, flung it back. Gertie smiled; she had suddenly realized that Callie Lou was one of the things she had missed in Detroit.

'Well, is he or ain't he a comen out?' Whit wanted to know.

Gertie realized that she and Cassie were about the only ones within sight of the Daly door who were not looking at it. Mr Anderson no longer seemed interested in righting the sled, but stared at the Daly door with the same look of all-consuming curiosity as must have been on the face of Lot's wife when she turned to watch the beginnings of the end of Gomorrah. Claude Jean, oblivious to the trickle of blood down his chin, stood at the end of the Meanwell sidewalk, watching, smiling a little, half afraid, but eager too.

He was joined in a moment by his older brother, Gilbert, only a year younger than Reuben but smaller, a tough and wiry child with hair the color of his pale skin, so that at a distance he seemed bald-headed, only now his head was splashed with crimson. Sophronie, seeing it, gave another low gasp, and pulled at the doorknob. Whit took another sip of beer and put his hand over hers as he said: 'You know better'n to go out an mix with them Dalys. Old man Daly,' he explained to Gertie, 'he's in good with th cops an th project manager.'

Sophronie blew a hard blast of smoke. 'Comen er goen he's allus got us. If'n our youngens gits help an licks his'n he'll go complainen to Mr Jergens—an Jergens threatened us last fall with eviction.'

'You didn't git a look at them two biggest Dalys,' Whit comforted Sophronie, but added, 'Some day, by God, me an you we're a goen to have us a little hole a our own, an they'll never be no more evictions.'

Sophronie took the bottle from him, took a long swallow, and handed it back, smiling. 'Whit, honey, th only hole a our own me an you'll have ull be in hell. Not six weeks after we're buried, no matter where it is—after we've got it paid fer with our insurance money—they'll come bulldozen that graveyard down fer a highway.'

'A factory site, you mean,' Whit said. 'Old man Flint'ull outlast me an bulldoze down my grave fer a coffin-maken factory.'

'He don't make coffins,' Sophronie said.

245

'He's put many a good man in one, though,' Whit said, and rubbed the pathway of the old wound across his cheek in a remembering, reflective sort of way. 'Old man Flint, he'll figger out a way so's a man when he drops dead can drop in a coffin on one end uv a 'sembly line an step right out in hell a shovelen coal on t'other end.' He squeezed his wife's hand over the doorknob. 'Don't worry none about old Jergens. He won't evict us no matter what that old communist says—we're both in defense.'

Sophronie, before he could finish, had begun an angry, troubled, sh-shushing. 'Now, Whit, you know he ain't no communist. If,' she went on in her usual low tiptoeing sort of voice, 'Daly knowed you was a callen him that, he'd git us throwed out fer true.'

'Sophronie,' Whit said, sighing, then taking another sip of beer, 'I wisht you'd git over bein so skeered. None a old man Flint's protection men is around a listenen.' He looked at Gertie, tapped his wife gently on the shoulder. 'She made me lose a job onct—back inu depression—frum talken in a store. But she couldn't hep it none. She didn't know they was a Flint man, one a them paid to listen an tell, right behind her.'

'Aw, Whit,' Sophronie said, looking ever more worried, throwing a quick, suspicious glance at Gertie, 'you oughtn't to say—'

'I ain't said a thing about nobody,' Whit said, looking out the door again. 'Sure, sure, Daly, he don't love communism no more. He ain't a bit like a guy I know wot left his wife. Allatime this guy goes around tellen wot a bad woman she was so's he can be certain he done th right thing an don't love her no more.'

'Emotionally involved?' Gertie said, then flushing, tramped on her tongue with her teeth. She was unable to explain to the startled, puzzled Whit that the words of the gospel woman had been running in her head for days, the way the Bible did or a piece of poetry. All the new Detroit words—adjustment, down payment, and now Whit's eviction and communism—would get into her head and swim round for days until she got them fastened down just right so that they lay there, handy to her thinking; like the stars when she looked at them told her the heavens declared the—

There was a sharp rise in the chorus of screams and cries from the alley. Gertie saw three of the smaller Dalys rush out of their kitchen and climb onto their coalshed as if to be prepared with a grandstand seat for some coming spectacle. Wheateye, holding a turnip by its top, peeling it with her teeth, jumped up and down on the Meanwell coalshed, and in between times screaming at the Dalys: 'Mother suckers, mother suckers; that's yer brothers, allus runnen home to yu old man. Why ain'tcha old man a comen out? Where's yu big-mouthed old man? He's drunk an inu jail, yah, yah. My brothers licked yer brothers, all yer loud-mouthed brothers. Christopher, Joseph, James, an John, Patrick, Michael, Francis, an Tom. Claude Jean an Gilbert, they licked um all. Mother suckers. Mother suckers.'

Hurling back Wheateye's words as if they had been balls were the little Dalys and the Bommaritas. 'Liar, liar, liar, hillbilly. Yu mom never had no shoes till yu come to Detroit. Yu mudder's a hillbilly son uv a bitch. Youse hillbillies come tu Detroit un Detroit wenttu hell. Waitansee, waitansee, hillbilly bigmouth whitehead, brother sucker, waitansee—'

'Them youngens. That Wheateye,' Whit said, looking at his daughter with a troubled headshake. 'Them bigger Dalys is up to somethen. Where's Gilbert?'

'He's baby setten, looks like,' Sophronie said, nodding toward Gilbert. He was strolling past Max's unit, eating a turnip with one hand, holding on his hip with the other the smaller of the two Japanese children.

'Yeah?' Whit said, looking again toward the Daly door. 'Looks like yer kids is into it, too,' he said to Gertie, satisfaction in his voice.

Gertie saw Enoch and Mike Turbovitch with Amos tagging at their heels. They walked slowly and proudly up the alley, conscious of the watching eyes. They passed the Daly coalhouse where the little Dalys were now mixing snowballs with the screams they flung at Wheateye. Enoch strutted yet more proudly. 'We licked yer big brothers, made em run to their mama.'

'Dat's wot youse tink,' the grape giver cried, flinging soft snow into Enoch's uplifted face, while another, even smaller, threw a tin can which he seemed to have been saving just for this.

'Run kids, run. Double, double cross. Run, Claude Jean. They're loaded down with icicles. Yu cain't fight um now. Run.' It was

Gilbert, who had run around the end unit, peeked, and run back again. 'Run. We cain't fight; we're all out a ammunition.' Gilbert smiled at the child, offering it a bite of turnip. When it refused, he took a large bite himself, and stood chewing, smiling at the little child like one who has lost all interest in fights and fighting.

Claude Jean and Mike disappeared around the unit at the further end of the building. Enoch, however, paused long enough to pick up the tin can and throw it back at the little Dalys.

He whirled to run after Claude Jean and Mike, but turned just in time to catch a hard thrown icy ball full in his face. Another, from the opposite direction, hit his shoulder. Gilbert cried, strangling on the turnip: 'They've gotcha cornered, kid. Git in frontaya door. Git atcha door. They'll kill yu.'

Enoch grabbed desperately for a handful of snow. But balls from every direction hit him—head, shoulders, and stomach. Bending low with his arms about his head and blood trickling down his chin, he dashed behind the Meanwell coalhouse. Gertie heard the cry, 'We've got um,' and saw three boys, all bigger than Enoch, running toward him across her walk. Gilbert, still chewing, holding the baby, warned: 'Don'tcha throw at me. Yu'll kill this kid.'

Cassie, whimpering with fright, ran up the steps and clawed at the storm door. Gertie started to open it, but Whit caught her hand and hung on with a grip surprisingly strong for such an old-looking man. 'Don'tcha start mixen in th kids' quarrels. Old man Daly'ull call th cops. An if it comes to callen th cops, let it be you.'

'I cain't stand an see em half killed,' Gertie cried. She shoved open the storm door and jerked Cassie inside just as a snowball whizzed past her outthrust head. She called to Enoch, but he, with a yelp of pain, and blood, looked like, running all over his head, jumped hard against the storm door and slammed it shut.

Gertie, still calling to Enoch, pushing on the door, stared through the glass. A second ago a Daly had been running across her walk with Gilbert watching, smiling a little as he patted the child. Gilbert was still smiling, but the Daly had gone sprawling hard onto the cement, like a galloping colt stepped into a sinkhole. Chris Daly was screaming. 'Yu tripped Mike, yu dirty bastard.'

248

'Oh, yeah?' Gilbert said, smiling down at Mike, writhing in pain. His smile widened when a tin can, thrown by the 'Oh, Lordy, Lordy,' crying Wheateye, hit the struggling Mike on the head.

Gertie still fought to get the storm door open. But Enoch continued to shove his shoulders hard against it, though it seemed to Gertie that all the Dalys, armed with chunks of icicles as well as snowballs, were charging upon him. The back of Enoch's head was pressed against the glass, and past it she saw one of the bigger Dalys spring to her bottom step. She saw the lifted arm and the red-lashed eyes consider the pane of glass behind Enoch. Enoch hurled an icicle. The Daly ball came hard, aimed for his head. Enoch ducked, and the ball landed in a shower of glass on the kitchen floor.

Gilbert, Wheateye, Claude Jean, Mike Turbovitch, and many of the neutrals began screaming: 'Call a cops. Call a cops. Kids breaken winders.'

Then all their crying seemed no more than a summer's breeze in pines when Max's door was flung open, and Victor boomed: 'I gotta sleep. Git home. I call a cops.'

There was at once quietness enough that Wheateye, now on Gertie's coalhouse, could explain, screaming: 'Timothy Daly broke out Miz Nevels' door light. Joseph tore down Miz Nevels' door an beat up on that little bitsy Nevels' girl.'

Complete silence fell in the alley when the Daly door opened. Wheateye, whose legs were nimble as her tongue, had leaped from the coalhouse and run toward the Daly walk the instant the door started opening. Like most of the others, she sighed with disappointment when, instead of Mr Daly, only Mrs Daly came out. She was clean and neat in her churchgoing clothes, with a boot in her hand as if interrupted in preparations for going out. She came on down the steps, and began a troubled looking about for her own when Wheateye began her screaming explanation. 'Miz Daly, Miz Daly, Timmy's busted th Nevels' door an beat up on that little bitsy girl. She was all bloody, awful bloody, when her mommie carried her in. I seed her. Lookut, lookut their door.'

So convincing was Wheateye's voice that Gertie gave a swift, searching glance at the unmarked Cassie, and Sophronie sighed, 'Them youngens, I allus dread th days when they ain't no school.'

Mrs Daly looked toward the broken door, but said nothing as the children, gathering round her steps in an ever thickening circle, chorused: 'Timmy done it. Timmy done it.'

And Timmy, defiant, shouted, 'Gilbert tripped Mike. They started it.'

'I ain't done nothen,' Gilbert cried. 'I'm a tenden to this kid.'

'Yu did trip me, yu dirty lyen son uv a bitch,' Mike, blood-smeared and limping, cried.

'Go crap on yu mama's neck,' Gilbert said, while Wheateye, seeing her father half in, half out of Gertie's storm door, ran toward it, chanting, 'Mike Daly broke out Miz Nevels' winder light an scooted up ina snow an bloodied his head an broke his leg an blames it all on Gilbert.'

Whit turned, picked up his empty beer bottle, shook his head. 'Them Dalys; their kids never does nothen. If'n one a our'n had broke their winder, they'd already be on their way to tell th office.'

Sophronie looked worried. 'Now, don't go a starten nothen. Mebbe they all need lickens but they've been hurt enough.' She turned to Gertie, sighing. 'Pore things, I want um tu have a good Christmas an as good a time as they can. Did I tell ye? That school nurse said they had bad tonsils, so's last week we carried um to th doctor an he said their tonsils all had tu come out. He'll do it Christmas vacation.' She shivered. 'I wisht it was me.'

'If it was jist you,' Whit said, 'jist one, that ole Doc Edwards couldn't finish payen fer his wife's mink coat.'

'It ain't like we didn't have hospitalization,' Sophronie said.

'No,' Whit said, 'that ole doc knows he is guaranteed his fifty a tonsil, cash on th line,' and he smiled at Gertie, fingering his scar as if the scar and the three operations were all one great big joke, funny still though on him.

'Git,' Sophronie said, pushing him toward the door. 'I've gotta hurry er I'll be late fer my merry-go-round, an if I don't git them kids fed an off to a movie they'll have another fight.' She had reached the bottom step, but turned, calling to Gertie: 'If your youngens are goen to th movies, they can go with mine. It jist a little piece, no through street but th one here, an I watch um acrost that. Jist twenty cents an it'ull keep em out a meanness till dark—an ginerly they like it.'

'No,' Gertie said, her mouth a firm line. 'I hadn't figgered on senden em.'

However, Enoch, just coming into the kitchen, heard, and at once began begging for all the alley to hear: 'Lemme go, Mom, lemme go. We're th onliest young—kids never sees movies.'

Gertie closed the door and looked at him. There was blood on his forehead, a bruise on his cheek, a swollen lip, a tear in his trouser leg, and a missing mitten. He stood an instant looking at her, gritting his teeth to keep from cying, then whirled away toward the bathroom. She called him back. 'I know it wasn't all your fault, son, but—you wasn't fighten fair. You was throwen ice like them. One a you could ha had a eye put out. An you didn't try to git inside. You stood by that door, a daren em, you might say, to throw. An I'm pretty certain I seen Gilbert trip that other'n. "Do unto others as . . ."'

'That don't work with them Dalys in this alley, Mom. One a them, he tried to git me in trouble. Out in th parken lot he got right in front uv a car an yelled at me, "Throw yu . . ." He called me a mighty dirty name, an I would ha throwed at him an broke that car winder, not thinken, if Gilbert hadn't grabbed my arm. "He's a tryen to git you in trouble so's he can call th cops." Gilbert, he says.'

'But son . . .'

'Now, Callie Lou, you gotta help sing; come on, Callie Lou—your voice is pretty like your hair.' And Cassie's thin trilling of 'Away in a Manger' came from the room with the block of wood.

Enoch frowned. 'Mom, you gotta make her quit that, talken to herself thataway. Some a th kids is a sayen she's cuckoo.'

'Cuckoo?'

'Yeah.' He tapped his head. 'You know, goofy in th bean.'

Gertie studied him, looked at him so long and so hard that his, 'Mom, lemme go to th movies,' was hardly more than a whisper.

Enoch had disappeared into the bathroom, and Gertie was listening, smiling, to Cassie sing when Clytie and Reuben returned from Zadkiewicz's, where they had been for eggs and a few other groceries needed over the week end. Reuben stalked away to his room, and Clytie plopped the basket on the table so hard that Gertie trembled for the eggs. 'Mom, don't make me carry this old basket no more.

251

Some youngens called us hillbillies an throwed snowballs. I think they was tryen to git Reuben to fight so's they could all gang up an half kill him.'

'I don't guess they meant any harm,' Gertie said, and put the ironing board under Clytie's bed. She was just coming back into the kitchen when the door was pushed open, and there was Clovis, home from work, and it hardly noon.

The children began their chorus of, 'Pop's home, Pop's got home,' while Gertie studied him in swift, troubled glances. She saw no bandages, no flush of fever to betoken accident or sickness, and though he looked more foolish and angry than sick, she asked, unable to think of any better question, 'You sick?'

'Do I look sick,' he asked, short-worded and surly, banging down his dinner bucket.

'But,' she went on, still more puzzled than angry when he offered no explanation, 'worken today would ha been time an a half fer overtime.'

'Do you recken I don't know that?' he yelled, all jangled up somehow, the way he often was when he got home from work, especially after a good-sized stretch on overtime. He had never used to be like that back home, even when a broken-down truck or flat tire made him past midnight coming in. Today he was angrier than she had ever seen him, and she remained silent, fiddling about the dinner getting to cover up her worry until he said at last, 'It was a walk out.'

'Walk out? What's that?'

'Everbody walks off the job. You gotta walk with em. What else could it be?'

The anger for something or somebody that had been kept shut down and still back there among the men flamed up now against her; when Enoch had a tough time in the alley he was sassier when he got home to her. 'It's kinda like a wildcat, I recken,' he continued, turning now to the puzzled children. 'They had one in th axle division day afore yesterday, but that didn't bother us none—somethen about a steward on the grievance committee was what caused it today.'

'What's that, this committee?' she said, for he seemed less angry now.

'Gert, darn it.' He flared up again. 'I didn't make the union— I pay dues, that's all I know. I heard em a talken. This steward, he beefed—complained—said overtime wasn't bein give out fair er somethen. He must ha had a kind a fight er somethen—I wouldn't know—he done enough th company laid him off fer three days fer a—a "disciplinary measure"—that's what they call it. So's this parts division I'm a machine repairer in had a walkout in sympathy.'

Gertie had opened the lunch box. Maybe she could eat the stuff for her own dinner, and save what would have been wasted food. 'But—Clovis.' She didn't want to make him mad again, but still she had to know. 'When them others walked off, couldn't you ha stayed? You need th money, an th war needs whatever it is you all are maken an . . .'

She stopped in the face of his angry, jeering glance. 'You want me to come home with a busted nose? When them others walk—you gotta walk.'

Enoch nodded wisely. 'Mike Turbovitch's mama, she works in a tire-maken place; they hadda walkout, an some didn't want a go, an boy, he said she said you oughta seen what they done to one a them that got sassy an . . .'

But Clovis had for the first time noticed Enoch's face. 'What in th dickens happened to you? Fighten again? You youngens has got to learn to git along without allus fighten.'

'Them Dalys started it,' Enoch said, beginning all at once to cry. He continued to sob as he went on: 'Me an the Meanwells an Mike Turbovitch an two a them little Miller kids was a playen peaceable on our hockey pond that we'd swept off ourselves. Them Dalys an that Bommarita kid, they come an grabbed our hockey sticks an called us names an started th hard snowballen. Pop, is a Protestant a heathen?'

'You know better'n that,' Clovis cried. 'It's th Catholics that's th heathen, a worshipen idols an th pope—an they know it. That's why they're allus a throwen off on people like us. That's why they hate us; we ain't—'

'Aw, Clovis,' Gertie began, 'not all—'

'How would you know, woman?' Clovis asked, his eyes blazing. 'You never have to git out an work with em, hear em talk about hillbillies.'

253

Gertie's anger shook her like a wind. 'You know I'd hunt a factory job in a minute, but you won't hear to it. I bet I could make mighty nigh—'

'Now, Gert,' Clovis said, soothing now, for more than once she had hinted at the possibilities of her getting a factory job, though the mere mention of it always angered Clovis. The anger always, like now, gave way to calm reasoning. He reminded her that she was too big for the factory machinery, set up for little slim women like Sophronie, and also that she was so given to wool gathering she might get a hand or her head smashed the first day. He gave his usual arguments, then shifted the subject back to Enoch, warning: 'But don't go around talken agin Catholics in this town. It'll git you in trouble quicker'n anything—they's Catholics ever whichaway, seems like. If a body went around talken agin priests an sich, they'd be called a commie.'

'What's that?' Enoch demanded.

Clovis turned toward the door. 'A red, I recken, but whatever it is you gotta learn to keep shut. Quit asken so many questions. You'll git in trouble.'

Gertie turned on him. 'Aw, Clovis, it ain't good fer people to go a bottlen their selves up thataway.' Her voice was like a cry as she went on: ' "I charge thee in th sight of God and of Christ Jesus—preach the word; be urgent in season, out of season, reprove, rebuke, exhort . . . " '

'If I recollect my preachers right, Paul said that,' Clovis said, smiling at her as if she had been a child.

She nodded, conscious that Enoch and Clytie smiled as their father smiled.

'You know,' Clovis went on, still smiling, 'what happened to Paul—an anyhow, he didn't have no family. Not even Jesus Christ had to put up with a Catholic foreman on one side, a yellen for you to go faster, an a Catholic steward a tellen you they's no need to break your neck a repairen a machine, that a minute's rest won't kill the tender.' He turned to Enoch. 'I wish you could ha heared a tool-an-die man Whit knows a talken onct. They'd had a big fist fight in th parts presses where I'm at. "Rabbits gits along," he says. They cain't fight. They don't run as fast as a heap a animals, an everthing on earth, frum birds to men with guns, is after them, but they keep fat an raise families."' And he stopped and looked at Enoch, asking, 'Why?' And when Enoch could not answer, he went on. 'They never make no noise till you kill em, an then jist one little squeak.'

He was through the door, calling over his shoulder, 'Miller down here's been a plaguen me to look at his car—idles too fast.'

They were just sitting down to a noonday snack when there came another knocking. Clytie sprang to answer with a guilty, confused air strange for Clytie. Gertie, trapped between the opened door and Enoch's chair, heard soft murmurings of girlish voices, and called as she would have called at home, 'Clytie, if it's company you've got, bring her in.' By bending over Enoch's chair and craning her head she was able to see on the stoop a blue-jeaned, short-coated, bare-headed, but warm-looking girl. Gertie was for an instant puzzled: so little clothing, so much warmth. She realized it was the red, curling hair falling past the girl's shoulders, a frame for red-brown eyes and red cheeks.

The girl smiled at her, looked at Clytie, giggled, and then said to Clytie, 'G'wan, ast her, cain'tcha?' And when Clytie only flushed and stammered, the girl drew a deep breath, and turned to Gertie again. 'Can Clytie go to th movies with me? Mom lets me go ever Saturday afternoon—if I help clean house ina morning an go to Sunday school on Sunday.'

Clytie's eyes were pleading as she stepped back in the shelter of the door and begged, whispering, so that the girl could not hear: 'Please, Mom, please, this onct. Mom—you don't know how it is. T'other day some a th girls at school was wonderen if Rita Gaynor had actually got a divorce from Bob Faith, he's her third husband. An I ast who she was, an they laughed at me.' She choked. 'You don't know—I could baby-sit an make money.'

'Can he go, Miz Nevels? They's gonna be a Western.' It was Claude Jean in a fresh, unbloodied shirt.

Enoch, unable to get out of his chair, was bouncing beneath the listening Gertie. 'She's goen to let us go.' Even surly Reuben was looking up from his plate, interested.

Gertie looked hopelessly about her. What would they do all afternoon, drive her crazy with the radio and quarreling in the house, or play and fight in the dirty alley? She shook her head wearily as she went for money. Did she want to be shet of her children, or was it that Clytie made her remember how it was to sit with company in her mother's parlor when the preachers came and they talked of God. She had sat in sweating misery, the only one a stranger to her mother's Christ the others knew so well. Maybe it was, for Clytie, equal misery to be the only one not knowing Rita Gaynor.

17

Gertie, busied with the tricky job of getting the part in Clytie's hair exactly straight, heard Cassie's laughter from the boys' bedroom, then her low toned chuckling talk. 'Oh, Callie Lou, look what my boot has went an done. Did you ever see such boots, Callie Lou, eaten my shoes this away?' Another boot went on amid more laughter, and then her booted feet were skipping over the floor.

'Mom, I wisht you'd make her quit talken to herself that away; th kids'ull laugh at her.' Clytie, without waiting for Gertie's opinion, lifted her voice in scolding: 'Quit that silly talken to yerself, Cassie Marie, an hurry an git th rest a yer clothes on. You'll make me late waiten fer you.'

'I ain't a talken to myself, an I don't need you to take me to school never no more.' A moment later Cassie came running through the passway, capless and mittenless. It was only when she held the door open, carefully, so that someone smaller than she might pass through that Gertie caught up with her. She was impatiently wigglesome while her mother pulled the snowsuit hood from under the back of the suit, found one mitten in a pocket, and shoved one bare hand, holding Gertie's little whittled hen, into the other pocket.

Gertie stood in the open storm door and watched her go. The bare hand holding the hen was out again, and under the muffled roar of the steel mill she heard: 'Run fast, Callie Lou, an you won't git so cold. Look at yer breath, Callie Lou. It's a cloud, a pure white cloud fallen down on you like Chicken Little. Hurry, mebbe we'll find that nice bubble-gum boy.' She was looking at the witch child instead of where she went, and bumped hard into a girl in a white scarf, hurrying in the opposite direction. The chicken flew from her hand, and Cassie fell face down in the icy alley.

Gertie ran out, but the bigger girl had already picked her up, and was brushing her off, murmuring, ashamed of having hurt a little one, 'I'm awful sorry.'

It was Maggie Daly. Gertie, remembering the fighting in the alley, was silent as she wiped Cassie's face and then the hen with a corner of her apron. But Maggie smiled, friendly as ever, and seeing the hen, cried, 'Lemme see,' and held out her hand. 'It's a chickun. I seen one once at u zoo. I like it better than a toy chickun Mom got for Santa.' She remembered Cassie. 'Got for Jimmy's birthday, I mean. He's plastic. Yu squash um down an u egg comes out. Where'dju buy this?'

'I whittled it.'

'Whittled?'

'Yes, took a knife an cut it out a wood.'

Maggie looked from the hen to her in wonder. 'Yu mean, yu made it?'

Gertie nodded, aware that Mr Anderson, who she had noticed left for work in suit clothes about the time the children went to school, was on his steps, listening and craning his head to see the hen. Their eyes met. He smiled, lifted his hat, and came on into the alley. His voice matched his neat clothing and hair when he said, 'You're Mrs Nevels, our new neighbor, I believe.'

She nodded.

'I'm Mr Anderson, from Indiana—an Indiana farm boy, like my wife.' He disregarded Maggie's giggle, but went on with the same look in his eyes her mother used to have when she would count the chickens over and over because she couldn't be certain whether one was missing or not, 'And you, I believe, are from Kentucky?'

She nodded.

'Your husband worked in a factory before he came up here?'

She shook her head.

'What part of Kentucky are you from, may I ask?'

'About th middle.'

'I mean, are you from the hills—the southern Appalachians?'

258

'I wouldn't know,' she said. He made her think a little of the man with the star. No, more like Maggie's Virgin Marys, smooth, with his neat shaven face, his cheeks rosy and plump below a high palish forehead, balding back into smooth, yellowish, oily-looking hair.

'I mean,' he was saying, vexation struggling with the chicken counting look in his pale blue, slightly bulging eyes, as if one chicken were missing, 'Are you from east or west Kentucky?'

She considered. 'I'd say about th middle.'

Two chickens were gone now, and he was vexed. 'But is it hilly?'

'Kentucky, th part I seen on th train, is pretty well hills all across—little hills, I mean.' She gave Cassie a little push. 'Run along, honey. Them safety boys'ull be gone an you cain't cross the streets.' Already the alley was empty of children except for Reuben, who always left last and walked slowly like a tired man going to a hated job. Cassie started away, but stopped and looked uncertainly at her mother when the man reached one pinky white hand for the hen, saying:

'May I see this pretty little thing? Mrs Ander—Lena said you carved.' He studied the hen, turning it over and over, until Gertie, embarrassed, said:

'It's jist some whittlen foolishness I made. An when th youngens wanted something fer to sell at the mothers' club sale at school I sent it. I figgered somebody might pay fifty cents—if anybody comes that likes sich tricks.'

Homer considered an instant longer. 'I'll give you a dollar for it,' he said. 'It will make an interesting conversation piece for my desk.' He reached into the breast pocket of his dark blue coat and drew out a wallet. From it he took a dollar bill and handed it to her, easy, as if money for foolishness grew on trees.

Gertie was conscious of Cassie's troubled eyes on the hen that had been meant for Miss Vashinski. 'You've already took her th jumpen-jack doll, and I'll git some cookies er somethin,' she promised as Cassie scuttled away.

'It's nice to have met you,' Homer said, lifting his hat as he turned back toward his doorway. Mrs Anderson, with the screaming Judy on her arm, had called to remind him that he'd be late for work. She, too, noticed the hen, and asked for a closer look. Homer handed it to her, frowning at the baby as he did so. 'Please, dear, must you spoil her? She must learn to cry it out.'

'But if she cries too long before feeding time, she burps so,' Mrs Anderson said, looking at the hen, her glance pleased and warm.

Maggie giggled. 'You two oughta git together. Mrs Anderson paints pitchers.'

Mrs Anderson gave Homer a quick, daggerish kind of look as she shifted the baby to her other arm. 'Not any more. There just isn't time or space—here.'

'Don't quit,' Gertie said, troubled by the woman's despair. 'Everybody needs a little foolishness a some kind.'

'My painting,' Mrs Anderson said in a low, tight voice, 'wasn't exactly foolishness.' The last word was almost drowned in a mighty banging clumping. She whirled back into the kitchen crying: 'Please, Georgie, don't—do let the ironing board stand up. Mother must iron.'

Gertie took advantage of the commotion to hurry home. Amos was alone. He might be sticking nails in the wall sockets or trying to light the gas or burning papers in the flame of the gas hot-water heater.

However, Amos was safe in his favorite refuge, the bathroom. There he never tired of running water into the washbasin and sailing the two wooden boats she had made for him, or of flushing the toilet, then leaning, elbows on the toilet seat and watching the water swirl in and out. Then, like one who has achieved great things, he laughed each time he heard the mysterious glug. He was bleached out and thinner than he had used to be. This morning he showed no sign of wanting breakfast, so Gertie suggested, as she often did when it was not too cold, that he play outside awhile like Enoch. But Amos only shook his head as he listened to the gurgle of the filling water closet.

She stood in the narrow space left from the shower, the hot-water heater, and other trappings of the bathroom, and studied him. She asked after a moment, 'Amos, honey, you recollect back home?'

'Huh?'

'You recollect back home, th trees, an runnen through th woods with Gyp, an a runnen down th hill to th spring.'

He finally lifted his head from the toilet and looked at her. 'Mom, Pop's goen to show me a boat, a great big boat, a real live boat on a heap a water.'

'You recollect Gyp?'

A train blew, sharp, hard jabs of sound followed by the roaring rush that rattled the windows and set the house atremble. Amos listened, smiling; and when the sound had swept on, he said, 'That train carries people.'

'You're a learnen your trains, son,' she said, and turned away.

She was picking up the ruckus left by the whirlwind rising and going out of the children when someone knocked. It was Maggie with the two least Dalys and a small paper-wrapped bundle. 'Are you awful busy?' she asked, smiling, taking her welcome for granted as she slid the children from her arms.

'Yes an no,' Gertie said. 'I'm in th worst kind a business—a tryen to make up my mind.' She fingered Mr Anderson's dollar bill in her apron pocket. 'This dollar frum th little hen belongs by rights to th school fer th money-raisen sale. Enoch an Clytie wanted to take cookies like th other youngens, but me an that stove ain't learned to git along. I'm a haten th thought a tryen to bake em, so that I've might nigh give in to tryen to buy um frum that—'

'Mr Zadkiewicz,' Maggie said. 'Th easiest way to manage him, Mama's found out, is to send all yu kids at once. He hates kids allatime messing around, specially little ones. He'll sell um anything he's got if enough goes, an yu know, pulls down stuff inu shelves. When our father's out a cigarettes, Mama sends um all but me. They tell him they can't go home without cigarettes. They hang around awhile, an pretty soon he finds some. I could go buy yu some cookies,' she went on. 'Mama hadda go out, an I hadda stay home with th little kids. For the dollar you could buy more'n three dozen plain sugar cookies. They'd look home baked.'

Gertie pondered. 'I mebbe ought to make em.' She looked uneasily at the stove.

'I could make um,' Maggie offered. 'It's not such a job. We could chill the dough in Mrs Bommarita's icebox and borrow

Mrs Schultz's cookie press. And I'll bet Mrs Anderson's got a lot a currants and raisins and stuff left from her fruit cake; they'd do for decoration. She loves to loan things on account u it gives her u excuse to ask questions for Homer. If you gotta buy sugar yu could git a stamp from Mrs Miller, on account u she works an her kids is so little she don't use all her ration points.'

'Mebbe,' Gertie said, 'we'd better jist buy um, but I'll go. Yer mama—'

'She wouldn't mind,' Maggie said. 'And p'raps while I'm gone yu could git a line on how to help St Francis. When I seen how good yu carved th little chickun, I thoughtcha might fix him.' She unwrapped the parcel, explaining: 'I saved his pieces, but du kids got into um un broke um up. John, don't take th woman's icebox bottom off. She won't like it. But Mom always liked um, so I saved um.'

John, somewhere between two and three, looked over his shoulder at his sister, then turned again to his job of taking out the little swinging piece of cardboard that hid the drip pan. Gertie examined St Francis, smiling a little at him or at what part of him was left. Whoever had whittled him had done a pretty good job, and used good wood, dark and fine-grained as the best black walnut root. His face, thin with wrinkles down the cheeks, made her think of Uncle John back home. She liked his high balding forehead, and his beard, long like that of old Amos. One hand was still safely laid against his bosom, but the other, that must have been lifted like that of a preacher giving benediction, was gone; and his legs were broken off at about the knees, she thought. It was hard to say, for, like the blue china doll in Max's house, he was draped in a long robe. 'How was his feet, honey?' she asked.

'He wore sandals that showed his toes; yu know, th way th saints do allatime. Butcha could make um barefooted; or if feet's too much trouble just let his robe fall down. Mostly I want him so's he'll stand up. And his hand—do yu think yukun fix his hand? He was blessing u birds, yu know. He had two birds, but Chris shot um with his BB gun.'

'I can fix him a hand easy. He's got one left to go by. But his feet? They'd look, I recken, like th ones next door.'

262

'Oh, no, no, not like that Polish stuff,' Maggie cried, turning toward the door. 'Lemme go git th blessed Virgin.'

While she was gone, and the children busied themselves with the icebox, Gertie went into her bedroom and got a narrow, slightly crooked, but thick little board of good black walnut. Back home she had saved it for years against the day when she might want some of it for buttons or the legs of a low three-legged stool she had always aimed to make. She had, when leaving, nailed it onto a crate, planning still on a little stool with legs carved prettily.

She was sawing off the needed piece when Maggie came running back with a china doll with a golden crown and a long robe falling past her feet. 'Like this,' Maggie said. Gertie paused in her sawing to study the figure, frowning a little. 'Ain't she pretty?' Maggie asked.

'Yes—but—'

'Don'tcha like her?'

Gertie finished the cut, put the saw away, and considered, studying the figure. 'That's Mary, th mother of Jesus?'

'Of course. Isn't she beautiful?'

'She looks like them on th Christmas cards,' Gertie said, and added slowly, 'Th other Mary, she couldn't ha been beautiful—at least not much beautiful.' She nodded over the robe, covering the feet. 'She never could ha done her work in a long-tailed dress like that. She was a worken woman an allus a goen here an yonder, like into th desert to see her cousin.' She looked at the smooth face. 'She seen too much trouble to look that away.'

Maggie was both sorrowful and angry as she asked: 'And how would she look, an how would you know? She's always looked like this.'

Gertie smiled, sorry she had hurt the girl by talking out on such a trifling matter. 'Law, I don't know, honey. I figger,' she went on, bringing out her knife, 'Mary would look like—like your mother.'

'My mother!' Maggie's hurt changed into astonishment which in turn dissolved in giggles as she repeated, 'My mother?'

'They both seen a lot a trouble, had a heap a youngens, an worked hard,' Gertie said, annoyed by Maggie's giggles, but more with herself for letting her tongue run away. The most she'd seen of

Maggie's mother was angry eyes above a broom handle, but she did work hard and keep her children clean.

Maggie was still giggling when she left to get the cookies, and Gertie was left to wrestle with St Francis and the young children. The baby climbed on the table and helped himself to some gingerbread she had baked the night before. John soon got up from his seat by the icebox and said, 'Lookee,' and held out the drain-pan cover as if it had been a gift.

Gertie, unable to think of anything else, said, 'Thank you, honey,' and laid it on top of the icebox. John walked slowly around the kitchen, searching for something else loose. He found the swinging panel on the cook-stove below the oven door, and sat by it, working, until it too was off. Then, after finding the heating stove too hot for his work, he leaned on Gertie's knee and watched her whittle.

St Francis took kindly to the strange wood, and by the time Maggie came back with three bags of cookies Gertie had the rough work done on his missing knees and feet. These she planned to fasten to the saint in a jagged seam that, once glued and held awhile in a clamp, would seem no more than a lighter band of brown around the robe.

Maggie went home to get lunch. The time had passed so quickly that the part of the morning Gertie dreaded most had come and gone without her knowing it—the moment the mailman passed her door. She would hope up to the moment of his coming. Maybe somebody at home had written her a nice long letter telling about everything and everybody. Each time the mailman walked on, not even looking in her direction, the quick death of her hope would bring a sharp thrust of homesick loneliness that followed her some days for hours. She heard at times from her mother. The letters were long enough, but they dealt chiefly with her mother's health, and were filled with advice and comments on religion, politics, and the weather.

Today it was noon before she hardly knew it, and time to get Enoch in from his alley play. Cassie came from school, racing ahead of the others to tell her that in school Miss Vashinski had showed all the youngens the jumping-jack doll she had taken yesterday. Miss Vashinski had said it was beautiful, very beautiful, Cassie said; her words the same, her voice like Miss Vashinski's voice.

Clytie and Enoch were pleased with the cookies. But Reuben, sitting silent as usual, spooning up beans and onions and bread, shook his head. 'I don't want no cookies,' he said.

'But Reuben, don't you want tu take somethen fer th bake sale? It'd be like not taken er not buyen a pie at a pie supper back home,' Clytie said.

'It ain't like back home,' Reuben said, his voice husky with feeling. 'Back home they ain't no youngens to giggle ever time I say somethen, an they never was a teacher as hateful as Miz Whittle.'

'But you like some a th teachers,' Gertie said. 'I've heared you say so.'

'But I've got that ole Miz Whittle more'n any uv em,' Reuben said, looking at her with the half accusing, half contemptuous look that had been new the morning her mother came crying on the white saddle mule. But the look was old now.

Reuben was less surly when he came from school in the afternoon, though it was Enoch who came running first with the big news. He'd seen the jumping-jack doll on a table with fancy work when he went at noon recess. There'd been a two-fifty price tag on it. Two dollars and fifty cents for a piece of his mother's old whittling! He stared at her in mingled shock and admiration.

Then Clytie came excitedly, calling: 'Mom, Mom, guess who bought that jumping-jack doll? Mr Spyros, an did he ever like it. He showed it to us in art class.'

'Oh, Law,' Gertie said, remembering the little man. 'I wisht he'd got the hen. She was a heap nicer.'

'An you sold her for jist a dollar,' Enoch chided. 'That ole Homer sure made a fast buck on you, Mom.' The admiration in Enoch's voice was for Homer now.

Clytie flicked on the radio, and the tearful voice of Nella Nottingham filled the place. This pure, but muchly persecuted one was trying, as she had been trying for the past ten days, to prove that her murdering of a former suitor was a frame-up, framed by a former mother-in-law. Enoch's special friend, Mike Turbovitch, called him into the alley, and Amos and Cassie went, too.

The two younger ones, after playing for a little while in the snowy alley, came in, wet and bedraggled, tracking snow over the forever damp floor. Gertie mopped up the floor, and added their wet clothing to the perpetually drying row of snow-soaked mittens, scarves, jackets, and snowpants on the gas pipe across the kitchen. As always, the clothing forced her to be continually ducking her head as she went about the supper getting.

The steamy, nasty smell of the drying, half rotten reused wool mingled with the gas smell, the chlorine water smell, the supper-getting smell, and became one smell, a stink telling her it was the time of day she had learned to hate most. The time she had loved back home, the ending when the day was below her.

Stopping over the too low gas stove, frying strange fish she had bought because it was cheap and unrationed, turning it in the scant grease she had been able to spare, she saw herself back home. The red ball of the winter's sun was going down behind the hills across the river. The cedar trees above the creek whispered among themselves in a rising night wind. The new milk was cooling on the porch shelf. Reuben was in the barn, the younger ones bringing in the wood and water, while Clytie fried fresh pork shoulder in the kitchen. On the stove hearth was a big pan of baked sweet potatoes, and pulled back on the stove where they wouldn't burn was a skillet of freshmade hominy and another of late turnip greens. It had been a good fall for the turnips she had planted. She was cutting up the soap she'd made that day from the guts of her big fattened hog. Every once in a while she'd step off the porch and look a little south, but mostly west; that would be above her father's house, where the new moon showed first. She couldn't see the moon, not yet, it was too early.

'Mom, Mom, make Clytie lemme have my turn on th radio. It's time fer Crime Fighters.' It was Enoch just in from his alley play, bringing in more dirt.

'But I'm listenen fer current events now. I gotta fer school.'

'The fifty-third wiped out a tank battalion. The screaming enemy trapped in their exploding—' Gertie tried not to hear, but the voice demanded that she listen as it went on, drooly with horror, like the voice describing the murdered man Nella Nottingham found. The voice was happy over the fine dish of news to be served tonight, loving it like old Battle John Brand loved the hell he made flame in the meeting house. But Battle John's hell was down in the bowels of the earth, the other side of being dead.

'Mom, have I gotta listen to that stuff—th ole war?'

In turning toward the squabbling children, a damp snowpant leg struck her in the face, then slid with seeming slowness, though she was never able to grab it, on down into the skillet of fish. She jerked the snowpants off the fish with one hand, and though she hadn't meant to do it she slapped Enoch with the other. ' "Th ole war.' You're worse'n that fool on th radio. It's a war with men a dyen, not a circus. Now git frum under my feet.'

Enoch, certain that he would not again be slapped, began sniffling. 'But, Mom, what can I do? You won't let me play out late like the other youngens.'

'Quit sassen, and git into yer bedroom. Clytie'—she realized her voice was loud, almost a screaming—'turn that racket off. That man ud . . .'

A plane came over, drowning the happy, gloating voice. The plane, like the man's voice, the trains, the heat, the smelly sticking fish, the damp grease-gommed snowpants, seemed inside her, clawing through her head, tearing her into pieces with gripping, many-fingered hands. There came a loud quick knocking on the door, but when she opened it the stoop was empty. Enoch, standing by the heating stove, quarreled: 'It's them Dalys, Mom—a knocken an a runnen away. All th other kids is still out. Cain't I go back, Mom? It's early.'

'Shut up.' She heard the crash of glass on the snow-covered sidewalk—ketchup bottles, beer bottles, everything, glass they had broken on her sidewalk. Enoch, listening, nodded, the same satisfaction, she thought, in his face as was in the news teller's voice.

'Mom, lemme go clean it up before Pop gits home.'

'You'll jist start a fight,' she said. She pressed her eyes hard down into her hands for a moment's blackness, peace from the downbeating hard white light that seemed a part of the heat, the noise, the closeness. 'It's jist a excuse to go outside.' She realized she was doing wrong. She'd told him to stay inside. She ought to make him mind; she couldn't; she was too tired.

Clovis didn't come. The fish grew limp and greasy waiting in the oven. The slaw wilted in the bowl; there wasn't room in the icebox for it.

Amos whined about being hungry, messed around with some molasses and margarine, and would not touch the strange fish. Clytie, glued to the radio, something now about a robbery, wouldn't come to the table, saying she wanted to wait until her dad got home. Reuben came, but instead of eating the cooked supper he ate bread and milk. Gertie tried not to watch as he finished an almost full bottle of milk, but when he got up for more milk from the icebox words burst from her, sharp and hard and stingy. 'Reuben, cain't you eat th supper I've cooked? It'll be all to throw out. Tomorrow we'll be runnen out a milk, and th milkman won't be comen till Sunday.'

Reuben shut the icebox door, looked at her, the look she had come to know, and now, as always when it settled on his face, he tramped stonily away.

She called to him, trying to make herself sound like the mother he had thought she was when they worked in the corn together; 'Now, Reuben, come on back an finish yer supper. If'n you don't like this fish, you know you're welcome to anything they is. I jist thought . . .' What had she thought? to save on Reuben's food?

She heard laughter, whooping, with trash cans thumping in distant alleys, and went out onto the stoop to see about Enoch. In the shaft of light from the kitchen door she saw the broom fallen slantwise of the snowy steps, pieces of shattered glass, and what at first looked to be blood, but after stepping closer she saw it was a broken ketchup bottle; the Dalys. She called Enoch twice, but instead of Enoch, Clovis was saying from out the darkness, his voice tired, quarrelsome, the kind of voice he brought home most nights now, 'Gert, you oughtn't to be a letten th youngens out this time a night.'

'I let him out to clean off th walk,' she answered, somewhat shortly, trying not to remember, as always, and hold it against him, that it was he who made her live like this.

He swore, and said a Sue Annie word, a thing unusual for him, when he stepped into the ketchup and glass; then, hardly glancing at her as he went up the steps, he commanded her to find Enoch and make him clean the walk.

Gertie had come out without her coat, and after the hot steamy kitchen the cold was beginning to send shivers down between her shoulder blades. But she walked on, now and then calling Enoch, and glad, in spite of the cold, to be out of the house. The always red-tinged twilight was brightening into wavering flickers of red light that sharpened the rows of squat chimney tops between her and the crimson sky above the steel mill. Behind her the snowy roofs grew warmly pink, and it seemed as if the snow must melt, and the red falling flakes hiss as they disappeared into the black alley shadow. She reached an intersection of alleys where no houses blocked the view of the steel mill. She had learned by now that a brightening of the light meant that a pour was being made. She called Enoch again, and then, both fascinated and repelled by the red light boiling up into the sky, stood a moment watching.

A voice, strangely familiar, came out of the darkness in the next alley: 'I tink yu kid's wit da Meanwells watching u pour.' A black shape, seeming too tall, too wide to be a man, was like a thicker darkness in the alley. 'Nummer three's coming off. Dey'll wait till it's over, du kids,' the shape said, coming toward her.

She was half afraid, for she could see no face, only the immense blackness. Still, she asked: 'How do I git there, to the steel mill? I'm hunten my boy.'

'He'll be awright,' the shape said, close now. 'It's shorter tu go by du tracks, butcha gotta watch out onu tracks. Kids gotta go du long way round bydu fence. Dey'll be awright. Steel's pretty when her pours. Kids like to watch.'

The voice in speaking of the steel had grown warm, yet wary, like that of a man speaking of a beautiful and beloved but deceitful woman. Gertie realized it was Victor, who until now had been mostly a voice behind the wall. She was no longer afraid as he came on to the end of the alley where she stood, but began to realize that she was cold. She hesitated, wondering if she should go on for Enoch, and watching and listening to the steel mill.

The light rose ever higher. Instead of red, it leaped now white, now blue like lightning, and with it there was a noise like one long roll of hissing, spitting thunder all mixed in with a kind of wordless

269

singing. The leaping light came bright into the meeting of the alleys, so that when Victor stepped into it he became at once a huge man in a peaked cap and strange monstrous gloves and heavy boots that seemed more iron than leather. Staring at the great sooty-faced man, smelling of burned cloth, singed leather, and sulphur, it seemed like one of Battle John's sermons had come to life and she had gone to hell and met a devil. But his voice was kind as he repeated, looking at her:

'Yu kid'ull be awright. Yu'll be sick coming out widouta coat.' But his glance on her hair was brief, as his blue, white-ringed eyes, bright in his sooty face, swung back to the steel mill. The light above the pouring shed was pure white now, so that all around it, in the drop-forge mill, the stripping shed, the other furnaces, the lesser lights, though all shades of quivering red, were dull beside the leaping brightness. Gertie shivered, suddenly determined to run home and get a coat before continuing the hunt for Enoch. 'Steel tonight, she behave like a lady,' Victor said, still looking toward the mill.

Gertie followed him a few steps, but the way seemed strange. She had turned many times in the coming, her mind on finding Enoch instead of noting the way. The black alleys were all exactly alike. All were bordered by the same long low buildings, even the patterns of light on the snow from the government windows were always exactly the same, and though there were numbers above the doors there was among the alleys no sign or name, for all were Merry Hill.

A great dog, his head lifted higher than her knees, ran growling and barking after Victor, but he walked on as if the dog were not there. Gertie, not having seen the dog on the way, hesitated while the beast circled, snarling, about her. Victor mistook her uncertainty for fear, and stopped and said, 'He won't bite.'

Gertie answered, feeling foolish and silly: 'Oh, I ain't afeared. I jist ain't certain this is th way home. I knowed you was my neighbor, and thought that by folleren you I could find where I live.'

'Hokay,' he said, nodding, waiting for her to come up to him. 'All a time people get lost inu alleys—cops, cab drivers, da good sisters. I wanta see yu on some business, but tonight I gotta hurry.

270

S'Max's night off. I got time off fu to take her tudu dance. Do her good.'

'Yes,' Gertie said, her mind jumping back to when she was a girl. How would it have been to have danced, and it not have been a sin, danced with a man bigger than she. Then she remembered and asked, 'Business?'

'Sure. Max told me yu carve good, thatcha could carve a crucifix like I been wanting fu my mudder, u genuine hand-carved crucifix.'

'Crucifix? Christ on a cross?'

'Sure. Allatime she want u genuine hand-carved crucifix—good wood.'

'But I don't know nothen about sich.'

'Max said yu carve good. I pay good. Fifteen—p'raps twenty dollars for one crucifix, no more danu foot—p'raps u foot anna half—high, good wood.'

'I've got a little walnut.' She tried to measure her piece of walnut, and see a Christ like that in Max's house. How had he been? 'Christ might have tu be in maple. But it's good maple.'

'Yu shape him up good, not make um too flat onu wood?'

'Oh, he'd be all there.'

They had reached their own alley, but he stopped before turning into the shadow. He looked again at the steel mill, then asked, 'Hokay?'

'Okay. I recken if it ain't no good you don't hafta take it.'

'It'll be good,' he said. 'Tomorrow I give you exact inches.'

Clytie had set up supper for Clovis when Gertie got back. He was, however, eating more bread and molasses than dried-up fish or wilted slaw. He looked up, tired and angry, and spoke shortly, telling her she oughtn't to let the children run wild. He interrupted her explanation of why she had come back without Enoch, with a disgusted rising from the table. 'Gert, that grub wasn't fitten fer a dawg.'

'It ain't my fault it set two hours,' she answered shortly, annoyed because he, unlike Victor, had not noticed that she was cold and damp.

He grew even more angry, and his voice rose. 'What ud you think I was a doen them two hours? Setten in a beer parlor er a shooten pool like a lot a men? I was worken, gitten overtime pay. I fin'ly git

271

home an th place is in a mess. One youngen off an gone, an nothen fitten to eat. Gertie,' he went on in a kinder tone, 'what's got into yer cooken? I know with all this rationen business an a stove you ain't used to it ain't so easy. But you've got plenty tu spend, an—'

'Spend!' she said. 'I've spent, not counten th milk, better'n twenty-five dollars fer grub this week.'

'Twenty-five dollars,' he repeated, angry again. 'You can't feed seven a us, all good big eaters, on twenty-five a week. That ain't four dollars a week apiece. Why, Gertie,' he went on, counting in his head, 'that ain't much more'n fifty cents a day apiece. Millions a men, maken no more'n I'm maken, spend better'n fifty cents a day fer beer an cigarettes.' He bent forward and looked at her, a long and ugly searching look. 'Gert, how much have you saved out a th money I been given you since we got up here?'

She swallowed. 'Clovis, I ain't got enough ahead to pay fer a spell a sickness in one a th youngens, an . . .'

'I got hospitalization,' he interrupted. 'How much money you got?'

She saw Clytie listening behind her father, interested, and accusing, too, as if the saving of a dollar were a sin. How much could she lie? She had to have something more than the money she'd saved for land ahead when they went back home. She had to have a mule—a cow and chickens.

Clovis seemed to read her thoughts. 'You've still got some a th money your mother give you in bonds. If'n I can't keep a job up here when th war's over, it's enough to move us back an make a down payment on a truck. Anyhow, we'll git by. We allus have.'

'I'm tired a allus jist getten by,' she burst out, 'an never haven nothen ahead. An pretty soon we'll be goen back home an . . .'

'What have we got to go back to? How much've you saved out a my wages?'

'What's th use a liven like this if a body cain't save somethin?'

'Save.' He was angry now. 'That's all I've heard since we've been married. Cain't you git it into yer head that millions an millions a people that make a heap more money than I'll ever make don't save? They buy everything on time. They ain't allus a starven their youngens.'

'I ain't a starven nobody, Clovis. I been—'

'You been a buyen th cheapest grub you could. You know that. An look at this place! Millions an millions a people live in places that ain't no bigger. Cain't you git it into your head you're in a city? Millions a youngens that has growed up in furnished rooms three floors up ud think a place like this with room fer youngens to play outside an automatic hot water an good furniture was heaven. An here you still ain't fixed it up none. Shorly you got money fer linoleum.'

'I bought curtains—an I mean to git more. I wanted to go to Ward's er some cash store.'

'How much cash you got, Gertie?'

'About—about fifty dollars,' she answered in a low voice.

'You mean,' he said, his tired face bleaching with anger, 'you mean, Gertie, you're a given us all grub like this an a letten this house go like a pigpen . . .' He looked about the kitchen, at the uncurtained shelves, the bare floor, the few battered saucepans on a shelf by the stove. 'Look, Gert,' he cried, his voice a mingling of sorrow and anger, 'all our life together I've wanted to make more money so's we could live better, so's you and th kids could have it kinda nice. I bet now I'm a maken more money than any man back home. An that cookware—look at it. If I recollect right, that's th same old beat-up aluminum pan yer mom give us when we married to make out with till we could do better.' In one swift stride he was across the kitchen, had grabbed the pan, and was flinging it through the door, almost hitting Enoch as he came up the walk.

Gertie hurried down the steps, her eyes searching for the shine of the pot in the murky light, and a woman's voice said: 'It's right here I do believe, on Mrs Bommarita's steps. Timmy, is that it?'

A moment later Timmy was thrusting the pot into her hand.

The Anderson inside door was open and there was light enough for Gertie to see Mrs Daly surrounded by her own boys and others. She realized they were all watching her and had seen the pot come sailing out, and that Victor was standing only a few feet away by his coalhouse door, stooping, a coal bucket in his hand. She saw the pot shaking; her hands made it do that.

273

She gripped the pot, trying to make it be still, determined to lift her head, straighten her shoulders, walk back into the house, and never let on to these strangers that there was any shame, anger, torment to hide. But she couldn't look up; she could only stand hunched and shivering. She saw another hand on the pot, small, much smaller than her own, but no child's hand, wrinkled, pudgy, ugly, red; Mrs Daly's hand pulling at the pot, her voice low, kind.

'Look, dearie, let me take da pan. When they've had a wee drop too much it's not good to bring da ting back in—that is, too soon. Leave um lay awhile. I'll just keep this till youse can keep it agin.' She sighed. 'An say a wee prayer to da Blessed Virgin dat pots an pans don't break like dishes. Ah, me, da Friday nights dat used to be.'

She smiled up at Gertie, a radiant smile, the smile of Maggie for the new feet of St Francis. 'He's taken Maggie tudu store—nine o'clock dere open now till Christmas—for a Christmas present fur me, c'nyumagine? When u stores close he'll take her to mass. To be sure, I'm happy—but allasame I hope it's not dishes.' And she giggled gaily as a child; then, as she looked up into the ugly twisting, agonized face above the battered pot, she began a soft patting and sh-sh-shushing. 'Don't cry—it makes um worse. An that old Homer is taken notes, I do believe. It's nothing. Only last week I was saying to Mrs Bommarita, wasn't I, Timmy? that Mr Nevels seemed a sober an dacent man; to be sure he'll have his drop, but . . .'

Gertie was at last able to speak. 'He ain't drinken—he jist wants some new pans. Leastways I don't recken he's a drinken. He never done it back home.'

'But he's a man, dearie, and a man is alla time changing.'

'Mom—' Clytie was running down the steps hunting her mother, trying hard to act as if nothing had happened—'Pop's awful tired; he's a feelen bad cause he got bumped. That means another feller'ull git his job an he'll have to work a midnight shift, but he'll be home all day. Won't that be fun? It's jist eight o'clock, an Pop said let Reuben stay with th little youngens—they've both gone to sleep, an Reuben don't want to go no how—an me an you an Pop an Enoch could do some Christmas buyen.'

Gertie turned slowly away from Mrs Daly, leaving the pot in her hands. 'You uns go,' she said to Clytie as she went up the steps. If she could only give the money in such a way that Clovis would never suspicion she had more than fifty dollars—fifty-four eighty it had been. But she would save the crucifix money; fifteen dollars would buy a sow.

18

Gertie stood with her head thrust out the partly opened kitchen door, and watched the gray brown sparrows feed on the coalshed roof. Twice she had spread crumbs for them, but once a gray alley cat had chased the birds and licked the crumbs, and when they were back again Tony Bommarita had covered their food with handfuls of the freshly fallen snow. The birds were ugly-voiced and dirty looking, but standing so, with the inside door shut behind her, there was for the moment a feeling of being alone with them, the way it had used to be back home, like the day she'd cut the hickory tree down on the Tipton Place. She had stood then, and watched two red birds. She closed her eyes. If she shut out the alley, she could smell cold creek water and cedar, the cedar smell strong and clean, like on a still, misty morning.

'Mom, Mom, make Amos gimme my auto! He got a big red wagin, an now he wants my little ole toy auto.'

Gertie turned back into the kitchen slowly, for in turning the red birds flew away, the smell of cedar faded, and there was the closeness, the noise, the overcrowding of all her family at home on Christmas Day. The radio could not cry again of so many shopping days left till Christmas. Everything was sold that could be sold. Millions and millions had bought like Clovis. Millions and millions of women would be happy to have a man like Clovis.

'Enoch, hand me that wrench on th table.' Clovis, taking the wrench from angry Enoch, smiled up at her from where he worked flat on his back under a large secondhand but bright white washing machine. 'I'll have this thing a worken pretty soon. An you can do a washen, old woman, with no work atall.'

She tried to smile. All morning that had been the hardest part, the trying to smile in the heat and the steam of the oven baking the turkey Clovis had bought. But she had smiled on everything, even on the dried-out Christmas tree that had no smell except one that made her think of shoe polish, for Clytie had sprayed it with artificial snow. It held no memory of earth or wind or sun or sky; a tree grown in a field, Clovis had said, just for Christmas. Lifeless it was, as the ugly paper wreath Clytie had bought. But still she had to smile, for the big gifts were for her. 'Mom, Mom, Cassie's climbed up an got the scissors. She knows she ain't supposed to have em,' Clytie quarreled from the passway. Then, with no permission from Gertie, she whirled and jerked the scissors from Cassie.

'Cassie Marie,' Gertie began, 'you know, you oughtn't—'

Cassie had suddenly dissolved into a heartbroken weeping. She quickly checked her sobs, but then, just as unusual for her as the crying, she tried to argue with her mother. 'I need um, Mom. I'll be real careful with them scissors,' she begged. She came into the kitchen and looked hopefully up at Gertie, the new fancy doll that Santa had bought clutched upside down in her arms.

'You'd ruin them sharp scissors, an they'd ruin you, mebbe,' Gertie said.

Cassie turned away, weeping again. She sounded so sorrowful that Gertie turned to pick her up and baby her a bit. But when Cassie went away to the block of wood, Gertie stopped by the kitchen table. Getting out of the kitchen seemed, for the moment at least, too much trouble. Never again could she walk straight into the passway, even with the table against the wall. The new washing machine took up so much room she could hardly slip her big body sidewise between it and the table. Amos began screaming again for the red plastic car, and Clovis shook his head in weariness.

'A body ud think them youngens got nothen. I thought Cassie was crazy over that new doll, an she did keep a talken about how pretty it was dressed.' He sighed, resting on his elbows by the washing machine. 'I allus hoped Clytie could have a nice store-bought doll like that—an now she's too old, an Cassie she ain't so pleased. An th money I've spent. What did she want?'

'Mebbe,' Gertie said, looking again at the hopping sparrows, 'she don't know. Lots a grown people never git an never know what they want. They spend money, hopen it'll satisfy em, like a man a hunten matches in a strange dark house.'

She nodded toward the alley where Sophronie's Wheateye was running down the steps. She wore a new pink rayon dress, and had an oversized doll on one arm and the box of red plastic dishes cradled in the other. Gertie watched a little saucer fall from a corner of the flimsy crumpling box and lie, a bright spot of red in the snow. She ought to call and tell the child that she had lost a dish, but she only shook her head. Did it matter? In a few days the box would be gone, the dishes broken, and nothing left but their price. Sophronie would pay that off at so much a week. $2.75 they had cost. How much was $2.75?

Clovis said, 'There,' in the pleased voice which meant that something he had meant to fit was fitted.

The sparrows flew away as Mrs Anderson, wearing her coat and boots, came down her steps carrying a bright red tricycle, and followed by a snow-suited Georgie. Then the Daly door opened and out poured the Daly boys. All seemed to have either fancy wheeled toys or new sleds, though soon she saw that two were on hockey skates fastened to special shoes, the kind Enoch had wanted. Even Reuben, who would have little to do with the alley games, had somewhat sheepishly said the other day that he would like to learn to skate.

Mrs Daly, steamy-faced, straggeldy-headed, her apron damp with dishwater, the least one in her arms, stood in the door and watched, smiling. Her glance leaped from child to child; each broadened the smile so that when she was at last able to tear her eyes away and look at Mrs Anderson, struggling to get Georgie face forward on the seat of his tricycle, her face was so full of smiles it broke into joyful laughter as she called, 'Merry Christmas!'

She flipped her apron about the baby and came on down the alley. 'Such a fine Christmas,' she said, beaming up at the plainly unhappy Mrs Anderson. 'Fresh snow. Nobody sick.' She glanced at the Bommarita door, then at Mr Anderson behind his storm door, and spoke more loudly. 'Our father home sleepen. He went last night wit Maggie tudu midnight mass. My, ain't she pretty? What's her name?' She was talking now to Wheateye, coming from the Miller door where she had been to show her doll.

'Sally Marie,' and Wheateye held up the great doll, demonstrated its powers of going to sleep and saying, 'Mama,' then ran to get the new doll buggy.

'That Santa Claus, he's sure got a failen fu kids.' Mrs Daly smiled on Wheateye as she had smiled on her own. Her joy even touched Mrs Anderson, who for a moment seemed what she was, a young and pretty woman, hardly thirty. Her voice was gay when she called to Gertie, now on her stoop:

'Your turkey smells good, sage in the stuffing like we always had at home. You almost never smell it here.' And after a wary glance at Georgie, still sitting backward on his tricycle, she came over and stood by Gertie's stoop, smiling up at her. 'If I shut my eyes here by your door, I can think I'm back home.'

'I'll give you some a mine I brung frum home.'

'Homer doesn't care for sage and red pepper,' Mrs Anderson said in the weary, talking-to-herself voice she often used, so that it seemed she was not the same woman who a moment ago had laughed in the alley. 'Homer doesn't care for fruit cake, either. The pediatrician would faint at the idea of letting Georgie taste it. I made fruit cakes mostly—I guess because I—' She reached for a pinch of fresh snow from the porch rail, watched the snow disappear, then looked at her empty fingers—'I wanted something that wasn't sensible and vitamic, just once, for Christmas,' she confessed all in a breath.

Wheateye was rolling a new and shining doll buggy, large enough for a live baby, down the Meanwell steps. She was being helped by a yawning Sophronie in a new housecoat, shinier and flouncier than the old had been. Sophronie nodded sleepily, but smiled as she returned the Christmas greetings the women called to her. No sooner had she gone back into her kitchen than Mrs Anderson began in a low, worried voice, her disapproving glance on Wheateye's doll carriage, 'Isn't it awful how they work at terrible jobs—have you seen Sophronie's hands lately—and then waste their money? That housecoat: what in the world does a factory worker with three children need with a flimsy rayon housecoat? And all that foolishness for the children. It makes it hard on the others with sensible parents.'

' "Man cannot live by bread alone," ' Gertie suddenly said in a surprised voice.

Mrs Anderson nodded. ' "But by every word that proceedeth out of the mouth of God." I went to Sunday school too, when I was little. But a flimsy doll buggy given by a mother who can't afford it to a child who won't take care of it has nothing to do with bread and God's word.'

Gertie was silent, her thoughts on bubble gum and shoestrings. She wished she'd got skates for Reuben—and maybe Enoch too.

The sound of a through train rushing by silenced Mrs Anderson. The smoke rolled and the cinders rattled down. Christmas seemed gone, sped with the train to some quieter, cleaner place. The smoke was still falling when Enoch's friend, Mike Turbovitch, came plunging and staggering on hockey skates, clumsy in the snow. He stopped at the bottom step and called: 'Oh, Enoch, come on out. Yu gitchu hockey skates?'

Enoch came running to the call, but stopped, his head around the storm door when he saw Mike's skates. He looked past him to the Dalys and their toys, and then saw Tony Bommarita pulling a long new sled. He turned quickly away. His choked mumble, 'I'd ruther listen to th radio an play with my builden set,' was cut off by the slamming door.

Mike looked after him with a shrewd but pitying glance, then turned to Gertie with a sharp, accusing look. 'Didn't he git his hockey skates, nor nothen?'

Gertie, conscious of Mrs Anderson's watching, listening face, said, 'Oh, sure, a builden set an stuff,' but Mike looked suspicious still, and after a moment's waiting and another call he staggered away.

When he had gone, Gertie called into the house and suggested to Enoch that he and Amos come out and play with the new wagon, but Enoch's answer was tearful and resentful. 'Wagins is baby stuff, Mom.'

Amos, roused from his boats in the bathroom, cried, 'I ain't no baby,' but an instant later he was in the living room, screaming because Enoch had the wagon.

There was a thumping and bumping of the wagon while Enoch yelled: 'You wasn't usen it. You an Cassie allatime play with my things.' There were more screams and thumps, and Clovis finally scolded. Though his voice was loud, it held the absent-minded tone of one taken up with some beloved pastime, so that his, 'Behave yerselves youngens, fore I git a hick'ry limb,' had no effect at all.

Gertie, embarrassed by the poor showing of her family on Christmas, turned to chide the boys, but Clytie screamed: 'Mom, make em quit! They're a tearen th place up, an I cain't hardly try on my new dress.'

'Merry Christmas.' It was Mrs Daly, who had at last managed to tear herself away from the sight of her children, going now into the next alley.

'We ain't so merry,' Gertie said.

'Sick on Christmas day?' Mrs Daly asked, coming up the walk.

Gertie shook her head. The screaming of Amos, the bumping of the fought-over wagon, and Clytie's shrill cries that they'd knock the Christmas tree over told Mrs Daly enough of the Christmas in her house without her adding words to it. The sounds proclaimed to any listening ears that Santie had brought to all the children only one real toy fit for showing up and down the alleys.

Mrs Daly listened and nodded as Clovis listened and nodded over the car's motor on a cold morning. She shook her head. 'Yu gotta git um all a big present apiece. Once I tried one sled butween Chris an Joe.' She sighed at the memory, then winked at Gertie and whispered, 'Yu least kid's Amos, ain't he?'

When Gertie had nodded, Mrs Daly stuck her face close to the broken-out pane in the storm door, and called above the tumult: 'Amos, it's too bad youse is too little to steer an don't know how. Yu could steer outside. Du kids is haven a kind a Christmas parade. An let youse brudder push.' She opened the storm door invitingly.

Another fight threatened over who should pull the wagon to the door. 'Now, now,' Mrs Daly cried, going into the kitchen. 'I generally git all th big toys tudu door myself. S'job in a crowded place. My, my, youse gotta big Christmas.' Her voice was warm with genuine pleasure as she went on: 'A refrigerator—such a big one an so fine—linoleum anu washing machine. An ina war when stuff's so hard to git.' As soon as she had put the wagon through the door, she must turn back and examine the great white icebox. It rose higher than her head and blocked most of the kitchen window, but her eyes were worshipful, pleased, Gertie thought, as if the thing had been her own.

Enoch forgot his quarrel with Amos and sprang to show Mrs Daly the wonders of the icebox. As soon as he was out of bed, he had put water into the trays. Then, it had seemed to Gertie, trying to get breakfast in the sharply contracted kitchen, that he had opened the thing at least a hundred times to see if the water was freezing. Now, trying as before to catch the light going on, he opened its door with a quick hard pull, calling to Mrs Daly: 'Lookee. Lookee. It's got a place fer butter an meat an vegetables an everthing.' He opened little doors and pulled out trays and drawers. The Icy Heart, as if trying to impress the little woman, flung out air so cold it made a fog in the hot kitchen. Next there came a soft purring, as if some strange kind of polar cat were curled in the heart of it.

'It's one of th finest I've ever seen,' Mrs Daly said.

'A 1942 Icy Heart with nine and three-tenths cubic feet,' Enoch said, putting his ear close the better to hear the white cat. 'Pop was real lucky to git it: no black market, taxes, nothen. He got it off'n a man he knows in th shop that got TB an is a goen to Arizona. He sold it an th washen machine—cheap.'

'His wife was sure a good housekeeper, not a nick on it,' Mrs Daly said, running a gentle finger down the blue and silver handle. 'Youse's lucky.'

Clovis warmed to her praise. 'The man gimme time an sold it some under OPA. Thataway, he said, them secondhand dealers wouldn't make a pile on him.'

Gertie carried the wagon down the steps. Conscious of Mrs Anderson's questioning glance, she tried to smile the way a woman with an almost new ten-cubic-foot Icy Heart should smile. 'I know you're awfully proud of your new things?' Mrs Anderson asked.

Last night, when she had learned what Clovis had done with the Henley money he had asked for a few days before, telling her then he only wanted to borrow it to pay more on his car debts, she had somehow kept down the bitter-tongued anger that seemed always rising in her of late. She had smiled last night for the children, all gay and excited with the surprise for her. It had been so hard then, it ought to be easy now. Cassie, gay again and singing one of her own songs, ran past her down the walk. Enoch next, and then Amos. Gertie turned away from Mrs Anderson on the pretext of getting the children started off with the wagon.

A plane went over, but too high to kill conversation with its sounds. The children were beginning to squabble now, especially Wheateye, who was screaming at some of the Daly boys for ruining her doll buggy with snowballs. Behind Mrs Bommarita, watching her children from her doorway, a radio was crying out the news of great slaughter in Germany. Somewhere another radio was singing Peace on Earth. Mrs Anderson noticed none of these things. She continued to watch Gertie and wait for her comment.

'I've lived a long time without sich,' Gertie said at last. 'An when we go back we'll have to sell em, mebbe fer less than we paid, an— it's more debts.'

'I'll betcha never asked fer one of them damn' big things. I seen it last night when they was moving it in.' It was Max on her steps, dressed in her Sunday best in a long coat with fur on the collar. The dark fur and a dark hat made Max's face seem gentle as some early spring flower blooming out of last year's snow-blackened leaves. The bluish rings under her eyes made them seem bigger and softer, her lips redder, kinder. 'Victor's mother,' she went on, coming over to Gertie's stoop, 'she buys th best—has got one exactly like it, only bigger. Always loaded down with enough damn' junk to start a delicatessen. All them drawers an shelves an trays to fiddle with an keep clean. An now Victor wants one.'

Mrs Anderson smiled. 'You're just jealous. Don't you know, Max, that every woman, that is, every American woman, dreams of the day when she'll own—'

'Yu mean have in her kitchen,' Max said, lighting a cigarette. 'Nobody in this alley owns nothen. When they get most a th payments made on something, it breaks down an they hafta trade it in on some more crap.'

'Now, Max,' Mrs Anderson said, still smiling a strange Whit-like smile, 'you're un-American—or else you don't listen to the radio. Every woman dreams of a ten-cubic-foot Icy Heart in her kitchen—Icy Heart power—Icy Heart. We must hurry up and win the war so we can all go out and buy Icy Hearts.' She had stopped, trying to remember. 'Last summer I knew it by heart; Mrs Bommarita had the Icy Heart program on every day.'

'I hope she's not listening to th news today,' Max interrupted. 'It's awful. A couple a them generals must have went on a drunk in Paris an left th war to run itself. Her man, he's a waist gunner.'

'It's the infantry that's so hard hit,' Mrs Anderson said. 'Sophronie has a brother somewhere over there in the infantry. I hope she isn't listening.'

'She ain't got time,' Max said. 'I hope Whit got her what she wanted. She'd set her heart on a housecoat she seen ina window at American Credit.'

'With flounces and lots of gold?' Mrs Anderson asked.

Max nodded, glad. 'He must a got it. Full-skirted, swishy?'

'You mean,' Mrs Anderson asked, 'she actually wants the kind of housecoat he gives her? But what in the world does a woman in her—in her station—'

Max dropped her arms from a long child-like yawn, smiled at Mrs Anderson. 'You've got me, kid, but she wears it, not me. Why did Jesus change water into wine? Water is a lot more healthful. Besides, you can wash your face in it, and it's cheaper, my pop used to say when Mom would quarrel a little because he'd brought home wine in th middle a th week steda just on Saturday night.'

'Was your father a minister?' Mrs Anderson asked.

'I don't remember that he ever called himself that but once or twice. I remember once somewhere down in North Carolina—it was spring and he wanted to stop awhile on the way north so he turned off on a gravel road. And somehow he said something to a farmer made the man think Pop could castrate pigs. The farmer begged and begged him. He thought Pop wouldn't do it on account he didn't have no money. So Pop castrated. He'd never done it, and Mom fussed and said he oughtn't to do it, for after he'd done the first pigs a lot a other farmers come. They paid us in hams, the best hams, an eggs an dried apples, and fresh-caught trout. Did you ever eat fresh-caught, fresh-fried trout with real young tender . . .'

'But, Max, what did your father say or do?' Mrs Anderson cried in an agony of curiosity.

'Why, he said, "Thank you," I guess.'

'I mean about being a minister or something.'

'Oh. When Mom complained because he castrated pigs when he'd hardly ever been close to a pig, he said, "Good lady, I minister to th wants and needs of all mankind." Yu want it for Homer?'

Mrs Anderson shook her head, and was suddenly interested in the whereabouts of Georgie, while Gertie asked. 'Did his pigs do all right?'

Max nodded, and Mrs Anderson sighed heavily. 'But Max, was he a preacher, like in a church?'

'I don't remember but once or twice, when we was real hard up. Once in West Virginia, by a mining town—th mines was running, but Pop couldn't mine—we'd even run outa gas, so he preached onu rich man going to heaven through that needle's eye. It made them pore miners feel good, I recken. Th money come rollen in, but he didn't like to take it; he said . . .'

Her words were drowned by Mrs Daly's calling from Gertie's doorway. 'It works—he fixed a motor. Can yu imagine?'

Clytie behind her, all in a jiggle of excitement, was begging: 'Come an see it, Mom. It's worken. Can I do a washen?'

Enoch, who had been pushing the wagon with Amos in it, heard and ran back to the house screaming, 'Lemme see! Lemme see!'

Wheateye, who had overturned her doll buggy in the snow while fleeing from snowballs, took up the cry of, 'Lemme see, lemme see,' and came running, as did the other children, who had by now marched down the other alley, around, and home again. Gertie got as far as the second step, but got stopped by the crowding children, and when Sophronie's Gilbert came running, his skate blade striking her shoe, she came down again and stood with Max

285

and Mrs Anderson. The three women by the house wall made an island of stillness among the eddying children, running now from distant alleys, drawn by the cries of, 'Lemme see.' 'What is ut?' 'Somethen for free?' Still others heard Mrs Daly call across the alley to Mrs Bommarita, 'Come and seedu Icy Heart.'

'Don't let it freeze the eggs an frostbite th lettuce,' Max said with a shiver. 'They're powerful things, them Icy Hearts.'

'Maybe I'm jealous,' Mrs Anderson said, 'but I don't like stuff so cold. Casimir does wake the baby and track in dirt, but an icebox was all we had in Muncie,' and her voice grew warm, warmer than when she spoke of her children. 'It stays on the back porch. I guess it is inconvenient, but we have the nicest back porch. There's a big maple—we have a big old frame house on the edge of town—right by the porch, too close, Homer thinks; he plans to have it pruned when we go back. But in summer the porch is always cool and shady, and in the fall, when you go out for the milk, the red and yellow leaves are all plastered on the floor, and it smells a little like the woods.'

'Mornens last fall when I'd go to th spring, th poplar leaves they'd be plastered thick,' Gertie said in a low voice.

'We seen th poplars yellow once up in th West Virginia hills,' Max said. 'But once in October, in Ohio someplace—I know Cleveland wasn't so far away—oh, them maples then. I remember Pop got us right in under one. Th leaves fell all over th roof—an he set ina door drinking coffee an watched um fall half th morning.'

'Max,' Mrs Anderson asked, after a polite pause to make certain the girl was finished, 'I was wondering the other day, where is—or was—your home and people?'

Max dropped her cigarette, clasped her gloved hands in front of her, and, like a child relating a thing learned so well there can never be a forgetting, said: 'From Earth, Lord, I come. That's one of the smaller planets; you would know it as a sister of Venus.' She choked and turned toward her door, remembered, whirled back, and looked at Gertie as she asked, her voice hoarse: 'A dream? I gotta have a dream; that's what I came out for.'

'Cedar,' Gertie said, realizing that through all the hubbub she'd heard a small child's troubled weeping. She found it on the other side of her stoop step, apparently lost. She picked it up and held it on her hip. It at once left off crying and began licking a purple sucker that had been stuck to the red plastic fish it carried.

Max was repeating, questioning the word, 'Cedar?'

Gertie explained. 'A little peaked cedar like grows by th creek on a limestone ledge. You know how they look fore sunrise on a summer mornen, with mebbe a little spider web er two, all white with dew.'

Max's gum was still between her front teeth while she considered. 'Yeah? Kinda. I'll take it. Seems like it was cedars we saw so much in Arkansas—but I don't remember any dew. Cedar's enough, though. I've gotta scram. Victor might wake 'fore I'm gone. I gotta be at work by two o'clock, an I want Christmas dinner first.'

Mrs Anderson clucked in sympathy. 'What a shame they make you work on Christmas day—and not get to eat at home.'

Max was hoarse again as she turned away. 'It wouldn't seem like home, dinner at home on Christmas day. Victor's mom's gonna have a fit when I don't show up. But I couldn't take it—all them Poles together, knowen one another, talken u same lingo. I *would* be lonesome then.' She looked back, her eyes lingering on Gertie like one lonesome now. 'I found a girl that wanted to be off—claims she's got kids. But I figger she wants to give her boy friend—her man's inu marines—a real good Christmas—present. Cedar, cedar,' and she went running up her steps.

Gertie looked about for someone who knew the child, though on her hip it seemed contented enough. There were plenty of children. Some satisfied with seeing, ran down the steps, bumping into others running up. There was a deal of shoving, joggling, and good-humored pitching of soft snowballs, while others pounded drums or blew horns. Most were also eating—candy, bananas, cookies, apples, oranges, and raw carrots. Wheateye, holding a bottle of pop in one hand, a horn in the other, the horn hand cradling her doll and one long spear of celery, divided her attention between blowing, taking little bites of celery and offering the doll the strings, and drinking, then handing the doll dainty nips from the bottle. At times she would wave the bottle and the horn and cry, 'Da biggest icebox ya ever seed—thirteen cubic feet an it costed a thousand dollars.'

The tide was thinning, the cries of 'Lemme see,' and 'What's cooken?' were giving place to comments, many admiring, some belittling. 'We've got a bigger one dan dat.' 'Who'd want a old secondhand junk heap?' 'We're gonna buy a brand-new one soon's the war's over.' And a jeering voice from a strange alley, 'Dem hillbillies, dey come up here an get all da money in Detroit.'

Mrs Anderson, listening, nodded as over a page in a book. 'That interests Homer a lot. He's working on his Ph.D. thesis in sociology, you know: The Patterns of Racial and Religious Prejudice and Persecution in Industrial Detroit.' Gertie blinked, and Mrs Anderson went on more rapidly. 'That,' and she nodded toward Mrs Daly coming out the door, 'interests him a lot. Almost nothing has been written about the hatred of the foreigner for many of our native-born Americans whose religion and social customs are different from his own. He's always finding evidence of it; it's interesting.'

'*Bein* th evidence ain't so interesten,' Gertie said, smoothing back the child's hair. She had such pretty hair, black and curly, soft, curly as Callie Lou's. She looked up as Max's door opened and Max hurried away, calling over her shoulder, 'Come out good; no sevens.'

Mrs Daly heard and asked, 'Does she still pick her numbers from da dream book?'

Timmy Daly looked up, wonderingly. 'Where'd her getta slip? Casimir ain't sellen ice today.'

And Mrs Anderson, with the puzzled look of a woman stepping into a fog at noon of a bright sunny day, asked her sharp, breathless questions: 'Why did she want a number? Oh, dear, I wasn't listening. Why did she want a dream? And what does Casimir . . .'

'Such a fine icebox, Mrs Nevels. I hope to be getting a bigger one soon. But it's like I tell Maggie, if I don't never save a down payment maybe du old can do till u war's over and dey'll take it fudu down payment. And Maggie, when she's married, will have a fine new one with a freezer chest all u way acrost u top like one I seen in u magazine.' She caught the mouth-open, wanting to ask questions glance of Mrs Anderson, and hurried on: 'Oh, how come

I could forget it. I wanta tell youse about Maggie's Christmas present—two towels, pure linen, hand-monogrammed for her hope chest.' She picked up the baby's sucker, fallen onto the snow, and put it back into its mouth, saying, 'Du snow was clean.' She turned again to Mrs Anderson, emphasizing her words with nods: 'Nobody, but nobody, can never say to my Maggie, "Yu had no dowry; yu've brought not one stitch u linen tuyu marriage." She'll have it. Linen, all pure linen, Christmas, birthdays since she was born—always one piece, two this Christmas, u linen, pure linen. Such . . .'

Georgie screamed from somewhere down the alley. Mrs Anderson had to hurry away, but Mrs Daly lingered a moment, looking after her. 'Books and schooling, nutten all her life but books an schooling—no wonder she don't know nutten. Does she think Casimir makes his liven out u ice?'

Mrs Daly, afraid her baby would get chilled, hurried home. Gertie started down the alley to hunt the owner of the child, a dark eyed little girl about two years old. She knew that she had never until now seen the child, yet she seemed strangely familiar. She was standing hesitant near the end of the alley, when Cassie came running, laughing, one hand outstretched. But instead of the witch child's hand she held an envelope smudged with licorice candy. 'Lookee, Mom, what that nice bubble-gum boy gimme, a Christmas card all for me.' She opened the envelope to show the wonders of a fat red-cheeked Santa Claus with big-eyed reindeer that looked like horned calves.

Gertie admired the card, held it up for the little child to see. She made a sound and held out her hand for it. Cassie, really looking at her for the first time, asked, 'Mom, how come you've got Mable?'

'Mable?'

'Uhuh, her's th bubble-gum boy's kid sister. His mom hadda work today. He's hunten her now. Lemme take her home. She walks good.'

Mable wanted down, and went away with Cassie while Cassie talked to her of Santa Claus and reindeer. Gertie stood a moment, smiling as she watched them go. At last she turned slowly back to her own door. She saw, at the foot of her sidewalk, the red wagon, no good for playing in the snow, and so deserted by her boys. She tried not to think of the twelve dollars the flimsy thing had cost as she walked past it. On the stoop she lingered a moment, hand on the storm-door knob. The alley was deserted for the moment, even by the sparrows. Still, her searching glance went over it; maybe behind some other door she might find the things not found behind her own.

Standing so, she heard the whirrity glug of the washing machine, Bing Nolan gargling away on 'Silent Night' on the radio, and then, more loudly, Clytie's outraged quarreling. Gertie hurried into the kitchen when she heard enough to learn that whatever it was it had been done by 'that mean, mean Cassie.' She saw then the bit of shiny blue rayon in Clytie's hands as she held it up for her father to see. 'Look, Pop, what that mean youngen's went an done. She's cut up th dress off'n that fine new Christmas doll and stuck it on a little ole makeshift doll Mom whittled fer her 'fore we left home.'

Gertie saw that the fine blue cloth was draped about the little hickory doll, the 'golden child' she had whittled by the Tipton Spring. She stood a moment looking, her eyes warm as if a sparrow had pecked a crumb from her hand. Both Clytie and Clovis, she realized, were looking at her with disapproval. Tightening her apron about her, she turned resolutely toward the Icy Heart to begin the last part of the Christmas dinner preparations.

While Clovis quarreled about the ravished doll, her own thoughts of Cassie demanding scissors helped her through the dinner getting. She felt sorry for Clovis. He looked so bleary-eyed and tired. He'd been getting less overtime since going on the midnight shift. But he was slow about learning to sleep in the daytime, and he'd spent a lot of his sleep time pushing his way through the hot, overcrowded, smelly department-store basements hunting Christmas for them all.

She kept her silence, but lost the warm-eyed look when, during the dinner that had cost so much, Clovis upbraided her ignorance of turkey cookery. Hemmed as it had been in the too small oven, the turkey had burned on the outside, scorching the breast meat, but they all came near gagging when Clovis cut into a thigh joint and blood ran out.

290

The real butter, that was to have been a Christmas treat with hot biscuit, had got so hard and cold from its stay in the Icy Heart that it refused to melt even on the hottest of biscuit, and butter and biscuit were chilled together. Clytie had the lettuce in the wrong place, and it was frozen. Reuben complained the milk was so cold it hurt his teeth. Clytie blamed it on Enoch, who'd turned down the cold controls; Enoch was angry; and Clovis turned sorrowful because the Icy Heart, like Cassie's new doll and the other things he'd bought, was unappreciated.

19

Somehow the dinner was finished, the dishes done, and one by one Clovis and the children either went to sleep during the afternoon or settled into quietness by the radio. Gertie had, some time ago, promised herself a Christmas gift. She would, she had decided, pleasure herself on Christmas afternoon with working again on the block of wood. But with all the children home there was so little room, and anyway she would feel guilty now, she thought, if she wasted time on the man in the wood when she could be making money by whittling out a Christ on a cross for Victor.

In order to escape somewhat from the radio and the heat, for she had put the turkey back for a further cooking, she stood by the storm door with the inner door open behind her. The pane broken by the Dalys let in a stream of cold air, and brought in but little noise, for the alley seemed deserted now of children.

There were only the Meanwell boys and a few of the Dalys, and even these were strangely quiet as they played a friendly game of forts and snowballs.

Gertie was yawning over the dull work of shaping the cross, absentmindedly listening to the boys, when she heard Gilbert Meanwell cry: 'Please, Miz Bommarita, we won't hitcha house an steps no more. They won't break nothen nohow. We ain't usen no hard balls.'

There was so much apprehension and piteous begging in Gilbert's usually untroubled voice that Gertie, troubled for the child, stuck her head around the door and looked into the alley. She saw Mrs Bommarita cross the alley and start up the Meanwell steps.

Gilbert sprang in front of her, and stood on the stoop. 'They ain't no use to knock. They ain't nobody home. We won't throw no more. Honest.' And the boy, cringing against the door, looked up at the large and angry woman as if he were afraid.

Claude Jean, the younger one, sprang from behind the trash can, a snowball dropping from his hand. 'They ain't nobody home. Git away an quitcha knocken.' A Daly ball splattered his pale hair, but he never noticed as he moved closer to Mrs Bommarita, his voice filled with a troubled beseeching. 'Please, lady, quitcha knocken. Everbody's—everbody's gone, I tell yu. Please.'

Mrs Bommarita hesitated, then went on up the Meanwell steps, asking in her low, always seeming sullen voice, 'An why for because don'tcha want me to knock?'

Gilbert pressed his back more firmly against the storm door, his arms wide spread across it, and begged again, almost crying now: 'G'wan back. They ain't nobody home. Pop's gone tu th bowlen alley—an Mom, too.'

'Yu don't wantcha mom to know yu've been dirtying mu steps again. Liars,' and reaching above Gilbert's outstretched arms, she knocked on the storm door with her fist.

There was a moment's silence after the loud and ringing knock. Gilbert twisted his head about and looked through an empty square where glass had been, his body tense. Claude Jean, who had been worriedly watching the door, cried, relief in his voice, 'See, they ain't nobody home.'

The Daly boys, too, were watching, not taking advantage of the unprotected positions of the Meanwells. Christopher, the biggest Daly, turned at last to Mrs Bommarita, and there was in his voice an echo of the Meanwell boys' troubled concern, as he said: 'Dey ain't nobuddy home. Honest. Look, if yu gotta tell tales, go tell mu sister, Maggie. She's—'

Mrs Bommarita knocked again, and Gilbert, still with his arms across the door, looked up at her, crying, an abject begging in his cry: 'Please, g'wan. I never knowed I was hitten yer—' He turned quickly and looked behind him when the inner door began a slow and careful opening. He jerked open the storm door and snatched at the knob, but his hand dropped when Wheateye squeezed

293

through the narrow opening, then immediately pulled the door shut behind her. Wheateye stopped between the doors and stood on tip-toe, her small face pushed through the frame of a broken pane. Gertie, who watched, and wondered, troubled for the children, saw that the child had been crying.

She did not look at her face again for staring at her hair. Wheateye's hair instead of being its usual pale, almost silvery color was—Gertie couldn't name the color; more purple than red in some spots, more red in others. All unknowing Gertie moved down another step to get a better sight of the hair. Mrs Bommarita stepped back, her voice loud in scolding. 'Yu kids. Youse oughta be ashamed. Yu mom works hard to give yu a good Christmas, and look whatcha done. You've ruined yu new dress. Look, it's all run over.' She pointed to streaks and blobs of purplish red on Wheateye's pink rayon dress, and quarreled on: 'Yu mom could git in bad trouble. She oughta know it's againsa law to leave kids by theirselves this away. Somebody might calla cops.'

'We'll be good,' Gilbert said, glancing uneasily at Wheateye's hair. 'We're gonna—' He sprang toward the door, opening again.

Wheateye whirled about and tugged on the doorknob. Her toes pushed hard against the door sill; her small body bent like a bow as she flung all her weight on her hands as they tried to keep the inner door shut. Gilbert caught the knob, but too late. The inner door began a slow opening. Mrs Bommarita leaned above the pulling children and pushed, scolding: 'Yu mean kids. Telling me lies so's yu mama won't know th meanness yu've been in.'

But when the door was only part way open, Mrs Bommarita's hands suddenly dropped away. She stood a second staring, then whirled and ran down the steps. She did not look back when Sophronie called: 'Come in, Mish Bommarita. Didja see Wheateye's hair? Don'tcha think it's pretty? Git out a my way, Gilbert.' Sophronie, with the strength that always seemed out of place in her puny body, gave the storm door a hard swift push that knocked Wheateye down the steps and Gilbert back enough so that she could get onto the stoop. She stopped, and stood sway-ing a little, but able to ask: 'Whatsa matter, Mish Bommarita? Runnen off?'

294

Mrs Bommarita only ran faster as she called over her shoulder, 'I gotta see about mu baby.'

'Baby?' Sophronie said. 'Baby shick?' Her wavering hands found the porch rail and clung to it as she came unsteadily down the steps.

Gilbert, near sobbing now, begged, 'Git back in, Mom. Please.'

Sophronie paid him no heed. She was apparently unaware that, save for her toeless slippers, her only piece of clothing was a black and flimsy nightgown with narrow straps for a top and a long and constantly lengthening tear up the front. Wheateye gave her mother one shame and terror mingled look, then scrambled to her feet and darted back into the house. But Gilbert sprang in front of Sophronie, begging, his voice loud, as if he feared she could not understand: 'Mom, yu fergotcha housecoat. You'll freeze.' He caught her arm and tried to turn her about. 'Please, Mom, git back in—' She gave him a hard slapping blow with the heel of her palm. He staggered, but clung to her arm; and unable to get her back up the steps, he walked backward in front of her, trying to shield her nakedness as he begged, 'Please, Mom, please—'

Sophronie seemed suddenly to realize that Gilbert was in front of her, blocking the way. She caught him by the shoulders and flung him hard to the ground. She then stood swaying, flinging her arms about in her efforts to regain her balance. Gertie thought hopefully that she was going to fall, and started toward her. If she fell and lay quiet, she could pick her up and carry her back into the house. However, Sophronie straightened at last, and stood holding herself stiffly erect while she looked about the alley in a fuddled sort of way. Mrs Bommarita's door slammed shut, and the sound apparently brought back her memory.

She called, 'Wait, Mish Bommarita. I'll look at yer baby,' and staggered on across the alley. Her tangled permanent-wave-crisped hair stood up like a wiry halo about her head. One strap of the nightgown slipped even further down her arm, and as she walked the tear in front continued to lengthen. The fallen strap entangled her arm, the lengthening pieces of the split skirt worried her feet. When she reached the Bommarita trash can, she stopped, said, 'Damn,' and then, seeming blind to Christopher Daly on the other side of the can, she stood on the nightgown tail and wriggled her body slowly, wearily, like a moth emerging from a cocoon. She went on up the walk, wearing nothing now but the red slippers.

Gilbert darted to pick up the nightgown, then called over his shoulder, 'Hurry, Claude, with the housecoat.' He ran after his mother, who was now pounding on the Bommarita door, calling in her thick, muffled voice:

'Yu want aspirin fer th baby?'

No one came to Sophronie's knocking. Gilbert waited a moment, then tapped on the door quickly, crying, 'Please let my mom in. She don't know what she's doen.' He began all at once to cry whole-heartedly, like a very young child, and stood slinging the tears away with his fist.

The smaller Dalys, who had been flinging swift curious glances at Sophronie, looked carefully away when Gilbert began to cry, and when Christopher called to them, 'Yu better scram, kids,' they turned toward the Daly door. Christopher, however, continued to stand and stare at a melting snowball as if there were nothing else of interest in the alley. He did not look around when the Bommarita door was opened enough to make a narrow crack and Mrs Bommarita said: 'If youse hillbillies don't git away I'll calla cops. I'll go to da pay station not a block away. G'wan, scram.' She hooked the storm door, then banged shut the inner door.

Sophronie blew a cloud of smoke. 'Who wants in a damned wop's house nohow?' She turned about, cursing again as she bumped into Gilbert. He stood as close to her as he could get, his tearful glance jumping from house to house as if measuring what help might come from each. He snatched eagerly at the housecoat when Claude Jean came running with it, but his mother shook it away when he tried to put it around her shoulders. He persisted, she grabbed it and flung it into the snow. 'I don't need a housecoat this time a day,' she said.

Gertie glanced toward her own door. Clovis was dozing in their bedroom. The children were mostly sleeping too. She started toward Sophronie, but in the moment of her looking away Sophronie had darted to the next stoop—the Andersons'. Gertie looked up in time to see one red slipper disappearing as Gilbert, picking up the house-coat, cried: 'Mom, don't go in there. Mr Anderson's home.'

Gertie stopped at the foot of her walk. She was relieved that Sophronie was behind a closed door, then worried, moving toward the sound, when from behind the door there came a short sharp scream—Mrs Anderson's. Gilbert ran to the door calling; 'Please leave my mama stay. She won't hurtcha none. She jist don't know what she's doen.' No answer came, but he continued to stand by the door, trying to make the new Christmas housecoat, mudstained and dye-spotted now, small in his hands.

Christopher saw Gertie, and after a moment's hesitation came to her. 'Mom's gone,' he said in a low voice. 'She could a managed this—but Maggie couldn't.'

'It's no business fer Maggie,' Gertie said. 'You'd better go home. I'll . . .' She stood pondering. What could a body do? She had never until now seen a woman drunk or human nakedness, save that of Clovis and her children.

'Please, Mrs Nevels, oh, please.' It was Mrs Anderson, brushing past Gilbert and rushing down her steps.

'If a body could git her to sleep. She was dozen off good when Miz Bommarita come,' Gilbert said, without leaving his place by the door.

'We'll manage your mother. Go on home now,' Mrs Anderson said, her voice sharp. Her cheeks were too pink, and her eyes too bright and glassy-like—like a body about to puke and cry at the same time. She motioned frantically for Gertie to come, then certain that Gertie was following she rushed back up her walk, again commanding Gilbert to go home.

Gilbert hesitated, but at last handed her the bathrobe, and with many backward glances started home. Mrs Anderson cautiously opened her storm door, and looked through the glass of the other door, her head tilted, listening. Gertie, behind her, heard in a moment Sophronie's question, insistent, as if many times repeated, 'Didn'tcha think it was pretty?'

A throat clearing, then the halting answer, 'Yes—yes, indeed—very nice.'

Mrs Anderson turned to Gertie. 'It's so horrible,' she whispered, 'so horrible. Homer was working—filing his thesis material—with his back to the kitchen door. I was on the floor helping Georgie

297

build a block house. I heard the door and looked up. There she was in the kitchen, naked, smiling that fuddled smile. What'll we do? She won't put on a stitch. I offered her a bathrobe. Homer's so upset. I've never seen him upset. He's so calm—always. When Georgie was being born, he left the hospital to look up something in the library.

'Georgie's in there grinning at her,' she went on, as Gertie continued silent. 'I've brought him up to have no horror of nakedness. Homer has learned so much about all the frustrations people get because they were taught false modesty. But Homer,' she added, getting more and more angry, 'with all the psychology he's had, he ought to be able to manage. But all he can do is sit there red as a beet and sweat.'

'You all are a doen enough jist keepen her in th house,' Gertie said.

'But we've got to go out. One of Homer's bosses took pity on us and invited us to dinner, or rather, as I understand it, one of the bigger bosses, a Mr MacSomething, too big to be bothered, suggested that this lesser boss invite us to dinner. Even the lesser one lives in Grosse Pointe,' she added, motioning toward her carefully done hair and the long-tailed dress. 'I'm sure he thinks,' she went on, 'he's doing us a great favor. You know, just like Christ—that is, if Christ had been so fortunate as to have a home in Grosse Pointe. Mr Turbi, our host, is very close to Christ—Mr Flint knows him by sight.'

'Give Mom another little drink er two an she'll doze off.' It was Gilbert, who, not trusting them, had gone no further than behind the trash can.

Claude Jean and Christopher watched and listened with him. Claude Jean only nodded, but Christopher said: 'Youse'ull have to get anudder baby sitter. Maggie her—can't come.'

Mrs Anderson, already angry, upset still more by her realization that the boys had heard all that she had said, bit her lip with exasperation at this last piece of news and looked ready to weep. 'Why didn't Maggie tell me sooner? I asked her days ago, and she promised.'

Christopher flushed and looked at Gilbert. Gilbert looked at Mrs Anderson. 'His maw—she's hadda go—out,' Gilbert said at last.

Mrs Anderson only looked puzzled as well as angry until Christopher explained in a low voice, 'Mu fadder.' Then angry at being forced to tell, he exclaimed, 'Hell. It's Christmas ain't it?'

'Oh—no,' Mrs Anderson cried, understanding at last. 'Oh, this alley—and all for Homer's thesis,' she said under her breath to Gertie, then more loudly to Christopher, 'But Maggie, so young; she'd be better here than—'

'That's th trouble,' Gilbert interrupted, looking after Christopher, who was hurrying away, his ears red. 'His old man ain't home. His mom's gotta find him. He was carryen th rent money.'

'And I used to think it was funny,' Mrs Anderson said. 'That song, "Father, dear father, come home with me now." Once we had a hired man, but we were never allowed to see him. My mother would pretend to us he was sick . . . when—'

'Has you uns seen Wheateye? Ole Homer, he's gotta see her.' It was Sophronie with her head stuck around the door.

Mrs Anderson whirled and stood in the opening, 'Oh—no—yes. Gilbert's gone to get her.'

'Thanks,' Sophronie said, pushing her head past Mrs Anderson to smile at Gertie.

Gertie looked into the pale blue eyes and tried to return the smile, but nobody was home in the eyes. The talking, though, was like Sophronie's as she said: 'I meant to give my youngens a real fine Christmas. Seems like I ain't hardly ever got time fer foolen with my youngens no more.' She smiled triumphantly. 'But today I fixed Wheateye's hair, shampooed an tinted it an give it a lemon rinsh, real good. Where's Wheateye?' She caught the storm door, and such was her darting speed that she was halfway through and had given one shrill call for Wheateye before Mrs Anderson and Gertie could get in and jerk shut the door.

'Wheateye's all right,' Mrs Anderson said in a breathless, jerky voice.

'But I wantcha tu see her hair. Oh, Wheateye,' and she screamed shrilly again, putting her face close to the glass, as if unable to see that Mrs Anderson's storm door, unlike her own, had all its panes.

'I'll go hunt Wheateye,' Mr Anderson said from the living room in a strange meek voice.

'No, no, dear, I'll go,' Mrs Anderson said, reaching for the doorknob.

Gertie felt a rush of cold air. 'I'm gone, dear.'

'Not through the front door. There isn't even a path cleared. You haven't even taken time to put on your boots. You'll have to walk all the way around.' Mrs Anderson's voice dropped to an angry hiss. 'He would go away and leave me.'

Georgie, grinning with delight at all the strange goings on, caught even his mother's whisper and cried: 'Poppa leave mama.' He made a song of it and circled around the tiny kitchen, pausing every few steps to look at Sophronie.

Sophronie had been groping over the kitchen table, apparently hunting cigarettes, for her last one, half burned, lay smoking on the floor. She saw the cigarette, bent to reach it, staggered, caught first a chair, and then the table. She leaned on it with both hands, smiling, 'It's like that merry-go-round,' she said.

Georgie studied her. His glance went from her red-nailed toes on up her body that looked like some gray, wrinkling sack filled with bones and muscles and joints. He considered her belly briefly, but it was only a row of wrinkles sagging between jutting hip bones, and above it her dry puckered breasts stood little higher than the ridges of her ribs. It was Sophronie's face that gave Georgie most satisfaction. Her lipstick wavered widely on one side of her mouth, and thinned suddenly on the other, so that when she smiled it was like half her face didn't move. Her eyebrow pencil was high and heavy, crooking down into the bright red spots of rouge smeared unevenly over her cheeks. All the colors, the pink, the red, the black, stood out boldly against the brick red of her neck and forehead, and the red flush, stopping abruptly as it did just above the hollows of her collarbone, looked painted on above the gray-white body.

'You're a Indian,' Georgie said at last, his glance on her upstanding hair.

Sophronie giggled. 'I'm a Indian on th merry-go-round—*yippee*.' Her voice rose into a wild screaming whoop that caused Mrs Anderson to press against the hooked storm door. She snatched once at Georgie as he dashed past, screaming with laughter. Sophronie looked toward her and smiled, her soft and blurry smile.

'I'm a Indian, all right—a Indian on a merry-go-round,' and began an unsteady stepping around the table.

'Merry-go-round, merry-go-round,' Georgie cried. 'I'm on a red horse with a gold bridle an you're on a blue horse with silver. I'm finer'n you an faster. I'm getting ahead, see,' and he pranced still faster.

'Wait,' Sophronie said, straightening, taking her hand from the table, but holding something in the air, as Cassie held to Callie Lou. 'On a merry-go-round they ain't no fallen back—no gitten ahead. You go jist as fast as it goes. See?' She was not looking at Georgie, but straight ahead, her soft but disobedient glance fighting to find something, somebody who could understand this thing. 'See,' she repeated, 'it's like thish—' and her eyes wandered so, groping like the hands of one newly blinded, that Gertie took upon her soul the sin of looking at a naked woman. She stepped in front of Sophronie and looked at her, trying to pull the wandering glance to herself. Anyway, the Bible, she thought, hadn't been thinking about nakedness like Sophronie's. Solomon would never sing of such.

Sophronie held to the table and swayed only a little as her eyes struggled to meet Gertie's glance. 'Recken I'll fall on the merry-go-round? If a body fell jist right, they'd punch out their eyes—but I missed.' She made an unsteady motion toward a band of sticky tape on her forehead. 'Missed,' she said, and started walking again, squeezing herself between table and wall.

'Why'nt you lay down an rest fer a few minutes?' Gertie said.

Sophronie took another unsteady step. 'I dasn't. My relief ain't come. You know a body cain't leave the merry-go-round er a moven line.'

'But yer relief's here,' Gertie said, and pushed Mrs Anderson up to the table. 'It's here—th relief,' she repeated, and hesitantly put her hand on Sophronie's naked shoulder. 'Come on, git over that dizziness so you can go back to work.'

Sophronie stood leaning on Gertie. Her great red clawlike hands with their calloused palms and bandaged fingers dangled by the puny gray-white body. 'I didn't fall,' she said, smiling, proud, 'but I'd better lay down.' She sagged completely into Gertie's arms, still smiling, proud as she mumbled, 'I never fell.'

Gertie laid her on the sofa, but she roused and looked wildly about her. 'Where's Wheateye? I wantcha tu see her hair.'

'I seed it,' Gertie said. 'It's real pretty.'

'I done it myself. I ain't hardly got time to be a real mother to my youngens no more.'

She was sleeping when Homer came tiptoeing up the steps and creaking through the kitchen door, peering in like a timid thief. 'You can come in now,' Mrs Anderson said. 'Mrs Nevels got her to lie down and go to sleep. And she,' with a cold emphasis on the 'she,' 'doesn't have at most more than an AB in psychology.'

'There's no discounting practical experience,' Homer said, and after telling Sophronie's children, clustering on the doorstep, to go back home and be good, he went on into the living room. He stopped by the heating stove, and with the note-taking look in his eyes, he studied Sophronie as she lay, covered now, on the living-room sofa. He turned to Mrs Anderson and reminded her that it was past time for them to be going. Mrs Anderson reminded him they had no baby sitter. Then both turned to Gertie, though it was Homer who did the talking. 'And we pay fifty cents an hour, just for sitting, no work at all,' he said, after a rather lengthy explanation of why they just had to go because they couldn't be rude and refuse a business associate.

'A boss, you mean,' Mrs Anderson corrected, and smiled at Homer as she continued, 'It would be seventy-five cents for a grown woman—a dollar an hour after midnight.'

'Oh,' Homer said, and looked at Mrs Anderson as if he would like to have a word alone with her, but he only cleared his throat.

'Seventy-five cents,' Mrs Anderson repeated. 'There'll be almost nothing to do but give Georgie his supper and Judy her bottle—it's all fixed—when she wakes. They should both be asleep again by eight.'

When they had gone, Gertie was at first more afraid of Georgie than of Sophronie. But Georgie, in turn, seemed afraid of her and gave surprisingly little trouble. He even stood by the door as she directed while she ran home long enough to get a piece of whittling and tell Clytie to set supper—turkey again, but maybe some of it would be good this time.

Both Georgie and the baby went to sleep before nine o'clock, and Gertie took out her knife and whittling wood. Back in her own kitchen she had reached for the cross that would, if it be made right, bring in a good bit of money. Her hand had touched it on the kitchen shelf, but after a headshake of disgust she had turned away. If she couldn't have the block of wood for Christmas, she would, she had suddenly decided, give herself the pleasure of a chickadee for Maggie to go with the St Francis, finished now. She began working on a little chunk of maple saved from the scrap-wood kindling.

The chickadee's belly was roughly rounded out, and a tail feather rising, when there came a knocking, gentle, as if the knocker knew that behind the door there were babies and a drunken woman asleep. It was Mrs Daly in her good churchgoing clothes, but snowy damp and rumpled as if from much walking about in the snow. She looked as if she had been crying, and her voice lacked the gay ring of the morning when she said, nodding toward the sofa where Sophronie lay: 'Christopher told me. Her kids is all right. Anyt'ing I can do?'

Gertie shook her head. 'I figger,' she said, 'that when her own youngens is good an sound asleep I'll carry her home. That is, if her man ain't back by then.'

'He'll set around up atta bowling alley or somewheres till time tu go tu work,' Mrs Daly said.

'I hope,' Gertie said, remembering his endless bottles of beer, 'he ain't off somewheres down an with nobody by him.'

'Not him—Whit ain't like some,' Mrs Daly said. 'He can take care a hissef.' She was still a moment, sighing, looking toward the living room where Sophronie lay. 'I come,' she said at last, 'to borrow Miz Anderson's electric heater. I know she's got one. I borrowed it last time Max set Maggie's hair. If yu don't mind I'll look inu bathroom where she keeps it.'

She was back in a moment with the heater, but stopped long enough to explain, 'When I got home anu kids told me, I went over dere. Wheateye wasn't gone tu bed fer cryen. She was before da looking glass looking at her hair. 'It was cake colorings,' she says. 'Momma couldn't see, an it won't never come out.' I went to work. I used everting—oxydol, yellow soap, shampoo soap, denna took

Roman Cleanser. It's like silver now, but she's wentu sleep, pore t'ing, anu head wet, anu fire out. I couldn't build upu big fire on accountu I gotta go out pretty soon. Yu kids, dey didn't see?' she asked.

'Nobody, I don't recken,' Gertie said, 'but that Miz Bommarita an me an th Andersons and your'n.'

Mrs Daly nodded like one relieved. 'Them, I imagine, will all keep shut. I told mine to keep shut. Anu cake colorings is outa du kid's hair. She'll never know. No use pushing it in Sophronie's face. It don't do um no good. If,' she went on, reluctant to speak, but lonesome in her trouble, 'feeling bad would make um quit, our father, he'd be home this night.'

Something about her voice and the way she looked going down the steps into the dark alley made Gertie think of Cassie, afraid of school but going on in spite of the fear. She wished she could think of something to say, and in a moment old Solomon did come to her help, ' "Give strong drink unto him that is ready to perish, and wine unto those that be of heavy hearts. Let him drink and forget his poverty, and remember his misery no more." '

Mrs Daly stopped on the bottom step to listen, then nodded. 'Ain't it u truth,' she said.

Some time around midnight there was another knocking. It was Max with a jar of cold cream and a nightgown. 'Mrs Daly told me she was out like a light, so I thought I'd clean her up good so's she won't hafta see drunk make-up when she comes to.' She yawned, the blue rings that had been under her eyes in the morning were bluer now.

Gertie whispered over the limber Sophronie: 'Couldn't I do it? You need yer sleep.'

'I'm okay,' Max said. 'I ain't sleepy. I forgot my caffeine pills. None a th girls had none. I've drunk so much coffee it's made me logy.' Then, gently, as over a sick baby, she began cleaning the worst of the make-up off Sophronie's face. Finished, she stayed with the children during the few minutes it took Gertie to carry Sophronie home and put her to bed.

The Meanwell unit, exactly like Gertie's except that there was one bedroom less, was even more cluttered than her own with the

304

celebration of the birthday of Christ. Empty beer and whisky bottles were mixed in with the broken and twisted ribbons and Christmas wrapping paper with its pictures of angels and candles and Santa Claus crumpled and torn into nightmarish little images. She saw a Santa Claus without his head, reindeer without feet, and wingless angels. The new doll buggy, snow-soaked and battered, cluttered the passway to Sophronie's bedroom.

Gertie put her to bed, then went to the other bedroom to look at the boys, sleeping together in the full glare of the unshaded bulb above them, their faces smeared with alley dirt and candy, and streaked as if from tears. Wheateye slept in a baby bed in the same room with the single bed that held the boys. The child's face was clean, but now and then she gave a kind of sobbing breath and her eye lids were swollen and red. Her hair lay silver white and almost dry across the pillow, moving gently in the warm air from the heater, which careful Mrs Daly had put a safe distance from the bed.

She went last to the living room, where most of the space was taken up by a Christmas tree larger than their own. There was a strong smell of scorched paint, for Sophronie, like Clytie, had sprayed the tree with store-bought snow; and the red and green and orange lights still burned, unwinking as the red lights by the railroad tracks when a train had stopped.

Gertie pulled the cord and the lights went out. Another pull and a newscaster telling of bombers dropping death on the enemy was still. As she walked across the alley, she saw Mrs Daly silhouetted in her doorway. She stopped when the little woman called to her, her voice thin and lonely-sounding among the tipped over trash cans and across the dirty snow, 'Dey okay?'

'Fine, everthing's jist fine. I don't see how you cleaned that hair.'

''Twas harder ona kid den me. She got Roman Cleanser in her eyes—pore t'ing.' Then, after asking Gertie if she would turn off the heater and lock the door on the children when she went home from the Andersons', she turned back into her doorway after a last long look down the alley.

Not long after, when Gertie had almost finished the chickadee's tail, she heard the Daly door open and shut, and then Mrs Daly's feet down the steps and crunching away through the snow. The door did not open again.

She must have drowsed over the chickadee, for Mrs Anderson was saying in a low breathless voice, as if she had been running 'You forgot to lock the door,' then asking, 'Is everything all right?'

'Fine,' Gertie said. 'They've slept like fresh-fed lambs. Georgie was good. I sung him to sleep.'

'Homer's studies indicate that rocking or singing a child to sleep is bad, very bad,' Mrs Anderson said, kicking off her slippers, then shaking their snow into the sink.

'What's bad?' Homer asked, opening the storm door.

'The weather,' Mrs Anderson said.

Homer glanced at her shoes. 'I'd have driven you to our walk instead of stopping at the parking place if you'd told me you'd worn your good suede shoes without rubbers. Snow ruins suede,' he said, bending to appraise the damage.

'So does old age,' Mrs Anderson said, looking toward the unlighted living room. 'How's Sophronie?'

'I took her home,' Gertie said.

'Lucky, lucky woman,' Mrs Anderson said. 'I thought of her all evening—with envy—peacefully sleeping, unconscious of the fact that two thousand years ago in Bethlehem of Judea, Christ was born. "Blessed are the meek: for they shall inherit the earth." That is so true—so true. One, in order to inherit, must first die. "Blessed are they which do hunger and thirst after righteousness: for they shall be filled." For in truth we are all brothers in Christ—But I'd better not say that. It's communists, don't you think? We all drink from the same cup—Dear me, that's worse yet.'

She had, after much groping, found the string for the living-room light. She jerked it on but continued to stand, her hand lifted to the string, her face upturned as it had been when she looked for the light in the dark. 'Homer, do you think it's possible that Joseph Daly in our alley and Mr Turbi in Grosse Pointe could have drunk from the same cup? Mr Turbi is one of Homer's bosses,' she explained to Gertie, still looking at the light. 'And he is in trouble—very great trouble. A Jew has moved into his neighborhood, only six doors away.'

306

She gave a shiver, turned away from the light. 'Isn't it horrible? He is certain other Jews will move into the neighborhood. Oh, I wept for Mr Turbi. The pity of it, to work so hard and be just a little man in a little house, then Providence—no, it was God—I'm sure it was God. No, it would have to be Christ, the Prince of Peace. Jews believe in God, and Mr Turbi wants nothing Jewish, but Christ was born to a Jewish mother. Dear God, whatever will Mr Turbi do? Make his own Christ in his own image. Isn't that what we all do? Here, Mr Turbi's Christ, the Prince of Peace, the decontaminated one, sent a war just for Mr Turbi's benefit. He got to be a big man in a big company in a big house in Grosse Pointe. The nasty war kept him from buying a new house, but everything in it is new. Sophronie would love it. All new, new, new. The early-American antiques in the living room are so new, everything a new tombstone for the old Mr Turbi— the poor part—and a Jew has dared, actually dared, move into a house only six doors away.'

She flung her hands wide and looked at Homer staring at her from the doorway. 'Oh, Homer, darling,' and she smiled the strange smile that, it seemed to Gertie, came only when the woman wanted to cry, 'isn't it terrible—the pity of it, poor, poor Mr Turbi!' She turned back to Gertie, who stood trapped between Homer and the stove, holding her coat. 'And Mrs Nevels, do you know about the Reds? They're taking over. The unions, Mrs Nevels, they're red, red, crimson like Christ's blood on Calvary we used to sing about in church. Did you know that some unions insist on treating coons like white men? Ugh.'

'Lena—darling. Please.'

She held up her hand, gave a slight giggle. 'Homer, darling, some day when you say "Lena" that way you'll forget the "darling" entirely. But maybe that time won't come until you start taking notes on me. You listened so respectfully while Mr Turbi discoursed on baseball, but all the same you are suspect. You did not know the batting average of Loy McGafferty. One shows ignorance only of lesser men like—Gandhi. They hadn't a book in the house.'

'Lena, you've had a cocktail or two too many. The Turbis have a library.'

'A room done in books, you mean,' Mrs Anderson said. She looked aggrieved. 'Homer, darling, your psychology isn't working today. Did you take it off and put your Christmas spirit on?' She stretched her arms, yawning. 'Oh, Lord, I want to be home. I know you're right. It isn't good for children to be separated from their fathers, but couldn't I go back and stay on the farm with Mom until—' She saw that Homer wasn't listening.

He was staring absent-mindedly at his desk, his fingers working through the part in his sparsing hair. 'I wonder what she or Turbi was? Italian? Jewish? I can't decide, for I must admit they are quite nicely smoothed over. If there were statistics available, one could write a most penetrating sociological study of Detroit's upper industrial class—its origins and its tastes.'

'But you seemed to find their tastes so interesting. I mean, not just as thesis material,' Mrs Anderson said, her voice lonesome-sounding.

'I am a man of many interests, my dear. And in business, you must remember, one has to make a few concessions.' He turned abruptly to Gertie, for he had never noticed that she couldn't go home until he moved out of the passway. 'Speaking of business,' he said, smiling as if he handed her a fortune, 'I have some for you. Your wood carving on my desk was noticed even by Mr Turbi. Mrs Turbi wondered tonight if you couldn't make some dolls, something unusual that one couldn't find in a store. She wants them—they must be different, of course—for the doll collections of two little girls; daughters of business associates, you know. Rather smallish, but nicely featured, and jointed at knees, elbows, and waist, and—Lena, did she say 'jointed at the head'?'

'She forgot that, but she didn't forget to say to try to get them for two dollars each. Five isn't enough for so much work,' Mrs Anderson said, looking at Gertie. 'Don't do it for less.'

'Three ud mebbe be about right,' Gertie said, yawning, moving toward the door, for Homer, taking off his overcoat now, had at last moved.

'Perhaps if they're walnut or some good wood and . . .' Homer's voice had grown more and more absent-minded, and at last stopped altogether as he considered his overcoat held in one hand for hanging. His speculative and slightly displeased glance went from the overcoat to the cuff of the dark blue suit he wore. 'You know, dear, we have to begin to think about getting some clothing. This suit—'

'It's practically new,' Mrs Anderson interrupted in surprise.

'Oh, it's new enough,' Homer said, his voice displeased as his glance, 'but—well, a dark business suit just won't do for every occasion; for casual wear everybody wears slacks and jackets. Mr Turbi's closets are full of—'

As she escaped through the kitchen, Gertie heard Mrs Anderson's lonesome-sounding cry: 'Everybody? Is Mr Turbi then everybody—for us?'

20

Early one Saturday morning during Christmas vacation, just as Clovis got in from work, a worried Sophronie came knocking. Her eyes were cold with fright above the rouge and lipstick as she asked if Gertie could watch Wheateye while she went with Whit to take the boys to the doctor, for it was their tonsil taking out day.

'Sure,' Gertie said, and offered to give Wheateye supper as well as lunch if Whit wanted to stay at the hospital late after Sophronie went to work.

Sophronie shook her head, and looked more frightened still. 'That doc—Edwards is his name—said they didn't need to go to no hospital.' She took a quick puff of cigarette smoke, and in her agitation swallowed it, then coughed long and hard into her closed fist. 'I tried to tell him about onct—it was when we had that place uv our own in Dearborn before Whit got laid off—they was a neighbor woman, she lived right acrost th street. Her little boy had his tonsils out, and she brung him home jist like I'm bringen mine. Nothen atall, her doctor said, jist like mine. I seed her little boy when she brung him home. He got stiller an stiller an whiter an whiter, but they wasn't no blood a body could see. Fin'ly he looked so still an kinda blue she went off to telephone. He quit breathen, they said, while she was a tryen to git th doctor on the phone. He'd bled to death and swallered th blood.' She shivered. 'I wanted mine in th hospital, but that doc wouldn't do it.'

'Maybe,' Gertie said, hunting words of reassurance, 'your youngens seems so good an strong he's a tryen to save you money by not putten em in a hospital.'

'That's what hurts,' Sophronie said. 'We got hospitalization. Had it ever since Gilbert got knocked down by a car an they wouldn't let us bring him home till we paid up. He'd broke one bone in his leg an hadda stay three weeks. We hadda git more on the mortgage, quick. But now th hospital could keep all th youngens one er two nights apiece, an they'd be safe if they started bleeden an—oh, Lordy.' Her hand shook so her cigarette hit her cheek. 'An now it wouldn't cost us a cent.'

Whit, still in his work clothes, had just opened the storm door, and now he smiled, his eyes sparkling up in his grimy face. 'An then that Doc Edwards couldn't git a mink coat fer his missus out a what he makes off a three tonsils and splitten two nights' hospitalization apiece with th hospital. They'll send a big bill to th insurance company an collect an then split.'

Gertie had hardly got Clovis fed and to bed and the kitchen straight when she saw that the battered Meanwell car was back. She saw Whit go alone up the walk in a kind of staggering run, as if drunk. She hurried out to help, and Sophronie, pale but no longer shaking, explained that the overpowering fumes of ether in the closed car had made Whit sick to his stomach. Gertie carried in both boys, squinching her eyes a little against the dripping blood, the strong smell of ether, the vomit-spewing, blue-lipped mouths.

Sophronie turned a shade whiter each time one spat blood, and if either lay stiff an instant she was bending over him, listening to the heartbeat, and holding her own breath, the better to hear his breathing. However, they seemed gradually to improve, and breathed more slowly and spat less blood, though when time came for Sophronie to go away to work, she lingered with them too long, and then had to run, looking over her shoulder, entreating Gertie, 'You'll watch em good, now, won'tcha?'

Whit had drunk two bottles of beer to settle his stomach, and gone to bed. He had not slept since coming off his shift, and must, like Clovis, leave again for work before midnight, so that it was Gertie who stayed through the afternoon and tended the boys. Clovis came to see how she was making out, and then with Clytie and Cassie went to the big store for the weekly load of staple groceries.

When he had gone, Gertie wished she had told him to round up all the children and take them. She had been too busy with Claude Jean and Gilbert to watch her own boys. She had hardly seen Enoch since breakfast, and now Amos was out of sight, and where was Reuben? The snow and the pale sunshine had tempted even him outside; though there was in him no meanness and he'd never been one to pick a quarrel, his bigness and his silence with that seeming sullen way of his, made it harder for him to take care of himself in the alley than for Enoch.

Max ran in with a package of pink ice cream for the Meanwells, but hadn't seen anything of Gertie's boys. She was on her way to work and hurrying, so that Gertie didn't ask her to stay with the sick children a moment while she hunted. Not long after Maggie Daly came, but she hadn't seen the boys, she said. She asked about Gilbert and Claude Jean, then held out a little board with holes. 'Buy a chance on this beautiful rayon taffeta bedspread. It costs forty dollars, and yucan perhaps get it almost for free, onie one dime. Yu can't lose. Your dime will help u good sisters build up our liberry.'

Gertie's mouth went thin and straight, but still she took a dime from her pocket. Maggie was writing her name on the little slip that came off when she punched the hole Gertie had picked, when Mrs Anderson came. She had a white shirt on one arm, the baby on the other, and her face was steamy red and weary. She asked about the 'tonsillectomies,' but hardly listened to Gertie's reply. She kept shaking her head and declaring that Sophronie should have managed somehow to get money to keep the children at least one night in a hospital. But before she could wait for Gertie's explanation, she remembered her own troubles. She held up the shirt, and begged: 'Oh, Mrs Nevels, do you know how to get a scorched spot off a shirt front? Oh, if he'd only wear colored shirts like he used to.' Gertie thought she was going to cry as she looked at the shirt, a beautiful thing of fine white cotton cloth. 'And right in the front it had to be.

'His bosses wear white shirts,' she went on, getting still more angry, 'and so he feels he should. I can't see the sense of it—and I have to do up the things.'

Maggie, finished with Gertie's punch, looked up in wonder. 'But he's gotta butter his bosses a little, don'tcha know? Yu oughta be glad he don't hafta get drunk with em. Pop knows a cop that drunk his way up to a sergeant's place, but he knowed plenty dirt onu inspector, and that helped him.' She bent to study the spot. 'Try Roman Cleaner. If it don't come off right away, soak it. Yu got any?'

Mrs Anderson shook her head. 'My husband is allergic to bleaches.'

Maggie was already going through the door. 'He won't be allergic if he don't know about it.' She called over her shoulder, 'Yu wanta beautiful bedspread?'

Mrs Anderson sighed, looked at the punchboard with disgust, but at last picked it up. She punched four holes with sharp, vicious jabs. 'I hate this,' she burst out, 'but worse than anything I hate and detest doing Homer's shirts. Back home we always had a hired girl. The laundering of shirts, alas, was not included in my education. But Homer thinks I should do the laundry. I suppose what he says is true. Many women whose husbands are in even higher income brackets than he is do the laundry, but if I could find a laundress, just for these cursed shirts, who could—well, why don't I say it? Slip it over on him.'

Gertie sat silent, aware of her expectant waiting. She had never taken in washing. Clovis wouldn't like it. But a dollar was—She heard Maggie's feet on the steps, and nodded.

The company was hardly gone before first Gilbert and then Claude Jean started vomiting again. She was so busy for the next half-hour that she had no time to worry over her own in the alley. Claude Jean, quivering with nausea, was leaning over the bed, blood dribbling down his chin, when his glance swept past the window that opened on the alley. His eyes, dulled with pain and nausea, were suddenly fixed, like the eyes of one dying, Gertie thought with fright. However, he managed to rise on his elbow, crane his head, and gargle, 'S'fight.'

Satisfied that the child was in no immediate danger, Gertie turned and looked through the window. She saw one of the bigger Dalys, bloody-faced, bare-headed, and with a torn coat, dashing for his door. He was followed at once by three of his younger brothers. Not far behind them came a snowsuited figure surrounded by a crowd of children. The boy came on with a sober high-stepping gait, like a woman in her finery walking slowly on her way to church so as to deprive no neighbor of the privilege of seeing her. It was Enoch, Gertie realized. She soon saw Amos, one in a swarm of little children, all looking up at Enoch as if he were God. Wheateye was racing for the coalhouse, and Cassie's friend, with Mable in his arms, came on more slowly.

The Daly door was flung open, and the bigger Dalys dashed back into the alley. The smaller ones, just getting home, turned and jumped on their coalhouse. There, they began hurling epithets toward Wheateye, now jumping up and down and screaming on her coalshed roof.

Then, his head rising above the swarming children, Gertie saw Reuben turn into the alley. There was blood dribbling down the side of his face; but from the way his shoulders humped and his hands twisted and clenched by his side, and the set look of his jaws, she knew the hurt inside him was worse than that on his head. The Daly door, as if waiting just for him, flew open as he came opposite it. A chunky man in suit clothes rushed down the walk, shaking his fist. His heavy jaw was outthrust, and he looked as if he had but one thought, and that to kill Reuben.

Gertie glanced once at the Meanwell boys to make certain they were all right, then hurried to the kitchen door. She was jerking it open when Whit, who seemed to have been watching through the glass, said: 'Now don't be a runnen out. He won't hurt th kid,' he reassured her as she pushed open the storm door. 'He's too smart fer that.'

Gertie stopped when she had her head around the door enough to see Reuben and hear Mr Daly's loud command of, 'Hey, youse, wait a minute!' Reuben only came on at a faster pace. This forced Mr Daly to run in order to get in front of him. When he did manage to stop the boy near the end of the Meanwell walk, almost in front of Gertie, he yelled: 'Stop, youse hillbilly. Wotta yu mean beating up on a little kid half yu size? I oughta see to ut that youse is put in u can fudu rest a yu life.'

314

Reuben stepped back from the waving fist. His eyes blazed, and anger bleached his face. His voice was a choked mumble. 'I never hit yer youngens.'

'Yu know yu did, yu lying hillbilly bastard.' Mr Daly's anger seemed suddenly to leave him. He smiled, and there were dimples in his smoothly shaven cheeks, going in and out like Maggie's. 'Youse is in Detroit now, mu boy. We've got law an order fudu likes a youse. Yu come up here an fudu first time in yu life you gitcha bellies full and shoes on yu feet, and it goes tuyu head.' Conscious of the watching alley, he made a grotesque and exaggerated motion of looking at Reuben's feet. He bent far over, shook his head in disbelief. 'So help me, yu've got shoes. How does ut feel tu have shoes on dem tough feet?'

A child's laugh rose shrilly from the ever thickening crowd of listeners. Mr Daly's blue eyes, so much like Maggie's, sparkled still more brightly when the laughter swelled into a mighty burst of whooping as a snowball, flung by someone in the crowd, landed with a splattering plop by Gertie's feet. Fragments of its dirty heart spotted her clean starched apron, but she, on her stoop now, did not look down at it. The cracking sound from the agonized pulling of her twisting fingers was unnoticed in the uproar, like Whit's hissing whisper behind her: 'Don't go a mixen in it, now. Keep shut. He'll call th cops.'

Reuben looked up, saw her, and started up the Meanwell walk. Mr Daly sprang in front of him, and stood, his outthrust stomach almost touching Reuben. Reuben stopped, and looked beseechingly at his mother. The crowd pressed close around him. The Daly boys were nearest, their bloody heads objects of observations, many delighted: 'Boy, dey fixed um.' Others were disgusted: 'Babies crappen onu old man thataway'; and not a few were aggrieved: 'Wotta's that big kid think he is, taken all u credit? It was a free-fer-all. He didn't do nutten.'

More children, and even adults, came running, drawn from distant alleys by catcalls and cries of: 'Dey's gonna be a real fight'; 'I'll bet her could lick um.' Word must have gone out that a little Daly girl had been beaten up by hillbilly boys and carried off to the hospital, for two boys came running around Max's end of the alley,

315

screaming: 'Didu cops git um? Where's u ambulance? Is her bad hurt? Show me du blood. Lemme seedu blood.'

Wheateye jumped up and down on the coalshed roof and screamed: 'Maggie Daly is a liar. She told her father she was dead. They ain't no other Daly girl. Maggie Daly told her father she was dead. Liar, liar, yellow bastard bitch!'

Mr Daly, smiling ever more broadly as the crowd thickened, continued to stand in front of Reuben. Gertie moved to the edge of the stoop, though Whit's warning whisper was shrill behind her. She stopped again and twisted her sweat-slippery hands. It would be easier to stand and see him beaten. He wouldn't look at her the way he looked now. She could fling that flabby-bellied— She saw Reuben's right fist shove hard into his jacket pocket, then the ripple of the cloth as the hand opened. She sprang down the steps, and in two strides had reached Reuben, just as he stepped away from Mr Daly, and stood, his eyes fixed on the man's chest, on the left side about where the overall buckle would be, had he worn overalls. It was like the game of mumblety-peg Henley had taught him. She had played it, too. You stood, your eyes on the target, opening the knife with one hand in your pocket; and at the word 'Go,' the knife came out in a hard swift whirl that carried the point deep into the target.

She caught his wrist just as it jerked upward. 'Reuben!' Her insistent, agonized cry rang out until even Mrs Bommarito, who had been watching behind her storm door, came onto her stoop. Mr Anderson, half in, half out his storm door, looked up from the pad and pencil in his hands. Gertie saw them, because she had suddenly remembered that she mustn't let her glance go again to Reuben's hand in his pocket. Only a city fool wouldn't know he was opening a knife. Up here there was a law against carrying knives. They might put him in jail for years, just for the carrying. Reuben struggled to get his hand out of his pocket. She held it down, and fought now with her eyes to make him look at her. But he'd only look at the smiling Mr Daly, his own jaws set, his cheeks white over the clenched muscles.

Reuben might hate her forever for this, but it was better than jail—and maybe a dead Mr Daly. 'Git in th house, son,' she said, and with one hand on his wrist, the other on his shoulder, she dragged him up the walk and over the steps. He struggled, his heels plowing through the snow shovelings, his blazing anger now for her instead of Mr Daly, whose belly rippled with laughter.

Somewhere a child exclaimed, 'Golly, her's strong.' It didn't matter what they said, for Whit, understanding at last, was opening the storm door. His voice was still a whispering, but worried now.

'Git in, boy,' he said, and grabbed Reuben's shoulder.

Reuben struggled against the hands trying to get him through the door, until Gertie caused another burst of laughter by picking him up bodily and shoving him across the threshold. He turned then and screamed at Mr Daly, his voice shrill and broken, unlike his own: 'I didn't tetch a one a yer youngens. They tried to gang up on my brother an some more little youngens. I tuck a rock away—'

Whit and Gertie together had managed to close the door, but Gertie was still outside. She looked once at Mr Daly, licked her lips, her palms rubbing on her apron. She remembered Whit's advice, and reached for the doorknob. A sigh of disappointment went up from the alley, then Mr Daly, by her bottom step now, was saying loudly: 'Listen, yu overgrown hillbilly; yu kid's lyen. He did too beat up on mu little kid. My kids don't lie—see.'

Gertie's hand dropped from the door, and she turned and looked at him. 'Th very first mornen mine went to school, yer youngen—'

'Huh? Youngen, whatcha mean youngen? In Detroit youse gotta learn to speak English, yu big nigger-loven communist hillbilly. Yu gotta behave. I, Joseph Daly, will see to ut yu do. I'm a dacent, respectable, religious good American. See?' Gertie opened her mouth, but shut it as he went on, laughing a little, one ear cocked for the audience behind him: 'Detroit was a good town till da hillbillies come. An den Detroit went tu hell.'

Somewhere down the alley a voice cried, 'Oh, yeah?'

Mr Daly gave it no heed. He came onto the bottom step, and looked up at Gertie, shaking his fist to emphasize his words: 'If one a youse touches one a mine, I'll have youse all inu clink, see. Du cops listen tu Joseph Daly, see. I letcha git by wit too much awready.' He straightened his shoulders, attempted to make his chest stick out further than his stomach, failed, but continued in his injured-good-citizen tone: 'An why for because didjas beat up mu wife, a great big overgrown hillbilly like youse on a little woman like mu wife? Why, because she barred da evil doctrine a communism from her door—yu call yuself a Christian, I prasume.'

Gertie gave a slow headshake. 'I recken I try tu be, but,' she went on in a low, choked voice, 'whether I'm a Christian or not is somethin' fer God to decide, not me.'

'So yu don't know, huh.' He laughed again, and the alley laughed with him.

The laughter somehow loosened her tongue. 'I didn't hit yer wife. I kept her frum hurten a woman she'd already haf blinded. Th woman was jist tryen to spread some kind a religion, an th Constitution says, "Congress shall make no—"'

'Communist,' he was screaming, waving his fist, and for an instant so choked with wrath he could not go on. 'Yu communists allatime yu gotta spout u Constitution. Don'tcha know they's a war? Oh, if u good Father Moneyhan could be President. He'd settle u likes a youse. Yu an yu Constitution, yu commies an heathen hill—'

A soft but dirty snowball splattered the side of his face. He whirled toward Sophronie's coalhouse, now covered with children, including Amos, Enoch, and Wheateye. 'Who true dat?' he cried, his grandstand manners lost in fury.

Wheateye screamed: 'I done it, Mr Daly. I done it. I'm sorry. S'it agin u law to throw snowballs? I didn't mean to hitcha.'

'She's jist a little girl an cain't throw straight,' Enoch said.

Daly strode toward the coalshed. 'Yu true dat, yu little liar.'

'Oh, yeah?' Enoch said.

'Yu need whatcha mudder needs an yu—'

Another snowball caught him on the ear. Gertie, sensing rather than hearing movement below the stoop, glanced down and saw Cassie's friend by the house wall. He was just bending to pick up his little sister Mable. He looked up at Gertie and smiled. 'Don't mind that great big liar, lady,' and Gertie saw the black snowball in his down-hanging right hand. He shoved it quickly behind Mable so that when Mr Daly sent a suspicious glance in his direction he saw nothing but a boy minding a baby.

318

Mr Daly whirled to face the alley when Wheateye began to scream: 'It was a little girl, Joseph Daly, another little girl like me; a little bitsy girl in a red dress, run run— Lookit, th cops. Lookit.'

Wheateye was already racing down the alley toward the Japanese unit, past Mr Daly's door. Other children had seen the scout car even before Wheateye, and all were running now or leaping from coalhouses and trash cans. Wheateye's cry had risen to a chorus, happy and excited: 'Da cops. Da cops is come. Dey're gonna take um to jail.' Gertie saw the black scout car coming slowly up the big alley that ran at right angles to her own. But she continued to stand, her back against the door.

'My wife's called du cops,' Mr Daly said. But his voice was uncertain as he added, moving toward the car but looking over his shoulder, 'Yu'll git a ride.'

Gertie pinched pleats in her apron and stared over the heads of the running children. The car stopped, a window was rolled down, and one of two burly men in uniform questioned the children. His voice was too low to carry through the tumult, but at once she saw heads nodding, and fingers pointing, seemed like in her direction. 'If it's me they're a hunten, tell em I'm right here,' she said in a low trembling voice.

But there was nobody left around her stoop to hear, except Cassie's friend, who comforted: 'Them cops ain't fu you, lady. Cops don't gitcha fu little ole quarrels.' He came onto the stoop and stood on tiptoe beside Gertie and tried to see the scout car, entirely surrounded by children. Mable was heavy, and he sank back on his heels when the car, instead of turning into the little alley, went on up the big one. 'See, they wasn't fu you.' But he was almost at once worried again, and stood on tiptoe, and tried again to see the disappearing car, a troubled wrinkle in his forehead as he said, 'Who they after, I wonder.' He turned to Gertie. 'Yu sure they wasn't no priest an no Red Cross in that car? Pop, we figger from his letters, is right inu middle a them Jap islands.'

'They wasn't no priest an no Red Cross. Your pop'll be all right,' Gertie said, and though she was not much given to caresses she smoothed his hair, then straightened Mable's hood that had slid over one eye. 'Yer pop, he'll be a comen home one a these days an—'

319

Cassie's friend never heard her. A swarm of children, Enoch among them, was running past toward the alley by the railroad fence. The boy cried: 'Whatsa matter? What is ut? Where yu going?'

No one answered his frantic questions until Mike Turbovitch, lagging so far behind he'd lost hope of getting a grandstand spot on a coalshed roof where he might see an arrest or even a fight with a cop, stopped. 'Them cops is crazy. It ain't u reg'lar patrol an dey don't know du project. Lookit, they've went all u way around, stid a going up u alley by du tracks to git tu 15411 Merry Hill.'

'That's me,' Cassie's friend cried, springing down the steps. He glanced once over his shoulder at Gertie. 'Yu sure dey wasn't no priest an no—' Panic choked him and he ran, Mable bouncing on his hip.

Gertie, still thinking of Reuben, had a moment's wish that she had held Mable while the boy ran to see what the cops wanted at his number. Nothing much, she guessed; police, she'd learned, came for all kinds of reasons, from barking dogs to drunken men. She went into the Meanwell kitchen, and comfort for Reuben took up all her mind, until Whit, opening another bottle of beer said: 'I don't reckon she's in any kind a trouble, that kid's mom. Sophronie knowed her. They was ona same 'sembly fer awhile.

'She'd drink some,' he continued, as Gertie, thinking only of Reuben, went into the hall. 'That is, accorden to Sophronie. I recollect onct she didn't hear frum her man fer a long time an her youngens all come down with th measles an she hadda quit work an got down in th mouth an drinken some when she got kinda hard run tryen to git along on them army wages. Soon's she could, she got her a job where she could git considerable overtime. She might a done somethen foolish er let herself git hurt on a little drink, er two. They go to some people's heads, specially when they're kind a tired frum overtime an—'

Whit's voice died as Gertie opened the bathroom door. Reuben was there, his face washed, but he continued to stand in the little place like a wounded wild thing afraid to leave its den. 'I didn't do nothen,' he said, glaring at her, more defiant and angry now than he had been with Mr Daly. 'All a them a laughen, an you a standen a taken his—' He choked, and she thought with terror that he was going to cry.

320

She tried to put her hand on his shoulder, but he brushed past her to the door. 'He's jist showen off, son—and, well, I thought I smelled whisky on his breath.' He was walking away as she talked to him, a thing not even Enoch had ever done. She followed, wanting to heal the hurt, determined that he should understand. 'Everwhere you'll find people with shoddy ways, son.' He only jerked open the kitchen door. She was afraid again for him, and spoke quickly. 'You'll have to quit carryen a knife, son. Detroit's differ'nt.'

He whirled and looked at her, his face white with fury. 'I've allus carried a knife. I ain't a quitten now. I ain't a maken myself over fer Detroit. I ain't a standen a taken nobody's lies—like you done.'

The door banged and he was gone into the alley. He wouldn't go hunt Mr Daly now, she thought, but still she hurried to the door, and was relieved to see him only a few feet away with Whit and another man she had never seen. She wanted to speak to Reuben again, or better yet hear him speak so that she might know he was not so hurt and angry as she had thought. She opened the outer door, and now, after the tumult of the children, there seemed a heavy stillness in the alley, as if it waited to hear again the blue-eyed smiling man call her names. Whit looked up, and waved his bottle toward her. 'Recollect that little boy with th little kid said somethen to you 'bout wanten a priest? His Mom, she got squashed to death in her press.'

Gertie gave a slow headshake of wonderment. That other woman hadn't done anything either except try to raise her children the best she could. She thought of bubble gum and shoestrings; maybe the woman had figured it all out in her head. She was staring straight in front of her, looking at the woman she had never seen, a woman pretty like her children, when she heard the sound of vomiting from the boys' room. Gertie, for the first time in hours, seemed like, remembered what she was supposed to be doing. But as she took the few steps to their room, she realized she couldn't have been away more than a few minutes.

Claude Jean was clearing blood from his throat when she got there, but he was able to look at her. There was disgust as well as pain in his eyes as he said: 'Jeez, couldn'cha a socked him onct, jist onct right in u puss? Couldn'cha, jist onct?' and he fell back, sighing, not heeding the blood on his chin.

Claude Jean was the only one who mentioned Mr Daly. The hush lingered in the alleys. Even the children were still, gathered in little huddles, not even shrill when Mrs Daly came, loaded with groceries, and they ran to tell her the news of the woman squashed to death. Whit, in for another bottle of beer, wished he could remember her name. Nobody did. Some thought it was Vermiglio, but they weren't certain.

Later, when suppers were over and the children in from the alleys, Clovis came to see, he said, about the Meanwell boys. But mostly, she thought, he wanted to visit with Whit. She wanted to ask him about Reuben, but did not. If Clovis didn't already know about the knife business, there was no need to tell him, at least not now. When not busy with the boys, she sat in the living room and worked on Victor's Christ while the men talked in the kitchen. They were joined soon by Andy Miller, once a service-station man in an Alabama town, but now a pitman in the steel mill. He lived with his wife and three small children in the last unit in Gertie's row. Not long after, there came a tool-and-die man from a place where tanks were made. He was one of Whit's old cronies, she learned soon, for he and Whit had worked together for old man Flint in what they called, smiling as they said it, 'the big house.'

He studied her hands a moment over the wood, and asked her what it was she made. 'A Christ,' she said.

He considered, his head tipped down. 'You could make a pretty good Christ with a jig saw,' he said in a moment, then turned away, for Whit was telling of Mr Daly's anger, laughing a little, like it was a movie he had seen.

Finished, he sighed a little, slumping in his chair. He was silent a moment before he said: 'It wasn't half what he said to Sophronie, onct.'

'Oh, him,' the tool-and-die man said, and the little trouble in the alley seemed forgotten. Over their beer the men talked of the woman dead in her press. A needless death, Whit said: her press had been the kind with a foot treadle, and it was too easy for a body to forget, being tired or sleepy, and tramp the treadle when your hands or your head was over the stock in the press.

They fell then into long musing tales of the things they had seen and heard of in factories when men got mangled or killed. Gertie

322

had never known there were so many ways for a workingman to die: burned, crushed, skinned alive, smothered, gassed, electrocuted, chopped to bits, blown to pieces. She heard tales of the ways of loose bolts or old belts with human arms, legs, and heads. She listened to stories of machines on a speed-up that, unable to bear the speed as did the men, flew with no warning into flying pieces of steel that blinded and crippled when they didn't kill. A fast-turning wheel or milling machine wasn't like a man; it wouldn't just fall down on the floor peaceable-like when it passed out the way a man would. Even worse, she thought, were Miller's stories of white-hot steel, but worse than anything were the foreman's fists and his iron-toed shoes in a man's behind.

Terrified, yet fascinated, she stood whittling in the passway the better to hear until Clovis noticed her and said, half jokingly, half chidingly, 'You'll scare my woman so she'll want to take me back home.'

Whit turned to her with a comforting smile. 'Th foremen ain't like that no more, leastways not right now. Th companies makes plenty a money now, with th war an cost plus. An we got th union.'

The tool-and-die man leaned back in his kitchen chair, tipping it far backward, for he, like the others, was a long man. 'Yeah, but wait'll th war's over. They'll bust th unions—when times gits bad an a lotta th men's got kids, not starving, but, well, you know, kinda hungry.'

'Oh, yeah,' Whit said, 'they'll hafta bust up a lotta men first.'

The tool-and-die man shook his head, his eyes reflective, remembering. 'But they're getten smart, them big companies. They've learned you can't bust a union by busten heads—not even if th busten kills a few men. Them companies has made so damn' much money outa th war they can do anything. I figger now they'll do it th smooth way, politics, no-strike laws, stir up things that'll bring trouble between th factions in th unions—kinda make the unions bust theirselves.'

'Oh, yeah?' Whit said, but the men were silent, staring less at cigarette smoke and the head on their beer than at the future.

Gertie wished Clovis would speak. He hated the unions as much as she. He'd grumbled more times than one about the dues he had to pay to a union he had never wanted to join. A man oughtn't to have to join anything except of his own free will. Free will, free will: only your own place on your own land brought free will.

The men left for work, but Gertie, after looking again at the boys, for Claude Jean worried her, he was so still, went back to her work on Victor's Christ. The figure was almost finished now except for the face and the nail holes. It was a drooping, ribby-chested Christ that made her think, faceless as he was, of somebody she had once seen, but could not name. He was no kin at all of the Christ she had seen in her mother's field. She sat a time and tried to see a face for him, but could see only Reuben's face, sick with hurt and anger, and in and out through Christ and Reuben there was the bubble gum boy's face and the worry of Claude Jean, sharper now that she was alone.

She went again and stood a long time by him, listening to his too-gentle-seeming breathing, and squeezing his hands that seemed cold. She snapped on the light. Still he did not waken, and it seemed to her his ears and lips looked blue, and there was no color in his cheeks. She kept pushing back Sophronie's story of the child who had died, swallowing his blood. But all at once she couldn't any more. Sophronie wouldn't be home for another hour, and by then Claude Jean could have bled to death like the other.

She grabbed the scrap of paper with the doctor's name and number, and hurried out into the alley. She'd never used a telephone and didn't know where the closest pay station was. She'd first have to find a neighbor to help her. She was looking frantically about for a lighted kitchen door, and wondering where first she should knock, when she heard a car come into the parking lot. It must be Victor, she thought, for with a car, and his work close, he got home much sooner than Sophronie.

She met him in the alley, and told him of her fears. He only shook his head. 'Yu couldn't git no doctor this time anight,' he said, and without taking the slip of paper turned back to his car.

She was listening to Claude Jean's heart when Victor came creaking through the door. 'Lookut um,' he said. 'If he's bleeding bad, we gotta call u cops.'

He handed her a flashlight, she got a spoon, and the two of them pried open Claude Jean's sleepy mouth. She could see no running blood, and Victor, wrinkling his nose at the smell of ether, also looked, but could see nothing.

They did, however, waken Claude Jean, who sat up and at once wanted ice, ice cream, and the answers to a great many questions, such as the time and how many kettles of steel had Victor unplugged on his shift.

Victor laughed and slapped Gertie on the shoulder as he went away. 'Quitcha worrying. Du kid's okay.'

Gertie had the nail holes finished when Sophronie came, breathless from running, but asking before she could get through the door, 'Is th kids okay?'

21

'Hu, Gyp. Hu, Gyp, come on now.' Gertie, holding a plate of breakfast scraps in one hand, unhooked the storm door with the other as she called the dog. 'Hu, Gyp, hu—' Wind screaming down the alley scattered her words and whirled the scraps away. An instant later it jerked the storm door from her, flung it hard against the wall, and sent powder-like snow into the kitchen. She caught the storm door, hooked it, then looked quickly and guiltily behind her. She was relieved when she saw no one had noticed her wool-gathering ways. Gyp was back home in Kentucky.

Clovis, finished with breakfast, was trying to sleep. Amos was in the bathroom, and Enoch, kept out of the alley by the weather, listened to the radio. In spite of the bitter wind whipping through the broken pane, Gertie continued to stand with the inner door open, and stare into the white desert of the alley. She looked down at the gray rubbery white, the flat yolk of the refused egg, the only scrap of food the wind had left. Maybe an alley cat, or a stray dog, or even a sparrow would come, just one sparrow to peck at the egg. That would be something alive that needed food in the hard cold, anything so as not to waste the egg in the garbage can.

However, nothing came but loose paper flying along with the whirling snow. She craned her head toward the Meanwell door. But, like the other doors, it might have been the opening to a tomb for all the life it showed. The steps, like her own, were heaped with snow in spots, clean swept in others, for no sooner did a body freeze herself to death to sweep off the thin, forever moving stuff, light as feathers, than it blew on again.

It seemed months since she had seen the Meanwells or spoken with anyone save her own. It just seemed that way, for the day that Wheateye's tonsils had been taken out was hardly three weeks ago, and Gertie had stayed with her as with the boys.

A louder shriek of the wind in the telephone wires caused her to close the inner door, but she continued to stand a moment, the saucer of scraps still in her hand. Maybe Max would come, asking for a dream, or Mrs Anderson, hurrying, a thief's look in her eyes, the bundle of Homer's dirty shirts small under her coat so that Georgie could not see and tell his father. She glanced at the clock. It was too early for the mailman, but there would surely be a letter. She had sent Christmas cards, and written to Aunt Kate and to her mother. Clytie, proud of the family's big Christmas, had written both her grandmothers; but still no letter for weeks, only cards from Mrs Hull and Aunt Kate.

She turned from the door at last and finished her kitchen work. Then, frowning a little, her lips folded tightly together with distaste, she took from a kitchen shelf a half finished doll, a kind of jumping-jack, smooth-faced thing, one of the two that Homer had ordered. Save for the face, Victor's Christ was finished, and since Victor wanted it only in time for Easter, she had laid it aside, hoping a face would grow in her mind while she filled Homer's order.

She sat now by the door and whittled, and watched for the coming of the mailman. Several times she glanced up hopefully, the beginnings of a smile warming her eyes, when she thought there was a shadow by her door as of someone looking in, or the sound of feet on her steps. But always it was either a wraith of snow flung near the glass, or some as yet unheard voice of the many-voiced wind, for Detroit's wind seemed like her people, a thing of many voices, many tongues.

Often she paused in the weary, lonesome work of whittling for money as another directed, head lifted, listening. Far away across the vacant land past the railroad tracks, the wind's whine mingled with the trains and the steel mill's roar. Then, there was the shriek of it as it leaped against her unit, poking and prying like a white cat determined to claw its way through the cardboard walls. Defeated, it would cry in the chimney, sob with a long woo-wooing by the walls, then be gone with a higher, shriller shrieking as it leaped through the telephone wires. Then would come the moments of silence, even worse now than formerly, for mingling with the ticking of the clock was the purring of the white cat in the Icy Heart. No matter how cold it was outside, the kitchen, unlike the rest of the house, was always hot, and the white cat purred.

It was almost time for the children to come home for lunch before she saw the gray shape of the mailman going slowly through the blowing snow. He did not look her way, but she continued to watch until he had passed into the next alley. There was always the chance he might have overlooked a letter.

She stood a long moment, lax-handed, staring into the swirling snow, before she remembered to look at the clock. She hurried then to start lunch for the ones coming home from school, and to get Enoch ready to go.

The afternoon was better than the morning. Instead of Enoch with the radio turned low, there was Cassie's whispering to Callie Lou in the block of wood, softly, so as not to awaken Clovis.

She had never had a letter in the afternoon mail, and so never watched for the mailman after his morning round. It was Clytie, coming home from school, who saw the letter through the glass. Gertie tore it open eagerly, for it was from her mother. She asked the children to listen to their grandma's letter, but the wind had lessened somewhat and Mike Turbovitch was calling Enoch into the alley. Amos was standing on the chair by the living-room door, to watch a train go by. Cassie, who thought of her grandma as the one who had hauled her on a sled, was telling the golden child a story of children changed into birds. Clytie had already turned on the radio, so that Reuben alone gave full attention to the reading.

' "Dear Gertie and loved ones. This don't find us so good. I'm glad, Gert, that after being so hard-run so long you have got plenty now. But don't let the big easy money go to your head. Don't let poor Clovis work hisself to death to pay for all your fancy fixings. When you are sitting in your fine warm place, pity your poor old mother dragging around in the mud. Your father complains a heap. He don't do much. But he won't sell the yoes. I want him to—" ' Gertie choked, and struggled to bring out the word until Clovis, wakened by the homecoming children, and now listening in the doorway, asked worriedly if the letter brought bad news. ' "—to sell th land." ' She stammered on. ' "He don't need a farm. We can live on poor Henley's insurance." '

Somehow she finished the letter, three more pages given over to her mother's constipation, the weather, and a long quarreling about factory workers who, she had heard, were striking and holding up the war effort while boys like Henley died. Gertie laid the letter on a kitchen shelf as she heard Clytie say to Clovis, her voice filled with pride, 'I'll bet there ain't nobody else frum back home has got a Icy Heart but us.'

Clovis nodded, but Reuben said, 'Who cares?' He turned to Gertie, and his voice was mean and sullen, the way it seemed so often now since Mr Daly's tongue lashing in the alley. 'If'n you'd ha stayed, I could ha hoped Grandpa with them yoes.'

Clytie corrected him as more and more she corrected them all. 'Reuben, quit saying "hoped" fer "heped." Don'tcha know th youngens—kids—'ull laugh atcha.'

'Shut up,' Reuben said, and Gertie thought he was going to hit Clytie, but after glaring at her he stalked away to his bedroom, slamming the door behind him.

Gertie tried to get supper, but thoughts of her father and of Reuben made her absent-minded. Reuben had not played in the alley since the trouble with the Dalys. When he had to go to school or the store, he walked more quickly than was his custom, huddling into himself, cringing before the expected. She had tried at times to talk to him, hitting usually upon school as a topic of conversation, but Reuben wanted no talk with her. His first dislike of his home-room teacher, a Mrs Whittle, had deepened since Christmas into a sullen hatred that made him speak with contempt of all things done in her room. Before the trouble in the alley, he had liked his other teachers, especially the woman who taught music, and Mr Skyros, the art teacher, but now he had no good word for anything or anybody at school.

Gertie in thinking of him felt more lonesome than when she had watched the empty alley. At last she opened his door, asking: 'Whyn't you git out an git some air, son? Th wind's kinda quieted down.'

He was kneeling on the bed, his face close to the window above it, and would not look around at her when she came in. She looked over his shoulder through the steamy, smoke-crusted double panes of glass that gave little view except the strip of earth between their building and the next. Unlike the alley, the place was forever empty save for two scraggeldy little half dead maples that stood with the forlorn air of things transplanted into unkind earth. She wondered what it was he saw in the ugliness. She bent above him on the bed and looked sideways past the gray railroad fence, and saw at last what she thought he had been watching. There was a coal car moving slowly through the switchyard, and in spite of the wind-curled smoke and the thickening twilight she could make out the words 'COAL,' and lower, smaller, 'Kentucky Egg.'

She was turning away when he said, still looking: 'I wonder how many yoes Granpa has got. Funny, a body ud never know it was mighty nigh lamben time.'

'Yes,' she said, cheered by his talk. 'It'll be spring 'fore you know it. An mebbe we'll be goen back soon enough to put in some corn. Th war news is good.'

'Oh, yeah?' he said.

She went back to the supper getting and worked with conscious carefulness, running the noisy water with half its force, never slamming the icebox door, keeping the radio turned low, shushing, always shushing the children, for Clovis had gone back to sleep. Now, as usual, it seemed there was bad sickness in the house to have a man abed when the children were awake.

Twice she called softly for Clytie to come cut cabbage for the slaw, but Clytie never heard for listening to the trials and tribulations of Wanda Waxford. Through Christmas vacation Clytie had gone more deeply into the world of the radio people. More and more she would sit on the floor, her arms about her drawn-up knees, her eyes drugged, unseeing, her lips soft, while she listened to tearful declarations of love, long amorous sighs, mysterious rustlings, wicked, forever wicked mothers-in-law, brassy-voiced villainesses, sobbing misunderstood wives, and noble cheated-upon husbands. The doctors, too, were noble; a body would think from the sick-room scenes they never charged a cent.

Just now, as always before and after and in the middle of Wanda Waxford, a husky-voiced man who could somehow talk so that a body felt you and he were alone together told Clytie to use Amber Soap because her shoulders after its use, her wh-o-ole bo-aw-dy, a-all her body, eeveery bit of her bo-aw-dy would be so-o beauu-uutiful, so-so-o-oft. The voice crooned on about the beautiful body Clytie would have until her eyes softened, glinted, and her lips moistened as she twisted her head about to consider the beauties of her arms and legs. Gertie, watching, thought now as always of Eve listening to the serpent, looking at her own body, becoming aware of the forbidden fruit.

'Clytie, git in here an hep set up supper.' Gertie knew her voice was too loud, too harsh. The child had done no wrong. She opened her mouth to say something that would soften the harshness, but could think of nothing. Clytie came, smiling, thinking of Wanda Waxford, untroubled by the harshness in her mother's voice.

A lonesomeness for the Clytie who used to be rose, sharp as a fresh sorrow. In this new life of hers she didn't need her mother. Somehow, while she sat lost in the radio world, she seemed further away than when she was gone to the movies that took her on Saturdays, or to the church on Sunday where she and the others, with the Meanwells and her girl friend, went in a bus. It was a good church, Gertie thought, but it was big and far away. The Girl Scouts that took her one afternoon a week were also good, but, like baby sitting, they somehow added to the lonesomeness.

Tonight, as on many nights, Clovis was late in awakening so that supper for the children was too late. The younger ones were already sleepy, but all had gommed and snacked around until they were not hungry when they came to the table; and anyway the food wasn't as good as it would have been an hour sooner. Gertie was relieved that Clovis ate it without complaint. She wished it were better. He looked so tired and was getting a peaked, whey-faced look. He didn't get enough sleep, she thought, for even while he ate he yawned.

After supper, when the radio was still at last and Clovis and the children had gone to bed, Gertie sat a while whittling in the kitchen. She finished one of Homer's dolls and began the rough work on

331

another. She soon got so sleepy that for some minutes she did little but nod and yawn and try to blink her eyes into wakefulness. Since Clovis had been put on this shift, she dreaded to go to bed even worse than formerly, for as soon as she got into bed she always came wide awake.

Tonight was no better than other nights. She lay rigidly still, inviting sleep, but it would not come. Half her mind wondered how soon the alarm would go off. The other half listened to the wind or, in the spells of silence between the sob and shriek of it, the night sounds of the city, lonelier seeming than by day, as if she lived in a world where nothing else lived. If in the silence she could hear the creek over rocks, the wind in living trees, the bark of a fox, the cry of a screech owl—anything alive, not dead like the clock and the Icy Heart.

She thought of their debts on the car, Icy Heart, washing machine, radio, dishes, curtains. Her mind kept wanting to add the total, reckon up the interest, that must be more, way more than John's 5½ per cent. She turned restlessly from side to side, but her mind wouldn't turn from the debts. What if Clovis got sick? She wouldn't think. She'd put herself back home. Pretty soon the war would be over and they'd be going back. She still had the more than three hundred dollars she'd saved in fifteen years. And she mustn't go back without a face for the block of wood. It must be a happy, laughing face even though she'd lost the Christ with the red leaves in his hands.

She was, instead of the laughing Christ, seeing Reuben's hurt and angry eyes when the alarm sounded. Clovis, whose hands always awakened first, reached and turned it off. Sleep pulled him back on the pillow, but Cassie awakened whimpering, and Clytie cried sleepily, 'Is it school time?'

Clovis protested as always that there was no need for her to get up. But as always she did, though his lunch was fixed, and there was nothing to do but make coffee. She'd rather be up in the kitchen than in bed unable to sleep for reading the sounds of Clovis—the opening of the icebox, hiss of the gas, slide of the lunch box across the table. Sound for sound that Whit made in the Meanwell kitchen behind the other wall. If she drowsed, the sounds might mix, and

332

Clovis, her man, would cease to be a man and become instead a numbered sound, known only by the number.

She thought of numbers still when Clovis was gone, and she was back in bed. Numbers instead of people. But she wanted people. People to call her 'Gertie.' If she could have an animal to nose her hand, a red bird to watch, even a potted plant. Something alive, she had to have something alive. Remembering roused her to lift on one elbow, smiling a little. She had forgotten the ice flowers on the kitchen window. This morning, before the wind rose to scatter the loose snow and make a body think there was another blizzard, the ice flowers on the glass had shone red as if alive when through them she had watched the sun rise between Mrs Daly's chimney and the telephone pole.

She was glad when two or three days later the children brought from school word that at the term end there was to be a thing called an 'open house' to which the mothers were invited so that they could see how it was in school and talk to the teachers about their children. It would be nice to see Mr Skyros, the art teacher, again, and she wanted to talk with some of the other teachers, especially Mrs Whittle, who taught Reuben.

He had come slamming through the door that same afternoon, his eyes blazing, not speaking, and it had taken three questions to find out what ailed him. He was to have 'that ole Miz Whittle' another term. Cassie, who would be six in February, had come home shivering. Next term she'd have to learn to read for true. She had to go into 'Ole Miz Huffacre's room,' the meanest teacher, Clytie had warned her, in the whole school.

'You'll learn to read same as th others,' Gertie had comforted Cassie, and to Reuben, 'You've jist got off on th wrong foot with her—keep a tryen.'

However, doubts tore at her as three days later she walked to the school after having accepted Max's offer to watch Amos and Cassie until it was time for her to go to work at four-thirty.

She would, she decided, go first to Miss Vashinski. Cassie liked her so, and maybe she would warn this Miss Huffacre that Cassie might have a lot of trouble in learning to read. Then it came to her that Cassie had only the one Miss Vashinski, but Miss Vashinski had a lot of Cassies, most of whom had been with her for months instead of only a few weeks. The woman wouldn't recollect her.

She was hardly prepared when Miss Vashinski right off gave her a great big smile and said: 'How do you do, Mrs Nevels. I hate to lose Cassie. She was so sweet.'

Gertie smiled. 'She hates to leave you, but how can you recollect all th'—Clytie didn't want her to say 'youngens,' but she couldn't think of the other word—'youngens,' she said at last, remembering too late the word Clytie liked was 'kids.' But she went on, flushing, flustered, 'Let alone recollect their mamas.'

Miss Vashinski laughed until her dangling earrings trembled. 'I don't always remember, but I remember you,' she said, savoring a victory. 'On Cassie's first day Garcia spoke, remember? I was almost ready to give up.'

'He must be talken right along now,' Gertie said. 'Cassie says somethen about him ever once in a while.'

'He's fine, just fine,' Miss Vashinski said. 'You should hear him and Cassie together. The other day we'd had a story about a little girl in Holland—I'd told the children Holland was a country across the ocean, and of course they started talking about countries—you know we have many countries here. Garcia said to Cassie, "My country is Mexico," and Cassie said to Garcia, "My country is Kentucky." Wasn't that sweet?' and she turned to the next mother, but after smiling, turned back to Gertie, who was saying, worried:

'Cassie's so afeared that she won't learn to read.'

'She'll learn,' Miss Vashinski said. 'She has a high intelligence rating; if she should have trouble, have her eyes checked right away.'

'Her eyes is good,' Gertie insisted. 'She can see th stars an she don't git up close; she backs off . . .' She had just remembered her father before he got his double-vision glasses.

Miss Vashinski had stopped in the middle of a great big smile after getting only as far as, 'How do you do, Mrs.—' She couldn't remember the other mother's name, and was glad to look at Gertie again. 'She could have a kind of farsightedness. I'll make a note.' She turned back to the other mother, a dark dumpling of a woman in a red and yellow scarf with blue roses, perspiring as she said slowly and timidly, 'I—Michael Ospechuk's mother.'

Gertie turned away. The woman looked too scared to talk. Maybe she had older ones like Clytie who didn't like the words she used and told her what to say. She followed a group to the basement, where in a little crowded, sweat-smelling room a great gang of children played with balls and jumping ropes. She realized she was looking at the 'gymnasium' of which Reuben had dreamed. Its ceiling wasn't high enough for even a basketball goal, and it was smaller than a classroom.

The teacher, a tired, middle-aged woman, smiled as the mothers introduced themselves, pretending like, Gertie thought, she remembered their children. She couldn't, because she taught all the children in the school above the third grade, and there were, she had heard, 642 children in a building put up forty years before for three hundred. This tired teacher looked as if in her time she had taught them all. But when Gertie introduced herself she smiled and said: 'Your son is so cute. At first he was so bashful, and he still won't do couple dancing with anyone but me. He's just getting to that age, you know; but in the folk games he's already one of the best—such a good sense of rhythm.'

'Seems like Enoch's smart in everything,' Gertie said.

'Enoch,' the woman said, looking disappointed, trying to remember an Enoch, 'I thought you were Reuben Nevels's mother.'

Gertie laughed. 'I'm Reuben's too. I just didn't figger Reuben 'ud be good at dancen.'

'Why? I'll bet you are,' she said, smiling, already turning to another mother who was wanting to know why her Eva Marie had got a *U* in self-control.

Gertie looked over her shoulder as she left the room. If she'd been a little girl here, her black sin would have been no sin at all. Clytie had been troubled the first time the gym class danced. Folk games the teacher had called it, she told her mother, but still it was dancing. She had been relieved when Gertie assured her that it was no sin, not the sinful dancing of which her Grandmother Kendrick had warned so many times.

Gertie tramped on up and down the building, a big perspiring woman in the crowd of mothers. The warm lights in her eyes grew warmer when she heard Clytie, the blue band of a traffic director on her arm, talking to the telephone in the principal's office easy as if she'd been born in a house with a ringing telephone. She was smiling widely by the time she had seen Enoch's home-room teacher and heard what a good boy he was, how well he had adjusted, and how quickly he learned his lessons. She felt proud and happy, remembering that until their coming to Detroit she, with help from Clytie, had given him most of the schooling he had had. She saw him sitting up near the front of the room with a book and some papers on his desk. She looked at him, smiling, until he lifted his head. He turned red, looked quickly away, then down, and began a furious scribbling. She stood an instant watching, her smile dying slowly.

Mr Skyros, with his questions about the head in the wood he had heard she was making, and his praise of Reuben's carving— for in art class he taught, along with lots of other things, carving in wood and soap, even potatoes—brought back a lot of the lost warmth. She lingered a while in the art room, studying the exhibits, and wishing her father could have seen such a room. A hound dog, a clumsy, ugly thing with too little chest and too much belly, made by Reuben, was there for everybody to see. She was ashamed of it and half thought to put it out of sight until two mothers admired it, and then she lingered reaping the nice remarks for a harvest for Reuben.

It was getting late, the children marching homeward through the halls, before she reached the one room she dreaded—Mrs Whittle's. It was empty save for one other mother just coming out, and a woman who Gertie knew was Mrs Whittle, for she was taking her purse from an open desk drawer. She hesitated in the doorway. She wished the woman, a tall, thinnish, middle-aged person with a pink and white face above a yellow stringy neck, would invite her in. Mrs Whittle did glance up briefly, but only turned sharp around to a cupboard in the corner behind her desk. Gertie studied her hair, so neatly and so smoothly fixed in rows and rows of little yellow curls that it made her think of the hard and shiny scallops on some piece of her mother's starched embroidery. She waited a moment longer, then cleared her throat and said, 'Miz Whittle.'

The woman opened the cupboard door and gave a slight backward nod as if to indicate that she had heard. Gertie watched as she lifted carefully off a paper-wrapped hanger a long dark green coat. She held the coat for an instant at arm's length, turning it slowly, inspecting it. She found something on a sleeve which she lifted off with the fingertips of one pale bright-nailed hand. She then put one arm into the coat, crooked the arm, and studied the coat over it for possible specks. The hand of the coated arm took the purse while she went through the same careful procedure with the other sleeve, then tied and buttoned the coat.

Gertie moved a step nearer and stood by the desk. The woman was now taking a dark green felt hat from a shelf and did not look around when Gertie said, 'I come to talk to you about my youngen—boy.'

Mrs Whittle, with a crinkling hiss of paper, was removing the hat from a green paper sack. 'You'll have to hurry,' she said, her voice somehow matching the paper. 'It's late and I've been teaching and talking to mothers all afternoon.'

'Th slip my youngens brung home said th teachers ud talk to us atter school,' Gertie said, speaking with difficulty, choked up at being forced to speak to the woman's back.

Mrs Whittle put the hat an instant on her head while she folded the bag and laid it upon the shelf. She then took the hat carefully between the tips of her fingers, and bending so as to get her face exactly in the center of a mirror affixed to the door, eased the hat gently onto the bright hair so that no one of the close-coiled ringlets was disturbed. The business required her utmost concentration, and she could not speak again until the hat was on and she was opening her purse, looking into it. 'The child's name?' she asked, bringing out her lipstick, turning again to the mirror.

'Reuben—Reuben Nevels.'

Mrs Whittle gave no sign that she had heard. The lipstick needed even more time and concentration than the hat. Gertie came round to the end of the desk, tried to see the woman's eyes in the mirror, but saw only their lids drooping over the eyes fastened onto the mirrored slowly shaping mouth. The precise red bow was finished at last. Mrs Whittle turned, looked briefly at Gertie, then spoke as she opened the desk drawer, and took out gloves, 'Well, what is the matter? Did your child fail to pass? A percentage do, you know.'

'No, he passed,' Gertie said, fighting to keep her voice smooth. 'But—but you're his . . .' She had forgotten the name, the kind of teacher. 'You've got him more'n th other teachers, an you'll keep on a haven him an . . .'

'Are you trying to say that I'm his home-room teacher?' Mrs Whittle asked, drawing on a glove.

Gertie nodded.

'Well, what is the matter?' She was smoothing the drawn-on gloves finger by finger now.

'He—he don't seem to be a doen so good—not in his home room. He ain't happy; he don't like school, an I thought mebbe . . .'

Her words, though halting and stumbling as they were, caused Mrs Whittle to glance up from the second glove, and for the first time the two women looked at each other. Mrs Whittle smiled, the red mouth widening below the old woman's angry glaring eyes. 'And of course it's his teacher's fault your child is unhappy. Now just what do you expect me to do to make him happy?'

'That's what I come to ask you,' Gertie said. 'He kinda likes his other classes, an back home he was . . .'

'Back home,' Mrs Whittle said, as if she hated the words, her voice low, hissing, like a thin whip coming hard through the air, but not making much noise. 'You hill—southerners who come here, don't you realize before you come that it will be a great change for your children? For the better, of course, but still a change. You bring them up here in time of war to an overcrowded part of the city and it makes for an overcrowded school. Don't you realize,' she went on, looking again at Gertie, looking at her as if she alone were responsible for it all, 'that until they built this wartime housing—I presume you live there—I never had more than thirty-two children in my section—and only one section.' She opened her purse. 'Now I have two sections—two home rooms, one in the morning with forty-three children, one in the afternoon with forty-two—many badly adjusted like your own—yet you expect me to make your child happy in spite of . . .' Words seemed inadequate, and she was silent while she reached into her purse.

'But I've got three more in school, an they git along an—'

'What did you say your name was?'

'Nevels. My boy's name is Reuben. Maybe you don't recollect him, but—'

'I don't what?' And she frowned as she might have at a child giving the wrong answer.

' "Recollect," I said,' Gertie answered.

'Does that mean "remember"?'

When Gertie continued to stand in choked silence staring down at her, she went on, after taking a bunch of keys from her purse and closing it. 'I do remember now—too well. Your children came up for discussion in faculty meeting the other day.' She stopped to select a key, a small steel-colored one. 'The others have, I understand, adjusted quite well, especially the younger boy and the older girl, but Reuben—I remember him,' and she looked up from locking a desk drawer, toward a back seat in the row farthest from her desk and the windows. She looked down, choosing another key, then bent to the other drawer. 'He has not adjusted. His writing is terrible—he's messy; quite good in math but his spelling is terrible. I'm giving him a *U* in conduct because he just won't get along with other children.'

'He warn't bad to fight,' Gertie said to the woman's back, for she had turned now to lock the cupboard doors.

'I have had one mother complain most bitterly. Her son had a toy gun. He was talking to Reuben, teasing him a little perhaps. You know how children tease—learning to take it is a part of their adjustment to life.' She took out a ring holding car keys. 'Reuben lost his temper—he's forever sullen with a chip on his shoulder—and bragged to the other boy that he wouldn't have a toy gun.' She shook one drawer to make certain it was locked, shook the other, but looked at Gertie the better to emphasize her revelations. 'He bragged he had a real gun all his own, and that he'd taken it off in the woods and hunted alone and that once he'd seen a bear. He never tried to kill it, just shot at it and it ran away, the boy said Reuben said. The boy, of course, called him a liar, and Reuben—are you certain he is only twelve years old?— slapped him down. The mother came to me. I told her to go to the principal.' She turned toward the door, jingling the car keys impatiently.

Gertie's face was pale. Her wide mouth was a straight line above her square, outthrust chin, her big hands gripped into fists until the knuckle bones showed white, her voice husky, gasping with the effort to keep down all that rose within her. 'Reuben warn't lyen. He's had a rifle since he was ten years old. They're bear an deer clost to our place back home. We're right nigh the edge of a gover'ment game preserve. One year the deer eat up my late corn.'

She drew a long shivering breath. 'I don't want any a my youngens ever a playen with a toy gun, a pointen it at one another, an a usen em fer walken canes er enything. Some day when they've got a real gun they'll fergit—an use it like a toy.'

Mrs Whittle smiled. 'Your psychology, and your story, too, are—well—interesting and revealing, but . . .' She stepped into the hall. 'I see no point in carrying this discussion further. He will have to adjust.'

'Adjust?' Gertie strode ahead, turned and looked at the woman.

'Yes,' Mrs Whittle said, walking past her. 'That is the most important thing, to learn to live with others, to get along, to adapt one's self to one's surroundings.'

'You teach them that here?' Gertie asked in a low voice, looking about the dark, ugly hall.

'Of course. It is for children—especially children like yours—the most important thing—to learn to adjust.'

'You mean,' Gertie asked—she was pulling her knuckle joints now—'that you're a teachen my youngens so's that, no matter what comes, they—they can live with it.'

Mrs Whittle nodded. 'Of course.'

Gertie cracked a knuckle joint. 'You mean that when they're through here, they could—if they went to Germany—start gitten along with Hitler, er if they went to—Russia, they'd git along there, they'd act like th Russians an be'—Mr Daly's word was slow in coming—'communists—an if they went to Rome they'd start worshipen th pope?'

'How dare you?' Mrs Whittle was shrill. 'How dare you twist my words so, and refer to a religion on the same plane as communism? How dare you?'

340

'I was jist asken about adjustments,' Gertie said, the words coming more easily, 'an what it means.'

'You know perfectly well I mean no such thing.' Mrs Whittle bit her freshly lipsticked lips. 'The trouble is,' she went on, 'you don't want to adjust—and Reuben doesn't either.'

'That's part way right,' Gertie said, moving past her to the stairs. 'But he cain't hep th way he's made. It's a lot more trouble to roll out steel—an make it like you want it—than it is biscuit dough.'

22

Saturday, Reuben had helped Gilbert and several of the bigger boys build a snow fort and had seemed to enjoy himself, as he did later in the afternoon when he went with them to a movie and saw a Western with much riding, shooting, and screaming of women, Gertie gathered from Enoch's description. He came home from the bus trip to Sunday school almost talkative. There was a gymnasium in the basement of the church, and his teacher was organizing another basketball squad, and it looked as if he would get to play center. His good humor lasted through Monday noon, for he had his special classes such as art, music and social studies of mornings now. But Monday afternoon brought silence and the slamming of the door.

Tuesday was even worse, his sullenness never lifting from breakfast on. Gertie, seeing the hurt under his still anger, tried to think of things to say, but could think of nothing. Wednesday he was home strangely soon, a good five minutes before the others, red-faced, unable to speak, hurrying like a chased wild animal to his room, then slamming the door. Clytie, coming next, was hardly through the kitchen door before she jumped into a long breathless account of what Reuben had done. He'd cut through the swampy vacant land by the railroad tracks instead of sticking to the patrol route, crossed streets where he wasn't supposed to cross, and walked by the tracks and that was against all rules; now he'd get reported and maybe have to go to the principal's office.

Gertie was silent, trying hard to iron and not show by her face she couldn't blame the boy. Her own feet cried for a path, earth

342

instead of dirty ice-covered cement. Enoch came soon after, his story much like Clytie's. He had seen Reuben turn off the sidewalk into the forbidden path through the vacant lot, had heard him sass the patrol boy who called to him to get back onto the sidewalk; and now he'd get a licking from the principal, a real good one, all the kids said; and Enoch's eyes sparkled in anticipation of the story he could tell of how the principal licked his big brother.

Gertie said only, 'Be quiet, now; you'll be a waken your pop.'

However, Clovis was already calling sleepily to know what was the trouble. Before Gertie could stop him, Enoch had rushed in to tell of Reuben's sins. She followed, declaring that after all walking off a proper road was not exactly breaking one of the Ten Commandments, but doubted if Clovis ever heard her, Enoch was chattering so, with Clytie throwing in more words.

Clovis lighted a cigarette and, sitting on the edge of the bed, listened in silence. He seemed more irritated by the world in general, as he always was when he hadn't had his fill of sleep, than angered by Reuben's wrongdoing. His voice was peaceful enough when he called Reuben to him, but his face hardened as he waited while Reuben took his time about coming. When Reuben finally did come, he looked surly and guilty, Gertie thought, as the other Reuben must have looked facing Jacob without Joseph—and her Reuben had done no wrong.

'What's th matter? You know you've got to walk where they tell you to walk. It's fer yer own safety,' Clovis began, kindly enough.

But Reuben, with a mean quick glance at Enoch, flared up as if Clovis had hit him. 'Frum th way you're all a carryen on,' he said, 'a body ud think—ud think I'd killed a man. All I done was walk a path.'

'You've got to walk where they tell you to walk,' Clovis repeated, beginning to flare up. 'What's th matter, anyhow? You're allus in trouble.'

'It ain't my fault,' Reuben cried, choking up. 'Th youngens don't like me. Miz Whittle hates me.' He turned to Gertie, all his disappointment for the lost farm, all the hatred for Mrs Whittle, Mr Daly, the hillbilly crying children turned on her. 'Now she hates me worse'n ever since you come a bawlen her out because I wasn't

343

happy. She said it right 'fore all th youngens—an some a them laughed their fool selves sick. Fer once she let em laugh. Things was bad enough 'fore you come sticken your big nose in—'

His next words were lost in the slap Clovis gave him, squarely on the mouth.

'Don't, Clovis—please; he don't know,' Gertie's voice rose like a crying.

'He knows enough not to sass his parents,' Clovis said, standing now, towering above Reuben, who stood bright-eyed and red-faced, not cringing or turning away or ashamed of the sassy words, too filled with the hurt inside him to notice the pain of the slap that had brought a dribble of blood to his mouth.

Clovis, as always on the rare times when he slapped a child, was sorry for what he had done, but afraid he would show his sorrow, spoke only the more roughly, and gave Reuben a little shove, 'Git back in that room an stay there till you can tell yer mom you're sorry. Whatever she said, she didn't mean to make the teacher mad.'

'Th rest a you youngens clear out—git on now—ever last one a you. I wanta go back to sleep.' He stopped as if to think, meanwhile looking at Gertie with more anger in his face than it had held for Reuben, 'Clytie, turn on th radio good an loud, it won't bother me none. It'll give Reuben in his room somethen to listen to.'

Gertie turned to follow, and opened her mouth to protest when the radio screamed, demanding that she go at once and buy one package of General Kapitan's cigarettes. But Clovis said, his voice low and mean, 'Wait a minute,' as if she were a mule to be ordered around.

Slowly her hand dropped from the doorknob, and she turned back to Clovis. It wasn't the way it had used to be back home when she had done her share, maybe more than her share of feeding and fending for the family. Then, with egg money, chicken money, a calf sold here, a pig sold there, she'd bought almost every bite of food they didn't raise. Here everything, even to the kindling wood, came from Clovis.

She understood in one second of time so many things—the trapped look in Mrs Anderson's eyes, why Max's radio played so loudly sometimes when she had an evening off and Victor was home. The rich had wide lawns and thick walls; the poor had radios. Now, under the sound of their radio, Clovis wanted to know why had she been such a fool as to go up to the school and raise a racket with a teacher. Didn't she know that Detroit had the finest schools of almost any city in the country? His voice rose, drove in the knife, and turned it round and round. 'You know you never was no good at talken. You allus look like you wanta fight. That's part a his trouble. He's big an tough-looken, an you've set him agin Detroit so he wouldn't like it now if you put him in a mansion in Grosse Pointe. You've got to git it into yer head that it's you that's as much wrong with Reuben as anything.'

She listened, stony-faced and silent, helpless in the face of his words as in the face of her mother's. When it seemed he had finished, she mumbled something about supper and hurried from the room.

Reuben wouldn't come when she called him to supper. She didn't try to make him. If he felt all choked up in his insides the way she did, he couldn't eat anyway.

Clovis, too, she thought, was troubled about Reuben, and sorry for the slap but unwilling to show it. That night he left for work with Whit earlier than common. As soon as he had gone, she went to listen by the boys' bed. She heard only Enoch's breathing, noisy as he snored up for a cold. The mound of covers over Reuben continued suspiciously still as she bent above it whispering, 'Reuben.'

The covers remained rigidly still, but she begged again, 'Reuben.'

'Go away,' he whispered.

She put her hand on his head. He shook it off. 'Git away. You'll be a waken Enoch.'

'Lots a your teachers at school likes you, an you liked Sunday school.'

He made her no answer, but after a moment of standing above him, she sat on the edge of the bed and tried to smooth his hair. When he had buried his head under the bed covering, she dropped her hands into her lap, but continued to sit by him. A steel pour was beginning; the red-tinged light through the drawn blind quivered, brightened, whitened, and made of her hunched body a grotesque shadow on the wall behind her. The thing trembled as if it shook

345

with laughter. She turned away from Reuben and watched her shadow as she fought for words. She gave up her own. They were never any good. She hunted through the memory verses in her head, the Ten Commandments; the blessings—blessed, blessed—Reuben had ever been meek and poor and pure in heart.

Blessed—blessed—he was reviled and persecuted, but not for Jesus. His sin was that he was Reuben. Amos cried to the rich about their treatment of the poor. Reuben had no need of Amos. He was the poor. Ecclesiastes: it would pass—all of it—'the rivers to the sea.' But Reuben's life was not a river to the sea to go on and on forever. His life would pass like her shadow, laughing less and less now, dimming. She watched herself melt. One moment there was a thin shivering shadow, then nothing but paleness faintly tinged with red. She held out her hand, moved her arm; nothing moved on the wall. It was like that, all living, Reuben's life. 'My days are swifter than a weaver's shuttle, and are spent without hope.' Reuben was living like that, for she had taken his hope away. A body couldn't live without hope of something.

'It won't allus be like this.' She stopped. How many times had she said that to Reuben when they worked the corn together, hill by hill, row by row. He had hoed while she had plowed, and they had gathered the corn together, two rows for them, two rows for John. Once, when he was little, he had cried when Silas Kennedy, it was then, had taken half their corn. She had comforted, 'It won't allus be like this.' She rubbed her arm hard across her forehead; his childhood had gone and the 'this' was with him still.

Or was it the 'this'? The trouble was that he was Reuben the same as she was Gertie. If she had taken her mother's Christ and Battle John's God and learned to crochet instead of whittle, and loved the Icy Heart and had never tried to talk to Mrs Whittle . . . Keep shut, keep shut, like the tool-and-die man's rabbit. If she had walked straight down the alley the day the gospel woman came, just watching Mrs Daly as Mrs Bommarita had watched, Mr Daly wouldn't have been mad at her and have taken it out on Reuben. The sins of the fathers . . .

She put her hand on his shoulder, and though he buried himself still more deeply under the bed clothing, she bent her face close to him and spoke in a low voice. 'Reuben, it's all your ole fool mammie's fault like you said. I've been stiff-necked an stubborn in the face uv . . .' What? She couldn't say God. 'Honey, try harder to be like th rest—tu run with th rest—it's easier, an you'll be happier in th end—I guess.'

He never answered, but after a little space of silence she struggled on. 'Reuben—recollect that creek at home—th one below th cove where you seed th bear? Recollect how them rocks way up high, by th bluff at th beginnens uv th creek, was rough an all shapes an sizes? An recollect th little round rocks down at th mouth by th river? They was mighty nigh all alike an round an smooth. They got that-away abangen agin one another a comen down th creek in th fallovers an . . .' She choked—she was no rabbit to beget rabbits. She remembered the look of Reuben's face in the alley, and went on: 'Nobody asked them rocks did they want to be smooth an all alike. You might like playen with a toy gun. Try it.'

He plunged still more deeply under the bed covering, jerking back from her until he rolled on Enoch, who muttered and seemed ready to waken.

She left him, closing the door. Though his bedroom door, like the others in the house, would not lock, it was like there was a locked door between them with the key lost.

Next morning when he sat at table, eating little, his slapped lip swollen, he was silent and sullen still behind the wall that more and more she knew that she had made. He went back to his room immediately after breakfast and stayed so long she was afraid he would be late to school. She called to him, trying not to let on to the already suspicious Clytie that she was afraid he would either not answer or else tell her he wouldn't go to school. However, he came quietly enough in a clean shirt and with his hair combed, more frightened now than sullen as he said, 'Mom, could you fix a lunch fer me—jist this onct?'

'Sure, son,' she answered, pleased that she could do for him some little thing, but Clytie cried, 'It's againsa rules, Mom; kids gotta have permission to take lunch.'

She turned to Clytie, an egg for frying in her hand. 'What's wrong with taken a little snack to school? He could eat it outside.'

'It's againsa rules,' Clytie repeated, adding, 'They's no place to eat it,' in the patient mother-to-ignorant-child tone that more and more she used with Gertie. Then, outside, her girl friend Iva Dean was calling, and she couldn't stop to argue.

Gertie started to break the egg into the skillet, but stopped, frowning. She whirled and jerked the door open just in time to see Clytie, snowpantless, as she had thought, disappearing into the alley by the railroad fence. She called twice before Clytie turned slowly back. The redheaded girl, also snowpantless, followed, and continued to follow as Clytie came slowly and ever more slowly back as Gertie commanded: 'You git back in here an git on some clothes. It ain't good fer a young girl like you to run around barelegged an no long underwear in all this cold.'

Clytie turned red at her mother's mention of long underwear. But Iva Dean, who wore a short jacket above a woolen skirt with a goodly length of blue shin beneath, looked sympathetic, her warm brown eyes going from Clytie to Gertie, lingering at last on Gertie as if her sympathies lay there.

Clytie stopped at the end of the walk and said, almost as brash as Enoch: 'Clothes, Mama? I'm smothered with so many clothes now.'

'Git in here an git into them snowpants,' Gertie said.

Clytie did not move. 'But Mom, I'm th only young—kid in my section that has got to wear snowpants like a little kinnergarden kid.'

'You don't want to come down with th flu an miss a lot a school,' Gertie said more kindly.

'Minnie Armstrong's mother—Minnie's in our section—makes Minnie wear um,' Iva Dean said to Clytie in an encouraging tone. 'An my own mom,' she went on reflectively, 'cried a couple a times last winter when I run off without th things, an she thought it was cold. It wasn't till this last cold snap that she give in. G'wan,' she said as if Gertie had not been four feet away, half through the storm door, 'if she's like my mom it'll take yu a whole winter to learn her yu don't need th things. G'wan, put um on—no use to hurt her feelens alla time.'

'You people borned an raised up here git used to this weather,' Gertie said, feeling grateful, wishing she could remember the girl's

348

last name. She'd heard her say it once; it sounded like she'd started to strangle, then changed her mind and coughed.

The girl gave a defiant headshake. 'Not me; my pop was, but when Mom got ready to have me she went back to Granma's in Isham, Tennessee.'

'Oh,' Gertie said, then added, not wanting to be pitied or thought a tyrant: 'I don't want to make Clytie wear snowpants all th time. Like t'other Saturday when you an her went to th movies, it was so warm I wouldn't ha made her wear pants—but you had em on.'

'I gotta wear blue jeans or snowpants to th movies allatime. Mom makes me but I'd do it anyhow. None a them guys that hangs around u movies ain't gonna run no hands up no dress tail a mine.'

Gertie said, 'Oh,' and let the storm door shut, and was still too startled when snowpanted Clytie swished past her to give a good-bye hug to Cassie running behind her. She glanced at the clock, remembered Reuben's lunch, and turned up the gas under the frying egg. He called from his bedroom to ask for a molasses and marga-rine sandwich. The margarine was too hard from the Icy Heart, the molasses too thin from the hot kitchen, so that by the time she had the lunch fixed she heard Clovis coming up the steps. She called to Reuben that it was so late his father was home and if he didn't hurry he'd be late, but Reuben answered that he had to go to the bathroom.

Clovis took off his jacket and hung it in the hall, and unable to get into the bathroom went into his own room to take off his shoes. A moment later she heard the opening of the bathroom door, but Reuben took his time about coming. She started to scold him for his slow ways, then saw his face, white and strained and frightened. She watched him to the railroad fence, and to the alley's turning, hoping he would turn just once and wave the way he had always done at home, but he only walked faster than common until the turning of the alley took him away.

She began to get a snack for Clovis. He soon came into the kitchen, grimy-faced and big-eyed; sleepy-headed, but not good sleepy like a man after a day's work. Fidgety—some part of him never wanting to go to bed because it was morning—and short-worded when he asked why Reuben was so late starting to school. She never knew

349

what to feed him when he got home from work—food that was neither breakfast, dinner, nor supper. Today, she fixed pork chops, eggs, fried potatoes, and toast. He ate right well, though his lunch, when she opened the box, looked as if it had hardly been touched.

Finished with his food, he leaned back smoking a cigarette, and seemed in such good humor that she tried her often asked but seldom answered question, 'How was it?' risking short words, some story of trouble with the foreman or the union steward, or worse, news of a wildcat strike or walkout in some other department that could tomorrow put him out of work. But it was worth the chance that he might tell something of what the people about him had said or done.

Today, though he looked more tired than usual, he smiled at her question and gave a little headshake. 'Boy, did I work, an I mean work. A body ud think I broke th danged machines th way that big-headed Polock foreman was allus on my neck. They ain't made to take that high production quota they put on Monday. An most a th dad-blamed fools that runs em has stood around an done nothen so long they cain't take it neither. An that dumb Polock foreman must be in Hitler's pay—th way he fixed th hands around.'

'Wotta yu mean, Pop?' It was Enoch, who, still on the afternoon shift at school, seldom bothered to get out of bed until his friend Mike came calling.

'Oh,' Clovis said, pushing his chair back and crossing his legs, 'if he don't like a feller's looks he puts him on a job he thinks he cain't do. He's like th Dalys an all th rest a these foreigners—he hates everthing an everbody that ain't just like hissef. An does he hate niggers! Calls em shines, an gives em th meanest jobs. Last night he put a spindly yaller gal, smart-looken too, on one a them bad kind a presses that works with a foot treadle, an they's allus th chance that if you git too tired er sleepy you'll tramp that treadle while you've got yer hands under.

'So last night when he puts this girl—a body could see she ain't never been in no factory before, th way she kept a wallen her eyes an acten skittish-like—he knows she won't last no time atall when he put her on this man-sized press with a foot control. He showed her how. She was smart an caught on real quick. But th stock's

350

pretty heavy, an it ain't so easy picken it up, putten it in, taken it out, wipen it off, layen it down on one side, reachen on t'other side, starten all over agin, allus a recollecten that old treadle right under yer foot. He watched her awhile an complains she's slow.

'That flusters her. Then he tells her she'd better not send out a piece a stock with a couple a her hands smashed in it. That flusters her some more, and she was a shivern an a sweaten. I could see big drops comen off her chin, an a couple a guys on some little presses that was out a stock was watchen her together with a stock boy. All that didn't do no good. But she didn't say a word.

'I was a tryen to git th air hose back on that blamed Bunken's press. I don't know how he does it, but it's allus somethen. An he's sich a fool, an allus so ashamed that a body, not even thet foreman, ain't got th heart to be much mean to him. This fool, Bunken, goes over to her press soon's th foreman's gone—he sells th numbers an it takes a heap a time—an tells her to watch fer th foreman an th steward, an he makes that ole press fly.

'Soon's I git his hose fixed I goes over to th girl an I says, "Lemme see if this press's runnen right," so I made her fly fer a right good spell. But that blamed gigglen fool uv a gal frum Georgie got her belt off agin—how she does it I don't know— an I had tu leave th yaller gal. But up steps that big Ukrainian feller I was a tellen you about—him on a little press with nothen to do. He hates everthing, niggers, hillbillies, Jews, Germans, but worse'n anything he hates Poles an that Polock foreman. An he is a good-hearted guy—he made that ole press fly so fast I thought it ud bust. An when th steward come around—that Ukrainian had put her up to it—this new hand, she says to him: "This press ain't doen right. It sticks an I cain't git the stock out when I go fast," she says. It ain't th steward's job to test th machinery, but he runs it—pretty fast.

'Anyhow, when that foreman fin'ly does git back frum sellen his numbers there was that yaller gal a leanen by her machine a poppen her gum. "What in th hell do you think you're a bein' paid fer?" he says.

'"I've been kinda wonderin," she says, poppen her gum some more an looken around easy-like. "I run outa stock a long time ago."

351

' "Jee-sus," that foreman says, an he whistles, then he's mad. "Th steward'ull be on you fer runnen over production," he says, an I thought that old Ponomarenko ud bust hissef a holden in his laughen—an that foreman never did ketch on.'

Clovis, good-humored now, got up stretching, yawning, ready for bed. However, as usual, he was hardly sound asleep before it was school letting out time. Cassie, first today, came banging through the door, shouting, 'Mommie, Mommie, I'm goen to wear glasses like Granma. A woman all in white had me a looken at pitchers. I wasn't skeered a bit. Miz Huffacre pinched my cheek an smiled at me. It's pinned on my dress,' and she began unzipping, unbooting, unbuttoning all over the house until Clovis groaned his awakening sounds, and Gertie was sharp with Cassie for her noise.

Clovis roused again when Clytie came running in to tell that she hadn't seen Reuben any place at school. 'Ain't Reuben home?' he called, concern in his voice.

'He took a lunch,' Gertie answered somewhat shortly. 'An eny-how, him an Clytie could go a week an never see one another.'

'But gineraly we pass in th hall,' Clytie said.

Gertie declared there was no reason why any of them should see him, as they had no classes together. Still, a growing uneasiness akin to panic laid hold of her, and to hide it she went outside for a bucket of coal. She stood staring up and down the alley until the dishwater spots on her apron froze, and a snowsuited child, drinking pop and eating a sandwich as he walked, stared at her in wonder.

All afternoon the uneasiness came and went in waves. One minute she was sweaty-handed, unable to keep her mind on the ironing, scared to death, certain he was not in school, but hiding out somewhere, afraid to face both Mrs Whittle and the principal. At other times, certain that he was all right, she tried to think up a face for Victor's Christ. But more and more she listened to Cassie as she talked with Miss Callie Lou. At last her lonesomeness and uneasiness overcame her and she took her whittling and went visiting, knocking on the door of the boys' room that held the block of wood, asking, 'How-do-you-do, ladies. How-do-you-do?'

Cassie, standing very straight and trying not to giggle, opened the door. 'Do come in, Miz Golden Shoe, an drink a cup a coffee with me an Miz Callie Lou: our men's gone off to make tanks fer Old Man Flint and Mr Griggs, so do come in an set a hour er two.'

And Gertie sat and drank coffee and ate 'little cakes with pink icen,' and discussed the weather and the school, never forgetting now and then to hand a bit more coffee and another cake to Callie Lou smiling at them from the block of wood. 'An how are your youngens in school, Miz Silver Bell?'

And Cassie's giggle, smothered in the primping voice of Mrs Silver Bell: 'Fine, jist fine, Miz Golden Shoe, but what do you think? My littlest girl has to wear glasses, but then she'll learn to read, read anything in th whole world. Miz Huffacre, that's her teacher, says so, an she is th finest teacher in th whole world.'

'Oh, I'm sure you have a very smart child, Miz Silver Bell,' and they visited a long while. The doll grew, and the sun, a little further north each night now in its setting, sent a long finger of yellow light through the window. It brightened the block of wood and made red glints in Cassie's straight hair. And Gertie thought she had never looked so pretty.

Then Joe was crying in the alley. The party had to end, and Gertie realized it was late, almost time for school to be over, and she was afraid again, thinking of Reuben.

23

Joe held out bananas for Gertie's inspection. 'Banana nice—today cheap. Ten cents.'

'They're frostbit,' Mrs Daly whispered, adding loudly enough for Joe to hear, 'They's nothing so deceitful as a frostbit banana.'

'Nice,' Joe repeated, not hearing, smiling at Gertie. 'Ten cents,' he insisted. 'Tomorrow eighteen. Today below OPA.'

Gertie studied the bananas. They looked good, and Reuben loved bananas. She drew a deep breath. 'Gimme four—no, make it five pounds,' she said, thinking, two apiece all around, and maybe one for Clovis's lunch left over.

'You'll be lucky if they's one pound that's good,' Mrs Daly whispered.

And Max, trying hard not to flirt with Joe's hungry-eyed nephew, said, 'Yu can't buy bargains on account a they ain't no bargains, kid.'

Gertie paid for the bananas, and hurried into her kitchen, uneasily aware that she alone had bought the bargain bananas. She forgot to examine them when she looked at the clock and saw that school was out. In a minute or so the first wave of children would sweep down the alley. Reuben would, of course, be with them. Clovis called from the passway, asking the time, and she made a great pretense of being so unconcerned she had not noticed. She looked again at the clock before she answered, 'Three twenty-six.'

'See any youngens comen home?' he asked.

She looked through the storm door, 'A few, jist turnen th corner—th ones that allus runs,' she answered easily enough. But, now unable to turn from the door, she stood and watched the alley. She was aware that Clovis had come up behind her, and that Cassie and Amos, somehow sensing the uneasiness, stood watching the children come home as she and Clovis watched.

Her eagerness to see Reuben, make certain he was all right, maybe even good-humored and happy again, made her want to run wildly down the alley searching. But she moved only to open the door for Enoch, who dashed in crying, 'Mom, I ain't seen Reuben,' and in the next breath, 'Mike wants me to come out an play hockey.'

'Say you've not seen Reuben?' Clovis asked.

'He don't allus see him,' Gertie said.

'But ginerally I see him when our section passes his section in th hall.' He saw the bananas, crowded past her, grabbed one and began pulling back the skin. Gertie continued to stand between the doors and watch the alley, brimming now with the full tide of the homecoming children. Her eyes snatched eagerly at each dark brown jacket, each head higher than the other heads. She did not look around when Enoch cried, 'This banana's rotten, Mom.'

And Cassie, troubled by the thought of throwing food away, said: 'Mine's all black and squshy inside, Mom. Must I eat it?'

Clytie came next, running up the steps, calling, 'Mom, I never did see Reuben.'

Gertie said nothing, and Enoch cried, disgust and derision in his tone, 'Mom's tryen to feed us rotten bananas.'

'She didn't know they was rotten,' Clovis said with some sharpness, and then in a kinder tone toward Gertie's discouraged back: 'But, Gert, you've got to watch what you buy. That sandwich meat you put in my lunch hardly had th taste a meat. More like corn meal an taters mashed an colored to look like meat.'

'Th man that makes it must make a heap a money,' Enoch said, admiration in his tone, then his voice nagging again like his father's: 'They're allus a maken a fast buck on you, Mom. Recollect them pork chops, two, three days ago. They all briled away into grease, like that hamburger an th sausage.'

'Grease at sixty cents a pound,' Clovis said, standing beside instead of behind her now. He put his hand on her shoulder, but his glance still searched the alley as he said: 'Yer mom ain't used to buyen. She's got to learn. It ain't easy. Like Cassie's dress; over an over that clerk tells me it's good cotton that'll wash an iron like yer mom wanted. She said they'd be a label if it was rayon. But th first time yer mom set a iron on it, it melted down like chewen gum.'

There was only one child going down the alley now and that a safety patrol boy. Still she watched; the turning away, the closing of the door would somehow be the closing of her hope that Reuben would come home. She clung to the hope, struggling against the mounting panic. What if he didn't come home by dark? She had caused him to do this just as she had wasted Clovis's money for rotten bananas and poor meat and all the other things they didn't know about—the box of pepper half full, the rotten eggs, the rotten oranges, the sweet potatoes bought as a treat one night but all black in their hearts, yet showing no sign from the outside, like Joe's eyes.

She gripped the door handle. She could raise bushels of sweet potatoes, fatten a pig, kill it, and make good sausage meat, but she didn't know how to buy. She could born a fine and laughing boy baby and make him grow up big and strong, but inside him all his laughter died. She heard screams and saw the Bommarita boy, his head hunched under his jacket as he raced home in front of the Daly ice balls. It was late when the Catholic children got home. But she continued to stand, unconscious of the cold wind whipping through the door. Then after what seemed a long time Clovis, his voice troubled, said, 'Me an th youngens is a goen to—to git some bananas. We'll look around a little fer Reuben, but most like he'll beat us home, fer we'll be gone a while.'

They were gone and the storm door shut. She tried to do her kitchen work, but in the spells of silence between the airplanes and the trains she heard the white cat in the Icy Heart, the clock tick, the wind scream in the telephone wires, and once Whit, by the girls' bedroom, moaned in his sleep and struck the wall with an outflung arm. She kept running to the door, but the alley was always empty.

The pale red glow of the steel mill had brightened as twilight deepened into darkness, and overhead the lights of airplanes glowed like wandering stars, before Clovis and the children came. They were too silent, and ate little of the supper of pork liver, fried potatoes, boiled beans, cabbage slaw, and cobbler made of canned peaches.

356

Clovis sat a long while stirring his coffee round and round, and when the older children had gone from the table and the radio was loud, said, 'I think I'd better tell th police, Gertie.'

'No—no.'

He was silenced by her terror, and nodded when she said: 'He'll come. I know he'll come. He wouldn't worry me thisaway. He's right around somewhere afeared to come home, afeared to go to school. He ain't never been afeared,' she went on, her voice rasping, broken. 'He don't know what to make of it—bein afeared.'

Clovis looked at her and she at him. Each saw the fear in the other but would not speak of it. At last Clovis, his face turned carefully away from her, said: 'But Gert, it ain't like back home. They's traffic—he could git hurt—an we'd never know. They's—they's mean men. You—you wouldn't know—quair mean. They's gangs kills a boy ever once in a while. We'd better git th police.'

She shook her head violently. 'No—no.'

'His knife missen?'

She nodded, and he did not urge her again; but seeing her restlessness, forever walking to the door with the drippy dishrag to stare into the dark alley, he said: 'Whyn't you wrap up good—it's mighty cold—take the flashlight an go look around. You can git to places we couldn't in th car.'

The wind tore at her coat, stinging her legs and her face, but it was better to be outside than in. The wind kept the smoke away, and on the side of the sky away from the steel mill she could see the stars. In spite of her worry she searched out the Big Dipper, though its bottom on the western side was washed away in the steel-mill light. As always she pondered on the highness of the north star here compared to home. 'The heavens declare the glory of God; and the firmament showeth his handiwork. Day unto day uttereth speech, and night unto night—'

She walked on. What was the speech to her but loneliness? The stars and the night sky spoke to no one around her. It seemed a long time since even Cassie had talked about the stars or watched the moon rise. The steel mill took the sunsets, the evening star, and washed out the pale young moon. Reuben had liked to look at the stars. Maybe he was now; crouching in the cold, freezing, looking up, crying at the coldness of the stars. She shivered and hurried on into the face of the north wind, trying to find the path into the swamp with the little trees.

She crossed the through street, turned the corner by the filling station, and walked on past the brightly lighted bowling alley and tavern. She went more slowly by their warm-looking windows, frosted like her own and double, but not too thick to let the juke-box music come seeping through. She passed a small factory where lights flickered blue behind the glass walls.

Just ahead of her a man in an overcoat and a woman in a long full-skirted dress got out of a car. They hurried, laughing, across the snowy sidewalk, then through a door that on opening flung out steam and music and laughter. She had a glimpse of a large dim room and couples dancing a dance quick and wild with much stamping of feet. A man almost as big as Victor, with a yellow-headed woman in his arms, was for an instant like a picture seen past the doorway. Gertie watched him as he stamped one foot, lifted the other high, threw back his head and cried out in laughter a strange and wordless sound. Past the dancers on a raised platform she saw dimly through the cigarette smoke the music makers; one worked an accordion, laughing as he played.

The door shut, but the shouts and the music and the laughter seeped through in one thin sound like the singing of a fiddle far away. Then there was nothing but the wind and the snow and the cars going by, their windows shut against the cold, dark inside so that it seemed they drove themselves.

She reached a vacant lot fringed with brush, where old newspapers stirred in the wind among shadowy mounds of drifted snow. Further, lay darkness where the yellow light of the street lamp on the corner did not reach. Reuben might have gone there. She plunged in and sank knee-deep in snow, but floundered on further and further from the light. She tripped over tin cans, struggled through piles of rub-bish, and slipped, falling at times, when she stepped onto one of the many little frozen ponds. Willow and alder brush and strange trees with unfamiliar twigs slapped across her face and tore at her clothing.

Here, the red light of the steel mill no longer warmed the snow, and overhead the stars were thicker, brighter than in the alley.

Detroit seemed far away. If Reuben were close by, he would be in such a place, as far away as he could get from the city. The brush rose above her head so that if a body stood still and didn't listen too hard, it was like being in a little woods where twigs instead of smokestacks and telephone poles stood between her and the sky.

She snapped on the flashlight, and at once the illusion of being away from the city was gone. The snow was trampled by the booted feet of children; a banana skin lay close to a bitten-into bologna sandwich; and under the willows was a tiny pond criss-crossed with skate marks.

A train thundered past, and through the willow twigs she saw fleeting squares of yellow light that held the blurred forms of people. The train was gone, and she was still, staring in its direction. She went back to her search and turned the flashlight off again. She had gone a few steps into the brush when she saw, half hidden in the willows, the figure of a man, the head dark above the snow-spattered shoulders. Reuben? Too thin, too tall—a tall man either wearing a closely fitting cap or bare-headed.

'Hello?' she said, but the figure continued still among the willows as if he held his breath. A man frozen dead standing up? A man followed her into the swamp? No man would follow her, so big, so ugly. A robber somehow knowing of the money in her coat?

'Speak,' she said, and flicked on the light. Old and rusty iron glinted dully. She walked up to it, and saw the bell-shaped down-curving top of an old lamp post, a fancy thing rising higher than her head, but grown rusty waiting for a light. A closely matted growth of vines and briars around the iron standard had given it the bulk of a man's body. She turned quickly away, stumbling over the rubble of a sidewalk that had grown root-cracked and wrinkled waiting for the feet that had never come to walk under the never lighted lamp to the houses that were never built.

She shivered, and hurried as if from a graveyard where the dead were only partly buried, plunging through snow and brush and tin cans toward the railroad tracks. Though the wind came more fiercely over the tracks than in the swamp, her numbed hands and face and legs felt it but little as she strode on, taking three cross-ties at a stride, not knowing why she walked the railroad and never asking where. Walking was the thing, for only by walking could she find Reuben. She would find him and he would be hers again, with no wall between.

She reached the switch leading to the steel mill, and hesitated, looking toward the switchyard. She saw only darkness, cut here and there by the slowly moving yellow eyes of engines. Reuben wouldn't be there. On a night like this he would want the warmth and light of the steel mill. Victor would be working now. Maybe he had seen Reuben.

She hurried through the opening in the high steel fence through which the trains went, remembering what she had heard of other factories; there might be guards with guns to keep spies away. But no one bothered her as she came up the track, past piles of smoking slag and irregular heaps of scrap waiting for the furnaces. She reached the stripping shed, and hesitated. While she stood there, wondering, the donkey engine passed, chugging slowly with its load of freshly poured steel, the uncapped tops of the molds glowing red, sputtering like dying firecrackers. When the engine with its light was safely past into the stripping shed, she stepped closer to the moving cars and felt the good heat of the hot steel on her chest and through her coat, for all the rest of her seemed frozen into numbness.

The last car passed, and she crossed the tracks and went over to the pouring shed. The great doors were shut against the cold, but through chinks and cracks the warm red light came, and it was like the cookstove back home on winter mornings before she had lighted the lamp. One pour, she thought, had just been finished, and another was almost ready. The ever rising roar and hiss and crackle of the electric furnaces muted all the other sounds—the blowing of whistles, the clank and rattle of the overhead cranes, and in the next shed the grating of the oven door, the muted clang of the drop-forge hammers, and at last the steel, crying, complaining, hissing, screaming in defeat as it went away under the great rollers.

Last Sunday afternoon she'd sat with Clovis and the children in the car in front of the forging shed, but mostly, instead of watching, she had listened shivering and wanting to go home. It would be warmer there in front of the pickling oven. Maybe she could find a man who would hunt Victor and ask him had he seen Reuben.

She started around the pouring shed, but stopped when the donkey engine came again, this time with stripped ingots for the oven. The tracks were close, and the fierce heat of the glowing cylinders of steel hurt her face, so that she quickly turned her back, pressing her body close against the iron doors.

The engine went on, and cold touched her again, but she continued to stand with her face against the crack between the hinges of the door, and through it she looked into the pouring shed. She saw a huge, cave-like room filled with smoke and flame; not flame either, more like the play of lightning about the four furnaces along one side of the wall. The lights were forever leaping, now blue, now red, now white; behind the shifting, trembling, leaping lights were dull glows and gleams. Above the furnace third from the front there was a wilder, brighter dance of lights, the thunderous hissing louder. Looking closer she saw through the smoke a giant kettle hung in front of it, waiting for the running steel, while on the other side of the shed a man who looked like Miller in the alley stood on a high platform and arranged molds that were swung into position with hooks and cables worked by an overhead crane.

The roar of the furnace grew even louder. It trembled as if with eagerness to spew out the fiery mass inside it. Then, on a narrow platform by it, so close it seemed that it too should melt, she saw, puny-looking as a paper doll, the figure of a man silhouetted against the brightness. He dissolved in the red-colored smoke, reappeared, vanished. She continued to watch, seeing sometimes his legs only, sometimes his shoulders, then all of him gone again; she pressed more closely against the crack, half afraid that he had flamed up and disappeared like a bit of paper flung into the fireplace. She saw him soon; now he seemed bigger than a man, an iron giant, distorted as he was by the smoke and the flickering lights.

She watched as he took an iron bar and punched it into the red side of the furnace, working quickly, with no air of skittishness, as if he knocked the bung from a keg of vinegar instead of eighty tons of running steel. A tongue of bluish flame leaped at him, and while he stood, seeming to watch, she realized it was Victor. Reddish steel came out, a thin uneven stream; he worked the bar again; white-hot steel shot out with a roaring hiss and a blinding brightness.

The stream widened, brightened, until she could see nothing but the steel. Even when she looked away, thinking of Reuben, wondering how to reach Victor, her eyes were like they had used to be when she looked too long at a bright sunset. Though now instead of suns before her eyes there were streams of steel, bright as the sun but not sunlike, more like a fiery fountain out of Revelation, springing in the land where might have walked the angel with the feet of burnished brass and the golden girdle, and above it the angel might have stooped to gather flowers. For out of the beds of flame and smoke the flowers came; long gracefully drooping stems would for an instant hang out of the kettle, lean earthward, blooming on the end into the blood-red flower, blooming, dying all in an instant, their seed a tiny lump of smoking steel.

She had not seen Victor again, and the furnace had begun its slow tipping over the kettle, when a hand tapped her shoulder and a voice said: 'Yu gotta git out, lady. Wives gotta stay behind du fence like anybody else.'

She turned to face a figure so wrapped and bundled and booted against the cold that she could see nothing except an old man's faded, watery eyes above a weathered red-tipped nose from which one drop, red like a jewel in the light, hung trembling, ready to add its weight to the frost on the muffler over his mouth. 'I'm not a wife,' she said, 'I want to see Victor—up there.'

'Lotsa women wanta see Victor,' he said, 'but dey gotta wait behinda fence like du wives. Git now,' and he gestured with his lantern toward the high steel fence between the mill and the road. She had not noticed or thought of the fence, coming in on the tracks as she had. It stood no more than fifty feet away, and behind it were the red eyes of parked cars.

'It's my boy,' she said, following the old man. 'Reuben, he's gone. I wanted to ask Victor had he seen him hangen around.'

'I watch,' he said. 'I never seen him. Kids allatime hanging round; but tonight, too cold.'

'I figgered he might come to git warm,' she said.

'Yu don't warm by pouren steel—yu burn.' He opened a gate, saying. 'Yu gotta wait like u rest.'

'Ask Victor has he seen him,' she begged, and began shivering again.

The old man answered nothing as he shuffled off toward the pickling oven that was opening now with a clanging and grating of doors, red light leaping out to show giant tongs fishing for an ingot. Gertie clung to the fence, shivering, hoping one minute to see Victor, the next afraid. He was her last hope; after him where would she go, whom would she ask? Close by her elbow a voice said, low-pitched and carrying through the noise: 'Yu gotta wear slacks in this weather. Yu'll freeze.'

Gertie looked around, and saw the outline of a babushka-covered head, the cloth white she guessed, but red now in the light, extending past cheeks and forehead so that she could see only the tip of a nose. 'I couldn't sleep,' the voice went on, 'an it was so cold I thought I'd bring th car an meet him. He gets mad—but no more'n a month ago th oil in a converter exploded. A first helper got killed—he was down in u empty furnace. It was a sight th way he screamed, Bo said, burnen up in th oil, knowen he couldn't git out.'

Gertie shivered again, making the fence creak, but did not answer.

The woman pointed toward the roaring glow. 'Lookut ut shine,' she said, and without taking her eyes from the brightness moved her hooded head closer to Gertie, asking: 'Yu know why they's so much light outside—now? They's a hole, a great big hole inna roof. You know how it come there? They was some snow inna scarp they filled number two with, a little ball of snow,' and she cupped her two gloved hands together to show the smallness of the snow. 'It stayed there alla time a turnen into steam while th steel got hotter. They touched—that white steel, that little bita snow—an number two blowed right throughda roof. They ain't had time to fix it. They never stop. They cain't stop—war's gotta have steel, this electric steel. It ain't enough to be alla time watchen out ferda steel—th juice gits um. I wish he'd never left that open hearth down in Birmingham.'

'You frum th south?' Gertie asked, not caring. Talking might help take her mind off Reuben.

'I'm frum all over,' the woman said. 'Wherever they's white-hot steel I'm frum. I was borned and raised in Arkansas, but I ain't seen none a my people in thirty years. Was it good an quiet tonight? He pours. I wish't they wouldn't shut them doors, but when yu work in steel th wind feels mighty cold. Sometimes it don't wanta go into th ladle an fights back and jumps all over. Sometimes it likes th ladle but don't wanna go ina molds an pours crooked—an when yu pour yu mustn't toucha mold. That steel'ull burn a mold right out, an molds is harder to git then men. He'd a had his leg burned off three weeks back but he had his asbestos boots on. An once th hoisten cable broke, but nobody was killed—burned some. Whena ladle fell, that steel, she spattered all over. He came home laughen about it. Was it good tonight?'

'Good, real good,' Gertie said.

'But th meaner it is, the better he loves it. An I foller him. Quit it, I says, when th war come. We was in Youngstown. Quit it, I says, yu can make as much in a factory. Let's go to Detroit, I says, they'll be factories. He come an they was steel. An I follered—never was a woman follered so.'

'It's what a woman's got to do, I recken,' Gertie said. 'Foller—take on a man's kind a life like Ruth.'

'Ruth? Ruth who? Some woman in u paper? Paper's full a pretty stories a women folleren their men up here, hunten houses, gitten lost.'

'This Ruth lived a long time ago; when her man died she took up with his people.'

'My man ain't got no family, but he's got people here in Detroit. Hunkies they calls em.'

'Da watchman told me bout da kid.' It was Victor, unnoticed in the noise, come to the gate. 'I ain't seen him,' he said, opening the gate. 'He wouldn't be here; behinda fence kids git chased away.'

'He's got to go someplace to keep frum freezen,' she said.

'Yu'll freeze yourself,' he said. 'Yu kid's gone back home, back toyu own people. Yu gotta come now an lemme take yu home. You'll do no good out in this cold. I've got mu car; I'll take yu home.'

She hesitated by the opened gate. 'You cain't leave yer work.'

'I'm gonna quit now. It'sa little early, but no more pours on mu shift nohow. Yu kid's gone; yu gonna kill yourself. Up here yu gotta

364

wear slacks.' His big grimy face, the eyes ringed with clean white where the goggles had fitted, smiled. 'If yu got trouble buyen um big enough, yu want I should loan yu some a mine? Come on, da kid's gone back to his own people.'

'He didn't have no money,' she said, coming through the gate. 'I counted mine. He knowed where I kept it.'

They had reached the car, newer and a finer make than Clovis's, the front seat spread with newspapers neatly placed so that the seat covers might not be touched with grime. 'Da kid'ull be all right,' he repeated, 'but yu'll kill yourself.' He opened the door for her, got in on the other side and started the motor, but sat a moment, head bent, listening as Clovis listened. 'Cold—but she runs good,' he said, then from his jacket pocket he took a vacuum bottle, poured coffee into the red plastic top, and handed it to her. 'Drink ut,' he said. 'Max's good strong coffee do yu good.'

She drank, and the strong hot coffee after the bitter tearing wind and the noise and scorching heat of the steel made the unlighted car with the windows closed seem a warm and kindly place with Victor, his shoulders broader than her own, filling more than his half of the seat. He rolled his window down a little and listened to the running of the steel mill. The down-bent listening face, with a nose and a chin and a forehead big and ugly as her own, made her think of old Uncle George Keith, the way he used to listen, nodding his head, reading each sound, when he was practicing up the choir for a big revival at Deer Lick. He had worked in one of Old John's mines, and for the choir practice his face was usually smudged with grime like Victor's now.

'She's runnen good,' he said, and rolled up the window and backed out of his numbered parking place, repeating, 'Du kid'll be all right,' then asking when they had turned into the street, 'Yu got mu mudder's crucifix finished?'

'All but th face,' she said and added: 'But I'm afeared she won't like it. It ain't pretty an it ain't smooth.'

'Dat'll be okay,' he said, pleased. 'It'll look genuine hand-carved—mu mudder all a time wanted a genuine hand-carved crucifix. Yu'd better be home carving on it—take yu mind off yu trouble.'

She never turned to answer for staring through the car windows. Her glance snatched at all things—garbage cans, clothesline poles, cardboard boxes, windblown paper, anything that could somehow change into the shape of Reuben. Her heart quickened as they turned into the alley. Maybe he was home. There was a light in the kitchen.

She rushed up the steps, thanking Victor with short, absent-minded words, giving no answer to his concerned command not to go off again, but to stay home and if she couldn't sleep, work on the crucifix. No one came to her first round of quick insistent knocks. Clovis must have gone hunting for Reuben. He wouldn't go to work and his own child gone.

'Mrs Nevels.' It was Mrs Daly in her kitchen door, her apron steaming as if wet from hot suds. She held a whitish cloth that might have been a diaper as she came down the steps, calling, pitying concern in her voice. 'Mrs Nevels, da kids told me at dark yu boy was gone. Maggie went quick, and over in Our Lady of All Help they's a candle burnen to St Jude. Nothen so good as a candle for St Jude when somebody's lost. An keep a callen da cops. You'll hear; I know yu will.'

Gertie thought of Mr Daly, and said, 'Yes.' She pushed on her kitchen door, for behind the blinds she saw Clytie's shadow. Clytie was only half awake, but still fully dressed, as if she had dropped to sleep on the couch. Her voice was complaining, disgust on her face as she looked at her mother. 'Mom, I thought you never was comen home. You fergot to fix Pop's lunch fer work. Th cops said wanderen around hunten a boy that age wasn't no good.'

'Th cops.'

And Enoch, fully awakened at once, as was his habit, was running in calling: 'Mom, Pop went to th pay station an called th cops. Two come in a car—a special squad, not jist th regular patrol. They've broadcast it; all th patrol cars is looken . . .'

He fell silent under her hard, accusing stare. 'It ain't somethen you're a hearen over th radio, Son. It's your own brother gone.'

'But, Mom, th cops said boys was allus—all a time runnen away,' Clytie said. 'They acted like it wasn't nothen at all. They was kind a hateful, asken had he done any meanness er been in any trouble, an did he have a gun er a knife.'

'Git to bed, youngens,' she said, and snapped on the living-room light. Reaching under her coat into her apron pocket, she brought out her knife open and stood, looking toward the kitchen shelf where lay the pieces of wood for the cross and the cross-like Christ, finished save for a face.

'Mom,' Clytie said, 'you're a shiveren. They's some coffee left.'

'I don't need it,' Gertie said, but roused and took off her outdoor clothing.

Though she lighted the gas in the oven and put her feet there, she was cold still, shivering so that the knife leaped about the dead Christ. After a while of useless trying, she went to the shelves across the end of the little hall and took down the jug of medicine whisky, poured herself half a glass, and drank it slowly, savoring its goodness, its warmth and the memory of old John Sexton, who in spite of new-fangled ways never made anything but good whisky, like in the old days.

Her hands were steady above the Christ, but still she sat a long time, her knife poised above the blank face. So many faces—a million faces she had seen in Detroit, but no face for Christ—not Victor's Christ or any Christ. The face of the Christ with the red sweet gum leaves was dim now, changed like a tree from which the leaves have fallen. She got up at last, went back to the shelf, got another drink and the Bible. She opened it and sat by the kitchen table and searched a long time, thumbing through Matthew, Mark, Luke, and John. Once she sat staring at the floor, her forefinger under the words of the other mother to her twelve-year old son: 'Why hast thou thus dealt with us? behold, thy father and I have sought thee sorrowing.' She began searching again through the worn pages, but most often she read: 'I have sinned in that I betrayed innocent blood. . . . What is that to us? . . . And he cast down the pieces of silver . . . and he went away and hanged himself.'

She read it for maybe the tenth time, each time thumbing away, but always going back. At last she closed the Bible with a quick abrupt motion, shoved it from her, and took her knife and the faceless Christ; and the knife, as if with a mind of its own, gave a tortured, furrowed face to the drooping head.

367

The face was finished and the Christ was on the cross with the tiny wooden spikes through his feet and his hands, and Detroit slept the restless growling sleep of the small hours when she heard quick feet up the steps and a key turning in the lock. 'Clovis!' She sprang up, her hands shaking again, but the gaiety in his face reassured her before he had time to speak.

'Gert, we're awful fools,' he began, jerking off a glove, reaching toward his inside jacket pocket. 'Reuben's all right.' And from his billfold he pulled a piece of ruled paper such as the children used at school. He held it toward her, not so much reading as repeating words he knew by heart:

'"Dear Pop: I took $20 to pay my way back. I hope it don't make you run short. I don't steel. I will pay it back. Back home I can make some money. I can trap and work for Granpa. I can't stay here no more. Your ever loving son, Reuben." You know,' Clovis went on, gay as if he'd found a fortune, 'I never seen it till I went into my billfold fer money to buy some ice cream. I figgered if he took money he'd git it frum you stid uv his old dad, an that if he wrote it ud be to you. He's took th money an put his note in this mornen when I hung my jacket by th bathroom. What's th matter? Ain't you glad?'

Gertie nodded. 'You know—I'm glad. Real glad.'

'I yelled when I seen it an all th men come crowden round. An that foreman told me to go home when everthing was runnen good—that fool Bunken had got a piece a stock stuck in his press. I got it out, but I have to have a man frum tool and die to put in a new plate. "You go home an tell yer woman," that foreman says to me. Who'd ha thought a blamed foreman would ha had that much heart?'

She was silent, staring at the crucifix, and he for the first time noticed what she had done. 'Aw, Gert, you've set up all night a worken on that thing,' he scolded, his voice disgusted, pitying. 'What a you want to take all that trouble to whittle out them logs, when you could ha made th cross flat out a little boards in a third a th time.' He took the Christ from her unresisting hand and considered it, frowning. 'An if wasten all that time on th cross wasn't bad enough, you've done worse by given away fifty dollars' worth a work a whittlen on this Christ. You didn't haf to make him out a

368

hard maple—an a have him a bowen his head an a showen his back this-away. You'd ought to ha left him flat an a glued him on, stead a foolen around with these little wooden pins.'

'You know what you need,' he said, pulling off his jacket, looking at her as she sat, lax-handed, head drooping above the Christ he had flung into her lap, 'you oughta have a jig saw. With one a them things a body can cut out anything—Christ, er pieces fer a jumpen-jack doll—it's all th same to a jig saw.'

Victor was so pleased with the crucifix that he gave her twenty dollars; and, much to Max's disgust, he let it hang for some days in the kitchen window where all the alley passing to and fro might see. Some, like Mr Daly and Maggie, only glanced at it and hurried on, but others, such as Mrs Anderson and Vegetable Joe, came up short at the first glance, went closer, then stood a time under the kitchen window, looking up at the rough log cross with the drooping figure.

Many, particularly Mrs Anderson, complimented Gertie on the fineness of her work; but she always answered only with a slow and painful smile. The crucifix, more than most things, put her thoughts on Reuben. Worry on how a boy so young could travel all alone had let her neither eat nor sleep until a card came, postmarked at the Valley, and written to Clovis to deepen the hurt. 'Dear Dad. Got here all right. It is a nice day. I am walking out to Granma's.'

Several days passed, and she had again grown half crazy with worry before there came a letter from her mother: two pages of her complaints, little news, no mention of Gertie's father, the last page and a half given up to Reuben. 'Gert, what have you done to Reuben? He looks so peaked. He said you didn't have much to eat. Poor Clovis is working night and day for you. And you are too stingy to feed and clothe your family.' She stopped, but after a while she read the letter on to the end, then laid it on the kitchen shelf where Clovis found it that evening when he awakened.

'I wish Reuben had ha gone to my people,' he burst out with a bitterness surprising in him, when he had finished the letter.

'He'll hope em git their wood an sich,' Gertie said.

'It ain't that,' he said. 'Th Hull youngens'ull help Mom, but your mom'ull turn Reuben agin us. She'll work him like a mule, give him no schoolen like she done you. I'll bet he never goes to school another day. An then when he's growed up knowen nothen but how to be a work hand on a backwoods farm, she'll be ready to git shet a him like she was you soon's Henley got big enough to work.'

Gertie flushed. 'But, Clovis, I allus thought you liked Mom. You allus got along so good with her.'

Clovis smiled the way he had used to smile when they were boy and girl in school together, 'If I'd ever a got along bad with yer mom, you would ha had a time. Recollect all them years she claimed they couldn't manage without you on the farm? I got to thinken she'd never give in, an was all set to go job hunten in Cincinnati. It was the first summer Henley was big enough to do most a th plowen. She heard about me leaven an writ right away. Recollect?'

Gertie turned quickly away, hoping he had not seen her shame and surprise. She had never known about her mother's letter. But Clovis never noticed. His eyes were on his memories as he said, 'She'll do no better by Reuben than by you.'

Gertie turned to comfort him. 'But Clovis, it won't be ferever. We'll be goen back home pretty soon, an—'

'Back home to what?' He was angry with her now. 'I can hear em all a sayen—specially yer mom, "Pore Gert, back agin with that tinkeren Clovis, an not a nickel to her name." "Tinkeren,"' he repeated. 'I'll show em they's money in tinkeren.'

'But, Clovis, th war'll be over, an when it is you'll be out uv a job, an—' She knew she ought to hush. That was a thing at which he would not look, the future, when men stopped making things to kill other men. She was glad of the knocking that came just then on the kitchen door, and hurried to open it. Maybe no more than some teasing child who knocked and ran away, but whoever it was had stopped her tongue. Instead of a child, she found in the still alley where the smoke lay unmoving in the twilight a strange woman on her stoop who asked in halting, broken English if this were the place where crucifixes were made.

371

Gertie nodded, and the woman asked how much for a Christ like the one that had been in the window. Gertie hesitated; it was a deal of work, but twenty dollars was a deal of money. 'Tell her thirty dollars fer one like that, but that you can make somethen cheaper,' Clovis was whispering behind her.

The woman heard, and disappointment touched her eyes. Still, she opened her purse, asking, 'What for, for ten?'

Gertie pondered. 'All maple—no walnut—plain sawed wood fer th cross—jist a few thorns in the crown. An fer ten dollars,' she went on, conscious of Clovis, 'I couldn't put holes in th hands an th feet an set in little pins—like I done in that other'n. But I could kinda make em look like nails.' She flushed, hating the conversation.

The woman, after a spell of silent considering, shook her head in disappointment. 'But why for because so high? Ten dollar—blessed? Nah. Gold-plated I can buy—blessed.'

'It's awful tedjus work,' Gertie said, turning again to the supper getting.

'Yeah?' the woman wondered, but held out a five-dollar bill. 'A deposit,' she said. Gertie took it and thanked her, but the woman's dark face darkened still more and she continued to stand, frowning, until Clovis said, 'She wants a receipt.'

She gave it, and the woman went away, but Gertie stood looking at the five-dollar bill, new and clean as if fresh from a pay envelope. 'Aw, Clovis,' she said at last, thinking on the unpleasant work ahead, 'Christ wasn't nailed on sawed lumber.'

'Aw, heck, what difference does it make? It ain't Christ nohow.'

'I know. But seemed like if I couldn't make a Christ fer Victor, I ought to make him a right good cross at least.'

Clovis yawned. 'They's millions an millions a crosses with a feller on em they call Christ; all out a sawed lumber with th Christ straight agin em, glued on, an now you want to change em. That's one a yer big troubles, Gert,' he went on when she had continued silent, 'you won't give in to bein like other people. But it's somethen millions an millions a people has got to do, an th sooner a person learns it, th better.'

He then launched into his perpetual quarrel with Cassie. 'She run right by me, a holden out her hand a jabberen away. They was

372

a youngen a yellen, "Cuckoo, cuckoo, talks to herself," but Cassie didn't pay her no mind. An she didn't watch where she was goen neither; recollect them glasses she's wearen ull break easy, an they cost eighteen dollars. You've got to make her quit them foolish runnen an talken-to-herself fits. Th other youngens'ull git to thinken she's quair, an you'll have another Reuben. An she cain't run back home. An th more you play act with her an carry on about how you hate th place, th harder it'll be fer her.'

Gertie turned away, her lips pushed tightly together. Last night, when she had finished the second of the dolls ordered by Mr Anderson, she had promised herself the pleasure of working on the chickadee for Maggie, making it to give away and as the knife willed. Then, she had thought, her mind forever winging away from the hateful doll, she would start again on the block of wood. The man waiting for her there could heal a little of the hurt and this hunger in her heart for Reuben.

However, tonight, as soon as she had finished the after-supper kitchen work, she took a chunk of the hard maple scrap and began on the ten-dollar Christ. Clovis lingered a time in the kitchen, and studied the way of her knife on the Christ. 'Gert,' he said at last, his face all smiley with his plans, 'I'll bet in this town a body could sell a million a them things if they was cheap enough. I do believe—that tool-an-die man, he'd help—that I can rig up some kind a jig saw, cheap, that ud do th work in a tenth a th time, everthing on th crosses, and they'd be smoother, an prettier, too. An with a saw like that you could do a heap a th work on th Christ. That other Christ took too long, an he was ugly anyhow.'

'Victor liked him,' she said.

'Victor's quair. He'd ruther set an listen to music than go to th movies.'

'But I don't figger Christ er enybody in th Bible was pretty. They seen too much trouble,' she said, trying to make the knife go faster.

Clovis turned away in disgust. 'You're allus wanten to change th wrong things! You'd better be a worryen over changen Cassie's crazy ways than quarrelen about how Christ ought to look.'

Gertie worked on even after Clovis had gone to work. She roughly shaped the figure, and began on the crown of thorns.

373

She remembered too late she'd promised the woman only a few. A feeling of guilt came over her, the same feeling she had used to have when in her girlhood she had waited by the spring until her bucket overflowed, and she let it flow on, lost in some whittling foolishness or just savoring the peace of the hillside. Now it was money she wasted when she whittled a thorn, a strand of hair, or a fold in the loincloth that didn't have to be there.

She remembered the thorns on that particular Christ for a long time. It was over a wasted thorn that she made up her mind to do away with Callie Lou. Clovis was right. Happiness in the alley with the other children was better for Cassie than fun with Callie Lou. If she couldn't have the witch child with the other children, she must be made to leave the witch child. But now in the wintry weather, when Cassie couldn't play much in the alleys anyway, it wouldn't hurt if Callie Lou lived for just a little while longer.

Reuben? Reuben was now. She stared a long time at the floor, the knife and work across her knees. She got up at last and put the ten-dollar Christ away. It was near morning before she got to bed, working as she had been at gathering up Reuben's things. Piece by piece she laid them on the kitchen table: the notebooks and crayons Clytie had brought from school when she told Mrs Whittle that Reuben Nevels was gone, his clothing, a ball—his only Christmas present—some marbles, and a length of rawhide string he had brought from home. Everything he owned, except the hound he'd made for Mr Skyros, and that she put away in her mother's round-topped trunk.

The next night she thrust the bundle that seemed surprising small when it was wrapped and tied, into Clovis's hands as he was leaving for work. 'When you git a chanct, mail it,' she said, choking, turning quickly away. She sat a long time that night working on the Christ, realizing later that she had put more work on the crossed feet than the feet of such a cheap Christ should have.

She made the cross and never argued further for logs instead of planks. She was silent now when Clovis talked about the millions, and complained of nothing, not even of the Icy Heart when it froze the milk and made the oleo hard as iron. Though Clovis at times complained of Cassie, he blamed her no more for Reuben. Still, she

374

knew that most of the trouble with Reuben was herself—her never kept promises, her slowness to hide her hatred of Detroit.

She moved Amos and Enoch into the room on the alley that she and Clovis had shared, and put herself and Clovis into the boys' room next to Victor. Though smaller, Clovis liked it better, for it was quieter than the other room. The children accepted the goneness of Reuben with no questions and little comment. Now and again she heard Enoch declaring in the alley that Mr Daly's lies had made his big brother run away. Other times she'd hear him brag that his big brother wouldn't take no sass off nobody; he'd run away before he'd go to see the principal.

Gertie spent long hours over the ironing and the tedious housework, trying to think up words for a letter—a letter that would make him understand she loved him. Then, unable to put the words together, she would think past a perfect letter, written. Suppose he knew she loved him; as Enoch would have said, 'So what?' Her love had ever been a burden, laying on him false hopes that, dead, weighed down still more the burden of his misery.

She missed him, but could never tell him how she missed him most. She hated herself when she lied, trying to make herself believe she missed him the way a mother ought to miss a child. In the old song ballads mothers cried, looking at tables with empty plates and rooms with empty beds. But how could a body weep over a table where, even with one gone, there was yet hardly room for those remaining. The gas pipes were still overcrowded with drying clothes; and eight quarts of milk instead of ten in the Icy Heart meant only less crowding, not vacant space. Two pounds of hamburger cost less than two and a half, and— She would hate herself for thinking of the money saved, and try never to think that living was easier with no child sleeping in the little living room.

She caught herself wondering one day in early March how it would have been with cross Reuben home after the cold soot-laden rains set in, when day after day, except for time at school, the children, even Enoch, were shut within doors; and the place seemed even smaller, smellier, more filled with steam and leaking gas and radio and quarreling children than at any time since their coming.

The hard-packed ice and snow changed soon into black water that, held up by the deeply frozen ground beneath, lay in a sheet, sometimes inches deep, over all of Merry Hill. There floated on it, mercifully hidden until now by the layers of ice and snow, all the debris of the winter—newspapers, paper wrappings, orange rinds, and other garbage, lost and broken toys, and the frozen feces of the many wandering dogs and cats. There was even one dead dog around which a bevy of mud-splattered children congregated, but it, like everything else after the long burial in the sooty snow, was sooty gray.

Slushy water lay boot-top deep along the curbs where the children had to cross with the safety patrols, and twice Cassie, like many of the smaller ones, had 'gone under.' And Gertie, washing the mud out of Cassie's boots, pondered on the powers that called men out of the hills and put them and their children into Detroit's swamps. But Victor, coming out for a load of coal, was comforting. It would all dry up by summertime, he said, and then there'd be dust instead of water. He waved his hand over the black lake of the alley. 'Dey hadda put u factory workers somewhere. Dis place it was too wet futu grow potatoes, mu Pop allatime says. He knows. Dey tried u subdivide but u sidewalks went under, an inu depression everting went under.'

Gertie, however, in spite of the ugly weather, gradually grew to look forward to that part of the day when Amos sailed ships in the washbasin, Clovis slept, and Enoch was in school. She could then be easy in her mind, knowing he was not fighting in the alleys or listening to what seemed worse than fights on the radio. Such times were islands of quietness, holding a little of the lost goodness of back home; for often she and Cassie played lady-come-to-see, and drank 'coffee' and discussed Miss Huffacre. Even the forever sassing, giggling Callie Lou, staying now in the living room because Clovis didn't like the block of wood in his bedroom, sat listening in respectful silence to the merits of Miss Huffacre, 'the best teacher that ever lived, an yu ain't kidden,' Cassie always said.

Callie Lou seemed less respectful when Cassie quoted Miss Huffacre, ' "Of course you're going to learn to read, but no child learns all at once. It takes hard work, you know." ' It was then usually necessary for Cassie to speak sharply to the block of wood. 'Recollect you ain't so smart, an ye needn't be a laughen yer fool self sick. When you're outside I hafta watch ye like a hawk er you'd git run over.'

Gertie would listen, smiling but feeling guilty in remembering what she had promised Clovis—and herself. The alley jeers of, 'Cuckoo, cuckoo, talks to herself,' had to go. Cassie had to—the new word—adjust. Her mind would jump past the trouble. Maybe by the time weather good for playing in the alleys came the war would be over and they would be home, a family whole again with Reuben, and only the trees and Gyp to hear the talk with Callie Lou.

Then, as if a piece of spring had somehow fallen into winter, the west wind shifted south and came more steadily, and at last the sun shone. The sheets of water dwindled into smaller and smaller pools, all set about with black, glue-like mud in which the children never tired of playing. The mud lay so deep in many of the alleys that even the patrolling police cars never tried to come through. On one glorious windy afternoon, just as school let out, a coalhouse only two alleys away caught fire, and the fire truck that came clanging stuck fast and stood helplessly roaring, smothered in children, while two women in housecoats put out the fire with water from their mop pails.

Cassie called the big middle alley the Street-of-the-Flying-Kites because children stood there, unconscious of the mud halfway to their boot tops, their faces lifted to the yellow, green, and gold kites tugging against their hands as they fought to go higher into the wind-washed sky. There in the mud was no danger that while your face was lifted toward the sky a car could come and send you there.

It was on such a raw and windy afternoon that Enoch came clamoring through the door: 'Gimme a nickel, Mom. Th popsicle man, he's come.'

Gertie wondered and stuck her head around the door. She frowned when she saw the cart with the ringing bell that drew children like the music of that Pied Piper in the old seventh reader. She frowned still more and shook her head firmly against Enoch's pleas when she saw what the children brought away; their nickels gone for nothing but little chunks of frozen, sweetened, brightly colored

377

water. The stuff was so cold it smoked, and so hard it sounded like hickory nut hulls when some, like Claude Jean, cracked it between their teeth instead of sucking. The popsicle man, as if he knew her mind, lingered at the foot of her walk and rang his bell while Enoch, helped now by Amos and even Clytie and Cassie, begged: 'It's jist a nickel, Mom. We ain't never had none. Jist a nickel. Gimme ut.' And then the whine that always hurt, 'We're th onliest ones ain't got none.'

Enoch jumped with joy when his mother shook her head in the weary gesture that he had come to know. Later, when the nickels were spent, Gertie lingered on the stoop, puzzled by some strangeness. The alley was filled with children, but among them all there was no fighting, quarreling, name calling, dirt throwing, or even screaming. She was puzzled still when Mrs Schultz, who lived on the other side of Sophronie with five on a fireman's salary, called in rueful laughter: 'I never can make up my mind. Is it worth it?'

'Them popsicle things?' Gertie asked.

'Oh, no. If I had my way they'd have to pay me to let my children eat the stuff.' She waved toward the alley, filled only with the blissful sucking, crunching, cracking, lip smacking, 'No, the peace. Five minutes for five cents. I think though,' she went on, turning toward her door, 'I'll freeze my own this summer. That twenty-five cents a day mounts up so.'

'An yu kids'ull allatime wanta buy like du other kids. I tried freezing mu own,' Mrs Daly said, the hint of a sigh in her voice.

Gertie turned back into her kitchen. The hateful work of doing Homer's shirts would just about keep her children in popsicles.

The popsicle man, the children said, was the first sign of spring; and it was true that next day the sun shone more warmly and the wind came less raw and chill. The good weather held even into Easter vacation, early that year. During this vacation the children brought in from the alleys more talk of things that Gertie did not understand. She could not answer their questions of what was Lent and Holy Thursday, and why did Maggie's mother let her starve herself for Lent until twice she fainted at early-morning mass.

Maggie, Gertie thought, had come to no great harm. She seemed chipper as ever when she came selling Easter cards. Not like poor

Max, who had forgotten and used all her ration points for steak for Victor on a Wednesday night. He had roared out at the waste of meat and money and declared she'd done it on purpose to make him sin. Max had cried again that night behind the wall, and next day there was an urgency in her voice as she came, red-eyed, asking for a dream.

The quick lengthening of the days brought sunshine early to the alleys, and with it came the children, even the very little ones who crawled more than they toddled, but big enough to play in the mud and water as they built dams, sailed boats, or just dug in the black dirt, using spoons, nail files, butcher knives, anything except the flimsy little shovels made for children's digging.

The older ones played wild running games of kick-the-can or cops-and-robbers, or tired of these, they rode—roller skates, tricycles, bicycles, wagons, and scooters. Then, suddenly weary of everything, they would run away to some forbidden land, usually the swamp across the railroad tracks, from which they brought home boughs of the slightly swollen pussy-willow buds. Many with factory-working mothers could not leave the sunshine long enough for proper eating, but ate as they played, always chewing peanuts or popcorn or candy or popsicles or some sturdier thing like a stalk of celery or a raw carrot, favorite foods of Wheateye.

Even the least ones wandered freely in the safe world between the through street and the railroad fence, but were always losing themselves or their possessions. Mothers and older children and even fathers would come hunting: a little girl in a green babushka on one roller skate, a little boy with a squirrel on the back of his jacket; or, 'He hadda blue tricycle an red boots on.' 'Her eyes is black but her hair's kinda like platinum inu movies.' Others hunted clothing: 'Almost brand-new, fourteen dollars fuda snow-suit anu kid loses u jacket.' Toys, usually toys on wheels, but sometimes other things also were hunted: a black teddy bear, big with blue eyes, and a bed-wetting doll. Still others hunted owners: 'Dis yu kid's shoe? Yu've got one about this size ain'tcha?' and a strange woman held up a small brown shoe, mud-crusted, but almost new. Mrs Daly, hunting children and toys, paused long enough to advise: 'Stick ut ona clothesline pole. Somebody'ull see an claim ut.'

Mufflers, mittens, scarfs, and even snowpants were shed all over the alley when the March sun came warmly down at noon. Little girls were little girls again, with skirts billowing above thin legs, white from long imprisonment in snowpants. Long hair, hidden through the winter under snow-suit hoods, flew now like the billowing skirts above roller skates, jumping ropes, or bouncing balls while voices chanted: 'A leansy, a clapsy, a whirl around to bapsy. I touch my knee, I touch my toe, and round and round, I go.'

Gertie often looked at the little girls and wished Cassie were among them. But in the pretty weather, when all the others were outside, Cassie preferred to be indoors with Callie Lou. Clovis, forever restless in his daytime sleeping, would hear her at times, and angrily command her to go outside and play. She would go, meekly obedient, but almost never did she play with the others in the running and jumping games. Mostly, Gertie thought, because Clovis and Clytie, and even Enoch, had warned her so much about breaking the glasses, which, they never tired of reminding her, had cost eighteen dollars. Cassie also missed the bubble-gum boy. She had gone twice to his unit. Once, nobody was there. The second time she found strangers who had never heard of him.

Gertie, however, learned one day that Callie Lou visited often with the boy and his sister Mable; and listened to a long story of how well the children fared. She had spoken her part of the conversation in whispers, guiltily conscious of Clovis in his bedroom. The real spring with grass and flowers and budding trees would come and Callie Lou would have to go away, but let her live now in this short false spring.

The alley mothers knew the fine dry windy weather was a fleeting thing, and took advantage of it. Day after day they were busy washing windows, scrubbing the winter's grime from stoops and coalhouses, while some, more optimistic than the others, took down their storm windows and stored them in their usual places of storage, under the beds. Clotheslines blossomed with rugs, bedspreads, curtains, and all the things unhandy for drying in the kitchens through the winter.

Mrs Daly washed every stitch of Maggie's hope chest, and though twenty women must have stopped to exclaim over the beauty and the wonder of the pure white linens Mrs Daly could always point out some as yet unnoticed cause for admiration such as the remarkable beauty of the rosebuds woven into a tablecloth.

Even Max, hurrying by with an armload of groceries for Victor, stopped to study the lace on a doily, when Mrs Daly, hanging diapers now, asked her if in all her travels she had seen anything like it. 'It's kinda like little waves,' Max said, standing on tiptoe, obediently peering up at the flapping doily, and trying hard not to shrug her shoulders at it. She turned sharply away, but as she came on up the alley, staring hard at nothing, she continued to repeat, 'A wave, I'd lufta see a wave, a great big wave.'

She looked so lonesome that Gertie, out rolling up her clothesline, smiled on her, and said in comfort, 'It must be kinda nice to recollect th sea, somethen like standen on a ridge an looken away at rows an rows a hills; only, them hills in th sea, they'd be moven.'

'Yeah?' Max said, considering. 'A big wave, all white on top but blue black at u bottom—like a cave—a little—no, not blue black. Hell, have I forgot th sea?' A look akin to terror came into her eyes. She came very close to Gertie, and looked up into her face whispering: 'I gotta see u sea. I just gotta. Victor's mom, she's never seen u sea. She don't wanta see th sea. She's never been outa Detroit. She don't wanta be outa Detroit. She's gotta stay stuck in Hamtramck—all her life.' She held her gum still, but at last chewed again, repeating slowly, 'All her life.'

'But if a body loves a place,' Gertie said, 'an it's all their own . . .'

'Yeah?' Max asked, turning to look back at the billowing hope chest. 'An allatime be a kind a watchdog over junk like that—like Victor's mom?'

Gertie went on into her kitchen, which, after the sunny, windy outdoors, seemed even smellier and more crowded than usual. She took from the shelf her current piece of whittling, opened the inside door, and sat to work with only the broken storm door between her and the alley. Less than a week ago, before she had finished the ten-dollar Christ, Homer had rushed straight from his work to her kitchen. There he had explained in his neat, carefully worded way with her, as if she were a not too bright child who should be pleased by a grownup's notice, that he had another doll order for her. This was not a doll for a child. Come to think of it, he didn't really want a doll. He wanted a figure, he had said, something of good wood, 'a bit of folk art. Say, a woman in a sunbonnet and apron, but barefooted of course; and not so broadly smiling as the jumping-jack dolls. It's for Mrs McKeckeran, you know.'

Mr McKeckeran, he explained without being asked, was a vice president. He was close, very intimate indeed with Mr Flint, and a most important man. Now, wasn't it odd that his wife, Mrs McKeckeran, should stop by his desk and admire the little whittled hen when she almost never came into the offices? 'Oh, no, Mrs McKeckeran did not ask for a doll,' he had answered to Gertie's rather harsh question. She had been in the middle of supper getting, and his shirts, which she had been afraid he might notice if she moved them, kept flopping in her face as she stirred the gravy.

He just wanted it ready to give Mrs McKeckeran when the opportunity arose. He had gone away only after telling her all over again exactly how he wanted the doll, and also reminding her in a voice that Moses might have used to speak of God, that Mrs McKeckeran was the wife of a most important man.

Gertie sat now and worked on the doll, using the last of her walnut wood. She tried to hurry so as not to have to work on it when Clovis was awake to watch. He would quarrel as always about the deal of time she took, and start again the planning for a jig saw and patterns. But the knife, as if remembering the old days when it worked as it willed, was slow and awkward, even contrary in the wood, so that the face seemed no face at all.

She grew more and more disgusted, more clumsy-handed. Outside, the wind blew, the children laughed and quarreled and screamed, and two airplanes, high and silvery against the clean blue sky, made a kind of singing with the children and the wind's cries and the steel mill. Mrs Anderson's Georgie was digging a gold mine by Gertie's walk, flinging black dirt onto her stoop.

She roused suddenly from her fight with the doll, and looked about her, wondering, sniffing. She got up, sniffed again through the broken pane, then flung open her door and hurried down the steps. She stood a long time staring at the black earth, rich-looking and alive. At last she squatted and bent her face close to it, and sniffed, her eyes warm as they had used to be when she set the first cabbage plants in early spring; this earth was black as soot, and strange, but the smell of it was much like that of other earth in other springs.

She sat again and tried to whittle, but thought instead of hens clucking over eggs, sage grass burning at twilight, the good taste of the first mess of wild greens, and early potatoes going into the ground. Potatoes? Good Friday was late enough for the first beans, and in this week was Good Friday. Hands, knife, and doll dropped into her lap together. She had known. She had watched the days on the calendar: time for the rent, the car payments, the curtain man, the Icy Heart; but she'd shut her eyes to spring, the real spring back home. If they went home tomorrow it would be too late to get a mule and a cow and do all the things she would have to do before she could make a corn crop or even a garden. Now, the money she had saved back home for land would have to go to get a start of livestock. Clovis had never been able to pay back the Henley money he had used as down payment on the Icy Heart and the washing machine.

They couldn't live back home unless she farmed—at least a little. If they went back in the late summer or fall, they'd starve out on what little Clovis would make with his truck. His truck? He didn't have a truck. She twisted her head from side to side in an unconscious gesture of agony. Another year—a whole year in this place, and without Reuben; he'd be grown so she wouldn't know him. He was maybe plowing today, but not his own land with his own mules.

She was whittling again, grim-faced and still when Mrs Anderson came, Judy on one arm, Homer's dirty shirts on the other. She studied the doll that Gertie made, and sighed. 'Spring; back home there's a pasture with woods behind it, and I've always wanted to paint it when the dogwoods are in bloom; after a rain it's best when the dogwood trunks are sooty black, and now—' She smiled suddenly, 'Maybe next spring.'

'Mebbe, fer all uv us,' Gertie said, trying to smile, for Mrs Anderson looked lonesome as Max a few moments ago. 'You oughtn't to feel so bad. You've got yer house, an you know you'll be goen back pretty soon, an—'

383

'My, my Callie Lou, you've got your lesson good, every word. Why, you'll be going to the bookmobile and getting books of stories in this coming summertime.' The voice, though low, was warm with love and admiration, yet somehow copied from one that Gertie had never heard, but the little chuckle that came after was pure Cassie. Gertie, her insides all torn from thinking on Reuben and the spring, took comfort from the happiness in the living room, and smiled.

She caught Mrs Anderson's listening look, saw her frown of disapproval. Clovis, when he chanced to hear such talk, frowned just as the woman frowned now. Gertie remembered her promise, and the smile died. Her voice was so harsh and hoarse that Mrs Anderson looked at her in wonder as she said, 'I recken a body has got to say it's spring.'

Mrs Anderson nodded in absent-minded fashion, for she was still the listener, looking toward the other room. 'Does she do that much?' she asked, whispering, but loud enough that Cassie heard, and there was silence. 'I've noticed her in the alley,' Mrs Anderson went on. 'Talking to herself so much is rather bad, don't you think? She ought to be out playing with the other children or she'll be like—'

She might as well have gone on and said it, Gertie thought; but smooth and polite the woman was, reminding her of what she'd done to Reuben without saying his name.

'You'll have to help her grow out of that dream world,' Mrs Anderson advised as Gertie continued silent. 'They are, Homer has learned, supposed to give all that up when they are three or four years old. The other children think them queer, and it gets harder and harder for them to adjust.'

'Yes,' Gertie said. She was glad that just then Georgie screamed and Mrs Anderson had to hurry away. She tried to whittle again, frowning on the feet, trying to recollect with half her mind if she had ever seen a barefooted woman in a sunbonnet. Maybe Sue Annie in her garden, when the ground was soft. The knife handle slipped in her cold, sweat-oozing fingers. She drew a deep shivering breath, sprang to her feet, the knife clattering to the floor.

'Cassie Marie!' The loudness, the anger in her voice, startled her. More like a cry than a calling, a cry for the smell of earth that was her

384

own, a weariness with the nosey, talkative woman, the piece of whittled wood that she had made contrary to the knife, 'Cassie Marie!'

She realized before the last cry was finished that Cassie stood in the passway staring at her, more puzzlement in her eyes than hurt and surprise at her mother's tone. Gertie looked at the child, then down at the whittling gripped in her hand. She'd made one foot too big. The ugly hateful feet; she had to have anger. 'Cassie Marie, you git outside an play. You're wasten a nice day a setten a jabberen to yerself in this shut-up smelly place.'

'But Mom, I ain't a talken to myself.' Cassie stared at her, puzzled.

'Don't be a sassen me. You know well as I do you're talken to yerself. There ain't no Callie Lou.' Reuben was lost to her, the alley had the others. Henley was dead, his money gone, the land lost, even the doll was Homer's. Giving up, giving up; now Cassie had to do it. 'Didn't ye hear me? Go on. Play with th other youngens. Git into yer snowsuit an stay out.' She was breathing hard, choked up inside, fighting down a great hunger to seize and hug and kiss the child, and cry; 'Keep her, Cassie. Keep Callie Lou. A body's got to have somethen all their own.'

Instead, she was still, knife in one clenched hand, doll in the other, as she watched Cassie move slowly backward, her frightened eyes fixed on her mother's face as she hunted desperately for some proof that Gertie scolded in fun, the way she had used to put a great black storm upon her face, pull her thick black brows together, and even stamp her foot to frighten Callie Lou. Gertie sat again, and tried to fix her glance on the doll that seemed somehow to have taken Homer's face.

She would not look up when Cassie, having dressed quickly, squeezed past her chair to get outside. At the door Cassie, so close her body brushed her mother's knees, stopped, and slowly turned back. Her dismayed, frightened glance touched her mother's face, went past it then to the block of wood, and Gertie saw the yearning, hungry glance. She opened her mouth, then closed it, the lips pushed hard together, and sat, head bowed over the whittling, while Cassie went through the door and down the steps.

She couldn't let her go like that. She flung the doll onto the table, and hurried outside. She had to hear Cassie's voice again; the sound of it would reassure her, tell her that Cassie wasn't killed by this killing of Callie Lou. She stopped at the foot of her steps when she saw Cassie a few feet further up the alley.

The child turned swiftly at the sound of her mother's coming, but after one glance at her face, stopped and stood a time in silence, looking half hopefully, half fearfully at her. At last she asked, in a low, hesitant voice, 'Mom—can I go in now. I'd be still, real still—an not wake Pop.'

Gertie would not look at her. 'You'd jist be a jabberen away a talken to yerself. You need a little air an youngens to play with.'

'I never talk to—' But, unable to find her mother's eyes, Cassie was still. She stood looking about the alley in a lost and lonesome way as if she knew nobody, nothing, not even her own home in all the place. Gertie with sudden swiftness strode up to her and pulled a pigtail from under her coat collar, then searched for the forever missing mitten in a snowsuit pocket; then as if taking courage from her mother's touch, Cassie asked, all in a quick trembling breath, 'Mom, don't you like Callie Lou no more?'

Gertie squatted by the child on the pretext of straightening her snow-pants, but her hands went instead to Cassie's shoulders as she looked into her face, and tried to smile. 'I'll bet you can see little girls in my eyes today; it's sunny.'

'Mom?' Cassie's voice was hoarse now close to crying. 'You don't like Callie Lou no more?' And Cassie never hunted little girls in her mother's eyes, but searched her face for trace of Callie Lou. Gertie got slowly to her feet, her hands straightening the snowsuit hood now, but absent-mindedly, wanting only to touch Cassie, hold her when the voice came again, abjectly begging now, 'Mom, why don't you like Callie Lou no more?'

Gertie's face twisted with a forced smile that made her seem as if she bared her teeth in anger to match the anger in her eyes. Her voice was hoarse and ugly as she said: 'Now, Cassie, you know there never was no Callie Lou. Back home you never did have nobody to play with but Gyp an th trees—so you thought up Callie Lou. But here, you cain't go around a talken to yerself; th other—'

The words so hard to speak were wasted, for Cassie was running away, not holding out her hand, or with giggle filled eyes peeping

386

over her shoulder, but with head down, arms pumping, running as if there were but one thing left to do in the world, and that to run.

Gertie, worried at first by her wildly running ways, spent much of the afternoon watching her in the alley. But Cassie never ran further than around the buildings or across the big alley to the railroad fence. She lingered longest by the fence, always alone, peeping, Gertie thought, between the cracks of the upright boards at the trains going by and the slowly moving engines in the switchyards.

That night at supper Clovis quarreled at Cassie because she ate so little, and advised her to get out and get more fresh air while the weather was halfway good, for it would most likely be snowing by Easter. 'She's been out,' Gertie said, her voice so snappish that Clovis looked at her in surprise. Cassie's almost untouched plate of food troubled her, but she mustn't let herself think it had anything to do with Callie Lou, or that some strange lonesomeness that hung about the overcrowded little place, as when they had first come, was there because the witch child had gone away.

However, by next evening Gertie worried less. Though the day had been chill, with a raw wind and black clouds piling in from the north, Cassie had spent most of it in the alley. True, she had stayed, usually alone, in the safe place between the alley and the railroad fence, but that night she seemed happier and ate a fairly good supper.

Sleety snow set in next day, but Cassie begged so hard to go outside that finally in the afternoon Gertie let her go, partly because she herself wanted to go to a store some blocks away where she had heard there was yellow soap and ham to sell. If she left them all in the house together, they'd maybe be fussing and quarreling enough to waken Clovis. A few minutes after Cassie had gone, Gertie was hurrying into the big alley when she heard from further down the alley the low murmuring: 'Don't cry, Callie Lou. You're a big girl now. Stay over there across th railroad tracks in them little trees. Nothen'ull hurt you. It's so cold I'll hafta go inside. Goodbye now an—'

Gertie stepped quickly back, but too late. Cassie, just turning away from the fence, saw her and looked so guilty and frightened, as well as cold, that Gertie pretended she had not heard. She was

387

meekly still, shivering with cold, as Gertie retied her babushka and advised: 'Honey, it's so cold an raw outside, you'd better git in. An when I come back I'll bring you some candy Easter eggs, all colors.'

However, after all the walking about in the damp cold, Gertie came home with the Josiah basket swinging empty on her arm, her brows drawn together in wonderment. The streets had been so still, more empty-seeming than on a Sunday, and this was Friday afternoon. She had tried three stores, and all were closed. At the third a woman had come to her rattling of the knob, but had only shaken her head, frowning fiercely on the basket as if the carrying of it were a sin.

She had her own door only part way open before Clytie met her with troubled lamentations, not unmixed with shame. 'Oh, Mom, I heard Miz Daly an Miz Bommarita a talken back an forth about you. They seen you go off in th middle a tres ore. I fergot, but looked like you would ha knowed—you're supposed to stay home an pray er go to church er some kind a movie through tres ore.'

'Huh?' Gertie asked, sliding the empty basket from her arm, remembering only that it was the Friday before Easter—time to plant beans back home. 'What, what is it now, this—'

Afraid some neighbor might overhear such ignorance, Clytie closed the inside door before she repeated: 'Tres ore. It's when Christ was dyen on th cross. They tell yu over th radio to keep it, an it's somethen yu gotta keep in Detroit or they'll call yu a heathen what never heared a Christ.'

'I ain't so certain Christ ever heared uv it either,' Gertie said, weary with the long walk in the cold, the angry woman, and now Clytie's quarreling. 'I'd lots ruther recollect him alive a goen to feasts an sich than on this . . .'

'Tres ore,' Clytie repeated.

Gertie, in time, learned the new word, though she sorrowed less for not having known it than for the one she should have known on Easter morning when Christ was risen. Amos cried, Cassie swallowed hard, and Enoch and Clytie were ashamed because on Easter morning their unit was the only one in the whole alley not visited by the Easter bunny.

25

Hardly a corner of the sandwich was gone, and the cocoa Gertie had made especially for Cassie because she, unlike the others, had never learned to like the city milk, was untouched, but Cassie pushed her plate away, and said, gagging a little: 'I'm full, Mom. Can I go out an play now?'

'Don't ye want a little 'lasses frum back home?' Gertie coaxed. The child's tired-looking, unhappy face troubled her. All the doubts and wonders that had at times tormented her since she'd done away with Callie Lou more than a week ago came over her now, though her reason told her that a little thing like a mother's scolding wouldn't make a child lose her appetite and be restless in her sleep. She was catching cold in this wintry weather after Easter was what ailed her. 'You've got to eat somethen er you'll be sick,' she said.

'But I'm full,' Cassie repeated, then asked again, anxiously now: 'Can I go outside, Mom?—I gotta go.'

'No, it's a spitten snow,' Gertie said firmly, and added with vexation: 'You ain't took off your snowsuit jacket. Time an time agin I've told you youngens not to set around in this hot place with all your outdoor riggen on. Take it off,' and she reached for the jacket.

Cassie sprang away and stood, her arms clasped tightly across the jacket bosom as if to hold it on while shame and fear reddened her face. Gertie stared at her in puzzlement until Clytie cried, 'She's a hiden somethen under her clothes, Mom.'

Gertie looked at the jacket, flat with no bulges, and then at Cassie's trembling chin and brimming eyes. 'You've got to let me take that off, honey.'

389

Cassie's arms dropped by her sides. She blinked rapidly and tried hard to hold her quivering lips together, but the tears came and with them the shamed and troubled sobbing, 'I ain't done nothen, Mom. Honest.'

Gertie never understood until, with the other children watching, she had undone the jacket and found the note pinned with a small safety pin to Cassie's dress collar.

DEAR MRS NEVELS:

I would like very much to have a talk with you about Cassie. Could you please, sometime soon, but at your convenience, come up to school? You may see me either during the noon hour or after school.

Gertie had not finished when Clytie, reading under her elbow, cried, 'She's been up to some meanness, Mom.'

'Hush,' Gertie said, her chin trembling almost as much as Cassie's, as she patted the child's shamed, bowed head. 'Her an Miz Huffacre have allus got along good together. An she's learnen to read. It cain't be nothen much.' She looked at the clock, 'If I hurry I can go right away an see her this noon hour.'

'Look, Gert,' Clovis, awakened as always by any sound, no matter how small, but out of the ordinary, yawned and struggled with sleep in the passway. 'You'll jist go up there an have another quarrel like you done with Reuben's teacher.' He studied the note. 'Most likely it's not much, but mebbe I'd better go—in a day er two. She didn't say they was any hurry.'

'I'd ought to go,' Gertie said.

But Cassie caught her apron, begging: 'Please, Mom. Don't go. I don't want Miz Huffacre mad at me like Reuben's teacher. I ain't done nothen.'

And Cassie cried so that even Clytie comforted: 'Aw, honey, it ain't much. Mebbe you've been a talken to yerself in time a school, er mebbe you fergot to blow yer nose. You're allatime a snifflen an snuffin.'

Enoch reminded her that 'ole Miz Huffacre' was the strictest teacher in school. But Cassie only cried the harder, her words between the sobs a heartbroken moaning, 'But I thought we liked one another so.' She went to the block of wood, and stood a long time by the chair that held it, looking up at it. Gradually, the sobs left her, but obediently she kept her silence with the wood, not even smiling on the being hidden there, only sighing as she turned away. She came again to Gertie, begging so with her voice and her eyes to go outside that Gertie at last let her go. After all, there were many other children playing in the alley in spite of the raw winds and half frozen mud.

Once outside, Cassie seemed much happier. Gertie, each time she looked out, saw her, usually in her favorite place, the little island of safety between the big alley and the railroad fence; at times she even heard snatches of laughter and singing, though no conversation. Callie Lou, she guessed, had really gone away.

Gertie let her stay until supper getting time, but once inside Cassie wandered about with a forlorn and weary air, so silent that Mrs Anderson, who dropped in a few minutes later with Judy, wanted to know if she were sick. Gertie answered somewhat shortly that nothing ailed her. Her 'No' to Mrs Anderson's question of did Cassie take vitamin pills was sharper yet. Still Mrs Anderson lingered; she had come, she said, to learn if one of these days Gertie could make a doll for Judy. Gertie wished the woman would go home; Enoch and Clytie were beginning their evening squabble over the radio, and it plagued her to have somebody sit and listen and at the same time watch the supper preparations.

She was glad when, as she was opening a can of corn, Georgie came pounding on the door, 'Mom, Mom—Pop's coming disaway. He see da shirts,' and he sprang inside and stood grinning happily at his mother.

Mrs Anderson bit her lip, 'Georgie, please, "He will see," not, "He see." But whatever are you talking about? Your father has seen lots of shirts.'

'Oh, yeah?' Georgie said, smiling at one of his father's shirts, freshly ironed, and hanging on an overhead pipe. He peeped through the door, then began jumping up and down in an ecstasy of joy. 'He did see me run in here. He learn about u shirts on account u I run in.'

Mrs Anderson gave the shirts one uneasy glance then looked about the kitchen in hasty searching, like one hunting an exit sign in time of fire. Her glance happened upon the fried potatoes that Gertie, hoping the woman would take the hint and go home, had dished up and set to keep warm on the open oven door. 'Judy's so hungry, could you please let her have a few pieces of potato?'

Gertie was so startled at the idea of Judy's eating fried food that she forgot to hold her head down, and bumped it on the corner shelf. Homer would—

'Is the figure finished?' he asked breathlessly, before the door was fully opened. His naturally round eyes, rounder now than ever, and bulging with excitement, were fixed on her face as if her answer were the most important thing on earth. She nodded, and wondered at his smile dripping face; pleased it was as Jacob's with his brother's birthright.

Mrs Anderson put another crispy round of potato into Judy's mouth and smiled at him. 'Whatever is the matter, dear. Don't you see us, all your family along with Mrs Nevels?'

'Of course, of course,' he cried, smiling, rubbing his hands. 'Mr.—'

Georgie began screaming: 'Lookut. Lookut, Judy's got fried potatoes. She'll be sick. They're not on her diet. I'm gonna have some,' and he snatched the few pieces left from the saucerful Gertie had given Mrs Anderson for Judy.

'Shut up,' Homer said, and Gertie thought he was going to slap his firstborn. Georgie thought so too, and ran into the passway where he stood screaming. Judy screamed because all her potatoes were gone. Gertie gave her some more, and Homer, unable to make himself heard in the uproar, fell silent and for the first time noticed the potatoes. And then he only shrugged his shoulders and smiled, explaining to the puzzled Georgie, quieted now with more potatoes, 'Over-rigidity in any training sometimes develops unpleasant consequences.' He looked at his wife, but got only a shade of disapproval through his joy. 'But now will she eat her purée of liver? This is her night for purée of liver, isn't it?'

Mrs Anderson nodded and shivered. 'And ugh, how I hate to see her eat that damned stuff.'

Georgie looked at his mother, and so great was his surprise, turning swiftly into admiration, that he could neither eat nor speak; but Homer only looked impatient, like one eager to talk, as Mrs Anderson continued, turning now to Gertie: 'That liver soup has the most horrible color. You know, I've often thought that if I could paint with strained baby foods I might get famous. The tints would be something unknown in nature and as yet unconceived by man.'

Homer never heard. He was saying, as he took the barefooted doll Gertie handed him, 'Come, Georgie. We must get home. Daddy and mother have to go out.'

Mrs Anderson leaned wearily back in her chair, crying, 'Again! Those terrible Turbis.'

Homer seemed ready to dance on his toes. 'The Turbis may be there. But we are going—the McKeckerans have invited us to their home.'

'McKeckeran! McKeckeran? You mean the people who practically forced us to go to that hockey match. The wife, you said, gave the tickets. Whatever in the world does the woman have against me?' and Mrs Anderson looked ready to weep.

But Homer was almost angry, 'Against you? It was a thoughtful gesture for the wife of a Flint vice president to make to a stranger and a—a subordinate.'

'Subordinate?' Mrs Anderson asked, her face reddening. 'Shall we kneel as before the pope or only curtsey as before the Queen of England.'

'Don't be facetious,' Homer said, reaching for Judy. 'It's just an informal gathering, nothing to get excited about; business, mostly, hardly social. Mr McKeckeran told me in person; we were to have this conference tomorrow morning, but it was decided that Mr O'Hara should go to St Louis early tomorrow—labor trouble— so Mrs McKeckeran suggested that we all meet in their home. Wasn't that thoughtful? He said just come as you are about seven-thirty or eight, and by the time we eat and you get ready—'

'Ready?' Mrs Anderson asked with an exaggerated showing of surprise.

'Of course.'

'But I'm honest. Come as you are, the duchess said; so I go as I am.'

'Lena, dear, you must put on a dress and different shoes.'

'You mean put on *the* dress and *the* shoes. This suit is okay; old, I bought it before I married, when I could afford nice things, but the cloth's good.'

'But it would look—well, disrespectful—an old tweed suit in the evening.'

Mrs Anderson followed him to the door, her eyes too bright, her jaw too hard. 'I will in this sweater and skirt be just as respectful as at Turbis'. In respectful silence I will sit and listen to talk of shines, kikes, and baseball. I may even smile on the jokes about barefoot hillbillies and ignorant ministers from the South. Ugh, I hate myself.'

They were gone at last, and Enoch, who had been listening from the doorway, said: 'Gee, Mom, ain't that somethen? They're gonna see a man that knows old man Flint hisself.'

'All th same,' Clovis, who had also been listening, said, 'I'll bet she goes as she is. She'll knuckle down so much an no more,' and his voice was envious.

Clovis was right. When Gertie went to baby sit, she found a restive, pink-faced Homer, freshly shirted and shaven, snappish, yet somehow subdued. Mrs Anderson, serene and pleasant in the sweater and skirt, was saying just as Gertie went in, 'Tell her, dear, that my mink coat and Paris creations are in storage—wheat storage in Muncie, Indiana.'

However, when they came back, less than three hours later, Mrs Anderson seemed curiously subdued, silent, until Gertie asked, 'Well, how was it?'

'I don't ex—'

But Homer, taking off his rubbers, cried behind her, his voice bubbly gay: 'Now, Lena, my darling, you know you had a wonderful time. Why, you were the hit of the evening. Mrs McKeckeran took to you at once, and asked you to help out with the refreshments. You two were gone so long in the kitchen, you must have had quite a conversation, though I must say I had expected highballs instead of tea.'

Mrs Anderson turned to Gertie, who was getting into her coat. 'It's really pathetic. The war has forced—not forced, either; nothing forces Mrs Mc—Bales—'

'McKeckeran,' Homer cried.

'Homer, dear, Mr Flint has sixty-two vice presidents. It's like trying to remember the names of both the major and the minor prophets. Anyway,' she went on, looking into Gertie's eyes, which had met her own on the name 'Bales,' 'this poor woman has through patriotism cut her staff by at least nine-tenths.' She clucked her tongue. 'She doesn't even have a full-time butler any more. He works in one of the Flint plants, and only helps out occasionally. They haven't even but one chauffeur left, I gathered. Isn't it pathetic?'

Homer, in spite of his beaming happiness, was looking slightly pained. 'You've made up your mind to hate Detroit's industrial leaders. You certainly can't compare Mrs McKeckeran with Mrs Turbi or Mrs O'Hara.'

'Poor ladies,' Mrs Anderson said, still talking to Gertie, 'they were like cheap rayon taffeta against hand-woven silk—a shade too shiny. Mrs Turbi was dressed as if for a bullfight—bare shoulders. Before the evening was over, her shoulders were one mass of goose bumps, and I think Mrs Mc—you know, Bales—'

Homer opened his mouth to protest, but Mrs Anderson rushed on: 'Our lady enjoyed every teeny-weeny bump. She was so kind when she explained—she wore a beat-up old suit, older than this but much, much better, something she'd had made, perhaps in London, years ago—she's well traveled. But anyway, she was so sweet when she explained to Mrs Turbi that she'd just got home from her war work and that since Pearl Harbor she'd never dressed for dinner. Isn't that terrible. And she was even sweeter when she explained to the bare-backed ones that in order to conserve oil she keeps the furnace at sixty. And she has the loveliest maid,' she added as Gertie went out the door. 'Her name is Johala. She got back from rolling bandages, she said, just as we were finishing in the kitchen.'

'How odd, introducing one's maid,' Homer said, opening the icebox as Gertie went down the steps.

She stood a moment on her stoop, searching for the stars, but a pour was crimsoning the sky, and there were none. She looked first at the clock when she got in, then hurried into the bedroom to waken Clovis. She saw that the alarm must have gone off, for he lay with the light on, one arm across his eyes, the other flung out of the bed with the silenced alarm clock gripped in his down-hanging hand. She could, she decided, give him five minutes more. He looked so tired. She gently took the clock from him, laid the hand back across his chest, squeezing it a little as she might have caressed Cassie's hand. He came suddenly out of his half sleeping and smiled at her. 'You a tryen to make love to me, Old Woman, when I'm sleepen.'

She flushed, dropped his hand, and backed confusedly away. 'I was jist a thinken, Clovis, that—that, well if all these years we've been a liven together I could ha seen Homer ever onct in a while—why I'd never ha quarreled at you atall.'

'Ain't it th truth?' he said, getting out of bed. 'Ever-time I look at that gigglen yaller-headed fool from Georgia that's allus a needen me tu fix somethen, I think what would I do if I had to live all th time with a woman like that.' He was suddenly thoughtful, pulling on a shoe. 'All th same, Gert, be nice to Homer. You don't know, he might some day hep me keep a job. Anybody that goes visiten that McKeckeran ain't peanuts. But,' he added quickly, 'don't be a sayen nothen to Whit an Sophronie; nothen gits a body in bad with them union stewards an sich than to let em think you're tryen to hug up to th foreman er somebody in the company.'

She nodded, wondering if she should tell him she had seen the other half of Mrs McKeckeran, but then maybe Mrs Bales, the poor and lowly gospel woman, was supposed to live in secret from all of Mr Flint's world. Then she forgot the business, in thinking of Cassie, who had been in the back of her mind all evening. 'Clovis, don't you think mebbe one a us ought to go see that teacher right away? She might mebbe want us to do somethen that ud hope Cassie.'

'Aw, Gert, I'll go in a day er two. I been aimen to git me some new Sunday shoes. I hate to go looken like a tramp in my work shoes. If you go, it'll be like that other trip. You cain't hep it, an some a these people up here thinks people like us is dirt under their feet. An anyhow, I figger it ain't nothen much. She'll most likely fergit about it in a day er two.'

Gertie said nothing more, but in the following days she often found herself wondering what the teacher could have wanted.

Cassie, who now spent most of her spare time outdoors, seemed happy enough in spite of her silence in the house, and Gertie had no wish to worry her again by discussing the letter. She thought at times of telling Mrs Anderson about the business. The woman would agree, she thought, that Clovis, since he insisted on going himself, ought to go now.

But with a body like Mrs Anderson, there was little chance to talk of anything except the double woman. Wonderings on the how and why of Mrs McKeckeran now occupied Mrs Anderson even more than her critical musings on the why and when of Mrs Daly's ninth baby, which had since Christmas taken up much of her mind. It seemed the woman couldn't think without moving her tongue. Homer's shirts gave her an excuse for dropping in on Gertie, so that it was Gertie who had to listen. 'You know,' she said, one morning three or four days after the McKeckeran visit as she pinched a bit of crust from a freshly baked banana cream pie, 'I am beginning to feel, just feel, of course, that it wasn't Mrs McKeckeran we saw in the alley. But I know of course that there can't be, just can't be, two women exactly alike, each with an exactly alike Johala.'

Gertie yawned over the ironing of a shirt collar. 'Looks like she would ha said somethen when you two was in th kitchen.'

'Oh, didn't I tell you about the kitchen? Homer would give his thesis to know. You see, she's no daughter of some man-killing day laborer turned mechanic like'—she looked swiftly about her—'like old man Flint. She's so very certain of her position, she can dirty her own hands in her own kitchen.

'Nothing happened in the kitchen except it must have been the way I looked at the little cakes laid out in the pantry. She asked me if I were hungry. Of course I told her that I'd been so upset at the idea of having to give up another evening to my husband's business that I couldn't eat. Funny, I could say that, but never ask her the one simple question that was burning a hole in me. I could even eat the large and luscious sandwich she fixed of all the things that Homer doesn't like me to buy and the children can't eat, but I never could say, "How's gospel work?"'

'It would ha plagued her,' Gertie said.

'She would have loved it. She would only have had to smile that sweet, sweet smile and say, "You're mistaken, my dear," and before all the others I would have been the mistaken fool.' Mrs Anderson drew a deep breath, her face reddened with anger. 'I'm certain she knew before I came that I was I. Perhaps from your carving on Homer's desk, or I might have given her my name; I keep trying to remember, but the children were acting up so. I think I even stuttered when the door opened, and there she was smiling, certain I would be the courtier's wife before the naked emperor, afraid to open my mouth and say that he was naked.'

'Mebbe not,' Gertie said. She pondered above the ironing, Enoch's overalls now. 'Mebbe she liked you th first time she seen you an thought you two ud git along good together.'

'But get along with which one? She's two people,' Mrs Anderson insisted.

Gertie considered Mrs Anderson instead of the ironing. 'Not exactly two people, maybe. Leastways, she's better off than some. She knows she's two people.'

'Du cops, du cops,' Georgie, Enoch, and others were screaming in the alley.

Mrs Anderson jerked open the door. 'And poor Homer will miss it. I'll bet Mr Karadjas is beating up his wife's boy friend again.'

'It was th boy friend done th beatin, er so I heared,' Gertie said, following her to the door, open now, filling the room with alley cries.

'Du cops, du cops is comen.' Wheateye was jumping up and down on the coalhouse crying: 'Dey're gonna git Mr Daly. Daly's gotta go to jail. He beat Miz Daly.'

Above Wheateye's voice rose the cries of the younger Dalys, running out their kitchen door: 'Cops is comen fu mu mudder. Little Sister, her couldn't wait.'

'Oh, my God,' Mrs Anderson breathed, then all sounds were drowned in the screaming of a siren, the sound that had at first thrown the children into ecstasies of joy, near now, louder and shriller than even the best ones on the radio.

Mrs Saito, the little Japanese woman who lived on the end next to Mrs Daly, came hurrying up the alley as if returning from an errand. Though she was the politest person Gertie had ever known, she took no time for knocking now, but hurried through the Daly door. She was hardly inside before a scout car whirled out of the through street into the big alley. Its siren came again in a long shrieking wail as it bounced and careened over the rough ground. The children squealed with joy as it skidded on the muddy gravel in turning sharply to get into the little alley and threatened for an instant to run right through the unit on the end, but disappointingly righted itself in time to stop with a squeal of brakes and a smaller skid in front of the Daly door.

A policeman sprang out just as Mrs Daly, neatly dressed, smiling, but walking with difficulty, came down her steps, followed by Mrs Saito with a small suitcase. The cop helped Mrs Daly into the car. An instant later she was gone, siren screaming, brakes and tires screeching, and the envious glances of all the alley children following after.

Mrs Anderson was for an instant able to say nothing more than, 'One would think that after eight she wouldn't be caught at the last minute like this.'

Sophronie, who like most of the other night shifters, including Clovis, had been awakened by the siren, stuck her head around the door and smiled, 'Lookut th cab fare she saves, though.'

Mrs Bommarita, staring wrathfully at her freshly scrubbed walk, spattered with mud from the whooshing scout car, shrugged her shoulders with disgust. 'Last time her done it, I just got in this place ana didn't know her so good. Yu know what she told me: her'd be glad her pains come on so fast her couldn't wait to call Mr Daly home from work. S'hard on him, she said. Can yu beat it?'

'Maggie is the one it'll be hard on,' Mrs Anderson said.

'We'll all hafta hep watch them little youngens,' Sophronie said. 'That Miz Saito, she works a midnight shift. She's gotta sleep some a th time,' and after yawning a moment she hurried down the alley calling, 'Hey, you,' to small Mrs Saito, struggling now to get a young Daly, who in the excitement had run out without his shoes, back into the house.

Sophronie and Mrs Saito were just getting all the little Dalys within doors when Mrs Schultz, who lived between Sophronie and the Millers, came onto her stoop, and called to Sophronie: 'I'll fix their lunch and watch them till Maggie comes home. I don't have to sleep like you two.'

Mrs Anderson continued silent, but Gertie, feeling guilty, called: 'I don't have to work away from home, an I ain't got no real little uns. I could watch em an feed em too.'

'Your turn will come, don't worry. She'll be gone at least three days,' Mrs Schultz said, smiling at Gertie, and Gertie smiled back, admiring the woman. She was held to be the best housekeeper in the alley, and in spite of five children, three of whom were under school age, she did all her own sewing, and often her marketing, for her husband was a fireman, and kept strange hours.

The little Dalys, when all were combed and in their shoes, disappeared through the Schultz door, from which came inviting smells of apple pie. The alley children came pounding back from chasing the scout car; and Enoch called to Gertie, just turning into her door: 'Mom, didja know that if she has it inu scout car she'll mebbe git her pitcher inu paper? An th baby's too.'

'No,' Gertie said, trying not to let Mrs Anderson see how much this talk of women having babies plagued her. Back home she had never heard the subject discussed at all until after she was married and had borne Clytie, and then only in whispers among the older married women. But here, all of Mrs Daly's symptoms, from her morning sickness to her fits of temper, were discussed by everybody in the alley, including Mrs Daly and her children, often in loud callings such as Enoch called now. Gertie, however, was saved from further embarrassment by Enoch's sudden remembrance of his perpetual quarrel with her: Why couldn't he go up to Zedke's and buy a Coke with Mike? Mike got at least one Coke every day and sometimes two, besides candy. Why was she so stingy?

Gertie sighed, and turned back into the kitchen, thankful that it was Judy's nap time and Mrs Anderson had gone. She looked at the clock; it was almost time to get lunch for the school children; and she glanced anxiously at the banana cream pie she had baked, mostly to tempt Cassie's lagging appetite.

Today, however, Cassie ate quite a bit of lunch. Later she played happily enough outdoors, and not always by the railroad fence, for she, like most of the rest of the alley, must be always running here and yonder, calling, hunting little Dalys. But in spite of them all, the stove wrecker slipped around to the front of Victor's unit where nobody ever played, and using a fork, a spoon, and a nail file dug a hole through Victor's living-room wall. Nobody knew until Victor flung open his seldom used front door and cried: 'But why for because yu gotta dig a hole in mu unit? G'wan, dig a hole in yu own house.'

But he slammed his door, defeated in the face of the derisive answer: 'Oh, yeah? Go cool yu can. Yu ain't me Uncle Sam. Nobody owns dis project but me Uncle Sam. Yu don't own nutten.'

'We'll have to build fences,' Mrs Anderson said when the tumult had quieted, and she went on to tell of the time last summer before Judy was born when Claude Jean Meanwell had dug a hole in her bedroom wall. She had been napping when she awakened to soft giggles, but unable to see anything except a small dirty hand waving at her from the wall; she had screamed so with fright, half awake as she was, that Claude had choked with laughter on his popsicle. He had turned blue and alarmed the alley, but the popsicle melted before the rescue squad from the fire department got to the scene.

Gertie wondered how the summer would be, and looked about for Cassie. She found her soon, off by herself again, by the railroad fence.

26

There was disappointment in the alley when, after all their troubles with her children, Mrs Daly did not get her picture in the paper. It was homecoming time for day-shift workers when a blurry-voiced, too stately stepping Mr Daly, dressed in his Sunday best, announced to all who wanted to hear that he was on his way to see his wife, who had been delivered of a daughter in St Theresa's Hospital at two fifty-seven that afternoon. He had gone high-stepping it out of the alley and, according to Mrs Bommarita, who'd listened through her wall, he hadn't got home until almost three in the morning; she knew because he'd wakened Maggie, and Maggie's crying by the wall had wakened her.

However, next morning, when Maggie stopped by on her way home from mass—she was staying out of school to mind the children but had to leave them long enough for mass—she was her usual smiling self as she offered Gertie a fifty-cent ticket to a bingo party with door prizes of china dinner plates.

Gertie shook her weary head against the dishes, and closed her door with relief. It seemed that she had run into the alley a thousand times to see about the little Dalys, two of whom had gone several blocks as stowaways on a milk truck and might have been gone all day had not the driver discovered them and hastily as well as angrily returned them to the alley.

She forgot about the Dalys when her own came home for lunch. Clytie was angry, splattered from head to foot with mud. 'An, boy, did them guys laugh when they whooshed right by th curb in that ole clunker an made us girls jump an scream.'

Worse than Clytie's trouble was Gertie's realization that Cassie was no place in sight. Frightened, she had run down the alley hunting, before she found her fooling along by the railroad fence. 'Your dinner'ull be cold,' she called in sharp scolding.

'I ain't hungry, Mom. Cain't I jist stay outside?'

Gertie, more troubled than angry now, hurried up to her, and saw that she had been crying, and at her, 'What's th matter, honey?' Cassie dissolved in weak hopeless tears, such as she had never shed.

Gertie picked her up as if she were a baby, and learned as they walked home that: 'I wet on myself, Mom. I done it right where all th youngens could see.' And the shamed and sobbing whisper, coming up from the face buried on her shoulder: 'An all th youngens they laughed at me. Don't tell Clytie, Mom.'

'Lots a little youngens has done sich at school. Don't feel so bad now, even if that ole Miz Huffacre did talk mean to you. One a these days . . .' She shut her mouth into a straight hard line. Promises, that was all she'd ever given Reuben.

'Oh, Miz Huffacre,' Cassie said, 'she said lots a little youngens had done sich when they didn't feel good er somethen. But, Mom, she asked me did you git her note. Mom, do you recken she's mad at me?' And Cassie cried again.

She continued to cry with a weary sobbing as Gertie changed her clothing, telling a little lie to the others that Cassie had fallen into a puddle. She was so miserable, not wanting any lunch, that Gertie picked her up and for want of a rocking chair sat on a straight-backed chair in the living room, and tipping back and forth, sang one of Cassie's favorites: ' "I've reached the land of corn and wine; and all its riches freely mine; here shines undimmed one blissful day . . ." ' Her voice, at first low, grew louder as the child snuggled against her, drowsing with half closed eyes, and on the chorus, "Oh, Beulah land, sweet Beulah land," her voice was forgetful, booming out as in the old days.

Enoch, eating a sandwich in snatches crouched by the radio, began complaining: 'Mom, you're a maken so much racket I cain't hear Silver Sam. Sing in her bedroom.'

'I'd mebbe wake Sophronie er your pop.'

'Well, sing in mine.'

'Victor's got to have his sleep, too.'

Clytie was calling in a shus-shushing, chiding voice: 'Mom, you're already a waken Pop. I can hear him a groanen.'

Gertie sat for an instant like one ready to rise. Let Clovis wake up and go now and see Miss Huffacre and learn what was this trouble with Cassie. She looked at the child, and began rocking her again, soundlessly, moving only her body now. Her face down in the crook of her own big arm looked so little and pale and tired, or lonesome, more lonesome than tired, she decided. Maybe she'd doze off and wake up happier; but if they all started talking about Miss Huffacre now she'd start crying again. Gertie continued to rock silently, looking down at the drowsing child, and wanting nothing except the privilege of holding her. But in only a few minutes Cassie came wide awake and looked wildly about her. She slid from her mother's lap, yawning, but asking, 'Can I go outside, Mom?'

Gertie cleaned her tear-smudged glasses. 'Whyn't you stay inside, mebbe take a little nap? It's so cold and raw outside, like a January thaw back home; er if,' she coaxed, 'you cain't sleep, you could show me how good you can read. You ain't read fer me in days and days.'

Cassie shook her head, glanced at the block of wood. 'That wouldn't be no fun. I hafta play. Cain't I, Mom?'

Gertie pondered, studying her; maybe a little running about would make her hungry, take her mind from what had happened at school. She said nothing as Cassie struggled into her snowpants, put on her boots, hurrying a little, her tired sleepy face determined, hard-pressed somehow, like Sophronie's on her overtime days, when she slept too late and had to fight the clock until time to go to work again.

Gertie, busy with a washing, saw her in the alley now and then, sometimes with Amos, but mostly alone, playing the game of airplane she had learned in kindergarten or singing little songs. The afternoon shift of school was over, and still Cassie played, in front of her own door now, where she and the smaller Dalys and Georgie built a school. Cassie became Miss Huffacre, the side of the coalhouse a blackboard, a piece of kindling wood a pointer. Cassie would point to a knothole and cry: 'That word is "skip." Now,

404

children, show what it tells you to do.' There were many words: 'run,' 'jump,' 'skip,' 'sing'; and the children amid much laughter and many shouts did the bidding of each word.

The fun attracted a little crowd; even Wheateye, eating what looked to be a quarter of a large-sized head of cabbage, watched critically for a time, but at last cried: 'That ain't no blackboard. An yu ain't no teacher—cuckoo.'

The bigger Dalys took up the cry of, 'Cuckoo, cuckoo,' and Cassie, after standing a moment, red-faced and silent, Miss Huffacre's smile frozen on her face, dropped the kindling-wood pointer and ran away. Wheateye immediately seized it, and holding it in one hand and the cabbage in the other, continued the school, amid much chewing of and at times strangling on cabbage.

The Dalys, weary of being pupils, repeated Wheateye's cry of, 'That ain't no blackboard, yu cuckoo kid,' turning it on Wheateye, who quickly crammed the remainder of the cabbage into her mouth, and so having both hands free, bopped the kindling-wood pointer hard against the seat of Jimmy Daly's pants, and then on the stove wrecker's head.

'I'm the principal, sillies,' she yelled, as they turned in retreat.

'Yu don't know nutten,' Jimmy cried. 'Youse don't learn nutten ata ole public school but communism. Da good sisters, dey hitcha ona hands. Come on, kids; da devil'll gitcha fu goen tuda public school—cuckoo—crazy.'

'Yu're expelled,' Wheateye cried. 'Git out,' she screamed, duck-ing dirt from Jimmy, a tin can from the stove wrecker, and at the same time getting in two good licks with the kindling wood, good enough that the Dalys retreated. She saw the Miller children of kindergarten and first-grade size, and called to them to come and play school, then looked about calling: 'Cassie, hey, Cassie, come on an play. Yu can be teacher an I'll be th principal. An bring yu girl friend, what's her name—Callie Lou. She can be th bad kid, an we'll make her stand in a corner like we done th other day. An these Millers can be th good kids. Ana Dalys can be th real bad kids wot comes an breaks th winder lights an throws th books ona floor when we're gone. Come on, Cassie.'

Cassie's smile at being called back to play was like a light across her eyes. Her mittened hand went out, seizing the witch child's hand, and her voice held the old burbling. 'Come on, yu mean youngen. Miss Huffacre's gonna make yu stand in the corner.'

Jimmy Daly watched her jealously. 'Nuts inu bean, hillbilly. Talks to herself. Nuts inu bean.'

Georgie, coming down his steps, his vigor renewed with a vita-min pill, a rest period, and the prescribed mid-afternoon snack, took up the cry, 'Nuts inu bean.'

Cassie dropped her hand and stood red-faced, looking uncer-tainly at Wheateye, who was only now swallowing the last of her mouthful of cabbage, tossing her head, wriggling her neck to make it go down in a hurry. The cabbage down, she twirled her kindling wood and cried to Cassie: 'Run, honey, run. Them wild mean kids wanta hurt yu little kid. Yu gotta stand up fu yer kid.'

The hand flew out, protective now, but Cassie, when almost opposite the door, looked up and saw Gertie watching, listening. Her mother was stern-faced and frowning, for she had been won-dering for the last five minutes if she oughtn't to tell Wheateye to be quiet, or else go somewhere else to play. They'd waken Victor again—and Clovis, too.

Cassie's hand dropped, her smile faded, as her mother's glance touched her, and ever an obedient child, she mumbled to Wheateye, her voice choked and guilty, 'They ain't no Callie Lou.' She ran then, and did not stop until she was out of sight around Max's corner.

No one came to Wheateye's calling, 'Come back, come back; we gotta have Callie Lou.'

Gertie went back into her kitchen to turn down the gas flame under the boiling beans. She bumped her head on the high shelf as she turned, but never noticed it for thinking on Callie Lou, smiling. All this business of doing away with Callie Lou had been a mistake. Suppose Miss Huffacre had heard the child talking to herself and felt about it the way Mrs Anderson did? Cassie could have Callie Lou at home. She, Gertie, couldn't kill her when already she lived in the alley.

She waited a moment on the steps, watching for Cassie, and when she did not come went to the end of the building and around

Max's unit hunting her, smiling. She'd call out, 'Lady, lady, bring that black-headed child in out a this raw cold,' or some such, and Cassie couldn't talk for giggling, and then she'd feel so good she'd eat a great big supper.

Cassie was not in the paper-littered water-soaked strip of earth between the front of their building and the front of the next, nor was she by the railroad fence. Gertie stood in the alley by the fence and looked about her, uncertain whether to go looking in the next alley or back to the other side of her own building. Quick-footed Cassie had most likely run all the way around as she often did. She wouldn't stay here in all this smoke, for on the other side of the fence a train stood on the side track. The switch engine was still in front of a long string of boxcars, broken apart at the through street. It had dropped off cars for the steel mill and was waiting, with smoke and steam flying up, to back across the street and pick up the caboose and the other cars.

The purring, steaming engine was far away and made but little sound. Fainter, like the buzzing of a horsefly, was the buzzing of an airplane, still high above, and almost hidden from sight, but she knew from experience that it would in a moment come in low for a landing in swooping circles of head-hurting sound. She savored for a moment the silence, when all Detroit seemed sleeping, and even the big engine was like something sighing and whispering in its sleep.

She had walked a few steps over the muddy gravel, still smiling thinking on how pleased Cassie would be to have Callie Lou back again, when she heard the word, hardly more than a louder whisper of the engine, but Cassie's voice, soft, yet warning, 'Callie Lou.' Gertie stopped dead still, puzzled. Memories of old tales of witches and warnings of names called down from the sky or up from a river came back to her. The wind, she'd always said, for the wind in leaves and by water had many voices. There was a little wind today, but the brassy-voiced Detroit wind could never whisper so. Machinery? A radio? She was still an instant longer, listening, looking about her, then walked on, for the airplane had swooped, circling, drowning even the sound of the engine.

She turned slowly about for a last look around before starting home. In turning, her glance, moving swiftly by the railroad

407

fence—for Cassie was plainly not by it—stopped, held by some strangeness about a crack between two of the eight-foot perpendicular boards—red-colored it had looked to be. It was a narrow crack, but wide enough for her to see, with one eye against it, Cassie's red babushka on the other side, so close she could have touched it could her glance have been her hand. Cassie stood between the main line and the fence, one hand holding Callie Lou's hand. Her head was turned sideways, cheek toward Gertie while her lips moved, laughing as she shook her head in some argument with Callie Lou, then nodded toward the boxcar on the next track.

Gertie called to her, 'Git away, Cassie, git away,' but the airplane kept her words from Cassie as if she'd been a mile away. Her calling more a screaming now, she could only watch the moment's argument that followed. Cassie shook her head violently and even shook the stubborn Callie Lou, who yielded at last and let Cassie step onto the shining rail of the main track. She stepped off it onto the crosstie and then walked the few steps to the next rail, on which she stood for an instant, looking down at the silvery shine below her boots.

She did not stop again until she had reached the boxcar on the next track, dull red, empty, with its sliding door invitingly open. Still swinging onto Callie Lou, she stood on tiptoe, peeping, but it was too high for much looking into, though she could touch it with the tips of her fingers. She found the great wheel, its shining roundness, almost as high as her head, more interesting. And unable to hear the terror-filled voice on the other side of the fence: 'Cassie, git back! Thet car's on a engine. It could move!' she put her hand on it.

Once she turned and looked about her, her eyes for an instant seemed like on the crack behind which Gertie pounded, but the airplane was low now, smothering the world with its crying. Cassie looked up at it briefly, for she hated the noise, then turned, put her hands on the edge of the boxcar by the wheel, arched her body as much as possible, shielding, Gertie realized, the smaller, more timid Callie Lou from the sound.

Gertie, still screaming, whirled away from the crack. Somewhere there was the hole through which Cassie had crawled. She hadn't time to run to the through street and around. She ran up and down, searching, calling, beating on the fence. She found the hole at last, so small and low she had twice run past it. She shoved her head through, though its lowness forced her to her knees; but heave with her shoulders, claw with her hands behind her as she would, she could not get her wide shoulders through, for the hole was the width of a board, broken off at the bottom and no higher than the stringer to which it was nailed on the other side.

She could only try to send her screams above the airplane that circled ever lower. Cassie had dropped to her knees on the end of a crosstie under the boxcar, and was holding out her hand, her lips moving in some reassuring burbling chuckle, her hair fallen across her eyes, as with a reassuring smile to Callie Lou she pointed to the boxcar above her head.

Gertie screamed more loudly, certain at last that Cassie had heard her, for the child seemed suddenly afraid, and sprang up. She looked once toward the fence, then down the track toward something Gertie had neither seen nor heard. It was the through train for which the switch engine had been waiting. Cassie stood an instant, her mouth open, her startled eyes bright with fright. Then, swiftly, she dropped to the ground, and as if hunting sanctuary from the oncoming train, crawled onto the rail and sat huddled close to the great wheel, waiting, her eyes squinched, Callie Lou cradled in her arms.

Gertie jerked her head from the hole. Cassie could never hear in all the racket. Why hadn't she thought to throw something—a pebble, a stick, anything would do to make her move away? She was little. She'd be safe between the trains. Why—why—hadn't she let Callie Lou live in the alley? Why hadn't she known that sooner or later she'd go away with Callie Lou? Why—why was there nothing to throw to make her move? The swampy earth held no rock—nothing. Callie Lou, you make her move. Feet away she saw a rusty tin can. She could jerk off her shoe quicker than she could run for the can. The can would have been quicker. The shoe was an oxford laced on her foot. Why hadn't she worn high-heeled pumps like Mrs Bommarita? Cassie had always wanted her to wear high-heeled shiny shoes. She jerked and jerked, turned at last toward the low hole, the shoe in her hand. She'd have to take good aim to throw through that low hole sideways to hit Cassie, and not able to get her head and arm through at the same time.

She bent far down and threw, and for an instant saw Cassie. Her legs were now over the rail, as she tried to get as far as possible from the oncoming train. Then the train shot past her, but still Gertie screamed for a moment longer, her head through the hole again, her shoulders fighting the wood. She knew Cassie couldn't hear, but still she screamed: 'Thet other train'ull move, too! Git *away*, honey! Git *between* em!'

She jerked her head back, turned, and ran down the alley toward the through-street railroad crossing. She had never run so slowly or so awkward seeming as in the one shoe. Her hair, jerked down from her struggles to get through the little hole, had fallen across her face. Blood oozed from her forehead, her neck, her shoulders, her ears, from her battle with the wood and her torn hands dripped more blood.

It was her eyes, she knew, made everything look blurry past the speeding train, like another train was moving on the other side, slowly, like the switching train. The switch engine tried to do as much as it could when another train was passing. Clovis had said that once when she complained because Cassie had to stand so long in the cold; but never so long as this while the train flew by. Something hit hard against her hip. She stared about her, unaware of pain, angry at being stopped. She saw the high dirt-spattered iron of a truck bumper, and wondered why it was there, and why did a red-faced man behind and above it glare down at her, his lips moving as if he yelled.

She turned to look at the train. Maybe if she looked away again it would be gone. Cassie had waited between the trains and would come running behind it. She would grab her up and carry her home, and they'd have school with Callie Lou and she'd send for ice cream for their supper.

There was a hard pull on her arm, and the same face that had glared at her was now looking up at her, the lips moving, but the eyes not hunting her eyes, fixed on the blood running down her coat. She realized even as she jerked her arm free that she had been out in the street running back and forth in front of the stopped cars. She ought to be ashamed acting so crazy, for Cassie would be all right. It was just that she had to be certain. She couldn't wait any longer. Why hadn't she thought of the place where the board fence stopped? It cornered so close to the tracks there was no room for a body to squeeze between it and a train. But she could crawl—there would be room between the fence and the wheels.

The man behind her was tearing her coat off, and around her there seemed suddenly a crowd of people, mostly children, but she was getting into the opening, like diving into a pool of noise. She could get through. Why hadn't she thought of it sooner? Then the last car shot past, and she sprang onto the track. Cassie would be on it—if she hadn't already gone back through the hole in the fence.

She was dazedly aware of cries and calls behind her, and from the other side of the fence, 'Wotsa matter? Who?' But mostly, as she ran down the track, she was aware of silence. The airplanes were still, only one going high and far away with a faint moaning so that after the roaring of the through train the world seemed still, so still that if she listened hard she'd hear again the low-voiced, 'Callie Lou,' and with it the burbling laughter. The backward-moving switch engine rolled slowly, so very slowly it made but little noise. Somewhere close behind her were pounding feet and a voice insisting. 'Easy now, da kid's gonna be awright.'

Then the switch engine stopped with a jerk that sent shivering knocks through all the cars. A man leaped down from the engine, crying to someone between her and the through street, 'Where, Chuck, where?'

She had come almost opposite the place where she had first seen Cassie, when the man who had cried out began running, his eyes fixed on something behind her. She turned and saw near the rail a child's boot, looked away from it, searching for Cassie.

The man's eyes, bulging, frightened, were fixed on nothing but the boot. She turned and stared at it again, a little boot that looked to be stuffed with something: torn cloth, oozing, soggy. She sprang toward it. The man behind her who had dragged her out of the street was crying, 'No—no, lady—please, lady!'

411

She heard then the frightened whimper. Cassie was safe. She was scared, that was all. The blood-oozing boot had nothing to do with Cassie. She, the trainmen, and the truck driver dropped by the sound together, and under the train she saw Cassie, white-faced, strange-looking, whimpering little begging cries of 'Mommie, Mommie.' Cassie was alive, moving on her hands and knees. Many hands reached, and there was begging, 'Please, lady.' But Gertie's arms were longer than the men's and she caught Cassie by the shoulders, her hungry hands gripping, pulling. She was alive, alive.

The truck driver was whispering 'Jesus,' and lifting carefully with the tips of his gloved fingers something else from under the train that dragged after Cassie as Gertie lifted her out. Gertie did not look at the bloody dragging thing, but laid Cassie across her knees. She squatted a moment holding her, looked down into her face, white, the eyes wide, straining, hunting, perspiration like a rain on her forehead. Her eyes tried to hold Gertie's face, but the head kept flinging itself about like the arms, flailing, striking her mother's chest with aimless beatings, while she cried in a choked, unnatural voice, 'It hurts, Mommie—oh, *Mommie!*'

The words ended in a gasping, inhuman scream, and Gertie sprang up, rocking her back and forth in her arms as she had done when she cried at noon; the twin streams of blood from the severed legs were like red fountains gushing down her apron, the blood-filled boot dangled, the toe turned backward knocking against her thigh.

Gertie looked once at the streams of blood, then dropped again to the ground, letting Cassie's head and shoulders fall into her lap while she caught the stubs of the legs, one in either hand, and sat holding them. She looked once at Cassie's white twisting face, touched now with blood from the frothing uplifted legs, then up at what seemed to be a whole forest of faces above her. 'Hep me, somebody, hep me try an keep down th bleeden. We've got tu stop it.'

There were cries and running behind her for cops, firemen, an ambulance; but no one stepped forward. The trainman's face was white, his glance unable to stay on the blood, spreading ever more over Cassie's body, congealing in bright lumps and sheets on Gertie's apron. He was not even able to look at Cassie's head, fallen backward across her mother's lap, the top brushing the cinders, twisting, writhing, the mouth open but no longer screaming, the whimper of 'Mommie' muffled, as if she had been running. No, not running, that would never make Cassie lose her breath—laughing did it—gasping from laughter and chattering and running all at one time.

'Here, lemme.' It was Victor, reaching for Cassie's legs. 'Yu git up,' he said. 'Start moving, quick! Cops, ambulance, somebody gotta take yu quick tuda hospital.'

Gertie held the child's body and Victor walked with her, holding the bloody stumps, one just below the knee, one just above, but even so the blood was still like brightly frothing fountains leaping over his hands.

Gertie tried to hurry, stumbling at times with eyes for nothing but Cassie, gasping more and more, no breath left now for screaming, each cry of 'Mommie' shorter, lower than the last.

The railroad tracks and the sidewalk were black and thick with people; many turned pale and looked away; many stood on tiptoe hunting blood, but all were silent, moving back, making a lane for Victor and Gertie as they hurried through. There was soon, from somewhere, the same wild screaming that had come for Mrs Daly. Gertie kept walking, hurrying, seemed like they walked forever to meet it, held up as it was by the train-bound traffic and the crowds of people.

She looked at the scout car surrounded by swarms of children, and shook her head, her voice thick. 'We need a ambulance with that stuff like blood.'

The man by the wheel in the scout car shook his head; the other, outside, pushed her a little. 'If it's plasma yu mean, a ambulance wouldn't have it. Yu ain't got no time tu argue—you gotta git quick to da hospital.' He helped her into the car, looked down at her feet as he did so, both bare now—the shoe she'd jerked first must have come off. 'Yu gotta go all away downtown—s'emergency.'

'I've got money,' she cried, but they never seemed to hear her. She never looked at the dangling boot or the blood again, still bubbling up, but more slowly, between Victor's clenched, unmoving fingers.

413

She had Cassie, her forever straggling hair over her arms, one hand with a mitten, one without.

They were all alone together. Seemed like the first time they had been alone, the two of them, since she'd made the golden doll by the Tipton spring. Cassie whimpered less and less; she was only gasping now, looking straight up, her eyes wide, frightened. Gertie looked into them, smiling, whispering: 'You're goen to be all right, Cassie Marie. We'll set all day, Cassie Marie, an have school an tea parties when you're gitten well—an ever day an ever minnit you can play with Callie Lou.'

Gertie wiped the perspiration and coal dust and cinders and blood from the face that never seemed to feel her hand, and repeated, her voice rising, shrill, so that the second policeman in the front of the car turned to look: 'Cassie, honey, you can have Callie Lou— allus an forever you can have Callie Lou. I'll never run her off no more—never. Hear me—Cassie—never, never—you can talk all you please.'

Cassie must smile. She must lift her head and know that there was Callie Lou. But Cassie, shivering like one freezing, struggled with some mighty effort to speak, spoke at last, her voice a low gasp of terror, the pupils of her eyes were big, so big they almost covered the lights and freckles in the dark brown eyes—greedy the pupils were for light and seeing—'I cain't see, Mom—s'dark.' The eyes were widening, straining.

'It's dark—real dark,' Gertie said, 'but even in th dark you can see Callie Lou.'

She thought Cassie smiled faintly. She knew she'd smiled. The main thing was to keep on talking. She mustn't stop talking. She mustn't look away. If she looked for just one little second, Callie Lou might snatch her, for the witch child wasn't dead. 'No— no, Cassie Marie—I'll bet old Gyp'ull be glad to see you. We'll be goen home pretty soon—real soon. It's spring—an you can climb trees agin an run. . . .' She choked, swallowed; for a long moment her voice wouldn't come—it was stuck inside her the way it had always been—but now she must talk—she must. 'Cassie Marie, you ought tu see all th cars piled up by th railroad tracks—a little thing like you a holden th cars still. Cassie?—'

She mustn't look away. 'Cassie?—look, I bet they's little girls in my eyes—Cassie—Cassie?—Marie?'

The turned around policeman what had he done? Cassie liked to hear about policemen. She'd been so proud to read about them at school, and always she had wanted one to speak to her like in the stories. 'Cassie Marie—honey—it's so funny—here's this policeman—he's took off his cap. Did ever a body see a policeman without his hat?

'Look—Cassie . . . Cassie?'

27

She let her hand slide from the knob of the closed door, but stood staring at the dark smooth wood before she turned slowly away. Her eyes hunted over the heavily carpeted, thickly draped room until they found the woman with the bluish-tinted hair. Then all the anger in Gertie's wild eyes dissolved before a great beseeching, 'Please—couldn't I stay—she couldn't abide a stranger a fixen . . .'

She couldn't keep the believing, the lying to herself that Cassie could care. She couldn't keep even the anger, at herself, the ways of trains, the hospital so far away. No more could she be like back at the hospital when they'd taken Cassie out of her arms and laid her on a table and rolled her quick like flying into a room marked 'emergency'; and she had stood on the other side of the closed door and waited, knowing that soon Cassie would come out to her. The policemen and Victor had waited by it and around her; it seemed like the policemen had asked her questions. Then quickly the door had opened and Cassie had come back to her, but as she bent over the cart, jerking back the sheet to pick up the too-short-seeming bundle, everyone—Victor and the policemen and a nurse and a doctor—all had cried, 'No.'

It seemed like she had cried back in answer, 'She's mine—mine—I can fend for my own.' Maybe she had not. It didn't matter; she had been with Cassie. The car, soundlessly running—smooth—smooth—like the door now; and the woman and back there the smooth-faced doctor had all cried out like a ringing in her head, 'No—no,' explaining the 'No' through endless halls and steps and elevators, all moving past her while she was still.

Their 'no's' hadn't mattered, for Cassie was there flying ahead on the cart. They'd mattered only when the other door had come, rising up at the end of a long and windowless hall. Even all whirled about and blown here and yonder as she was by the wave-like bursts of understanding, sucking her under, whirling her away, even through all this she had felt the coldness under the white light in the narrow hall, the coldness rising out of the opening door, touching Cassie on the cart. But she had been able even then to hold the believing, to cry out against the knowing, 'No, no—cain't I take her back with me?'

'Wait,' they had said. 'It's better,' somebody had told her, the Negro man rolling the car, 'to take a little time about such things.' They would keep it till morning. 'For free, maybe,' and he had nodded toward the bundle on the cart.

She had barred the way of the cart into the coldness, repeating, 'No, no,' wanting Cassie away from the cold seeping door, for the place was the place in the Bible: 'And where the light is as midnight.'

Then Clovis had come, trembly-handed, white-mouthed, not touching, but somehow seeming to lean on Whit, who was with him; and Whit, like the black man pushing the cart, had said: 'They'll keep her—a little while. Give you uns a chance to look around. When yu lose a kid, them undertakers murders you,' and his beer-drinking smile, the smile that was never mirthful, had played across the cart. 'When a body's all tore up, they'll go in debt tu spend everthing they'll ever have an . . .'

Gertie for the first time had understood that money would bring Cassie out of this windowless place by the cold seeping door. She had shoved her hand down into the blood-encrusted coat, crying, 'Money? Clovis, I've got money—all th money—all them years.' And she had laid it in his startled, trembling hands: the old bills, the ones in balls, in tiny squares, the bill with the pinpricks through Lincoln's eyes, the dominecker-hen money, the molasses money, the man-with-the-star money. She had put it all into his hands.

One of the policemen, waiting, watching, had at once stepped up and begun a low-toned conversation with Clovis. Whit had put his face close to the policeman's and listened, his mirthless smile widening, chilling his eyes. Victor had not moved but continued to stand, arms folded, back against the wall, watching, listening, frowning, shaking his head over the loose heaped-up money spilling from Clovis's hands.

Gertie, forever being whirled about, losing herself in the rushing winds, the roaring waters tumbling over her, but somehow standing upright, clinging with both hands to the cart that seemed always ready to move, to fly from her, had heard without listening, just as she had seen without perceiving, a wadded bill fall from Clovis's unwatched hand while he was listening to the one policeman. She saw the other policeman bend quickly under the black man's watching eyes, and his hand was closing, going toward his pocket when Victor's great hand, open palm upward, came under the other's face, and Victor said, 'T'anks.'

'For what?' the policeman said as his closed fist went into his pocket.

The Negro smiled, a smile like Whit's, his black eyes for an instant matching Whit's blue ones.

The reaching hand, the closed fist, she had seen, but they had had nothing to do with her. She had continued fishing with one hand in her coattail; there must be money—money—and she would have Cassie—hold her. She was impatient with Whit, who was shaking his head, his soft voice imploring Clovis, yet cautious, coming somehow as if he would send it past the policeman under the sound of the wind, but his voice never got past the policemen. The one who had been talking to Clovis said sharply to Whit: 'He'sa kid's father. Wot's it tuyu?' And his voice was like Mr Daly's voice; she remembered Reuben, and was in a great hurry to be home with Cassie, have Reuben again, all of them together. She'd found another bill, a wadded one, low down in the corner, and shoved it at Clovis.

'Won't it do—ain't it enough? We can take her now.'

She'd wondered if they'd heard. The wind spinning her round and round, the noise, the crashing—they would frighten Cassie; but through it all the policeman's voice had come, friendly now, urging, 'It's a good place.'

She had reached for the bundle, but the cart had fled from her in a hissing, crying wind, and she had fled after it down through the rushing, choking halls, past smooth and silent doors; in the car, through dark streets where red lights and green lights and brightly lighted windows had whirled around her. But through it all Cassie had never been her own again. All the money gone, and she had not held her in her arms.

She stood now by the last door, the smooth door through which she could not follow. Seemed like she'd been by it a long while. Clovis behind her was saying, 'It ain't like back home, Gert.' She turned slowly about, and pushed back her hair with a bended arm. The lie was worn out, torn in pieces; she couldn't make herself believe that Cassie there behind the door could feel the cold or huddle up in fright at stranger fingers through her hair. This now, it was the then—the then that might have been after the hunting in the dark for Reuben; if the knife had slipped on Amos; it was what came for Henley. What had she told herself then: 'And there the weary are at rest'?

Not that; there was no weariness, only smoothness: the rubber-tired wheels, smooth-running, like the policeman's voice, the smooth-eyed young doctor back there, too eager to show that a dangling boot, a bit of blood, could not make a rough spot in his smoothness—everything smooth, like the woman now with the white, bluish-tinted hair, nodding slightly toward Gertie, polite, her glance lingering only an instant on the bare feet, the torn and bloodied coat, the tangled hair, smooth-voiced as she said: 'You both have had a terrible shock. Tomorrow is time enough for you to select the'—she hesitated delicately, the way Jethro Coffee had used to do when he recited pieces at school, then brought it out softly, but firmly—'the casket and the clothing. You will want to get in touch with the family pri—' She studied Clovis an instant. 'Minister.'

It was early, not much past supper getting time, when Gertie walked from the parking lot down the alley and up her steps. Another train was thundering by, the sky was crimson with a steel-mill pour, and the heavy early-evening traffic made a growling scream on the through street; but Gertie's alley seemed still. A great gang of children, gathered in the twilight at her coming, made lanes of silence drawn back against the coalhouses as she passed by, and no one, not even a Daly, tittered at her bare feet, though just as she started up her steps the stove wrecker darted from some shadow in the deeper darkness, crying, 'I've got a little sister at home.' Then some voice was calling, but soft in its calling: 'Sh-sh-sh. Come back here, now.'

Mrs Anderson opened the door, but Gertie turned quickly about and started down the steps. If she could walk now, walk all night, walk and walk, forever; if she had corn to gather, like for Henley, even a cow to milk, some gentle cow that would let her lean her forehead . . . Clovis was saying, pushing her a little: 'Now, Gert, try to git some rest. An git—cleaned up.'

Clytie and Enoch, who had been listening to the radio, sprang up. Clytie started toward her but stopped in the doorway and stared at her, then slowly backed away, her mouth open, her eyes wide, unable to leave the twisted, soot- and blood-streaked face that seemed not a face at all, more like a mask such as children wear at Hallowe'en to frighten other children: and out of it blazed the eyes that from being gray and forever calm were black now, glittering, fighting all things, even the children.

Enoch stood white-faced, peeping at her, frightened, yet somehow curious, as if one of the nightmarish creatures, embodiment of murder and theft and torture of which the radio told him, had come alive into the room. Amos, dressed in his nightclothes, looked once around the bedroom door, then shut it quickly. Mrs Anderson, still by the kitchen table, littered with the dishes and food of a scarcely touched meal, said as if to make some sound in the silence, 'Clytie's girl friend's mother—Mrs Ku'—her voice stumbled against the name, stopped altogether, then rushed on—'came when she heard. They live in a private house, lots of room. She suggested that Clytie come for the night.'

She looked at Gertie for some sign of her having heard, but the black blazing eyes had leaped once at her and then away, and were now hunting back and forth across the living room, leaping about as if they were hands tearing the place to pieces.

Mrs Anderson looked beseechingly at Clovis, but he had eyes only for Gertie's back, and she stood silent, pressed into the corner between table and icebox while her glance searched about the kitchen as if there might be words dangling from the light, or on the uncurtained shelves. She found words under the sink and drew a sharp quick breath. 'Max found them, your shoes. Don't you want your shoes?'

'Huh?' Gertie asked in a hoarse, guttural voice, choked like that of a swimmer just risen free of a crushing wave, her glance still searching the living room as she repeated 'Huh?' the word loud, as if between her and Mrs Anderson there were long distances filled with walls and waves of tumultuous sound through which voices could not carry.

'Your shoes,' Mrs Anderson repeated, almost crying, looking now at the open knife in Gertie's hand. 'Your shoes—don't you want your shoes?'

Gertie's brows drew close together and made a black line, mingling with the soot and the dried blood on her forehead. She did turn and look as Mrs Anderson pointed, but it was plain she never saw the shoes. She turned swiftly back, asking, 'Where is it?' and stared angrily at Mrs Anderson. 'Who took it away?' She shook her head like one flinging water out of her face. 'I want tu work awhile. Th wood—where is th block a wood?'

'We put it back in th bedroom,' Clytie said, shivering, beginning to cry. She shrank back in terror as Gertie strode through the door way, the knife uplifted; but her mother never saw her; in two swift strides she was down the hall and into the bedroom, though for all her haste she closed the door softly, as if somewhere a baby were sleeping.

The quivering red light seeped through the blind enough that she could see to find the light string. She jerked it, and at once saw the wood back on a chair as it had been when they first came and the boys slept in the room. Quickly, she stacked the chairs on the bed and made room for herself and the wood on the floor together, then kneeling by it, knife in hand, she considered the bowed head.

She'd known exactly how the back would be, the hair falling down, upcurled at the ends, parted over the neck bones, leaving the neck bare, framed by hair, but not in curls like Callie Lou's, not at all like Callie Lou's. All her life she'd needed time for this, and now

421

she had time only, years and years of it to get through; but the man in the wood was strong; he could pull her through the time.

A train blew with a loud long screeching, and she sprang up. The knife clattered to the floor. Her whole body quivered as if the sound were waves of wind shaking her; and for an instant she was again by the fence, tearing at the boards, screaming, reaching; her arm was long, long; she had reached Cassie.

Then the train sound was dead, but she was still leaning across the bed, pushing, pulling, fighting the narrow windowsill; behind her one of the piled-up chairs toppled from the bed and fell, clattering in the narrow space. She had turned without taking her hands from the window to stare, wondering at the racket, when the door opened and Mrs Anderson, trying hard not to show any wonder at the fallen chairs or at Gertie crouched on the bed by the window, held out a glass of what looked to be pinkish water. 'Drink this,' she said, and went on with a swift chattering, as if to hide embarrassment. 'It's phenobarbitol—something like what they gave you at the hospital when—lots of women use it. Mrs Turbi told me about it when I complained that city living made me nervous; she just couldn't live without it, she said. Even if it doesn't put you to sleep, it's like a hot iron smoothing out the wrinkles—everything.'

Gertie got off the bed and drank the stuff, partly to please the woman, she looked so troubled, but mostly to make her go away. But hardly was she gone before Clovis was in the doorway, peering at her, jabbing her with quick troubled glances as he said, his mouth all a tremble, 'Gert—honey, you'd feel better to take a good hot shower—an change clothes.' He hesitated, studying her face and neck, uncertain about the dried blood he saw. Was it her own or Cassie's? 'Looks like you've hurt yerself—pretty bad,' he said.

'Ain't you goen to work, Clovis?' she asked, after watching him a moment, her forehead puckered, her eyes puzzled as if she made some great effort to understand what he had said.

'But, Gert, I hadn't meant to go to work—not tonight.'

'Your mom would ha worked,' she said, turning toward the block of wood. Mrs Anderson, who seemed to have been listening in the hallway, called Clovis; some talking passed between them, then Clovis was back again, looking at Gertie kneeling again by the block of wood, her knife lifted. 'Gert, I guess I will go—you take a shower an change clothes, an git some rest. Tomorrer—' but his voice hoarsened, choked, and would not go past the tomorrow.

'We ought tu git a early train, so don't work overtime,' she said, smoothing back her hair with a bended arm; then the lifted hand was still while she, looking upward and slantwise of her eyes, sniffed the blood crusted sleeve so close to her face. She sprang up, looking wildly about her as she lived again the losing battles—all the battles: to have the land, to make Reuben happy, to reach Cassie, and the last big battle—to hold the blood—nothing left to lose.

Clovis was asking harshly, loudly, his voice almost a crying: 'Train? You don't think we're goen home?'

A little of the misery, the brokenness in his voice got through to her and something like pity stirred under the anger, the hatred for herself who had caused it all. 'But, Clovis, honey, th money, all that money, recollect, they's enough to take—take her back amongst her own kin.'

'Things like—this, costs a heap,' he said, not looking at her. 'It ain't like back home, an—they'd be th train ride there—an back an—'

'Back? But I couldn't leave—'

'They wouldn't be nothen else we could do. I ain't got no truck; you wouldn't have time now to git in so much as a garden—an I'd be losen time frum work—I wisht it was different, Gert,' he turned away, choked up, and soon after she heard the closing of the outside door.

She was still squatting by the wood, one hand on the bowed head, the knife idle in the other, when Mrs Anderson came with another glass of pink water, chattering as always. 'It's better here,' she said. 'She'd be close—and it's much—'

Gertie gave a low whimpering, clutched the block of wood as if it alone could keep her from sinking even lower on the floor. 'But—she wouldn't like it. Back home on my father's land they's

423

the family graveyard—all th old uns, an Henley they'll bring back—
sometime. It's high, an a body can look out an down an see—an
see—' She reached for the pink water, drank it, returned the glass,
and looked steadily at Mrs Anderson, 'I keep fergetten—th dead,
they cain't see.'

The man in the wood at first seemed far away, walled off like all
other life about her by furious sound of wind and water and the
whole earth shaking; the knife fumbled, a lost knife hunting a lost
man in the wood; no, not lost, hiding, forever hiding. But gradually
the thing in the wood came closer and yielded itself, and chips and
shavings fell. The hair grew, taking up the whole world, everything
in the world; and there were moments like a drowsing dreaming
when she and the wood were alone, alone in her mother's house,
though sometimes she looked up, frowning, annoyed by the strange
brightness of the lamplight that made the shadow of her moving
hand fall blackly on the wood. Then would come the remembering,
and the knife would be lost again while she sat helplessly fumbling,
once more far from the man in the wood, tossed and whirled about
as she was in the ringing, roaring fury.

Next day more than one person come through the funeral parlors
looked curiously at the big woman with the smoothly combed,
neatly parted hair above a bruised face and bandaged neck. She sat
still and straight in a too small chair; her mouth a bleak straight line
of determination under eyes that were bewildered as a lost child's
eyes, some strange child who, even as it begs to find the way home,
knows there is no finding the way, for the home and all other things
at the end of the way are also lost.

There were at times murmurings around her and to her: a
red-headed woman came and wrung her hand and said, her
voice holding faint traces like memories of the voices back home
Gertie had known, 'S'tough when yu can't take um home.' Max
came and patted her knee and said, 'Don't trytu find no answers,
kid, for things like this; they ain't none,' and brought word from
Mrs Schultz not to worry about her boys. Mrs Anderson came,
opening a box to show a white thin dress, and over it Gertie nodded uncertainly, as if wondering why the dress was there, then said

424

with rough loudness in the smooth still place, 'Th shoes—she allus liked pretty shoes.'

Then it was morning in another day, and she wore a new coat; it kept worrying her, for there was no hole in the pocket; she kept pushing at the skimpy, flimsy pocket while she sat in the car with Clovis and the three children; their faces, like everything else, came to her like the faces she had used to make in the sunset clouds—alive one minute, unreal and far away the next.

They sat in a row; in front of them was the coffin, covered with a white cloth and mounded with flowers. Once, she bent forward and peered at the cloth stretched over the wood; she wished she could see the wood; it ought to be good wood. Vague memories of the money came, so much money; it seemed like she had told Clovis to spend as much as was needed—the cloth above the wood must be firmly woven and lasting.

Words came down from above the casket, kindly words floating out of a kindly face—the preacher where Clytie and Enoch went to Sunday school. She heard sniffling and looked about her in impatient anger. Why should any of them cry? She, Gertie, had killed her. She turned around and frowned over an oldish woman with tears running down into a handkerchief held under her chin. Who was the woman and why should she cry? By the old one, a younger stared straight ahead, blinking back tears. What right had she to cry? She was a young woman neatly dressed in a dark tailored suit. Chicle—a child reaching and a big painted mouth smiling: this woman belonged to that somehow.

Then it was over and she was looking at Cassie again; not Cassie either. She had never been so still, so neat, so smooth, her little secrets always showing in her eyes; the smoothness and the neatness now kept well the secret of how she died.

More riding in the car, through heavy traffic, past thunderous trucks and trains into the still cemetery where between the endlessly winding drives the grass showed green under thin scatterings of April snow. She had wanted very much to see the earth—real earth, something real—but there was a green thing like paper spread over all the good earth. The casket in the cold rays of the broken sunshine looked flimsy and cheap, and under the too shiny cloth

425

the wood was maybe sappy. She wanted to cry out, to tear off the cloth, see the wood, touch the earth; but the preacher was murmuring, and Clytie, watching the coffin go down, was beginning a great weeping. Then everything was drowned, blotted out by an airplane coming in low and loud, for, as Clovis had promised, the cemetery was close to the project. She took a quick step forward. She couldn't leave her like this—in the cold, with that flimsy little dress—and all this racket.

28

She lifted her glance from a fold of the cloth drawn over the shoulders, and, the knife open in her hand, stared at the window; rain mixed with snow made a moving sheet against it. She watched it, her brows drawn together in puzzlement. Then, the look of wonder deepening, she looked upward, sidewise, an ear turned ceilingward, and listened, frowning, wondering why she could not hear the rain. Then gradually the ceiling drifted into shape, and became the sickly green cardboard, smoke-grimed and darker now at the ending of the winter. The Detroit home shut out the sound of the rain.

Strange, she hadn't noticed the rain on the window until now. Back home she would have known it: a spring rain blown in on a red, windy dawn with thunder growling far across the ridges, the pines crying out the warning, and the sugar tree flowers blowing down the hillside all when the poplar blooms were like yellow lilies unfolding. But better than anything had been the sound of the rain on the roof shingles when the early potatoes and peas and lettuce showed, and the early cabbage was set. Tomorrow she would hunt wild greens; wild sweet potato vine would be high by the creek banks, and she would linger, listening, watching the white water—

A train blew. She shivered, the knife clattered to the floor, but no longer did she go springing toward the window. She only backed away and stood a long moment, her body pressed against the door, her hands pressed hard against her eyes. She was able at last to look again at the window, gray white under the moving sheets of rain. Seemed like the last time she had looked, the window had been a square of quivering red light. It was daylight now—another night was through—and now another day.

She lay down and stared at the gray sheet; a solid sheet like ice, but never the same sheet, moving, always moving, a slow sliding that wouldn't stop. The day would be like that—a long gray thing sliding past—tight like a tunnel, but she must somehow squeeze through. A long business, and she was tired. She looked about her at the unmade bed, the shavings on the floor, the rumpled coat, linted from the sheets, a smear of alley mud on the hem. The sheet was grimy black; Amos must have walked on it when she made him stay by her. She ought to change it, maybe even wash it, but she was too tired.

She realized the light was burning. She switched it off, and lay and watched the window, put all herself into the rain sheet, held herself there, and soon she could hear creek water, the creek below the Tipton Place.

She sat straight up in a fury of disappointment—always and always they were taking it away. Now it was Clytie, with her head stuck around the door like she expected a bear to jump out and grab her, and her eyes tiptoeing from the bed to the shavings on the floor as she asked, her voice tiptoeing like her eyes, 'Mom?' and when Gertie only continued to stare at the window under her lowered lids, she said, her voice trembly troubled now, 'Mom, don't you think you'd better let Pop git a doctor like he wants? You ain't—well.'

'No,' Gertie said, without moving her head.

Clytie continued to stand half in, half out the door, but turned and held a troubled whispering with someone behind her. Gertie remembered, and lifting her head, called wildly, 'Amos. Amos.'

He came at last and put his head around the door, but after one quick peep at Gertie, he, swallowing hard and fighting to keep back tears, turned to Clytie. Gertie called him again, and he buried his face against Clytie's waist, and broke into a wild frightened crying. Gertie, angered by his strange ways, screamed in a voice unlike her own: 'What a you bawlen about? Cause you cain't go outside? You mustn't go outside. You'll git hurt. Stay close to Mommie.'

He clung all the harder to Clytie, and Gertie with the nimble swiftness she had known in the woods leaned far out of the bed,

428

and jerked him roughly to her, her voice loud now, shrill, rising above his screams. 'I didn't aim it that away. You know I didn't. I didn't send her off to be killed. I didn't aim to kill her when Mom made me come. It was Mom an—' Her voice was an incoherent screaming, and she shook Amos, knowing it was Amos she shook, but unable to stop while thinking of her mother, the Tipton Place, Cassie alive this minute and running down the hill. No, not her mother, herself, herself—only, she couldn't say it. She ought to have stood up to them all—if she had thrown the shoe sooner; maybe had she tried she could have climbed the fence.

Words came from the other side of the wall, 'Easy, now—yu ain't done nutten. Yu gotta sleep some. Go tu sleep now.' The sound of the voice more than the words held her and she marveled that Victor had a baby. Her hands dropped from Amos, and he sprang away, but stayed by Clytie, half in, half out the door.

She glanced at him again to make certain he was safe, then drowsed back into the sleep that seemed less a sleeping than a stupor. She awakened again; maybe it was that morning, maybe some other morning; the rain was gone from the window, but her coat was still on the foot of the bed, and there was the same tiptoeing in Clytie's voice and eyes as she asked: 'Mom, cain't I bring you somethen to eat? I've give th kids their breakfast.'

Clytie waited, but when her mother neither moved nor answered, she turned away, then stopped at once, eager, hopeful, when Gertie called, 'Don't let it out when you're openen an shutten th icebox door.'

'What?' Clytie asked, her eyes widening with fright.

'That cat—what else?' Gertie answered, her voice rough with weariness and anger. She thought she heard frightened weeping. It didn't matter. She'd started off through the long tunnel of the day. She had reached a cool and foggy valley when the white light snapped on, leaped against her eyes, and a voice from far out of the bright whiteness called to her:

'See if you can do it. It comes crooked fer me. You'll have to set up to do it.' She saw then, just under her elbow, a round and shining thing cut through the middle with a crooked white line. She tried to pull herself together—in pieces seemed like she was, floating every which way in a heaving, blowing world.

She rubbed her eyes, and Sophronie, with a cigarette in her mouth, the brush in one hand, comb in the other, was smiling at her, eyes squinted against her cigarette smoke. 'I'm sorry if I woke ye,' she said, 'but I cain't never git this right.' And the round thing became Clytie's head as she knelt by the bed for her mother to part her hair. Gertie took the comb, and the familiar and trying task of parting Clytie's hair brought the world somewhat together. She remembered Amos, and called him.

Sophronie somewhat sharply told her he was in the bathroom, and then said, 'Whyn't you git up, an come out to th kitchen an be a setten up when Clovis gits in—make him feel better.'

'Is he feelen bad?' Gertie asked, listening now to a sound she hated. 'Turn it off. It hurts my head,' she said.

'What?' Sophronie asked, working on one of Clytie's side braids.

'That racket—that clothes-washen thing.'

'When clothes gits dirty—they gotta be washed.' Sophronie hesitated, then said: 'A woman like you with a family, they—well—they jist cain't lay down an give theirselves up to nothen. Kids gotta have somebody.'

Gertie flopped over and faced the wall. If she stayed still, real still, they would maybe go away. If she had corn to plant, or wood to split, or a cow to milk.

But hardly were they gone before Mrs Anderson was floating over her, carrying another glass of what seemed a million glasses of the pink water. 'I do believe you've been asleep,' she said, smiling, holding out the glass.

Gertie drank to make the woman go away, but she stayed chattering a moment, her words blowing in and out, now near, now far, like a wind in April; no, more like a hound dog crying across a hill: Homer had a job; she had to hunt a house, or maybe it was Mrs Daly had to have a house; seemed she had a baby.

She left at last, and Gertie snapped off the light, and lay, too tired to move. It seemed only a minute later that the light was on again and Clovis was looking down at her, a little white-wrapped package in his hands, a frightened, backing-away look in his eyes.

'How're you a feelen, Gert, old girl?' he asked. 'I'm late gitten in,' he went on when she did not answer, 'but I thought I'd better see a doctor. I told him—well, how you was—an he had me git this. It's a goen to hep you a sight, old girl.' He had busied himself unwrapping, and then unscrewing a bottle of red liquid, but now as he sniffed the medicine his face clouded with disappointment. 'I swan. It looks an smells like th same kind a stuff Miz Anderson's been a given you—only,' he sniffed again, puzzled, 'a body cain't git this 'thout a prescription. An this doc,' he went on, his troubled glance on her coat now, 'he said you'd ought to come in an let him see ye. Them places on yer neck. They look swoll' up to me, and they could be a given you a infection, he said, er layen around lifeless this away could be th flu, that doc—'

Gertie had roused enough to lift on one elbow and glare at him. 'Aw, Clovis, spenden good money fer— Money,' she repeated the word slowly, her face twisted with a great effort to remember something. Her wandering glance went about the room, paused on the block of wood, went on, and came at last to her coat; there it stopped. She frowned over the coat an instant, then seized it, and began a frantic searching through the pockets. She found at last the right pocket, the one that would let her hand go deeper, fishing, hunting.

Her brows were contracted still with the great effort to remember, but the lost thing seemed less a memory of her mind than of her hands, for it was not until she had searched through the coat and stared a moment at her empty hands that she asked, hesitantly, as if she did not wish to speak of it to Clovis, but must, to still some panic rising now in her eyes: 'Didn't you put it back, what was left? They was so much it couldn't ha tuck it all.' Her words grew thick and struggling. 'She's got to have a marker—right away. So many others—she'll be lost.'

'They's no danger a that,' Clovis said, and it seemed he had been standing there for days, saying this to her, over and over, 'but all th same we'll git a marker.'

She began the frantic searching through the coat again, frowning, whispering, 'I couldn't ha lost it.' She looked at Clovis, angrily demanding: 'Give it back. What's left; I'll keep it till we git th marker.'

Clovis had turned toward the door, his shoulders sagging wearily, but he turned slowly back when her voice rose in an insistent

431

crying: 'Give it back, Clovis, what's left. You might lose it 'fore we git th marker.'

'Gert—you're too sick to worry over sich. We'll manage.'

She sprang up, caught him by the shoulders, and searched his face as she shook him, demanding: 'You ain't lost it, Clovis? You ain't?'

He could not look at her, but tried to back away, his voice discouraged like his eyes as he said, 'Whit warned me—an Victor, too; but when Victor had a chanct tu tell me, it was too late; he'd seen one a them cops—Enyhow, them two cops, they see a heap a accidents—an when they see, well—people in trouble like us, they've got a place er two they send people like us—you know, not knowen nothen—to—' He licked his dry lips, his soft eyes glittering like her own. At last he drew a deep breath and plunged on. 'An ever time they send some dead—some customer—they git a little somethen frum th undertaker. Leastways, that's what Whit an that tool-an-die man told me. An th places th cops recommends—they ain't so—good.'

He backed away from Gertie's boring eyes. 'Ain't so cheap, I mean. Like I asked th man fer a pretty good casket—like you wanted, nothen cheap an shoddy. He showed me one an told me th price—a th casket; an I told him you didn't want no fancy funeral with a lot a cars—like you said—jist somethen decent. An he said th funeral allus matched th casket—an he didn't say no more about th cost. I ought to ha knowed when he asked all about where I worked an how much money I had an how much I made; but he was all smoothy sighs.

'Enyhow, when it was all over, th cost was twict as much as what he told me th casket ud be. He got real mad when I kinda complained. Half fer th funeral, half fer th casket, he said. You've gotta take a kind a fancy funeral with a halfway decent casket; an that doubles it.'

Gertie had been silent, watching his mouth and his eyes like a deaf person or one other-languaged. But at last bewildered concentration gave place to angry disbelief. 'You mean, Clovis—' Still, her hand would not believe, and began again its frantic searching down into the flimsy cloth which she had at some time or other opened

432

with her knife or restless fingers until the pocket was a deep and secret thing hidden in the lining. Her hand was still when she said, 'They ain't nothen left fer a marker? Nothen?'

He tried to fill his voice with an easy certainty, 'We'll git one pretty soon, that is, th down payment.'

She was tired, her hand unmoving, her body slumping on the bed, but after a moment she said, still hoping, 'You're lyen, Clovis. You've lost th money. People couldn't be so mean.'

Clovis picked up the bottle wrappings, 'Gert, honey, I didn't lose it; don't take it thataway. I recken it's like th tool-an-die man said— cops don't make a lot a money less'n they've got jobs where they can git shakedowns. But them accident men, all they can git is a little kickback fer senden somebody—'

She frowned over the strange word. 'Kickback?'

He nodded. 'Everbody does it. I've heared em say in th shop that these big men that owns these plants, why, they give kickbacks to them gover'ment men that gives em contracts at high prices. An then th men that ain't so big—well, kind a th size a this McKeckeran—why, they git kickbacks in money er favors frum th people they give a good parts-maken er scrap contract to. Them kickbacks comes outa taxes in th end—they say; but this un—it come out uv us.'

She looked at him, for an instant the old Gertie. 'Oh, Clovis, don't be a throwen off on people jist cause they've got more money than we've got. Look at Uncle John—he's a good honest man.'

'He's worked mighty hard,' Clovis said, and seeing her more like herself, he reached and patted her shoulder, 'You've saved onct— we can agin—enough to finish payen fer all this an git th marker.' A look of awe came into his eyes. 'Jist think, back home when you had all that money, an th money yer mom give you frum Henley together with what I sent, you must ha had six, seven hunnert dollars. Why, that was enough to buy you a little patch a land like you'd allus wanted. I've heared say,' he went on, seeing that she was listening, and glad himself to talk about back home, 'that John would ha sold th Tipton Place fer less'n that.'

He backed away from the rage, the torture in her glance, her eyes blazing, glittering like those of a trapped wild animal, penned for easy torture. He hesitated, half frightened, but tried again to smile and talk and fix her thoughts on back home. 'Why, if I'd ha knowed you'd ha had all that money, I'd said buy a place an wait fer me. I'd ha worked up here jist long enough to git me a pretty good truck, an soon as th war was over I'd come a rollen home an a fixed me up a good road a my own like I'd allus wanted, an never a had to fix up somebody else's washed-out road no more an—'

'But you never wanted a farm—Mom didn't want me to—Oh, Lord.' After the screaming words she dropped back upon the bed and turned her face to the wall.

He cleared his throat, studied her as she lay with her legs drawn up, her head pulled down as if she would hide herself. 'I wanted you to have what you wanted, Gert. It was jist—jist that I didn't see no way a saven up fer a farm, an I hated to see you an th youngens a worken an a heavin', allus a given haf a what you made an—' Her unmoving back silenced him, and he stood a long time looking down at her, but reached at last to pick up her coat.

She turned swiftly, raising her hand as if to strike him, crying: 'Git away. I allus thought you'd want my money fer a truck— She'd still been alive.'

She dropped upon the bed again; and after a long time of watching, opening his mouth, then closing it, he went away.

She heard his feet, and then the sound was lost in the steel mill, the traffic, the wind, the trains. She wanted to look at the window again, but she was too tired. No, she wasn't tired; it was just that there was no reason at all why she should turn over and look at the window. The wall so close to her eyes was just as good, almost the color of the window, sooty gray, tinged with green.

She was back on the old Ledbetter place on the ridge top, cleaning up a patch of brush to make a new-ground cornfield. The wind rocked the pines, the creek was aroar from the white rain that had brought the wild plum to full bloom all in one night. Cassie was the baby, but big enough to walk hanging on to Gyp; she couldn't hear her chatter for the wind, a kind of begging, crying wind, scattering the redbud flowers, but still a voice crying: 'How yu comen? I gotta have a dream, kid.'

Gertie opened her eyes. Early-afternoon sun slanted through the window, falling on the dirty, disarrayed bed, the shaving-littered

434

floor, and showing each speck of grime and dirt on the four sides of the window panes. So much ugliness she shut her eyes, and pulled a corner of the quilt over them. She tried to bring back the roaring pines and the redbud flowers, but the voice would not go away. 'You'll smother in this room, kid. Th sun's took a notion to shine, an considering it's in Detroit it's doing pretty good. Yu need a little air.' And Max knelt on the bed and reached across Gertie and after some struggle lifted the inside window, then raised the little board across the three holes in the storm-window sash. She leaned back on her heels, smiling on Gertie, her gum still. 'Listen. Yu know what it is.'

Gertie heard Detroit. She awakened more fully, and all the things came back again, and lay like black cats choking her; she pulled the quilt higher; if she could hide from them all.

Max pulled the quilt away, tipping her head toward the three little holes, commanding, 'Listen. Yu gotta listen.'

'Where's Amos?' Gertie asked, starting up.

'Victor's got him by th hand. Listen,' the girl insisted, and went on, smiling, her eyes soft. 'I recollect onct about this time—no, it was earlier—we was on our way back from Texas, an we hadda stop somewheres in Ohio, an them big fields was one big puddle. That night Pop couldn't sleep for listening; said he counted eight different voices, an th frog eggs he got me hatched in Pittsburgh.'

Gertie had ceased pulling at the covers, for now she heard, now faint, now a swelling chorus, the voices of the frogs—thousands and thousands it seemed like, more frogs than she had ever thought could be. She halfway wanted to listen, but Max was all a jiggle on the bed, laughter in her eyes, laughter in her voice. 'It's spring, kiddo,' she was saying. 'Th war's about over. I said to myself last night: "You're young an alive, kid; quit th crappen an leave this damned alley; you'll never learn to make them damned Polish dumplings." Ugh. Th first time I bit into one a th things at Victor's mom's—you know, innocent, not looking for cabbage—it was all I could do to keep from loosing th rest a th junk under th table.'

She bent above Gertie, looking down into her face, ' "And why for because," I asked myself, "should I spend my life making what will never be no good nohow?" "Who inu hell," I said to myself,

435

"wants to try to make pies like Mother makes when it's so much simpler to let Mother make um inu first place?" ' She jiggled Gertie's elbow. 'But I gotta, just gotta have a dream. "You're lucky," I said to myself th first time I seen yu. You're still my luck, but they ain't much time. We're buying furniture, an pretty soon we gotta own our own home like Victor's people. See? Be good an respectable an go to church, an be stingy as hell so's yucan buy a lotta crap for th house; an a good fur coat like his mom's got, so's you'll hafta wear th same damn' coat for years and years, an be allatime wearing your wits out, wondering is it keeping good inu summertime. Ain't that liven? Spend all your days living with that crap you've saved like hell to buy—six lamps Victor's mom's got in her living room.' The words had come tumbling over Gertie as if she were just a piece of something to catch the tumbling words.

'If I could a lied allatime an kept most a mu tips; but I ain't no good at lying. See? Not when I thought I loved th guy. He wanted to save, so's I give him most a what I made; he banked it in both our names. He's a good honest guy.' She sprang up. 'Look, I gotta have a dream.'

Gertie turned her head so that she could see the window; lying flat like this, the whole window was filled with sky—not even a telephone wire across it—blue with white clouds; blue like the wild iris by the creek. But Max didn't want wild iris or white water. She must give Max what she wanted. The sky was so endless, the white clouds sailing: I saw a ship a sailing; a sailing on the sea. 'Sea,' she said, not looking away from the sky, knowing it was what Max had wanted, for Max was taking the dream, carrying it toward the door, crying:

'I gotta go—I'm so late now I'll hafta call a cab.' She turned for one last glance at Gertie, then stopped, studying her with narrowed eyes as she bent above her sniffing. 'Wotta they given you? Goof balls a some kind. They'll drive you crazy.' She sniffed again. 'Pink stuff in water, huh? Quit it. Medicine won't help what ails you. Mom, they doped her up so to keep her quiet when she learned what had happened to Pop when that drunk colonel run into um that she, well—you know, went like Pop. Yu gotta git outa here. You'll go nuts.'

'They's no place to go,' Gertie said, 'cept to Cassie, an they won't let me.'

'Go ask Homer questions; I've never had th time. But whatever you do, quit that stuff. It ain't putten yu to sleep—s'maken yu goofy. Hell, kid,' she said, straightening the bedspread, 'we've all got holes—an they all gotta be stuffed with something—liquor, like pore Sophronie, or religion an liquor—it takes em both—for Daly; or phenobarbital, like somebody Mrs Anderson knows. She's th one give it to yu, ain't she? She giggled too much ina alley when Joe come yesterday, but Mrs Bommarita—she's a hateful smooth-faced bitch, you never tell when you hear people cry—she said Mrs Anderson cried a lot.'

She remembered the time, and hurried to the door, calling over her shoulder: 'I'm comen over tomorrow and clean this room up. An yu'd better hurry up an eat something or I'll tell Victor's mom an she'll bring yu galombkis—ugh—an you'll hafta eat em while she watches to make certain you enjoy um.'

When Max had gone, Gertie lay and once again forced all her being toward the sky; and the clouds, instead of being ships, were clouds only, and below them in the land she could not see were high pines with wild pansies blooming at their feet, and lower in the foggy valley were sugar maples red with bloom, and the poplars flowering in the coves where the earth was black, pure black, with hundreds of years of fallen leaves, and lower still was the white water; she kept hunting the white water, but the fog and the spray covered it; she couldn't see it, though it was loud, so loud—

A fast train roared by, and she sat bolt upright. Telephone poles, a row of chimneys, smoke, and an airplane tore apart her sky. She pressed her palms hard against her ears, and rocked her head from side to side to drive the sounds away.

When the train had gone she sat a time and looked at the block of wood. She wanted to work on it, but she was too tired. She was hot and sweaty, but to do anything about it was beyond her. She wanted a drink of water, but the bathroom was too far away. She lay down again; but now the sky was only something above telephone poles and the steel mill. Then, like an onrushing wind, she heard the first wave of home-coming school children—whooping, laughing, kicking tin cans, and soon Enoch's feet up the steps and the door banging open.

In a moment he was asking from the doorway, 'You feelen better, Mom?' and without waiting for her answer rushed on to tell of how the project office was giving grass seed and fertilizer, and loaning rakes and spades so that the project people could grow grass and flowers.

'Flowers—in this place?' Gertie asked.

'Yeah. It's spring, Mom—or mighty nigh.'

But Gertie could only repeat, 'Spring,' and stare vacantly, never so much as looking at Enoch as he rattled on:

'Can I go to th office, Mom, an git some a that stuff for free? Claude Jean an Gilbert's goen—an Mom, Victor said we gotta have a fence—th kids is punchen his place full a holes.'

'Fence,' she repeated. 'You cain't grow stuff without a fence.'

'Goody,' he said, 'that's what I told um,' and he was gone.

Then Clytie was asking from the doorway, her voice a careful whisper, 'You feelen better, Mom?'

And when Gertie nodded, she came on into the room. 'Mom, we're jist about out a everthing. Can I go to th store? My girl friend's waiten. We'll take Amos an hold both his hands—but they ain't nothen to cross.'

Gertie nodded, drowsing, dreaming of fence. 'If you don't have enough—' Her hand went into an imaginary pocket in the old familiar gesture; she awakened, and the hand dropped, loose-fingered, on the bedspread. 'I hate fer you to have to wake yer pop—'

'Oh, don't worry, Mom. Zedke's been awful good to us. He give me credit when I asked. You an Pop was gone—an we was out a everything.'

She was gone, and Gertie repeated, 'Credit; credit.' Something a man had given Clytie, but nothing was for free, and whatever it was it wasn't a bargain. Debts. She wanted the fog and the white water, and shut her eyes, squeezing them up tighter and tighter, but like last night, or maybe a week ago or forever, other things came unbidden behind her eyes. She saw a rotten box sunk in a pool of black water, half covered with flat, limber, water-soaked leaves; she kept wondering what was in the box and why it was there, and all the time she knew it wasn't there.

438

In front of her was an old, old quilt; in it were squares of white calico set with black sprigged flowers from the dresses her grandmother had worn after her grandfather died. The box was gone; in its place was the spring path at home, a little cedar tree, two limestone rocks, and a loose sheepskull rock in between, and the path yellow dusty. It wasn't there, only the quilt. But she had to follow the path, for it led to her father's barn, and Callie Lou had run around the barn corner, her red dress and black hair flashing past the corners of her eyes, always just going away, swifter than her eyes.

She opened her eyes wide, and Callie Lou skipped past their corners; she rolled them, turned quickly in bed so that she could see the door, but Callie Lou had just gone through it. If she hurried she might catch her in the kitchen; there was nobody in the house but Callie Lou; it was so still. Gertie ran on tiptoe, the nightgown billowing behind her, her tangled, unbrushed hair scattered over her shoulders and half hiding her face. But hurry as she would, Callie Lou flitted out the kitchen door as she was taking the few steps down the hall. There was so much racket in the alley was why she hadn't heard the opening and closing of the door.

She opened the inner door, but stopped when she looked through the storm door into the alley. The overflowing trash and garbage cans, the shreds of cardboard dripping from the walls, the gray clothesline poles with their gray sagging ropes, the mud-splattered children, all the debris of the winter—the ugliness clear in the white spring sunlight, for the windscoured sky was clean of smoke.

And seemed like she had never known there could be so many children: digging with shovels and spading forks from the project office, laughing, eating, quarreling, crying; but Callie Lou was not among them. She had slipped out of sight, and was waiting, laughing, hiding just around the end of the building. Soon, she would bring her back; like last night she'd hunted her all the way to Cassie's grave, and then brought her home only after much trouble. Tonight, like last night, she'd have to wait until Clovis was gone. Children's cries blew through the broken pane. How had it been last night? Someone had followed her, then led her home. She rubbed her eyes hard with a thumb and finger. There was no Callie Lou, only children in the alley.

She was tired, and the bed was far away. She leaned against the doorframe and watched the children. Most were congregated about Gilbert as he struggled to connect a hose to the outside faucet under Max's bathroom window. But in spite of a great deal of advice and much help, he was unable to screw it on so that it did not leak; little boys were constantly reaching behind him to turn the faucet, and still others opened the hose nozzle so that water squirted here and yonder. More than one child got wetted, and Gertie's yard became a bedlam of screaming children, most joyful as they threw mud, fought for the hose, or ran in mock terror from its spray.

Supper getting mothers began to glance uneasily from their kitchen doors, and some even called to their own. Claude Jean Meanwell grabbed the hose, turned off the nozzle, and sprang to the top of Gertie's coalhouse. 'Look, kids, we gotta behave; they won't let us have u hose no more,' he screamed above the uproar. 'I know a real good game we can play; yous'ull like it.'

Georgie, hearing the word *game*, sprang onto the garbage can and began to climb onto the coalshed, screaming: 'I'm gonna play. I'm gonna play.'

Claude Jean kicked his hands away. 'Everybody's gotta line up ona ground in front u me. Come on, kids, lotsa fun,' and his voice was enticing, inviting.

Gilbert Meanwell looked up from his tussle with the hose connection; his eyes on his younger brother were for an instant half admiring, half afraid. Then he, too, smiled and began to call the children to come and play a good game.

Francis Daly, older than the others, who had until now been a bystander, watching the water fights over a bottle of pop, began to giggle; but after throwing his emptied bottle into the alley he smothered his giggles enough to cry: 'S'u real good game, kids. Lots u fun; butcha gotta line up an push—hard—real hard, like they was a door in front a yu an a fire behind yu.'

The children, especially the younger ones, flattered by an invitation from older boys to play, came flocking. Soon the mass of shoving, giggling, pushing children stretched in a wide band from Gertie's coalhouse almost to the Meanwells', with Francis Daly behind them, his arms widespread as if he herded sheep. They

440

were even more eager when Gilbert, by the water throttle, called to Francis: 'Yu wanna be old man Flint? We gotta have him inu job-hunten game.'

'Sure, but I gotta be a plant protection man, too,' Francis said. 'S'fine game, kids,' he added, talking now to the children, his voice reassuring, for some had begun a backward pushing, eager to get out of the shoving mass. Others, though still pushing toward the coalhouse as directed, looking anxiously up at Claude Jean who was smiling, standing suspiciously near the hose nozzle, though it did not even drip now, for Gilbert kept his hand on the screwed-down valve.

Gilbert gave an uneasy glance toward Mrs Bommarita, watching suspiciously from her stoop. He screamed to Francis, 'We gotta git a playen,' and to Claude Jean who seemed ready to burst with sound-less giggles, 'Yu gotta git set.'

Francis stretched his neck, made himself as tall as possible. He, then, commanded in a loud, unnaturally deep voice, heavy with anger and authority, its wrath turned on Claude Jean, 'Yu gotta send dese men home. Gitum outa du way.'

'But Mr Flint, dey ain't done nutten,' Claude Jean answered; and he too tried to make himself tall and deep-voiced, but failed in the face of his giggles. 'Daisies jist waiten tu git jobs. Dey been here all night.'

'Dey ain't no jobs. Daisies inu way. Git um out. Out,' and 'Mr Flint' screamed, waved his arms, jumped up and down, waved his fist, and in general so beguiled the children with his fit of anger that most, looking behind them now at 'Mr Flint,' forgot their suspicions of Claude Jean by the hose. Many were choking with laughter when Wheateye, forever wary of her brothers, saw Gilbert's quick hand on the valve, and screamed, 'We'ses gonna git drownded—we—'

Her words were cut off by the hard beating stream of water that came with full force through the lawn-sprinkling nozzle that Claude Jean had opened wide. The children set up a mad, squealing, shov-ing, fighting scramble to get away from the cold hard stream while Gilbert and Francis, bigger than the others, waved their arms, shout-ing, 'Yu gotta go out bydu gate—youses can't come inu plant.' And

441

they herded the children into the water that Claude Jean, laughing his flat-eyed, soundless laugh, squirted impartially here and there.

Gertie suddenly stiffened, then crouched, and put her face close to the broken-out pane, for above the clamor of the children and the angry screams of the hurrying mothers she heard Wheateye's shrill screeching: 'Callie Lou, Callie Lou; are you okay, honey? Call th rescue squad, quick. Yous'es has put out th fire but my kid's smothered an drownded. Git me u ambulance, quick.'

Wheateye screamed still more wildly, and sprang into the kindling shed. 'Send um back. She's all right. She started u fire herself a playen wit matches. Oh, yu mean, mean kid,' and Wheateye lifted a knee, and began spanking the long carrot she had been nibbling.

Gertie crouched a moment longer, listening.

29

The whispering went off and on like the sound of the shoals in the Cumberland when the wind was gusty from the west; she struggled, wanting the wind, but wakening, took the whispering. She saw the window filled with the late spring sunshine, strange sunlight, blurred and moving like rain. She realized it was her tears that made the window move; she mustn't cry; she hadn't cried since her mother gave her some of Henley's money; no, not since the afternoon she'd learned the bigness of the alley, the kindness; big enough and more it would have been for Callie Lou—and maybe Reuben, too, for the alley and the people in it were bigger than Detroit; no, it was another afternoon, that time when she had gone out to bring Callie Lou back from the dead.

But when was all this? When had she stood by the kitchen door and watched the children? She pondered: yesterday, a week ago, today maybe? Spring it had been, or somebody had said it was spring; no greenness, and the wind she'd sniffed through the kitchen door had been raw and cold as from a field of ice. She called Amos. The whispering came again, and then Clytie's answer, 'He's a watchen his tadpoles ina kitchen, Mom,' and the whispering started up again, fierce arguing now.

She looked about for her coat; it was gone from the bed. She dropped her head back upon the pillow; it didn't matter about the coat; the pocket was an empty hole. Everybody had holes, but a body had to live with holes, fill them. The light made her head ache; she closed her eyes; she ought to brush her hair, but what was the use of it? And it was like she had weights on her hands

443

and rubber in her elbows. 'Mom, didn'tcha say I could have a fence?'

It was Enoch, run up to her bed, disregarding Clytie's angry, 'I toldcha not to be a waken her.' Clytie turned to her mother for support. 'Mom, yu oughta see th mess he's maken inu yard. Him an th kids has brought junk frum all over—loads an loads a them little sticks frum the scrap wood—'

'They're pickuts, I tell yu,' Enoch screamed. 'We're goen—'

'You're not gonna do nothen. You can't cut up them old wore-out clothesline poles th maintainance man give yu fer free. An Victor won't hep none.'

'He's aimen to. He hadda work overtime a heap,' Enoch, almost in tears, said.

'Him an Max, they're gonna move away soon's they can find a place,' Clytie reminded him, then turned to Gertie with her tale of Enoch's foolishness. 'He hadda go an buy some seed up at school t'other day; he done it jist cause th other kids was buyen em—a heap a th people around's a putten out winder boxes, an some in privates has got gardens; an inu project here yu can rent a garden.'

'Pop won't,' Enoch cried.

'Whit rented him one last year, an th ground was pure sand where they give em gardens, an th dogs an cats nastied up what little stuff he did grow; said he didn't make back his seed,' Clytie reminded him.

'That's why we gotta have a fence,' Enoch insisted.

'Silly, Pop's already said it ud cost too much.'

'But I'm tellen yu that what I've spent on seed an fencen I got myself by goen to the store an sich fer people,' Enoch was screaming again.

Gertie roused enough to make a shush-shushing sound. 'Pop ain't tryen to sleep,' Clytie said, and added quickly when Gertie stared at her, 'Thet punch-press division had a little layoff—jist about a day, they think, on account a parts shortage.'

'Why?' Gertie asked, pushing herself up with one hand, swinging her feet to the floor.

'They had a wildcat somewheres where they make um,' Enoch said.

444

'It'sa teamsters' union, walked out over seniority; an they couldn't git um hauled,' Clytie corrected.

'Aw, heck, yu don't know nothen; th teamsters ain't got nothen to do with this un; it was another'n,' Enoch argued. He remembered his original quarrel with Clytie, and turned again to Gertie. 'Mom, didn'tcha say we'd build a fence—jist yesterday? Me an Victor, we'll saw them posties,' and he hurried away while she was trying to think up words in which to tell him he couldn't build a fence.

When the children had gone, she continued to sit on the edge of the bed. She ought to go see what the child was up to, but it didn't seem worth the trouble. She studied an elbow come since yesterday out of the block of wood, and gradually the night grew in her mind like a quilt block partly put together: they'd quarreled at her because she wouldn't take the pink medicine; most of the night she'd worked on the block of wood, smothering with the man in the wood the trains and the dangling boot and all the other things that came behind her eyes when she tried to sleep. She touched the top of the head, gently, as if it had been some human to whom she would show gratitude.

She had her hair parted in the neat straight part that made a white line across her head, but was still brushing it when Mrs Anderson came, pink-cheeked, bright-eyed, and smiling as she held out the glass of pink water. She was playful, shaking her finger. 'You're way behind on your medicine.'

Gertie gave the woman's too bright eyes a critical glance, then frowned and shook her head.

Mrs Anderson set the glass on a chair. 'You're better,' she said, still smiling; and when Gertie made no answer, but only nodded under the curtain of her hair, she turned to the block of wood. One side now was no block of wood at all, but the cloth-draped shoulders of someone tired or old, more likely tired, for the shoulders, the sagging head, bespoke a weariness unto death. Mrs Anderson touched the top of the head, fingered the hair where it fell apart over the bent neck, a strong neck with muscle and bone rising out of a fold of the cloth, careless cloth, as if the wearer were too lost in uneasiness or sorrow to think of cloth, consider its color or quality,

445

only pull it blindly about him and hold it because one must hold to something. 'It's beautiful,' she said. 'I've seen pieces take prizes not half so good. You must finish it—finish it,' she repeated slowly and emphatically, as if the finishing of it were a job that could be done only with great sacrifice and determination.

Gertie looked up at her through the curtain of hair, and spoke slowly, as if the words were stones to be pried one by one from the hard earth. 'I aim to—allus I aimed to finish him, but never had th time. But now, seems like, they's nothen left tu me—but time—an she allus begged me. I wish I'd tuck th time.'

'But how does one take time when—' Mrs Anderson had stood an instant, her hands clenched by her sides while the bright smile that had seemed ready to burst into giggles slid somehow with no movement of her mouth into a big-teared, soundless crying. She dropped all in a heap on the floor, bent her forehead against a wooden shoulder, and wept fully and completely as her Judy wept when she was hurt.

Gertie watched her a moment, puzzled, then began patting her shoulder and smoothing her down-bent head.

The woman sprang up as suddenly as she had flopped down. 'I should cry before you,' she said, her eyes on the man in the wood. 'But sometimes I wonder—why raise children? Why give your life up to them—everything—if—if their lives will be as miserable as your own? Why?' The last 'why' was a hesitant whisper, as if she were afraid to believe that she had asked such a question.

'Why can't I be like Mrs Daly?' she went on, her voice loud and angry now. 'When her ninth baby was three days old, her husband sobered up enough to bring her home from the hospital—a cab hired with money borrowed from Zedke—put it on the grocery bill—bringing her ninth child to temporary housing, designed by a space-stingy government—at least for workers' housing—for four children at the most. And is she happy? She was standing on her steps this morning—it must be all of ten days old—yelling details of its birth to Mrs Schultz, who's looking forward to her sixth. A person would think that for twenty years she had prayed to the Blessed Virgin for just this one child. The stupidity of so many children! Homer, on the basis of a fairly good sampling, estimated

446

some time ago—when he was interested in such things—that this project already had roughly twice as many children as it was set up for.'

She stopped for breath, then rushed on: 'And what will they all do when the war's over? Homer used to think about things like that before he tasted the—what is it in the Bible?—my grandfather used to use the expression a lot, but somehow I can't think so well.'

'The fleshpots of Egypt,' Gertie said, remembering she would try again to read the Bible—seemed like she had tried but the words had blurred—'or else,' she went on, 'th birthright fer th mess a pottage. Samuel ginerally preaches on both together, but I never thought he ought—a body can, I recken, taste th fleshpots 'thout sellen their birthright.'

'But not Homer,' Mrs Anderson said. 'Just think, he was just a poor, socially conscious government worker running a little employment office until he got some workers for Mr Turbi—the Flint people were of course grateful, for nobody has yet thought up a way to make money without men. They held out the fleshpots for a sniff; Homer claimed he was curious, and snatched and gobbled—but he never sold his birthright—he thinks he's found it. But he stole mine.'

Gertie pondered, pinning up her hair; the woman thought she was still drunk on the pink stuff. 'I guess,' she said, speaking with difficulty, thinking of the Tipton Place with Cassie, 'we all sell our own—but allus it's easier to say somebody stole it.'

Mrs Anderson walked to the door and back again. '"Steal" is perhaps not the right word. What does a woman do? I'm not Max; I have children. Her baby died; now she is free to—' Her thoughts seemed to wander, and she smiled, the homesick smile of Christmas Day. 'I wish I'd painted Max. Do you know that all these months I've lived here and wandered the alleys after Georgie and collected statistics for Homer, I've ached inside to go on with my painting; Indiana fat farms and cattle—and flowers—a sort of Rosa Bonheur—Grant Wood—you know, I rejected modernism, surrealism, Marxism, and all the rest for life in Indiana as I saw it—that is, of course, I rejected everything but Homer.'

Gertie shook her head, not understanding, but Mrs Anderson rushed on; a cloud had to drop its rain; Mrs Anderson had to drop her words. 'Always I hated it, this alley, the ugliness, the noise—there wasn't time or quiet in which to paint—and of course nothing to paint only statistics for Homer. I never saw them—the pictures; Wheateye standing on the coalshed roof with a popsicle in her hand—Homer had wanted airplanes for thesis background, so I set out to count the airplanes going over; many children helped, but especially Wheateye; strange I never saw her then, but I do now; dirty with popsicle juice dribbling down her chin; Sophronie worked overtime a lot last summer and couldn't give her children much of anything but money; there'd be flies buzzing round, and the gray houses and the dirty trash cans, always spilling, and the black steel-mill smoke, but there she would stand on the coalhouse looking up at the clean, silvery airplanes.'

She shook her head wearily. 'But I never saw her, any more than I saw Victor when he came home tired and dirty with goggle marks around his eyes after a double shift in the steel mill, sixteen hours. But he didn't look, you know, proletarian tired, exploited; he looked happy; Max was pregnant.'

She looked at the pink medicine she had set on a chair. 'Are you certain you don't want this?' She reached before Gertie finished shaking her head, drank it quickly, shivering a little, then stood a moment, staring at the block of wood. She straightened her shoulders at last, and smiled at Gertie. 'You'll have to get well—quick. Somebody has to watch the children while I house hunt.'

'But ain't you got a house?' Gertie asked, weary of the woman. While she had rattled on, something almost pleasant had come into her head, something she had thought she wanted to do, tired as she was; now it was gone.

'Oh, that thing in Muncie,' and her voice was a mimicry of Homer's, 'we're selling it, of course. But I thought I'd told you; when a farmer buys cattle he looks them over first. Well, the other evening the great McKeckeran was looking Homer over—and his wife too; that's me. Two or three days later Mr McKeckeran called him in—' She stopped, frowning. 'He spoke, but somehow I think his wife, that Mrs McBales, is behind it all—why—but anyway, the great one said, "We'll need well trained men in your field after the war." '

She smiled at Gertie as she turned toward the door. 'The strong-arm, up-from-the-ranks, shirt-sleeve, rough-house stuff is out; everything is smooth, smooth, smooth. Moses had only the Ten Commandments when he came down from his visit with God on the mountain, but Homer after his lunch with McKeckeran had the Promised Land— only, I'm the one has to find the house there.'

Gertie nodded, the last hairpin jabbing firmly down into the great smooth knob. 'I'll watch yer youngens. I'm better, lots better,' and when the woman had gone she began to dress herself and straighten the room. There were long moments when she would sit drooping, or even flop onto the bed, tired to her death, all living useless, wondering why she moved at all. Then she would think of Mrs Anderson flopping around, weeping over nothing. Once her fumbling fingers found the knife, had opened it, and she had turned to the block of wood before she stopped, frowning—something else tonight.

The children and Clovis had finished supper, and the late spring twilight was red-washed with the steel-mill light, before she was clean and dressed, her bed made, and the room straight. All were overjoyed to see her come walking, calm and neat, into the kitchen. Clovis, hunched over a little contraption on the kitchen table, smiled up at her, and begged her to eat some supper. Amos came running, crying, 'Lookee, Mom, lookee,' and pointed to a cake with white thick frosting on a shelf behind the stove, and then brought from under the sink a fruit jar filled with water and half grown tadpoles. Mrs Schultz, she learned, had sent the cake, and Victor had helped Amos get the tadpoles.

Her knees shook and the floor seemed a weaving slippery hill, but she stood up long enough to rummage through her chunks of seasoned maple wood on the kitchen shelf to find a piece that was suited to her needs—the pleasantness of whittling a little fat doll for the new Daly baby.

She sat by the table, and Clytie, seeing the knife and the wood, was reminded to tell her: 'Mom, two or three days ago a girl at school—she didn't know about Cas—our trouble. Her mom seen th crucifix you'd made fer that Hungarian woman, and her mom wants one, too. She keeps plaguing me to ast you.'

449

'Yer mom ain't able to be a doen all that whittlen now,' Clovis put in quickly. 'That tool-and-die man an me, we're riggen her up a contraption. I got this little old vacuum cleaner motor today cheap. It needs new brushes an th wiren's shot, but soon as I fix it, it'll be good as new. An th tool-an-die man's riggen up a saw tu go with it.' Clovis picked up a tiny wrench and bent over the motor again, his washed-out yellow face less tired, his eyes warm with satisfaction as piece by piece he took it apart.

'I could do it now—start it,' Gertie objected, her hands hesitating over the piece of wood, one end already growing into a bald, baby-shaped head. 'I could make a cross—quick,' she said.

'You can turn em out by th dozen when I git a saw set up,' Clovis promised.

She stared at it a moment, her brows puckered in a disapprov-ing frown, but she did not shake her head. After a time of working slowly and ever more slowly on the doll, she laid it aside and took instead two short straight lengths of wood that when put together would form a cross. Shaping the pieces exactly alike in width and thickness, and trying to figure in her head just how long the arms should be, were dull and tedious after the baby's head. There were moments when her hands fumbled, and she seemed to wander on creek banks through wild ginger leaves and above frothing water— it would be nice now to make a wild ginger flower in wood. She realized that all of them, even Enoch by the radio, were watch-ing her, their sneaking, tiptoeing glances touching her face and her hands, the way they had done when they came to the door; and she was silent, going meekly away when Clovis suggested that she go back to bed.

Enoch left Pat McDougall of the FBI and followed her into her room where he lingered to tell her in low tones that Clytie could not hear, of the wonders of his fence. Did she know that he had dug three holes in just a little while? Easy; here in this country of no rocks all a body had to do was screw out the dirt with a thing like a big corkscrew; he'd left some holes undug, and if she got to feeling real good and strong she could see what he meant, but she wouldn't have to be strong, not real strong; the work was that easy.

He went away, and a little eagerness for the next day stirred within her. She'd look at Enoch's fence the first thing. She shook her head over the strangeness of her children. Enoch it was who, given the job of sticking the pumpkin seed into the hills of corn, had hidden them instead in a hollow stump where they had grown and told of his lazy ways.

She shut her door, and looked hungrily toward the block of wood. But she was still fumbling, determined to work on the cross that would bring in money, when she heard the tool-and-die man in the kitchen. His voice was familiar; seemed like she remembered it through Callie Lou's running, her dreams, and the trains, saying always much the same things it said now: 'How's everything? I just dropped around to see is there anything I can do.'

Whit came soon, and not long after the two men left together. Clovis, idled by the walkout, went to bed with Amos, as he had been doing lately, she thought, for Enoch seemed always to be in the living room. She struggled with the cross, but the things were moving behind her eyes again, and with the little holes in the storm window open, the sound of the trains came more clearly. There began again that continual reliving of the last few moments of Cassie's life when over and over she would put the picture together again piece by piece like one methodically laying hot coals on her own body.

She turned at last for comfort to the wood; gradually, her own torture became instead the agony of the bowed head in the block of wood. The arms grew tonight, not fully, but enough she knew the hands would not be reaching out, but holding—holding lightly a thing they could not keep. The head was drooped in sorrow, looking once at the thing it had to give away. Who gave and what gift, she wondered. Jonah with a withered leaf from the gourd vine— Esau his birthright—Lot's wife looking at some little pretty piece of house plunder she could not carry with her—Job listening to the words of Bildad and wondering what next the Lord would want. And what had Job said?

She got the Bible, and thumbed through it quickly, then read, knowing the words were there; but something forced her to read as it forced her always to remember: 'For there is hope of a tree, if it be cut down, that it will sprout again, and that the tender branch thereof will not cease. . . . But man dieth, and is laid low . . . and the river wasteth and drieth up: so man lieth down, and riseth not.'

She closed the book and laid it on a chair, and stared at it, her hands twisting across her aproned lap. Amos, and the old preacher—she'd comforted the children with him for Henley—and Solomon, and Jesus, and John the Baptist, and Jonah pitying the gourd vine, and Jethro's daughter bewailing her fate in the mountains; but all—all of them could not change Job's words.

She couldn't either. Her head drooped, and even the wood was wood only. A train came, jerking her to the window to watch, to listen, to live it over again. She fled tiptoeing from the sound into the kitchen. She snapped on the light, and the bottle of pink medicine above the sink caught her eye. She grabbed it, jerked out the stopper, turned toward the one drawer in the place for a spoon; she didn't need a spoon, half the bottle, all the bottle, anything to get her through the night, bring her, if not sleep, a little forgetting. She stopped, the bottle halfway to her mouth; Callie Lou, seemed like, had just flitted through the door, past the corners of her eyes.

Seemed like? Wavering a little with weakness, she set the bottle on the sink rim; if she took enough of the medicine Callie Lou would be there; she'd go running, flitting, always a corner, an alley-turning away. She rubbed her hand hard across her eyes. Did she remember, or was it like Callie Lou—only something seeming—a hand bigger and stronger than her own, pulling her. She had struggled against it, angry because Callie Lou was past the next turning, hidden in the dark, laughing at her, the soundless-seeming laughter; but the voice that commanded had been troubled. 'Yu gotta git in; yu gotta git some sleep an I've gotta sleep; I can't be allatime watching yu. Nobody yu need tu hunt in u alley; yu kids is home sleeping.'

'Not all,' seemed like she had said. She remembered nothing more, only the man's voice kept running through the soundless laughter; it had held pity for her, and kindness—she, Gertie Nevels, had never needed pity—and what was kindness? She looked at the little bottle, full of lights and gleams under the light; if she drank it Callie Lou would come alive, and she herself would sleep and

452

dream to waken at times and work on the block of wood. The block of wood? She might ruin it. Gertie Nevels must whittle it, not some weak and weeping smoothed-out creature; she couldn't flop down and cry like some; she had to make money; a cross waited to be whittled, and—a train came, and for refuge she went to a hand of the block of wood.

The crimson light grayed up for dawn, and in the shaving-littered room she slept, but wakened soon, half dreaming still of earth and trees and hills and running water. Dreams, she told herself, and got up and dressed, and then remembered. Not all of it was dreaming; she had the earth. The earth at the bottom of Enoch's post hole, how had it looked?

Still, it was late morning and she was caring for the little Andersons in the alley before she had a chance to look at it; dark and rich it was, with more sand than that on top, and smelling even more like the clean earth back home. She would liked to have touched it, but she had Judy on her other arm; her weak knees trembled with the weight of the child when she bent above the scattered earth.

She set Judy on the coalhouse roof and leaned against it resting. Mrs Bommarita was hanging out clothes, Sophronie was taking down storm windows, and past her the Schultz baby carriage poked through the storm door. Then Mrs Schultz, neat and starched as always, and with her hair in curlers, came behind, guiding the carriage down the steps. She called gaily to all the women, including Gertie, then left the carriage on the walk, and from her coalhouse dragged out a large trough-like box. 'Ain'tcha starten farmen kinda early this year?' Sophronie called, on seeing the box.

'Why, it's spring,' Mrs Schultz answered. 'Joe's been selling pansies; and if they weren't so dirty I could pick a ton of dandelion greens. Do you think nasturtiums would grow in a window box? I love to smell them so, but they do take up a lot of room. Perhaps I'd just better stick to pansies and petunias. You'll have a fence,' she was calling now to Gertie. 'You grow some nasturtiums and I'll come smell them.'

Gertie smiled, but shook her head over Enoch's beginnings of a fence. It was in truth what Clytie had said it was, a mess: piles of little kindling-wood slabs that Enoch meant for pickets, and a

453

great line of junky, oddly shaped posts stretching between her place and Sophronie's, across her narrow strip of yard and two sides of Victor's place on the end, enclosing in all a good-sized piece of earth.

Worse even than the posts were the would-be stringers, heavy, crooked, nail-scarred old oak planks. Enoch must have bought cheaply at the scrapwood place, for they were unfit for either kindling or lumber. Mrs Bommarita looked at the mess with a head-shake of displeasure. 'Yu'll never keep th kids out—last summer they ruined my gladiolus; they'd started out real pretty.'

Mrs Schultz, rolling the baby carriage and with two little ones tagging after, reminded Mrs Bommarita that the children had always left her window box alone, and that some of Sophronie's marigolds, even without a fence, had bloomed. But Mrs Bommarita remembered how the Dalys had made mud pies out of a pot of just-getting-started-good delphiniums Mrs Anderson had put to sun on her stoop step, planning to set them on the other side of her house where the children played less often.

Sophronie reminded the dour woman that no child had ever bothered her sweet-potato vine; and she'd forgotten it once already and left it sunning on the coalshed roof when she left for work. There followed an animated discussion of Sophronie's wonderful way with a sweet potato, but Gertie was silent, feeling ashamed; seemed like she was the only woman in the alley who had no growing thing—even Max had some ivy in a little glass dish. She wondered about Max. Why hadn't she come for a dream, either yesterday or today?

Mrs Bommarita was complaining now that the Dalys threw banana skins in her yard, and Gertie wondered aloud on the color of hair the new little Daly had. 'Oh, that's right, you ain't seen her!' Sophronie cried. 'She's th cutest thing.'

Gertie looked longingly toward the Daly door, and Mrs Schultz, careful not to let her eyes linger on the scarred face or bandaged neck, looked at Gertie. 'I saw her only three days ago, but the stingy thing still wouldn't let me see her eyes—and I hate to be always running in. Yu know, yu don't feel too good when a baby's not two weeks old. But couldn't we all go at once? Be better than somebody always running in—and nobody's got a cold.'

They all turned toward the Daly door, but Mrs Schultz gave a last lingering glance at the fence, her blue eyes slightly narrowed, pondering. 'Yu know, I think perhaps we'll have a fence. I never know what to do: save every cent for a down payment on a house or spend it all as you go along—a long spell of sickness could take all you've saved—but kids, they'd always remember a yard with flowers.'

'I tried th saven onct,' Sophronie said, then added slowly, 'but mebbe th war'ull be over pretty soon, an with a lot a people outa work things'ull git cheaper an—well, you don't have to worry none—firemen they don't hafta go on strike er git laid off . . .' Sophronie's voice had grown more and more halting, more troubled; plain it was she did not like to think of that time—for herself.

Mrs Schultz frowned, uncertain. 'But what if they take off OPA?'

They reached the Daly door, all its lights broken now but one. Just as they had got up the steps, Mrs Daly flung it open and stood smiling on them all, especially Gertie. 'Come in an see du baby, but please don't look an mu house,' she went on somewhat wistfully as Mrs Schultz, the best housekeeper in the alley, stepped through the door.

'Ugh, you ought to see my place,' Mrs Schultz said. 'I can't bear to look at it myself,' and she, no more than the other women, appeared to see the crowded, cluttered kitchen, nor did they let their glances stray into the still more rumpled living room that served as living room and nursery by day and bedroom for four little Dalys by night. Mrs Daly, young and happy looking in a new cotton housecoat, had eyes only for the bundle which Maggie, as if to be finished quickly with the visitors, was hurriedly bringing into the kitchen.

Mrs Daly took it with an eager smile, and sat down somewhat carefully on a chair with a broken seat while the women crowded round her, their eyes expectant, smiling. She pulled the blanket from the reddish, puckered face, and at once the place was filled with soft 'Oh's and 'Ah's,' and uncounted cries of: 'Oh, that hair. I do believe she's got jist one dimple.' 'One dimple; ain't that somethen?' 'Ain't she big? Lookut, she already knows th way to her mouth. Ain't she strong, though?'

There was a moment's silence while the five pairs of eyes watched the baby's eyes; for, as Mrs Schultz had complained, she held them stingily squinched, sucking one fist, waving the other, frowning, uncertain of whether or not to cry. 'She's kind a little to look around much,' Gertie said.

'But she's been—' disappointed Mrs Daly was beginning when the baby, like a good child, opened her eyes wide and smiled. The women fell into a chorus of wondering exclamations over the beauty of her wide, dark blue eyes, as if until now they had never taken that first look into any baby's eyes.

Sophronie's exclamations were almost at once swallowed in giggles as Mrs Daly, the better to display the wonders of the feet and body, unwrapped the baby. 'Lordy, I didn't think you'd put it on her,' Sophronie cried, picking a speck of lint from the green crocheted jacket the baby wore.

'Put it on her!' Mrs Daly exclaimed, for an instant able to take her eyes from the baby's face. 'Lookut what Sophronie gimme. She knowed it ut be a redheaded girl. Canyu imagine?'

Sophronie flushed at such praise. 'Back when I was gitten Easter clothes fer th kids down at Union Credit, I seen this green baby sweater—I'd never seen no green baby clothes before, but I thinks to myself, "That little Daly she won't look good in pink." I was afeared the green ud made Miz Daly mad, but it was so cute I bought it.'

'Mad,' Mrs Daly said, looking at the baby. 'You had more sense'n me. Till I seen her, I had my heart set on another girl like Maggie—but there was this green, ready waiting. Maggie,' she said, glancing toward her oldest but beaming as on the baby, 'is th only one has got hair an eyes like her fadder.'

'She'll always be th prettiest one, I bet,' Mrs Schultz said, smiling at Maggie, who through all the goings on over the baby had stood silent in the passway as if she would hide the mess behind her that too plainly showed the family's torn sheets and tattered blankets. Her eyes were unsmiling when she glanced briefly at the baby, though when Mrs Schultz complimented her she did smile, that is, her lips went away from her teeth, the dimples leaped into her cheeks, and she tossed her head enough to ripple her dark curls.

'An no matter how pretty she gits, she cain't never be no better than Maggie,' Mrs Daly said, smiling on first one daughter and then the other. 'Wudju believe it? Not one little cross word for having to miss school—and even, one day, mass.'

'She'll give yu black-headed, blue-eyed grandchildren,' Mrs Bommarita said, studying Maggie. 'A dozen—could be fourteen.'

Mrs Daly, at the thought of fourteen grandchildren, all black-headed, bounced with delight until the baby jiggled on her knees; then she was hoping she could get a few more pieces for Maggie's hope chest first and, it would be nice for Maggie to finish high school, then let her marry, 'an raise as many babies as th Blessed Virgin sends her, like any Christian woman ought.' She smiled at Maggie again, but Maggie had turned her back on her mother, and gave no sign that she had heard.

There was a banging on the kitchen door, and a chorus of children's voices, Amos among them, all crying, 'Georgie's gotta buggy widu kid in ut.'

It was Mrs Schultz's baby, left for an instant by the Daly door. No harm had come to it on the wild bouncing ride down the main alley before fleet-footed Sophronie rescued it. But even she, the silent one, joined in the chorus of condemnation and gazed wistfully upon Georgie. 'Law, wouldn't it be fine to spank him, jist onct!'

'Summer, summer,' Mrs Schultz said, sighing, putting the baby carriage by her stoop, hunting with her eyes through the alley until she found the two-year-old and the four-year-old. She was, however, soon in her usual good humor again, and called to Gertie as she walked slowly past with Judy, hunting Georgie: 'Yu know, I think I'll crochet a cap and bootees to match that green sweater— it costs so much to give all the new babies around something, but since it's a girl and she's so proud and all, I'd like to give it something.'

Gertie nodded. 'I figgered I couldn't spend no money, so's last night I started it a little whittled foolishness.'

'I wish I could carve,' Mrs Schultz said, turning back to her spading, but had lifted only one shovelful of earth into the window box before she was calling, like a child, 'Lookee, lookee.'

Gertie went closer, but at first could see only a little mound of broken pebble-strewn cement; then between the rock and the house wall she saw the violet leaves, still blue and rolled against the cold;

457

but living leaves. 'I never thought they'd pull through,' Mrs Schultz was exclaiming. 'I put that rock around them to keep the children from squashing them to death, after they'd brought them to me from that vacant land on the other side of the railroad tracks. And now they've pulled through,' she repeated, her voice triumphant.

Amos came calling to tell his mother that Georgie had run away toward the steel-mill fence, and Gertie followed. Today, with the warmer weather, there were many people in the alleys: women doing much the same things the women in her own alley did, and quite often men also were rolling carriages, washing windows, changing storms for screens, or even hanging out the wash; for most three-to-twelve-shift workers were by now astir. A man polishing his car smiled at her, and up near the steel-mill fence a youngish man, with a bad limp, who was putting up a little square of fence on one side of his stoop hurried away before she had hardly finished her question of had he seen a little boy dragging a red wagon upside down. The man was back in a moment, pulling Georgie in his wagon.

While Georgie was in sight, Gertie rested a moment on a covered garbage can, but soon he disappeared at the next turning, and she followed. People smiled at her; some praised the warm spring weather, others remarked that Judy was a pretty baby, but none noticed the bandages on her neck or the scars on her face. A small child with black eyes and white hair on a red tricycle fell in behind her, while back and forth and round her went a large and long-haired dog who now and then wagged his tail and licked the face of some passing child; and Gertie surmised that he, like the gray cat she fed sometimes, belonged to the alley.

She found Georgie again near the corner of the project where the railroad fence and the steel-mill fence came together. Nearby was a unit with a child-dug, toy-strewn bit of earth that had no beginnings of grass or fence or flowers, but on the stoop a dark dumpling of a woman with broken teeth and a mustache bent lovingly over a crepe-paper-swathed pot in which a dusty gray and prickly cactus stood. The woman lifted her head and smiled at Gertie. 'A whole new leaf it gives, since Christmas,' she said.

Gertie's knees were weak, and the ground seemed all awhirl; she stopped to rest on the woman's steps, and though there was some trouble—one hardly able to understand the other—some talking passed between them; the weather, and flowers, and children mostly. The woman, Gertie thought, had four, but she wasn't certain; maybe it was four and the baby trying to crawl through the door.

Georgie came, but only to tell her that now Amos was missing, though Georgie thought he had gone home. Gertie hurried down the alley by the railroad fence, trying not to look at the place where the hole had been, mended now with a whole new board, unpainted yet and too plainly showing among the dull sooty green of the other boards. Seemed like she couldn't get past the place; it was like she stood still, sweating, shivering, going closer and closer, but never able to get it behind her. What would there be now on the other side of the crack?

There came a soft calling, half crying, half laughing; and Max came running through her seldom used front door, then looked over her shoulder as if afraid of being seen. 'Amos is onu other side with Victor,' she said in a calling whisper, and came running on, one hand pushed down into her housecoat pocket.

'It come up—see—th number yu gimme,' she whispered when she was close to Gertie. 'Just like always, I got th page number it was on in Mom's old dream book, added th number on th third check I give out at work, and give it to Casimir next morning—an it come up—it come up.' She was half laughing, half crying, all bouncy on her toes, as if by bouncing she might hurry out the whispered words. 'I couldn't sleep all night for thinking on how I'll scram. Butcha gotta keep it till I go—I ain't taking no chances on going soft and showing it to Victor. I played um big. Yu got a pocket handy?' And after glancing swiftly around her, her hand came up out of her housecoat and shoved the thickish roll of what looked to be twenty-dollar bills down into Gertie's apron pocket, 'About 830, I think, in all. I put in some tips I'd saved.'

She was hurrying back to her door, her housecoat billowing about her, her hair blown over her face as it had been when she first came asking for a dream in the snow, 'Don't tell nobody—he might hear ut.'

Gertie took a swift step toward her. 'Honey, you'd ought to give him this money. Don't go; he's a good steady—'

Max, her hand on the doorknob, whirled toward her in exasperation. 'He's in u yard trying to nail fence. He'll hear us. I gotta go. He's allatime been after me to go to mass. I said I would—now.'

'Now?'

'Sure.' Max was still, with her hand on the door handle, her face turned skyward as she waited for an airplane to come lower and smother the sound of the closing door. 'I can be kinda nice to him now. See? I ain't afraid no more. When my number come up, I knowed what I hadda do. See? But—well—if I wanta make him feel kinda nice s'okay now, on account I know he can't soften me up none. But it'll hafta be quick. I gotta scram pretty soon on account a we're—he's gonna move soon's the war's over, see?' The airplane circled down for a landing, and under cover of the sound Max slipped through the door.

Gertie went on to the alley where Victor, red-faced and covered with sweat, looked mad enough to eat the three nails he had crooked in the wood. She handed Judy to Enoch and considered the nails and Victor. She was so weak, with her legs all atremble, and her arms, too, just from carrying Judy, she knew she couldn't drive a nail in seasoned oak. But what were the words for telling a body how to drive a nail? She pondered, shaking her head.

She took the hammer; the feel of it, the same old hammer she had used back home, was good in her hand. Victor held the stringer, and she set another nail by the three he had crooked. It wasn't easy; the post jiggled in the damp sandy soil, and wouldn't stay firmly against the iron-like oak stringer; and worse, it seemed like all the alley watched her wrestle with the contrary mess. However, it was only a moment until a great yell of triumph went up from the watching children. She rested, and then worked on until she got four stringers nailed and Victor could start putting up the flimsy little pickets.

The yells and commotion in general awakened Clovis, who came to the door; and Enoch ran up to him crying, 'We're gonna have a fence, a real fence, Pop.'

'But won't it cost a heap? Recollect we'll have to pay our part,' Clovis said in a low voice meant only for Enoch and Gertie; but Enoch, sticking out his chest almost as much as Mr Daly, told his father that he had already paid for more than their part with money he'd got for running errands and such, and anyway, he'd managed to get a lot of the stuff for free.

Gertie looked at Clovis with wonder; strange it was for open-handed Clovis to worry about the bit of money the fence would cost. 'You short on money?'

He shook his head. 'Not bad. My pay checks ain't been so big, missen time like I've been. This week that wildcat'ull make me short ag'in—but I recken I can meet all th payments. Th grocery bill at Zedke's is mebbe gitten kind a big so's I mebbe cain't finish it off, but—' He licked his lips and studied her as if loath to trouble her with bad news, then spoke quickly, as if to be finished with the business: 'Th trouble is, they's a heap a talk out at th shop about a speed-up on a parts assembly line—an, well—they's a bunch a hotheads yellen fer a strike, and everybody in my division ud most likely hafta go out in sympathy. Jist another wildcat, but—' He looked at her worriedly as she continued silent, wiping back her hair with a bended arm. 'Gert, you oughtn't to be out a doen sich. You ain't able to mind that woman's youngens, let alone build fence.'

Gertie had been resting on the steps, but now she got slowly up, glad to feel that some of the quivering was gone from her knees. She turned toward the door; it was almost noon; Judy was hungry and Enoch's ears were dirty. 'I'll never git my strength back a layen in bed—an already I'm so behind in everything I never will git caught up.'

30

The house hunting went slowly. Mrs Anderson usually got home late, tired and angry, near tears at times. 'One hundred fifty dollars plus utilities for an apartment no bigger than our unit here—no place at all for the children to play. They did us a great favor even to consider taking the children. . . . Three hundred dollars for a house like that—furnished they call it; it's so filled with junk there'd be no place for my piano. . . . But we have to have a place to live—but even after selling the place in Muncie there still won't be enough for a down payment on the house and all the furniture we'll have to buy—nineteen thousand they want—it's almost new, one of the last houses built before the war—but ugh—the decorations: black roses in one bathroom. And it's all so tiny, just a brick box big enough to hold the gadgets; no place at all for me to paint.' She sighed. 'But Homer likes it. Why? The great Mrs McKeckeran herself found it; it's in the poorer section of her own neighborhood; and is Homer flattered?'

The woman might have talked all through supper getting had not Joe come calling, and she remembered she was out of vegetables, though as usual she quarreled at having to buy them from 'that smuggler,' as she sometimes referred to Joe, or from 'that smuggled one,' by which she meant Joe's nephew. Gertie went out for potatoes and turnips—cabbage was high now, but turnips, with the tops good enough for a bite of greens, were cheap. Joe smiled at her, and the nephew smiled; he wanted to say something, and studied her face an instant, smiling, hunting the word, but in the end snapped his fingers, laughing at his failure as he said, 'No seeck.'

'Well,' she said, and he nodded, pleased, repeating the word slowly, but it sounded like 'weal.'

It was a cold day with a mist of rain and at times a spit of snow, but Joe's truck was piled high with flowers for setting which he sold along with the vegetables. Among them were some tiny lavender flowers such as Gertie had never seen. They made her think of the wild sweet Williams back home—something wild for Cassie's grave; then Enoch was begging, and Clytie, too: 'Buy flowers, Mom. Buy flowers. Miz Schultz has already put pansies in her winder box.'

Gertie touched the flowers, but firmly shook her head. Cassie's marker came first. The nephew saw her glance and said, 'Flowers,' slowly, smiling as he took a box of marigolds and bent above them sniffing, then held them out for her to smell. She shook her head again, and said the two words Max had told her to say when she wanted to be rid of a peddler, 'No money.'

He pondered a moment, looking past her to the fence, half finished now, with the earth behind it spaded. He turned, and after some consideration selected a box of pansies and a box of the little lavender ones and turned to Joe. Some talking in their language passed between them with Joe at first frowning and shaking his head, but at last he yielded to the insistence of the nephew, who turned to Gertie with a smile of victory as he set the flowers in her basket. 'For free,' he said. 'Not so hot.' But it seemed to Gertie that the flowers were only a little battered, a little wilted; the roots were damp and living.

She wanted to thank him, but Max came running down her steps, and as always the nephew had eyes and tongue only for her. It was on Max that he had tried, one by one, the new, important words he gleaned from America; 'credit, car, installment, movies, Coke, down payment, priest, mass,' along with the others, such as 'dollar,' he seemed always to have known. He would watch her lips, smiling a little as she corrected his pronunciation.

Enoch begged to set the flowers in a safe place close to the house wall, and where they would get the morning's sun; but that night at supper Gertie felt guilty about the gift. Her words of, 'No money,' to the nephew seemed like begging now when Clovis suggested that she buy more. 'But I thought you was afraid you'd have to go out on a strike,' she said.

He shook his head; some shut-down anger slipped across his eyes. 'Not now; that steward that was a tellen us we ought to strike he got—well, kind a hurt an he's in a hospital.'

Gertie marveled that he seemed so little pleased; it was bad for anybody to get hurt, but if it had to be somebody she was glad it was the man who had wanted a strike. She started to ask about his hurt, but the children were all in a clamor of talking, and anyway she was tired with her mind wandering. More than anything she wanted to be alone with the man in the woods; but he had been moved again into the living room, for with screens instead of glass the bedroom on the alley was too noisy for Clovis to sleep in by day, and her lately acquired habit of working on the block of wood in stray moments of time through the day disturbed his sleeping.

She, with Clytie helping, hurried through the hateful kitchen work, but still it seemed hours before the place was quiet, with the children in bed. Then, she was disappointed, angry, too, when just as she had readied herself for the man in the wood with a clean apron and freshly combed hair, the tool-and-die man came. Tonight, he held out to her a strange contraption of steel. 'A gift for you,' he said, but looking round her to the block of wood as he went on to explain that the contraption was a part for the jig saw he and Clovis were making for her. This was the piece on which she would lay the wood for sawing. He'd made it in a parts place owned by a man he knew, and now he had a little hand work to do.

She nodded, and tried to show some gratitude for this beginning of a gift; and hoped a little that he would never get it finished, for with the war everything in steel was hard to come by. Conscious of his curious glance on the man in the wood, she turned from it and got down the Christ for the unfinished crucifix, and worked on it while the two men sat by the kitchen table and worked on the jig saw. Tonight, they seemed wrapped in some dour troubled silence until Whit came, asking, 'You uns seen th paper?'

'I seen *him*,' the tool-and-die man said.

The other two looked at him with interest. 'What'd he say?' Whit asked.

'He say anything about who he thought done it?' Clovis asked.

'He couldn't talk,' the tool-and-die man said. 'Th papers didn't tell th half a it. They didn't use a rubber hose on him—knucks, lead pipe, and truck tire chains, I'd say.'

Whit whistled. 'Th paper said that when his wife come a runnen, she seen four men jump into th car. You talk to her?'

The other shook his head. 'She was there, but all she could do was bend over th bed and look at him, then turn around and walk back and forth like a crazy woman. "What's he ever done?" she'd say. "He's always been such a good, sober, steady man," she'd say to th man in th next bed—like that had anything to do with it.'

Whit finished his beer, set the bottle on the table. 'You'd ought to a reminded her they killed Jesus Christ,' then added, as the other continued silent: 'They's a heap I think ain't sorry; some's a sayen he was a commie, or leastways close kin to one.'

The tool-and-die man lifted his head quickly at that. 'You know he wasn't a commie; he did fool around with th Trotskyites a little. But mostly some hate him on account he couldn't keep his mouth shut—always he hadda pop off on th Black Legion, th Silver Shirts; an one day he tore up some a Father Moneyhan's literature. That was enough to make him a commie right on th spot.'

'You think,' Clovis asked slowly, guardedly, 'it was somebody in th union afeared he'd egg us on to strike that done the beaten?'

The tool-and-die man was angry now. 'If th company can get enough good union men like you believing some union men half killed another union man, it'll be fine—for th company.'

Whit pondered, twirling his beer bottle. 'He was ina right, too. They've set the production quota way too high.'

'Sure he was ina right,' the tool-and-die man said. 'Old man Flint knows we got a no-strike pledge. He didn't raise th quota; he just took a few men off a line and let th rest do more work—a little a what he done in th depression.' He sighed. 'It's bad, but talks no good, not now; it ain't safe. I tried to tell that to Bender, but he won't shut up; he'll be next, an they'll kill him.'

'Mebbe,' Clovis said, 'th police can find who's doen these beatens. Three union big shots beat up and half killed since February—all complainen about worken conditions; th police must be looken hard.'

465

Whit broke into derisive laughter, and even the tool-and-die man smiled as he said: 'Th police. You think they wanta find out who beat up some a old man Flint's hands?'

Not long after, they went away, and Gertie worked on the block of wood. Callie Lou was still tonight, so that she worked in peace, mostly on the cloth-covered shoulder; the shoulder drooped too much, she thought; so tired, so sorrowful. Why so sorrowful, so tired? The world, the block of wood were not herself. She realized that for a long time, maybe all the while she worked, she had been listening; it wasn't clear two walls away; Detroit, even in its sleep, was too noisy to let human crying come so far, but still she knew it was Max who cried.

This was different from her crying on the night Gertie had rubbed Enoch; no lostness now, only sorrow—sorrow because her number had won the money. Why so much sorrow, like the man's wife shivering and crying? What had he done, the man, that they beat him so? She hadn't bothered to ask, but he couldn't be much if he ran around with men who got drunk and beat him up. Mrs Anderson was most likely crying by her wall, sorrowful because she had a man and children. Mrs Bommarita cried by her wall because her man was far away—maybe he flew tonight, a waist gunner, she'd heard say. And the pretty little Japanese woman so far from her home—maybe she cried, too.

She realized she was tired, so tired the folds of cloth were blurring. But when she got into bed there was the crying still—plainer now—pure sorrow, like Cassie crying for Callie Lou; and she came wide awake, remembering, reliving, swung about by the tides of anger that made her want to walk the alleys, to pound the walls, to do anything but lie still while her mind went on and on, refighting all the battles lost. If she tore herself from Cassie, there was Reuben waiting, and if from Reuben, the lost land called, and then became a lost life with lost children. She thought of the pink medicine; take enough of it and maybe the anger and the hatred would leave her; she lifted on one elbow, but in a moment lay down again; with the anger and the hatred, the medicine would also take herself; and she had work to do, such a deal of work—the crucifix to finish, baby sitting, the fence to build.

Next day and on the following days until it was finished, she worked on the fence in what time she could spare from her other work. Victor, who was now forever gay, whistling, or bursting into snatches of songs the words of which she could not understand, though the joy came clearly through, helped in the late afternoons as did the children. Girls as well as boys begged often for the privilege of driving a nail in one of the little pickets or of using the saw. Gertie, working always in a swarm of children, learned soon to keep her hammer in her hand and her nails in an apron pocket, for if she left either hammer or nails loose they were gone with the children.

She was nailing pickets around by Victor's corner one morning when she heard a train bell over in the switchyard begin a noisy clanging. She hammered hard to kill the sound, shivering, trembling, crooking the nail, but pounding on until it smashed into the wood, crook and all. Still, the sound, instead of dying, grew louder with the blowing of a train joining in. If the train could have blown for Cassie—she jabbed blindly into her pocket for another nail, but stopped, hammer uplifted when other railroad whistles began a loud, long screaming. These were joined almost at once by the cars and trucks all around her; even Casimir, stopped in front of Sophronie's, ran out and began to blow his truck horn. Somewhere bells were ringing, then Enoch came shouting, 'Mom, Mom, they've beat th Germans!'

Mrs Bommarita ran down her steps crying, 'It's over in Europe. Joe will come home.' She stopped suddenly and stood in the middle of the alley looking about her, speaking to no one but herself. 'Th place where he hadda job sold out.'

Mrs Schultz, her baby on one arm, its bottle in her other hand, called to Mrs Daly, 'Maybe things will get cheaper now, an they won't want so much for a down payment on a house.'

'Ain't it grand?' Mrs Daly called from her stoop. 'I'm hoping I can hear dear Father Moneyhan again; they hadda have more room for th war news so's he went off du air. Wasn't that patriotic now? We need men like him tu make du country turn around an clean up them communists while we're at it—that's what Mr Daly says.' She nodded her head knowingly as she came on into the alley past the trash cans. 'Du red squad anu FBI, dey'll listen to um now.

Oh, da t'ings Mr Daly knows,' and she looked at Sophronie, who through all the bedlam had continued to hang clothes on the line. Jabbing home the last clothespin, she turned to Gertie, sorting slabs for pickets now, and smiled her timid, fleeting smile. 'Well, I recken we'll all be gitten laid off pretty soon.'

The shouts of the children and the noise of the bells and whistles and horns gradually died, but the uncertainty, the wonder of what next, lingered in the alleys, and instead of joy there seemed to hang a heavy, troubled stillness. That night at supper Clytie wondered what the depression had been like; she'd heard some of the kids talking at school. Clovis, more silent than usual, told her somewhat shortly it was a time when there were about ten times as many men as jobs. His voice was so short and so troubled, too, that Clytie said nothing more; but at last, restless in the heavy silence, she turned to Gertie with talk of the lilac bush in her girl friend's yard. 'Tall as th two-storied house might nigh, an full, completely full, of buds for flowers. Mom, do you recollect any lilac bushes back home? Donna Mae's mom says th smell, specially on a kinda still rainy day, beats anything you've ever smelled.'

Gertie shook her head. 'I don't recollect any, but whatever they are I bet they cain't beat wild plum er honeysuckle.'

A few days later, however, Gertie had to admit that, though the smell of lilac flowers was maybe a shade too sweetish, it was stronger than any flower smell she had ever known. Clytie had brought an armload from her girl friend's house, and that night in the smothery closeness the smell of the lilacs rose stronger than the chlorine water smell, dwarfing at times even the gas smell. The alley children brought sprays and boughs from the giant bushes set years before in the subdivision by the rusty lamp posts, so that the sweetness hung over the alley like the steel-mill smoke.

It was on such a day, warmish and still, with a little mist of rain, that Max, dressed as if to go to work, came hurrying, softly sneaking through the front screen door. She stopped on seeing Gertie, and held out her hand, empty, asking, but her glance wandered to the fruit jar of lilacs by the radio. 'Them lilacs got me,' she said. 'Boy, yu oughta see an smell um in New England—better than them in Ohio.' She wiggled the fingers of the heldout hand. 'I gotta go. We looked at houses some more yesterday—one kinda nice—oldish, u pretty yard, th biggest lilac bush, full a bloom. Haven a lilac bush allatime could be nice if it could be allatime spring with warmish rain. Yu lost it?'

Gertie thought the child looked hopeful, as if, learning her money was gone, she would turn around and go back to bed, and move in time to Hamtramck, into the house with the lilac bush; and in afteryears the girl would thank her, and Victor too, for Max would some day tell him. Their children would laugh in the springs when the lilacs bloomed over the old tale of how Mama once might have run away when she was young and sad because she'd lost that first little baby, and could have been a homeless tramp upon the earth, wandering among men and cities into a lonesome old age—only, the big fool woman she had trusted with her money had lost it.

Eight hundred dollars was enough to pay their debts; the war was almost over. She could maybe sell the washing machine and the Icy Heart for enough to buy a mule. John would let her rent the Tipton Place; there would be enough left from the eight hundred, maybe, to get a cow and some chickens after they'd moved back; it was too late for a corn crop—but her father would let her save some of his wasting hay—her father. She took a step forward as if he were somewhere out the door and she had only to go walking to see him. If he would only write to her. They would take Cassie back; and Reuben would be there. How did he look now? Her mother in her last letter had said nothing of him; she'd only written of what a sweet child Cassie had been; and told of how nightly she prayed to God that Gertie would take better care of the others, and look upon this death of a loved one as an act of God chastising her for her stiff-necked . . . 'Yu lost it?' Max was repeating, with no anger, no worriment.

'Oh, no,' Gertie said. 'I allus keep it right by me,' and she unpinned from down in her apron pocket an old tobacco sack into which she had stuffed the roll of bills.

Max seized it, jammed it down into her purse without looking, and after fishing a moment in another part of the purse, brought out a new and shining twenty-dollar bill. She shoved it into Gertie's apron pocket. 'Buy flowers for yu garden. He likes flowers—his mom's allatime messen around in her yard.' She turned swiftly away, opening the door.

Gertie stared after her with the struggling, wide-eyed look that was often on her face now, then caught Max's arm. 'Child—ye cain't go like this. You don't know where you'll sleep tonight.'

'Sh-sh,' Max said, glancing toward Victor's bedroom window. 'In a bus headed fer th sea, I'll sleep. I gotta see th sea. I gotta go to sleep an awake up an hear wheels a rollen under me.'

'But they's a heap a seas,' Gertie said. 'You ain't twenty years old. You—you need somebody. Ain't ye got no people, nothen, nobody?'

Max's chin lifted; she jerked one shoulder toward the window. 'I learned there—I didn't need nobody.'

'But ain't ya taken nothen—clothes?'

'Leave him th clothes. His stingy mom cain't never say he spent one nickel on me—my tips I saved is in his bank. When yu got money yucan buy, and I've never had no trouble picken up a job. That gospel woman put some heart in me.' She glanced worriedly toward the window. 'He worked double shift last night, an oughta sleep late. I figger if a jerk like Homer can get next to a job that'ull give him grub without so much as dirtyen his hands, they's hope for a girl like me. I think I'll take a business course—to hell with this barmaid stuff. Th big tips ain't worth th rubben an th pinchen.'

'I know some people by th sea,' Gertie whispered, reaching from the doorway and pulling Max back up the steps. 'They're a little kin a mine—they went to Hampton Roads, Virginia, to build ships by th sea. They're good people. Wait, now; I want ye to have their address,' and still holding Max, she got the Bible, and from between its leaves took the paper that held the addresses. Among those once together back home, but now scattered by the war, was that of Laurie Tompkins; no more than a cousin on her father's side, but after Meg went away the closest thing to a sister she had ever had.

Max took the slip of paper on which Gertie wrote, and after glancing hastily around as if afraid of being watched, opened her purse, and from it took a thin sheaf of papers, held with a rubber band. 'I'll put it here with me,' she whispered.

'Me?'

470

'Yeah; it's all a me; see. This I was born; I gotta high-school diploma—Pop taught me more'n I'd ever learn in school, but he wanted me to have one a th things; he read inu paper once about a little school in Alabama wot burned an lost all records—so's I graduated from it—year before it burned; I was smart at seventeen. I gotta social security number—when I got this last job I never bothered to change it—s'lucky thing.'

Gertie glanced at the little paper. 'But you've been married, Max—'

Max closed her purse, turned away. 'Not me, kiddo—his mom alla-time said we wasn't—so's I'll take her word for it—that's alla me.'

'I'll bet if he come a beggen this minnit, you'd go back,' Gertie said, grabbing at her again to put the twenty-dollar bill into her hand.

Max's, 'Oh, yeah?' was weak and trembling. On the bottom step she suddenly turned back, flung her arms around Gertie, and gave her a quick embarrassed kiss that landed on her jaw. 'I wish you'd been my people,' she said, and was gone, flinging the bill back to Gertie, then crouching low as she ran past Sophronie's window, never turning her head to Gertie's calling whisper, 'But, honey, we're kin, close kin,' and more loudly, 'Victor's a good man, such a good steady—'

That night was the worst Gertie had had in many nights; there was some comfort in a hand of the block of wood, a hand cupped, but loosely holding; behind the blank wood above it she could sometimes see the face, eyes peeping through the wood, looking down upon the thing, hard won, maybe, as silver by Judas, but now to give away; the eyes were sad or maybe angry with the loss; it was hard to say, for Callie Lou was flitting again; she was restless, hunting Cassie; lost like Victor. In the late afternoon she'd heard his singing as he moved about the place, maybe drinking the coffee Max had left ready to perk when he flicked a switch. She must have also left a note, for after a time there was silence broken only by the restless tramping of feet. She'd been out in the early twilight watering the marigold bed when with never a word he'd gone down his walk in his Sunday clothes and to his car.

He came home late, long after his going-to-work time; and while she lay alone in her forever too short bed in her place close against the wall she heard him twist and turn in his bed only a few inches away; but still, small sounds, she thought, to keep a tired woman awake; maybe it was the smell of lilacs kept her awake—maybe it was the lilacs wouldn't let Victor sleep. He and Max had brought home a great armload when they came back from house hunting together. Maybe he didn't know he smelled them now; but tomorrow he would know, and then it would be too late to throw them away; he could fling them in the through street and let them be crushed by a million cars or he could bury them deep in the earth, but still there'd be the smell—like the train grease on her hands. She hadn't smelled it then, but now she knew it would be forever on her hands.

Next day, while watching the Anderson children, she lingered much among the flowers she had planted by Victor's wall; so little, the old maids and asters and cosmos and marigolds, most without even the beginnings of buds, yet over them hung the heavy sweet odor of flowers. It was the children who found the great, unwilted lilac bouquet, pitched pot and all into Victor's trash can. The children broke the boughs into many little sprigs and made a garden in the spaded ground, trampling it so that Gertie was tempted to warn them the grass would never grow, but did not. Children needed earth as well as grass and flowers.

However, the grass grew; each afternoon, when the house shadow fell over it, the children fought for turns at sprinkling it with the leaky hose borrowed daily from the project office. Many passersby and peddlers—like the home furnishings man, who still came weekly with an outstretched hand, but since, learning of their trouble, now kept his suitcase closed—stopped to admire the beginnings of grass and the borders of flowers by the fence and the house wall.

Only Victor never saw the grass and flowers; he came and went on many double shifts, and spoke to no one. The alley quickly learned about his trouble; Mrs Anderson thought Max had done the proper thing, but Mrs Daly shook her head and sighed and told him one day to burn candles to the Blessed Virgin and also to

472

St Jude on the chance that Max was lost. He maybe listened, for he was still, looking at the woman as she spoke, though he stalked away without answering.

Gertie pitied him, but wished at times that he would take a little interest in the fate of the flowers he had wanted so. One afternoon a gang of boys broke several of the flimsy pickets right in front of his window, and he never even knew about it, though he was home awake. It was Enoch who noticed the broken pickets when he and others played hide and seek among the cars in the parking lot at twilight.

Victor never even yelled any more at the little youngens coming in, not to play, but for pure meanness to pinch buds and pull up flowers. Georgie, Gertie guessed, gave most trouble, but there was only one of him; there were so many little Dalys, and for all the attention they gave her outcries she might have been the wind; or if they answered her at all it was with jeers and cries of: 'Yu got no right tu fence dis, mu pop says; he's gonna see du project manager; he's in good wit him; du gover'ment's gonna make youse tear dis fence down.'

One Saturday morning when Gertie had done a big washing and had just got the first part of it almost dry on the outside line, Amos came running with the news that the Dalys had pinched all the buds from the cornflowers and dug a ditch in the marigold bed, all on Victor's side where she hadn't seen them. Gertie sighed in particular over the loss of the cornflowers; they had with their early buds promised enough flowers for Clytie a bouquet at eighth-grade graduation, and they would have looked so pretty on the white dress Iva Dean's mother was making for her. She said nothing, but Enoch ran after the Dalys and ordered them out of the yard; but just as they were going through the gate, Jimmy, the one a little bigger than Amos, grabbed up a handful of wet marigold bed by the fence, and threw it, marigold and all, so that it dirtied two of Homer's white shirts hung on the line to dry.

He and his brothers ran home, but Gertie, not wanting the sight of the despoiled flowers, turned wearily back into the kitchen, where Clovis was eating breakfast. A moment later Enoch came banging in, screaming, almost crying: 'Mom, yu gotta stand up fer

473

yer rights. Mr Daly'ud have us out a th project if we throwed mud on their washen.'

Clovis nodded, and Clytie nodded, and all of them looked at her. She hated the washing of the fine white shirts about as much as she loved the flowers. She hesitated a moment, then whirled about, strode through the door, took the muddied shirts from the line, and went on down the alley toward the Daly door. Her own children followed, and Wheateye ran ahead gathering recruits with her cries: 'They's gonna be a fight. Miz Nevels is gonna beat up on u Dalys.'

Gertie was just going up the steps with children flocking round the Daly stoop, when the screen was flung violently open and Mrs Daly, redfaced and angry-eyed, glared at her, screaming, 'Listen, youse nigger-loven—'

Gertie never knew whether Mrs Daly meant to call her communist or hillbilly; Mrs Daly had for an instant looked past her into the alley, and had seen something that made her hands drop from her hips and smiles of welcome sparkle in her eyes; she at once opened the screen door wide as she said in the voice she used when she was walking home from mass: 'Do come in, Mrs Nevels—a little Roman Cleanser is all them shirts needs—but do come in an have some coffee. My, ain't it a beautiful day?' and she smiled past Gertie into the alley with such joy in her eyes that it seemed the uncombed and grimy children screaming among the overflowing trash and garbage cans were little angels, clean and well mannered, floating by a green and shaven lawn in heaven.

The disappointed children gave a gasp of wonder, and Gertie, mystified, went through the opened door, but could not get into the kitchen, crowded with children and a glugging washing machine, enough to let the door close completely. Mrs Daly, with a shoe-polish dauber in one hand, for she had apparently been blacking the shoes of Mr Daly, who sat reading a religious paper in the living room, pushed Maggie closer to the table, pulled Gertie in a little more, and so was enabled to close the screen against the flies; she then looked through it, giggling with satisfaction. 'Aint' he th disappointed one now? Yu thought yu'd take notes on my way a tucken, huh?'

474

Mr Daly cleared his throat in disapproval, and Mrs Daly fell silent, but for a moment longer feasted her eyes on the sight in the alley. Gertie, unable to turn her body without moving the washing machine, twisted her head enough to see Homer moving away from what must have been his listening post by the trash can.

Homer's disappointed back put Mrs Daly in high good humor, and before Gertie could protest, for she had only wanted Mrs Daly to see what her children had done, not wash the shirts, the little woman had seized them, held them an instant under the faucet, and pitched them into the tub where a white wash went round and round in a sea of suds and smell of Roman Cleanser.

Gertie was not allowed to leave until time enough had passed for her to have a cup of coffee, but as the pot was empty and no one could get to the stove without first moving the washing machine, and anyway as Mrs Daly said, 'Nobuddy wants coffee nohow this time of day,' Gertie passed the coffee-drinking time in admiring the baby that Maggie was feeding by the kitchen table. The little one had grown enormously, produced already three freckles, and gave promise of having even more abundant and redder hair than even the stove wrecker.

In spite of the ruination of the cornflowers, Clytie had a bouquet for eighth-grade graduation, though she was annoyed because Gertie could not remember to call it a corsage. Iva Dean's mother fixed Clytie one of delphinium spears and pink rosebuds, just as nice as the one she fixed for Iva Dean, doing it in the same unasking way as she had made the white thin dress and petticoat that Clytie wore, getting only what help Clytie could give. The two girls had been talking of graduation dresses the day Cassie had been hurt; and later, when Gertie had no mind for anything, the red-headed woman had taken Clytie's dress upon herself, not even asking Clovis to pay for the cloth, though of course he had.

Gertie sat beside her in the hot, overcrowded place they called the auditorium, though it was little bigger than a classroom, and served as such by day, so small the parents only could be invited to the graduation. It was during the singing that Gertie, who had been staring straight ahead, trying not to think of the last time she visited the school when she had four children in it, heard a faint sniffling, turned, and saw the tears in the redheaded woman's eyes. She caught Gertie's glance and blinked them away. 'I was just thinken,' she whispered when the singing was finished and the girls, Clytie among them, were filing off the stage, 'th boys come—one's on Saipan, one's in England now—when times was pretty good; but she was a little accident—come in 1931—Little Depression we used to call her. We hadn't had our place long, an we never did know where th next payment was comen frum—Ivan lost his job. But they was a job in a little restaurant—cooken—not much, but some leftovers was throwed in—an I hadda wean her.'

The redheaded woman's husband, a large man with blue eyes and scarred hands, squeezed her with the long arm around the back of her seat, and smiled at Gertie. 'Listen to her take all a credit. I hadda raise th kid.' And then to his wife, 'Recollect when you was worken how I'd . . .'

The principal came onto the platform. Gertie was silent, staring in front of her as if she saw and heard all that was said; but the bright lights made black spots swim before her eyes, and the heat and the closeness were worse than in her project kitchen.

She was glad when it was over and wanted to hurry away; but it was the way it had used to be back home after church, little knots of people talking, lingering, blocking her way; the girls gigglesome and gay in their white dresses, the boys stiff, with toothy grins in good new suits they would outgrow before high-school time in the fall.

Many knew the redheaded woman, and with her exchanged compliments of children. Two men whom Gertie did not know spoke to Clovis, and as she was standing, feeling sweaty and plagued because all around her people were talking and she knew no one, a voice she had heard before spoke out of a little knot of people, 'How do you do, Mrs Nevels. Aren't you proud to be the mother of such a smart, pretty girl?'

Gertie jumped with startlement, but found soon the owner of the voice, and smiled, and nodded and wished she could remember the teacher's name; someone who taught one subject to all the children. She forgot the woman when she saw a face she remembered—it was turned sideways to her now as it smiled up at a tall girl with tightly curled yellow hair. The other time it had had a handkerchief to its mouth to catch the tears it had no right to shed. She stared hard at it, and soon the owner turned. Then as if to answer her angry question of 'Why did you cry?' the woman said slowly, reluctantly, 'I'm Miss Huffacre.'

'You teach th first grade,' Gertie asked, the words coming out roughly, accusingly.

'Yes,' and now the other was able to smile. 'For forty-two years I've taught first graders.'

'What had she done?' Gertie asked, moving closer, and it was as if they were alone.

'Oh,' Miss Huffacre said, and there was sorrow, trouble in her voice, 'you didn't think she'd misbehaved when I sent for you.' She hesitated. 'She seemed unhappy—and was so still. She used to giggle and wiggle and have the best time. Oh, I don't mean she created a disturbance; she was always very quiet but—well, I used to look at her—and you know how the world is so much troubled—two of my boys in one week, neither nineteen—the battle of the Bulge—and you look at them and—well—wonder. Anyway she was so happy, so good to look at there in her own world. I've had others like her—always very bright children. Gradually, of course, they grow out of it—gradually. But all at once she seemed so unhappy, and was . . .'

'Like she'd lost something?' Gertie asked in a choked voice.

'Yes. When I sent the note I only wanted to ask if something . . .' She turned her head, for a girl was calling:

'Lookut, Miss Huffacre—a genuine orchid I got—lookut. It smells—it ain't paper.' Miss Huffacre sniffed the outthrust shoulder, smiled, as the girl said: 'Remember what a time we had? I never thought I'd learn to read, let alone graduate with a orchid.'

'And soon you'll graduate from high school,' Miss Huffacre said, adding, 'You girls sang beautifully.' She turned slowly back to Gertie, who had never left off staring down at her, an angry stare, and puzzled, too, with her brows pulled together in perplexity.

'How many in yer class?' she asked, her voice harsh.

'Forty-one of mornings; forty of afternoons.'

'Allus?' Gertie asked.

'Not always—part of the time I've had only the one class—but during the wars and afterwards, for a little while, there are more children.'

'An you don't teach em all year.'

Miss Huffacre tried to put some lightness into her voice, take some bleakness from the hurt eyes. 'No, as I often say, I am the beginning of the assembly. You know, I only teach them one term—beginning reading.'

Gertie shook her head violently, angrily. 'It ain't like a factory— not a bit—more like th sparrer bird.'

Clovis was pulling her, Miss Huffacre was looking troubled, but still Gertie spoke, yielding to Clovis as she turned. 'I'd think God would have a easier time watchen all th sparrers fall than you—with so many little youngens—thinken on one.'

31

It was near mid-July with a heat wave settled down before the Andersons' new home was ready; the gadget box, Mrs Anderson called it, for Homer after looking at a few other houses had settled on the house Mrs McKeckeran had found and recommended. Judy cried when Mrs Anderson, wearied with her last-minute chores of moving, came to get her from Gertie. 'She knows it's the end of one thing and the beginning of something else,' Mrs Anderson said, and Gertie thought she was going to cry.

They stood in Gertie's yard, bald spotted and dug by children, but dotted with the green of grass, and brightened by borders of flowers just beginning to bloom. Mrs Anderson's glance went slowly about the alley, which, as always for anything the least bit out of the ordinary such as a fight or a scout car's stopping, was crowded with watchers—more grownups than usual, and many like the children, barefoot and scantily clad against the heat, and all sleepy-eyed, for last night had been too hot for sleep in the low, unshaded bedrooms where the top halves of the windows were nailed shut.

Mrs Anderson looked once at scraggeldy-headed Wheateye dressed in an outgrown bathing suit, strawberries spilling from her cupped hands as she ran down the walk, then turned sharply away. 'I wish I'd looked sooner,' she said. 'This alley could keep a thousand artists busy a thousand years—and now there'll never be any time—it takes time to be a pillar of society.'

'You'll have more room, an mebbe—' Gertie began.

'Room? What do you think you can get in a modern brick house with a two-car garage in a good neighborhood for nineteen thousand—but we couldn't just couldn't go in any deeper—Homer has to have a good car.'

'But he's maken good money—an mebbe you'll learn to like it,' Gertie comforted.

Mrs Anderson slapped at a fly with a vicious swing. 'That's what I'm afraid of—and what she hopes—It won't be enough that I quit painting in the struggle to keep up with the neighbors—I must quit wanting to paint. And always,' she went on, her voice vicious as her hand slapping at the fly, 'she will be there, waiting to see if I will ever be anything but the perfect courtier's wife, but pretty certain that I shall be—that I will always cry, "See the emperor's new clothes," that I will always be afraid to try to give her secret away.'

'Mebbe she's kinda lonesome herself an wants tu be—kinda kind.'

'Kind? Her husband is a Flint vice president; and if God were lonesome he'd order somebody to talk to him. I'm not certain, but it—all this interest in an underling—is more like a bribe to keep shut. Say, I've intended to ask you: Homer was wondering—how is the man who was beaten, you know, by thugs? I imagine your husband knows him?'

Gertie's eyes on her were steady. 'My man don't know him—but seems like one a th youngens was readen in th paper—he lost one eye.'

'Oh.' She turned sharply away. Homer was calling her to come look over the place to see if anything had been forgotten; he had already looked but two pairs of eyes were better than one. He came and took Judy, and told Gertie good-bye, then lingered, waiting for his wife, his frowning glance fixed on the fence so long that Gertie felt ashamed of it, such a raggeldy, taggeldy piece of business it was with its strange shaped posts and crooked stringers.

'It ain't much, but it's better'n nothen,' she apologized, and added, hoping he would understand, 'I recken everybody wants a little piece a land fenced up an all their own.'

He pondered, then spoke quickly, for Mrs Anderson was hurrying toward the car. 'I wouldn't say that; not everybody. If people are hungry, that is quite hungry for a long time, they can be satisfied with food, even plain bread.'

They were gone and Mrs Schultz was laughing. 'They got out— maybe there's a chance for the rest of us.' But Mrs Daly sighed and shook her head, 'Pity du neighbors wot's gotta put up with Georgie.' Sophronie smiled as if a great burden were gone; but Mrs Bommarita was troubled for the future, wondering if it would be some family with half a dozen children and the parents given to drunken noise and fighting; while Enoch hoped there would be a lot of new children, none of whom knew the job-hunting game.

Gertie pulled a few weeds from the asters, and said nothing. The shrill voices of the children, rising all around her, made a buzzing in her ears, for the argument between her boys and the Meanwells on one side and the Dalys on the other about the tent they had been trying to build together in the corner formed by her fence and the Meanwell coalhouse, was starting up again. She saw that in their fussing and jarring they had got onto her side of the fence and trampled the petunias; she opened her mouth to protest, then shut it. What else was there for the boys to do; back home now Enoch would be at work and having a better time than he was now. There was a place for playing ball in one corner of the project, but it was across the through street, and the two times Enoch and the Meanwells had tried to play there, bigger boys had chased them away.

She squinched her eyes against the heat waves dancing on the garbage cans, shut her lips tightly against the gassy smell of a passing milk truck, but at last turned wearily back into the kitchen where a bleary-eyed, yellow-faced Clovis in nothing but his underpants sat sweating over a cup of coffee, and from the looks of his plate the only thing he'd touched.

She sighed over the wasted food; he ought to have told her he wasn't hungry; but he looked so nearly white-eyed and so disgusted with it she had no heart to chide him, and instead said: 'Honey, you've got tu git some sleep an rest. Why don't you an Whit an Miller all go off to a park an sleep like you done on them real hot days last week?'

He shook his head wearily. 'I cain't spare th gas an they cain't neither. An anyhow it warn't no picnic; they's allus about a million

481

others a tryen tu do th same thing; ever place else is jist about as noisy as this place; a little cooler mebbe, but in a halfway shady place th mosquiters is worse.'

Gertie wiped her sweat-dripping forehead, and wished for a city with many parks holding picnic places and trees for shade like the children had read about back home. Here, within walking distance and past many through streets, were a few little dusty, sun-baked playgrounds, but the closest park of any size was better than half an hour's drive away through heavy traffic. The children, especially the boys, were always begging Clovis to buy a black-market stamp and take them someplace: to the closest big park with trees; the zoo that was for free; or Belle Isle, a place in the river where a body could see boats go by, but so crowded on the two times that Clovis had taken them, a body could hardly find walking room let alone a bench or a picnic table. Gertie had gone on only one such excursion; the crowding, the cigarette stub, popsicle-wrapper-strewn-earth had depressed her as much as the hot drive through the noisy traffic, and if a body tried to sit a moment on the dirty earth under a bit of crowded shade, the mosquitoes settled in biting, buzzing swarms.

'Looks like,' Clovis was saying, lighting a cigarette, 'I'll have plenty a time for sleepen pretty soon.' He told then of a walkout in the paint department after more than twenty had passed out with the heat; not just the heat either: the ventilating system had gone bad and the guys said the place was full of fumes, so full that Bender had got the whole trim department to walk out in protest. The company hadn't fixed the ventilating system, mended it a little was all; everybody knew it would kill a man to work in such, but a damned steward had come through the parts place where he worked, and reminded them of their no-strike pledge, and said it was just Bender's talk had caused the walkout in the paint department. 'Like men passen out with th heat an th air full a paint spray had nothen to do with it,' Clovis commented bitterly, then added, 'That steward must be in company pay; we all oughta go out in sympathy.'

Gertie, gathering up his dishes, looked at him with surprise. 'But Clovis, you ain't hurten none—you been a sayen all th time th place where you work is cooler than this—and they's a war—What's the good—'

She was silenced by his blazing eyes. 'You're a thinken jist like old man Flint. Sure, I ain't a hurten; I work midnights; it's cooler then; an I ain't in that trim department. But it's like Bender says, If th union lets th company git by with all this, what'll we do when th war's over an times is mebbe kinda hard? In a union, yu gotta hang together.'

Gertie was silent, wishing she had not spoken; but more short pay checks when they were just getting caught up on their payments; she thought of the money in her pocket she had made from whittling and baby sitting—enough for Cassie's marker. She felt almost rich, and was able to act interested and pleased when Clovis, after a wary glance toward the screen door where children were so often congregated with inquisitive eyes and noses pushing against the screen, whispered, 'I got a surprise fer you, old woman.'

She followed him into the bedroom, after he had turned up the radio to drown the sounds he might make, and watched in silence while he took the contraption he had finished last night, when she was helping Mrs Anderson pack, and plugged it into the wall socket. She tried not to back away or show her hatred of its noise and ugliness when he set it on a chair, flicked a little lever, and bent above it smiling as he watched the busy little saw and listened to the motor. 'Now look,' he whispered, and showed her a piece of thin smooth board on which he had sketched a short-armed cross; he flicked the lever and the saw stopped; he put the board on the flat piece of steel, turned on the saw again, and by turning the board as the blade ate into the wood, he had in a moment a cross exactly to his knife markings.

He held it up for her to see, and whispered: 'Look at th time you'll save. We're goen to fix some other blades, an already I've got a thing to put in that'll bore holes in jumpen-jack dolls. When you learn to work it right, it'll cut any pattern you want—a Christ—a fox—anything; they'll all be flat, a course, but you can round em off with yer knife an they'll look genuine hand-carved, an'ul take less'n a fifth a th time. But,' he warned, 'you'll hafta be careful an

483

not saw a finger, an not let on to them Dalys what we're doen—it's againsa rules to use electricity in these gover'ment places fer anything but household use an they mightn't—'

He turned quickly to shut off the motor when there was a banging on the kitchen screen, followed at once by the opening of the door; but it was only Enoch and Amos come in to beg popsicle money, for a popsicle bell was ringing only two alleys away now. They both began clamoring for Clovis to run the saw for them so they could see the manner of its working. This time he drew a heart, and cut it quick as cloth with scissors. Enoch nodded in approval. 'I bet I could learn to run it,' he said.

Clovis considered, smiling, looking at first Gertie and then the boys. 'Tell you what, we'll start us a factory,' he said. 'Yer mom can be th pattern maker; I'll be toolmaker, tool-an-die man, an repairman; you, Enoch, can be machine operator; Clytie can run th trim department; an Amos—well, on jumpen-jack dolls, fer instance, he can be a 'sembly hand—run the strings through the holes.'

The boys laughed with pleasure. Enoch suggested that they put a sign over the bedroom door, 'Nevels' Wood-working Plant,' then at once wished it wasn't against the rules and they could put it over the kitchen door for everybody to see; only it would be better to put No. I after the name so that people passing by would think there was more than one Nevels plant.

Gertie let Enoch and Amos each have a nickel; it was so hot and maybe the chunk of colored ice would keep them still until Clovis could drop off to sleep. He had to use ear plugs now with the windows open; they cut the noise, he said, but their strangeness made it harder for him to go to sleep, and sometimes loud noises straining through gave him nightmares.

There was a little time of peace while the children sat in the ever narrowing band of shade by the western wall and sucked their ice. Gertie frowned a moment at the jig saw that Clovis had put on a hall shelf, then turned abruptly away, her hungry fingers opening the knife in her pocket. It had been so long, almost a week ago, and then seemed like she couldn't leave the fingers of the cupped hand. What did it hold? Was he just getting or just giving away? The answer was not in her head, but something for the knife to find, like the face buried in the wood.

The knife brought out a wrinkle in the knuckle joint of the little finger, but still she heard the crying of Mrs Schultz's baby, broken out with heat rash, like all the other babies. Gradually, however, the growing knuckle joint walled away the bedlam of children and machinery—even the shrill quarreling and screaming of a bunch of little girls playing house on Sophronie's steps, and the screeching whoops of a gang of older ones having a water fight in front of the building across from her.

She worked on, though the Miller radio played mountain music with a loud, nosey twanging that she hated; Mrs Schultz quarreled shrilly; and only a few feet from her front door, where the scraggeldy maple had finally died and the project office had unloaded sand in which the little ones were supposed to play, two mothers quarreled and seemed ready to fight over some trouble between their children. She glanced once toward the sand pile; most children got spanked if they dug there, since it was the favorite bathroom for all the alley cats and dogs and even some of the very small children; the older ones had tossed in rubble from the alleys and on the rubble had broken jars and bottles so that the place was unsafe for bare feet. Amos was not there, but in the house wall shade with Enoch. She started another wrinkle, and a child, nose pushed against the screen, said, 'Whatcha doen, lady?'

'Tryen to whittle out a finger,' she said, but the child, a little boy in nothing but a pair of blue jeans with the legs torn off high above the knees, continued to watch and suck ice cream on a stick; others joined him at times, and then drifted away. She heard soon the hesitant opening of the kitchen door, then bare feet on the linoleum; and looked behind her to see a small one in nothing but his underpants, looking about him in mystification—the rooms, the walls, the furniture were exactly like what he had always known, but still it was not home. Gertie smiled, and the toddler went away. Once, there came low giggles and whispers, and she looked up to see legs dangling from the roof edge, and went and pulled their owner, about the size of Amos, down. 'You'll fall an git hurt, an ruin th roof into th bargain,' she said, and went back to work.

A few moments later Wheateye came screeching enough to wake the dead, 'Miz Nevels, th milkman's horse has went to th bathroom inu next alley!' and Gertie, less for need of the manure than to quiet the child, got the scrub bucket and the little ash shovel and hurried down the hot alley and got the manure before Mr Bommerinkoff, one alley over, got it for his flower beds.

She had buried the manure by the hollyhocks, told a picture selling woman she had no money, told a black-robed nun, 'No,' when she came knocking, asking if anybody in the household had been baptized in the Catholic faith, and got back to the second knuckle of the little finger when she heard Enoch's outraged, angry voice: 'Naw, yu don't. I won't! It's all a great big lie.'

'Who do yu think you're calling liar, hillbilly?' a Daly voice asked.

'Don'tcha be a hitten that kid.' Gilbert Meanwell's command was mixed in with the sound of a slap, followed by a scuffle.

Then all was drowned in Victor's angry roar, 'I gotta sleep.'

A moment later Enoch came banging through the screen door, red-faced and angry, forgetting to tiptoe, and keep his voice low. 'Mom, ain't it all a lie that less'n you wanta burn ferever in hell yu gotta have a priest to pray yer sins away?'

Gertie considered, her knife poised above the wood. Enoch had brought so many questions home, especially since school was out and he spent more time in the alleys; there'd been the words she didn't know, like 'wop' and 'kike' and 'shine' and 'limey'; and why did big Chris Daly say hillbillies worshiped rattlesnakes? He'd never known anybody who worshiped rattlesnakes, and was it the truth that the public schools were never any good, with most of their teachers bad women?

Now, while her mind thumbed through Christ's words, Enoch rushed on with other questions: 'Mom, ain't it a lie that all Protestant preachers ain't no good, and that priests never does bad?'

'Hush, you'll wake yer daddy,' she said. 'I don't know all th answers, but we both know what John said: "Whosoever believeth on him should not perish, but have eternal life." Jesus would hate tu see you youngens a fussen an a jarren around so. I guess, mebbe, they is some mean preachers, but—' She thought of

486

Samuel and now the people at the big church where the children, and even Clovis sometimes, went; they were kind to her own. 'They's good preachers, real good, like they's good priests an bad, too. But don't go arguen; talk about somethen else.' What was it she had said to Clovis, years ago it seemed like now? 'Spread the word,' she had said. 'Keep shut,' he had said. She looked longingly toward the unfinished finger. 'We've all got to live together,' she said.

Enoch went away, and there was a moment's peace, though the knife was by now uncertain in the wood. Now and then Gertie glanced through the door, knowing as she looked that she would see only bare, sun-baked earth, the cardboard shedding walls of the next building, and above these the black roofs where the heat waves danced and trembled until the steel-mill towers and the telephone poles were twisted and dancing like things seen under water. Today, as on other heat-shimmering days, her eyes, hemmed in by the glaring closeness, cried for long looks across green hills. If for just one minute her eyes could go looking through long blue distances, and not always have to look at things so close they seemed behind her eyes! Once she tried looking at the sky, but it was low-hanging and pale, like a tin roof holding the heat down; and so from time to time she shut her eyes tightly; blackness, even blackness broken by the sights that lived eternally behind her lids, was better than the blinding glare of the dancing heat waves.

She was about ready to give up; sweat kept running into her eyes and oozing from her hand onto the knife, when through the kitchen door behind her she heard Mr Daly speaking loudly, as if he wanted all the alley to hear. 'Listen, yu kids; now I'm not mad, see. I know youse don't know no better. Yu public schools an parents an preachers dey don't teach yu no Americanism. Don'tcha know it's un-American tu tell lies an persecute minority groups? Youse oughta be ashamed telling mu boys they's bad priests and tucken like the Church could be wrong. Don'tcha know that's th way communists talk? But youse can't help it—youse has been listening—youse fadders ain't too careful a du company.'

'Oh, yeah?' Gilbert cried. 'What'sa matter with mu pop's friends?'

'Yu'll find out, m'lad. Justyu wait till Joseph Daly goes tudu red squad. I know a lot. See?'

'Go some'eres else to crap,' Gilbert jeered. 'Our dads is sleepen. Victor run us away frum t'other side; now yu gotta come yellen, an we'll git run away frum this tent shade—yu kids gotta keep their mouths shut if yu don't want um to hear th truth.'

'Du truth,' Mr Daly roared, angry now. 'An wot is du truth? Dey's somepun in mu house yu oughta read—if yu'd learned tu read in yu public schools. It'sa great big scrapbook wot Maggie helped me make; an it's nutten but u truth; du little bit a truth wot comes out in u papers about u doings u yu Protestant ministers; headlines, I got; everthin—drunkenness, stealing, traffic violation, ignorance, immorality, killing people wit rattlesnakes; everthin. An I've got enough clippings futu make two books,' he went on, the same relish in his voice as when he had talked to Reuben, 'all about rottenness in u public schools; du papers is full a it; parents allatime complaining du kids learn nutten; teachers gitten drunk. Yu tink I got mu education inu public school? Yu betcha life I didn't; du good sisters, dey taught me everthin I know, see.'

Gertie had by now come into her kitchen, but as she had no wish to let Mr Daly see her she stood listening behind the half-open inner door. There was a moment's silence, and she thought with relief that he had gone; but, peeping, she saw that he had only stopped to get new wind and wipe sweat from his face and neck. Then, as if he felt her eyes upon him, he looked at her door as he resumed:

'An when anybody tried tu tell me or mine that Protestant preachers an public schools is fit fu decent, God-fearing Americans, I tells um, "Well, I never say nothing bad about nobody, butcha oughta read u papers an listen to Father Moneyhan."' He raised his voice. 'How many clippings yu tink I got about priests that breaks u law, or parochial schools wot ain't no good, or criminals wot has graduated from parochial schools? Not one. Yu can read u Detroit papers year in an year out, an yu can't find one priest, one good sister, wot's done wrong; not one com—'

'Oh, yeah?' Gilbert interrupted, sticking his head out of the play tent. 'G'wan; I'll bet—'

He was silent when Sophronie, her voice low and worried, called: 'Shut up, Gilbert. You uns'ull be a fighten.'

Mr Daly smiled. 'See, yu own mudder knows youse is a liar.' He went back to lounge in the shade by his western wall, and Gertie, watching, thought he smiled to himself like one tasting victory; she had kept silent; she had not stood up for the boys; Enoch must have repeated what she had said to him, and because of his belief in her he and the others were called names.

She turned to the block of wood in the other room, but three children stood with their noses pressed against the front screen door. One, seeing her, called, 'Wot's he gonna do?'

'Give it back,' she said, and grabbed her old blue split bonnet and fled to Victor's part of the yard at the end of the unit. A train passed, and as always she trembled at the sound, but at least she was out of sight of Mr Daly. Maybe it was about him the child had asked, not the man in the block of wood. She was pulling weeds out of the moss-rose bed, the seed of which she had brought from home, when Enoch came, and she saw that his lips were quivering.

'It ain't th truth, what that ole Daly says, is it, Mom?'

'Law, no,' she said.

'But—it's th truth that they ain't no mean priests inu papers, an that th good sisters never does bad things like some school teachers, an that they ain't no criminals ever graduates frum parochial schools. If it ain't th truth why—'

She bent above the flowers to escape his glance; his eyes were like Reuben's eyes—they wouldn't believe the way Cassie's eyes had believed. 'Why didn'tcha talk back to him, Mom?' he was asking; and after a moment's silent waiting for her answer, went on, his voice yearning, 'I wisht I could find a piece, jist one little piece in u paper, about a bad priest er somethen.'

'You won't,' she said, 'an if you did it wouldn't make you no better. You don't want to be like that man, all th time throwen off on people.'

'Sure,' Enoch said, 'then he wouldn't throw off on us an Pop's friends. Mom, Gilbert said it was that tool-and-die man ole Daly was throwen off on, an that he has been up to some kind a meanness; Sophronie don't want him to come visiten their house no more. Gilbert said she'd have a fit if she knowed he was comen around so much.'

'You must a heared Gilbert wrong,' Gertie said. 'Sophronie herself told me onct he'd allus been good to them; he ain't got no family.'

'Oh, yes he has,' Enoch said. 'Sorta. He hadda wife an two kids; but they started a tryen to strike out at old man Flint's big place an he got th offer a bein a plant guard; but he wouldn't take it er be no scab; but his wife, she wasn't much; when they got a little hard run she upt an left him, went back to her own people in Pennsylvania. He's allus sent money fer th kids, though, Gilbert said. But Gilbert wouldn't say what he'd done, th meanness. What's he done, Mom?'

'Nothen,' Gertie said. 'Run an play now—we'll be a waken Victor.'

'Victor's gotta leave,' Enoch said. 'Mr Daly, he went up to th office—yu know, people without families, they ain't allowed to live inu project—an Mr Daly, he told that project manager, they're good friends, that Victor didn't have no wife now an—'

'I have, too, gotta a wife,' and Victor, his blue eyes blazing, a new burn on one cheekbone a livid red, glared at them from his living-room window

Enoch scuttled away, and Gertie flushed and bent low among the flowers; she ought to have known that in the heat and the children he would be trying to sleep in the living room with its fenced-off northern wall. She pulled weeds from white flowers by the house wall whose names she did not know; many so trampled by the children their stems lay on the ground, but still they opened their little spires of pure white bloom above the cindery earth. She wished she could call such valiant creatures by name, just as she wished she could somehow help Victor. She straightened at last and stood close to the window and found his glance still upon her. She thought of Samson with his hair cut off, but only said: 'Whyn't you go tu yer mother's long enough tu git a good sleep? I've heared she's got a big house in a big yard; it ud be cooler an quiet, too.'

'Max might come while I was gone,' he said.

'But she— You could leave a note with me,' she said, but he seemed not to have heard, and she went back to the weeding of the flowers. There was still a narrow band of shade by the northern wall, but the heat rising up from the parking lot between the fence and the big alley was like air from a bake oven, and the noise worse than within doors.

She was just turning toward her door, when she stopped, troubled by the uproar of a man's screaming, children's crying, and a woman's hysterical scoldings that came from the unit across from Victor's. She'd never got acquainted with the people except for chance meetings in the alley; the woman, young, with three youngens, none big enough to wander in the alley or play with her own, had been living there, she thought, since the middle of winter. The man had come only lately, and of him she had heard Mrs Bommarita talk in whispers, and Mrs Daly sigh with pity; a discharged soldier—they'd ought to have kept him in the hospital longer, Mrs Daly had said, for he was worse than wounded, and Mrs Bommarita had frowned and tapped her head. 'An we gotta have th likes a him around,' she had said.

Gertie now saw the girl-like mother come out the kitchen door, carrying one baby, and dragging another about a year old by the hand. They went to the northern end and sat on the ground amid weeds and broken bottles and rusty tin cans, the woman putting her back against the northern wall, drawing her feet up to make her body fit the narrow band of shade. She rocked her body back and forth and tried to quiet the baby, but it cried, and the other one with her cried; the man roared again from the house, something fell on the floor; then the child still in the house began a shrill, frightened screaming. Gertie, glancing quickly from the corners of her eyes, saw that the woman was crying too, her tears falling on the baby, naked save for a diaper and red with heat rash.

She took her knife and cut a fair-sized bunch of flowers, and risking Mr Daly's curious glances she went around and through her gate and across the alley. 'Hold um up in front a you,' she said, 'an they'll shut out th sight a that parken lot an th railroad fence, an mebbe you can think it's cooler.'

'Thanks,' the girl said, reaching for the flowers. 'I ain't never got time to notice the heat; it'sa kids it's hard on.' But she sniffed the flowers before she waved them by the babies, and even smiled a little, though the tears on her cheeks were hardly dry. 'I kinda git a kick looking at them flowers you've got—an grass,' she said, her voice still quivery. 'I don't know nothen about such, an mu kids don't leave me a minnit's time, but someday—mu husband's not been home long outa th army—I'm gonna fence us up a little place; that is, when he gits him a job. It goes hard on a soldier when—that is—they ain't a thing wrong with him, honest, but his discharge wasn't medical.' All at once she began crying again; Gertie lingered a moment longer; she wanted to say something, maybe advise her to try baking soda on the baby's heat rash, but the man roared out again, and Gertie went home.

Like Victor, the weeping girl had made her think of Max and the letter, come three days ago, waiting, hidden, for her to read again and answer. She managed to get her letter finished just as the boys came in for lunch, though there was hardly time enough to seal and stamp it, and shove it down into her apron pocket. Sometime late in the long twilight she would sneak off to the mailbox two blocks away on the through street.

It was while they were eating lunch that Enoch suggested they all go to the scrap-wood place and hunt boards good enough to make dolls and crosses on the jig saw. Gertie hesitated; she didn't think she'd ever use the ugly little thing; it was like a monster from some fairy tale that, instead of grinding salt, spewed ugliness into the world. But Enoch insisted; they could take the shortcut through the vacant land, he said; it would be cool by the pools of water and through the little trees.

'Brush and scummy ponds, not trees an pools, son,' Gertie corrected him, but couldn't make her voice scornful, and hurried through the dishes.

She put on a clean apron, her sunbonnet, and taking the red wagon went out into the alley, which seemed even hotter than within doors. She found herself at once in a great gang of running children, all, she gathered, on the way to a kind of playground in a corner of the project where the steel mill and railroad fences came

492

together. She hurried on through the dancing heat waves, worried as always when Amos was out of sight.

She learned after a little questioning that Amos was with Enoch, and that all the running was to see a drunk man, in nothing but a ragged pair of shorts, sound asleep in the full sun by the chinning bar. There was a good chance, the children said, the cops might come and there would be a fight.

Gertie walked more slowly, wondering if the man were sick or dead; he would be if he lay for long half naked in the sun. The heat of the shadeless alleys was beginning to make her head whirl, and when she passed the unit where the woman with the cactus lived she hesitated, looking wistfully toward the narrow band of eastward-creeping shadow on the woman's stoop. The cactus was there, but the door was closed, and while Gertie walked slowly past, watching the door, hoping it would open, a woman feeding a baby on the next stoop explained: 'She hadda go to du hospital. Her man, his millen machine blowed up—hit um onu head.'

'I hope he ain't bad hurt,' Gertie said, and walked on to meet soon a disappointed Enoch; some kid had laid ice cubes on the man and he'd got up and walked off; his shorts had been so torn a body could see 'his you-know-what,' and he couldn't walk straight; but now the cops wouldn't come like they'd done last week for the man two alleys over, who'd been stretched crosswise of the road.

The three of them went on down the alley by the railroad tracks. Amos kept lagging behind to stare at the new board; he still cried out in his sleep at times, and Gertie had learned without ever asking that he had been in the crowd that had seen Cassie. She was glad that when they reached the vacant land he soon found a skinny, big-eyed frog, and laughed and followed it across piles of rusty tin cans and rotting papers until it jumped into a puddle of black swamp water.

The mosquitoes were bad and so were the flies, and the whole place smelled like a garbage can on a hot day when the collectors are a week overdue, but Gertie gathered a bouquet of tall-growing red flowers that grew by an evil-smelling pool of black water, and then she stood a while under the smoke-blighted, cinder-battered leaves

493

of a cottonwood sprout; if she kind of shut her eyes and forgot the smell, it was a little like having a whole tree between her and the sky; and save for her own children the place was still of humankind.

The children had used to sneak away and come here as late as lilac-blooming time, tempted by the frogs and the flowers and the aloneness, but lately even the big bold boys such as Francis Daly seldom came. Men, sometimes with their britches only part way down, but often naked, had chased children; one had caught a little girl and hurt her badly, but the cops had never found him.

Rested somewhat by the stillness and the leaves above her head, and the wild flowers already wilting in her hand, Gertie, with the boys pulling the wagon behind her, went on to the scrap-wood place; a trip which, although she had already taken it three times hunting wood for whittling and the fence, she still dreaded. The owner of the place was a squat, surly-seeming man who almost never spoke; in fact there had been for a time in the alley wonderings as to what language he did speak. Victor had tried him in Polish and scraps of Hungarian; Mrs Zola from the next alley had used French; Mrs Bommarita had tried Italian; Clytie had told of how the mother of one of her girl friends had tried him with Russian. The most that anybody ever got from him was a shrug and a stare until Gertie came one day carrying the Josiah basket; and the man had looked at it, touched its fat sides, and almost smiled as he said, 'Oak splints.' But when, hoping he was from someplace at least close to back home, she had tried to talk with him, he had acted like Joe when Mrs Anderson asked him questions.

Today the man was silent, watching from his little shed that held a power saw, as they wandered through the mountains of scrap wood and discarded furniture and packing cases from the war plants. He watched Enoch in particular, but turned away like one not interested when Enoch, after some looking about, came running to his mother, though plainly the child's face betrayed the joy of a great discovery. He'd found away over behind that mountain of old factory work benches, some big, box-like things that he was certain were solid maple wood under the dark green paint.

'But Mom,' he whispered, 'don't let on yu want um bad. That man ud put th price up; lemme do it,' and he ran ahead of her to the man, his face blank of everything but surliness as he listened to Enoch's quick talk. 'Mister, I'm a Cub Scout, see—a little Boy Scout, yu know; and I wanta little scrap wood, cheap, futa build a little house—den house, yu know—so's couldn't yu give me some-then ain't much good? They's some old green boxes—no good atall, all smashed up an tore apart. Couldn't I have some to build us a little den house? They ain't fitten fer nothen an—'

'Son,' Gertie began, unable to hold her conniving silence longer.

'Why, Mom,' Enoch spoke with conviction, 'they're all full a nail holes an—well, kinda splintered, yu know,' and he looked at her, his face smooth as half melted butter, then turned and ran toward the spot to which he had pointed.

The man looked after him an instant, then turned to Gertie. 'Smart kid, yu got. Kindlen wood he bought off me—sold it fer fence pickuts.' He waved toward a pile of wood topped by a sign. 'No more,' he said.

Gertie considered the sign, *Fence Pickuts Cheep 10¢ a Piece*. It was the same kindling wood they had bought last winter, paying twenty-five cents for the red wagon heaped full—that much now would be a dollar—worth more now because the people needed them to build little fences that would hold babies out of the alleys or dogs away from flower beds. She remembered now that seemed like back when she was sick, Enoch had had a lot of money to spend on the fence and that he had been gone a lot with the wagon. 'But you buy em fer scrap still,' she said, looking hard at the man, 'an th youngen thought it up hissef.'

He smiled and shook his head. 'I don't buy nothen; I git paid fu trucken u stuff outa du plants; you gotta git it out—fire laws.' He squinted one eye at the wagon, and said: 'That wagon full a whatcha kid wants—one dollar. S'good wood—gover'mint grain bins—solid maple, boards morticed, glued; corners screwed. Splintered? Naw.' He smiled faintly. 'Maple fudu army horses—cardboard fudu gover'mint workers—u wagon load, one dollar. An I don't loan hammers er screwdrivers.'

Gertie nodded, smiling a little. 'Okay,' she said, and took the wagon to the pile. He came to watch, and his face continued expres-sionless as she after a survey of the grain bins, which were in truth of

495

solid maple, or morticed and glued boards, screwed at the corners, but so big that one would have more than filled the wagon, took her knife; and using the little blade loosened screws until the boys could turn them with their fingers. The boards being truly sawed and straightly seasoned, stacked well. She continued to take the boxes apart until they were stacked on the wagon as high as Amos's head, stopping then only because she was afraid the wagon might break down.

They were hardly off the through street before children came flocking around to know why they hauled so much kindling wood in the summertime; and Gertie, though she hated herself, kept silent when Enoch explained that they had just happened to find a good bargain in boards that his mother liked to keep handy to mend the fence or make 'hand-carved' dolls. Once home, Enoch couldn't wait to try out the jig saw on the new boards, and kept teasing Gertie to draw some pattern—a doll, a chicken, or a Christ, anything to try out the jig saw.

Gertie, more for amusement than anything, carried the scissors, some newspapers, and a pencil out to the kitchen stoop, shaded now in the late afternoon. There, with a slab of government grain bin across her knees, she set to work on a pattern, but at once a child came begging to borrow the scissors, another wanted the pencil, and one, a small stranger, pulled and tore the newspapers until she must send Enoch for more. All the while there were at least a dozen bigger ones, barefooted, hair plastered, dripping from play with the hose, swarming round her, asking questions, trampling the flowers, jiggling her hands, her knees, their hot wriggling bodies pressed against her shoulders when they tried to see what it was she did; for an instant the longing for silence and aloneness made her forget what it was she had tried to do.

She could think only of what she would do after supper, when there were no delivery trucks and few cars about so that the children could play in the alleys, with less danger; she would then walk up to Cassie, a short way on up the through street and across another railroad. She would be alone, but even then there would be people, the strange people who ever added to her loneliness, for the living crowded round the ever more crowded dead.

496

She roused; somewhere a child cried, a lonesome cry, frightened; maybe another lost one; lost children were always wandering by her door. She saw him then, all alone on her coalhouse roof, a fat, white-headed, black-eyed child, his sun-bleached hair so much lighter than the rest of his fat sunburned body that in spite of his weeping he made her feel that a jumping-jack doll patterned after him would make a baby laugh.

She sent Enoch and Mike Turbovitch away with him to find his home, which Mike was certain was four alleys over, then went to work on a pattern fashioned in his likeness, trying as she worked to answer at least a few of the questions. 'Whatcha gonna do? Yu gonna whittle?' 'Lemme see yu knife. Yu gonna make a cross?' while somewhere a little boy wailed, 'Please, lady, lemme go tuyu bathroom. I just gotta.'

Clovis gave up trying to sleep, for with the sun beating in from the west the house was like a bake oven, and he like most of the other night workers was covered with sweat and bleary-eyed. He tried lolling on a pallet in the shade of the house wall, but the children, the noise, the flies, and mosquitoes drove him within doors. He lingered behind the screen door and watched her attempts at pattern making, reminding her there was no need for a lot of pieces; joints at the knees and elbows maybe, and even the waist, but no need to make a floppy head and hands as in the ones she had whittled; oh, yes, and she mustn't make a lot of little fingers, for the saw wasn't fine enough for such work. He said no more, for Enoch, returned from taking the child home, made a great hissing, and Clovis remembered he mustn't speak of the saw before the children.

She'd wanted to work more on the pattern; it didn't look a bit like the child, but Enoch in his eagerness rushed with it to Clovis for sawing when she had to stop work to get supper. Clovis took the saw and wood into the bedroom, turned up the radio until recordings of Bing Nolan flooded the alley. Bing Nolan was still not finished when Enoch, with Clovis behind him, came with the doll, sawed, bored with holes, strung, and jumping on a shoestring.

Gertie cried out at its ugliness, but when she saw how hurt Clovis was by her hard words she tried to make him feel better. 'When I

497

git his face an his hands an his body kinda whittled out, he won't look so bad.'

'Law, Law, Gert,' Clovis said, too pleased that the contraption had worked to be real quarrelsome, 'you jist want somethen you can make ina hurry an sell cheap; they could be money in sich. Sell em, say, around Christmas; that hand carven takes too long ever to make much; I'd say about all this needs is to git that ole paint off an put on some more—real bright.'

'Paint?' Gertie cried. 'Cover up that pretty wood?' and she put the forkful of salmon salad she had lifted to her mouth back onto her plate.

Nobody noticed. At mention of the word 'paint,' Enoch had gone into an animated discussion with Clovis on the various colors of paint they would buy and use. Then Clovis remembered they couldn't get paint at the grocery store and it would take cash. 'I can mebbe make some more money pretty soon—if I can think up somethen like th pickets; but I bet Mom's got a little cash,' Enoch said.

'Mebbe,' Gertie answered, 'they'll be a little bit left frum Cassie's marker.'

A silence fell on them all, and Enoch spread his elbows on the table as if noticing that, from having once been crowded, there was a whole side for each tonight; but he would, by widening himself, hide the emptiness from his mother. All were glad when Clytie came, running up the steps, pleased because she'd earned four dollars baby sitting for a woman whose little boy, in the hospital with rheumatic fever, was so sick the nurses let her stay with him all day. Clytie was full of talk about the home, a private in the same neighborhood as Iva Dean's and with the prettiest yard. The woman had given her a great bunch of blue delphinium and red columbine, and Clytie before she sat down fixed a bouquet for the kitchen table.

Amos complained that it took up too much room, and Clytie chided him, 'Yu need flowers worse in a little ole smelly place like this than in a big pretty place; that's what Mrs Schultz says.' She turned to her mother. 'Mom, it's too late now, but next year could'ntcha fix up some window boxes like Mrs Schultz; it keeps u flowers away frum u kids. An when her window's open it's like haven um right inu house.'

Gertie nodded. 'I been thinken on it.' She added, smiling a little: 'Mebbe I'll have a garden. They's a woman two alleys over's got little tiny onions.'

'Chives,' Clytie corrected.

'An some lettuce an some curledy stuff.'

'Parsley,' Clytie explained. 'But still, I wanna put th garden in front u th bathroom an flowers fer th kitchen.'

'An where'll we have th corn crop?' Clovis asked, smiling in spite of the sweat running into his eyes.

'Under th west winder so's it'll shade us,' Enoch said, and they all laughed a little.

32

The sticky heat wore on, and tempers grew even shorter. Riot weather, Mr Schultz the fireman called it; for with most people unable to sleep or even stay in their stifling, overcrowded homes, streets and parks, like the alleys, were continually crowded with weary, sleepy, trigger-tempered men, women, and children. Quarrels, and even fights, were constantly flaring up between the grownups as well as the children. Gertie's own boys quarreled, cried, and fought; more than one mother screeched at her in hysterical scolding for some wrongdoing of her children, usually about some little thing that in a cooler, calmer time would have passed unnoticed.

Still, Gertie, like many of the others, minded the heat, the fights, the never ceasing noise of the children less than the silence of the forever patrolling policemen who in the 'riot weather' watched the people more closely. They drove more slowly and more often through the alleys now, never speaking, not even nodding to any one save Mr Daly and Casimir the iceman; but always watching, hunting with their hard, unsmiling eyes.

Late one hot afternoon, when all the children were in the alleys, two cops in a scout car, patrolling an alley not far from Gertie's, had to stop the car so that one could get out and move a tricycle left in the middle of the alley. The cop in his anger hurled the toy over a fence; it landed in a marigold bed, and barely missed a baby in a pen, or so all who saw it said; two women—the tricycle owner and the baby's mother—rushed from their stoops and bawled out the cops. The racket had caused a small dog, a little harmless, flop-eared thing that Gertie had fed more times than one, to come barking from still another unit. The dog had been so noisy and so little that the children, coming in an ever growing swarm, had laughed to see it take the part of the women against the big, surly cops.

In front of the laughing children, one of the cops had fired three shots into the dog, but by then so many children had gathered he wouldn't shoot any more; a vicious dog, both cops had answered to the enraged and sorrowful outcries. They had driven away, and left the dog to die all through the long hot afternoon; it had at first run round and round, dragging its fly-covered intestines and spreading blood, lying still only when its legs could no longer hold it up—but always it had whined and cried. And all around were the watching children, many crying like the dying dog; others cursing the cops, the black words flying up in loud boldness, the speakers knowing that no mother would chide now for dirty talk.

Nobody had had the heart to kill the little dog in front of the children; and as always, in the crowding and the heat, it was the children who got hurt the worst. In the heat everybody fussed at them; nobody wanted a gang of kids close by with a ball to break windows or a hose to wet babies, and no matter what they did their noise was always awakening babies and nightshift workers.

Gertie grew to look forward to the long twilights, when there was usually a bit of coolness outside; and during the lingering half-darkness, when there were no delivery trucks and fewer passing cars, the children played more freely. All, even big girls like Clytie and Maggie, joined in great games of hide and seek or kick the can, while their elders, with the babies, sat on the stoop steps or, like Gertie, worked among their flowers.

The children's tumult of calling and laughter drowned all other sounds but those of the trains and the loudest airplanes, dying only after the long twilights had thickened into darkness, and hurrying mothers and fathers with worried voices had gone up and down the alleys calling—Mary, Joseph, Rudolph, Casimir, Rita, Teddy, Herman, Josephine, Jesse, Sharon, David, Julius, Geraldine, Zigmund, Waleria, Theresa, Emil, and a Zygmunt forever answering from the next alley on.

It was Zygmunt's mother who, one twilight when Gertie was watering the asters, lingered after listening to the answer of her son, and said, with a little headshake, 'Ain't ut awful, dut atom bomb?'

Gertie nodded, vaguely remembering family talk of news on the radio and in the paper; but in spite of the bomb and the heat and the swarming children and the watching policemen, she'd been lost for most of the day in the block of wood. She was working now on the empty hand, the one held palm downward above the other; the slow cogitations on how the fingers of the empty hand should be, followed her always, and were with her now among the flowers. She roused enough at last to wonder, but the woman had gone on, hunting her child.

A few minutes later Wheateye stood on the coalshed and took a paper sack of water, colored red and mixed with Jell-O to make it stick, and dropped it on a little Miller's head; and when he ran screaming home, uncertain himself that the gooey red stuff streaming over him wasn't blood, Wheateye called after him: 'Don't cry, honey; don't cry. You've been hit by u atom bomb.'

Gilbert, pulling the Schultz baby in an orange crate, sneered, 'When yu've been hit by u atom bomb, silly, yu don't cry.'

But Enoch, swinging on the wire that braced the telephone pole, thought differently. 'Why, yu know they'd be some wot cried. I figger that ole bomb jist kills th ones real close right away; them on u edge gits bad burnt an crawls around awhile—Mom, recollect back home when we'd git rid a th tater bugs by knocken um off into a can with coal oil in it, then when we'd git a lot we'd drop a lighted paper inu can? You allus wanted u big fire an burn em all up right quick; but no matter how big a fire we'd have they'd be some that'd jist git scorched, an they'd crawl like crazy ever which away till they died. They'd be bad swinged, but they couldn't die—not right away. Now, I figger them Japs around u atom bomb is kinda like them bugs.'

'Mebbe so,' Gertie said, and though she had meant to water Victor's flowers she shut off the hose and went to the block of wood.

There was another atom bomb; then a few days later the train bells rang again and the car horns blew for the ending of the war. Gertie was sitting on her stoop taking the old paint off the leg of a

502

jumping-jack doll sawed from a piece of government grain bin; she paused a moment, startled by the noise, then, understanding, she tried to work more swiftly. She'd need dolls to sell, now; Clovis most likely wouldn't have a job tonight; but job or no, the hands would still come reaching, this week, next week, and all the weeks after. The Tipton Place was waiting still. If only she had stayed and held out against her mother for these few months only, Clovis would be coming back to them—back to all of them—Cassie maybe the first to go running to meet him, with Reuben as always lagging behind, but even he, hurrying a little, to see the new truck, a good secondhand truck, paid for with all the money they'd saved; and the farm all their own, and—

She could not be still, and remembering only to call Amos, she walked blindly through the alleys, the sawed doll's leg gripped in her sweaty hand. She walked a long time, took many turnings, and seldom answered the children. 'Yu maken a doll, Lady?' 'Some time, Lady, make me a horsy.' 'Yu gotcha man finished, Lady?'

Many grownups spoke to her. A few said: 'Well, wotta yu know? It's over,' and often they mentioned by name some friend or kin who would be home; others sighed, and also spoke a name, but said, 'It come too late for him.' Most, however, had thought only for the future, asking, 'Recken everting'ull shut down now?' or, 'When u soldiers all come back tudu rightful jobs, somebody's gonna be laid off.' The woman with the cactus, her husband behind her on the stoop, bandages still on his eyes, said, 'I don't guess a woman can ever find a job, now'; and in her voice, as in all the other voices, Gertie could hear no rejoicing, no lifting of the heart that all the planned killing and wounding of men were finished. Rather it was as if the people had lived on blood, and now that the bleeding was ended, they were worried about their future food.

Dust and heat and weariness turned her homeward at last. As she went into her own alley she saw a little knot of women congregated by her gate, and walking on, she heard Mrs Daly's shrill but troubled whisper, 'Don't youse be laughing and carrying on; it'll make her feel worse.'

Gertie hesitated, stiffened; she had ever hated pity; she didn't want it now—let them be joyful; it could not darken her sorrow.

She went slowly on up to the women as Mrs Schultz, some sewing in her hands, one foot moving the carriage with the whimpering baby, said: 'Butcha know she's glad it's over; things will maybe get cheaper now and a down payment won't have to be so big on a house—and won't they let her go home now? I've heard they had a place in California.'

'No, I live in—' Gertie was beginning, when Mrs Daly turned to her.

'I wonder,' the little woman said, 'wouldju mind to give me some flowers—a bouquet—fu her?' and she jerked her head backward toward the unit next her own where Mrs Saito lived.

'But wouldn't they make it—well, you know, seem like a funeral—flowers?' Mrs Schultz asked, whispering like the others.

Mrs Daly firmly shook her head. 'I tink she'd like um. Her kid said something once about flowers back home in California.'

Mrs Schultz looked at her baby, and gave a little shiver. 'I wonder if her people—got the bomb, or was she just—well, crying for them all.'

'Watsa difference?' Mrs Daly asked. 'T'other night when u first bomb fell, an I wasn't right certain her was crying—that is, I wasn't certain right away—I got tu thinking—that is, when I was certain. I ain't never seen mu mudder's country, onie what she'd tell to me, but—'

Mrs Schultz nodded. 'I don't remember—my older sister used to tell me: my mother could speak nothing but German, and in the First World War it was dangerous to speak German on the street—and she had so many cousins on the other side—she used to hide and cry.'

Mrs Daly sighed, 'Yu gotta realize that it ain't like them Japs was good white Christians; as Mr Daly says, them Japs is pretty near as bad as them communist Russians—but,' and she looked about her and spoke softly, guiltily, as if her words were treason, 'yu still gotta say, people is people. Why them Japs lives something like this,' and she waved her hand over the flowers, the low houses, the child-flooded alleys, the babies, 'all crowded up tuged-der inu towns; little cardboard houses kinda like what we've got; and maybe lotsa—you know—kids.'

Gertie had long since opened her knife and turned toward the flower beds, not now too filled with bloom, for when a passing child begged for a flower or even a bouquet she usually gave it. Following Mrs Schultz's suggestion of 'not too much white,' she collected the brightest of her zinnias, marigolds, and cosmos; and when it was finished the women all agreed it was the prettiest bouquet that had ever come from her yard.

Mrs Daly, after first thinking up words for offering the flowers so that she would not make Mrs Saito think she had heard her crying, hurried to her neighbor's door, while the others scattered to their stoops and tried not to act like women watching as Mrs Daly knocked and with much nodding and smiling gave the flowers. They turned away, satisfied, when, after a weakish headshake, Mrs Daly disappeared into Mrs Saito's kitchen.

That evening the children played less in the twilight, but stood about and listened to little groups of men and women talk in low, troubled voices. Many, like Clovis and Whit, were worried about layoffs through the changeover, followed by more layoffs for strikes, model changes, inventory, walkouts, and—the worst time of all, as Whit said—'plain hard times when cars don't sell.'

Miller, the steel worker, was unworried, for the steel mill would have no changeover, but of them all, only he planned to go back home. 'I'm stayen jist till we use up Nancy's unemployment insurance,' he said. 'She'll git laid off; that little jigger she's been a spot welden steady fer three years now won't be needed no more with th war over.'

'You can mebbe work overtime a heap an save some more while she's a drawen it,' Whit pointed out. 'They've gotta have steel fer them new cars everbody's wanten. You're lucky, man, a goen back home with all that money saved.'

Miller nodded. 'Ain't it th truth? Jist about ever cent my wife made, we saved, an some a my overtime pay. But if they hadn't been no nursery school or she'd a been caught with another kid er I'd had a accident in th steel mill, we'd a been stuck here fer th rest a our lives, mebbe never gitten ahead enough fer a down payment on a house. It took my regular wages an most a th overtime jist fer liven; we did swap in our old car on one a little younger, but that's all. An all that steel-mill money went,' and he stood, a chunky man with wide brown eyes, as if overcome by surprise, only now realizing the money was gone.

'Leave it tudu women. They can make a man's money go,' Mr Daly, who had been forecasting a clean-out of the reds to Mr Schultz, said to the group by Gertie's fence.

Miller shook his head. 'That's th dickens uv it. I done all th buyen. Nancy couldn't, an keep her job an do th cooken an th housework.'

When Mr Daly had gone, Clovis, speaking hesitantly, like one on uncertain ground, asked, 'I wonder if times gits bad will they try tu bust th unions like some's a sayen?'

Even Miller, with all his money, was troubled, thinking ahead to a possible depression when the filling station he was buying might make nothing at all. Mr Schultz, however, was more afraid that there'd be a kind of boom with OPA taken off and everything going sky-high—except a fireman's wages. The fireman went away, and Whit looked after him a moment, smiling a little, then turned back to Miller and Clovis, and spoke in a low voice: 'Aw, quitcha crappen; maybe we uns can all scrape along somehow. Things might boom so's we could trade in all our secondhand cars an sich fer secondhand stuff a little younger, an taste ham meat a few times fore th next war.'

'War?' Clovis asked.

Whit's voice dropped to a whisper, and he drew still closer to his listeners. 'Yeah, th Catholics has gotta have their war; th pope wants to lord it over them Russians.'

'That's commie talk—some says,' Clovis said.

'Oh, yeah?' Miller said, and fell to whispering, a low but bitter hissing that made Enoch stand on tiptoe the better to hear.

Gertie turned away. Enoch would listen and believe, but he would like herself keep shut when Mr Daly talked in the alley; there was a poem in one of the old readers—'I was angry with my foe; I told it not, my wrath did grow.' Her mind searched, but could not find any more: something about a poisoned apple.

She finally got Enoch indoors and under the shower, but he was slow about going to bed. He never mentioned Catholics or future wars, but asked innumerable questions about depressions, sitdowns, and speed-ups, and why did Whit and Sophronie once have nothing to eat? Gertie could find no answers, but Clytie answered everything.

'Whit didn't have no job, an no money, silly.' Then Clytie was worried, wondering if baby sitting would be hard to get now when so many women were being laid off; she seemed ready to voice other worries, but fell silent after a slow searching of her mother's face, and then said, turning away for her nightly shower, 'Law, Mom, lotsa men git laid off allatime—an they git by.'

When the children had gone to bed, Gertie worked awhile at sanding pieces of some jumping-jack dolls Clovis had cut; but the dull work left her mind so free it went swinging back and forth through trouble, and worse than thoughts of trouble were the memories that came unbidden: sights and smells and sounds sharp and clear as her shadow on the kitchen table. The railroad tracks and the smell of grease on her hands mingled with the heat and the closeness of the kitchen and the particles of old paint she sanded off, sticky on her sweaty hands. She nodded, drowsing over a doll's head, and dreamed she had reached Cassie, for her arms were long, long— then Clovis was saying, 'Gert, go tu bed. I figger I'll have plenty a time to help you with th things. Whit an me, we're leaven kind a early,' and he was gone.

She roused, but instead of bed turned to the block of wood; for more than her walks through the alleys among the tumultuous sea of children the man in the wood gave rest and peace from thoughts of the things lost behind her and the things ahead she feared. Tonight, however, seemed like she'd worked on the lifted hand for only a little while before she came wide awake with listening; it seemed the faceless man was whispering, 'There's no money in me.'

She gave it up, but could not face the dolls again, and so got into bed. The western bedroom was too hot for sleep, a close and muggy place where her body's sweat, enough to dampen the sheets, brought no coolness; and through the window came the growl and mutter and roar of night-time Detroit; worse than this were the sounds of the people trying to sleep outdoors; babies wailed and whimpered and men cursed and groaned.

She drowsed at last, and there was the curtain man, smiling, holding out his hand; there was no money for his hand; then Joe

507

was calling through the alleys, and the nephew came, holding out to her the cheapest thing he had—cabbage—Amos was crying for it, but the nephew was taking it away because she reached for it with an empty hand; and Mr Daly watched and smiled. She got up.

She was working, sweating, something frantic in her eyes as she tried to rub the dark green paint from a doll's leg, when Clovis came back. He stood a moment, trying hard to smile. 'If we'd a listened we'd a heared over th radio. We seen th sign on the gate. They'll call us back when they want us—th sign said.' He stood a long moment, droop-shouldered, lax-handed, before he remembered to put the unopened lunch box on the table.

He noticed at last the work she did and after reminding her that it was past midnight and she ought to be in bed said: 'Don't worry so; they's thousands an thousands in th same boat. I'll go down an sign up fer that unemploymint right away.'

'But we couldn't live on about twenty a week an pay rent,' she said.

'Yu could pay th rent an breathe, an have a little left over fer milk an stale bread—half-price.' It was Whit, who, drinking his beer on his stoop only a few feet away, had heard their troubled talk and come to comfort.

Whit and Clovis talked again of depressions, wars, and relief. When Whit had gone, Clovis quarreled at her because she wouldn't leave the dolls and go to bed; but he wasn't sleepy either, and went rummaging around, looking on shelves until she asked what it was he hunted. 'Th pattern,' he said. 'I didn't cut but parts enough fer three—an now I can't find none a th pattern pieces.'

Gertie's hands, still busied with a doll's leg, dropped into her lap. 'You mean, make em all alike—exactly? I throwed that ole pattern in th stove.'

Clovis began a methodical searching through the trash left in the heating stove against the day when it would be cool enough for burning; she'd filled it because in the summer, when there were no ashes, the trash cans were seldom emptied. 'Law, Gert,' he explained as he searched, 'look at all th time it ud take to be allus maken new patterns; an you'd all th time hafta be worried about gitten th parts mixed. First thing,' he went on, fishing out a crumpled right leg, 'is to make a good strong pattern out a cardboard er plywood.'

508

She watched with wide, strained eyes, but did not protest. She even kept silent next day when, after much help from the children, the parts of ten dolls were sanded clean, and she got out her knife to round out thumbs and ears and cut faces. Clovis saw what she was about, and said: 'Gert, you cain't take th time to do no whittlen. Th next thing's tu paint em. You an Clytie can draw up some faces while I go git some paint an some strings to put em on.'

When he had gone they all drew faces, even Clytie's friend Donna Mae, who knew about the secret of the saw. But the day was half gone before there was a face that suited Enoch, whose job it was to haul them through the alleys in the wagon. 'You gotta make stuff that'll sell,' he kept saying. He settled at last on a face that Donna Mae drew; the mouth big and wide-lipped, the brows short and thick above round, sidewise-rolling eyes. Clytie colored it with crayons left from school; Gertie looked at it and turned away, but Enoch pranced with joy.

Clovis came home with many little bottles and cans of paint, even gold that, he explained, was for the hair. Gertie shook her head over the ugly, too bright colors; but all through the hot afternoon she painted; slowly, painfully, she followed Clytie's marked lines, the lines forever the same, though the colors could be different. Some had red hair, some black, and two with gold; the clothes were changed about in color, but in the end it was always the same— ugliness on the pretty, fine-grained maple wood. The work of creating ugliness was worse than the sneezy, stinking job of getting off the old paint; the new paint smelled more strongly than the old, and, try as she would, she could not keep it off her hands; the feel of the sticky stuff, especially the bright, bloody red, nauseated her. She could not work outside because the dust and mosquitoes and flies would ruin the finish; the heat and the smell made her dizzy, and the kitchen door by which she worked was usually blocked by children, noses pushed against the screen as they asked her what she did; and Wheateye lingered, quarreling, declaring that Gertie should first have finished the man in the wood.

Whit came to watch, unworried now, at least for the moment. Both he and Sophronie could draw the unemployment insurance, and already he'd found a job setting pins of evenings in a nearby bowling alley; and anyway everybody would be called back to work for the times would boom—for a little while.

Gertie sighed for quietness and coolness, but worked on, straight-mouthed, grim-eyed; her hatred for the ugly dolls fading at times as she enumerated in her head all their needs against the opening of school and winter quickly following.

It was two or three days later before the dolls were painted and dried and strung, and Enoch, in a fury of impatience to test his salesmanship, loaded them into the little red wagon. Hardly were they loaded before Mrs Schultz left off hanging up her wash to come and study the dolls. She took one and jumped it, smiling. 'Isn't it cute—kinda different. I'll bet my Kathy would like it.'

'Genuine hand-carved maple,' Enoch said. 'An a kid cain't tear um up—an they's nothen on um tu hurt a baby—genuine enamel—none a yer cheap lead paints; an nothen tu come lose an choke em. An lookee, even a little kid can make um jump.' And he jerked the string and bounced the doll, then set it upright in the wagon.

'How much?' Mrs Schultz asked.

Gertie cleared her throat, remembering the cake with thick white frosting, remembering the family argument only a little while ago about what the price should be; two dollars she'd thought was scandalously high for some little pieces of painted sawed scrap wood, but Clovis had held out for three; in the end they'd compromised on two-fifty; Clovis had thought they might not sell well through the changeover but there was no use to give them away.

Now, Enoch, as if not trusting his mother, said quickly, 'Two-fifty, an it'll last a lifetime.'

'But son,' Gertie said, 'when that paint comes off it won't be no doll.'

'It won't come off,' Enoch said, plainly angry with his mother, but smiling at Mrs Schultz. 'It ain't like they was cheap plastic things.'

Mrs Schultz continued to linger over the dolls, wistful, yet half apologetic, like one who cannot buy. 'So far I've made about all th toys my children used when they were babies. Toys—anything good like those wooden educational toys—cost so much; but'—she picked up a doll, shook it, watched it jump—'I guess I better not.

510

I've been saving a little toward sheets—and there'll be plenty of sheets pretty soon, an maybe cheaper.'

'This doll'ull outlast a sheet, lady,' Enoch said, impatient, pulling the wagon away, followed already by a crowd of admiring children, with Amos walking importantly behind, pretending to push the wagon, smiling, and nodding when Enoch began his cry: 'Dolls—genuine hand-carved dolls. Solid maple, safe fer a baby—unbreakable string—safe fer a baby.'

The Miller door opened and Mrs Miller, who between factory and housework had seldom been seen in the alley, called to him; and after jumping several and a bit of considering, she chose one. She paid the exact change, and as she turned back into her kitchen held the doll toward Sophronie on her stoop, explaining, 'Lookee, I figgered it's th last thing I'll be buyen in Deetroit.'

'I thought you'd stay long enough to draw your unemployment,' Mrs Schultz, hanging out clothes again, said.

Mrs Miller shook her head. 'That steel mill ain't a stoppen. Andy's worken overtime—big money. I figger if we wait too long we might git out a th notion a goen back an lose th chanct he's got to buy into this garage—s'good place—if he don't change his mind,' and as if the thought frightened her, she hurried swiftly through her door.

Sophronie glanced after her with wistful eyes, and Mrs Schultz wondered why they didn't stay. 'They've got way more'n enough for a down payment,' she said.

'She's been awful jumpy ever since that last pitman got burned up alive,' Sophronie said.

'I wonder what she'd do if she was a fireman's wife,' Mrs Schultz said.

The women were silent, but Gertie continued to stand a moment longer listening, 'Genuine hand-made dolls—genuine . . .' An airplane blotted out the sound.

She went into the house and stood by the block of wood and stared at it for a long time in what she thought was silence before she realized she was saying, 'But they's not any real whittlen on th things.' Then the unfinished empty hand, turned palm downward, that had been calling to her, impatient, while she messed with dolls, called her now; the wrist would be loose like Mrs Schultz's wrist, as she held up the doll she wanted but could not buy.

She lost herself for a time in the wrist, but the dolls had made her behind in the housework. Clytie was gone to the bookmobile with Donna Mae, and the breakfast dishes still unwashed and the beds not made. She went into the kitchen, stared a moment at the mess that no matter what she did would be there again tomorrow and all the days after, then turned sharp about and flopped upon her own unmade bed. She lay and looked at the ceiling—she was so tired she wished she could lie forever and never move or think. What was the good of trying to keep your own if when they grew up their days were like your own—changeovers and ugly painted dolls? She remembered Amos, gone with Enoch. What if for one little second he forgot and ran in front of a car—or if somebody drunk sped through an alley, as often happened?

She sprang up and hurried outside, but had only got as far as the big chughole alley—the street of the flying kites, Cassie had called it—before she heard Enoch's long drawn cry, 'Gen-u-ine maple dolls—hand carved.'

She stared through the quivering heat waves toward the sounds until guilty thoughts of the dirty dishes drove her home. She had the beds made and the kitchen clean, ready to start dirtying again for lunch, when Amos came banging through the kitchen door, screaming that he was hungry and they'd sold five dolls.

The others went more slowly. It was at twilight three or four days later that Enoch came running home with the empty wagon bouncing behind him. He was near speechless with running and exultation, and for an instant stood gasping, thrusting money into his mother's hands. 'Guess what, Mom,' he cried at last. 'A cop took one, a real honest-to-goodness cop inu scout car. An boy, did he like it.'

'You done good, real good, son,' Gertie said, straightening bills, arranging change. 'Yer pop's not worken, but this money's goen fer clothes fer you, an you git a dime fer ever doll you—' She began to count the money again, and looked at Enoch when she'd finished. 'Son, if you sold all four a them dolls they's money fer one a missen—an yer pop told you not to give credit.'

512

'But Mom, I toldcha a policeman took one,' Enoch said, proud as if he'd got ten dollars for the doll. 'I give it to him—he's onu regular patrol. Don'tcha worry, I'll sell um; when the changeover's done an it's clost to Christmas I bet I could sell a million—well, a couple a hundred enyhow—right around here inu project. A lot a people likes um but they say they ain't got no money.'

'And so you give one to a cop that's got money,' Gertie cried, anger darkening her eyes. She remembered how Mrs Schultz had wanted one, and she hadn't given it to her.

'Yeah, Mom,' Enoch said, still proud. 'That regular patrol car, it went by me real slow, anu one a driven he ast me where I got th dolls an what I was a doen. I told him my pop was outa work an we'd made um an I was sellen um fer to git money to go to school. An I jumped one fer him, an he took it an jumped it an acted like he kinda liked it; an I says, "Wouldn'cha like one fer yu little girl?" An he says, laughen kinda, "How'dju know I hadda little girl?" An I says, "I jist figgered." An him an that other cop, they both laughed, but he kept th doll un said, "Watch traffic an short-changers, son, an don't go into strange houses er strange neighborhoods by yerself."

'An, Mom, he ast me my name an where I lived—recken he'll recollect; an I'll have a cop speaken tu me by name just like some does to Casimir er Mr Daly.'

Gertie's anger choked her, but Whit, taking the cool of the evening on his stoop, called: 'You're maken a fine beginnen, boy. They won't be allatime a watchen yu now—pesteren yu about sales tax an sich.'

'That's what I figgered,' Enoch said. 'I don't guess they is a—a—a peddler's protective association like they is for—they call um fruit vendors—you know, like Joe. That Bommarita kid, I heared um a braggen one day that nobody never bothered Joe—he belongs to this association. He don't hafta pay no dues to no union ner nothen. Joe an his kind, they don't fool with jist cops; they've got um a councilman—that kid said.'

Whit smiled, listening too intently. 'I wonder does th teamsters know all that—them teamsters, why they've got a state congressman.' He added, cautiously, 'So I've heared.'

'But ole man Flint's got him a congressman in Washington, an a newspaper broadcaster on u radio says whatever he pays him to say,' Enoch said, then remembered to add quickly when Clovis looked at him, 'So I've heared.'

'So what?' Whit said, smiling. 'Didn'tcha know that these big automobile companies is gonna buy um a man an sell him tuyu fer President someday jist like they sell new cars.'

'Not me, brother,' Enoch said.

Clovis, who had been draped over the fence listening, guessed they'd better get busy and make more dolls. Gertie continued silent; the thumb was just barely touching the man's chest, for his elbow was close against his side—kind of huddled into himself like Max when she went away—maybe the thumb oughtn't to be touching. That might throw his elbow out too much. She fled from the plans for more dolls, and from Whit who now that he was not working seemed almost to have become an extra member of the household; she was watering the flowers, having picked up the hose that at first had seemed such an unhandy thing, while her thoughts went round and round the man's empty hand.

She smelled the marigolds and the wet earth above the garbage can smells, and smiled on the white asters beginning to bloom under Victor's kitchen window, dark, like the rest of his unit. She'd seen little of him since the war had ended; cars were crying for steel and he was working many double shifts. She stepped onto his bottom step to water the asters and Victor said from the darkness behind the kitchen screen door, 'You an her was friendly. She say anything tuyu about where she'd go?'

She saw his outline dim behind the screen; he sat huddled into himself on one of the too small kitchen chairs, well back from the screen like a man trying to hide. 'If I could find her,' he went on when she did not answer, 'she'd come back tu me. S'funny t'ing—twice she went to mass wit' me—pretty soon she'd married me—that is, wit' u priest—them other marriages ain't nutten. If I could find her, she'd come back to me.'

'Yes, she would,' Gertie said, and added, 'She wanted th sea.'

'Which sea? What sea?' he asked in anger. 'I gotta pick out one—an go.'

'They is a heap a seas,' Gertie said, turning away, watering other flowers, and for a moment it was quiet and she was alone; children still played in the hot steel-tinged twilight, but they were in alleys other than her own. The aloneness lasted only a moment, then a voice was calling, 'Mrs Nevels.'

She answered, and Mrs Schultz, her voice gay and brisk as always, said, 'I was watering my window box, and I thought you were in your flowers,' and she came on, explaining that she had thought it over, and would take a doll after all; it wasn't easy these days to find anything substantial and well made. She couldn't buy new sheets yet anyway, so now she would use some of her sheet money, and if she got a chance at sheets she'd take their money out of the house down-payment money.

Gertie pushed back a strong impulse to give her one, but in the end offered only to paint it and fix it just as Mrs Schultz directed.

She told Clovis of the doll order when she went indoors, and he was pleased. 'You could have a little steady income—if you can make th things cheap enough but still nice enough that a lot a people'ull want em.'

'Yes,' she said, but with no enthusiasm, studying now the thumb of the uplifted hand in the block of wood. She held her own just below her breasts, then dropped it quickly; her hand would never be like that; she had two hands now, one reaching out making people drop into it money that might have gone for down payments. She felt heavy and tired and old.

Some life returned to her next day in the excitement of a car with a telegram: Clovis was to report for work on the three o'clock shift that afternoon.

33

The heat wave went as suddenly as it came, and she was cold now in the twilights watering the flowers—cold in late August; and she told herself it was only a spell of cool weather, but she knew in her heart it wasn't, for by the parking lot and in the vacant land the wild asters and the goldenrod had long since bloomed, and now stood smoke-darkened and dried. She would think at times of the closeness of winter, when she would be forever shut up in the steamy, smelly indoors, with snow above Cassie, the wind crying in the telephone wires, and the Icy Heart purring and purring. She would shiver, then remember the block of wood; this winter was the time for which she had waited so long; she would bring the man's face out from its long hiding.

Here and there were vacant units from which people had moved away, but there had been no great rush of workers to go back home. Many families had at least one jobholder, such as Mr Daly or a steel man like Victor, unaffected by the changeover. Still, there were idle men in the alleys, and many families had no one working, but lived on unemployment insurance. More and more as the unemployment mounted, Gertie was aware of some thing among many of the people around her that, if not envy, was close to it.

The new woman who had got Mrs Anderson's unit, two bedrooms for her four children, sometimes gave her sharp envious glances, and one day in Gertie's hearing remarked in her broken English to Mrs Daly that Detroit certainly loved the hillbillies: there was a hillbilly family close by with only three kids, but they had three bedrooms, and the man hadn't had to go to war, and now he was working through the changeover. But Mrs Daly sighed, and said only, 'Maybe that family lost some kids.'

Mr Daly, however, was one of the loudest of the many who complained about hillbillies in Detroit. One afternoon, when he had finished somewhat early his work of driving a garbage truck, he stood in the alley almost in front of the Miller walk, and loudly remarked, 'They's plenty a native-born Detroiters walking a streets without jobs, while hillbillies wot don't belong here works.'

Mrs Miller, who, as if vacationing from the three years she had spent almost continually within doors, either in the factory or over the housework, was now much in the alley, gossiping and watching her children, heard and cried: 'Oh, yeah? You never did see them ads an signs an letters beggen all th people back home to come up here an save democracy fer you all. They done it ina last war, too. Now you can git along without us, so's you cain't git shet a us quick enough. Want us to go back home an raise another crop a youngens at no cost to you an Detroit, so's they'll be all ready to save you when you start another war—huh? We been comen up here to save Detroit ever since th War a 1812.' She stood, hands on hips and looked at him, a proud defiant woman—and strong. She hadn't missed a day from sickness in all her three years of factory work. 'I almost wish I was stayen. I'd help make Detroit into a honest-to-God American town stid uv a place run by Catholic foreigners.'

Mr Daly turned white with fury; Mrs Bommarita, cleaning her garbage can, stopped transfixed with lifted broom, while Mrs Miller continued to stand hands on hips, smiling, 'You think I don't know who runs things, even th schools an—'

Miller was thundering through the screen, 'Nancy, shut up an git in!'

Mrs Miller smiled and turned to her husband. 'What'sa difference? We're goen home; we don't have to have jobs no more. I made up my mind all that time I hadda pay dues to a union I hadda join an listen to a priestquoten steward, an be bawled out by a foreman with a cross under his shirt, I'd tell off—'

She slammed the door behind her; and the alley, even Mr Daly, was for a moment still. Sophronie's hands, taking clothes off the line, went faster as she gave Mr Daly a swift sidewise glance, as if afraid

517

he might read in her what she was thinking. Gertie stared down at the doll she was sanding; she wished Nancy Miller had kept still; there'd be more fighting and fussing among the children, and Clovis would quarrel at her a little more for 'huggling up' to Mrs Daly. It was the first time she'd ever heard the word 'Catholic' mentioned aloud in the alley. The things Mrs Miller said, and worse, were dealt with in whispers under the noise of radios. If the tool-and-die man chanced to be around when Whit and Miller and Clovis had such talk in the kitchen he would shut them up with a: 'Cut it, boys. Talk like that's a good way to bust th union. We all gotta hang together. Not all Catholics are Joseph Dalys.' They would be still, though Whit's smiling silence at such times was worse than any words he might have said.

Only a few minutes after Nancy Miller's outburst, Clovis came home, though he hadn't been gone three hours. 'They was some kind a walkout—electricians jarren around claimen th machine setter-uppers was a doen part a their work—so they sent us all home. That danged old man Flint,' and he looked so pestered, so disgusted, that Gertie did not press him for further explanations. Only yesterday he had said it looked like steady work for him; there were rows and rows of small lathes and punch presses out of the grease and onto the floor waiting for him and other repairmen. She only sighed and set up supper.

Like most workers on the three-to-twelve shift, Clovis ate a hearty meal around two o'clock, and so was not hungry at the family's regular suppertime; but tonight he sat with them and sipped coffee, and gradually some of the anger left him, and he talked enough that she learned what ailed him. ' "Yu tryen to git in good with that foreman?" he asks me, hateful-like. And I hadn't knowed that little piece—two screws an a bolt an she's on—was tu be put on by a tool-an-die man. I thought th foreman when he showed me had it under machine repair. "Foreman sucken, huh?" that steward says. "Tryen tu save th company money doen tool-an-die work on a repairman's pay." '

'Mebbe you'll git shifted agin,' Gertie comforted.

Clovis yawned, all the anger gone from him. 'Then I'd most likely git a mean foreman agin. Th one I've got now's a good feller—but that steward, they's a election comen up an he wants his faction in, an Bender's out; that steward, he claims Bender an his bunch is all commies, allus crappen around, th steward says, wanten us to take a strike vote, some's a sayen.'

'Why?' Gertie asked.

Clovis shook his head wearily. 'Gert, time an agin I've told ye I don't know nothen about the union's business. Mebbe they oughta strike—Whit thinks so, an so does that tool-an-die man; they're both buddies a Bender's frum away back.' He got up, and went for the evening's paper, spread as usual on the floor, open at the comics. 'I'd sooner take Bender's word fer things than that steward's; Bender's got a right to crap; he's on a grievance committee.'

Gertie wondered what was a grievance committee, but kept silent. The fear that always came over her when Clovis did not work his regular hours had laid hold of her so that she could not eat. She could hardly wait until the meal was finished so that she could clean up the kitchen and begin sanding the pieces of a new batch of dolls Clovis had cut some days ago.

However, tonight Clovis frowned on the sanding and told her to leave it be; the tool-and-die man was fixing her up some sanding wheels. They could work from the same motor as the saw, and not only was there a set to get off the old paint and smooth up the wood but one that would round off the sawed edges and make the dolls look more genuinely hand-carved.

'I hope you're paying him fer all his trouble,' Gertie said, and in spite of all her hatred for the contraptions he made, she suddenly wished the tool-and-die man would come tonight. Since Clovis had gone on the three-to-twelve shift, she had seen the man but seldom, and strangely enough had missed him, though he had never talked much with her. Still, he had been kind, always asking about herself and the children, even about Reuben sometimes, and lately he had taken more and more interest in the man coming out of the block of wood. The last time his words had made a joke and he had smiled, but his eyes were thoughtful, fixed on the hands. 'Well,' he had asked, 'can't he make up his mind? Will he keep it or give it back?'

'He's thinken about it,' she had said.

He had given a little headshake, still studying the wood. 'I'll bet he already knows he's made up his mind to give it away,' he had said.

It was Saturday evening, three nights later, with Clovis home on his regular time off, before the tool-and-die man came up the alley from the parking lot. Gertie was out watering flowers, though it was late with most of the children in from the alleys; and even as she smiled toward him she wondered all at once why it was that on all his visits he had come only after dark; and if it were true that Sophronie would not let him come to her place, for now that she was laid off and home of evenings he never went there.

She called to him in greeting as he came through the gate, and they stood a moment talking about the weather and the flowers. He turned then toward the kitchen door, but just as he stood on the stoop, caught in the shaft of light through the screen, a voice called: 'Well, well, if it ain't mu old pal. I thought yu'd be in Moscow.' It was Mr Daly, a blur of white shirt front and dark trousers by Gertie's gate.

The tool-and-die man turned, his voice easy, pleasant. 'No,' he said, 'I never got that far. England mostly, and then Africa, till they sent me home.'

Mr Daly laughed. 'Ain'tcha th disappointed one? Yu stunk so wit politics th army couldn't stand yu no longer.'

'I wouldn't know,' the other said. 'Mostly it was shrapnel in my leg—and my age,' and he started to open the door, but stopped and turned about and listened as Mr Daly said:

'Back in mu ole sinful, foolish days I always liked youse—in spite u yu color—now.' He stopped, laughed, then spoke more loudly. 'I don't wanta say it out loud where so many can hear—might give some people u bad impression a wot kind a friends some a th hill-billies in this alley keeps—but I jus wanta give youse a li'l friendly warning.' He stopped, then spoke more loudly. 'Youse commies hadda picnic true du war—but just youse wait an see. Du red squad ain't dead—an Father Moneyhan, he'll be warning his people agin. I'll be selling his literature—an them that tears it up now, why we can call um bydu proper name—commies.'

Those who had missed the earlier part of the speech, heard the last, and certainly the last word, for Mr Daly flung it over his shoulder in a great shout as he went on up the alley on the way to his regular Saturday night's amusement, followed by mass, if he were sober enough, in the early hours of Sunday morning. The tool-and-die man was still a moment, looking after him, then said as he went through the door, 'And they told me Hitler was dead.'

Gertie, still watering her flowers, heard Sophronie's troubled whispering as she stood in her darkened kitchen door; there were sounds of a muted scuffle and heavy breathing, then Whit came down his steps and around and through her gate, and his voice was gay and ringing as, without waiting to open her screen, he called a greeting to the tool-and-die man.

She lingered a long time among the flowers, though the spraying hose was so cold it hurt her hands, and all her body grew ashiver from the evening's chill. She did not want the whispers or Whit's hate-filled glittering eyes, but when she did go in it was as if Mr Daly had never spoken in the alley, for the men were deep in talk of union politics.

They never noticed her, and she went on into the living room, but even there she heard their troubled talk, mostly now about Bender. Whit thought he ought to have a bodyguard; in fact he felt it so strongly that after a little further talk he said: 'I could drive slow ahead a him fer a few nights; he lives on this side a town, an I'm ginerally through setten pins before he comes off his shift.'

Gertie waited, but could hear no word of dissent from the other two. She wished Clovis were not on the same shift as this man the others liked so well. Then Whit was saying: 'Let em kill Bender; we'd still go out on strike. Th—'

Gertie gave one last yearning glance toward the block of wood on which she had hoped to work, and fled to the bedroom by Victor. She shut the door, and stood trying not to think of Meg's letters from Harlan years ago when the big battle for the union was on. Meg had written of fights, killings, bombings, and what seemed worse—hungry children, the men out of work so long. Her mother had gone around sniffling, declaring that if a man didn't want to work and went on strike and left his children to starve he ought to be shot.

She had agreed with her mother then, and wondered at Meg, who had seemed to take the idleness of her man for granted. But now? Suppose a man didn't want to strike after the vote was taken? Could he work? Or suppose the men in the mines hadn't struck, and one man alone stood up and said, 'I won't work because the pay's too low, the timbering's bad, and too many men have already died from bad air and you won't fix the fans . . . .' To that one man or the dozen men or the hundred the company could have said, 'You're fired.' Then what?

She had in her trouble turned all unknowing to her knife, now open in her hand, while, hardly knowing what she did, she looked about the little room for a piece of whittling wood. There were, she thought, on the top shelf of the doorless closet, some little chunks of seasoned maple scrap. Reaching, her fingers touched some bit of rounded wood; puzzled as to what it could be, she pulled it out and saw the bald-headed baby in maple she had meant for the least Daly. She had always aimed to do a little more work on it, put at least a little curl in the hair, but even unfinished it was still much nicer for giving than the two-fifty dolls. Close by was Maggie's chickadee, finished, but forgotten until now. Once, little and made of poplar as it was, it had seemed a thing too cheap and shoddy for a gift; yet, looking at it now, she thought Maggie would like it.

She went sneaking and tiptoeing through the living-room door with the gifts hidden in one great hand, in case Clovis looked up to wonder where she went and what she gave; but no one noticed her going, absorbed as they were in talk, whispers now between the huddled heads.

She hesitated by the Daly screen door, not wanting to startle a lone woman by a sudden knocking. Mrs Daly might for a minute think something bad had happened to Mr Daly, who wasn't expected home till Sunday morning. She had walked heavily up the steps, but no one seemed to have noticed her coming. She peeped at last through the door, and saw Mrs Daly by the ironing board, her shoulders hunched as she pressed down the iron. Gertie knocked gently, but still the woman did not look around.

She looked more closely and saw scallops such as her mother had used to embroider and realized it was a piece of Maggie's hope chest Mrs Daly ironed. She remembered that a day or so ago, Mrs Daly had washed it all again, and Mrs Bommarita out by Joe's truck had said, 'She wants u new people to see her fine linen.' Mrs Schultz had wondered why she didn't at least wait until Maggie was home to do all that laundry; Maggie had gone someplace visiting, and her mother had such a time when she was gone and nobody to help her.

Gertie knocked more loudly, and at last Mrs Daly looked around for an instant, but turned back to the ironing before she said, 'Come in,' and when she spoke it wasn't like Mrs Daly's voice at all, neither laughing, nor cursing, nor quarreling, but still, just saying things like any other voice.

Gertie felt awkward, holding the chickadee and the doll, opening the door slowly and slowly making her way across the cluttered kitchen to the woman who wouldn't turn her head to look at her. 'I been wanten tu give yer baby one a my dolls,' she said to the woman's back. 'Somethen it can chew on an git no splinters—and no pain,' Mrs Daly still ironed and gave no sign that she had heard, but after a moment's waiting Gertie continued, 'An a long time back, I made Maggie a chickadee—a little chickadee to go with her ma—saint that blessed th birds.'

Something about the shoulders, too still, too stiff, as if they fought to keep from sagging down upon the unironed linen, made Gertie think of Job's wife, a woman she had lately pondered much upon. The iron went slowly and ever more slowly, and stopped at last on a scalloped hem. Gertie said, 'It'll burn, Miz Daly,' and took the iron and set it endwise on the scorched folded paper that served as pad; but even so, there was on the embroidery a faint yellowing of scorch. Mrs Daly turned at last and looked at her, and Gertie saw her eyes, dried out and old-looking, ringed with red as if the weeping were finished only because there were no more tears. 'You're worken late,' Gertie said, looking quickly away from the tell tale eyes to the bushel basket half filled with dampened things.

'I gotta hurry. I hafta quit when Mr Daly comes home,' Mrs Daly said, her voice low and level dead. 'It would make him feel bad, dear man, to see all her tings spread out—an her not needing um no more.'

'Oh?'

Mrs Daly turned back to the iron, nodded above it. 'Maggie's gone away to be a nun. Dey'll never be no turning back for her while she can turn back, like they's some that'll say. She'll take her vows when her time comes. Such a girl was Maggie,' and her voice was defiant, a little of the old Mrs Daly. ' "Wot'ull yu do wit'out her—an all that hope chest?" some says, like his sisters. But I'm proud, real proud.'

Gertie backed away, not answering, wondering if she ought to tell the woman her tears would spot the linen; tears were not like plain water, not a bit.

34

Back home it would be hot, with the little goose-craw beans hanging plump and green among the late corn, but here in late September there was the chill of frost in the air, and already the alley lay cold and blue in the still dusty twilight, though it was early, with Clytie not yet home from high school. Gertie lingered, looking for her, head craned around the door, glass again in place of screen. 'Yer flowers done real good.' It was Sophronie speaking from her kitchen stoop, nodding toward the marigolds by Gertie's fence.

And Gertie, too, smiled on the dwarfish, child-battered plants covered with their many petaled flowers all shades of gold and bronze and brownish red. There was something frantic in their blooming, as if they knew that frost was near and then the bitter cold. They'd lived through all the heat and noise and stench of summertime, and now each widely opened flower was like a triumphant cry, 'We will, we will make seed before we die.'

Sophronie's still, forever troubled eyes were on the flowers as she said, 'That strike talk's gitten worse—comen in over the radio now.' Then added as if Gertie didn't already know, 'I been looken fer a telegram an a listenen on th radio all day, but Whit ain't got no call back. They let him work jist long enough to make him lose that bowlen alley job an th unemployment.'

'Well, leastways they ain't made you lose your unemployment compensation.' The long strange words came slowly, and she spoke haltingly, feeling guilty, somehow, before Sophronie. Whit had been sent home before he'd had a chance to draw even one full pay check; a parts shortage, the company had claimed; but Whit and

525

others claimed the company lied; there were whispers of mountains of parts; the company just didn't want to assemble the parts into cars until the OPA went off and cars could go sky high.

Sophronie turned back to listen to her radio, but Gertie went out onto her stoop and continued to watch for Clytie. Clovis had lost a lot of time from wildcat strikes and walkouts caused by the workers, and even more from mysterious work stoppages, and one disciplinary lay off by the company. Still, they had been able to meet their payments, start Enoch and Clytie in school, and lay in a ton of coal against the winter. She oughtn't to complain, for times were none too good for many; she could see that in the peddlers flocking through the alleys; many ex-servicemen, all knocking on her door, holding out books, magazines, photographs, clocks. 'Lady, yu need luck; lemme sell yu this genuine electric clock in a horse-hoe, onie twelve ninety-five,' Others sold dancing lessons, clothing of all kinds, imitation jewelry, an endless assortment of pots, pans, brushes, gadgets for what use she could not even guess, radios, and toys. 'But, lady, it's onie eighty-eight days till Christmas.'

The last had been said to her today—another Christmas, another winter. She wanted to run from time that took her life, her days, and left only trouble in return. There was no place to run, so she went slowly down her walk, looking for Clytie. Her glance happened upon some tiny lumps of coal, spilled from the coalhouse door. She squatted and began to pick up the pieces; a moment later a voice asked, 'Lady, what must we do to be saved through Christ?'

She looked up and saw a young man in a worn soldier's coat, bent above her by the fence. There were so many sellers of Christ in the alley; He was offered on Christmas cards, punch boards, rosaries, revivals, bingo parties, books, Bibles, and pamphlets. Now the teachings of her childhood came with no bidding, and she answered, reaching for a lump of coal, 'Believe.'

'One of our own,' he said, and held out a card with the name and address of a church.

'But what if a body cain't believe?' she said, still squatting, looking up at him. There was a scar on his forehead, disappearing into his hair, and his face had the whitish faraway look of a soldier's long in a hospital.

'We must believe,' he said, smiling, believing.

'But God give us a mind that can or cain't believe.' She shook her head over an old wonder she had never spoken aloud until now, 'but not even God can make us believe.'

'Pray,' he said, 'and come to church; we want your soul, not your money.'

'But you have tu believe first before you can pray,' she said, but he was gone toward Sophronie's door.

He limped, she saw, and looked tired; she ought to have invited him in for a cup of coffee; he maybe didn't have a dime ahead. She was ashamed of herself being always afraid; it was the strike hanging over their heads; always and always the strike talk, even the children at their schools. A strike vote was coming up soon: Whit wanted it to win, Clovis was silent, and Sophronie was wearily certain; certain, too, that the strike would be long and hard and bitter; the first big strike since the war, with the whole nation watching, or so the tool-and-die man said, to see if the union could hold what it had won through the war. Gertie heard other talk, the whispers, mostly of women in the alleys—the strike was made by the union big shots who wanted to show their power.

She forgot the strike and drew a breath of relief when she saw Clytie coming up the alley. Clytie came and went on the streetcars with her girl friend, but even so she seemed so young to wrestle with Detroit. The girl came closer, and Gertie smiled on her, and all at once her child seemed grown and far away as she so often did, now that her mother didn't raise her any more. She looked like any one of thousands of other girls Gertie had seen; she wore like a uniform the white head cloth far back on the head, the straight, hip-length, dark blue jacket of cheap, reused wool, the plaid skirt, and the low shoes with thick white socks, perpetually wrinkled so that her ankles looked thick and ugly. Gertie never complained about Clytie's choice of clothing; after all, the child had bought most of it with babysitting money.

Gertie had wondered at times what high school was like and how her teachers were in the great school all in shifts so that sometimes Clytie never left until nearly noon, but some mornings she had to leave so early it would be dark in winter. She pondered much on the things Clytie told her—of the place where she could learn to drive a car when she was older, of the tough guy who knocked down a teacher, of the strange girl who'd offered her lunch money one day when her girl friend was eating on another shift and she had lost her own. There were many stories of the boys who didn't go to school, many still in soldier's uniforms, who waited on back corners to offer the high-school girls rides. Boys with cars were the especial worry of Iva Dean's mother, who had warned her own daughter, and Clytie, too, so much about boys and men with cars that Clytie was wise, though she had already learned much from the men. ' "Little girl, you'll freeze in this cold rain; lemme take yu home,' he says to me, an boy did I run.'

But that had been two days ago; tonight there was another story. 'He opened that car door right in mu face an says to me, "Little girl, yu know I know yu pop; he's a friend a mine." ' And Clytie gave word pictures of herself smiling, but backing away, then safe out of arm's reach across the sidewalk, asking, ' "Mister, yu must work at Griggs?" "Sure, girlie, yu know me—come on, lemme take yu home," he says to me.

'An, boy, did I laugh. "Oh, yeah, wise guy?" I says, "My ole man works at Flint's." I thought he was gonna jump out a that car, an boy was I glad when I seen Donna Mae an a bunch a kids waiten at the corner! I'd forgot my algebra book an run back by a shortcut alley to git it was how it happened. One a th big girls, when she heard me tellen Donna Mae, told me not to go off by myself that away no more; if yu stay with a gang or even just one er two they never bother you none.'

Gertie nodded, grim-faced. 'Stay with th crowd,' she said.

Clytie never saw her mother's sick-hearted eyes for she had found the evening's comics, and a moment later was laughing shrilly over a strip showing a wolf trying to snuggle up to a pretty girl. 'Boy, did he git his comeuppance,' she cried, and added from her wisdom, 'Yu gotta treat um that away, jist like Clare Bodell on u radio.'

Gertie nodded again; and the evening was long, as if eternity looked through the window, while she got the evening's work done and the children to bed so that she could find cleanliness and

528

strength and truth, too, seemed like in the uplifted hand of the man in the wood. However, tonight the work went but poorly; she was tired, kneeling by the wood, and realized that instead of whittling she was leaning on him.

She looked at the clock; almost midnight and not much use to go to bed, for soon she would be awakened by Clovis's homecoming. No matter how he tiptoed she always came wide awake, but worse, were the nights when he didn't get home on time. She would awaken, frightened, knowing he hadn't come, but rushing to the kitchen in her half-sleep, hoping to find him there. She would stand and watch the alley through the darkened kitchen door, her mind jumping from traffic accident to fight, for lately in the electioneering for and against the strike vote there'd been several fights between the factions.

Tonight she watched the red light from a steel pour, heard many empty streetcars going home, and had fallen into a shivery, restless pacing from kitchen door to living-room door before he came. He was unhurt, and somewhat angered by her sleepless, worrying ways as he explained that he had had car trouble. She answered nothing to that; did not even point out that used to be he had ever bragged he never had car trouble; he'd always been able to see trouble coming and keep a car running, even the oldest of his trucks. Maybe he'd had a flat tire; but she did not ask. She tried instead to put her mind on the flowers; maybe she should have cut a great bouquet tonight; it had seemed so cold.

However, it was not until three evenings later that she went out to cut the flowers in the cold still twilight. She was bent above the asters searching out the finest buds when she stopped, knife uplifted; a gurgling, inhuman scream, the kind the radio made when an Indian died, had come from the Meanwell kitchen door. She whirled to see Wheateye race through her door and down her walk, then spring, monkey-like, from garbage-can top to coalshed roof. She held a large bunch of purple grapes, and in spite of chewing and swallowing she began to scream again while she went round and round on the coalhouse roof in the jigging, bouncing step the alley children used when they played Indian war dance; her hands were ever clapping at her mouth, but Gertie, listening, frowned.

The words, though gargled and broken with the grapes she chewed and swallowed, were plainly not the usual Indian words heard on the radio.

Gertie went closer to the small thin figure that in the red-tinged half-darkness looked like some poorly sawed jumping-jack doll dressed in outgrown clothing so that it seemed all skinny legs and arms, for since there was so little money coming in, Sophronie's children, like Gertie's, wore their good clothing only to school. But Wheateye's cry was not of nakedness nor hunger, but joyful; and when Wheateye's brothers and other children took it up, Gertie understood the words: 'Old man Flint is dead—dead—dead. Old man Flint is dead—dead—dead. Globba—lobba—lobba. Old man Flint is dead, dead, dead; globba, lobba, lob.'

Whit, who had been shifting his car wheels in the parking lot, came running, a wrench in his hand, asking, joyfully, unbelievingly, 'Honest?'

And when Sophronie called from her stoop, 'Yeah, it come over th radio; sudden up at his fall home,' the joy in even her forever troubled tiptoeing voice was reflected in his own as he stood smiling, looking about him, but unable to say anything but, 'Well, I'll swan,' followed by a low whistle of exultation.

There was a great calling back and forth across the alley, some wanting to know if the news were indeed true, with others giving joyful confirmation. Mr Daly, listening to the radio, had heard it all, Mrs Daly reported, walking down the alley, speaking loudly above the chanting of the children. 'He hadda bishop by him when he died. Cunyu'magine, a bishop fudu last rites? They was vacationing tugedder.' And some of Mrs Daly's old self came back as she pondered on the future of old man Flint; with all the money he had and a bishop by him when he died, he wouldn't have to spend hardly any time at all in purgatory. She hoped she could go to the funeral; if she could get a baby sitter she was certain she could get into the cathedral; Mr Daly knew so many cops. There would be bishops at the funeral mass, and maybe even a cardinal. Just think of it, and she shook her head in wonder. Democracy did it, for Mr Flint had been an immigrant boy who'd used a pick and shovel to dig out railroad beds.

Gertie offered to mind the children, and almost a week later, when the city had paid full tribute to Mr Flint with lowered flags, throngs filing past the dead, the papers each outdoing the other with pictures of his many homes, his many children, his collection of ruffled petunias on which he had spent more than a hundred thousand dollars and said to be the finest in the world, his many grandchildren, and his old, bejeweled wife, who had not been with him when he died; after all this Mrs Daly went to the funeral. She came home disappointed. There had been no end of bishops and priests, and cops directing traffic, but still the funeral was not so fine as Short Joe Menazzi's. Oh Gertie, of course, hadn't been in Detroit in the days of Short Joe Menazzi; he was king of the rum runners all through prohibition; but somebody—a cop would never have been so mean—shot him when he came out of one of his banks. Yes, he'd bought a lot of banks, and he'd been a fine man, openhanded with cops and the Church and a bitter, bitter enemy of communism.

Even the weather had seemed to consider the burial of old man Flint; the cold fall rain that had threatened all day never started in earnest until even Mrs Daly had her children home from Gertie's. The sooty rain fell on the frost-blackened flowers, and Gertie watched it with a heavy heart—the beginning of winter. The radio ground in her head, funny tonight with a drunk man, then above it Enoch squealed with laughter and cried: 'Lookee, Clytie, didja see this—th old woman with a mule? Boy is she haven herself a time!'

Gertie, thinking of Aunt Kate driving a sled because all her sons had been taken for the war, turned and looked over Enoch's shoulder. She saw a woman, not so old as Aunt Kate, barefooted and sunbonneted, driving a raw-boned mule fastened to a home-made sled. They were going to town, and the woman on the way changed her bonnet for a silly looking hat with a big bird and a little long-stemmed flower; the old mule looked round and bucked and knocked down the woman.

Gertie knew, even as her palm shot out, it wasn't Enoch she wanted to slap; he was a good boy—everybody said he was good. Her palm came against his cheek, but not too hard; and he, used

531

now to the falls and blows in the alley, was more angry and startled than hurt, yelling at her, 'Mom, cain't a guy laugh at a funny picture?'

'It made me think a yer Granma Kate,' she said. She wanted to apologize for the slap, but was unable to make her voice kind as she said. 'It wasn't funny.'

She strode to the block of wood, knife open in her hand. The radio was talking by it, something about the strike vote coming up at the Flint plants in three more days. She retreated to her bedroom. She ought to work on the dolls, but she couldn't, not tonight; she couldn't bear the eternal sameness of the ugly things. They needed the money, but she'd wash, she'd iron, she'd do anything.

She closed the bedroom door and stood with her back against it so that the forever curious, solicitous Clytie could not come in. At last she put a chair against the door, then knelt upon the bed, her face close to the window; when she held her face so and listened hard, she could faintly hear the rain against the glass. If she could hear it on a roof—fall rain on the roof shingles of a barn when the animals were fed and the fodder and hay still smelled of summer—and Dock to drive. Where was Dock? He had been so kind; he wasn't broke to saddle good when Amos took sick, but seemed like he had understood and let her ride him. To have Dock in a barn, even a rented barn, and around her food for the winter, and then be able to stand in the barn hall and listen to the rain while she held the night's milk . . . and above her on the hill would be the house with her children, all her children, safe. To live that way, without debts, unions, boys in cars, foremen, traffic; to be free from the fears, forever at her back— How long would Clovis work tonight, next week? Would the strike vote pass? What if he got sick? Doctors here, she'd heard it said, wouldn't come unless they knew they'd get the money.

She realized tears were falling on her twisting hands. She had never cried for Cassie, but now she cried for a mule, a mule that wouldn't recollect her, but with him she had been so free, so unafraid.

The children went at last to bed, the radio was still, and Gertie worked on the block of wood. Tonight she chose again the cupped hand; in her haste to be finished with the general shape and bring out the empty one above it she had finished only the upcurving backs and tips of the fingers, so that the hand seemed overfull with riches heaped above the fingertips and slipping down between the fingers.

She worked a long while dividing fingers from the thing they held. She grew tired, but still she knelt, working. The knife stopped at times over the ball of the bent thumb; the ball must be flattish, hardly rounded at all, for the hand had done much work, maybe worked all its life for the thing it held, and now she took it away. What did the hand hold, heaped so high, so full it slipped between the fingers? Sandy earth from her father's river-bottom fields? She dreamed of the coolness and fog by the river and the sound of the shoals and the rustle of corn, ready for cutting; and while she dreamed one finished finger of the hand tapped on the window behind her. Her head lifted; no, the tapping was a maple bough like that by the doctor's window; it kept tapping and tapping, but mixed in with the rain as it was, she could hardly hear it.

She realized the knife was drooping in her hand, and that she was drowsing, kneeling by the wood. She rubbed her eyes; there was no maple bough; the window was, as always at night, covered by the pale blind; the rain was hard tonight, tapping so loudly. She got slowly to her feet, frowning over the stiffness of her knees. She forgot her knees and turned swiftly toward the window as the tapping came again, and she knew it wasn't rain.

She reached for the doorknob, but hesitated as she remembered the warnings of Clytie and Clovis and the neighbors: never, never open the door at night to a strange knocking—crazy men, drunk men, thieves, and murderers. She tiptoed to the window at the end of the sofa, and lifted the shade enough to get her head under it. She dropped it again behind her, and when her eyes had grown accustomed to the dim light she saw the rain washing down the storm window glass, faintly pinkish in the steel-mill light, dull now, as if no furnace were ready for a pour.

The tapping was repeated, and she jerked her head back in surprise, for, close as she had been, she had seen nothing. The sound came again; she pressed her face against the glass, and looking down she saw a long thin hand, a man's hand, but seemingly all alone, with no man behind it as it rose out of the darkness by the house wall and tapped her window again.

Fear twitched her face, but she did not move; she at last made out the dark blurred shape of a man crouched close against the house like one who must hide even when there is no place to hide. She hesitated, then at last tapped softly on the glass; a man's face rose swiftly out of the shadow, but stopped when it had come just high enough to let her see it through the glass. She drew back, staring; rain fell on the uplifted face, but not enough to wash away completely the smear of blood on one cheek. She stared a moment in fear and wonder before she realized it was the tool-and-die man; his lips moved, made words without speaking while his head jerked side-wise, then frontward; she understood that she must turn out the light and open the door.

She jerked the light string, and with her throat choking, her breath a hard thing hurting her chest, she moved a chair, pulled back the locked thumb latch, and opened the door slowly, with no creaking, and then in the same cautious way opened the storm door. No one was there. She went out onto the top step and looked about her, unconscious that rain from the unguttered eaves was splattering on her head.

She saw, at last, what looked to be a thicker blot of irregular darkness moving out of the parking lot at the end past Victor's unit. She hurried toward it, hugging the wall, crouching in the shadow as the tool-and-die man had done. She was past Victor's windows when in the murky light she saw enough to know that the moving darkness was a huddle of man shapes, hurrying now by Victor's fence. They came on so strangely, hurrying but staggering like drunken men, that she hesitated, half afraid; but her fear for Clovis was greater, and she went on, hurrying, but crouching even lower, for here the street light two alleys away made the gloom less thick. A few steps further, and she understood it was only three men walking, staggering because they carried another man.

She sprang forward, peered into the faces of the three walking, and not finding Clovis, looked down to the one carried. She didn't need to see the face; the smudged shape was enough. She gave a whispered, terrified, 'Oh,' and bent lower, searching for his face. She found it, a black, featureless mask in the dim light. Why so black? She sniffed, and knew without touching him that his face was covered with blood.

She must have made another sound, for the tool-and-die man gave a whispered, 'Sh-h.' He was close against the house wall, holding up one shoulder while a slight thin shape she did not recognize held the other shoulder, and Whit came behind with the feet; all three moved clumsily, stumbling at times and bumping against the wall in their haste. Gertie caught the sagging waist, and walked a step or so, stooping, hurrying like the men. The fresh blood smell brought back Cassie: she should have run faster, much faster—a few minutes sooner to the hospital . . . Hospital—that was where Clovis ought to be going—go now, and it wouldn't be too late, like for Cassie.

She stopped so suddenly that, holding him as she was, the men staggered, 'We've got tu git him to a hospital,' she said, forgetting to whisper.

'Keep moving,' the tool-and-die man begged, pulling on Clovis while she held back. 'He's not bad hurt,' he whispered.

It could not have been more than five minutes from the time she heard the tapping until they had him through the door and on the cot in the living room. But to Gertie it seemed hours before she could bend above him, hear his breathing, a mumbled groan, and then the thickly spoken words, 'What th heck?'

'Yu passed out 'fore we got tu th car,' Whit whispered, his voice more disgusted than sympathetic; then, as Gertie jerked on the light, he was worried, asking, 'Ain'tcha got a little lamp a some kind? People'ull notice this.'

Gertie did not answer; she was looking at Clovis, or at what little of his face she could see for the blood. She was too dazed to help Whit, grabbing newspapers now, commanding, 'Git somethen under him; yu don't want blood all over.'

Whit and the tool-and-die man shoved the papers under his bloody head, and by him on the floor, for his eyes were bulging, his stomach writhing like one who had to vomit. He did, mostly blood, it looked to Gertie, and the tool-and-die man, seeing her frightened glance, explained: 'They got him in u jaw. He's swallered blood's all. Some wet cloths an a towel might help.'

She roused from her stupor of terror and got water and towels and washed his face and neck and hands while the tool-and-die man took off his shirt and looked for body blows. There was none, and some of the trembling went from Gertie's legs when she saw that though there was much blood, his wounds seemed no worse than Henley had used to get in some drunken jamboree of fist fighting back home. He was lucky in a way, for a little more and he would have lost an eye; there was a deep, though short, gash just above his left eyebrow.

One jaw was cut and bruised inside as well as out, and that was why he kept spitting blood, or maybe he had a tooth loose or even lost. She wanted to ask him, but didn't. His jaw hurt him more and more, stiffening so that he spoke with difficulty. He lay wracked with nausea from his own blood, and stared at the ceiling, his good eye blazing, the one under the cut blackening up and swelling shut but blazing still, while through his clenched teeth came terrible whispered oaths such as she had never heard from him, for he had joined the church before they married.

'Don't take it so hard,' Whit said, gathering up the dirtied newspapers. 'It wasn't nothen personal.'

Clovis twisted his head, the terrible anger like a blindness in his eyes. 'I ain't to say hurt. It's th blood, th damned, damned blood, an th fool I was.'

He vomited again. Whit spread more papers, laughing a little like one who has come from a gay and pleasantly remembered party. He tried again to soothe Clovis, reminding him that he could have been blinded or had his skull crushed. 'It was lead pipe,' he said, considering the cut on the forehead, 'endwise, but he never got a good swing.' And over the jaw he shook his head; a poor swing too, for the jaw was not so much as fractured, bruised some, but so little he couldn't tell if the wound came from a poor swipe with a tire chain end, or maybe nothing more than a ring on the bare fist of a short-reached fighter.

Clovis flopped down again. He was silent, the wounded eye almost closed now, his rapidly swelling jaw making speech more and more difficult, but the one good eye kept swinging about the room, saying things that Gertie had never thought could be in Clovis. 'Don't take it so hard,' Whit repeated, wiping blood from his shoes. 'We was all lucky; we could all git away on our legs. That's more'n they could do.'

'I wonder if,' the stranger said, and stopped when they all turned and looked at him. Gertie saw that he was young enough almost to be the son of any of the other three. His face, though unbloodied, was deathly pale, and his dark brown eyes, wide like a child's eyes, were neither angry nor frightened; they were dead, glittering, maybe a little puzzled. Still, they were familiar; she remembered at last the blue eyes of the young soldier who had wondered about hunting and who had seemed to belong to the man with the star. These eyes, like the blue ones, saw things behind them, the way she saw Callie Lou and smelled the train grease in the stillness and the dark. It wasn't dark and it wasn't still, but this child saw them now.

He looked at Whit, licked his lips, opened his mouth, and stood an instant so. 'I wonder,' he began again, his voice struggling like his glance, 'if that one you hit—well, he was so still—and when they dragged him off he was like the ones I used to see—you know, in th war.'

He began to shiver. Whit's eyes on him were angry and disgusted. 'Sure, it's like th war. I got in some good licks with mu jack handle, an—'

The tool-and-die man spoke quickly. 'Aw, kid, nobody's gonna die that easy.'

'Sure,' Whit agreed, 'right onu back a th head like that, they pass out easy.'

The boy's eyes were still accusing. 'But you hit more than once—I thought; you kept on and on after he fell. I can—could—hear it.'

The tool-and-die man tried to smile. 'Aw, kid, you're imagining things. If you'd stayed in th car like we said, we'd have their number now an—butcha didn't; that's that. But hell, no matter what happened, they ain't no rules fer stuff like this. It ain't high-school basketball.'

Clovis rocked his head from side to side, in anger and disgust. 'Th kid done as good as me. He was supposed tu watch—I was supposed tu fight. I didn't.' Anger and the pain of speaking made him fall again into a whispered curse.

'Butcha done good, real good, for th first time,' Whit said.

'But I didn't have no sense,' Clovis said, swinging his feet to the floor as he attempted to sit up. 'I gotta pretty good look at th kid comen at me—it wasn't so dark but what I could tell he was scrawny—not to my shoulder.' He stopped to spit blood, and went on, his good eye squinched against the pain of speaking: 'I thought to myself, "That kid an them three others is jist aimen to skeer Bender; all four a them wouldn't jump on one lone man." Then he swung at me 'fore I could make myself swing on him with that big wrench—him a little guy, mebbe jist a kid.'

'But frum what I seen, yu didn't stand still fer him,' Whit said.

Clovis dropped his weary head into his hands. 'Naw, but somehow that wrench got away frum me; the next thing I knowed I was a comen down on him with my hands an my teeth like when I was young, fighten back home. I recollect a thinken, "If I cain't kill him, I'll mark him up good." So's I gouged at his eye an chewed on his yer. I'd know him now in a million, an I'll allus recollect th way he sounded—damned dago.'

'Sicilian,' the tool-and-die man corrected with a quick silencing look at Clovis, and a troubled glance toward the young one who stood, his eyes on Clovis without seeming to see him.

'Aw, don't take it to heart so,' Whit said. 'That kid that gotcha, he didn't have nothen agin you; he hadda chance to make a fast buck's all. Somebody hired him; mebbe th same feller smuggled him into th country, fer all we know. If he gits killed, whatsa difference? He didn't live here inu first place; cops cain't hunt a feller that never lived—an enyhow Bender's still safe.'

The tool-and-die man's sigh came loudly in the silence, and he looked old, older than Whit. 'That's what hurts,' he said. 'Yu know we could a done away with all four a them after Bender, an never hurt th real one—th one that hired em—saved him money. I guess he pays for the beatings, not the tryings.'

'A lot a good union men don't wanta strike an hate Bender,' the young one said.

538

The other three turned as one and looked at him, their eyes accusing. 'Boy, if you're hinten at what I think you are, you're plum crazy,' Whit said, angry, mean.

'You're tired, kid,' the tool-and-die man said, his voice kind. 'Somebody inu company hired these thugs; th war's over; they don't mind a little labor trouble. They ain't in any hurry for final assembly, but they don't wanta full-scale strike now; they'd like to git a lotta cars ready for final assembly—but sell um when OPA goes off.'

'An recollect th war's over, they're out to bust th unions—if they can,' Whit said, his voice low, but like a battle cry.

Gertie folded another newspaper, dirtied with blood from Clovis; she straightened, thinking of Meg's man in Harlan, the redheaded woman in the station, Mrs Miller, and now this. 'But a body's got a right to be free. They oughtn't to have to belong tu nothen, not even a union.'

There was a moment's silence; the words had come almost without her knowing, an over-flowed weariness with the dues, the numbers, the badges, the meetings, the walkouts, the strike talk, and now blood.

'Aw, Gert,' Clovis said at last, ashamed of her, 'you don't know what you're a sayen. Shut up.'

'Yes, she does,' the tool-and-die man said. 'A man oughtn't to have to pay dues an belong to a union to get a decent wage—but th way things are he's gotta.'

The young one, who seemed to be recovering from his stupefaction, nodded. 'I know. Pop's told me things—an when I was little I used to see things like—well, like my mother crying. Pop quit telling her things, but he'd tell me; he saw a man die on th 'sembly right by him—speed-up—August—no fans.'

Clovis for the first time looked at the young one and seemed to understand that he had been hurt more than any of them. 'Gert, git some cawfee. Tony there, he'll be wanten to go home.' He made a brave show of sitting up, but dizziness overtook him again, and he let his shoulders sag against the wall.

'Yeah, you'd better be gitten home,' Whit said, and he too was kind, as he added, 'You're lucky like the rest uv us not a—'

He stopped suddenly, his glance fixed on the young one's neck, 'Say, ain't that blood?' He added quickly when the other began a frightened fumbling: 'It's off a Clovis most like. Nobody got in a good lick at you. One turned an might ha swung when you come runnen up, but I got him frum behind—he kinda grabbed atcha when he went down; yu could be scratched a little.'

Whit's voice had grown more and more reassuring, while the other's fingers reddened with blood as they hunted under his shirt collar. Suddenly, the fright growing in his eyes, he jerked off his jacket, and then his shirt, so impatiently that a button popped off. His hand searched frantically over his undershirt as he craned his head to see his shirt. 'It's gone,' he cried. 'My Christopher medal, they got it. All through th war I wore it—on Wake Island, in a hospital. I'm home, and—' He turned blindly about as if to run, but the washing machine by the passage into the kitchen barred his way. He flopped down into a chair at the end of the kitchen table, buried his face on his outflung arms, and fell into a hopeless, homesick weeping, the sobs like hands jerking him to pieces.

Gertie started toward him, stopped. She had never heard a man cry—soundless tears and sniffles at funerals, tears in church when men wept for their sins—but not like this. She wanted to touch him, to smooth his hair, but he was a man, a soldier. And if he cried for this, what would he do when real bad luck hit one of his own?

The men, too, were silent, embarrassed, looking first at the boy, and then at each other, and lastly at Gertie, as if she, being a woman, must act like a woman and stop the man's crying. 'Don't wake their kids,' Whit whispered, and then to Clovis: 'His medal would ha been on a little chain. That un I hit grabbed at th kid—s'funny all that feller wanted soon's I got in that first good lick was somethen to grab holt on—an then he hadda git th kid's medal.'

'He oughtn't to ha come, a kid like that,' Clovis whispered.

'Nothing else would do him,' the tool-and-die man said. 'His dad was all set to help us—fool-like he told th kid—so th kid took it on hisself to come. "My dad's too old for this," he said.' He turned again and looked at the weeping one, disgust on his face.

Whit's eyes sparkled. 'Wouldn't it ha been something now if old Luigi hadda come?'

'You're enough,' the tool-and-die man said. 'If Luigi hadda come an done like you, th ones left couldn't a dragged th other two away; police find a dead man by Bender's back door that strike vote woulda been defeated for true.'

'He wouldn't ha had no union card, an anyhow we could a dragged—' Like the others, Whit had turned to look at the living-room door, for behind it there was a low but insistent tapping. 'Th cops?' he asked in a moment, losing something of his look of pleasure.

'Cops don't knock thataway,' the tool-and-die man whispered, studying the door.

The tapping came again. Gertie lifted the blind, and saw Sophronie, crouching, only her face in the light with the lips moving, commanding, 'Lemme in.'

She slipped swiftly in, the rain-dampened housecoat pulled tightly about her. She pushed the door softly shut with her back, and just as softly reached behind her and tested the catch, all the while her eyes searching over Whit, his head, his face, his body. Satisfied with him, her frightened glance considered Clovis, then went on to the crying boy in the kitchen. 'You unsoutta be ashamed,' she said, all her anger coming out in a whispered hiss, 'letten a kid like that mess around in this.' And then her hopeless weary whisper: 'I've bagged yu an bagged yu tu quit messen around. Yu'll git in more trouble, an be losen another job.'

Whit smiled. 'I was hunten a job when I got back in at old man Flint's. I figger th union's worth a little trouble.'

'Trouble,' she said, 'yu hunt it,' and she looked at the tool-and-die man.

'Aw, Sophronie,' Whit said, flushing as her angry, accusing eyes swept the other, 'yu gotta have a little—little faith. Recollect, yu quit believen they'd ever be a union at Flint's.'

'It took a war,' she said. 'All that fighten an passen out lit-erature an paraden with our faces covered—that didn't do no good. An atter all people like us has done, them sitdown strikes an all—' She drew a deep breath, then spoke all in a rush: 'You know what they're sayen, I heared plenty 'fore I got laid off, th ones that done nothen er hardly nothen, never had to dirty their

541

hands, why they're sayen them that pulled th rough stuff is red—commies an—'

'Sh-sh,' Whit hissed, nodding toward the bowed head, and then more loudly: 'You've jist been hearen a little fussen in th union. We've got a union, we'll keep it.'

Sophronie sighed. 'In th end it'll jist be somethen else to mind, like—' She had for the last moment or so been watching the boy, still lost to the world in his weeping, his hand hunting again over his bare chest. 'He bad hurt?'

Whit cleared his throat, looked at Sophronie, and then away. 'He kinda got hurt.'

'Mostly he's broke up; he lost his medal—saint something,' Gertie said.

'Medal? Saint?' Sophronie asked, and her eyes grew still more frightened. She stood an instant, terrified, staring at the back of his head as if it had been a rattlesnake, coiled and ready to spring. She turned suddenly to Whit, begging, 'Git him out; git him away.'

Whit looked at Gertie. Gertie looked at the boy, hesitated, then walked resolutely up to him and put her hand on his shoulder. 'You'd better git home son; an keep out a sich. Fighten around, taken sides—in this—it ain't no good an—' She choked; maybe he didn't want to be a rabbit, either.

Her touch on his shoulder and her words in no way checked his crying, but did loosen his tongue. He moaned, his face still buried on his arm: 'Somebody's gotta take sides. Allatime I was inu army, I stuck up fer th union. Lotsa mu buddies hated th unions on account a they'd read th papers from back home; th papers give um th notion that union men and women never done nothing but strike, and that every factory worker just worked at his job to keep outa th army—an why have they gotta make us hate each other so? An now this,' and he dissolved again into incoherent weeping.

The tool-and-die man came to Gertie's help. 'Look, kid,' he said, bending over the boy, 'it wasn't a union man tried to kill you.' And when the boy did not answer, but only sobbed, he added impatiently: 'Don't take it so personal; yu gotta remember them men was getting paid to beat up Bender; you got in their way; they hadn't

542

anything against you—or Bender either. They was hired; it's like hating th gun that—'

The boy lifted his head, and his voice after all the whispering was loud. 'That's it. I had nothing personal against the Japs. See? Somebody told um to try an kill me. Somebody give me a gun and told me to try to kill them. Now, I'm home—peace. An it's allasame.'

His voice had risen so that all around were the troubled, whispered shushings. Sophronie nudged Whit. 'Git him out.' Then, in a louder whisper: 'You'd better tiptoe around an turn our kitchen light on—you ginerally have it on way 'fore this. Somebody'ull be suspicionen. Anybody see yer car?'

Whit shook his head. 'Th kid drove his'n,' and he nodded toward the tool-and-die man, now helping Tony into his jacket. 'Th rest a us rode ahead, like we've been a doen, a little piece behind Bender in his'n,' and he nodded toward Clovis.

Sophronie was silent as she snapped out the light, opened the door for the three men to go through, then closed it again, softly, her shivering sigh of relief that the boy was gone loud in the dark. 'Old man Flint's dead—but they's still people around a watchen, a listenen, a runnen with tales tu make a man lose his job—or git hit on th head. That Catholic kid, he'll be runnen to his priest an th police an—oh, Lord—I figger th union, it mebbe watches an listens too. They're agin rough stuff—now.'

'Mebbe everything'ull be all right,' Clovis said, but he sounded troubled, his whisper low as Sophronie's.

35

Gertie stood, the sweaty slip of paper in one hand, the sweaty nickel in the other, and stared at the telephone. If this were the kind like back home where a body asked for a number and didn't have to dial—she began to read the directions slowly, seeing with difficulty in the dim light, increasingly aware of the growing impatience of the people behind her; she ought to have come sooner than Clovis said, for already she had waited in line. She wished the thing were in a little boxed-off place like one she'd seen one Sunday when Clovis had taken them into a drugstore for ice-cream cones—such a waste of money. Why had she let him waste money so? It was after they'd paid for Cassie's marker, and she'd felt rich somehow.

She rubbed her arm hard across her forehead, then suddenly stepped aside, flushing, ashamed, hardly able to look at the woman next in line. 'You go ahead,' she said. 'Seems like I'm kinda mixed up.'

'Butcha gotta git used to th things sometime,' the woman said. 'Me, I never seen nothing but that other kind till I moved here.' She glanced at Gertie's slip. 'Yu just gotta make a sick call?'

Gertie nodded, cleared her throat. 'My man, he's got th—flu,' she said, her eyes narrowed a little, watching the other's face.

'Ain't it awful?' the woman said, reaching for the receiver. She listened a moment, took Gertie's nickel, dropped it in, and after listening again, held the phone to Gertie's ear. 'It's sounding awright, so's yu gotta begin.' She looked at the slip, and with her eyes on it she dialed the two letters, the five numbers, slowly, repeating each to Gertie like one teaching a child its numbers. 'Now,' she whispered finished, 'when somebody answers yu say this,' and she pointed to the next number, 'Line 371.'

A voice, flat, like a machine speaking, said in her ear, 'Flint Manufacturing Plant Number Ten.'

And Gertie repeated the line number very slowly and so loudly one of the project office girls looked in her direction. Another voice was in her ear, and flustered now by the strangeness, she said, 'My man, Clovis Nevels, he's sick.'

The woman behind her was whispering, 'Nah, not thataway; not his name.'

The voice in her ear said, 'His division, please.'

She read the next number. Sophronie, familiar with such things, had written it down; she answered more questions with other numbers, finishing at last with the one on his badge. The numbers must have answered all the questions; the voice never asked for the name or was Nevels spelled with one *l* or two, but after the questions said only, 'Call each morning at this time when he is ill.'

Something clicked; the phone was still; and the woman behind her, whom she had forgotten, was saying, reaching for the receiver, 'Yu done good fudda first time.'

She hurried home, but once there, tried to walk slowly and unconcernedly up her steps, remembering not to look around and betray any concern as to whether the neighbors watched or no. Clovis seemed asleep when she stuck her head through the bedroom door. His eye was black and swollen shut from the wound above it, and his whole face was misshapen from the bruised and swollen jaw, but sleeping so he looked more peaceful, more like himself than last night. She turned to tiptoe away, and he roused, started to turn in bed, struck his sore jaw on the pillow, and came wide awake, remembering, anger brightening his good eye. He saw her troubled face, and asked thickly, for he had more difficulty in talking now than he had had last night: 'What'sa matter? Sick call okay?'

She nodded, looking at him—all the millions and millions of other numbers; they were men, too, and—'It was easy,' she said, wanting to ease the worry in his face. 'You was jist numbers—to them.'

Her words angered him, for he spoke, lifting his head a little in spite of the pain: 'If it wasn't fer th union, I wouldn't be nothen but a sick man, wonderen if I hada job.' He forgot his anger with her in the bigger one brought back by the pain. He twisted his head from side to side like one in unbearable agony, whispering through his clenched teeth: 'I'll find him, Gert. I'll find him if it takes a million years.'

She stood, her mind, as always, stumbling around, picking up words, laying them down. Not personal, the tool-and-die man had said, but that was all a lie; everybody was a person. Judas was a person; he fulfilled the prophecies made hundreds of years before he was born, and in so doing he sinned, and like any other man he suffered for his sins—and Clovis would most likely suffer for his; only, they were all together, he, she, and the children.

She timidly went up to him and felt his forehead; it was hot, and some of her fear of the future dimmed in the face of her immediate concern for him. She tried again, as she had tried earlier in the morning, to persuade him to let Whit take him to a doctor, but now as then he was angry at the suggestion. A doctor might get suspicious, and call the cops, he said. It hurt him so to talk, she came away. Maybe Whit was pretty certain he had killed a man.

She washed the dishes, made the beds, quickly, briskly, to drown her thoughts; then she whittled a new boat for Amos to keep him in the bathroom, since the day was cold, with a mist of rain, and he could not go outside to play. She warned him again of the dangers of catching the flu if he went into his father's bedroom. The bed was against the wall, with the low foot facing the door; and it was she who had thought to have Clovis lie with his head by the footboard so that if Amos chanced to look in he would see his feet more quickly than his face. Clytie and Enoch she had told—a little. She had made a floundering tale of union fighting and drunks, or started to, but it had suddenly seemed to her that they had known more about the business than she. Maybe last night they'd been awakened; maybe Enoch had learned things from Gilbert Meanwell.

She was just coming out from giving Clovis another aspirin when someone knocked. She closed the bedroom door swiftly but silently before opening the other. Nancy Miller, holding a loosely wrapped package, came in and closed the door before she said: 'Buckandy knowed all about it, all along. Is they anything I can do?'

Gertie shook her head. 'I'm a tryen to git him tu see a doctor.' She heard snorting, muffled sounds from behind the bedroom door, and opened it.

Clovis was sitting up in bed, calling, 'I wanta see Buck.'

'He'll drop around a little later; it ud look funny him comen early inu mornen like this,' Nancy said, studying his face, then feeling his forehead. 'He feels kinda feverish,' she said to Gertie, 'but I wouldn't worry none. If he gits too bad, I'll take him to a doctor. I can drive.'

Clovis made a mumbled sound of disapproval, and she turned back to him. 'I cud throw yu inu car, an go tu a doctor off a piece— he wouldn't hafta know who we was. I'd tell um I got drunk an beatcha up. Yu gotta lie when yu gotta lie. But,' she turned to Gertie, 'from what I heared his insides ain't hurt none. I know a druggist that'll sell sulfa pills 'thout a prescription. They're handy; I keep um allatime fer th kids. Try a few on him, an th aspirin; an if he don't git better I'll take um.'

'I don't want no doctor,' Clovis was insisting. 'Stid a gitten me a doctor, git me th man that done it.'

'Don't think Buckandy an a couple a guys he knows ain't a looken; one's mu cousin goen back home with us—an he knows a feller that's comen up pretty soon with a load a—yu know—liquor. That guy knows his way around. He'll be a looken fer a dago with a bunged-up left eye an a tore-up yer.'

Mrs Miller turned back to Gertie. 'Don't look so worried,' she consoled. 'But, Lord, don't I know they's nothen worse than bein worried crazy over a sick youngen er a sick man? But if he gits real bad I'll git um to a doctor.' She remembered the package she still held, thrust it quickly into Gertie's hands in a shy, ashamed sort of way. 'It's a cake,' she said. 'I ain't much uv a cook—an I'm plumb outa practice. Lots a times while I worked, specially on overtime, I didn't hardly have no time to do any real cooken. I hada use bakery goods, and I hated um—made out a rotten eggs an weeveldy flour, I allus figgered; but ever since I got laid off I been on a baken spree.

547

Buckandy laughed when he seen this. "You're practicen up on a neighbors," he says.'

'Law, you're mighty nice,' Gertie said, adding as she removed the paper: 'An so's th cake. Ain't it pretty?' for it was covered with pink frosting.

'It's mebbe kinda deceiven, though,' the woman said, looking again at Clovis, then turning toward the door. 'He don't look so bad,' she said to Gertie in the kitchen. 'I'll bet his feelen's hurt worse'n his head. If I was him I wouldn't rest easy till I give that foreigner plenty fer what he done tu me—funny talken, like he hadn't been over long, Whit said. That's th kind allus a comen over here to run th country. Them Catholic foreigners owns them factories an runs them unions, an they're all in cahoots together.'

Gertie remembered the boy's head on the table. 'I don't think . . .'

'Yu ain't never had tu work with th things, keep still an listen to um throw off on everybody from th South. I hadda keep shut one day while th steward told a joke about a fam'ly come tu Detroit, an they rented um a place an they was supposed to a asked, "But where's th eaten trough?" A maken out like we don't so much as have dishes. But you say somethen to one a them, boy, that's different! A girl inu washroom, she says somethen to me one day, complainen tu me because at th place where she hadda eat an them sandwich wagons they didn't sell nothen but fish on Friday and Wednesday—it was in Lent. An this other girl, she heared her an she upt an says, "Commie, huh, haten Catholics"; an that kid, she'd never heared a commies till she hit this town, no more'n me. I told that girl she'd better keep shut. "My people back home," I told her, "they hated Catholics frum away back—an they ain't never heared a commies; but boy, if anybody went around a callen my people commies on account a they don't like Catholics they'd git their heads knocked in, an nobody ud wait to round up bedsheets fer to do th job in—they'd do it onu spot," I said, "without waiten tu mess around with a lot a KKK's." That's somethen else,' she went on, apparently talking now to Gertie instead of to the girl, 'they're allus talken about Klan-loven, nigger-haten Southerners, but I'm tellen th truth, they're more nigger haters an Klan lovers up here than ever I did know about back home; an th Black

Legion—Lordy, I just recollected I left Buckandy's biscuit in the stove,' and she was gone.

Clovis stuck his head around the door. 'Don't pay no attention to that fool woman,' he said, 'shooten her lip like she owned the world—big-headed cause she's saved some money. Close tu ten thousand dollars they've saved . . .' He stopped, blinking at the sum.

She tried to get him back to bed, but he declared he felt better and wanted more coffee, which he drank carefully with a teaspoon from the unhurt side of his face. He stayed in the room, but was restless, listening to the sounds of the alley through the window which she had opened an inch or so at his request. He wished some of the men would come visiting, and asked so many times and so wistfully if the mail had come that at last she told him: 'They won't be none no how. I jist answered Mom's last letter two, three days ago, an yer mom, she hardly ever writes.'

He wondered on the ones back home, staring at the ceiling, shaking his head at times, as if by much talking, much thinking, much moving around, he could forget the man who'd tried to kill him. His brother Jesse and others of the soldiers were coming home, and Clovis wished he could see them, wished he could go fishing. At last he said, trying hard to sound as if it didn't matter: 'I bet coal haulen's gitten good. It allus does along about now; an with no gas rationen an th mines able to git stuff to work with, I could do good—real good.'

'But you wouldn't have no truck, Clovis.'

'Law, I was jist thinken. Cain't a body think about how nice it ud be if'n you'd ha bought that Tipton Place an I'd a cleared out a this town soon as V-J Day come an put my car in on a pretty good truck. Then I'd a come rollen home in it—had a good truck might nigh paid fer by now—an you . . .'

She couldn't listen any more. Mumbling something about food left cooking, she hurried away and shut the door behind her. She stood by the kitchen door and watched the thin gray rain and wished for some excuse to take her walking through it, up and down the alleys, up and down, and wear all thought away. She ought to work on dolls. She'd have to make dolls, and sell them too. This year Enoch went all day to school.

She reached for the pieces of pattern, put carefully away on a shelf, but her hand dropped and she turned swiftly into the living room. She couldn't work on dolls, not now; they matched Mrs Miller's voice and her own words, the lie she had told Amos about his father's sickness, the lies she had told the voice on the phone, the sneaking, the hiding, the fear.

She felt clean working on the block of wood. The boy weeping on the table, the man dragged away in the dark, the wonder of how they would manage while Clovis was laid up, memories of the Tipton Place in the rain before the poplar leaves were gone, faded as she worked on a fold of the cloth, low down below the hand. By the time school was out in the afternoon, she was calm enough to say to Enoch, 'I'll buy er make ye some kind a Hallowe'en outfit somehow.' Enoch had been worried. The other kids had big plans for Hallowe'en.

She was getting supper and Enoch was listening to the radio when Clovis pounded on the kitchen wall. She hurried in to find him crouched below the window, listening; his eagerness to hear, his fear of being seen like two fists knocking him in different directions. 'Be still, real still,' he whispered, angry at the noise she made opening and closing the door. 'Mebbe I'll hear it again.'

She listened and heard faintly down the alley a cry she'd often heard, 'Fresh fruita, vegetable—homa-grown tomato-oes.'

'Sounds jist like him,' Clovis whispered, 'jist like that bastard—almost,' he added, disappointed when the cry came again. 'I meant fer you to run out an look—but it ain't th same.'

'You'll drive yerself crazy,' she said. 'It ain't nobody but Joe th vegetable man—mebbe one a his boys, er his nephew.'

'They sound a heap alike,' he said, still crouching as he came back to the bed. There was a bead of perspiration on his upper lip; she guessed the aspirin had done that, and started to ask him how he felt, but the vegetable cry came again, and he lay there whispering curses she did not want to hear.

Two mornings more she dialed numbers, repeated numbers into the phone. After that there was no need, for Flint Plant Number Ten was closed. The strike vote had passed; by law the men should have worked a few days longer, but Plant Four, that made small parts for the parts assemblies in Number Ten, went out on a wildcat, and since a strike would stop everything soon anyway, Flint management closed all plants.

Sophronie sighed when she heard the strike vote news. What was the good of striking? she said; if the men got more wages, better hours, things would only go higher; a body couldn't win. Whit was proud of the vote to strike, though he bemoaned the old days when a strike was a strike and a man had to fight scabs, city policemen, and company guards; now a man wasn't allowed even to hang around the token picket lines, unless it was his turn to walk. This strike, though, might be long, real long, he said; and even if a striker couldn't get the unemployment compensation there was relief—relief if a man were able-bodied enough to work at street cleaning or shoveling snow. He could, maybe, make enough to keep the rent paid; a factory hand could usually get grub enough together on credit to keep from starving, but not rent, especially in these government projects where there was never any fooling around about evictions.

36

Clovis was over the worst of his wounds by the time the strike vote passed, but the scars and bruises lingered and kept him in the house, so that it was Whit who brought his last pay check. Though his wounds had cost him only one day's work in that pay week, walk-outs and work stoppages had made him lose so many hours the check was for only $37.23. Gertie figured that after the November rent was paid, and rent-paying day was less than two weeks away, there would be almost three dollars left.

She would think of all the payments falling due and all their needs against the winter, and the next minute try to silence her fears by reminding herself how lucky they were—compared to the Meanwells and others. They had a ton of coal paid for; Clovis was getting well without a doctor; their credit was good at Zedke's with the bill down almost to nothing when the strike started. She had always paid the milk bill on time, and credit for milk should come without trouble. True, the children would need more clothes before long, but what they had were paid for, not bought on time like the Meanwell clothes. And anyway, she had money, over and above the last pay check; she had counted it after the last telephone call—$34.86. Clytie would make a little money now and then from baby sitting, and Enoch was always getting a nickel here and a dime there from running errands.

Still, in spite of all the brave talk to herself of her riches, she worked frantically on dolls, thought frantically for some combination of colors she had not yet tried. She decided that one all solid red with a white face and yellow hair might sell; she'd never tried that combination, somehow hating the yellow and red together. She carried the pieces before they were dried and strung in to Clovis for him to see, but he only glanced at the new combination of colors with absent-minded eyes.

His eyes were often like that now, unworried by the payments falling due, blind seemed like to everything except his memories of the man who'd tried to kill him—a slight, youngish-seeming man with a torn left ear and a bruised left eye, and with a voice and an accent that Clovis would know in a million if he could only hear them again.

With no pain of wounds to distract him, no work to use up either his mind or body, Clovis let the little man grow until he was big, bigger than all the rest of the world. When Whit or Miller or the tool-and-die man dropped by, his first questions were not of the strike or the chances of his picking up an odd job, but: 'Have ye seen anybody? Have ye heared enything?' And it seemed to Gertie that many men, all close friends of Whit and Miller, were looking.

It was, however, the voices of the many fruit peddlers, who now tried frantically to sell the home-grown peaches and other produce that could not be kept overlong after frost, that threw Clovis into his most frenzied fits of anger. Many times, after crouching below his window to listen, he had pounded on the wall for her. Reluctantly she had gone and listened to his whispered commands to go look at the seller of fruit. 'It sounds so much like him,' he'd say.

Sometimes she would go hesitantly into the alley, and stand, twisting her apron, searching the face of some dark-faced peddler who in his language, and looks, too, seemed kin of Joe. More often she argued. 'These peddlers,' she would say, 'mebbe they do sound like th man that hurt ye—they've got a right to; most a them come frum th same little place acrost th waters, I've heared—but that don't mean nothen. To people up here we'd sound jist like th Cramers back home; but we're all different, mighty different; an Joe an his boys an that nephew, mebbe they do sound like that man; but they're good hard-worken people.'

He would be silent; listen sometimes; maybe even look at her, but his glance on her was that of the wise for the stupid. Enoch, who with no bidding was always running to scan the face of some foreign sounding peddler, would, like his father, keep silent, but the 'Oh, yeah?' was plain in his eyes.

Sometimes it seemed to Gertie that even Clytie watched and hunted. She was certain Mrs Miller was suspicious of all Sicilian fruit peddlers, even Joe, with whom the Millers had never used to trade, for both had hated the 'foreign-talken swindlers.' But now Mrs Miller was always running to buy a bit of fruit from every passing truck.

Gertie, out one afternoon to buy a dime's worth of the cheap overripe peaches from Joe, found Mrs Miller looking over and around the heaped-up, open-sided truck as if she expected to find something more than fruits and vegetables. However, in spite of the busy season, there was no one with Joe but his latest 'nephew,' a small child, not much bigger than Amos, whom Gertie had first seen on the truck some time during the summer. Mrs Miller considered the little one, and asked: 'Ain't they no Catholic school today? Is that why he ain't in school?' Joe acted as if he had not heard, but Mrs Miller insisted: 'Where's your nephew, Joe? You need a helper.'

Joe jerked his shoulder toward the child, and the child, as if aware of being watched, turned and smiled shyly at Gertie. She tried to return the smile, then swiftly began to consider the cheap home-grown potatoes. The child's eyes were black as Callie Lou's, and something in his timid glance from under the long dark lashes made her think of Cassie. He could speak no English, so there was about him, too, a lostness that had been Cassie's after she had done away with Callie Lou.

Gertie, as usual, was the last to buy the bruised and overripe peaches, but Mrs Miller lingered, and watched Joe drive away, her eyes narrowed and suspicious. ' 'S'funny thing,' she said, whispering, glancing about to make certain no one but Gertie heard, 'th way them dagoes gits rich so quick.'

'Rich?' Gertie asked. 'They work awful hard fer real rich people.'

'Yeah? Didn't yu see his nephew—must a been five er six weeks ago—he come driven down th alley, slow, then stopped by Max's place. He didn't git out a th car, one a them big '42 Olds—th kind you cain't git without black market an a big down payment. He set there in that car, an looked at Max's door, hopen she'd see him. He didn't know, I recken, she'd already cleared out, an I kept a wishen that big Polock ud see an come out an knock his head in. But he never did. Now, Buckandy an me, an a heap a th others, we'd like to know how yu can make money on a fruit truck enough to buy a car like that.'

'I guess he puts ever cent he can scrape together on it,' Gertie said, shivering, hurrying up her steps, for a cold wind came out of the north, promising thick ice and a heavy frost if it stilled through the night.

Next morning she stared a long time at the frost, like a thin snow on the coalhouse roof; she thought of outgrown children's boots, ragged, too short coats, and sleazy snowpants, already twice mended. She built a fire in the heating stove, the house was so cold, remembering only after she had poured on better than half a bucket of coal that she should have done as Mrs Daly did when her coal was low—kept the oven going full blast. But a body had to be careful and stay close to the kitchen door in case somebody from the office came snooping—it was against the rules to use gas for anything but cooking. But it was like Mrs Daly said; a person could always forget to turn the oven off after making toast or something—and a ton of coal wouldn't last forever.

The weak sun in the smoky sky had hardly touched the frost by the time the milkman came, and thinking on the winter ahead Gertie found it a little easier to ask for credit. Still, she was so sweaty-handed and flushed up as she stumbled over the words, that the milkman, forever hurrying, paused long enough to ask, 'Yu trying tu ask fu credit, lady?'

She nodded, hanging on his answer, and when he gave her none, she said: 'Make it jist four quarts ever other day, stid uv th six I've been gitten. My man's been sick, an now th strike—it's come.'

He looked disgusted as he wrote her new order in his little book. 'If it's Flint, it oughta come sooner,' he said, half accusingly, as if he read her doubts, then added words she had already heard from many: 'It's gonna be a long un—butcha'ull pull through. I been on some tough uns muself—teamsters.'

He gave her courage to look at the shelves and into the little cupboard at the end of the sink. Since Clovis had got hurt she'd been buying as little as she could; now everything was running out: no more than enough flour for a batch of biscuit, coffee low—she'd have to mix in even less new with the old grounds—the last cake of soap half gone, a bit of sugar, a dust of meal, and that was all. She ought to buy more meal; mush for breakfast instead of oats would be cheaper.

She pondered above an empty oats box; all groceries would have to come from Zadkiewicz on credit. How long would he give so much credit? Maybe it would be better to do as Sophronie did: buy stuff on credit from different people. Sophronie had credit with the bakeryman, Vegetable Joe, the milkman, and a clothing store in Hamtramck. She had bought so little from the bakery man, she could only ask credit of Joe; the bill would get so big at Zedke's he might cut them off before the strike was over.

She mustn't worry so, she told herself as she got the noon meal. As soon as the scars on Clovis healed a little more, he'd get some kind of job, tinkering, maybe, like back home. She was ashamed when meal time came. The food was worse than they'd ever had back home, even late in the winter after a poor crop year: boiled beans scantily seasoned with a little bacon grease, sliced overripe tomatoes, and peaches, raw, because cooked ones needed sugar. However, the children ate it with no comment; and Clovis, who'd always quarreled if she seemed the least bit stingy about food, ate the meatless beans without a word.

She could have fed him sawdust just as well, she thought, taking his dishes away, for he still wouldn't risk Amos's questions and maybe his talk in the alley about his dad's scars, but continued to eat in his room, feeding mostly on anger. Today, as always, he'd asked Enoch the minute he got home from school, 'See anybody?'

Enoch had shaken his head, weary of the hunting, tired of his father's anger. 'Aw, Pop, fergit it. Nobody can't never find him.' He had, then, repeated Whit: 'He didn't have nothen agin yu nohow.'

There was little but beans and bread and scanty milk until the next night at supper when she served fried potatoes, using the last of the potatoes, the last of the lard. Lard would have to come from Zedke's on credit, but more potatoes she would get from Joe—or at least she would try to get credit from Joe. He came through twice a week, and tomorrow was his day.

All afternoon, next day, she listened for his calling while she sat by the kitchen table and drew around patterns laid on the grain-bin maple for another batch of dolls. Amos was playing outside so that Clovis enjoyed the freedom of the whole place, and lingered in the kitchen waiting for her to finish, for he had caught up with her in the sawing. It was almost school letting out time before she heard Joe, still two alleys away. Her hands grew sweaty over the pencil, and her mind went leaping back and forth for easy credit-asking words, but Clovis never noticed for listening to the sound of Joe's voice. As always he ran to the window, peeping, cursing, repeating, 'Sounds a heap like him.'

Gertie forced herself to work on until the truck had stopped, then waited by her gate until the other women had finished; she wanted to be alone with Joe when she asked for credit. She saw that he had put up his truck sides; winter it was when Joe boxed in his truck and started his little charcoal stove to keep the produce from freezing. It was curious, she thought idly, that he did all that today when the weather, though cloudy, had warmed up since the hard-freezing frosts had browned even her bit of grass.

She pretended to be busy pulling up the dead flowers while Joe waited on the other women, but she saw with swift glances from the corners of her eyes that he had help, for she saw a hand reach out with sacks of things. She wondered a moment if it could be the nephew, whom she had not seen in some days, then forgot him in thinking on how it would be to ask Joe for credit. Mrs Bommarita, the last customer, was paying now, and Gertie, in her embarrassment and eagerness to be done with the business, hurried through her gate, and spoke too quickly and so loudly that Mrs Bommarita looked around. The woman stopped and listened as Gertie, the empty Josiah basket twisting on her arm, began, 'Joe—' She was even more embarrassed when she remembered that Joe was maybe not his name. Max had called all peddlers Joe. 'Yu gotta call um something; they're people,' Max had said.

Whatever his name, he was studying her confusion now, his dark eyes smooth as ever, 'I got—' she began again. 'We're gitten kinda hard run.' She'd better not say Clovis was sick; credit would come harder to a sick man than to one just on strike. 'My man's out on strike. Could I git credit?'

He considered her a moment longer. 'Hokay,' he said, the words almost a sigh, his face angry, the long wrinkles in his cheeks twisted as when he had bawled out the nephew.

She moved nearer, fumbling over the potatoes; a smear of their black dirt stuck to her sweaty palm. Did it always come so hard, this credit asking? It was Clytie, she remembered, who had asked credit of Zedke. 'Home-grown,' Joe was saying over the apples. 'Cheap. Sweet potatoes, nice—' He remembered, and never named the price; a striker's wife on credit could not buy the always expensive sweet potatoes.

She bought a peck of the cheapest Irish potatoes, and he called in his own language into the back of the truck, apparently for his helper to weigh the potatoes, for he waited motionless for her next order. Gertie's flustered glance wandered over the produce displayed near the letdown tailgate, and then for the first time it chanced deeper into the truck. She saw then among the fruits and vegetables the moving brightness of a boy's jacket, shiny green with red sleeves, all of smooth rayon such as that of children's snowsuits. The nephew, she thought, for he loved bright clothes.

'Cabbage,' she said, taking her glance and her thoughts away, 'that is, if it's kinda cheap, an good solid heads. A big head I'd ruther have, an then some onions—jist them little cooken kind.' She looked at the abundance spread in front of her, as Joe called to his helper in the back of the truck. The purple home-grown grapes were so cheap—but she couldn't ask for a penny more credit than what she just had to have.

She felt water come into her mouth, staring as she was at the grapes. Seemed like in the summer a body got so hungry for all the raw stuff they could eat; it was fall now and none of them had ever had all summer his fill of good fresh fruit and garden truck. A large cabbage was thrust between her and the grapes. She took it, looked at it, hefting, considering. 'How much?' she asked, and lifted her head.

The nephew took the cabbage as he smiled at her, then turned toward the scales. She knew she must, but she could not take her eyes away. It was so dark in the truck, she was imagining there was a bruise about the nephew's eye; and anyway it was on the right side. She brushed the back of her hand across her eyes; his head was sidewise to her now, bent above the scales, but still the bruise was there, and more plainly the bruised and once-torn ear, covered with some whitish salve, but the wound still showed—like the first time she'd tried to mark a pig's ear; its pitiful squealing had unhanded her.

'Lady, yu wanta white onions?'

She turned quickly to Joe; the boy studying the scales had never noticed her glance. 'White,' she said, remembering Clovis's, 'They all sound alike.' The boy would know when she spoke that she talked like the man he had hurt and who had hurt him. He and his people were looking for Clovis as Clovis looked for him; but Whit and Clovis both declared they hadn't so much as grunted; the tool-and-die man had warned them against it.

'How many, ladee?'

She kept her eyes steadfastly on the vegetables, and tried to remember how many of what. 'A gallon,' she said at last. The cabbage was below her face again, and the boy, proud of his English and his mastery of the scales said, 'Twenty-one cents,' then adding, smiling, 'nice—cheap.'

She looked at him again, not meaning to. He smiled, a warm smile, like when he had given her the flowers. She turned confusedly away, and grabbed the Josiah basket into which Joe had dumped the potatoes to save a bag, then realized the boy had been holding out the cabbage all this time. She reached for it and would not look at him as he reminded her, saying, 'Cabbage.'

She darted toward her door, but stopped when Joe said, 'Wait, ladee.' She turned part way back and waited while he took a little worn notebook from a pocket and, after looking at her load, wrote numbers while she stood trying hard not to look at Sophronie's door or Miller's door, or even her own, and whispering somewhere below sound, 'Please, Lord, get the boy out of the alley, quick.'

The book closed, and she turned, remembering she must go slowly and not act afraid. But Joe again said, 'Wait.' She could not, and, still moving, looked at him over her shoulder. He was smiling like old John when he told her she could have the land. 'Ladee,' he said slowly, no longer the seller of vegetables, but a friend, 'allatime people gotta strike. Yu gotta strike. Th union.' And in his mouth the word was like a curse, but for her he smiled. 'Yu not starve. Credit good. Times good.' He turned and said something to the nephew.

Gertie, though understanding that Joe was not yet finished with her, continued to move toward her door, watching him over her shoulder. The boy handed out a bushel basket half full of overripe peaches. 'Take du peaches. Tomorrow—no good. Spoil,' Joe said, taking the basket from the boy, shoving it toward her. He saw that her arms were burdened, the filled basket on one, the large cabbage on the other. He gave a quick command; the boy came, and stood hesitant on the tailgate. He glanced swiftly around him like one half afraid, and Gertie saw he looked palish, as if he had been sick or some time indoors. Joe gave a swifter, sharper command, and the boy sprang down, took the basket, smiling up at Gertie as if to say that whatever dangers lurked about for him there could be none with her.

'Automobile—accident,' Joe said, seeing her eyes flick the boy's face.

She was unable to thank Joe, unable to think of anything except that in another moment the boy would be on her stoop with Clovis just behind the kitchen door. 'No, no,' she burst out, springing away, 'I don't—he mustn't—'

Joe patted her arm. 'Now—ladee—no charitee—gift. Yu kids lika du peaches.'

She dashed up the walk, the boy behind her. She glanced quickly at her kitchen door, the inner door ajar just as she had left it, but the blind was pulled; it hadn't been when she came out. Amos came scooting through a hole in the fence, leaped up to see what the boy carried in the basket, then at once began crying, 'Peaches; Mom's gotta lot a peaches.'

Gertie set her own basket quickly on the stoop, grabbed the basket of peaches just as the boy started to open the kitchen door, 'Thanks,' she gasped, 'you'd better hurry back to—'

'Bring backa da basket,' Joe was calling.

She heard her own hard breathing as she opened the storm door, and went through the partly opened inner door. 'Wait,' she said over her shoulder, struggling with the word, it came through with such a choking. 'I'll git somethen tu put em in.'

The basket scraped against the narrowly opened inner door, but the door would open no wider, for Clovis was behind it, his long thin body crouched as he looked through the crack the door made in its opening. In one swift glance she saw the side of his face, teeth clenched, still, like the terrible stillness in his crouching body. She looked wildly about for a box, a pot, a sack, anything to hold the peaches. She could see nothing. The boy, she thought, was coming into the kitchen, for he held the storm door part way open. She dumped the peaches onto the floor. They made a little banging thumping, but Clovis did not move, not even his eyes. She shoved the basket through the door. The boy took it, but still he lingered, looking toward Max's door now, smiling. 'Peaches—nice,' he said, moving only when she came through the door. She could neither nod nor answer, and he looked troubled and disappointed, then said again, even more slowly, more clearly, 'Peaches nice—cheap. For free.'

She nodded, and he smiled, pleased that she had understood. 'You'd better git on,' she said, low-voiced, almost whispering. 'Joe—won't like it.'

He smiled as if he understood, but was slow in turning about and looking at Joe, who had finished putting up the tailgate and was bending now to look for children's legs on the other side of the truck. The boy nodded toward Victor's stoop. 'Max—sick?'

'Gone,' she said. Clovis was gone too, now. She had felt him move behind her, for he had made no sound; and with the door half shut as it was, the boy, even had he been looking into the kitchen, could not have seen Clovis go.

She stood, unmindful that Amos and a whole swarm of little children had gone into the kitchen and were messing round in the peaches spilled over the floor. She continued to stand after the truck had disappeared around the end of the alley, nor did she lift her eyes when an airplane screamed overhead, nor shiver when a moment later a through train roared by; but the sound roused her enough that she went within doors.

She was like a person moving in her sleep as she got the children out of the kitchen, put the peaches into the other split basket, and cleaned the floor. In time she even remembered what it was she had been doing when the truck came. She finished marking out the board of dolls' legs, then sat a moment, lips mumbling, head lifted at times as she tried to hear the words she would say to Clovis to take all his suspicion away.

She took the board in to him after Enoch came from school; and she wasn't certain but she thought it was the first time he had forgot to ask Enoch if he had seen a marked-up man. He was lying on the bed, his folded arms under his head, his eyes on the ceiling. Looking at him, she thought his face was wiped clean of the blind anger; now, it was as when he had worked on the washing-machine motor, a strange business, but a satisfying one, his face said, for he would puzzle his way through it, put it all together, make it work.

'Clovis,' she said, laying the board on a chair, 'that boy—' She stopped in the face of the effort to hear her own voice; she mustn't sound troubled and excited, but easy and off-like—smooth—that was the word. 'That boy, Clovis, he's been in a car wreck.'

'Huh,' he said, coming a little out of his machine up there in the ceiling.

'That bo—kid, he's been in a car wreck.'

He looked at her without moving his head, seemed to ponder, and said at last, 'Huh—what kid?'

'Th one come tu th door.'

'Yeah,' he said, then quickly, 'sure, sure,' and flopped away from her, his face toward the wall.

She stood a moment longer, staring at his back, her lips moving, trying out words. She turned away at last. His voice had been so easy, so soft, the way she'd wanted hers to be, but not meaningless, no, not quite; a Detroit 'Yeah,' she had learned, almost never meant yes.

The machine in the ceiling did not hold Clovis long. He'd found a way to solve it, she thought, for by the time Clytie was home from high school he was restless, pacing the floor, the dolls' legs left uncut. That night for the first time he came out and ate supper with them all. 'Nothen much ails me no more but th scars,' he said, and added a little worriedly, 'I'm marked like a sheep.'

Clytie giggled. 'I bet I could fix yu up with a good make-up base an that liquid stocking stuff like Roland O'Rourke. He played a

562

gangster, but allatime you could see he was a right guy. Anyhow, his sweetheart fixed up his face so's he could go out—that is, in a car atter dark.'

'That's better'n nothen,' Clovis said, his voice gay almost as it had used to be when he got paid for a ton of coal he'd given up for a bad debt.

There was a quick silence when Amos, who had been studying his father, said, 'How'dju git hurt, Pop?' He left his food and came and stood by Clovis the better to see the red mark above the eyebrow and discolored jaw.

Gertie tried vainly to think of something to distract the child's attention, and then sat silent while both Enoch and Clytie, with a little help from Clovis, explained to Amos how the flu sometimes scarred up people. Enoch turned to her for confirmation. 'Mom, yu recollect wotta time Granma Nevels had when last winter—winter before now—her jaw swole up, and her eye turned black with th flu.'

Her nod was slight, but still a nod, and it seemed to her that Clovis, watching, smiled. He was still gay when, after making certain the early autumn dark had fallen, he went over to the Meanwells' unit. Whit had been so good to visit him, he thought he'd visit Whit for a change, he said.

Clovis came home early, and soon after, she thought, but couldn't be certain, she heard the Meanwell car leave the parking lot. She forgot to wonder when, after the children had finally gone to bed, she began to work on the man in the wood. Then late, very late, there came a tapping on the door, and Clovis, as if he'd been expecting it, hurried to let the knocker in. It was the tool-and-die man, whom she had not seen since a few nights after Clovis was hurt. He smiled at her, and studied the fold of cloth on which she was working. 'You'll have more time now for th man,' he said, and held out the sanding contraption he had apparently just assembled.

She mumbled some unenthusiastic words of gratitude. He kept looking at the man in the wood, and seemed ready to talk of him or ask her questions, but Clovis was impatient, calling from the bedroom door, 'Come on, an let's see if them sanders is any good.'

He turned away and closed the door, as if he already knew it must be closed.

Feeling ever more guilty at the time wasted on the man in the wood, she quit at last and worked again on the dolls. She sat by the kitchen table in the place where Clovis ate, with her chair pulled out into the passway, so that the bedroom door was less than a hand's reach away. She kept the sandpaper scraping over the old paint on the wood; she knew she didn't want to try to eavesdrop; there was nothing to hear but the test run of the new sanding machine. Clovis sanded pieces of the dolls in his bedroom with the door closed; working so, there was less danger of letting the neighbors know what he was about or of awakening the children. Tonight was no different from other nights; Clovis was always eager to try out a new machine.

Once the machine stopped, and she was still, the sandpaper still as she sat, breath held, head tipped toward the door, for the tool-and-die man was saying, a weary arguing in his voice: 'Butcha gotta be certain. I'd forget it; th kid was a hired hand doen a job. If we could learn something . . . Butcha could kill one and he wouldn't talk—he couldn't talk to us, not English. If we did do something an it ever got out into th papers, th cops, everybody, would say th union was behind it. Yu gotta keep th union clean. Yu gotta—' The sanding machine had started up again.

She was so tired, she leaned her head against the door, and through the buzzing on the other side there was, she thought, the arguing still. She got soundlessly to her feet, and went again to the block of wood, and was working by it, kneeling, when she heard a resigned sigh; she looked around, and the tool-and-die man was in the passway, leaving for work.

Next day, as she came up the alley from hunting Amos, she passed Mrs Daly out airing the new baby in the old carriage. The little woman looked at her and said, 'Yu mustn't take ut so hard.'

'What?' Gertie asked, realizing at once that she had turned too quickly, and spoken too worriedly, for Mrs Bommarita, hanging clothes, was listening.

'Du strike ana sickness,' Mrs Daly said. 'Yu look like youse was comen down yuself from worry.'

Gertie tried to smile, but knew she was only pulling her lips back and showing all her teeth. Still, Mrs Daly sighed and shook her head, then declared that Clovis had been in bed an awfully long time for just the flu, while behind her Mrs Bommarita watched and nodded. 'It's settled in his face—his teeth—his whole face swole up,' Gertie said, and wondered if they noticed her voice or that her heart pounded so it quivered her dress.

'Don't I know?' Mrs Daly was saying. 'Last fall I gotta toothache an it quit, but wudju believe it? Mu nose got as big as three noses, an mu eyes—yu oughta seen my eye—black. I hadda let Mr Daly take me tudu doctor.'

'I'm goen tu make Clovis go—if it don't clear up pretty soon,' Gertie said, breathing easier, moving on toward her gate, then remembering to stop again and say: 'It ain't like he could work. With that strike on an jobs scarce right now, I figger he might as well stay in an take care a hissef.'

37

Clovis whistled now at times, and she wondered at and often feared his gaiety, not gaiety either, just peace, for the machine in the ceiling was put together. He still spoke sometimes of how he would like to find the man who had marked him up, but he could never get back the old ring of helpless anger, and talked mostly, she thought, for the benefit of Enoch and Clytie. Yet, she could not be certain; there were days when he was restless and angry, frowning for long moments into Clytie's mirror as he studied his scars.

The marks still held him within doors by day, so that it was she who paid the rent for November. She came away from the project office, fingering the three one-dollar bills, the seventy-three cents left from the last pay check. She counted in her head their total savings; less than thirty dollars now. She did not know exactly; Clovis had taken three one-dollar bills for gas; he planned to go job hunting soon and would need the car. She'd had to buy socks for Enoch; Zadkiewicz didn't carry socks, and anyway they already owed him close to a hundred dollars. She was still, twisting her head over the sum; it was like a tight collar choking her—more than she had got back home for both Dock and Betsy. She walked again: November was so short, the rent for December wasn't much more than four weeks away; the rent she had to have seemed bigger than the debt for groceries—and some said the strike might last till Christmas.

She went home and found the kitchen floor covered with her baskets, old cardboard boxes, her pots and the coal bucket, all heaped with apples, overripe peaches, tomatoes picked against the frost when green but ripening now, peppers, celery, even onions and potatoes. She was gaping at the welcome mess in wonder when Clovis stuck his head around the bedroom door to explain that Bunkin, who had just gone, had brought the stuff because he had no place to store it and it wouldn't keep any longer.

'That Bunkin,' Clovis said, shaking his head half enviously, 'he bought him a piece of uv a old farm, four, five acres, somewhere outside a Detroit, soon as him an his wife could scrape enough together—she's worked some a th time. He allus aimed to stay, he said. That was more'n three years ago. He's put him up a garage—all paid fer, an fixed so's they can kinda batch in it in th summer—an now while th strike's on he's a starten on a house.'

'I allus thought you said he was kind of foolish,' Gertie said, still glad of the vegetables, but remembering that this was the day for Joe. Now she couldn't go out to him and see— What had she wanted to see? Of course she would see the same thing she had seen last time, the nephew, smiling, weighing vegetables. Trouble and worry had sickened her mind so that she was always imagining silly things, she told herself, as she sat by the kitchen door and marked for painting some pieces of dolls that Clovis had sanded. Still, when she heard Joe's calling she sprang up and stood watching until the truck had stopped and she had seen the long but young-looking hand give a grapefruit to Mrs Miller. She was worried, wondering if Mrs Miller, who had been gone the other day, noticed the boy's face now; but today Mrs Miller was so busy gossiping and laughing that she seemed to notice nothing.

Next afternoon she was painting a dozen left legs a bright and shiny red when Sophronie came tapping. She stood in the kitchen, throwing quick, worried glances about her, like some little hopping tree bird that never feels safe on the ground. 'They're pretty,' she said of the doll parts, with a loudness unusual for her. She gave an uneasy glance toward the bedroom where Clovis stayed, then asked, still more loudly: 'Have you got any sage? I'm a tryen tu fix a stuffed beef heart—they're cheap and real good if you stuff um right.'

Gertie got down the sage, old now, but still better than the stuff from stores. Sophronie gave a swift, uneasy glance about her, then

567

came very close to Gertie and whispered up to her as she took the sage, 'Come out on th stoop.' Then loudly again, for any listening ears, 'Have you seen Miz Bommarita's new winter coat? She's got it out a airen on her line.'

Gertie followed and closed both kitchen doors, though the radio was going, loud, for Clovis was running the sanding contraption. She realized as she went onto the stoop and pretended to look at the coat, that Sophronie had come just now because of the covering sounds. She listened, staring at the coat, while Sophronie stood a little behind her and whispered rapidly: 'That Miz Miller she's invited me tu go to a midnight show, downtown, double feature that'll make us gone most a th night. I gotta go—Whit's maken me. She's gonna ast you. Don'tcha. They're up to somethen; too much's goen on. You stay an— That shore is pretty. I wisht I had one like it.' Mrs Bommarita had come out onto her stoop, and Sophronie, after some loud remarks about the goodness of home-grown sage and the beauties of the coat, hurried home.

Mrs Miller came that afternoon. 'I'm gonna celebrate,' she said. 'We're leaven pretty soon. I don't think we'll stay to git all my unemployment money. I'm gitten jumpier and jumpier when Buckandy's gone to th steel mill—another cable broke last night, an one pitman got it pretty bad.' She went on to tell in her loud rushing voice of how she wanted to take Gertie and Sophronie to a real fine show; her husband would chauffeur them there and back and in between times act as baby sitter, tomorrow night, his night off.

Gertie shook her head, and tried to smile. 'Law, I ain't got no time tu go to a show. I wouldn't know how to act in one a them big downtown places.'

Mrs Miller only nodded, 'I don't neither, butcha gotta learn some time. I told Buckandy I jist hadda go. Yu know, back home people'ull ast me, "How was Detroit?" an I'll hate to say, "I never did go down to lookut it." Honest to God, I ain't never been downtown. I've allus kinda wanted to, an if I don't while I've got th chance I'll allus wish I had. Like now, I already wish I'd learned wot I made in u shop. Fer almost three years I hadda same job, welden five little jiggers on a little piece a steel; somebody said they thought they went somewheres inu battleship, but I know they ain't battleships enough inu whole world tu use all them little pieces I welded.' She remembered the object of her errand, pulled her chair closer, insisting, 'Come on now, yu gotta, yu jist gotta go.'

Clovis heard, and came begging Gertie to go, grew more and more insistent, and was for an instant surly when she would not promise. Then he was like a man remembering to put on his Sunday behavior as he pointed out that she needed to get out and have a little pastime once in awhile.

He fussed at times even after Mrs Miller had gone, and worse, he told Clytie when she came home of the chance her mother was throwing away to go downtown to a real movie palace. Clytie whined most of the evening because Gertie wouldn't go; she had long wanted to see the real downtown Detroit, but like many of the alley children she had never been there.

Next day Clovis began his persuadings again, though it seemed to Gertie he was careful not to act too interested; and he was meek as could be when she turned on him. 'Man, what ails you? Here I am tired to death with all kinds of work to do, dolls, an some patchen jist has to be done, an you tell me to rest my self by goen to a movie. You know I wouldn't like th movies no better than th radio. I'd swap em all fer a walk in nice clean woods, an enyhow I've got a headache.'

He looked worried at that, for there was between them no memory of her ever having mentioned pain. 'You ain't comen down?' he asked.

She sighed windedly, 'No. Mostly, I recken, it's stayen inside too close with th gas smell an th paint smell frum these dolls, an I've been stayen up too late. Tonight I'm aimen tu go to bed early an git a good night's sleep.'

He said no more, but she could see he was dissatisfied and restless. He tinkered with and cleaned up all the contraptions in the house, and oiled all the door hinges. Finished with that, he tramped around the house and quarreled about being penned up with a black eye. Then he was still for a long while in Clytie's room, and she thought he was fixing the inside window so it would work better, but when he came out to her, smiling a little, she jumped in startlement. He had a hat jammed low on his forehead to hide the mark above his eye, and different from his usual neat ways, he hadn't shaved for days, so that his whiskers covered the bruise on his jaw. Going closer, she saw he had powdered his forehead; the mark showed less, but his whole face had an odd look.

It pleased him that he looked strange to her. 'Pretty soon,' he said, 'I can job hunt an take my turn in u picket line. Th union'll be thinken I don't care nothen about th strike.'

'You ought to tell th union what you've already done fer it,' she said with some bitterness. 'If they hadn't been no union, you wouldn't ha been hurt.'

'Tellen th union ud be might' nigh as bad as tellen th cops. They're allus screamen their heads off fer law an order—them higher ups. An anyhow, Whit wasn't certain, but—' He was suddenly interested in a passing moving van.

She never asked him to finish what he had started to say; the boy who had been a soldier wouldn't cry over a few black eyes. She tried to put her mind steadfastly on the dolls' arms she was painting now. But the work gave her mind nothing to hold to. It kept swinging away to Cassie. She'd wanted to set some bulbs this fall for flowers come spring, but—; she'd think of the next rent paying day, and from that her mind would jump back to the last letter she'd had from her mother. Mostly, she had written complaints of Reuben: he'd run off to a play party given for some wild soldier boys who'd been spared to come home when her Henley was dead, and there'd been banjo music and drinking with some wild dancing, she'd heard. Her mother thought Reuben had had a dram or so, maybe even danced, and she'd written half a page about the sins of the fathers, explaining it could also mean mothers, being visited upon the children.

Her mind swung back to the other boy away from his mother, Joe's helper. Why did Clovis and Whit want their women gone tonight? She sprang up, getting a smear of red paint on her apron; she had to talk to someone. Who? She thought of the man who had talked over Cassie; he'd looked honest and stern as well as kind. She realized she was out on her stoop with a half painted doll's right arm gripped in her hand, searching down the alley as if she expected someone. Who? Maybe the gospel woman would come again. She could tell her and she would understand. What would she tell the gospel woman? She didn't know anything. There wasn't anything except her own wicked imagination.

Her uneasiness blazed up again like a smoldering fire when Clovis, after eating almost no supper, grew more fidgety than ever, and though he tried to hide it he was like a man waiting for a train. Clytie whined again because Gertie hadn't taken the trip downtown to the movie that was all for free, but Clovis told her to shut up. 'Yer Mom ain't feelen so good. She's goen tu go tu bed right after supper?' he said, looking at Gertie.

Gertie nodded, but continued to paint dolls, the hair now, bright yellow above red-spotted cheeks, even after Clytie had gone to bed. She was just thinking of putting the smelly work away, when she heard the slamming of the Meanwell kitchen door, followed by Mrs Miller's loud laughter. 'There they go, an you could ha been with em, Gert,' Clovis said, half accusingly, then added, as he went for the bottle of turpentine in which he kept the brushes, 'I thought you was goen to bed early.'

She only nodded, but when he had put the brushes away he said, turning toward the closet at the end of the hall: 'I ain't sleepy. I think I'll go keep Whit company.'

Gertie felt the cold sweat on her hands as she pressed them hard against her weary eyes, but her voice seemed level enough, uncaring, as she said, 'Miller'ull most likely be with him; he ain't stayen fer th movie.'

'Miller's got to stay home with his little youngens,' Clovis said. He took his hat and jacket from the hall closet, and with no more words for her went away.

She took a shower, hot, that put clouds of steam in the little bathroom and made water drip from the windows. The sound of the shower as always drowned all other sounds, but seemed like she heard the opening of the kitchen door. Frightened as she had never used to be back home, where doors where never locked, she turned off the shower, stuck her head past the curtain, and listened, but the place was still.

She stayed a long time in the shower; the noise and the water beating on her body somehow made all the world about her, even Clovis, seem farther away. She thought of hills and of home where the yellow poplar leaves would be drifted knee-deep on the ridge sides; the children, Cassie among them, would come running home from school, for with the war over there was school. But Reuben wasn't going. He didn't care for school, her mother had written several weeks ago. He'd liked it well enough in the beginning, for she'd been able to do without his work for a few weeks in the summer; then she'd sent him after corn-cutting time for a while, but now after corngathering time he didn't want to go. It was the same letter in which she had hoped Gertie's father would get some sense and move into town and quit trying to farm. What then for Reuben, Gertie wondered—the coal mines—a factory hand? He wouldn't like it underground, and he had her hatred of machinery.

There weren't any answers, and her mind jumped back to Clovis. She looked out the kitchen door when, as was her custom now before going to bed, she made certain it was locked; she saw the square of light from Whit's kitchen door, and felt better. She felt still better when, while testing the other door, she looked down toward the parking lot and saw Clovis's car and Whit's car side by side with another she thought was the tool-and-die man's.

She went into the bedroom between her kitchen and Sophronie's where Clovis slept now, and lay as he did since he had been hurt, with her feet instead of her head close to the Meanwell wall. However, she at once came wide awake; the place was stuffy, steamy from the family's nightly showers, and smelling too of gas and paint from the dolls mixed in with boiled beans and cabbage.

The wall in front of her made a faint glimmering in the dim light from the alley. It was so still behind the wall—too still. Whit's beer bottle should be clicking on the table; there'd be talk, and maybe the slap of cards as the men played setback. They wouldn't sit in dead silence.

572

She got up and stood in the narrow space between the foot of the bed and the window. She heard now, only after much listening, the creak of a chair as if one man sat there.

She fled from the still wall into the living room. A steel pour was coming up; the red light flickered on the drawn blind; the light grew brighter; the block of wood made a faint shadow on the floor, trembling like her own shadow when she had sat by Reuben's bed. She mustn't work on the block of wood; though for days she'd been wanting to finish the lifted hand that lingered longingly above the money in the other hand; for it was money—taken—but soon to be given away. The man, then, was Judas; but she didn't want Judas. Christ had had no money, just his life. Life and money: could a body separate the two?

What had Judas done for his money? Whispered a little, kept still as she did now. No, it wasn't Judas. She'd bring the face out now, prove to herself it wasn't Judas. She jerked on the light. She had to work on the block of wood.

Barefooted and in her nightgown, she stepped into the hall, and without looking reached on the top shelf. It was higher than the children could reach, and just above the place where she hung her coat. She had put the knife there on the first day of her coming, for it was a handy place and safe from even Clovis. He never carried a knife, but sometimes he borrowed her own, and he had a heavy hand with a knife; could dull the blade in no time. Once, back home, he'd jerked it up, and used it for a screwdriver, needing a little one.

She rose on tiptoe, reaching still further. The knife had been pushed to the back of the wall was why she couldn't feel it. She had no memory of laying it there, any more than she remembered putting her clothes over the foot of the bed or the leftover beans in the icebox. It was just that she always did such things.

She snapped on the hall light, got a chair, and stood on it and looked. She searched, at first slowly and methodically, then frantically through all the shelves in the hall, in the rooms where the children were sleeping, the kitchen, the pockets of her clothing. The knife was gone. She hadn't lost it. She would have noticed, walking around, the weight gone from her pocket. Clovis had borrowed it again. Why? He wanted to use it again as a screwdriver while he and the tool-and-die man worked on some contraption. The tool-and-die man kept a kit of tools in his car; but that was only some talk of the children.

The need of being certain that Clovis had the knife, that he was sitting with Whit on the other side of the wall, became an overmastering torture. She slipped into her coat and shoes, hurried down the steps, and up to Whit's door.

He must have heard her coming, for he was opening the door before she'd finished knocking. He stood in the doorway, one hand on the knob, and when she pushed to come in to speak to Clovis, it would open no wider than Whit's shoulders as he stood barring her way, smiling, but not pleased. 'What'sa matter?' he asked, whispering.

'My knife—it's gone.'

'Now who would want a knife at one o'clock in u mornen?' and he laughed his soundless, shivering laughter.

'I want tu whittle,' she said. 'Clovis has got it. It wouldn't be lost. I've never lost it or mislaid it in all these years.'

'Yeah,' he said, not moving.

'But ask Clovis has he got it,' she begged, trying to see past him. He seemed alone. She brushed her hand across her eyes; she wanted to think of her father—of anything. Whit was alone in the place except for the sleeping children. But Clovis had to be there. 'Ask him,' she repeated, pushing on the door, but whispering still. Why did she whisper? It was no uncommon thing in the alley to hear people talking at any time of the night, for many worked strange hours.

'Law, woman,' Whit said, not moving, not smiling, 'I ain't got th heart tu wake him. Some baby sitter he is—passed out, him an that tool-an-die man. One's in my bed, one on the sofa. You'd better git home an git some sleep. That fool Sophronie forgot her key. I've got tu be up tu let her in. No need a waken him now.' His voice had grown softer and softer; and now she didn't hear it at all because the door was shut, soundlessly, with no squeaking like her own.

She was afraid now, and turned off all the lights and sat on the edge of her bed and brushed her hair, and when she could no longer

574

sit still she tiptoed from window to window, watching, listening. The street light on the corner made some light in the alley, but if they came in the other way, hugging the housewall, slipping in on the noise of a train or an airplane, careful to pick a time like now, when there was no steel pour coming off, she could neither see nor hear them.

She stood a long time in the dark living room, her head between blind and glass, but saw nothing, heard nothing, except trains and airplanes.

Weary of these, she sat on the chair at the head of the bed by Sophronie's kitchen wall. She couldn't say exactly when it was, but some time very late, she felt more than she heard people behind the wall. Then all at once, and quite loudly, as if the tool-and-die man wanted everyone to hear: 'Well, boys, I'd better get on. Thanks for the nice evening, but remember, it wasn't a Dutch treat—it's all on me. My notion in th beginning started it, see.' And the door opened.

She heard Whit, wistful now, 'Lord, I wisht they was some way a letten Tony know it wasn't no un . . .'

The tool-and-die man's angry, hissing 'Sh-sh' was all she heard, except his feet down the steps.

She heard a few minutes later Mrs Miller's loud laughter in the alley, and was in bed, her face turned to the wall, when Clovis came soon after. He called softly: 'Gert, Gert. Old woman, are you awake?'

She lay still until she remembered she did not know how she seemed when asleep. 'I recken so,' she said trying to sound sleepy.

'I'm sorry about th knife,' he went on, undressing rapidly. 'I come back an got it when you was taken a shower. We hadda keep a score fer setback—an would you believe it they wasn't a sharp pencil er a knife fer sharpenen in that house? You told me you was goen to bed er I'd a brung it home.' And he sprang into bed, drawing close to her, repeating, 'I hadda sharpen a pencil.'

She wanted to knock him out of bed, to cry, 'No,' to remind him that Sophronie's children used pencils for their homework—they sharpened pencils with Sophronie's kitchen knives. Why did he need a knife with a blade that was long and thin—but strong?

The window was graying up with dawn before his breathing came regularly enough that she dared get out of bed. He had for a long time been restless, talkative, like a man greatly excited, gay almost, as if some weight of trouble had lifted, letting him spring free. Twice she had tried getting up, but some watching deep within him that never stopped even in his sleep made him mutter worriedly, then lift for an instant on an elbow and stare vacantly about him.

The knife was in its proper place on the high shelf. She took it into the bathroom, and standing under the strong overhead light opened it blade by blade. She saw at once that it had been washed: a body couldn't dry a folding knife—not right away—that is if the handle had been in water. The water got down into the blade pockets and wetted the blades when they were folded back into the handle. Somebody had done a pretty good job—that is on the big blade; it was the little blade that came out dampish.

She stood staring at the open blades; they seemed to move; her hand was trembling; she was tired, was why it trembled. She studied the washbasin; it was speckless white from Clytie's scrubbing of the night before. She put in the plug, turned the faucet only part way so that the water would come with no sound, and ran in an inch or so of water.

She laid the knife into it; watched, rubbed her eyes, looked again. It had not gone away. Yes, it had; nothing was there. Some red rust, maybe, coloring the water, faintly pinkish, spreading up from the handle at the place where the big blade folded in. The knife had gone deeply; some blood had got into the handle. No, no, it wasn't blood; man's blood on her knife. She turned the water on full force; it frothed and bubbled white in the basin, pure white; there was no stain—no stain at all. Why should she think such things? His clothes, hung as always in the hall closet, reassured her; his overalls were clean, like his jacket and his shoes; in stories on the radio there were stains on shoes.

She studied his shoes, his work shoes, stained with oil or grease from the factory, but clean as always; brushed and clean; neat Clovis always had neat shoes, even the soles clean.

She sprang up. Why was she squatting here studying his shoes? There were in the crevices between the thick soles and the uppers a few grains of white sand, glittering and clean. It was like the sand she'd seen by the lake. That was a long time ago—funny the sand had stuck until now. Funny she choked so and her hands were cold; it was the bad air and the coldness of the place, for it was cold now, getting close to winter.

38

She knew she didn't watch; she saw them without watching—the scout cars driving through the alley. Clovis, she thought, watched too, in the same carefully careless way he would notice his hand when it strayed, as it so often did, to feel the scar on his forehead. It was only a mark now, more white than red, but a clear and noticeable thing that could not be covered by his hat; and seemed like now it worried him more than when he'd first got it. Seemed like, too, the scout cars went more slowly and more often through their little alley than they had used to do; she couldn't remember, but she was almost certain that back in the summer and in the winter too, the cops had driven mostly through the main alleys.

But maybe she only imagined all that, the way she imagined Clovis noticed his face. It was well, and he'd even got one odd job of tinkering. He'd taken out the engine block of a run-down car, but like back home there hadn't been much money in it. The man was a friend of Bunkin's and lived on the other side of town, and for all his traveling and the two days' time Clovis had charged only twelve dollars. He'd got just half of that in cash, the rest on time, for the man was laid off because of the Flint strike; whatever it was he helped make used Flint parts.

Clovis had left home around five o'clock for three mornings and waited in long lines of men and women in front of factory gates, the lines so long and so early forming, the few workers needed were taken before Clovis ever got through the employment gates. The factories weren't hiring many to begin with, and with so many soldiers returning, so many Flint men on strike, still others not yet called back after the changeover, and all roaming the town for work, jobs were scarce.

The dozen dolls they had made were stacked in the living room. Enoch had been out several times and sold none. But always he had come home cheerful enough, and filled with reasons for his failure: things didn't sell well after school because most of the women were busy getting supper, and anyway with the strikes and changeovers, money was a little short.

It was Saturday now, afternoon, and the alley still, for there had been money enough, even in those families affected by the strike, for the afternoon movie. Clytie had earned hers by baby sitting, and Enoch, though he had declared it was a gyp, had helped an older boy deliver papers, working better than an hour running from doorstep to doorstep for only ten cents. But in three afternoons he had made enough for the movie and a sack of popcorn in yellow cellophane, which, he had explained to Gertie, made a body feel that the popcorn was lathered with butter—that is, if he opened and ate it in the dark of the movie.

Gertie was by the sink, thinking of butter as she washed the dishes from the lunch of potato soup and toast. The children had loved the soup, made with some of Bunkin's onions and potatoes and milk. They'd be out of milk before Monday, and Enoch would want to run up to Zedke's for more. She wouldn't let him go, for even with credit from Joe and the milkman, and being as chinchy as she could, Zedke's bill must be close to a hundred and fifty dollars now.

What did a body do when the grocer cut off credit? She stared at the shelf above the sink, and the shelf stared back at her. Next week she'd have to buy more stuff from Joe. Bunkin's vegetables were all gone, for they had eaten them quickly, eating little but bread and vegetables. The boy would be there smiling at her, proud, showing off his English words like Cassie when she came from school. She hadn't seen him lately, but that was just because she hadn't bought anything and hadn't watched so closely.

She couldn't stand any longer and stare at the wall; she'd work on the block of wood, and late in the afternoon, just before dark, she'd walk up to Cassie. Not so many people came when the flowers were dead and the days cold.

Turning away from the sink, she saw, without really looking through the glass in the door, the scout car coming slowly down the big alley past Daly's unit. A policeman had his head stuck out as if he hunted someone.

Mr Daly, on his stoop picking his teeth, turned to look at the policeman. The policeman must have spoken to Mr Daly, for he came eagerly down his walk, and the car stopped. Gertie had by now opened the door, soundlessly, and only wide enough to hear Mr Daly, speaking loudly, say, 'Right there he lives.' She heard, too, the satisfaction in his voice as he pointed to her door.

She continued to stand a moment longer; not wanting to be seen; only her eyes slipped sidewise through the glass of the storm door, which she had not opened. She saw the policeman look toward her unit and the police car go on up the big alley, but Mr Daly stood looking at her door, his face expectant.

She came softly away, leaving the inner door ajar. She remembered her hands were wet from the dishwater, and stood a long time drying them on the kitchen towel. She drew a deep breath, and turned into the passway and looked at Clovis. He was sprawled on the sofa, reading the day-old paper that Victor, after a brief reading, put on their doorstep because strikers never bought papers. Twice she cleared her throat, but even so her words were hoarse and trembling. 'Clovis—th police, they're hunten us.'

He dropped the paper and sat bolt upright, his hand flying to the mark on his forehead as he swung about to look at her. Then he was rigidly still, only his hand dropping from his forehead as he sat staring straight in front of him.

She saw the fear sweat on his face and cried, not meaning to: 'He was so young, Clovis, he didn't know; like if a bunch a men got Reuben into—'

He turned on her, his eyes blazing. 'What a you talken about?' he cried, amost screaming. 'Who was young?'

'Him,' she said, her own voice shrill, 'th one you—' She wouldn't say it. No, she couldn't—tongue-tied she was by him as by her mother. Would she in time feel toward him as toward her mother? She couldn't live with him and feel that way. She stood silent, hands pulling one the other, as she watched him lie down again with the back of his head to the passway as it had been. He remembered to pick up the paper, so that once again he was a man stretched at his ease, reading the paper.

She turned back to the kitchen door; the police, she told herself, didn't always want people for— They came for all kinds of things. She rushed through the door, down her steps, and into the alley, almost bumping into Mr Daly. 'Du cops is wanten youse,' he said.

'I know. I heared you,' she gasped, running now past Victor's unit, toward the big alley by the railroad tracks down which the scout car would come. 'Did they say,' she called over her shoulder, 'was it a accident? My youngens was—'

His smile frightened her again for Clovis, and she stopped and turned part way round and looked at him as he said: 'Naw, it wasn't no accident. It's yu kid, that biggest boy, they want. Yu gotta learn to keep a tight hand on yu kids.'

'But Enoch ain't—'

'Youse wouldn't know,' he interrupted. 'Inu public school thataway they're alla time gitten into meanness—no proper Christian teachings.'

She was weak with relief; some little meanness like a broken window or a rock-dented car. She stood smoothing her apron, looking up the alley, and beginning to be conscious of her shivers, for she had run out without her coat. 'No use tu stand an wait,' Mr Daly said. 'Don't worry, du police'll find youse—anu kid, too. Dey cun jerk him outta that movie an clap him inu detention home.' His words made her back away with her troubled eyes on him as he went on, explaining, 'A detention home's a place fu real bad kids.'

'But—but he's ten years old,' she said.

' 'S'plenty old fu trouble,' he said.

Clovis was calling through the broken pane in the storm door, his words an angry hiss. 'Gert, git in here you'll jist, jist'— It seemed a full minute before he could think to add—'freeze.'

'Looks like youse's both scared,' Mr Daly said.

'Of what?' Clovis asked, speaking through the broken pane.

'Yu know—cops wanten yu kid.'

'My kid ain't done nothen,' Clovis said.

Scared as Gertie was for Enoch, she wondered if Mr Daly had noticed the relief in Clovis's voice. She started through her gate, but stopped when Mr Daly said, 'Yu needn't run now; dey're coming.'

She whirled and saw the car, just turning into the alley. It held two big mean-looking men; hard-hearted men who let her trouble wait while they followed their regular beat round by the steel-mill fence and down by the railroad. She ought to go into the kitchen and wait behind the storm door with Clovis. Then she was running past Victor's unit again, and had almost reached the corner of the fence when the car came slowly past her with a window rolled down and a policeman craning his head toward her door: 'I'm Miz Nevels, th boy's mama,' she said, turning about, matching her pace to that of the car for the moment or so before it stopped. 'Is it anything bad? He told me you was hunten us,' and she nodded toward Mr Daly without taking her glance from the one who had been driving; he was a heavy-jawed man with the same flat icy-blue eyes as Whit.

'Huh?' he asked, staring at her and then at Mr Daly while his hand reached into a coat pocket. 'Oh,' he said, still fumbling in his pocket. She moved backward against the fence while he finished his fumbling and brought out his hand, the fist closed, 'Look, lady,' he said, 'don't be allatime looking fu trouble. Yu gotta bad deal once—but that's no reason yu'll git more. Twice I reported that hole.' He stopped and studied her too white face with the boring, blazing eyes under the forehead, wrinkled in spite of the tightly drawn-back hair, with a great effort to understand.

She shook her head slowly, her eyes on the fist, opening now into a cupped palm, thumb and finger pinched together over two one-dollar bills and a fifty-cent piece. She still did not understand as the policeman said, 'I betcha kid thought he hada dead-beat cop.' He shoved the money toward her, smiled. 'Mu kid got su mad 'twas a sight to see. She tried right off tu take it apart, and when she couldn't she throwed it at me.'

Gertie's 'Oh,' of understanding came at last in a long relieved sigh, but she did not lift her hand for the money. 'He wanted you to have it,' she said. She struggled for words, pulling her fingers. 'It ud be kindly hard fer you to understand—but back home in their readers, they was stories about policemen on corners an walken th streets. They'd—that is, them in th stories—why they'd talk to little youngens, an hep em across streets to school. An he thought they'd be sich here. But th policemen here—they're different, way different frum th books. An so it made him awful proud, you speaken to him thataway.'

They had both listened, patient with her stumbling words, but the policeman was impatient when he said, 'Yeah, kids all crazy over cops, but I couldn't take nothen, not from a kid.' He brushed her hand with the money, and the other, silent until now, glancing now and then at Mr Daly who had come closer, said:

'Look, mu wife kinda wanted one to send to her little niece fu Christmas—only, she wondered if yucud make it plain, no paint, like a old man used to make um back home.'

'Back home?'

He nodded, smiling, and the other smiled too. 'Force's full a down-homers; he's from Pikeville, Kentucky.'

Gertie also smiled. 'A body ud never know it frum th way you talk.'

'Been gone too long,' he said. 'But couldcha make a doll—plain wood with a little whittled face like they used to be—but not for free. Him an me neither, we don't want no dolls for free.'

Gertie nodded, and the other, still offering the money, motioned toward Victor's unit. 'Didn'cha carve that crucifix we seen there last winter?' And when she had nodded again, he said, 'I'd like one like that—some time.' He gave her a quick speculative glance. 'But it looked like it was all done by hand. Must a cost a lot?'

She pondered, remembering the jig saw, the sander. 'I could make one cheaper, a little less handwork, hard maple stid a walnut, er mebbe I could find some walnut. He liked it so good he give me twenty dollars; but he makes big money in th steel mill.'

The cop nodded sourly. 'Can work a double shift on overtime, I bet.' He frowned, studied the address, then spoke to the other, 'He'sa one.' He turned back to Gertie. 'All them wages, an he's got neither chick nor child.'

'It's not his fault; his wife, she—He's a good man,' she said.

'Sure, it's th good ones they run out on,' the down-homer cop said.

'Pretty soon,' Gertie said, eager to change the conversation, wondering if Victor had tried to get the cops to find Max, 'I'll git some good wood—somehow. I figger I could make a right nice cross fer five, six dollars, an if you didn't like it you wouldn't have to take it.' She would make a cardboard pattern, and Clovis could saw one cross, a hundred crosses—and Christ, too; cheap crucifixes might sell better than cheap dolls.

'Look, lady,' the other cop was saying, 'yu make me a crucifix an him a doll—but we may not want um 'fore Christmas. Take this money; we can't stop all day.'

'But he'll be disappointed,' she said, reaching. 'It made him so proud talken to a policeman.'

'We'll be seein him,' the driver said, easing his foot from the clutch, moving slowly away as the other said:

'Tell th kid hello for us; he's a smart kid.'

The driver nodded, stopped the car again, and stuck his head out. 'But he's little, though, just a kid. Don'tcha let um go selling dolls after dark, an—well, kinda warn him, yu know, about going into strange houses or off by hissef, an taking car rides with, yu know—men. Tell um never to go much by hissef.' He was moving again so that his last words were an over-the-shoulder calling; 'We've had some pitiful cases—little kids, sellen things.'

She didn't need his loudness, for plainly she heard the mutterings of the other: 'She's hadda rough deal already. Wotta yu wantu scare her more?'

That night she told the children about the nice cops—one from back home, or close to back home. Maybe Enoch, when he'd gone all the way through high school, could be a cop, she said.

'Who wantsa be a cop? They don't make no money, less'n they've got a beat where they can git shakedowns like a feller Jimmy Daly's pop knows. Why, cops don't make as much as a plain 'sembly hand.'

'An they ain't got no union,' Clovis said.

'But th work's regular,' Gertie said pondering. They'd always looked so fine in their cars and uniforms, way finer than factory hands, so she had supposed they had more. 'It wouldn't be sich a bad callen,' she insisted, looking at Enoch. 'Seems like some real nice men gits into police work.'

Clytie tossed her head. 'All a same you've got to watch um. They's a girl at school, she's gotta sister, see.' She looked at Enoch, who had looked up quickly at mention of the word *girl*. 'This big girl, she hadda work a three-tu-twelve shift; an one night walking home frum u streetcar she got scared, see. Then she seen a scout car driven slow behind her, an she told um she was scared, an they said; "Git in. We'll take yu home." But they didn't take her home—they—yu know—and then they says to her, "Girlie," they says, "yu better not start crappen around about what th cops has done tuyu. We'll run yu in an lock yu up fer"—yu know, Mom. Wotta yu call it, soliciten?'

Gertie flushed, Enoch's eyes had dropped to his plate, but Amos was looking at his sister, ready to ask questions. Clytie saw his curiosity, and said, 'Want some more milk, honey?' and dumped the little bit in the bottle into his glass, quickly, so that a few drops splattered on the table.

Enoch cried, 'Don't waste milk.' And it seemed only a few days ago that he had been getting into the icebox for milk to feed an alley cat.

Gertie realized that when she told him of the money the policeman paid, he had said nothing of the dime he had always received from the sale of each of the other dolls. He asked now, cheerful, as if such things were an expected part of life, 'Mom, how long doyu reckon we'll have to live on beans?'

'We ain't a liven on beans,' Clytie cried. 'Whatcha crappen about? They's potatoes an bread an cooked peaches an—an all kinds of things—Mom, ought I to start walken? Some a th kids has gotta, an when I bought my lunch today some girl, an boy, was she hateful—I hadn't bought nothen but soup an a little candy bar—she was inu line ahead a me, an when I started past her she looked at wot I'd got an says, "Are you onu diet?" "My pop's onu strike," I says. "I can't buy out u whole cafeteria," I says. "Huh," she says, "it must be some strike. You've still got lunch money. When I was little inu depression," she says, "we lived on nothen but stale bread fer six weeks. So quitcha beefen, kid," she says to me. An I hadn't made one little beef,' Clytie said, looking persecuted.

'Aw, she was just shooten her lip, I bet,' Enoch said. 'Some a th kids tells all kinds a tales. Gilbert said onct they didn't have nothen but a sack a dry beans, an th water an th electric was all cut off, an Sophronie—'

'Miz Meanwell,' Gertie corrected.

'Anyhow, she was a setten an a cryen—Wheateye was a baby then—Gilbert don't recollect it so good; he jist knows frum a hearen um tell it—his mom was a bawlen away a maken big tears, an Whit says tu her, "Put them beans under yer face, honey, an we'll have biled beans stewed in tears." "We wouldn't have no ketchup, nohow," Sophronie says, an kept on a cryen—Pop, is tales like that th truth?'

'Some a these people that has been up here a long time can tell some tall tales about th depression an layoffs an sitdowns an evictions an standen all night in th rain er th snow in front u employment gates so's to be first in th mornen. An I've heared some tell how they'd seen great swarms a men hangen around behind restaurants an bars an sich, a waiten fer garbage to be put in th cans so's they could git it. They've mebbe made their tales a heap bigger; an anyhow,' he added quickly, catching Gertie's troubled eyes, 'they warn't no unions then.'

'The unions cain't make jobs,' Gertie said.

They were silent, the same silence that came when something said brought back Cassie and her laughter, or when Clovis talked of back home as he often did here lately, with a wistfulness and a hopelessness strange for him. Now, as at such times, they seemed to draw closer one to the other, silent as if they listened to Detroit, sounding, as always, through the place. Tonight, supper was earlier than when Clovis worked, and the going-home traffic at its heaviest while they ate, so that it came from the through street in a long roaring growl, drowned at times by the scream of an airplane, or a louder blast from the steel mill. The sounds, as they often did, made Gertie think of some many-voiced beast out there, hungry, waiting for them all.

Next day she went early to the project office, carrying the Josiah basket with two of the brightest dolls. She hoped that someone might ask if they were for sale while she did her business, which was

586

to put up a sign she had rewritten three times the night before while the others were in bed: 'For Washing, Ironing, Cleaning, Gertie Nevels—18911 Merry Hill.' But her hands hesitated as they tacked it on the bulletin board near the rent-paying window; it was the last of several rows of such notices; she saw, 'Sophronie Meanwell—Ironing, Wall Washing,' and further down, but from the looks of it put up some days ago, 'Clytie Nevels, Baby-sitting, Housework—'

She turned away, her reading of the little sign unfinished, but still she lingered near the office. She held the Josiah basket on her arm, swinging it a little, as she looked hopefully past the rent-paying windows to the people who ran the project—two office girls, two young men, the gray-haired project manager, and his gray-haired secretary. None of them looked at her, for there was another woman on Gertie's side of the rent-paying window. Gertie, like the office help, gave her a quick sidewise glance, then looked away as the old project manager talked to her in a low flat voice touched with impatience and weariness. 'It's a government rule. You had your hearing. There isn't anything else I can do. I neither own the project nor make the rules.'

The others in the office were uncomfortable, fidgety because of the woman, and seemed relieved when she turned suddenly and rushed away. Gertie followed her, and wished she could say something; she looked so young, but had the large breasts and the largish stomach of a woman with a very young baby, and her crying was like that of a woman so tired she couldn't care for much of anything, a wet and sloppy crying that had seemed out of place in the neat bare office with its adding machines and typewriters.

Gertie was halfway home before she remembered she had planned to walk to the closest big store, almost a mile away, and buy a beef heart and some pork liver. Zadkiewicz sometimes had such, but the big store was always cheaper on everything; it could afford to be; it never gave credit, never delivered, never waited on a body like Zedke.

She turned about and walked more slowly, holding the basket well out from her body so that the dolls would show. She lingered a moment by the tavern and bowling alley; there would be money in such a place. People came and went, but nobody noticed the dolls.

The big store, as always, made her head whirl; so many, many things in packages, but it wasn't easy to tell what was behind the pretty pictures, and she thought of the money she'd wasted, letting herself be fooled by the pretty pictures. Today, though she rolled a cart slowly up and down the aisles, looking, she bought none of the packaged things. She bought only the beef heart, too big, with the little fat on it yellow like from an old cow; she knew it would be tough and that it wasn't fresh, but it was the only one left. The pork liver was all gone, but she did buy two loaves of bread from the day-old pile—half price. Sixty-eight cents, the machine said, and then the tax; with the tax money she could have bought— What could she have bought? A sucker each for Enoch and Amos, but had there been no tax she wouldn't have bought the suckers anyway.

She walked slowly home, swinging one of the dolls, jumping it at times. She hesitated where the path turned into the vacant land; she ought to walk on the sidewalk where people could see the swinging doll, but the walk alone through the swamp would be nice. The brush was leafless now, blighted by frost and smoke, for it was getting deep into November, and rent day close again. Clovis had kept the six dollars he'd earned; he had to have the money for gas to hunt a job.

Lingering among the leafless willows and the tin cans, she told herself that she was tired, just taking her time, resting herself with a few smoky twigs between her and the sky. She wasn't staying away because it was Joe's day to come into the alley. There was in her pocket enough for the rent and enough to pay him. The boy would be there, weighing vegetables, smiling at the customers. Two times now the truck had been by since the night Clovis had borrowed her knife to sharpen a pencil, and she had got so worked up she couldn't sleep. Wasn't that silly.

She hadn't seen Joe's nephew since that night; he was there, of course; she just hadn't looked real close. If Joe had not already gone by the time she got home, she'd buy some little squashes from him—they were cheap.

Still, she took her time, and tried hard to think of nothing; but her feet kept coming under her glance, and gradually she fell to thinking of her shoes; she couldn't buy new shoes—not now. But soon as the weather got bad, she could wear the high boots; they'd cover her shoes, and the holes in her stockings, too.

A child screamed, 'Scab, scab,' and seemed like all at once a million little youngens, some smaller than Amos, were all around her. One swung onto the basket, two had her coattail, while half a dozen, looked like, jumped up and down in front of her, all pulling, pretending great anger, but many helpless with laughter, unable to cry with the others: 'Scab, Scab. You've crossed a pickut line!'

She stopped, realizing that instead of the vacant land she walked through a corner of the project, and that she had got into a game the children played. 'I didn't see no signs,' she said, smiling. Cassie would have loved such a game.

'Yu gotta walk over there; yu've crossed u pickut line,' one, a little bigger than Amos, said. Another, slyly smiling, pointed to the empty air above the sticks he and the others carried that looked suspiciously like the missing slats from her fence. 'Can'tcha read, lady? Don'tcha see our signs, these great big signs?' he asked; then, giggling, he pointed to the empty sticks and 'read,' 'Strike. Keep off,' and lastly in a very loud voice the sign above his own shoulder, 'Ole man Flint is mean.'

She nodded. 'It's a fine big sign,' she said, 'only Mr Flint, he's dead.'

'Quitcha kidden,' the child said, and she walked on.

If she'd only spent a minute longer with the children, Joe would have been gone. She didn't honestly need squash, but he might think it funny if she paid him off and didn't buy anything. He looked old, she thought, like John after he sold his timber. He did not even say 'Nice,' as he held out three oranges for Mrs Miller's inspection.

Mrs Miller nodded briefly over the oranges, her glance fixed mostly on the inside of the truck. 'I'll take um,' she said, 'an three pounds a sweet taters.' She was silent while Joe climbed into the truck and got the sweet potatoes, but when he had finished with her and was making change, she asked, 'Where's yu nephew, Joe?'

'California,' Joe said, turning to Gertie.

'He leftcha, huh?' Mrs Miller asked, 'after yu smug—got him over here, an taught him th fruit business. But,' she went on, as Joe held out a handful of the cheap little Irish potatoes for Gertie's inspection, 'people has allatime got tu be on the go, looks like.' She glanced at Gertie. 'I reckon you know th Millers is leaven—early in th mornen.'

Gertie nodded, and the woman hurried away. Gertie's wistful eyes followed her. Such luck the woman had had—all her children and ten thousand dollars. Her eyes dropped at last to the potatoes over which Joe was sing-songing, 'Potatoes, cheap today.'

She shook her head, and bought only three little acorn squash, fifteen cents. She held out the one dollar bill and the change. 'I better pay you,' she said. 'I hate bein in debt.'

He studied her, not taking the money. 'Credit's good,' he said.

'I hate debts,' she said.

He considered, his glance falling below the outstretched money down to her shoes; there, it stopped an instant, then wandered up again to the basket on her arm. 'How much?' he asked.

She had forgotten the dolls. She wanted only to pay him, to get away from the truck that, crammed as it was with baskets and crates of fruits and vegetables, still seemed empty. 'Oh,' she said at last, 'th dolls—why, two-fifty I've been gitten.'

He pulled out the greasy black book, counted, nodded over the squash, then reached into his pocket. He dropped a dollar bill, a quarter, a dime, and a penny into her lax cupped hand. 'But yu credit's good,' he said, and picked up a doll.

39

The days ticked by: Sunday—a nickel apiece for the children to take to Sunday school, money that came from Clytie and Enoch. Monday—the first rent day; she waited in line, gripping the two tens, the two fives with sweaty fingers. Ahead of her a woman paid for two weeks only. She considered—it would be good to have sixteen dollars for two weeks in her pocket—but suppose she lost it, or one of the youngens took bad sick and she had to have a doctor. Victor, somebody, would maybe let her have doctor money, but rent money was different; she fished slowly in her coat pocket and brought out the rest—the ones, the fifty-cent piece.

She paid and came away; there was still $1.36 in her pocket. Clovis was going to try for credit in one of the stores that sold clothing on time. Enoch had to have shoes, and Clytie, boots; any day now the weather could turn cold and snowy like last year when they came.

Clovis, working on another sanding gadget, looked quickly at her bleak face, and then away. 'Look, Gert, it could be worse. When it's all over I still won't be in so deep as a heap. Whit an Sophronie, 'tween his pin setten an her unemployment money, they're a keepen th rent paid, but they're in debt fer most a th grub they've had since th changeover, an fer ever stitch a clothes they've hadda buy fer their youngens since school started.'

'But, look how they've wasted their money,' Gertie said, 'all that beer fer Whit an cigarettes fer th two uv um, an her never a sewen a stitch, an—'

'So what?' Clovis interrupted, angry, more trigger-tempered lately than he had ever been. 'Supposen they had a saved ever cent they could, never a penny fer cigarettes er beer. How long would it ha lasted now, through th changeover an a big strike like this? Th danged company called him back and let him work jist long enough to lose his unemployment; they done a heap that way, figeren a strike might maybe come.'

Gertie flicked a speck of dust from a shoulder of the man in the wood. She looked hard at Clovis, opened her mouth, then shut it. Why wouldn't he speak first? He knew what he had to do. 'Clovis, you'll have tu see about gitten credit at a drygoods store; th young-ens jist has tu have clothes if they stay in school.' She'd brought out all the words in a loud, breathless rush that, when ended, left the room strangely still.

Clovis bent his head over the contraption, and did not answer. She waited, and he turned to her at last. His hand came up to the scar; he noticed, frowned angrily, and dropped his hand. 'Yeah,' he said. 'I'll git some—something to do. Th last two places where I asked about work—fillen station was one—they ast me had I been in a fight. Seems like now—with the war over, I mean—they look at a man mighty close.'

'But we need credit now,' she insisted. 'An them ads in th paper, they claimed a factory worker didn't need nothen but his badge to git credit.'

'Mebbe not,' he said, measuring sandpaper against the wheel. 'I'm—I was behind in my car payments—jist five more an I'll be out—that went—woulda—gone agin me asken fer credit, but I'm pretty certain I can git credit—now.'

'Now?'

He nodded, but would not meet her glance. 'It ain't like back home, Gert. They won't wait if you git overdue on a car. I've heared a two strikers that had a let their cars go—company come an took em right out a th parken places beside their houses; they wasn't a thing they could do. I knowed they'd want mine; it's about paid fer an it runs good an— Oh, heck, Miller let me have money fer this month's payment so's maybe I can git—'

His voice trailed away. She tried to make him meet her eyes, but he would not, and sat guiltily with hung head as she said, 'You've tried fer credit—an couldn't git it, Clovis.'

He mumbled something at last about 'th danged ads that lied,' but she never answered. She had suddenly begun working on a fold of the cloth where it lay above a forearm. Clovis after a while began talking again, and kept on talking and talking as if to kill his thoughts, mostly it was about the Meanwells: when times started getting good at the beginning of the war, they'd had nothing but debts and three little youngens; they couldn't get credit, and were living in one furnished room on Grand River; but look at them now; their car paid for and plenty good enough for a down payment on a lot newer car, most of their furniture paid off, more clothes than they had ever had, plenty of credit, even credit with a doctor.

He ran out of words, and they had been for a long time silent, working, when someone knocked. She hurried to open the door— maybe it was a woman with a big ironing. It was, however, only a little Daly, asking if Mr Nevels couldn't come fix his mother's washing machine; it wouldn't work at all. Clovis hesitated, looking at Gertie, his hand jerking toward the scar. 'They wouldn't be any money in it,' he whispered, 'and she'd be nosen around like them I ast fer jobs.'

'It's him that's the nosey one, an he ain't home,' Gertie said; and Clovis crammed his hat low on his head and went, taking Amos, who had heard the knocking and wanted to see his daddy fix the machine.

Gertie continued to work on the block of wood; but the fold of cloth could not drive the boy away, for when she was alone he came between her and all the rest of the world—even trouble. Of course the boy was in California. Clovis was just jumpy from that fight, and worrying about money was why he seemed so afraid; he wasn't afraid. He drove around town often—after dark; tomorrow or some time he was going to another tinkering job.

She tried to work faster on the uplifted hand, held close against the chest. Gradually the man in the wood brought some calmness to her; he was alive; the hands, the head, even the face were there;

she had only to pull the curtain of wood away, and the eyes would look down at her. They would hold no quarreling, no scolding, no questions. Even long ago, when only the top of the head was out of the wood, below it had seemed a being who understood that the dancing, the never joining the church, had been less sinful than the pretending that she believed, and— She never heard the knife strike the floor, fallen from her hands; instead, she heard her moans, her words, like from another's mouth; her tongue ashamed, too ashamed to use her own speech, but crying in the words of the alley, 'I stood still fer it—I kept shut—I could ha spoke up.'

The wood was strong, holding her up, understanding, for what had Judas done but whisper a bit and keep still; no, it wasn't Judas. She was still, wondering if she had cried, 'No, no!' The silence of the wood loudened the memory of her own cry, and she peeped about her, crouching by the wood as if to hide. Had anybody heard? And what was there to hear, she asked herself, picking up the knife, smoothing the cupped overfull hand. She worked again, and a mound of chips and shavings grew about her feet.

The whole thumb of the empty hand was out, such a good thumb, and strong; and then she heard the knocking, not Sophronie's kicking or the rough knocking of a child or peddler, but dignified and gentle: this time surely a woman with a big washing—five dollars.

She sprang up just as the door opened and Mrs Anderson called, 'Hello—I was afraid you'd moved away.' She came on in, smiled once at Gertie, but after that had eyes for nothing but the wood. 'It's magnificent,' she said, walking all around it, touching each hand with her gloved hands, pausing at last with her hand on his shoulder. 'It would take a prize—and,' she looked at last at Gertie, 'it's much more effective like that without the face. It's all so plain,' she said, and was silent, looking.

Gertie had backed against the chair in front of the door. She was a little flustered; this woman all in new clothes, her hair no longer braided but skinned back, tight as her own hair, though the knob was low, low enough to make her neck ache; and got up in gloves, lipstick, and a hat, wasn't like Mrs Anderson from across the alley, but somebody else from a world that didn't know strikes or beef hearts. It seemed a long while they stood so; Mrs Anderson looking at the wood, Gertie looking at Mrs Anderson; finally she remembered to ask, 'What's so plain?' and then, 'Set down.'

Mrs Anderson only walked around the wood, squeezing herself between it and the sofa for a closer look. 'That he won't keep still and hold it. He'll give it back,' she said.

'A body cain't allus give back—things,' Gertie said, filled suddenly with a tired despair; the wood was Judas, after all.

'I'm glad it's good, really good,' Mrs Anderson said, sitting down, taking cigarettes from her purse. 'It was my undoing.' She held the unlighted cigarette, explaining: 'I remember when I first saw it at Max's—I didn't want to look. "There's a woman," I thought, "who's never had a lesson in art, but with five children and nothing but a block of wood and a pocket knife, look what she's done. And look at me." I wish Mrs McKeckeran could see it.'

'Mebbe she'll come through agin sometime,' Gertie said.

'Perhaps,' Mrs Anderson said. 'Did Max come back?'

Gertie shook her head, and answered other queries about the alley, for Mrs Anderson was hungry for talk and curious as ever. She answered so many questions that she grew absent-minded, trying to think of something she could ask that would turn Mrs Anderson's thoughts from her own life; she thought of old man Flint at last. Clovis had read in the paper that those who took over after his death had made some changes, and so she asked if things were any different since he died.

'Not basically,' Mrs Anderson said, 'but smoother—much smoother; no rough stuff, at least nothing the public can see. Business has gone holy, if you know what I mean. Businessmen are like saints in stone—hard, but smooth as my hair. You haven't said a word about the way I look—the skinned-onion look. You know, an onion never stinks till you cut it. No, more like little pretty garlic cloves. Everything is like that—smooth, no smell. The big companies are so wealthy from the war they can buy lawyers, maybe judges if they need them. Congressmen, you know, for a few laws, can be had within reason. They are all so rich they can even afford religion—now.' She stopped, her glance on the down-bent covered face; shook her head. 'He couldn't though.'

'Homer,' she went on, as Gertie continued silent, 'is happy. The company, mostly Mr McKeckeran, wants him to finish his thesis and get his Ph.D. The thesis has given him no end of trouble. He finds all manner of prejudice, but he'll have to make his own pattern. Not all prejudice is so honest as Mrs Daly's—you know, I'm beginning to admire the woman—even prejudice is smooth now—and there are so many kinds, the kind you've felt, and others never mentioned; but whatever kind it is, it's always smooth. The shirt-sleeves-up-from-the-railroad-section gang is out; our leader Mr Flint has left us, not for a ribband to stick in his coat, but for heaven with a golden crown. All his crowd are dead or old. Their granddaughters were brought up by finished mothers. They belong to junior leagues and are the alumnae of the best schools money can buy. They don't want rough stuff; they want to be good, very, very good.'

She looked at Gertie. 'We go to church—now. Homer hadn't been to Sunday school since he rebelled in high school, but he teaches a class now—adolescent boys. Sooner or later, I suppose I will. I used to teach art, you know. I was so ignorant then about everything, especially art, real art. The real art is living so as to fool the neighbors, easily, smoothly, and never drop a hint to anyone that we've gone in so deeply we have to spend the salary before we get it. We had to have a house, furniture, a better car—order already placed for a new one—clothes; we hadn't any. Anyway, the neighbors must never, never guess that in order to squeeze out the dollars for a laundress-cleaning woman two days a week, I have to have a stew or hash or something cheap like spaghetti at least three times a week. But, of course, there's money for liquor and baseball.'

She sprang up, walked restlessly to the window. 'I wish the steel-mill light would show. I liked to look at it and dream sometimes of painting it at twilight when the red was like blood on the children. Once, I drove by a few weeks back and watched a pour so long I was late. Do you know what I was late to? A baseball game. It was before the Turbis were out. He's out, you know—cold. Homer, if he knows why, has never told me. Turbi, I think, hinted too much of the shirt sleeves they want to forget; he pulled some kind of rough stuff—I never did know what. But whatever he did it was what the company wanted; he just wasn't smooth enough in the doing. Poor

596

man, he must have suffered when he learned he hadn't pleased the company.

'Anyway, I had to put in an appearance at a baseball game—it's only those high up like Mrs McKeckeran who can refuse the royal command to attend a baseball game. Fortunately for me it wasn't cool enough for mink—such a pity for the others. But now at football time it is. Next week there's an invitation to go by special train, or maybe just by private coach. Who knows? I may sit next to a bishop; it's a Catholic university. A business couple who detested sports and drunken spectators would be held subversive—so I grin like a fool—ugh.'

She stopped long enough that Gertie, weary of her talk, could ask, 'How's the youngens?'

'They're adjusting,' Mrs Anderson said. 'That is, to the neighbors—such nice people: among them all there isn't one who'd let her house get mussed or her children go—well, a shade too grimy—and paint— You don't by any chance have any pink medicine left—you remember it? I don't need it, really, but driving in this traffic has unsettled my nerves.'

'I let most a it spill in th sink one night,' Gertie said, getting up, 'but they's a little left.'

There was more than Gertie had remembered, but Mrs Anderson took it all, shivering as always at the taste, then smiling, explaining: 'I've grown accustomed to the pills—they're easier to manage. Georgie was beginning to— What would you do if you'd learned you'd raised your children all wrong?'

Gertie fidgeted, thinking up an answer; Clovis might at any minute get back from Mrs Daly's, and she didn't want the woman to see him. A faint smile suddenly brightened her troubled eyes. 'I recken if somebody told me that, I'd think about my youngens like I think now—take credit to my raisen a them fer th good they've got, an give th devil er what was born into em credit fer th bad.'

Mrs Anderson shook her head to that, and rushed into another shower of words. 'Mrs McKeckeran suggested this pediatrician. He's very busy, but his office is shabby, and I wonder about him. There was a Negro woman with a baby in his office. It was the first time I've seen a Negro in a doctor's office in Detroit. He was almost hateful. "Your children," and he had really given them a going over "are healthy and normal"—Homer had thought perhaps Georgie should be taken to a child psychiatrist, and I tried discussing the matter with this doctor, and he was quite rude. "Try for a change," he said, "to think of them as human beings instead of problems. Let the boy eat when and what he wants." And he didn't even give me a diet sheet for Georgie. Homer is terribly worried because we'll have to keep him; Mrs McKeckeran recommended him—they're friends and I have a suspicion he's—'

The door opened. Gertie looked up anxiously, and Mrs Anderson turned and smiled at Clovis as if glad to see him. He smiled in return, then his hand lifted, but stopped with a jerk halfway to his face, then rose more slowly and he stood, covering the dark spot on his jaw with his hand moving as if he only rubbed his face. Mrs Anderson, still smiling, looked hard at him. 'You've been sick? You look pale.' She moved closer, 'Or was it an accident—your head's scarred.'

Gertie spoke quickly, for Clovis seemed tongue-tied. 'A little a both,' she said.

And Clovis asked, 'How're you liken your new place?'

'Fine, just fine,' Mrs Anderson said, still scrutinizing Clovis. She turned abruptly again to Gertie, then looked down at the litter of chips and shavings on the floor. 'I'll bet you want to get on with your work,' she said.

Then, with her eyes too bright, and her ever widening smile threatening at times to burst into giggles, she told quickly, as if in a hurry to be gone, why she had come. It was about the Christmas bazaar she was helping plan for the church. Homer had decided they should select the church of her maternal grandparents, a splendid old faith he had said. She had agreed that it was perhaps better than either of their childhood churches—of course, the fact that Mr McKeckeran was a deacon in the church hadn't a thing to do with it.

Anyway, Mrs McKeckeran and others of the leading women in the church had decided that this year the Christmas bazaar should put less emphasis on baked goods and ordinary bits of sewing, and more on other handmade things of a more artistic nature. Mrs Anderson was contributing a good many hand-done

Christmas cards; another woman was making place cards—
'flowers done with tweezers and glue and tiny shells—ugh.' She
hurried on; others were contributing all manner of dolls, and
stuff from their looms and pottery kilns. Everything was to be
artistic, even the crocheted pot holders. They would in addition
have things made by the blind and the mentally deranged, and
Mrs McKeckeran had thought—'She looked at me, smooth as butter, and wondered if any of us knew where we could get some
wood carvings. She thought we should be able to sell three or four
dozen smallish carvings of animals or figures or birds, real handmade things of good wood what could be bought for around $4.25
and sold for $5.00 each.

'I nodded, of course—she knows now that never, never will
I speak out of turn or even hint about her other half—and I said I
knew a woman who might take such an order; and she said, was it
the one who made her little hill woman, not batting an eye, and I
said, "Oh, yes," not batting an eye; and she said, "How lovely."
I was forthwith appointed a committee of one to negotiate the deal;
but the bazaar is close—and can you make anything like three or
four dozen in that time? Such a deal of work.'

Gertie nodded. She leaned forward, watching, as Mrs Anderson
opened her handbag, and continued: 'She must have good wood—
everything about this church is good and sound. She must have
walnut or cherry or dogwood or holly.'

Gertie's brows drew together in a troubled frown. 'Wood like
that's kind a hard tu find. Mebbe none at all in th scrap-wood lot,
an if they was he'd make it high.'

'Oh, Mrs McKeckeran thought of that, trust her.' Mrs Anderson's
eyes were even brighter now and gigglesome she was, as she kept
fumbling in her purse. She brought out first a slip of paper, then
began to pull out bills. 'She commanded me to give you fifty in
advance for the buying of the wood. Here's the address of a picture-
framing place downtown that also keeps wood for art classes and
such,' and she held out the slip of paper and three bills, clean
and crisp with the pretty, useless look of new money.

Gertie stared at the money, but swallowed and backed away.
'What if I didn't git them dolls finished in time, an . . .'

'You can certainly finish fifty dollars' worth; that's only about a dozen, fast as you work. And—oh, yes; if you have time you might make a few crucifixes; not big expensive ones like you made for Victor; but we might sell three or four ten-dollar ones—less commission, of course.'

She was holding out the money, but looking at the block of wood, her eyes too bright, her mouth twisting in the giggly smile. She turned away and shoved the money into Gertie's hand. 'Oh, I'm glad, so glad, that somebody . . .' She looked once more at the wood, and was gone, calling but not looking back, 'I'll be back soon to see how you're making out,' and Gertie, looking after her, wondered if she laughed or cried.

Gertie was still by the wood, staring down at the bright greenness in her hand, when Clovis came out of the bedroom. 'I heared her,' he said, and he sounded like a man from whom a great burden has been lifted. 'A hundred—even fifty dollars ud mean a lot to us right now.' He came and looked at the money, touched it as he said, 'Recken it'll take all that fer enough wood tu make what she wants. Whyn't you,' he went on with more enthusiasm than she had seen for days, 'git ready an let me take you right now to that place an see about th wood; they might hafta order it.'

Gertie pondered, looking at the money, and then at Clovis, his eyes so pleased and shiny. He'd been worried, bad worried. 'Shorely,' she said, 'it won't take all this.'

'Good clean walnut with no sap wood'ull come ungodly high. I don't guess a body can buy cherry, that is, seasoned an ready to use. I've got gas enough to git there an back.' He touched his forehead, not noticing. 'I could go into th place with ye; they never ask no questions when they're sellen you somethen. Jist when you're asken for work—er credit.'

'She noticed,' Gertie said.

'She was allus nosey,' he said, and was silent, glancing once at the wood, then turning away to look through the door, his glance for the outdoors wistful, she thought, and troubled.

'This order fer th dolls is a piece a luck,' he said, turning back to her. 'You make up—well, say about six differ'nt patterns. Wouldn't that be enough? An I'll cut em when we git th wood—about eight uv each, I'd say. She'd want um kind a chunky, nothen cheap fer her. But I could cut em two ways on th jig, take pains, an then on th little sander I can do a sight.' The motor-listening look was on his face. 'Supposen it's a pig—you make real good pigs—mark out th bottom a each foot, an I'll grind right up between em an in a minute you've got legs. Nothen to do but finish it; but it'll take good hard seasoned wood that won't splinter.'

'Yes,' she said, and went for her coat. 'I think I'll go look around th scrap-wood lot; they might have somethen. An mebbe on th way I can sell a doll.'

She met Mrs Daly hunting children through the alleys, and eager to tell Gertie to tell Clovis the washing machine ran like a dream now, and to tell her that a letter had just come from Maggie, and Maggie had got the chickadee and had it by St Francis and liked it a lot. Maggie had thanked her and asked how was the Virgin Mary coming out of the wood.

'Fine,' Gertie said; it wasn't the mother Mary, but if Maggie wanted it that way she might as well have it. 'Go in an look at her,' she suggested, 'then you can write her exactly how she is. Tell her Miz Anderson asked about her,' and she hurried on through the nearby alleys that made her world and that of her children. Past these the people were mostly strange to her, and here she went more slowly; the basket, with a doll propped up against the handle, on one arm; another, the brightest of all, red and yellow and orange, jumping from its string in her other hand.

She knocked on two doors: at the first a woman opened it a crack, whispering, 'Mu man's asleep.' At the other, the woman wearily shook her head, 'Dolls? But I'm laid off an he's ona pickut line.'

Gertie, feeling a kinship, tired, wanting to linger, and wishing the woman would ask her to sit down, said, 'My man's picket turn ain't come up yit.'

But the woman, there were three little ones squalling around her, only looked at her with envious eyes and said, 'S'good you've got a way a picken up a little money—s'more'n I've got.'

And Gertie went on. Once, she tried calling, 'Dolls, dolls, pretty jumping-jack dolls, hand-carved,' but her voice sounded strange and squeaky to her ears, and no one came to her calling. She tried again, saying only, 'Dolls, dolls.' On the first call her voice boomed so it startled her; the second 'doll' was low and hoarse like a croak. A child on a tricycle stopped to stare and then to giggle, the only thing in the alley that gave any notice of her calling.

She turned and walked swiftly away, and went again through the familiar alleys where she had walked in the summer while caring for the little Andersons. She realized she was close to the place where the cactus woman lived—maybe her man was well and working; and they would meet and the woman smile. She might even buy a doll.

She frowned in puzzlement when, upon entering the alley and looking toward the other end, she saw a great stack of junk by the woman's coalhouse. She went closer, and saw that it was furniture. She stood looking, shaking her head, furniture out like this when it looked like rain, though a body could not tell what waited in the sky on such a still and smoky day.

She walked again, but more slowly, remembering only when she was halfway down the alley to jiggle and bounce the jumping-jack doll. She stopped behind a woman carrying a tricycle up her steps and asked, 'Want tu buy a doll?'

The woman turned and shook her head, 'We gotta take up a collection,' she said, and nodded toward the pile of furniture, 'Eviction.' She waited, studying Gertie an instant before speaking again. 'Her man got hurt—way back inu summer—inu head. His milling machine exploded; but th company doctor, when e put um out a th hospital, said his eyes was jist still swoll' from th lick on his head, was why he couldn't see. He never did see; stone blind, an cain't git a penny. He signed some papers, couldn't see wot he signed, an they didn't tell him; he hadda learn it hisself. His unemployment run out a long time ago. We was taken up a collection.'

Gertie fished in her pocket, felt the strange smoothness of new money; she went deeper and her fingers touched coins. The dime or the quarter? She held out the quarter.

The woman shook her head. 'When I toldcha about u collection I wasn't hinten none. Don'tcha man work at Flint's? They're talking around that th strike'll last till Christmas.' She hesitated again,

602

her eyes on Gertie's shoulder. 'Somebody saidcha didn't have no insurance when yu— Yu keep yu quarter.'

Gertie shoved the quarter into the woman's hand gripped on a tricycle bar. 'I'll be maken money frum my whittlen. Where'll they go?'

The woman glanced uneasily toward the piled-up furniture, whispered: 'She's over there kinda in behind th coalhouse. We divided um up last night—kinda crowds a person, butcha gotta do somethen—them little kids, an it cold. They's a shelter place run bydu welfare; an th man next door—he's out on strike—he's took her man there now to see if they's room.'

Gertie walked on. She saw the woman huddled behind her furniture in a rocking chair with a blanket-wrapped baby across her knees. 'I been wanten tu see yu,' the woman said. 'Ain'tcha du one wot grows such pretty flowers? I been t'inking—couldcha keep mu cactus? I've had it su long; it's older'n mu kids. Yu'd unnerstand wot it needs better'n most around.'

'Sure,' Gertie said. The woman was going to cry, she thought. But the woman made no sound as she, still holding her baby on one arm, got up and went for the cactus, placed carefully under the stoop, safe from running children. 'You've got nice furniture,' Gertie said, wanting to comfort.

'Yeah, an all them payments finished,' the woman said, but looking only at the cactus, fondling it with her eyes, 'but u icebox. They come an got that a good while back, but not su quick as they got th car—onie three more on it and we'd been through—I'm afraid it got stunted last night; it was so cold.'

'It'll be all right,' Gertie said. She dropped the doll into the basket, and reached with both hands for the cactus, hurrying, for one of the woman's tears had fallen on a leaf. 'I'll take good care uv it, real good,' she said.

'Keep ut warm an not too wet,' the woman begged.

Gertie was past the next unit before she remembered to say, calling over her shoulder: 'You know where I live. I like it—allus did love potted plants—but you come er send eny time when you git a place fer it.'

'Yeah,' the woman said, sobbing, rocking the baby again.

Gertie was going up her walk with the pot, large and wrapped in silver foil, held carefully in both hands, when she remembered the scrap-wood place; she'd been on her way there when she passed the cactus woman. She stood a long time, holding the pot, looking at her door. She went in at last, and Clovis, listening to her explanation of how she came by the cactus, looked hard at her, started to speak, hesitated, but interrupted at last, 'Gert, you look—funny—kinda pale. You don't want tu be gitten sick again—not now.'

'I'm all right,' she said, but sat down in the middle room by the block of wood. She sat a long time looking at it while Clovis talked; he had good news. Bunkin had been around; there was a guy—a real honest-to-goodness farmer—had about two days' work for a good mechanic. His stuff was old and he'd run it so hard it was all breaking down. He wouldn't pay more than five or six dollars a day; he'd want about fifty dollars' worth of work for twelve; right now he wanted somebody to help rig up a stump-pulling machine. He was cleaning up an old apple orchard. Bunkin had wondered if Gertie wouldn't like some apple wood for her whittling.

Gertie looked at him, and he repeated what he had said, then added: 'Gert, don't look so—well—like you'd lost th last friend you'd ever had. We'll git by till you git some money frum that whittlen. I'll git credit in a department store. Zedke'ull carry us fer groceries. Main thing's th rent; these gover'mint places gives credit fer so many days an no more—but we'll borrie—er somethen.'

'Yes,' she said, and continued to sit by the block of wood until even Clytie was home from a late class and Enoch in from Cub Scouting. She roused then and got supper—spaghetti covered with a can of tomato soup, and smeared on top with a little dab of cheese. It didn't look too good, she thought, and never ate any— A good thing, she decided later, for the children and Clovis ate it all. Nobody complained of the scanty supper, and when Amos asked for a second glass of milk Enoch chided him: 'Don'tcha know, kid, yu pop's on strike?'

Amos did not ask again, and Gertie did not offer; the milkman wouldn't come again till next day noon, and there was hardly more than a pint left for the breakfast mush. Eggs for breakfast instead of mush or oatmeal ran the grocery bill up so.

She hurried through the dishes, and without waiting for the children and Clovis to be out of the way, began work again on the block of wood, the unfinished palm of the uplifted hand; working so steadily, so swiftly, that Clovis complained, 'You'll wear yerself out on that, Gert,' and when she made no answer, added, 'You ought to be worken on them patterns, so's we'll be all ready.'

'They's time,' she said, not looking away from the wood as she crouched, head tilted, knife swiftly bringing out a line in the down-curving palm. The one line finished, she moved on to another with no stopping, as if time were running out and this were the one thing she must do with her time.

The children went to bed and Clovis went to bed, but she worked on. Victor went to the steel mill, Whit came home from the bowling alley, the fast passenger that had always used to waken the children with its long screech for the crossing, passed, and still she worked, her face gray now and lined with tiredness, her legs stiff from the long kneeling; for though she had put him in a chair she still must, on the empty head, work kneeling, crouching with uptilted head.

The late autumn dawn was still far away, but the dead time of night had come when the traffic on the through street was thinned to single cars passing and the streetcars far away had the lonesome sound of emptiness, before she rose slowly from her stiff knees, dropped the knife into her pocket, and went to bed.

She could not sleep, but lay and watched the red steel-mill light behind the drawn blind pale, then change slowly into gray dawn. She got up, made coffee, but it still wasn't time to waken the children. She went into the living room, and sitting by the block of wood, took down her hair, dropping the pins into her lap, widened by her knees, outspread a little. She combed her hair a long time, pausing now and then to touch the block of wood—the head, the hands, the cloth about the shoulders.

Clovis wakened, grumbling because she had not got him up; he'd wanted to be through town by daylight. He looked at her as he ate the breakfast mush. 'Are you all right, Gert? You look kinda big eyed an peaked.'

'I'm fine,' she said.

Clytie asked her the same as she fixed margarine sandwiches to take to school, but when her mother answered, 'Fine,' the girl continued to study her.

'You're bad worried, Mom,' she said. 'Would it help if I give yu my carfare? This week's already in tokens, but I've got money laid by fer next week in case I don't git no baby sitten.'

Gertie smiled. 'Honey, th shoe leather you'd wear out on that long walk ud be worth more'n th money.'

'Mebbe I can sell a doll atter school,' Enoch said, 'an I know that soon's it gits a little closer tu Christmas I can sell a heap.'

'We're all right,' Gertie said. 'Better off than lots. Recollect I've got a big order fer whittled goods an yer pop's got some work.'

The older children were gone, and she dressed Amos and washed his face and combed his hair. 'We've got tu take a trip,' she said, 'an you've got tu be neat an clean.'

'Th graveyard?' he asked.

She shook her head. 'Jist th—' Her tongue fumbled, and he stared at her; his mother's eyes were bright and somehow twisting like her hands, 'jist th scrap-wood lot,' she said at last, adding as she put on her coat, 'an I'll need tu borrie yer wagon.'

Amos brought the wagon out of his room, and she carried it down the steps and onto the walk. Wheateye, eating a carrot, racing down the alley on a borrowed scooter, saw, and called, 'Where yu goen?'

'Th wood lot,' she said; and to Amos, 'Wait, now; we've got to take a load.'

She went into the living room, and stood for a moment smoothing the wood and looking down at it, then took it in her two arms as if it had been a child, and carried it to the kitchen door. She stopped there and looked back at the room; it seemed empty now—of what? A block of wood could not make such emptiness.

She turned quickly through the door, and the children, who had gathered to Wheateye's crying, began asking:

'Whatcha gonna do, Miz Nevels?'

'Lookee, lookee, ut's a man.'

'It's a woman.'

And a little Daly, running up, cried, 'It'sa virgin,' but the stove wrecker thought it was a saint.

There were as yet no grownups about in the alleys, but there were many children, for the weather was warm for November; still, with a low weak sun in a pallid, smoky sky, so that the children came running as always to anything strange. Many followed after her, fussing at times over who should have the privilege of helping Amos pull the wagon, for the load was a heavy one. Wheateye left the scooter and pushed; a little Schultz and a Daly helped her, so that there was a little procession with Gertie walking in front, the Josiah basket on her arm, a doll in her other hand. She stopped at times to match her pace to that of the children, but never seemed to hear their questions: 'Watcha aimen tu do wid dis? Yu gonna sell um? Don'tcha like um eny more? Why don'tcha fix his face?'

And when she did not answer, Wheateye and the others fell to talking to the block of wood.

'Whatcher name?' they'd cry.

'Where yu goen?'

'Why's yu face all covered? Yu shamed tu show yu face?'

'Lemme see yu face.'

The little Schultz reached high and struck the down-bent head, but others cried, 'Aw, don't hit him; he ain't done nutten.'

Gertie turned, and her voice was supplicating, 'Don't be hurten him, now.'

She heard the saw in the scrap-wood lot, and stopped and stood, her head bent; but the pushing and pulling children bumped her, and she walked again.

The saw was singing loudly so that the scrap-wood man did not hear their coming. It was only when he chanced to look up that he saw them all, watching him, waiting, the block of wood in the wagon, in front of Gertie now. He stared at the wood, studying it, then stopped the saw, and came round to the hidden face, turned away from him toward Gertie. He bent and studied it a moment, then looked up at Gertie. 'Christ?'

She shook her head. Her eyes were wide and black under her tightly pulled-back hair, and they fondled the wood an instant, the hands, the head, the covered face. 'Cherry wood,' she said at last,

607

slowly, loudly, as if he had been deaf. 'I want him—it—sawed into boards fer whittling.'

'Oh,' he said, and looked at her, then back to the wood. 'They's a lot—a lot a work in ut.'

'Jist pastime,' she said, not moving, steadfastly looking past the wood. 'I'd like it sawed—now.'

'Yu'd oughta put a face on him,' he said, still studying the wood, 'ud been nice tu seen ut.'

She was silent, her lips tightly shut together, her hands clenched a little, the forgotten basket slipped down her arm, but her eyes were now unable to stray from the wood, the hands and hair so clear out here in the pale sunshine, the wood so bright under the pallid sky.

He studied it, and shook his head. 'It's too big,' he said. 'Th way it is, yu'll hafta split ut.'

'Oh,' she said, the 'oh' like the beginning of a cry, but smothered at once, and she was still, considering; while the children, troubled, gathered round, and looked first at the wood and then at her. She was so still; it was as if by steadfastly looking at the wood, she, too, had changed into wood.

She took it from the wagon at last, and looked about for a level spot.

'Quarter it,' he said. 'That'll be enough.' He reached for an ax, lifted it, hesitated, looking at the wood, his glance long on the bowed head, the empty uplifted hand. 'Yu'd better do ut,' he said, and handed the ax to her.

She stood above it, the ax lifted, her eyes on the top of the head. She hit it, and the man laughed as the ax leaped back from the swirling hair.

'Yu'll hafta do better'n that, lady,' he said.

She swung the ax in a wide arc, and it sank into the wood straight across the top of the head; and she stood so, the ax motionless, deep in the wood. She breathed heavily, and there were beads of sweat on her forehead.

He brought a wedge, and a large hammer he used for knocking down heavy crates.

She struck the ax with the hammer, but weak she seemed, her sweat-slippery hands sliding from the hammer, her hands forever

608

fumbling; but at last the wood cried out, opening a crack wide enough for the wedge. She brought the great hammer hard down upon the wedge, again on the ax. The wood, straight-grained and true, came apart with a crying, rendering sound, but stood for an instant longer like a thing whole, the bowed head, the shoulders; then slowly the face fell forward toward the ground, but stopped, trembling and swaying, held up by the two hands.

A great shout went up from the children.

The man reached for the fallen face, righted it so that she might strike the head again, but his hand did not immediately come away. He touched the wood where the face should have been, and nodded. 'Christ yu meant it tu be—butcha couldn't find no face fu him.'

She shook her head below the lifted ax. 'No. They was so many would ha done; they's millions an millions a faces plenty fine enough—fer him.'

She pondered, then slowly lifted her glance from the block of wood, and wonder seemed mixed in with the pain. 'Why, some a my neighbors down there in th alley—they would ha done.'

Afterword

This brutal, beautiful novel has a permanent effect upon the reader: long after one has put it aside, he is still in the presence of its people, absorbed in their trivial and tragic dilemma, sorting out their mistakes, rearranging their possibilities, pondering upon the fate that makes certain people live certain lives, suffer certain atrocities, while other people merely read about them. Because Harriette Arnow's people are not articulate, we are anxious to give their confusion a recognizable order, to contribute to their reality, to complete them with language. They are assimilated into us, and we into them. *The Dollmaker* deals with human beings to whom language is not a means of changing or even expressing reality, but a means of pitifully recording its effect upon the nerves. It is a legitimate tragedy, our most unpretentious American masterpiece.

First published in 1954, *The Dollmaker* tells the story of a dislocated Kentucky family during the closing years of World War II. The Nevels family comes to Detroit, so that the father can contribute to the 'war effort' by working in a factory. The war is always a reality, though at a distance: real to the Kentucky women who wait anxiously for mail, dreading the arrival of telegrams, real to the workers of Detroit who dread its ending. But the 'war' itself becomes abstracted from common experience as the Nevels family gradually is accommodated to Detroit and its culture of machines, the radio being the means by which war news is always heard, and also the primary means of entertainment. In the foreground is a life of distracting, uprooted particulars, everything dependent upon everything else, tied together magically in the complex economic knot of a modern industrial society. How can the human imagination resist a violent assimilation into such a culture? In Kentucky, the Nevels are themselves a kind of domestic factory, producing their own food; in Detroit they are the exploited base of a vast capitalistic pyramid, utterly helpless, anonymous cogs in a factory that extends beyond the brutal city of Detroit to take in the entire nation. They are truly American, as they become dehumanized—Gertie Nevels is encouraged to make cheap dolls, in place of her beautiful hand-carved figures, and her children are enthusiastic about selling themselves in various clever ways, knowing that one must be sold, one must therefore work to *sell oneself*. A pity they can't put up a sign over their door, they say, declaring this three-bedroom apartment to be the 'Nevels' Woodworking Plant Number I!' The enthusiasm of the children's acquiescence to the values of a capitalistic society is one of the most depressing aspects of this novel.

It is a depressing work, like most extraordinary works. Its power lies in its insistence upon the barrenness of life, even a life lived in intimacy with other human beings, bound together by ties of real love and suffering. Tragedy does not seem to me to be cathartic, but to deepen our sense of the mystery and sanctity of the human predicament. The beauty of *The Dollmaker* is its author's absolute commitment to a vision of life as cyclical tragedy—as constant struggle. No sooner is one war declared over than the impoverished, overworked citizens of Detroit anticipate the start of another war, the war against 'communists,' particularly those in Detroit!—no sooner is one domestic horror concluded, one child mutilated and killed, than another horror begins to take shape. The process of life demands total absorption of one's energies, there is no time to think, no time to arrange fate, no time to express the spiritual life. Life is killing, a killing of other people or of oneself, a killing of one's soul. When the war is over, concluded by the drama of the atomic bombs, 'Gertie could hear no rejoicing, no lifting of the heart that all the planned killing and wounding of men was finished.

Rather it was as if the people had lived on blood, and now that the bleeding was ended, they were worried about their future food.'

It is a fact of life that one must always worry, not about the 'planned' killing and wounding of men, but about his own future food.

The Dollmaker begins magnificently on a Kentucky road, with Gertie in her own world, knowing her strength, having faith in her audacity—a big, ungainly, ugly woman astride a mule, ready to force any car that comes along to stop for her. She is carrying her son Amos, who is dangerously ill, and she must get a ride to town in order to take him to a doctor. Her sheer animal will, her stubbornness, guarantee the survival of her son; she is not afraid to cut into his flesh with a knife in order to release pus. She succeeds in stopping a car with an army officer in it and she succeeds in overwhelming this man by the determination of her will. But it is her last real success: after the novel's beginning, everything goes downhill for Gertie.

Basic to her psychological predicament is a conflict that has been an obsession in the American imagination, particularly the imagination of the nineteenth century—the twin and competitive visions of God, God as love and God as vengeance, a God of music and dollmaking and domestic simplicity, and a God whose hell quivers with murderous heat. The God of hell is the God worshiped by Gertie's mother, who is responsible for the tragedy of the novel. If the God of this hell rules the world also, and it is Gertie's deepest, helpless conviction that He does, then all of life is forecast, determined; and the fires of Detroit's steel mills are accurate symbols for Gertie to mull over. Gertie, like Judas, is foreordained to sin against such a God. The novel resolves itself in a bitter irony as Gertie betrays herself, giving up her unique art in order to make herself over into a kind of free-lance factory worker, turning out dolls or foxes or Christ, on order; she is determined to be Judas, to betray the Christly figure in the piece of wood she never has enough time to carve out, and the Christly figure is at once her own and that of the millions of people, Americans like herself, who might have been models for Christ. They do not emerge out of the wood, they do not become incarnated in time, they are not given a face or a voice. They remain mute, unborn. Man is both Christ and Judas, the sacred, divine self and the secular, betraying, human self, the self that must sell itself for 'future food' because this is the foreordained lot of man.

'She thought she was going to cry. . . . So many times she'd thought of that other woman, and now she was that woman: "She considereth a field and buyeth it; with the fruit of her own hands she planteth a vineyard." A whole vineyard she didn't need, only six vines maybe. So much to plant her own vines, set her own trees, and know that come thirty years from now she'd gather fruit from the trees and grapes from the vines. . . .' Gertie's only ambition is to own a small farm of her own. In order to live she must own land, work the land herself. The owning of property has nothing to do with setting up boundaries (there are no near neighbors); it is a declaration of personality, an expression of the profound human need for self-sufficiency and permanence. Wendell Berry's *A Place on Earth*, also set during the closing months of World War II but dealing exclusively with those Kentuckians who did not leave home, is a long, slow, ponderous, memorable novel of praise for a life lived close to the earth, to one's own earth, a 'place on earth' which is our only hope; the earth and human relationships are our only hope. In the government housing project in Detroit this desire is expressed feebly and pathetically in the tenants' planting of flowers, which are naturally trampled and destroyed, though a few somehow survive—the tragedy is that this desire lies beyond the reach of nearly everyone, and therefore identity, personality, the necessary permanence of life itself are denied. To be 'saved' in this culture one must remake oneself entirely, one must sell oneself as shrewdly as possible. One's fate depends not upon his sacred relationship with the land, but his secular, deceptive relationship with society.

There are great works that deal with the soul in isolation, untouched importantly by history. Sartre's *Nausea*, which concerns the salvation of a historian, is an ahistorical work, a work of allegory; Dostoyevsky's *Notes from the Underground*, neurotic and witty and totally subjective, is nevertheless a historical work. It seems to me that the greatest works of literature deal with the human soul caught in the stampede of time, unable to gauge the profundity of what passes over it, like the characters in certain plays of Yeats's who live through terrifying events but who cannot understand them; in this way history passes over most of us. Society is caught in a convulsion, whether of growth or of death, and ordinary people are destroyed. They do not, however, understand that they are 'destroyed.'

There is a means of salvation: love, particularly of children. But the children of *The Dollmaker* are stunted, doomed adults, destroyed either literally by the admonition 'Adjust!' or destroyed emotionally, turned into citizens of a demonic factory-world. There is another means: art. But art is luxury, it has no place in the world of intense, daily, bitter struggle, though this world of struggle is itself the main object of art. Living, one cannot be saved; suffering, one cannot express the phenomenon of 'suffering.' Gertie Nevels is inarticulate throughout most of this novel, unable to do battle effectively with the immense hallucination of her new life, and her only means of expression—her carving—must finally be sacrificed, so that her family can eat. So the social dislocation of these Kentucky 'hillbillies' is an expression of the general doom of most of mankind, and their defeat, the corruption of their personalities, is more basic to our American experience than the failure of those whom James thought of as 'freed' from economic necessity, and therefore free to create their own souls. Evil is inherent in the human heart, as good is inherent in it; but the violence of economic suffering stifles the good, stimulates the evil, so that the ceaseless struggle with the fabric of the universe is reduced to a constant, daily heart-breaking struggle over money, waged against every other antlike inhabitant of the city, the stakes indefinable beyond next month's payment of rent or payment on the car.

If the dream of a small farm is Gertie's dream of Eden, the real 'Paradise Valley' (a Negro slum section of Detroit) is an ironic hell, and the 'Merry Hill' to which she and her family come to live is, though segregated 'by law,' no different. Detroit is terrifying as seen through the eyes of this Kentucky farm woman. The machines—the hurrying people—the automobiles—the initial sounding of that ugly word 'Hillbilly!'—everything works to establish a demonic world, the antithesis of the Kentucky hills. There, man can have privacy and dignity though he may be poor; in the housing development money appears and is lost, there is no privacy, everyone intrudes upon everyone else, the alley is 'one churning, wriggling mass of children.' The impact of this dislocation upon children is most terrible: Reuben, the oldest boy, becomes bitter and runs away from home, unable to 'adjust'; Cassie, deprived of her invisible playmate Callie Lou, is killed by a train in the trainyards near her home. I can think of no other work except Christina Stead's *The Man Who Loved Children* that deals so brilliantly and movingly with the lives of children, and Mrs Arnow has chosen not to penetrate the minds of the Nevels children at all but simply to show us their development or deterioration from the outside. It is a fact of slum life that children dominate in sheer numbers. The more impoverished the neighborhood, the more children to run wild in its streets and on its sidewalks, both powerful and helpless. The fear of anarchy, shared by all of us who have been children, materializes in the constant struggle of children to maintain their identities, striking and recoiling from one another: in miniature they live out tragic scenarios, the pressure upon the human soul in our age, the overcrowding of life, the suffocation of the personality under the weight of sheer numbers, noise, confusion. Yet no dream of wealth, no dream of a fine home in 'Grosse Pointe' is too fantastic for these people to have; corrupted by movies, by the radio, by the mystery of the dollar, they succumb happily to their own degradation, alternating between a kind of community and a disorganized, hateful mass that cannot live in peace. Neighbors cannot live in peace with neighbors, nor parents with their own families, nor children with children. The basic split in the American imagination between an honoring of the individual and a vicious demand for 'adjustment' and conformity is dramatized by the gradual metamorphosis of the surviving Nevels children. Gertie is still Gertie, though profoundly shaken by the loss of Reuben and Cassie, but her other children have come a long way, by the end of the novel, when they can laugh at a cartoon of a woman with a mule, having learned the proper contempt for a 'hillbilly.'

Gertie's husband, Clovis, with his liking for machines, adapts himself easily to the new culture. He takes pride in buying his wife an Icy Heart refrigerator (on time) and a car for himself (on time) and in 'hunting Christmas' for his family in smelly department-store basements. It is part of the moral confusion of life in Detroit that Clovis, essentially a good, 'natural' man, should become a murderer, revenging himself upon a young man hired to beat him up because of his union activities. There is no time to assess properly Clovis's act of murder—Gertie has no time to comprehend it, except to recoil from what she senses has happened. But the struggle continues; nothing is changed by the murder; another thug will be hired to take that man's place, by the mysterious powers with money enough to 'hire' other men; at the novel's conclusion Clovis, like millions of other men, is out of work and we can envision his gradual disintegration, forced to look desperately for jobs and to live off his wife and children.

It is part of the industrial society that people of widely varying backgrounds should be thrown together, like animals competing for a small, fixed amount of food, forced to hate one another. Telling an amiable anecdote about factory life, Clovis mentions a Ukrainian: 'He hates everything, niggers, hillbillies, Jews, Germans, but worse'n anything he hates Poles an that Polack foreman. An he is a good-hearted guy. . . .' Catholics hate and fear non-Catholics, spurred on by their famous radio priest 'Father Moneyhan,' but Irish Catholics hate Polish Catholics. However, the hatreds seethe and subside, especially in the face of common human predicaments of drunkenness and trouble; at any rate they can be easily united into a solid hatred of Negroes, should that need arise. Living in fear more or less constantly, being forced to think only of their 'future food,' these people have no choice but to hate the 'Other,' the constant threat. What a picture of America's promises *The Dollmaker* gives, and how unforgettable this 'melting-pot' of economic democracy!

Mrs Arnow writes so well, with so little apparent effort, that critical examination seems almost irrelevant. It is a tribute to her talent that one is convinced, partway through the book, that it is a masterpiece; if everything goes wrong, if an entirely unsuitable ending is tacked on, the book will remain inviolate. The ending of *The Dollmaker* is by no means a disappointment, however. After months of struggle and a near-succumbing to madness, Gertie questions the basis of her own existence; inarticulate as she is, given to working with her hands, in silence, she is nevertheless lyrically aware of the horror of the world in which she now lives. Behind her, now unattainable, is the farm in Kentucky which her mother talked her out of buying; all around her is the unpredictable confusion of Detroit. What is the point of having children? 'What was the good of trying to keep your own [children] if when they grew up their days were like your own—changeovers and ugly painted dolls?' Throughout the novel Gertie has been dreaming of the proper face for the Christ she wants to carve. She never locates the proper face: instead she takes the fine block of wood to be split into smaller pieces, for easily made dolls.

The drama of naturalism has always been the subjecting of ordinary people to the corrosive and killing facts of society, usually an industrial one. *The Grapes of Wrath*, so much more famous than Mrs Arnow's novel, and yet not superior to it, is far more faithful to the naturalistic tradition than is *The Dollmaker*: one learns a great deal about the poetic vulgarities and obscenities of life from Steinbeck, and this aspect of life has its own kind of immortality. *The Dollmaker*, however, is not truly naturalistic; a total world is suggested but not expressed. Mrs Arnow, like Gertie Nevels, flinches from a confrontation with sexual realities. The frantic naturalism of such a work as the recent *Last Exit to Brooklyn*, superimposed upon this little Detroit epic, would give us, probably, a more truthful vision of Detroit, then and now; but such naturalism, totally absorbed in an analysis of bodily existence, is perhaps equally unfaithful to the spiritual and imaginative demands that some people, at least, still make. So Gertie is an 'artist,' but a primitive, untheorizing, inarticulate artist; she whittles out figures that are dolls or Christs, figures of human beings not quite human, but expressive of old human dreams. She is both an ordinary human being and an extraordinary human being, a memorable creation, so real that one cannot question her existence. There are certainly greater novels than *The Dollmaker*, but I can think of none that have moved me more, personally, terrifyingly, involving me in the solid fact of life's criminal exploitation of those who live it—not hard, not sentimental, not at all intellectually ambitious, *The Dollmaker* is one of those excellent American works that have yet to be properly assessed.

Joyce Carol Oates, 1971